SAUCER COUNTRY

SAUCER COUNTRY

Become our fan on Facebook **facebook.com/idwpublishing**

Follow us on Twitter **@idwpublishing**

Subscribe to us on YouTube **youtube.com/idwpublishing**

See what's new on Tumblr **tumblr.idwpublishing.com**

Check us out on Instagram **instagram.com/idwpublishing**

Ted Adams, CEO & Publisher

Greg Goldstein, President & COO

Robbie Robbins, EVP/Sr. Graphic Artist

Chris Ryall, Chief Creative Officer

David Hedgecock, Editor-in-Chief

Laurie Windrow, Sr. VP of Sales & Marketing

Matthew Ruzicka, CPA, Chief Financial Officer

Lorelei Bunjes, VP of Digital Services

Jerry Bennington, VP of New Product Development

ISBN: 978-1-68405-095-6   20 19 18 17   1 2 3 4

Originally published by Vertigo as SAUCER COUNTRY issues #1–14.

For international rights, contact licensing@idwpublishing.com

WRITTEN BY
PAUL CORNELL

ART BY
RYAN KELLY

ADDITIONAL ART BY
**JIMMY BROXTON, GORAN SUDZUKA, DAVID LAPHAM,
MIRKO COLAK,** AND **ANDREA MUTTI**

COLORS BY
GIULIA BRUSCO, LEE LOUGHBRIDGE, AND **CRIS PETER**

LETTERS BY
SAL CIPRIANO

SAUCER COUNTRY CREATED BY
CORNELL & **KELLY**

COVER ART BY
RYAN KELLY

COLLECTION EDITS BY
JUSTIN EISINGER AND **ALONZO SIMON**

COLLECTION DESIGN BY
CLAUDIA CHONG

PUBLISHER
TED ADAMS

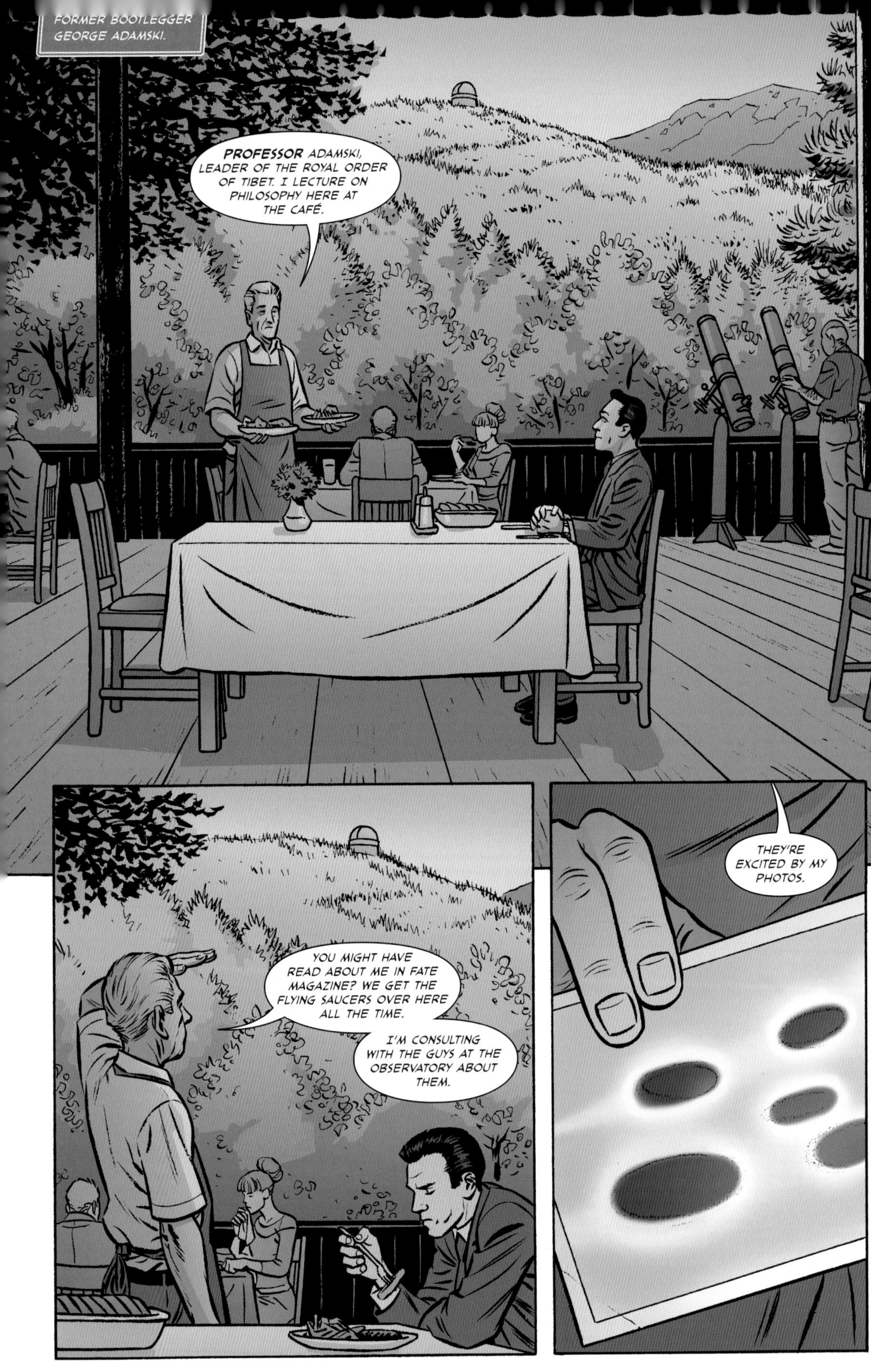
FORMER BOOTLEGGER
GEORGE ADAMSKI.
PROFESSOR ADAMSKI, LEADER OF THE ROYAL ORDER OF TIBET. I LECTURE ON PHILOSOPHY HERE AT THE CAFÉ.
YOU MIGHT HAVE READ ABOUT ME IN FATE MAGAZINE? WE GET THE FLYING SAUCERS OVER HERE ALL THE TIME.
I'M CONSULTING WITH THE GUYS AT THE OBSERVATORY ABOUT THEM.
THEY'RE EXCITED BY MY PHOTOS.

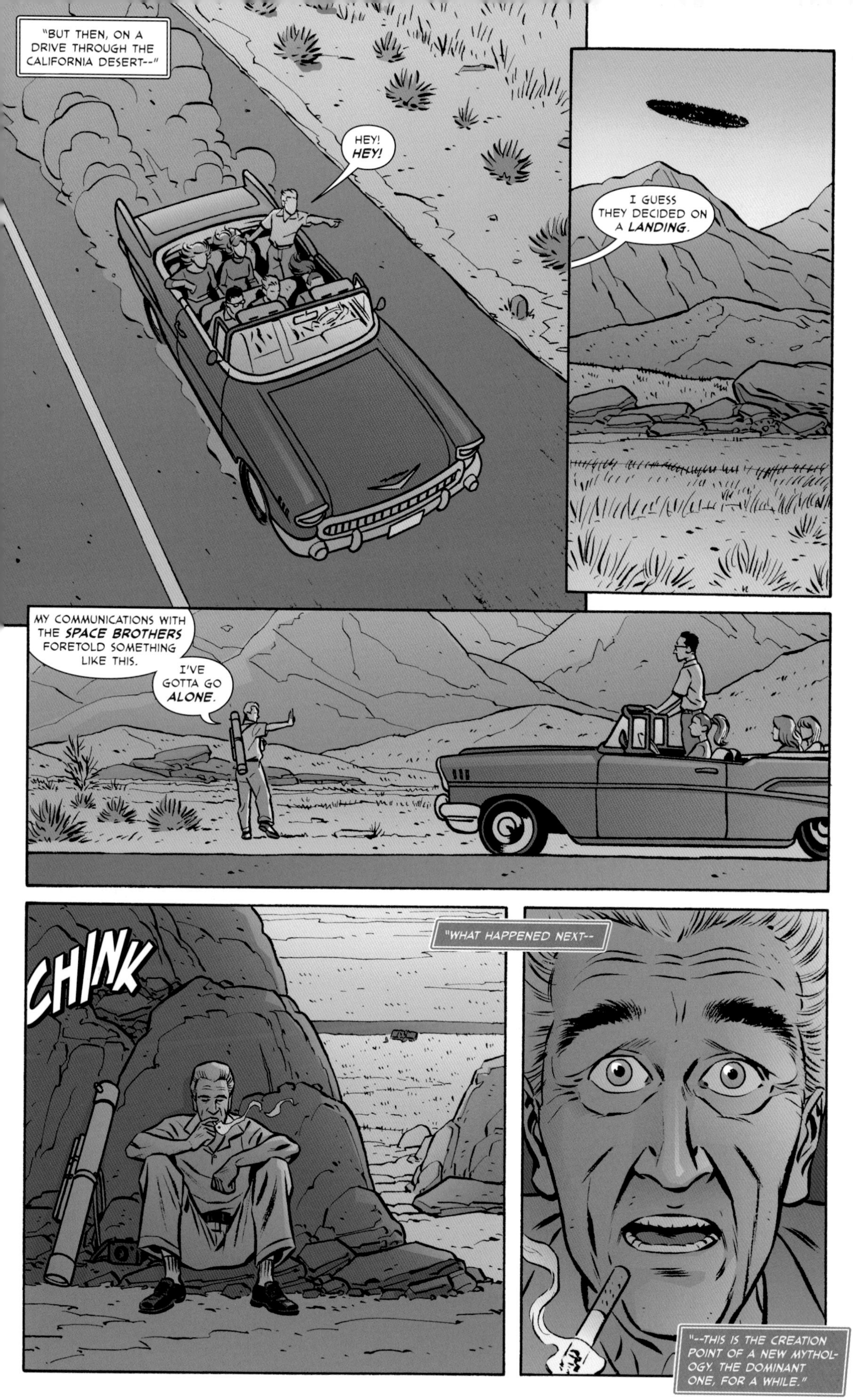
"BUT THEN, ON A DRIVE THROUGH THE CALIFORNIA DESERT--"
HEY! HEY!
I GUESS THEY DECIDED ON A LANDING.
MY COMMUNICATIONS WITH THE SPACE BROTHERS FORETOLD SOMETHING LIKE THIS.
I'VE GOTTA GO ALONE.
CHINK
"WHAT HAPPENED NEXT--
"--THIS IS THE CREATION POINT OF A NEW MYTHOLOGY. THE DOMINANT ONE, FOR A WHILE."

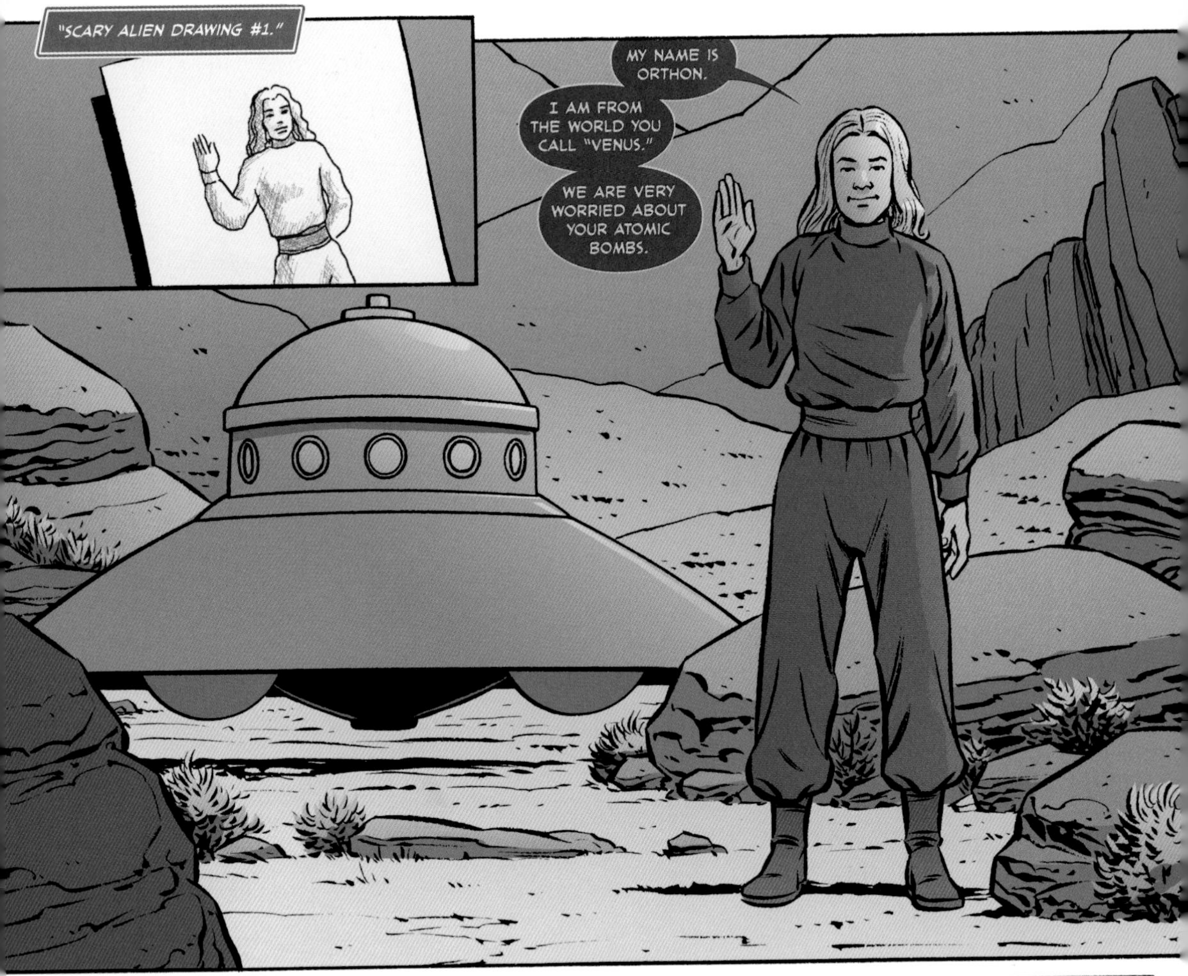
"SCARY ALIEN DRAWING #1."
MY NAME IS ORTHON.
I AM FROM THE WORLD YOU CALL "VENUS."
WE ARE VERY WORRIED ABOUT YOUR ATOMIC BOMBS.

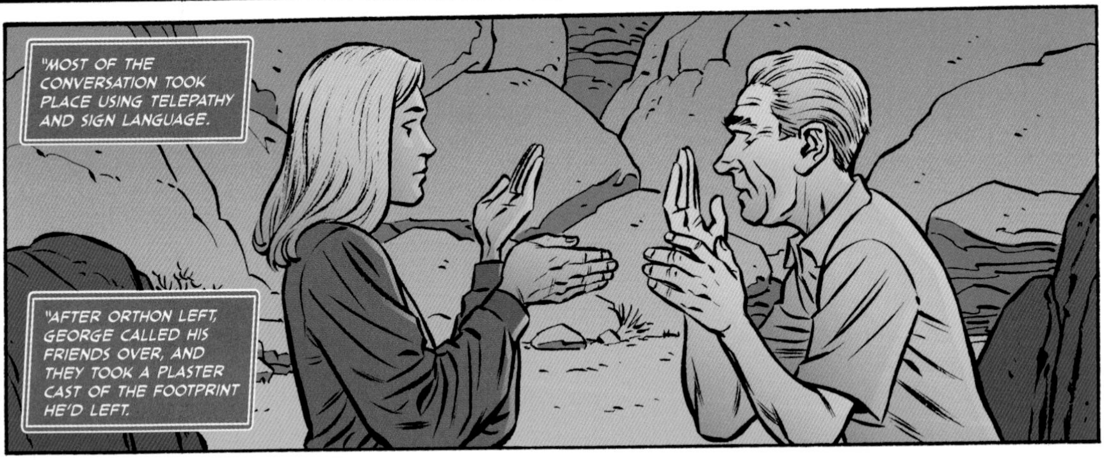
"MOST OF THE CONVERSATION TOOK PLACE USING TELEPATHY AND SIGN LANGUAGE.
"AFTER ORTHON LEFT, GEORGE CALLED HIS FRIENDS OVER, AND THEY TOOK A PLASTER CAST OF THE FOOTPRINT HE'D LEFT.

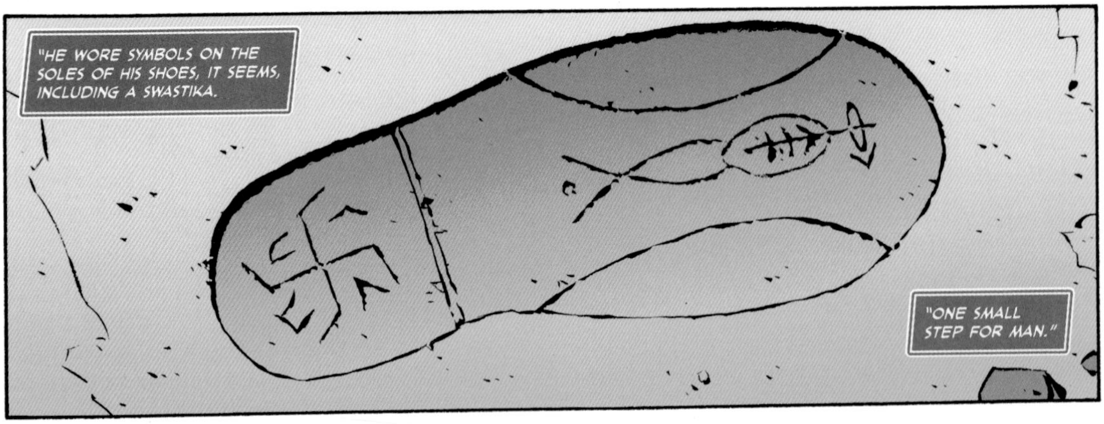
"HE WORE SYMBOLS ON THE SOLES OF HIS SHOES, IT SEEMS, INCLUDING A SWASTIKA.
"ONE SMALL STEP FOR MAN."

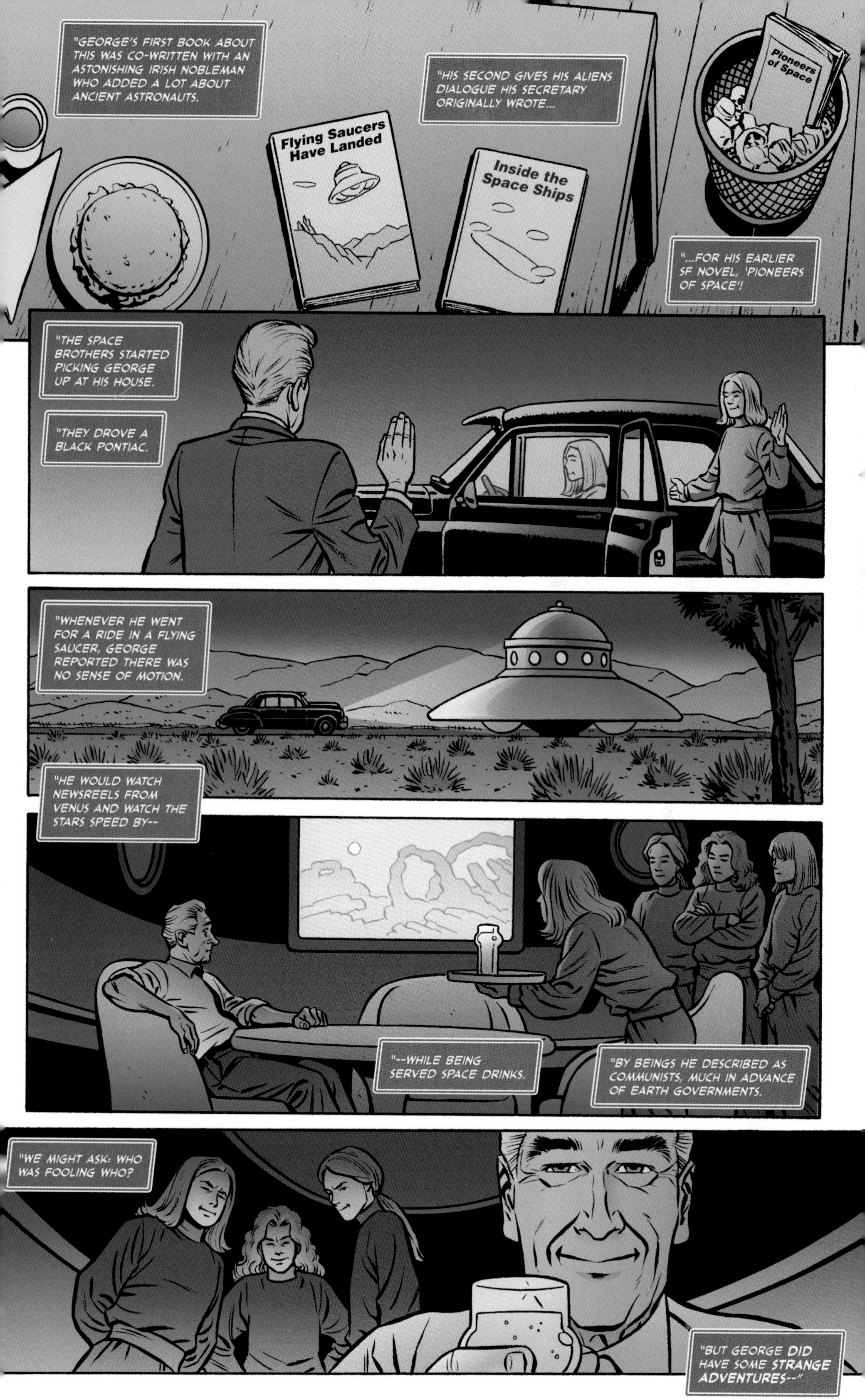
"GEORGE'S FIRST BOOK ABOUT THIS WAS CO-WRITTEN WITH AN ASTONISHING IRISH NOBLEMAN WHO ADDED A LOT ABOUT ANCIENT ASTRONAUTS.
Flying Saucers Have Landed
"HIS SECOND GIVES HIS ALIENS DIALOGUE HIS SECRETARY ORIGINALLY WROTE...
Inside the Space Ships
Pioneers of Space
"...FOR HIS EARLIER SF NOVEL, 'PIONEERS OF SPACE'!
"THE SPACE BROTHERS STARTED PICKING GEORGE UP AT HIS HOUSE.
"THEY DROVE A BLACK PONTIAC.
"WHENEVER HE WENT FOR A RIDE IN A FLYING SAUCER, GEORGE REPORTED THERE WAS NO SENSE OF MOTION.
"HE WOULD WATCH NEWSREELS FROM VENUS AND WATCH THE STARS SPEED BY--
"--WHILE BEING SERVED SPACE DRINKS.
"BY BEINGS HE DESCRIBED AS COMMUNISTS, MUCH IN ADVANCE OF EARTH GOVERNMENTS.
"WE MIGHT ASK: WHO WAS FOOLING WHO?
"BUT GEORGE DID HAVE SOME STRANGE ADVENTURES--"

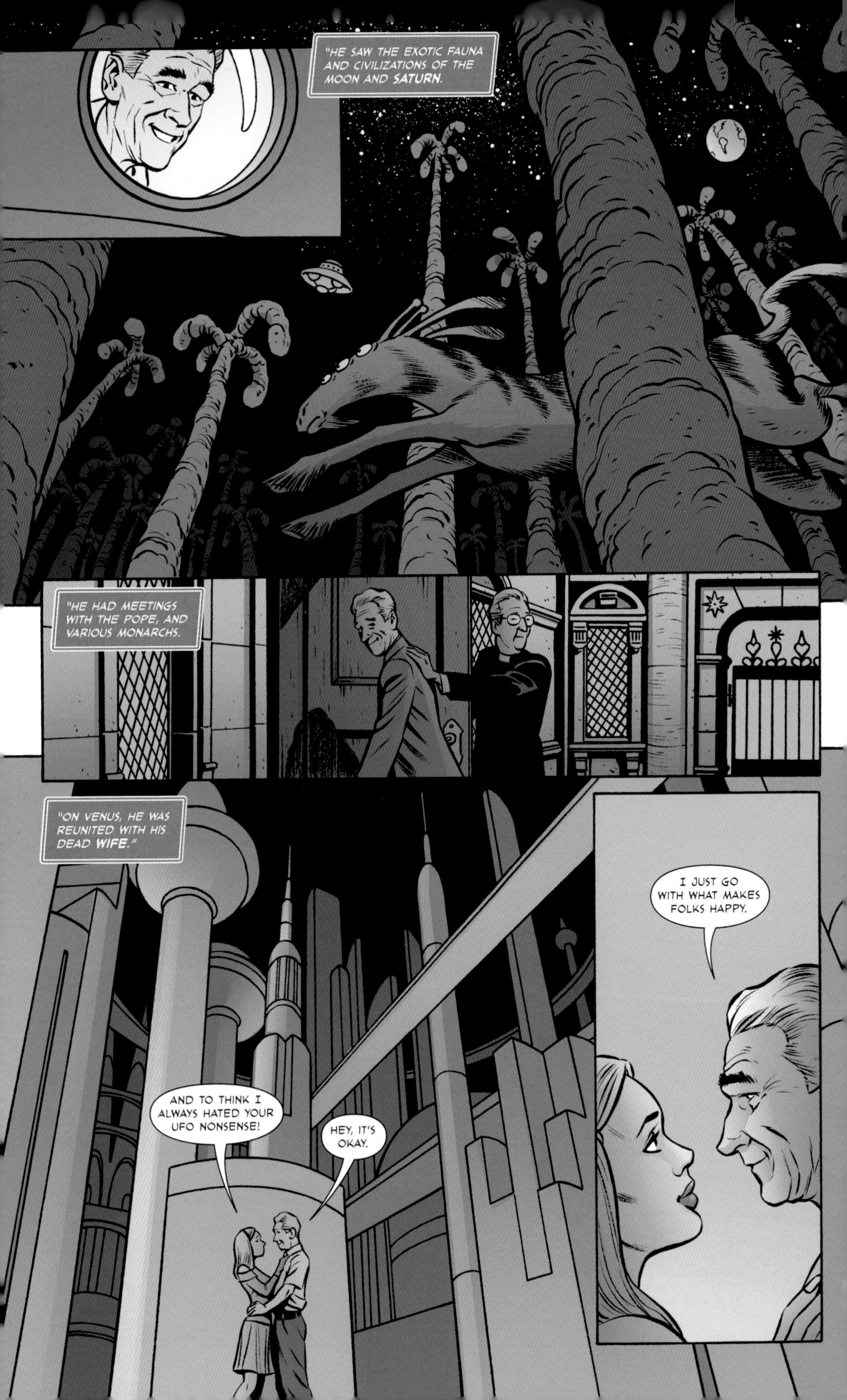
"HE SAW THE EXOTIC FAUNA AND CIVILIZATIONS OF THE MOON AND SATURN.
"HE HAD MEETINGS WITH THE POPE, AND VARIOUS MONARCHS.
"ON VENUS, HE WAS REUNITED WITH HIS DEAD WIFE."
AND TO THINK I ALWAYS HATED YOUR UFO NONSENSE!
HEY, IT'S OKAY.
I JUST GO WITH WHAT MAKES FOLKS HAPPY.

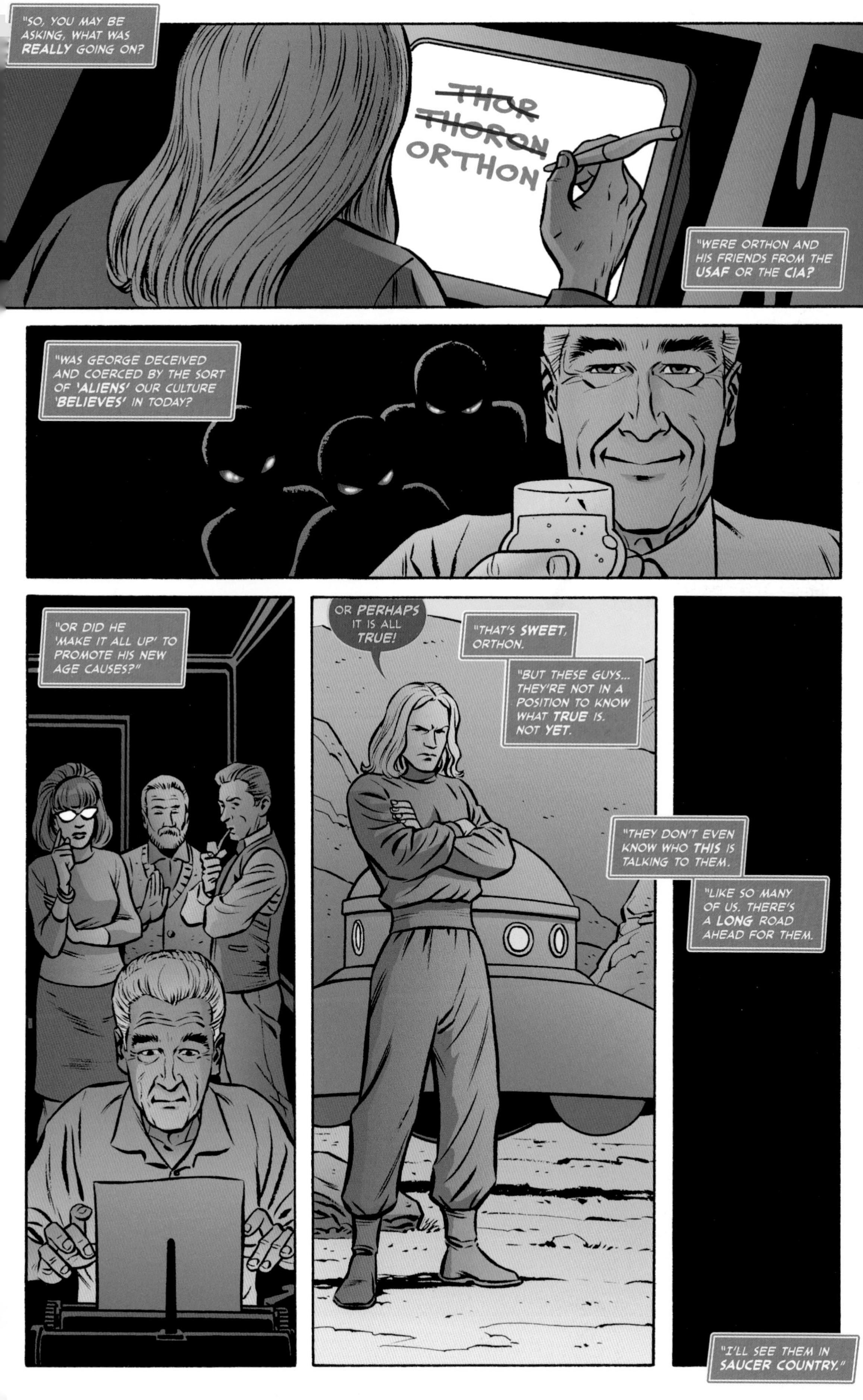
"SO, YOU MAY BE ASKING, WHAT WAS REALLY GOING ON?
THOR
THORON
ORTHON
"WERE ORTHON AND HIS FRIENDS FROM THE USAF OR THE CIA?
"WAS GEORGE DECEIVED AND COERCED BY THE SORT OF 'ALIENS' OUR CULTURE 'BELIEVES' IN TODAY?
"OR DID HE 'MAKE IT ALL UP' TO PROMOTE HIS NEW AGE CAUSES?"
OR PERHAPS IT IS ALL TRUE!
"THAT'S SWEET, ORTHON.
"BUT THESE GUYS... THEY'RE NOT IN A POSITION TO KNOW WHAT TRUE IS. NOT YET.
"THEY DON'T EVEN KNOW WHO THIS IS TALKING TO THEM.
"LIKE SO MANY OF US. THERE'S A LONG ROAD AHEAD FOR THEM.
"I'LL SEE THEM IN SAUCER COUNTRY."

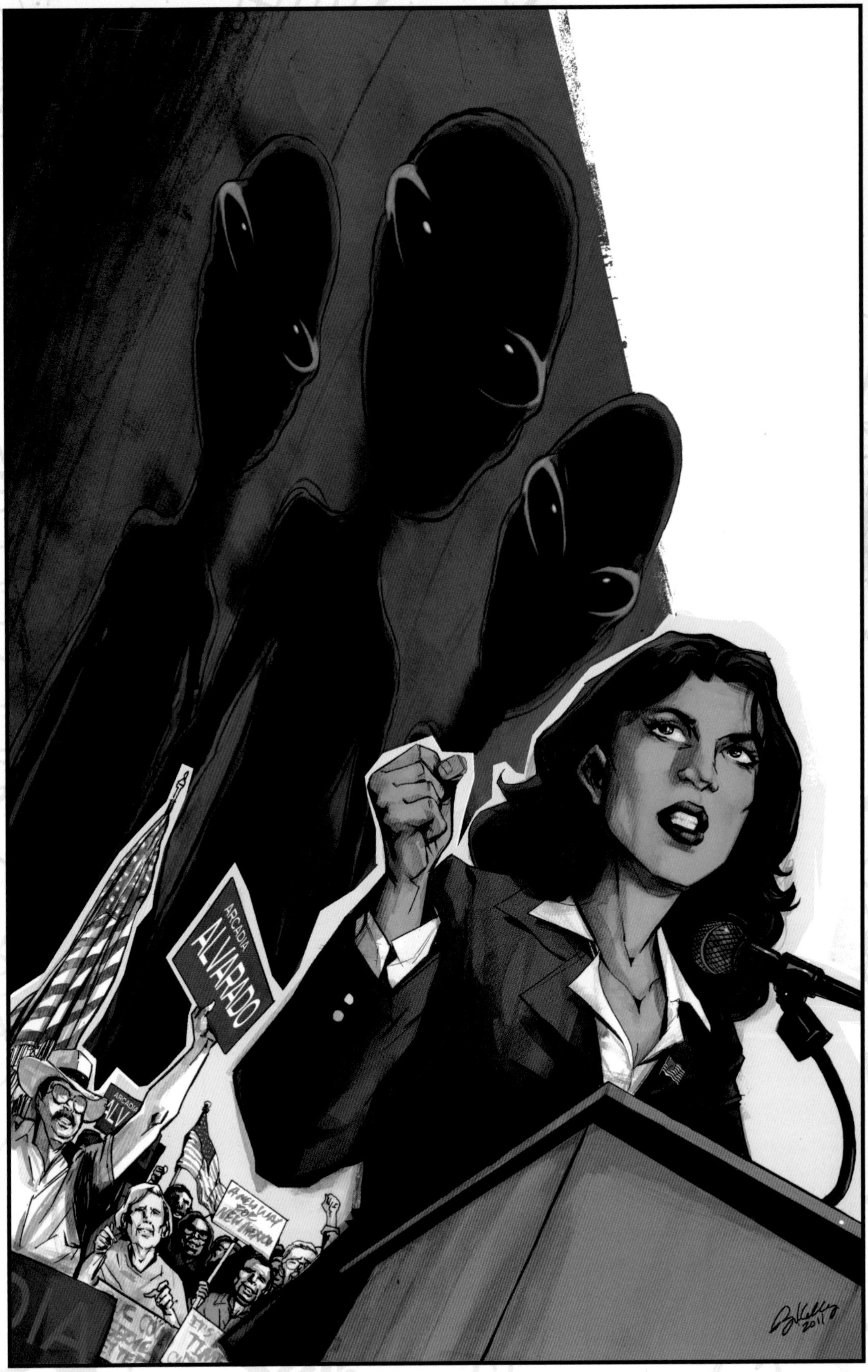
ARCADIA
ALVARADO
ARCADIA
ALV
A NEW WAY FOR NEW MEXICO

COVER ART BY **RYAN KELLY**

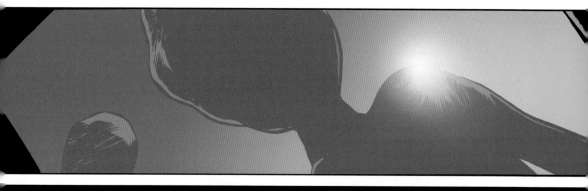

ABORTED FETUSES, MONKEYS USED IN LAB EXPERIMENTS, THE CHILDREN OF BELSEN...

DOES *ANYONE* ACTUALLY BELIEVE *ANYTHING* ANYMORE?

I THINK THERE'S... SOMETHING...OUT THERE. BUT ANY TIME ANYONE TRIES TO PUT THEIR FINGER ON EXACTLY WHAT...

LOOK WHO'S HERE TO SEE YOU!

STAY ASLEEP.

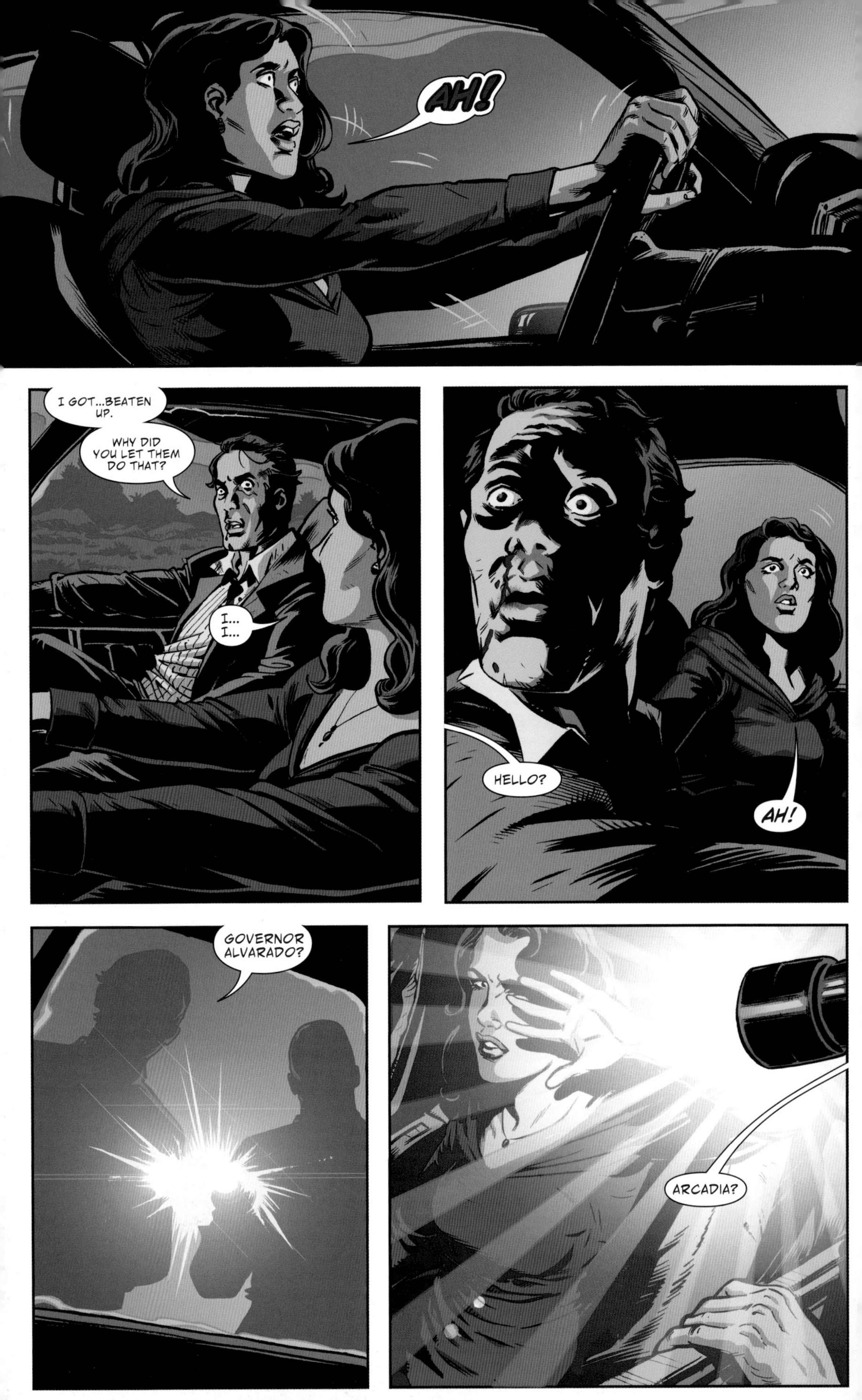
AH!
I GOT...BEATEN UP.
WHY DID YOU LET THEM DO THAT?
I... I...
HELLO?
AH!
GOVERNOR ALVARADO?
ARCADIA?

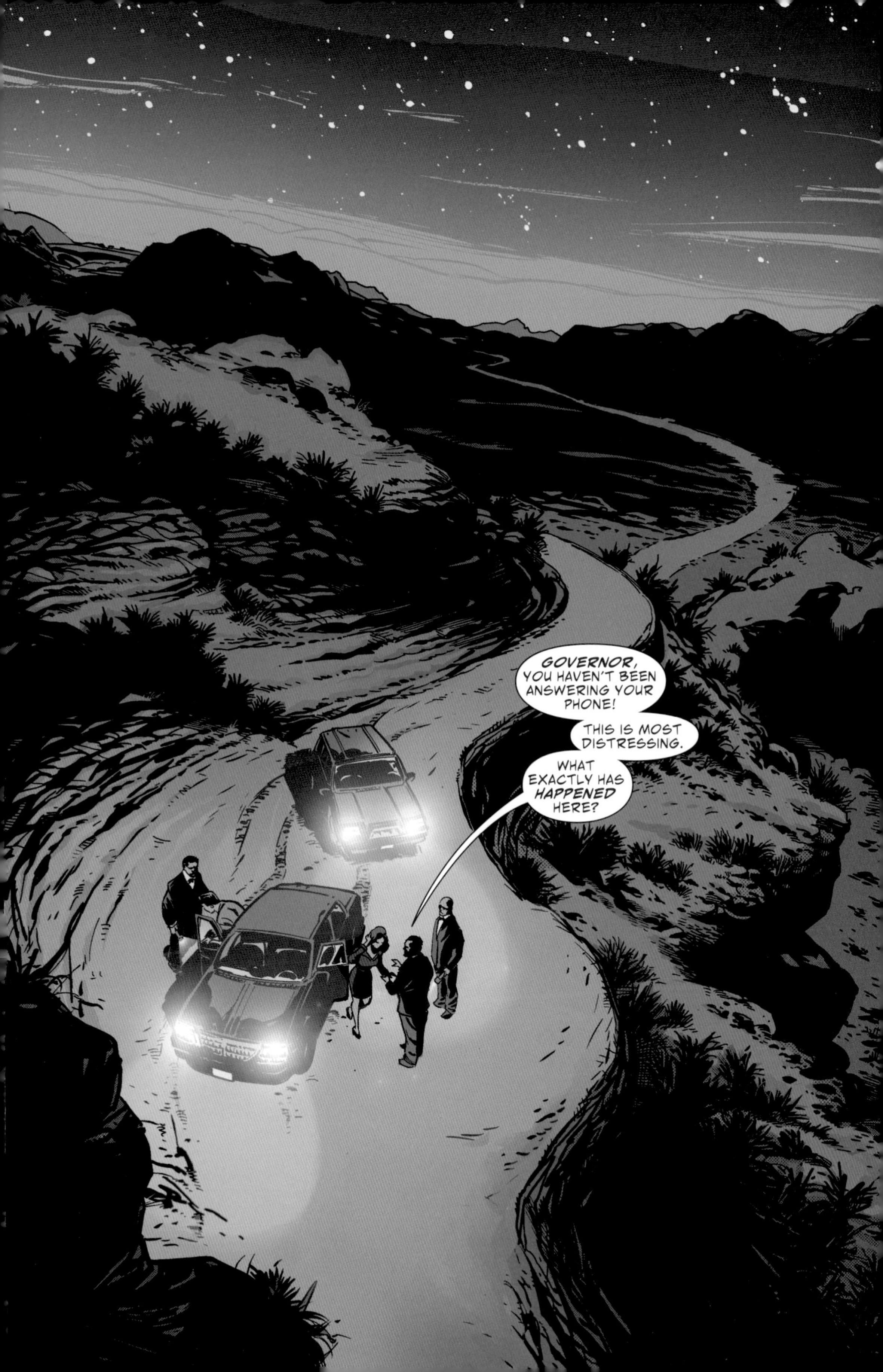
GOVERNOR, YOU HAVEN'T BEEN ANSWERING YOUR PHONE!
THIS IS MOST DISTRESSING.
WHAT EXACTLY HAS *HAPPENED* HERE?

IT'S TYPICAL OF YOU TO WANT TO PROTECT YOUR EX-HUSBAND.

...

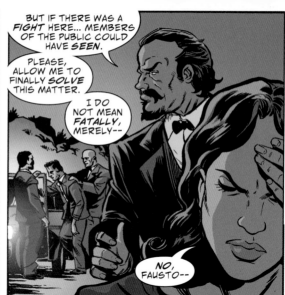

BUT IF THERE WAS A *FIGHT* HERE... MEMBERS OF THE PUBLIC COULD HAVE *SEEN.*

PLEASE, ALLOW ME TO FINALLY *SOLVE* THIS MATTER.

I DO NOT MEAN *FATALLY,* MERELY--

NO, FAUSTO--

--*I* DROVE MICHAEL BACK FROM THE PARTY... BECAUSE WE HAD SOME... PRIVATE MATTERS... TO DISCUSS.

WE...WE MUST HAVE... FALLEN ASLEEP.

PLEASE... DRIVE ME BACK TO THE MANSION.

THANK YOU FOR COMING TO FIND US--

--AND NOT GETTING THE *POLICE* INVOLVED.

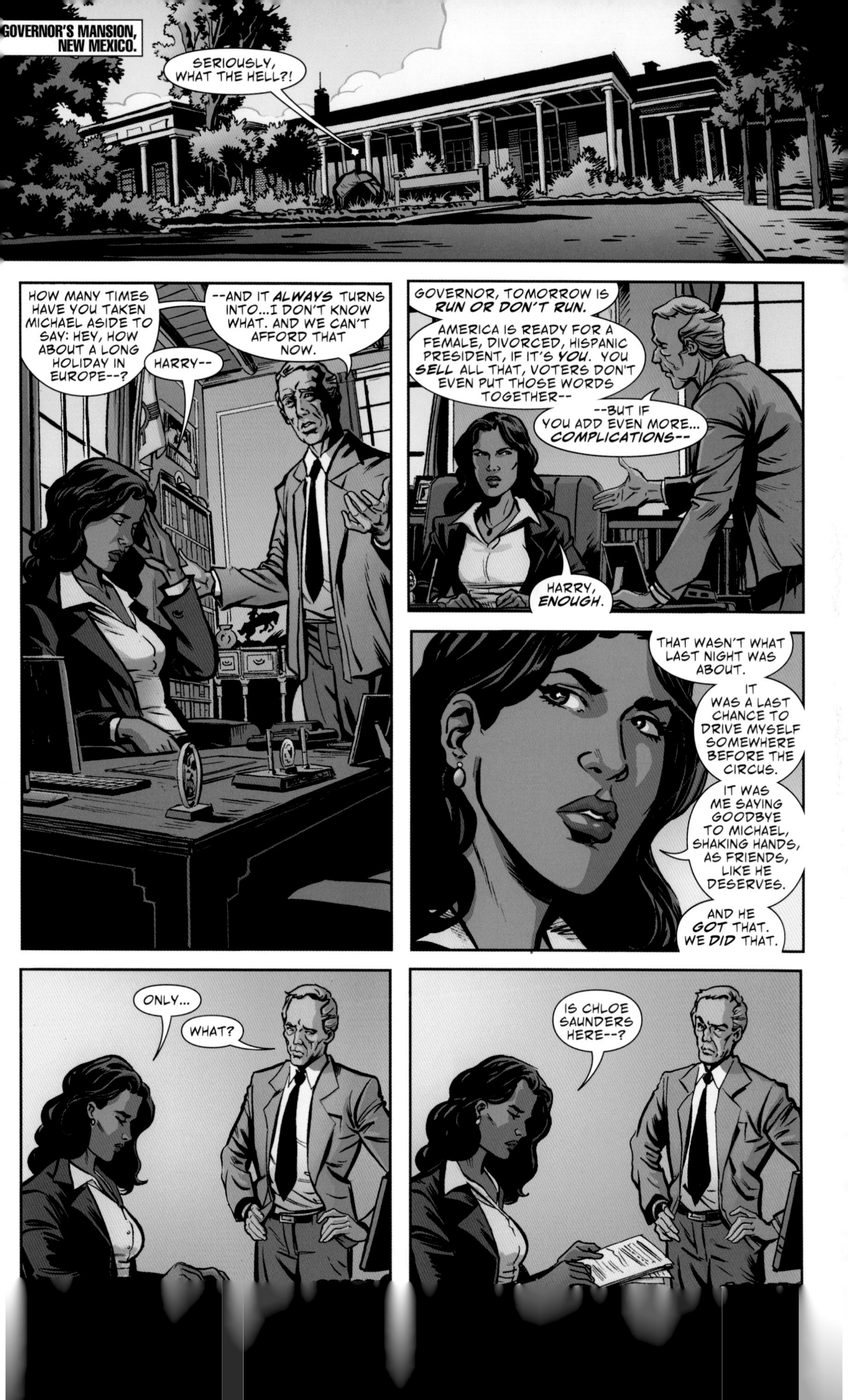
GOVERNOR'S MANSION, NEW MEXICO.
SERIOUSLY, WHAT THE HELL?!
HOW MANY TIMES HAVE YOU TAKEN MICHAEL ASIDE TO SAY: HEY, HOW ABOUT A LONG HOLIDAY IN EUROPE--?
HARRY--
--AND IT ALWAYS TURNS INTO...I DON'T KNOW WHAT. AND WE CAN'T AFFORD THAT NOW.
GOVERNOR, TOMORROW IS RUN OR DON'T RUN.
AMERICA IS READY FOR A FEMALE, DIVORCED, HISPANIC PRESIDENT, IF IT'S YOU. YOU SELL ALL THAT, VOTERS DON'T EVEN PUT THOSE WORDS TOGETHER--
--BUT IF YOU ADD EVEN MORE... COMPLICATIONS--
HARRY, ENOUGH.
THAT WASN'T WHAT LAST NIGHT WAS ABOUT.
IT WAS A LAST CHANCE TO DRIVE MYSELF SOMEWHERE BEFORE THE CIRCUS.
IT WAS ME SAYING GOODBYE TO MICHAEL, SHAKING HANDS, AS FRIENDS, LIKE HE DESERVES.
AND HE GOT THAT. WE DID THAT.
ONLY...
WHAT?
IS CHLOE SAUNDERS HERE--?

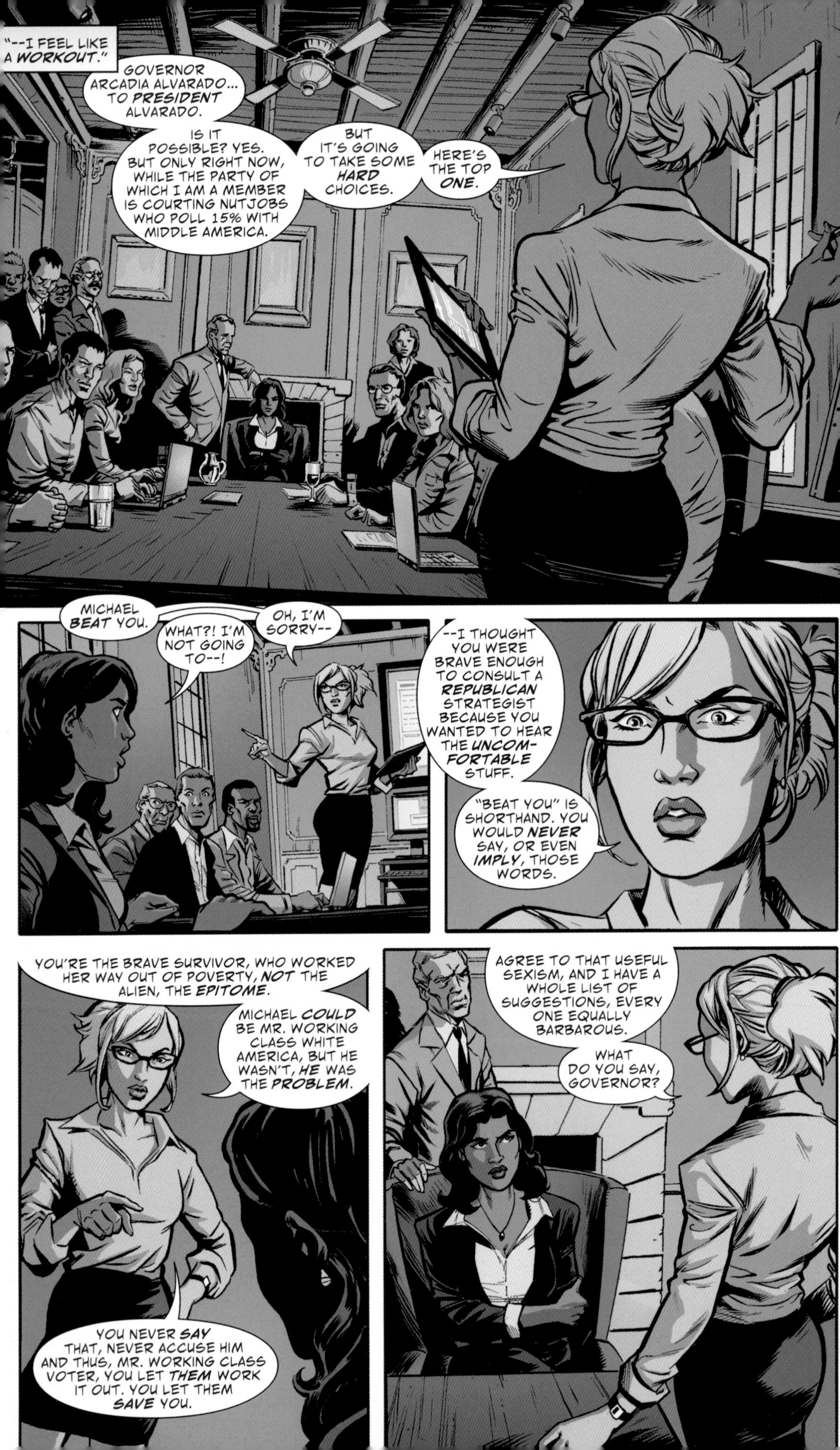
"--I FEEL LIKE A WORKOUT."
GOVERNOR ARCADIA ALVARADO... TO PRESIDENT ALVARADO.
IS IT POSSIBLE? YES. BUT ONLY RIGHT NOW, WHILE THE PARTY OF WHICH I AM A MEMBER IS COURTING NUTJOBS WHO POLL 15% WITH MIDDLE AMERICA.
BUT IT'S GOING TO TAKE SOME HARD CHOICES.
HERE'S THE TOP ONE.
MICHAEL BEAT YOU.
WHAT?! I'M NOT GOING TO--!
OH, I'M SORRY--
--I THOUGHT YOU WERE BRAVE ENOUGH TO CONSULT A REPUBLICAN STRATEGIST BECAUSE YOU WANTED TO HEAR THE UNCOMFORTABLE STUFF.
"BEAT YOU" IS SHORTHAND. YOU WOULD NEVER SAY, OR EVEN IMPLY, THOSE WORDS.
YOU'RE THE BRAVE SURVIVOR, WHO WORKED HER WAY OUT OF POVERTY, NOT THE ALIEN, THE EPITOME.
MICHAEL COULD BE MR. WORKING CLASS WHITE AMERICA, BUT HE WASN'T, HE WAS THE PROBLEM.
YOU NEVER SAY THAT, NEVER ACCUSE HIM AND THUS, MR. WORKING CLASS VOTER, YOU LET THEM WORK IT OUT. YOU LET THEM SAVE YOU.
AGREE TO THAT USEFUL SEXISM, AND I HAVE A WHOLE LIST OF SUGGESTIONS, EVERY ONE EQUALLY BARBAROUS.
WHAT DO YOU SAY, GOVERNOR?

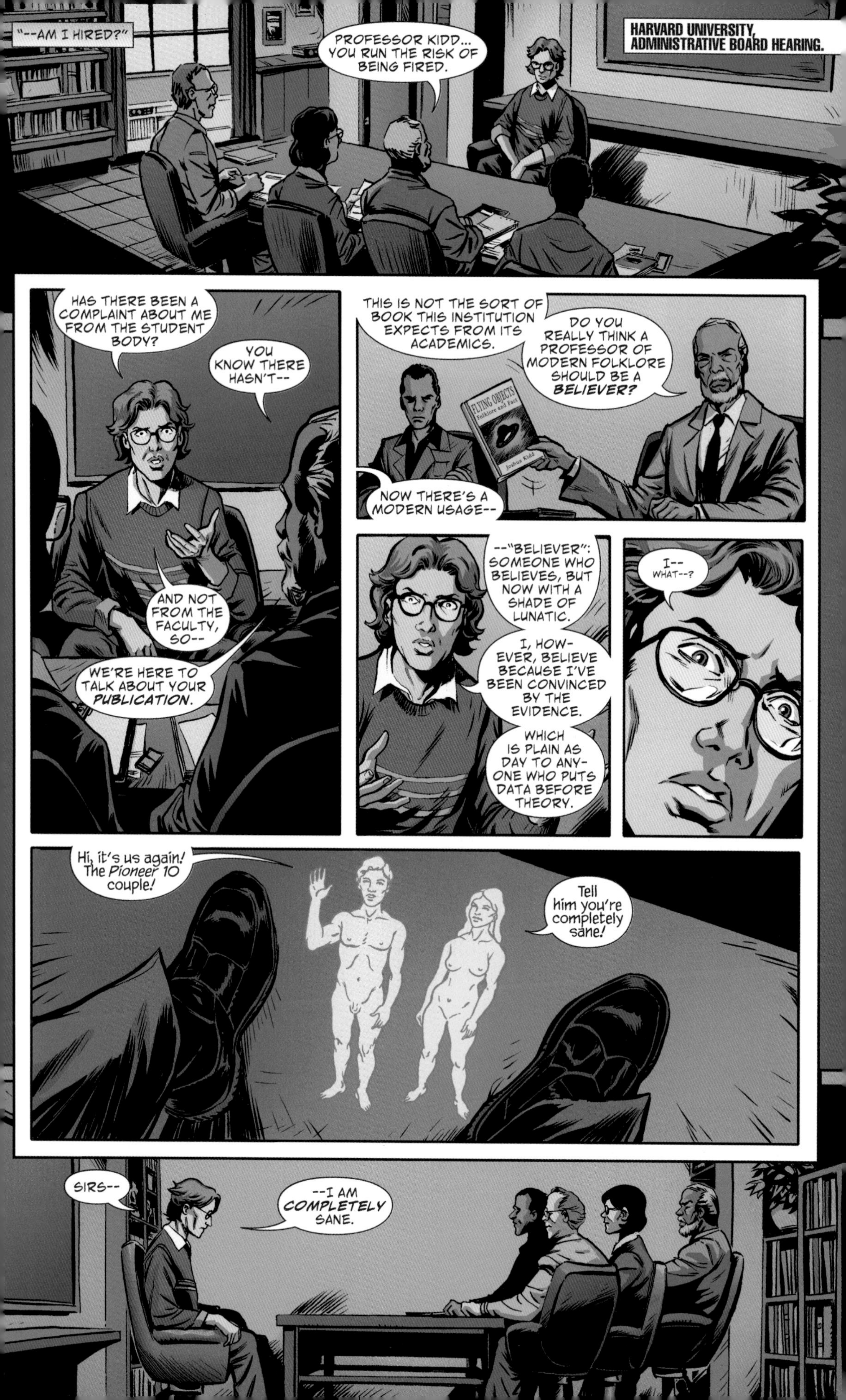
"--AM I HIRED?"
HARVARD UNIVERSITY, ADMINISTRATIVE BOARD HEARING.
PROFESSOR KIDD... YOU RUN THE RISK OF BEING FIRED.
HAS THERE BEEN A COMPLAINT ABOUT ME FROM THE STUDENT BODY?
YOU KNOW THERE HASN'T--
AND NOT FROM THE FACULTY, SO--
WE'RE HERE TO TALK ABOUT YOUR *PUBLICATION*.
THIS IS NOT THE SORT OF BOOK THIS INSTITUTION EXPECTS FROM ITS ACADEMICS.
DO YOU REALLY THINK A PROFESSOR OF MODERN FOLKLORE SHOULD BE A ***BELIEVER?***
FLYING OBJECTS
Folklore and Fact
Joshua Kidd
NOW THERE'S A MODERN USAGE--
--"BELIEVER": SOMEONE WHO BELIEVES, BUT NOW WITH A SHADE OF LUNATIC.
I, HOWEVER, BELIEVE BECAUSE I'VE BEEN CONVINCED BY THE EVIDENCE.
WHICH IS PLAIN AS DAY TO ANYONE WHO PUTS DATA BEFORE THEORY.
I-- WHAT--?
Hi, it's us again! The *Pioneer 10* couple!
Tell him you're completely sane!
SIRS--
--I AM ***COMPLETELY*** SANE.

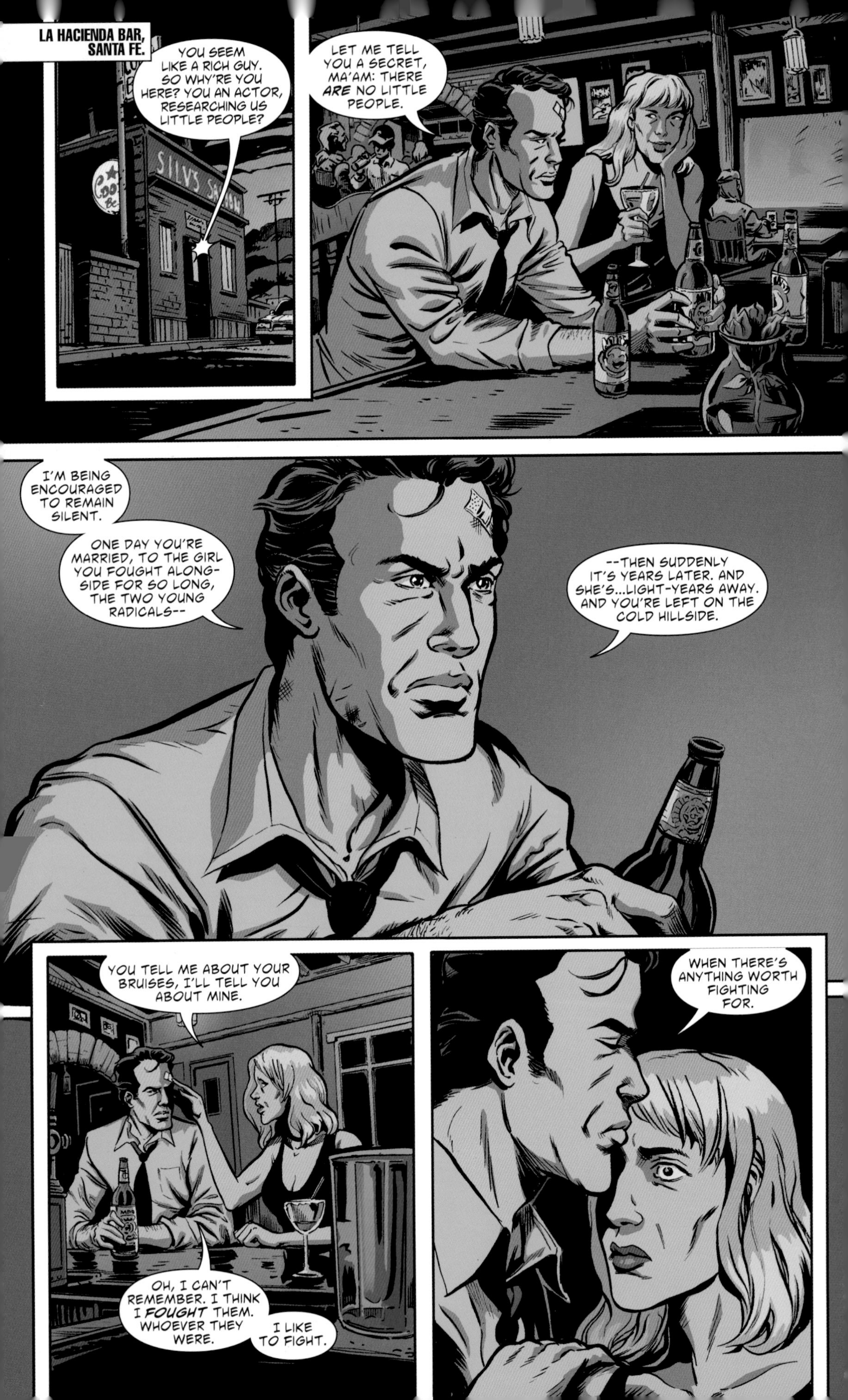
LA HACIENDA BAR, SANTA FE.
YOU SEEM LIKE A RICH GUY. SO WHY'RE YOU HERE? YOU AN ACTOR, RESEARCHING US LITTLE PEOPLE?
LET ME TELL YOU A SECRET, MA'AM: THERE ARE NO LITTLE PEOPLE.
I'M BEING ENCOURAGED TO REMAIN SILENT.
ONE DAY YOU'RE MARRIED, TO THE GIRL YOU FOUGHT ALONG-SIDE FOR SO LONG, THE TWO YOUNG RADICALS--
--THEN SUDDENLY IT'S YEARS LATER. AND SHE'S...LIGHT-YEARS AWAY. AND YOU'RE LEFT ON THE COLD HILLSIDE.
YOU TELL ME ABOUT YOUR BRUISES, I'LL TELL YOU ABOUT MINE.
OH, I CAN'T REMEMBER. I THINK I FOUGHT THEM. WHOEVER THEY WERE.
I LIKE TO FIGHT.
WHEN THERE'S ANYTHING WORTH FIGHTING FOR.

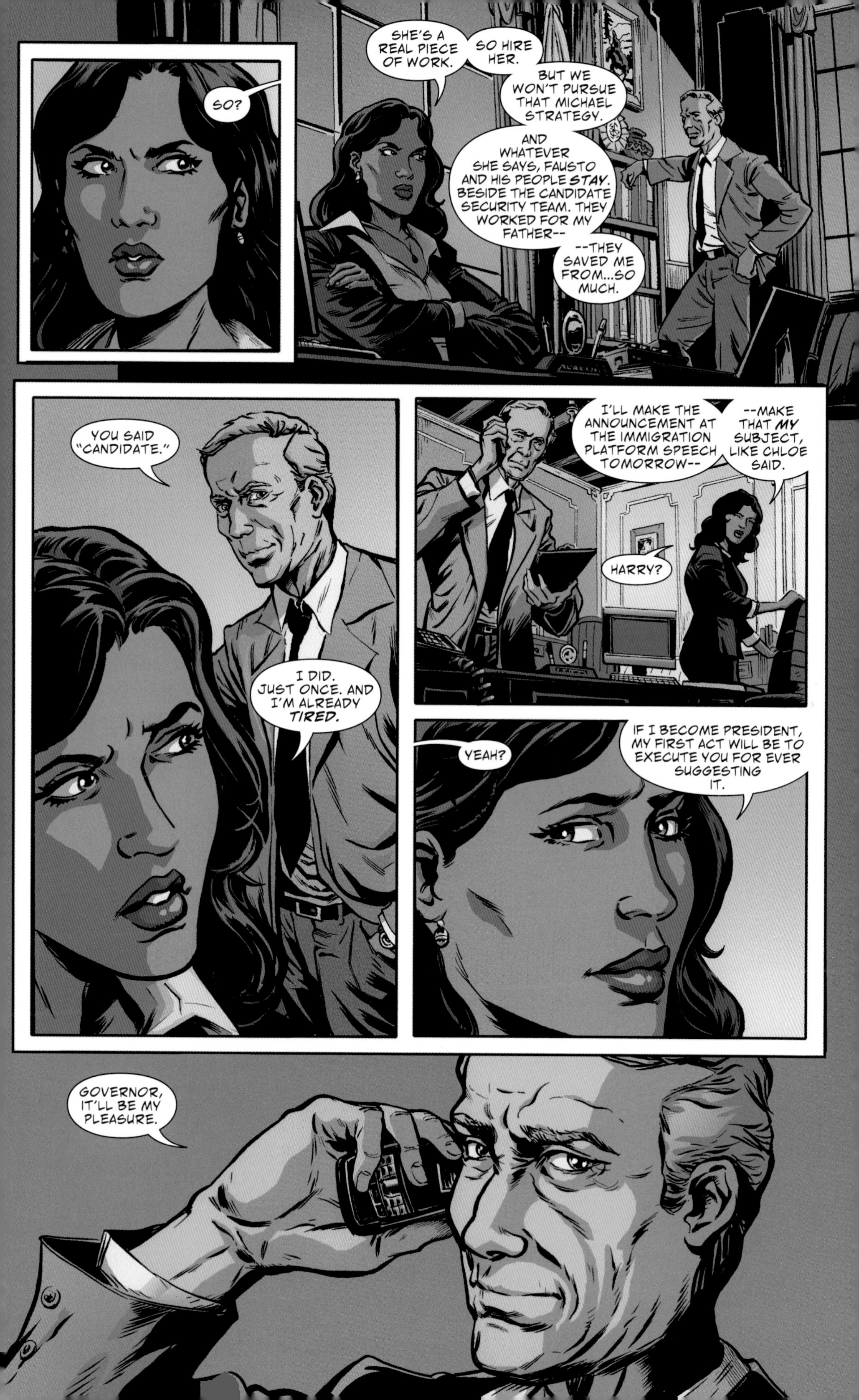
SO?
SHE'S A REAL PIECE OF WORK.
SO HIRE HER.
BUT WE WON'T PURSUE THAT MICHAEL STRATEGY.
AND WHATEVER SHE SAYS, FAUSTO AND HIS PEOPLE STAY. BESIDE THE CANDIDATE SECURITY TEAM. THEY WORKED FOR MY FATHER--
--THEY SAVED ME FROM...SO MUCH.
YOU SAID "CANDIDATE."
I DID. JUST ONCE. AND I'M ALREADY TIRED.
I'LL MAKE THE ANNOUNCEMENT AT THE IMMIGRATION PLATFORM SPEECH TOMORROW--
--MAKE THAT MY SUBJECT, LIKE CHLOE SAID.
HARRY?
YEAH?
IF I BECOME PRESIDENT, MY FIRST ACT WILL BE TO EXECUTE YOU FOR EVER SUGGESTING IT.
GOVERNOR, IT'LL BE MY PLEASURE.

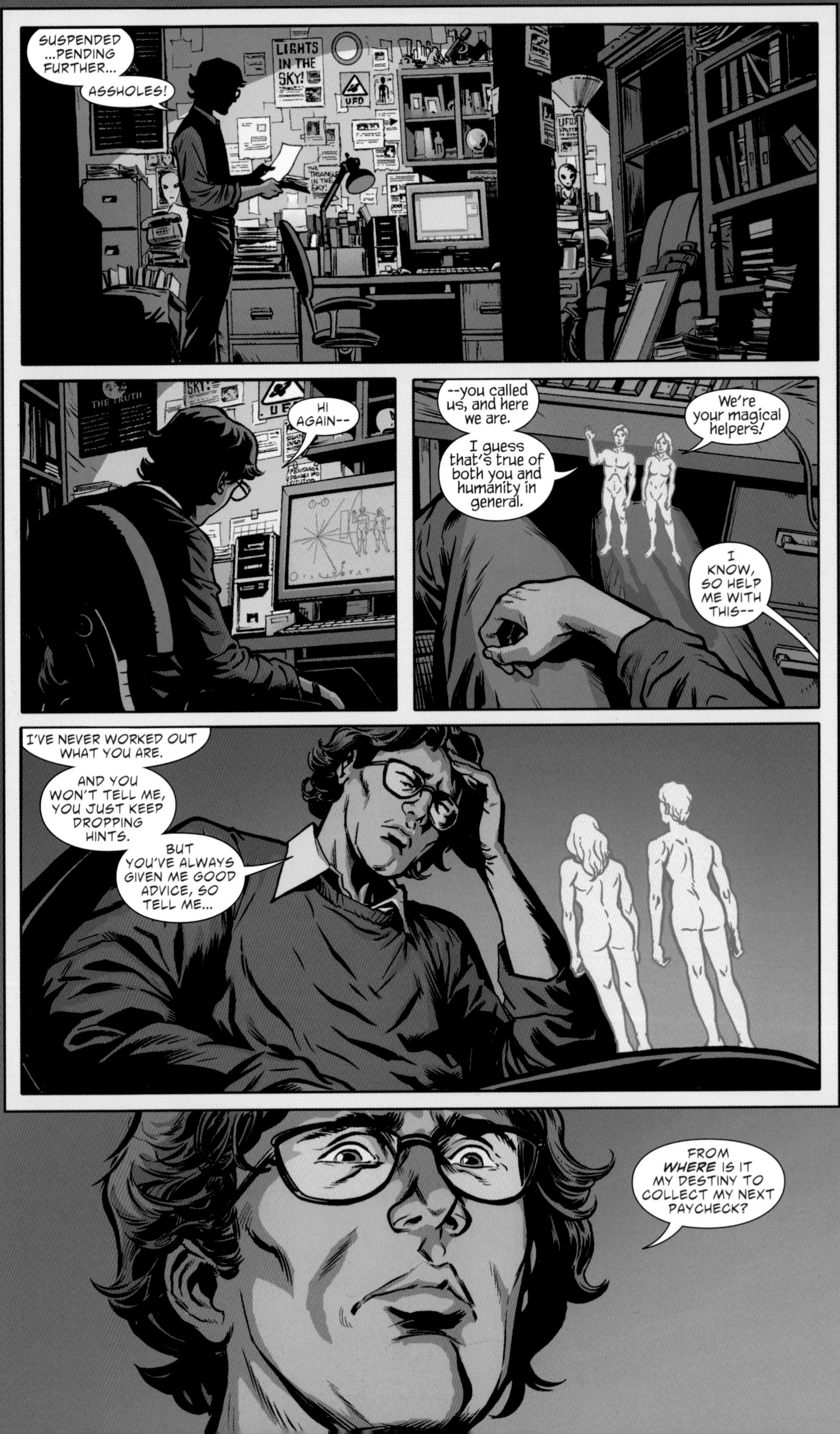
SUSPENDED ...PENDING FURTHER...
ASSHOLES!
LIGHTS IN THE SKY!
UFO
HI AGAIN--
--you called us, and here we are.
I guess that's true of both you and humanity in general.
We're your magical helpers!
I KNOW, SO HELP ME WITH THIS--
I'VE NEVER WORKED OUT WHAT YOU ARE.
AND YOU WON'T TELL ME, YOU JUST KEEP DROPPING HINTS.
BUT YOU'VE ALWAYS GIVEN ME GOOD ADVICE, SO TELL ME...
FROM *WHERE* IS IT MY DESTINY TO COLLECT MY NEXT PAYCHECK?

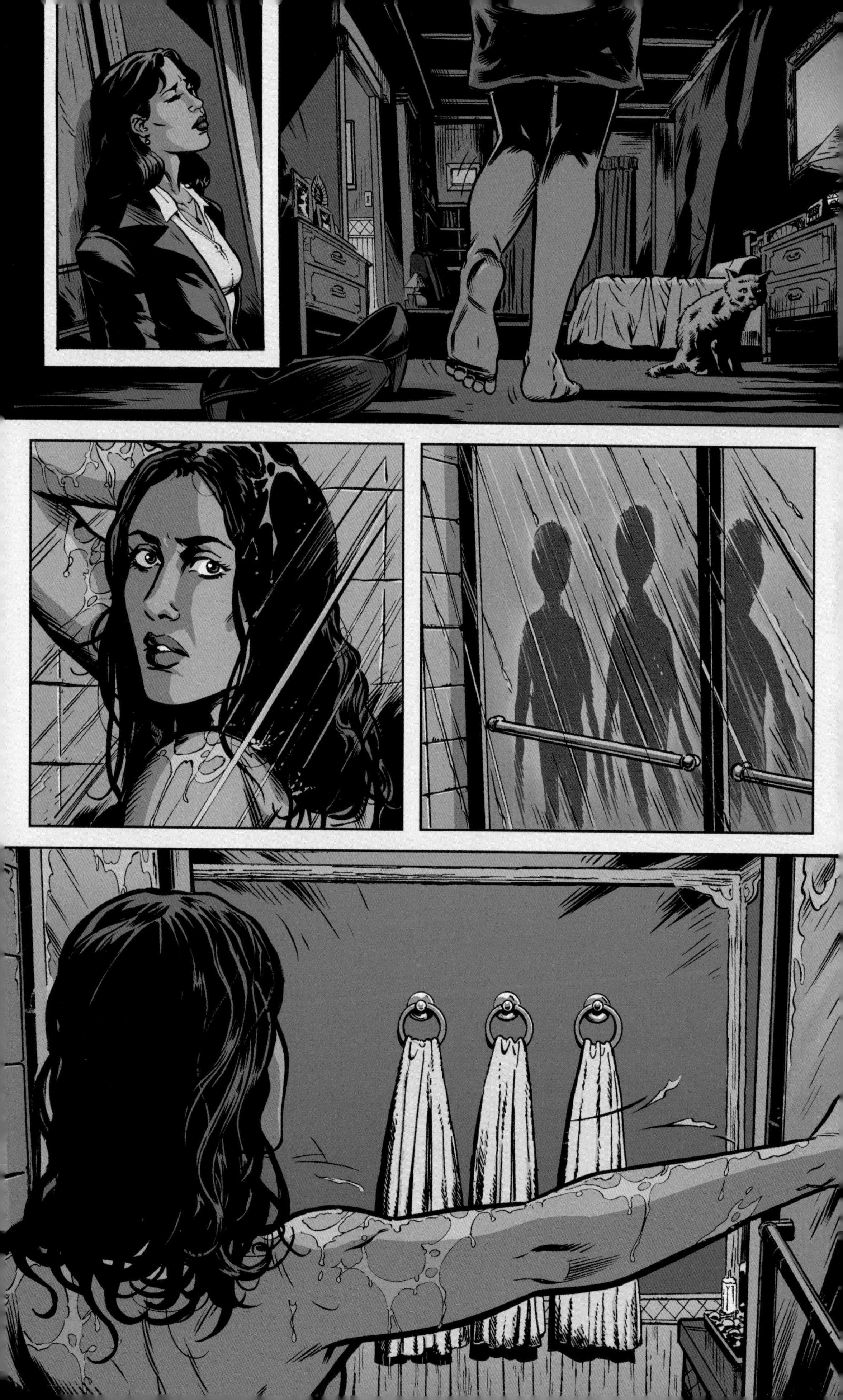

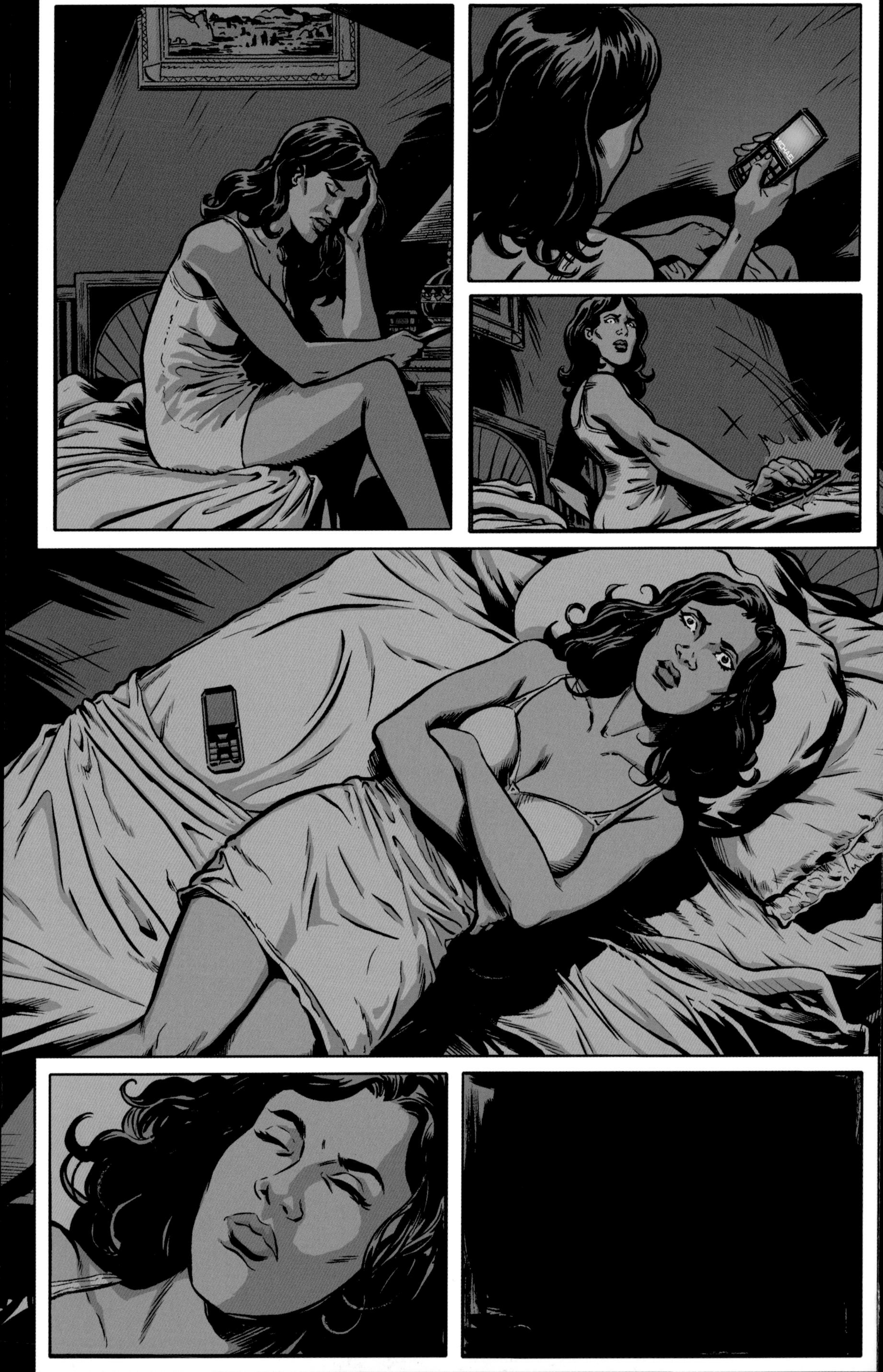
MICHAEL

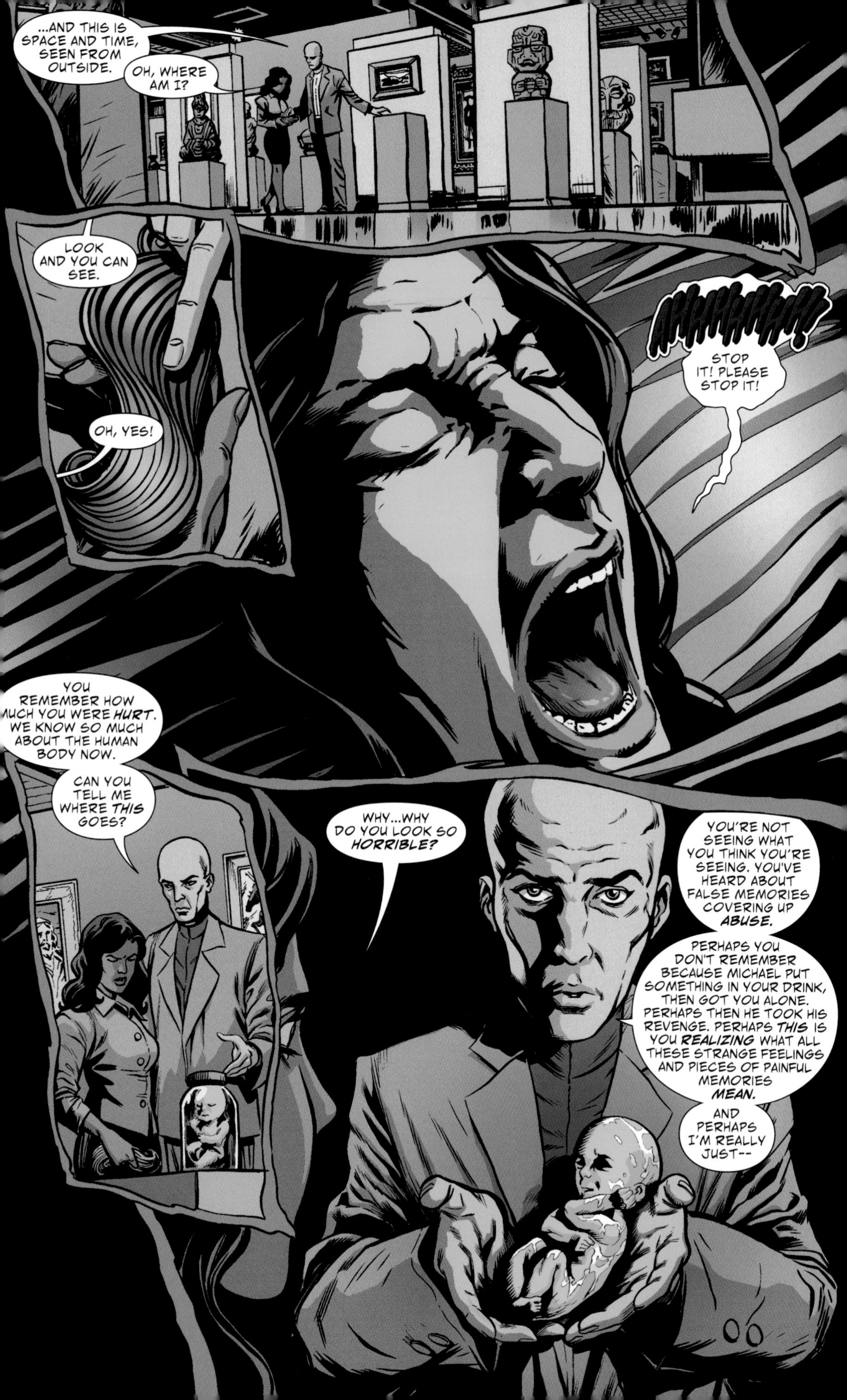
...AND THIS IS SPACE AND TIME, SEEN FROM OUTSIDE.
OH, WHERE AM I?
LOOK AND YOU CAN SEE.
OH, YES!
AHHHHHHHH!
STOP IT! PLEASE STOP IT!
YOU REMEMBER HOW MUCH YOU WERE *HURT*. WE KNOW SO MUCH ABOUT THE HUMAN BODY NOW.
CAN YOU TELL ME WHERE *THIS* GOES?
WHY...WHY DO YOU LOOK SO *HORRIBLE?*
YOU'RE NOT SEEING WHAT YOU THINK YOU'RE SEEING. YOU'VE HEARD ABOUT FALSE MEMORIES COVERING UP *ABUSE.*
PERHAPS YOU DON'T REMEMBER BECAUSE MICHAEL PUT SOMETHING IN YOUR DRINK, THEN GOT YOU ALONE. PERHAPS THEN HE TOOK HIS REVENGE. PERHAPS *THIS* IS YOU *REALIZING* WHAT ALL THESE STRANGE FEELINGS AND PIECES OF PAINFUL MEMORIES *MEAN.*
AND PERHAPS I'M REALLY JUST--

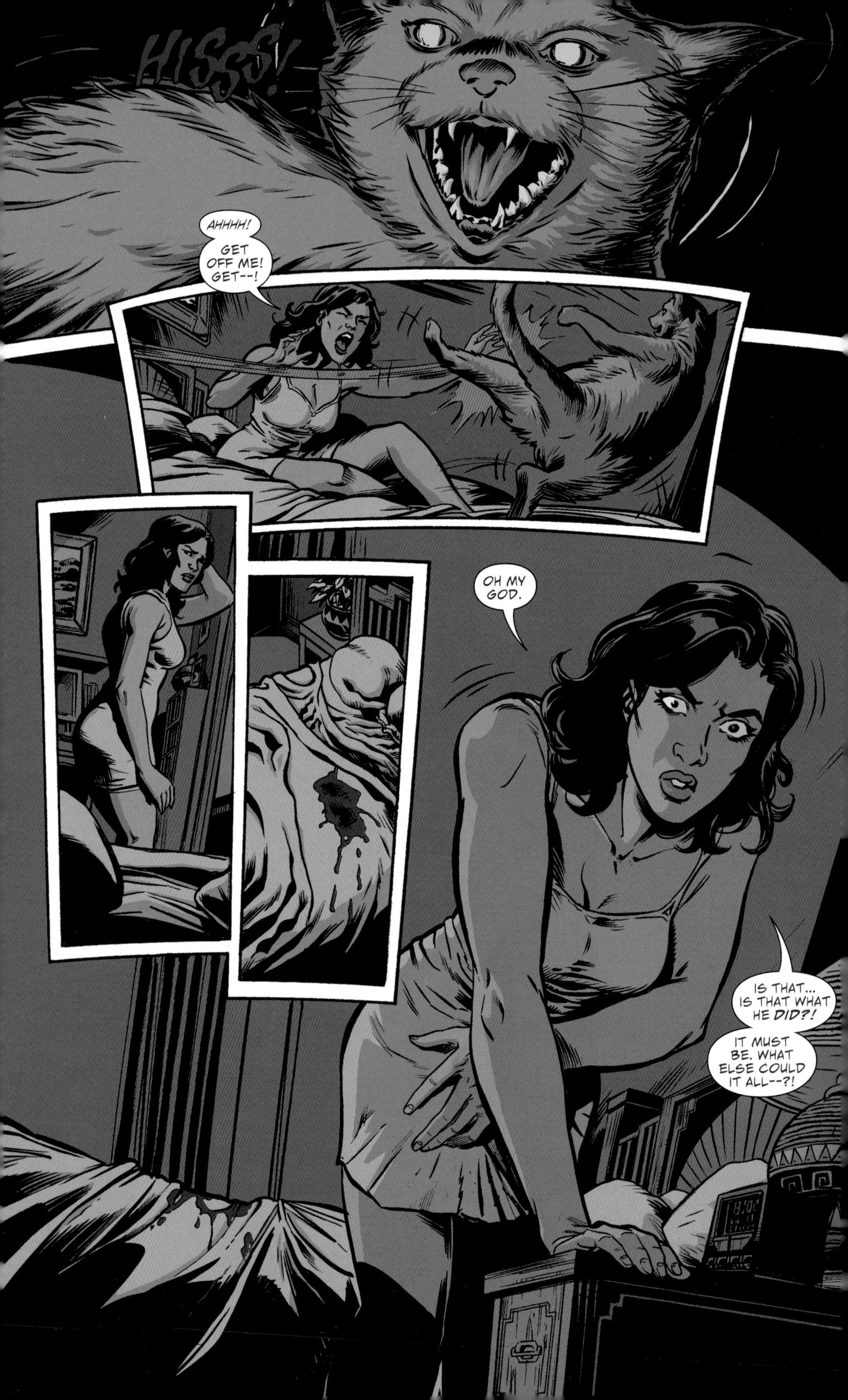
HISSS!
AHHHH!
GET OFF ME! GET--!
OH MY GOD.
IS THAT... IS THAT WHAT HE DID?!
IT MUST BE. WHAT ELSE COULD IT ALL--?!

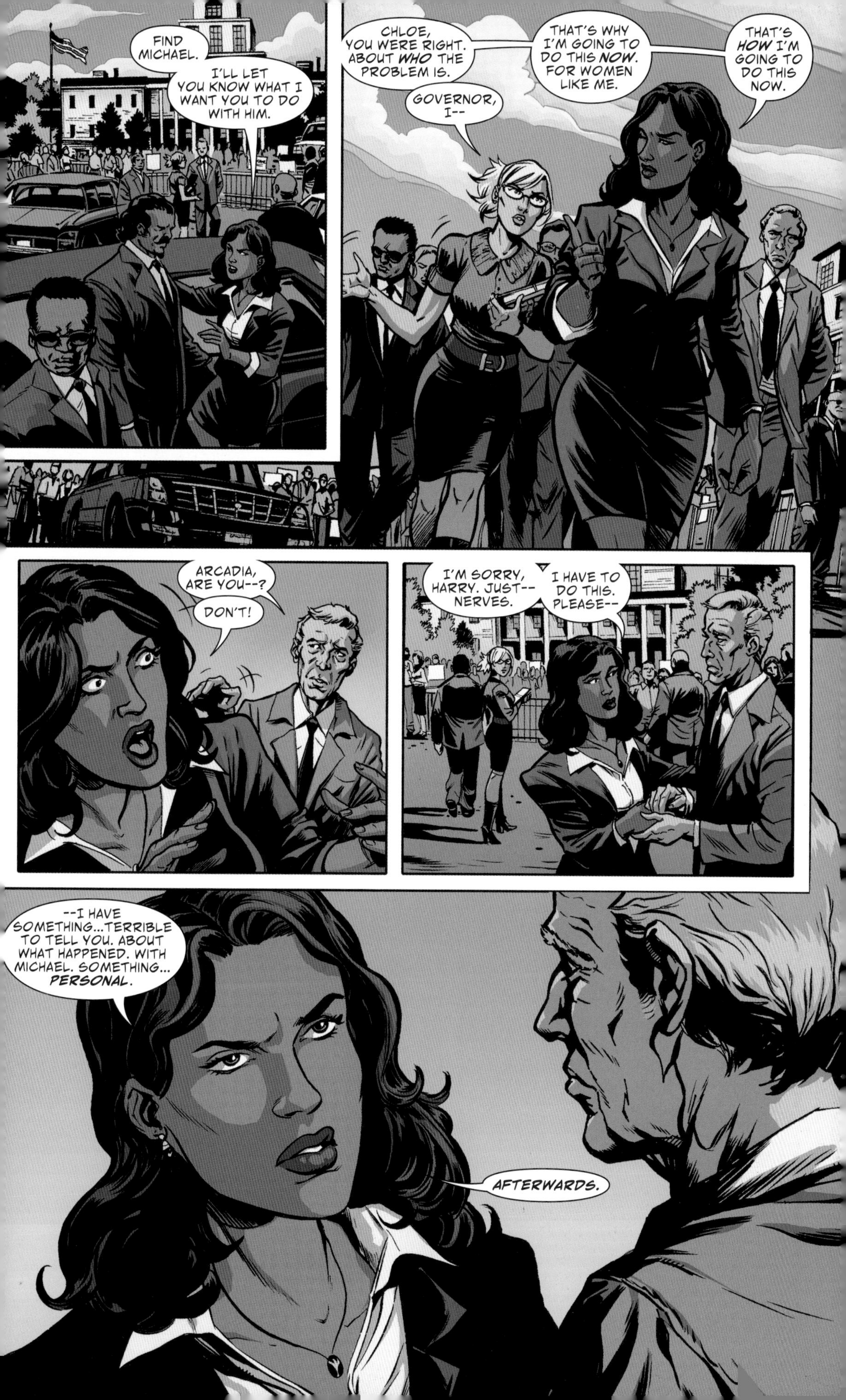

FIND MICHAEL.
I'LL LET YOU KNOW WHAT I WANT YOU TO DO WITH HIM.
CHLOE, YOU WERE RIGHT. ABOUT *WHO* THE PROBLEM IS.
GOVERNOR, I--
THAT'S WHY I'M GOING TO DO THIS *NOW*. FOR WOMEN LIKE ME.
THAT'S *HOW* I'M GOING TO DO THIS NOW.
ARCADIA, ARE YOU--?
DON'T!
I'M SORRY, HARRY. JUST-- NERVES.
I HAVE TO DO THIS. PLEASE--
--I HAVE SOMETHING...TERRIBLE TO TELL YOU. ABOUT WHAT HAPPENED. WITH MICHAEL. SOMETHING... *PERSONAL*.
AFTERWARDS.

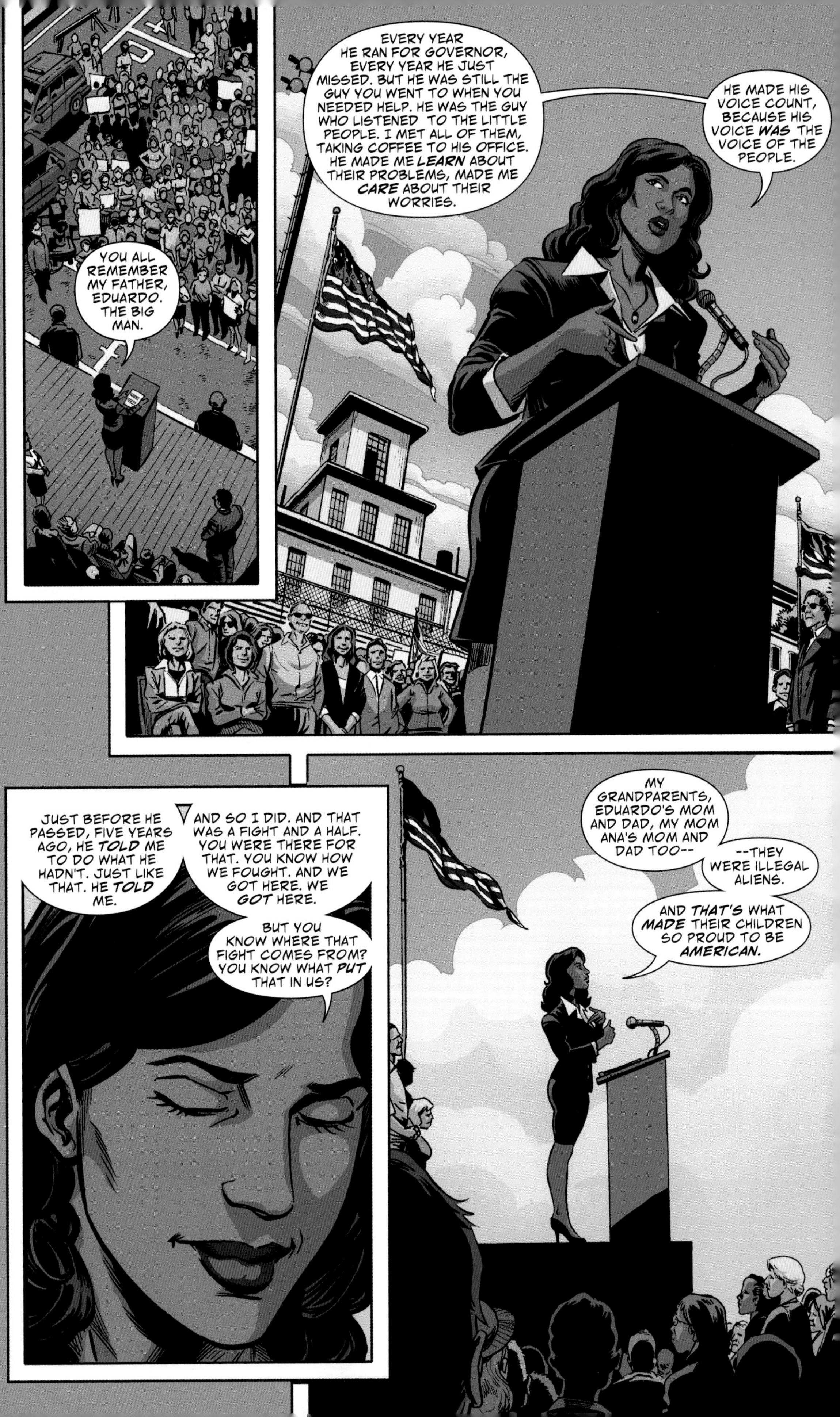
YOU ALL REMEMBER MY FATHER, EDUARDO. THE BIG MAN.
EVERY YEAR HE RAN FOR GOVERNOR, EVERY YEAR HE JUST MISSED. BUT HE WAS STILL THE GUY YOU WENT TO WHEN YOU NEEDED HELP. HE WAS THE GUY WHO LISTENED TO THE LITTLE PEOPLE. I MET ALL OF THEM, TAKING COFFEE TO HIS OFFICE. HE MADE ME LEARN ABOUT THEIR PROBLEMS, MADE ME CARE ABOUT THEIR WORRIES.
HE MADE HIS VOICE COUNT, BECAUSE HIS VOICE WAS THE VOICE OF THE PEOPLE.
JUST BEFORE HE PASSED, FIVE YEARS AGO, HE TOLD ME TO DO WHAT HE HADN'T. JUST LIKE THAT. HE TOLD ME.
AND SO I DID. AND THAT WAS A FIGHT AND A HALF. YOU WERE THERE FOR THAT. YOU KNOW HOW WE FOUGHT. AND WE GOT HERE. WE GOT HERE.
BUT YOU KNOW WHERE THAT FIGHT COMES FROM? YOU KNOW WHAT PUT THAT IN US?
MY GRANDPARENTS, EDUARDO'S MOM AND DAD, MY MOM ANA'S MOM AND DAD TOO--
--THEY WERE ILLEGAL ALIENS.
AND THAT'S WHAT MADE THEIR CHILDREN SO PROUD TO BE AMERICAN.

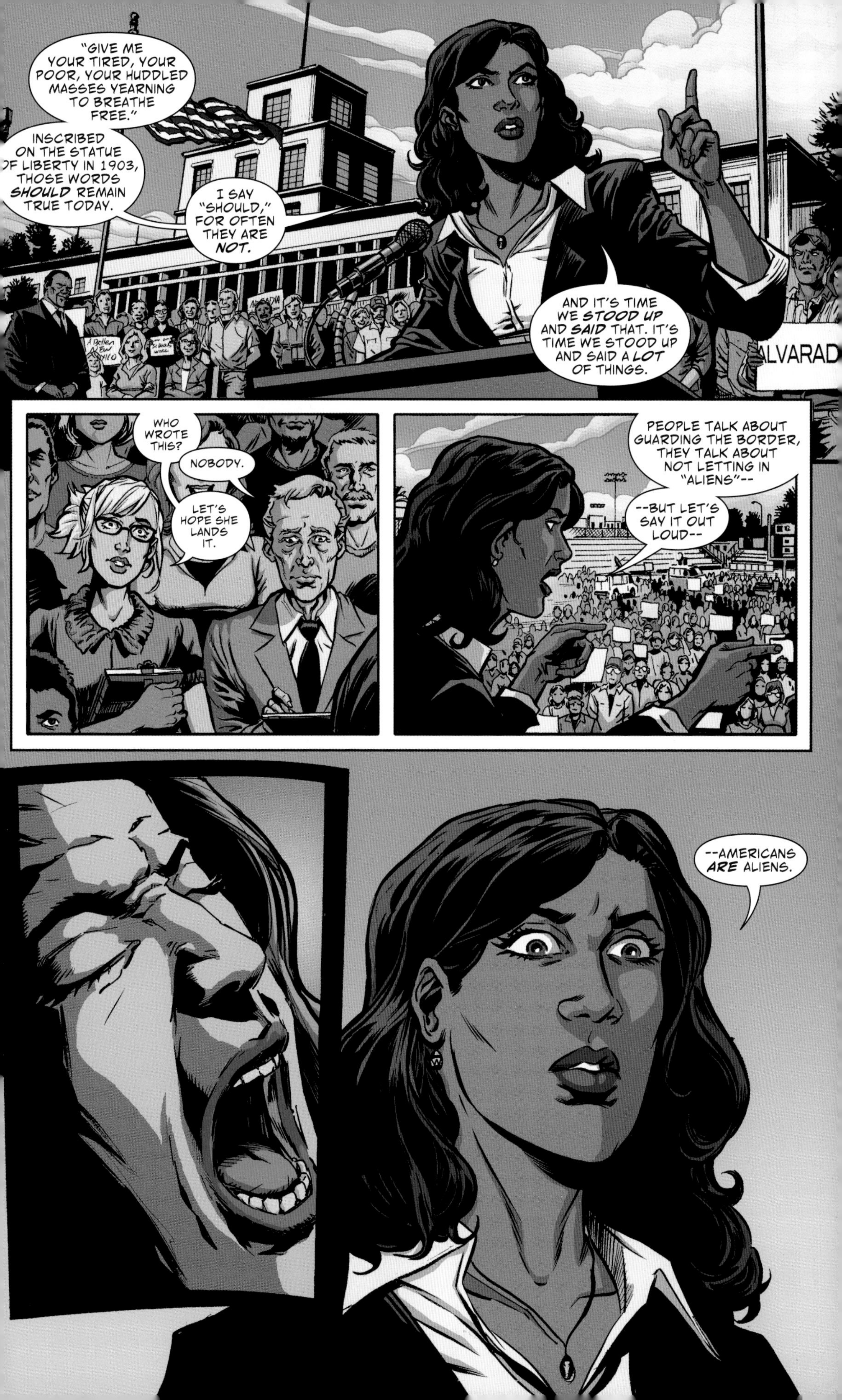

"GIVE ME YOUR TIRED, YOUR POOR, YOUR HUDDLED MASSES YEARNING TO BREATHE FREE."
INSCRIBED ON THE STATUE OF LIBERTY IN 1903, THOSE WORDS SHOULD REMAIN TRUE TODAY.
I SAY "SHOULD," FOR OFTEN THEY ARE NOT.
AND IT'S TIME WE STOOD UP AND SAID THAT. IT'S TIME WE STOOD UP AND SAID A LOT OF THINGS.
ALVARAD
WHO WROTE THIS?
NOBODY.
LET'S HOPE SHE LANDS IT.
PEOPLE TALK ABOUT GUARDING THE BORDER, THEY TALK ABOUT NOT LETTING IN "ALIENS"--
--BUT LET'S SAY IT OUT LOUD--
--AMERICANS ARE ALIENS.

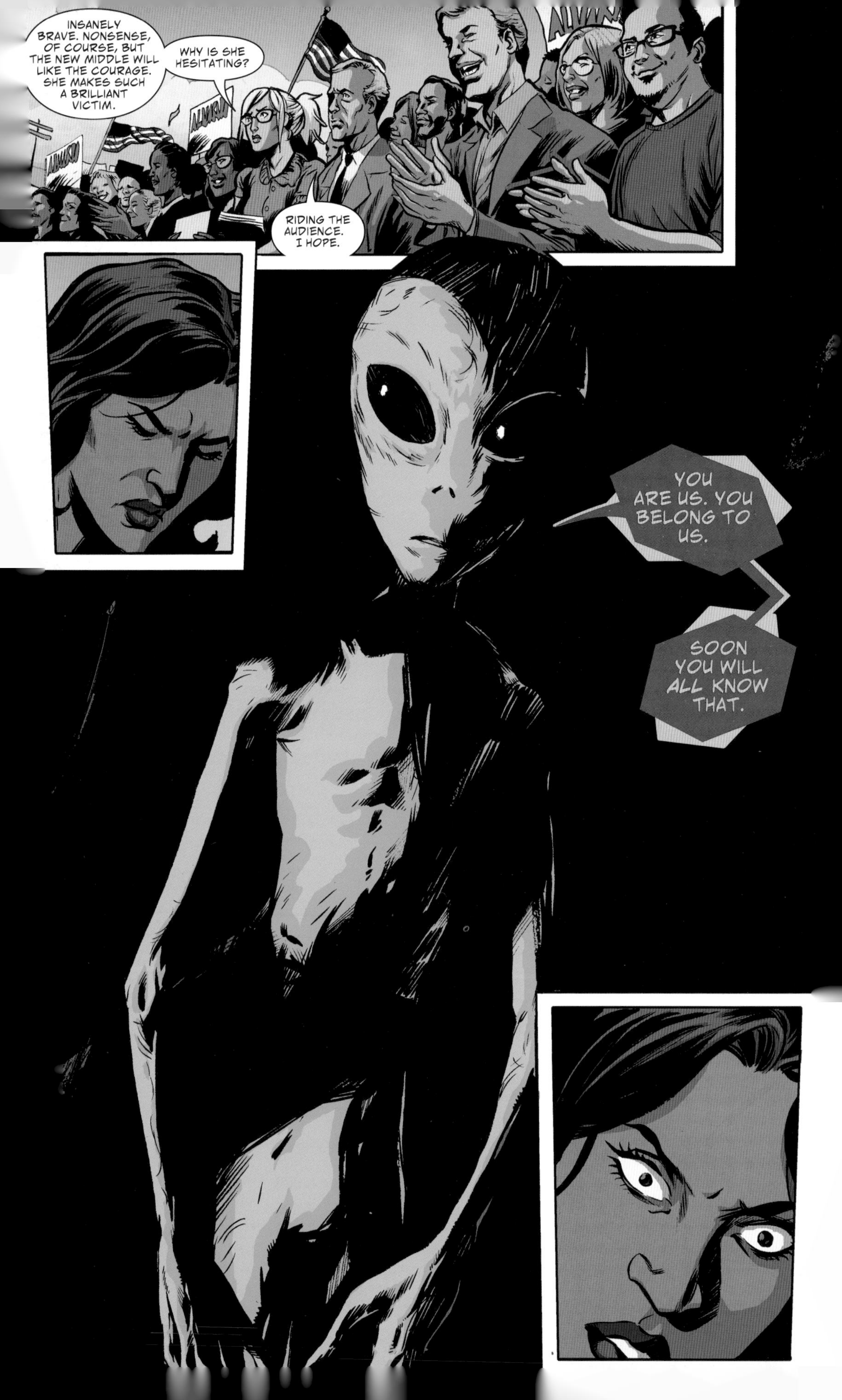

INSANELY BRAVE. NONSENSE, OF COURSE, BUT THE NEW MIDDLE WILL LIKE THE COURAGE. SHE MAKES SUCH A BRILLIANT VICTIM.
WHY IS SHE HESITATING?
RIDING THE AUDIENCE. I HOPE.
YOU ARE US. YOU BELONG TO US.
SOON YOU WILL ALL KNOW THAT.

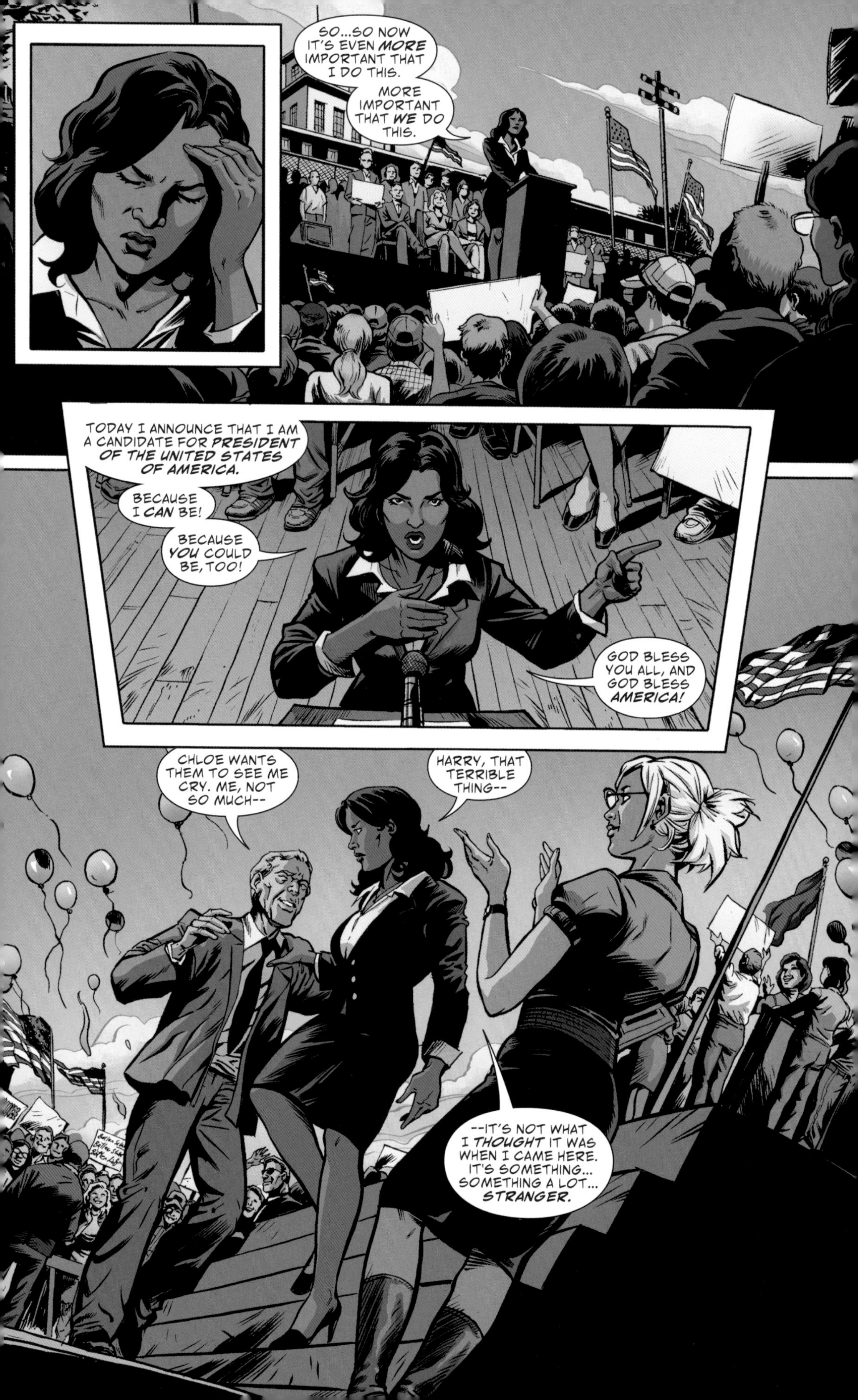
SO...SO NOW IT'S EVEN MORE IMPORTANT THAT I DO THIS.
MORE IMPORTANT THAT WE DO THIS.
TODAY I ANNOUNCE THAT I AM A CANDIDATE FOR PRESIDENT OF THE UNITED STATES OF AMERICA.
BECAUSE I CAN BE!
BECAUSE YOU COULD BE, TOO!
GOD BLESS YOU ALL, AND GOD BLESS AMERICA!
CHLOE WANTS THEM TO SEE ME CRY. ME, NOT SO MUCH--
HARRY, THAT TERRIBLE THING--
--IT'S NOT WHAT I THOUGHT IT WAS WHEN I CAME HERE. IT'S SOMETHING... SOMETHING A LOT... STRANGER.

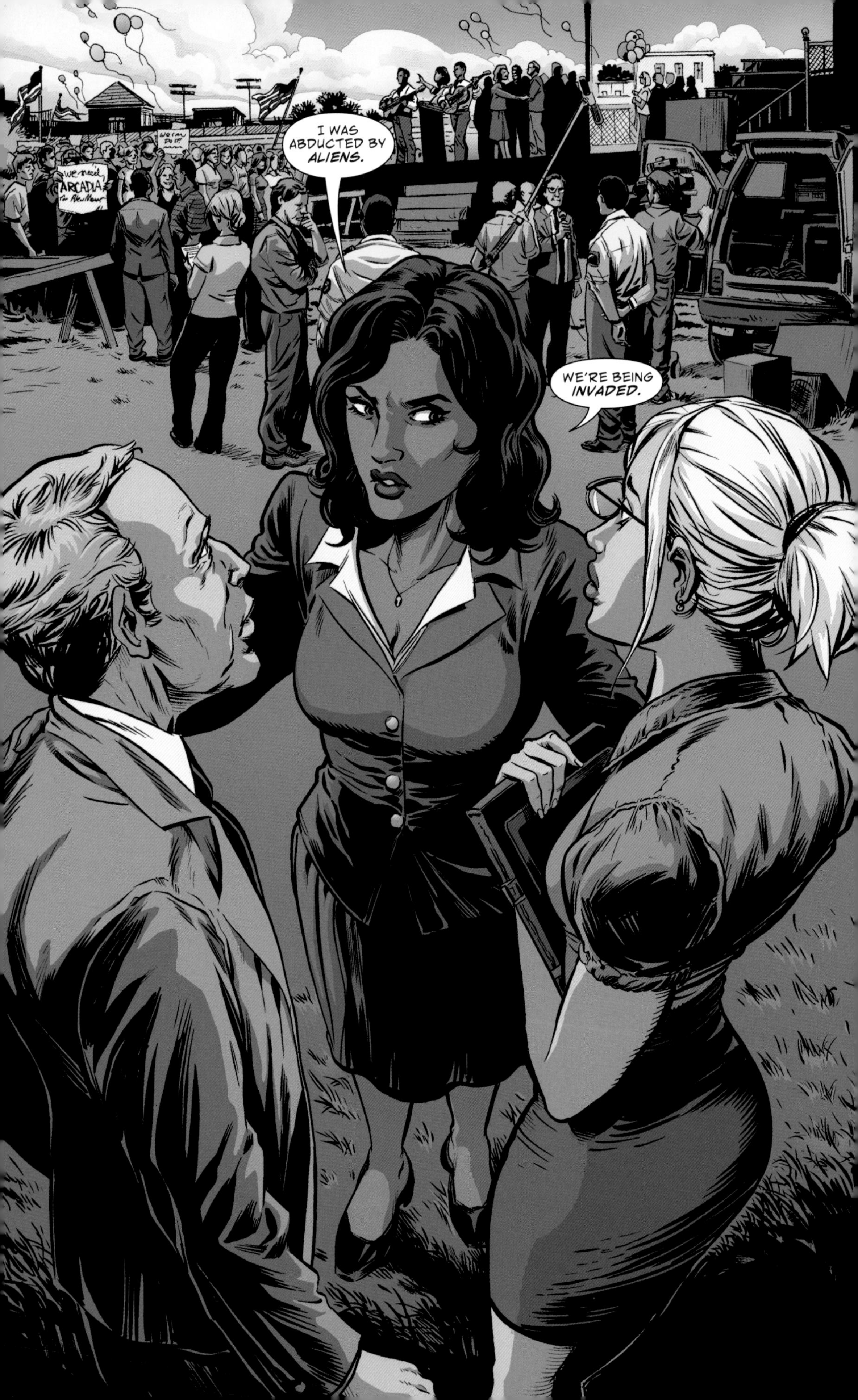
I WAS ABDUCTED BY ALIENS.
WE'RE BEING INVADED.

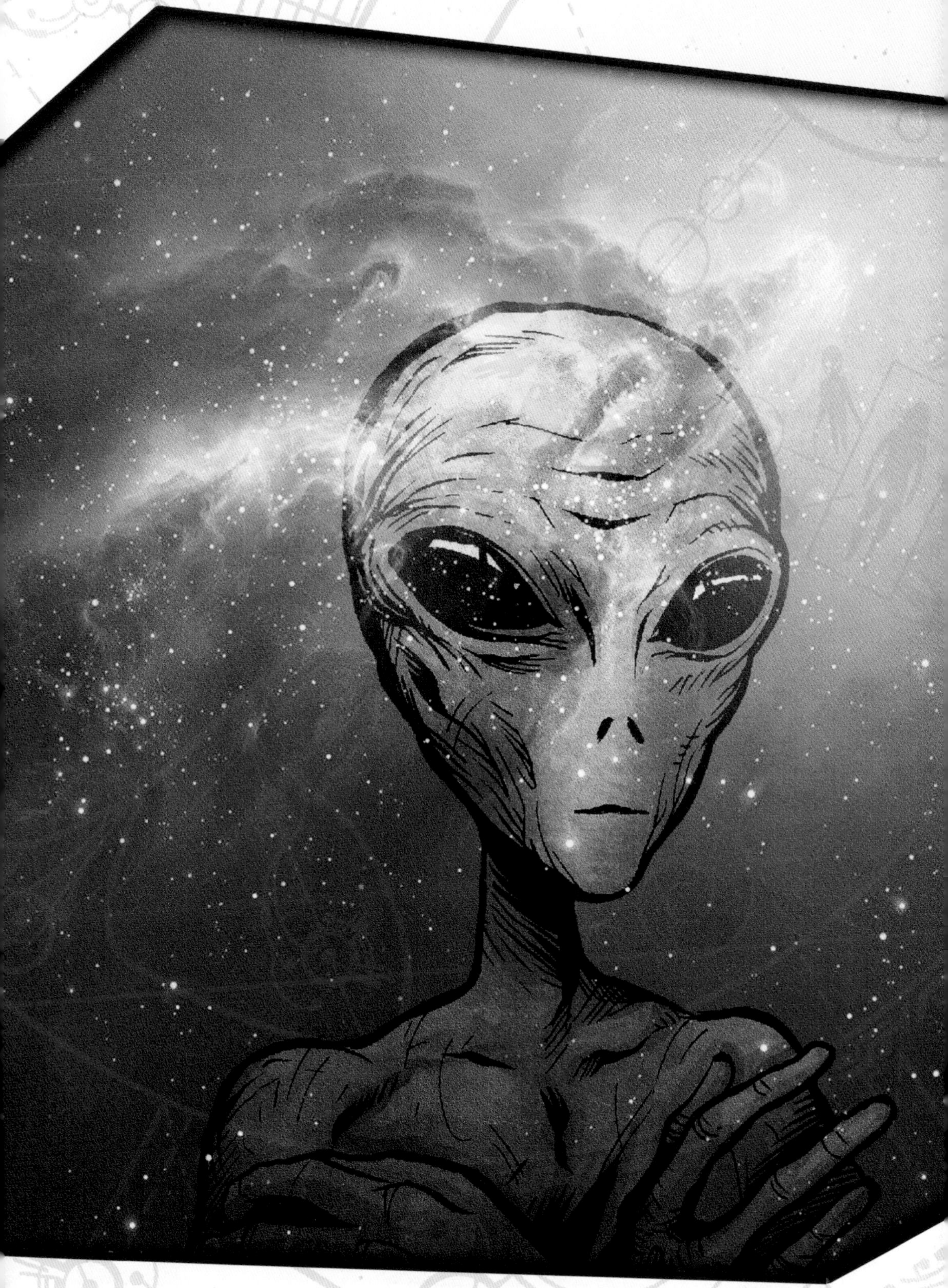

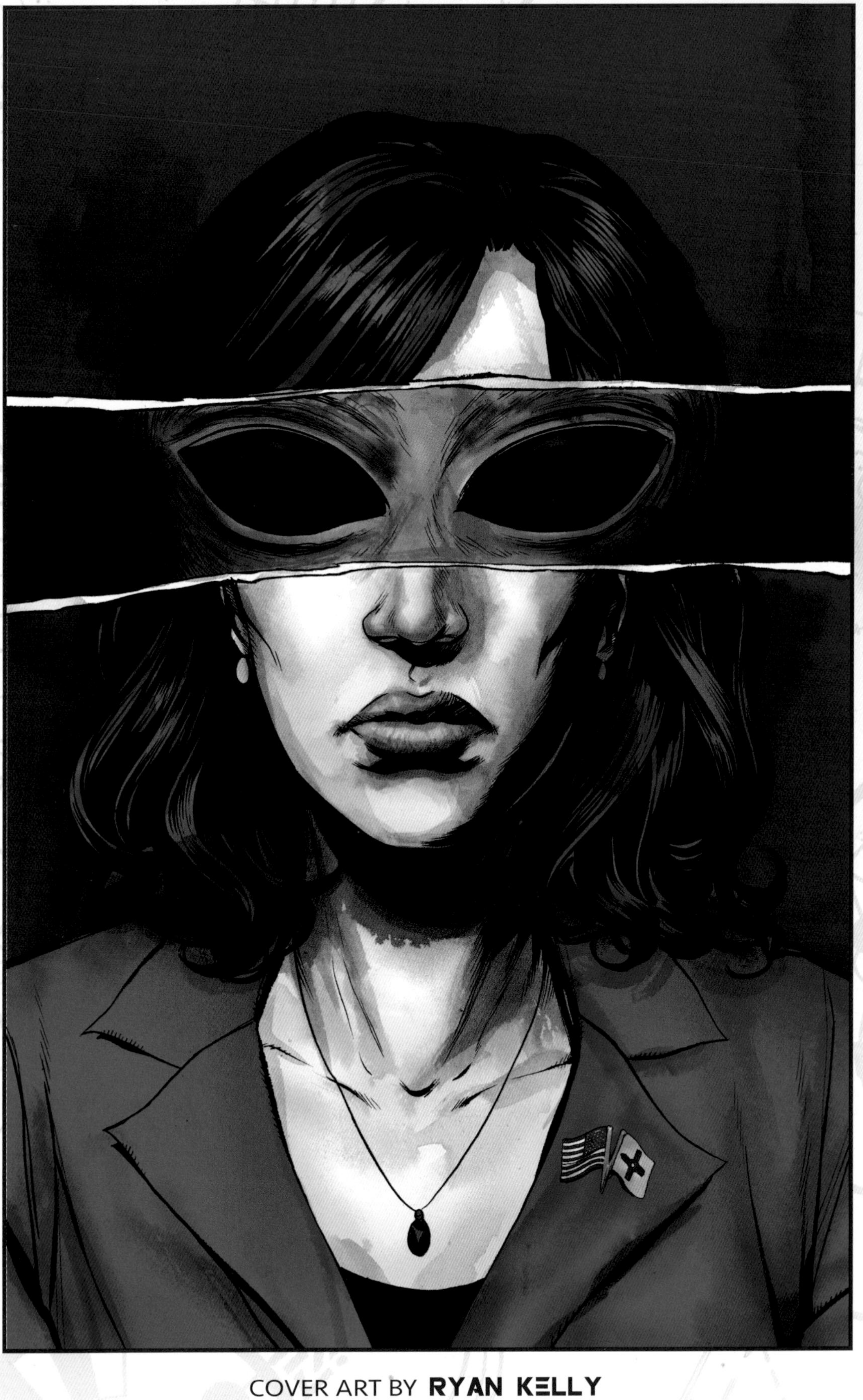

COVER ART BY **RYAN KELLY**

"WHEN I WAS A KID, ME AND MY SISTER USED TO GO PLAY 'UP THE TOP FIELD.'"

"'COS THAT'S WHERE OUR FRIENDS WERE."

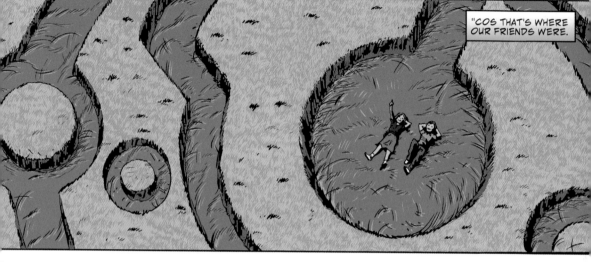

"CAPTAIN LARK AND MISS PERCIVAL AND THEIR GANG."

"I MEAN, OKAY, THEY WEREN'T REAL--"

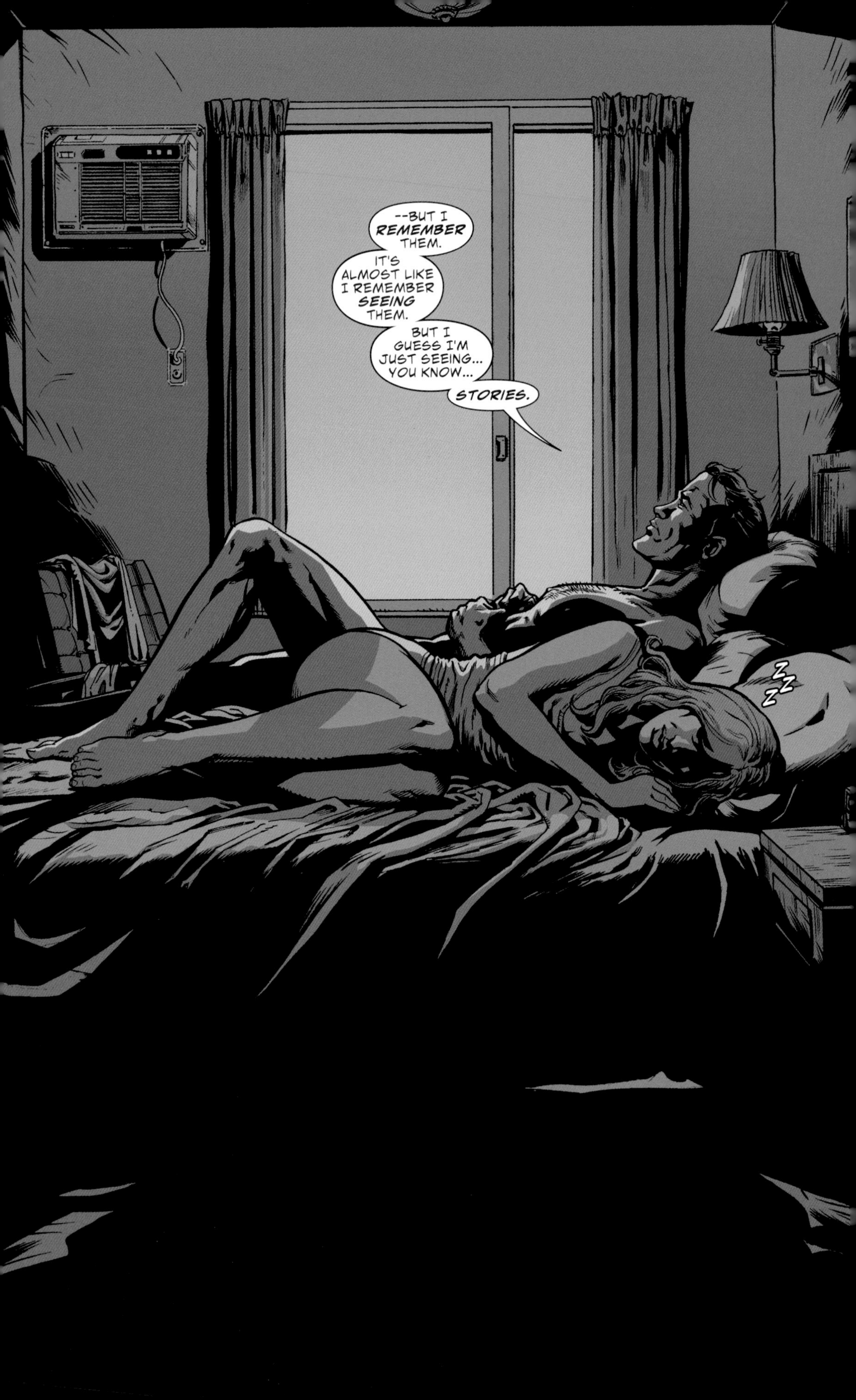
--BUT I **REMEMBER** THEM.
IT'S ALMOST LIKE I REMEMBER **SEEING** THEM.
BUT I GUESS I'M JUST SEEING... YOU KNOW...
STORIES.
Z Z Z

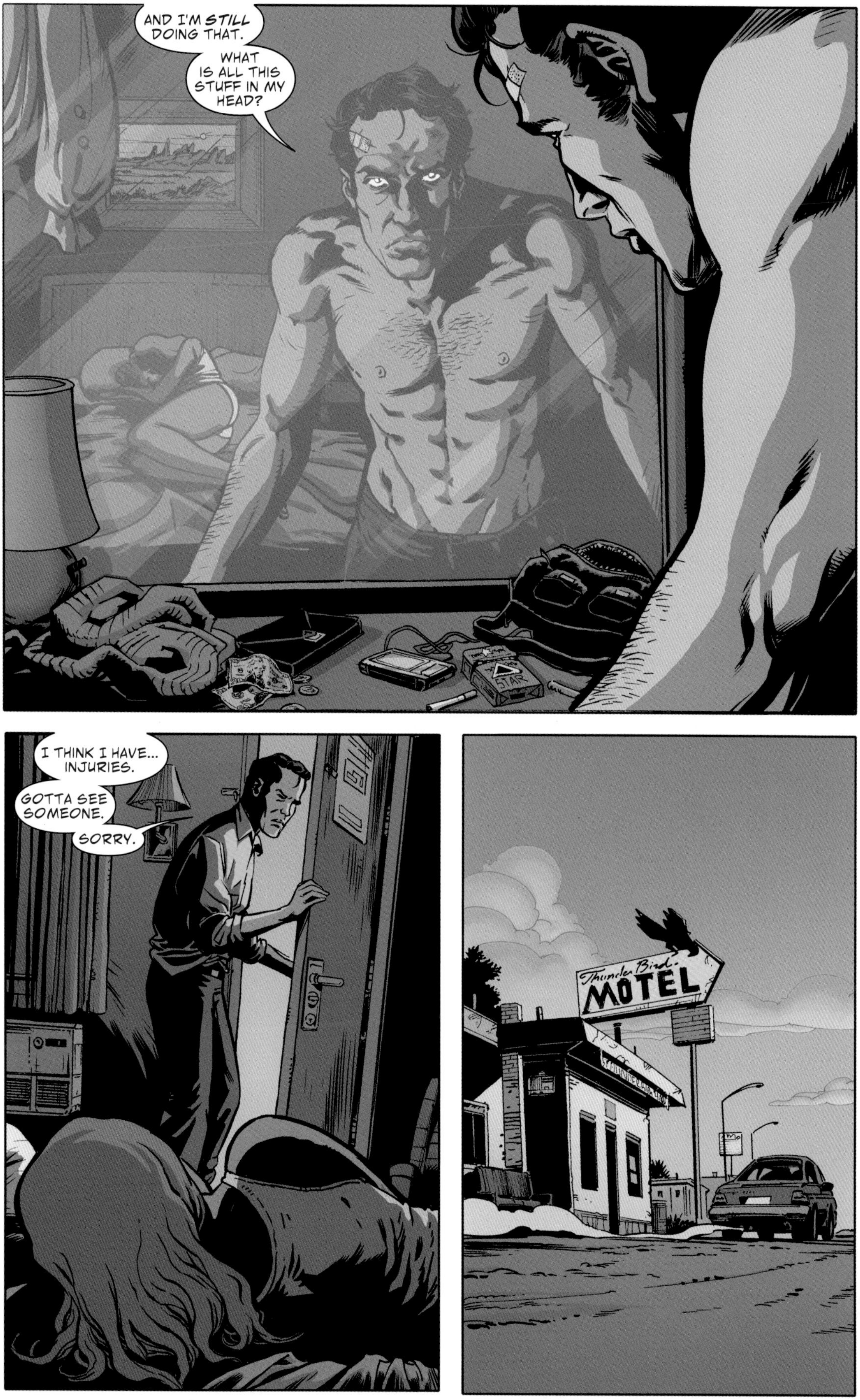
AND I'M STILL DOING THAT.
WHAT IS ALL THIS STUFF IN MY HEAD?
I THINK I HAVE... INJURIES.
GOTTA SEE SOMEONE.
SORRY.
Thunder Bird
MOTEL

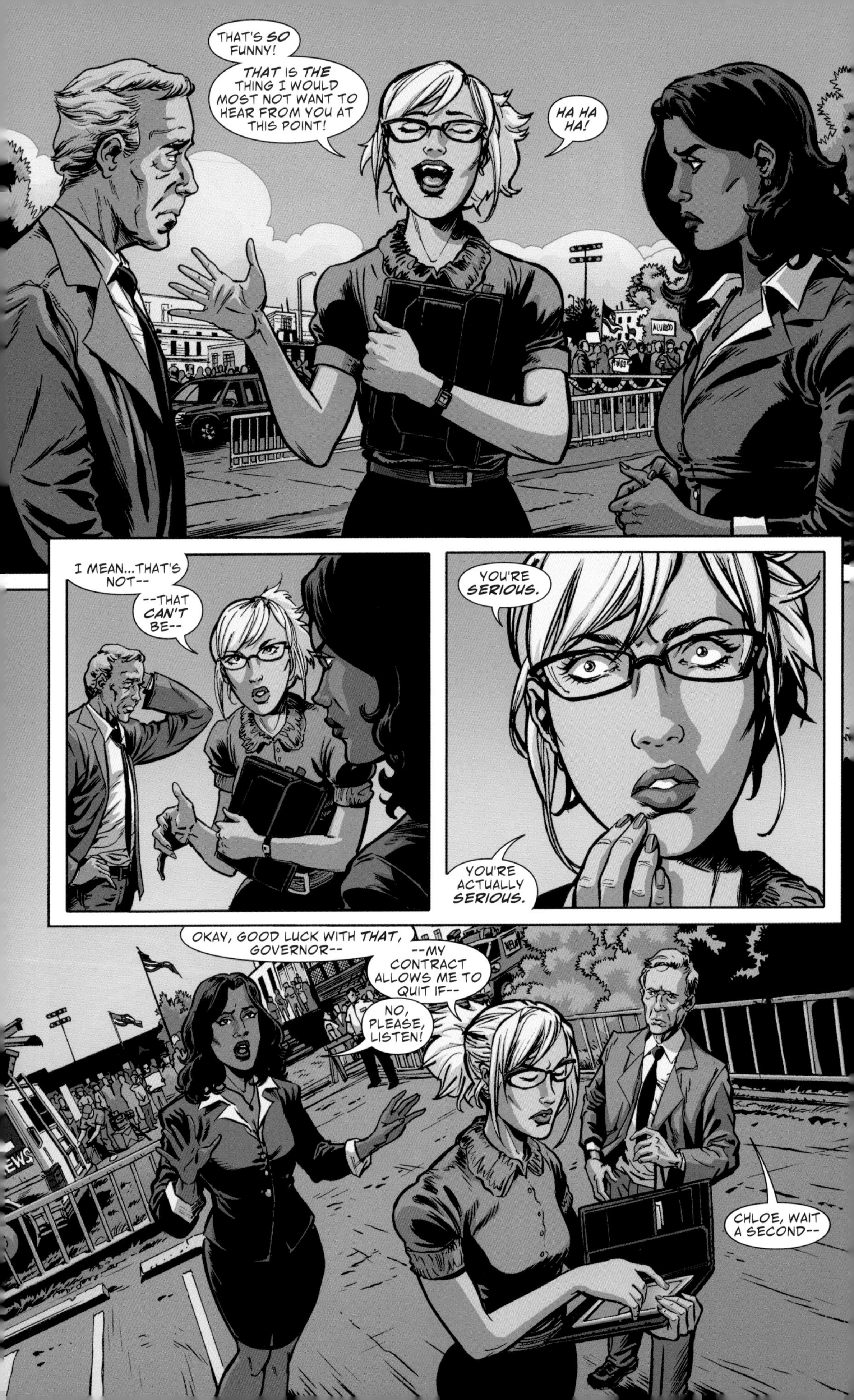
THAT'S SO FUNNY!
THAT IS THE THING I WOULD MOST NOT WANT TO HEAR FROM YOU AT THIS POINT!
HA HA HA!
ALVARADO
I MEAN...THAT'S NOT--
--THAT CAN'T BE--
YOU'RE SERIOUS.
YOU'RE ACTUALLY SERIOUS.
OKAY, GOOD LUCK WITH THAT, GOVERNOR--
--MY CONTRACT ALLOWS ME TO QUIT IF--
NO, PLEASE, LISTEN!
CHLOE, WAIT A SECOND--
NEWS

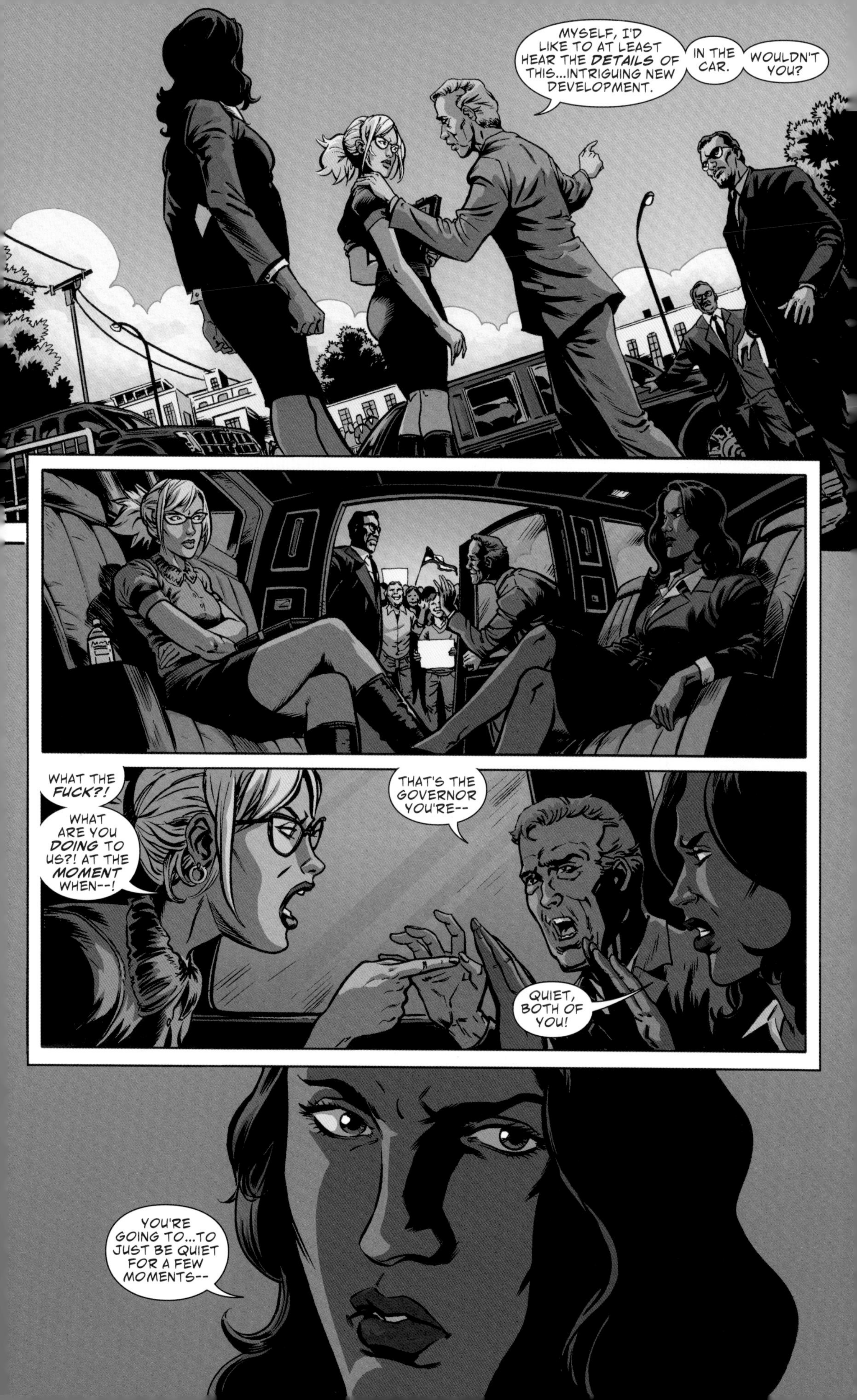
MYSELF, I'D LIKE TO AT LEAST HEAR THE DETAILS OF THIS...INTRIGUING NEW DEVELOPMENT.
IN THE CAR.
WOULDN'T YOU?
WHAT THE FUCK?!
WHAT ARE YOU DOING TO US?! AT THE MOMENT WHEN--!
THAT'S THE GOVERNOR YOU'RE--
QUIET, BOTH OF YOU!
YOU'RE GOING TO...TO JUST BE QUIET FOR A FEW MOMENTS--

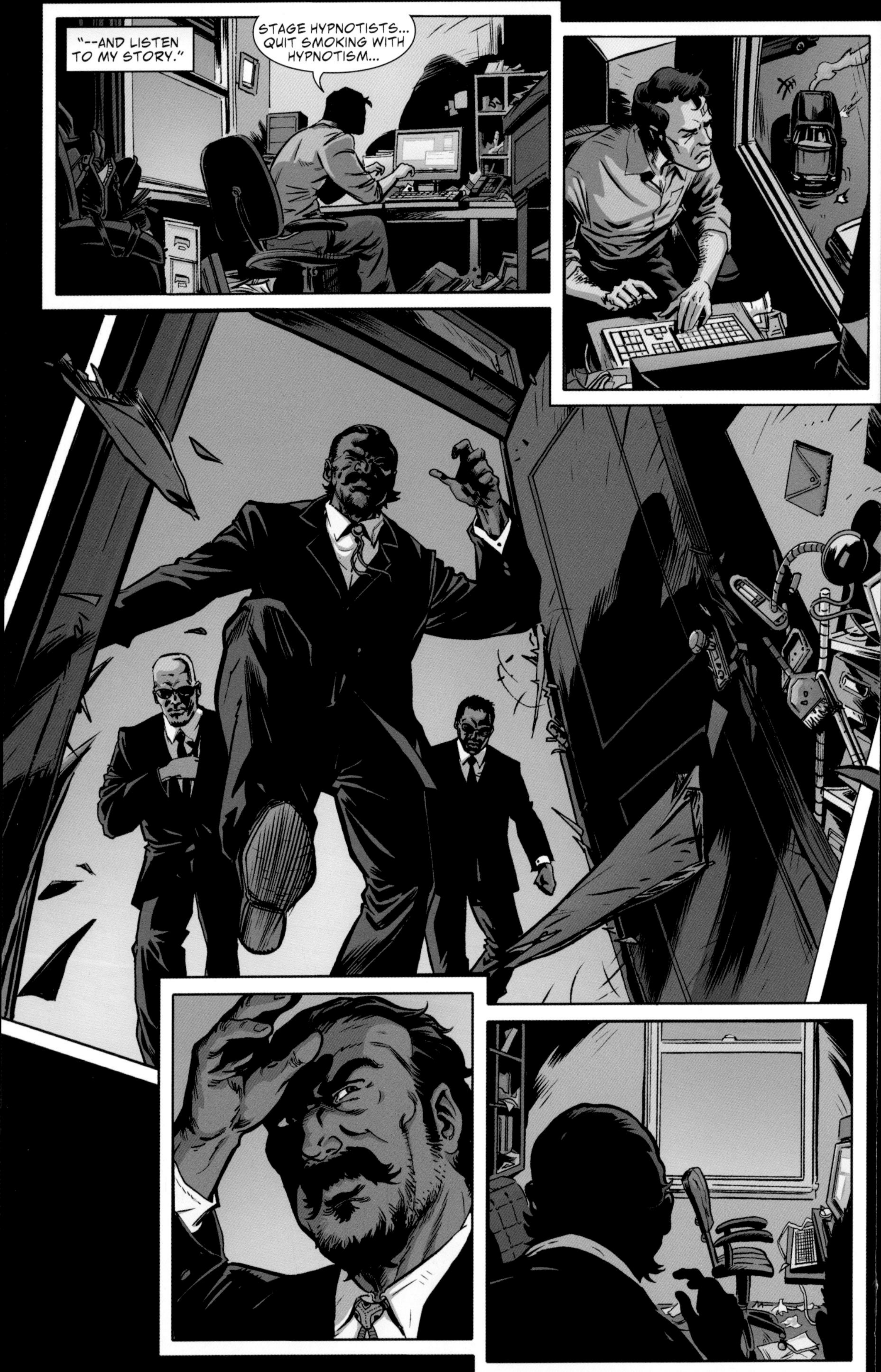
"--AND LISTEN TO MY STORY."
STAGE HYPNOTISTS... QUIT SMOKING WITH HYPNOTISM...

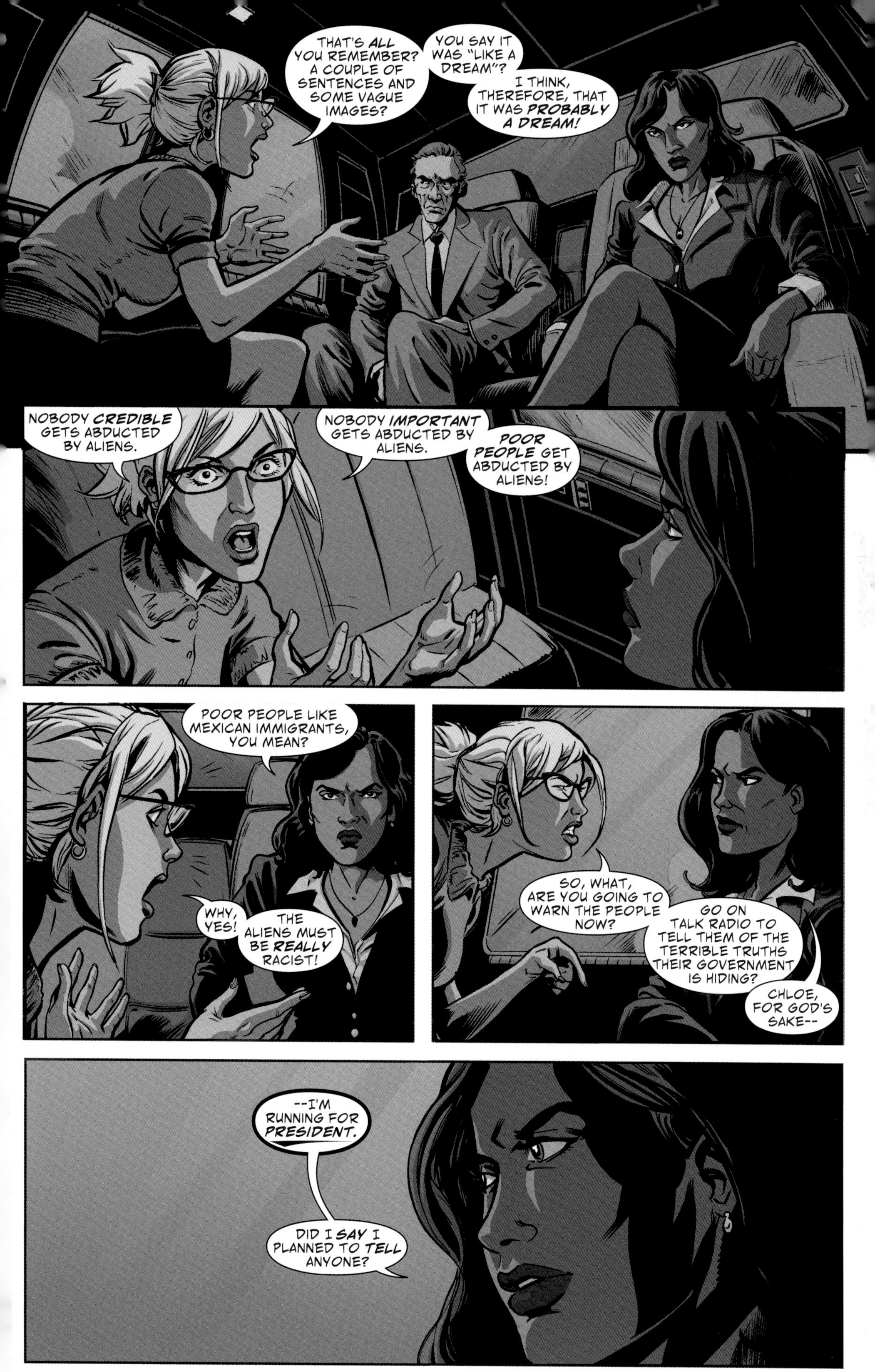

THAT'S ALL YOU REMEMBER? A COUPLE OF SENTENCES AND SOME VAGUE IMAGES?
YOU SAY IT WAS "LIKE A DREAM"?
I THINK, THEREFORE, THAT IT WAS PROBABLY A DREAM!
NOBODY CREDIBLE GETS ABDUCTED BY ALIENS.
NOBODY IMPORTANT GETS ABDUCTED BY ALIENS.
POOR PEOPLE GET ABDUCTED BY ALIENS!
POOR PEOPLE LIKE MEXICAN IMMIGRANTS, YOU MEAN?
WHY, YES!
THE ALIENS MUST BE REALLY RACIST!
SO, WHAT, ARE YOU GOING TO WARN THE PEOPLE NOW?
GO ON TALK RADIO TO TELL THEM OF THE TERRIBLE TRUTHS THEIR GOVERNMENT IS HIDING?
CHLOE, FOR GOD'S SAKE--
--I'M RUNNING FOR PRESIDENT.
DID I SAY I PLANNED TO TELL ANYONE?

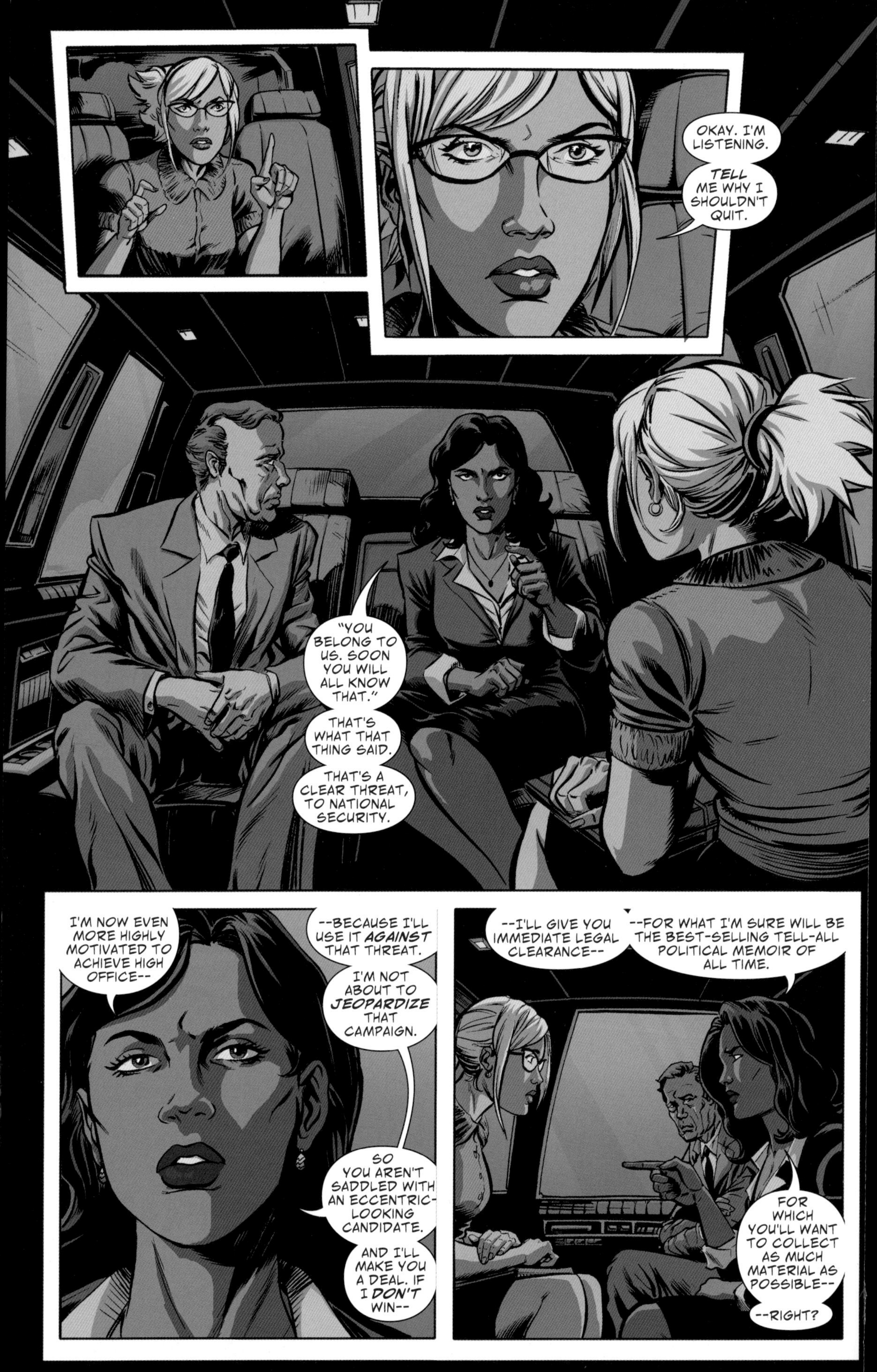
OKAY. I'M LISTENING.
TELL ME WHY I SHOULDN'T QUIT.
"YOU BELONG TO US. SOON YOU WILL ALL KNOW THAT."
THAT'S WHAT THAT THING SAID.
THAT'S A CLEAR THREAT, TO NATIONAL SECURITY.
I'M NOW EVEN MORE HIGHLY MOTIVATED TO ACHIEVE HIGH OFFICE--
--BECAUSE I'LL USE IT AGAINST THAT THREAT.
I'M NOT ABOUT TO JEOPARDIZE THAT CAMPAIGN.
SO YOU AREN'T SADDLED WITH AN ECCENTRIC-LOOKING CANDIDATE.
AND I'LL MAKE YOU A DEAL. IF I DON'T WIN--
--I'LL GIVE YOU IMMEDIATE LEGAL CLEARANCE--
--FOR WHAT I'M SURE WILL BE THE BEST-SELLING TELL-ALL POLITICAL MEMOIR OF ALL TIME.
FOR WHICH YOU'LL WANT TO COLLECT AS MUCH MATERIAL AS POSSIBLE--
--RIGHT?

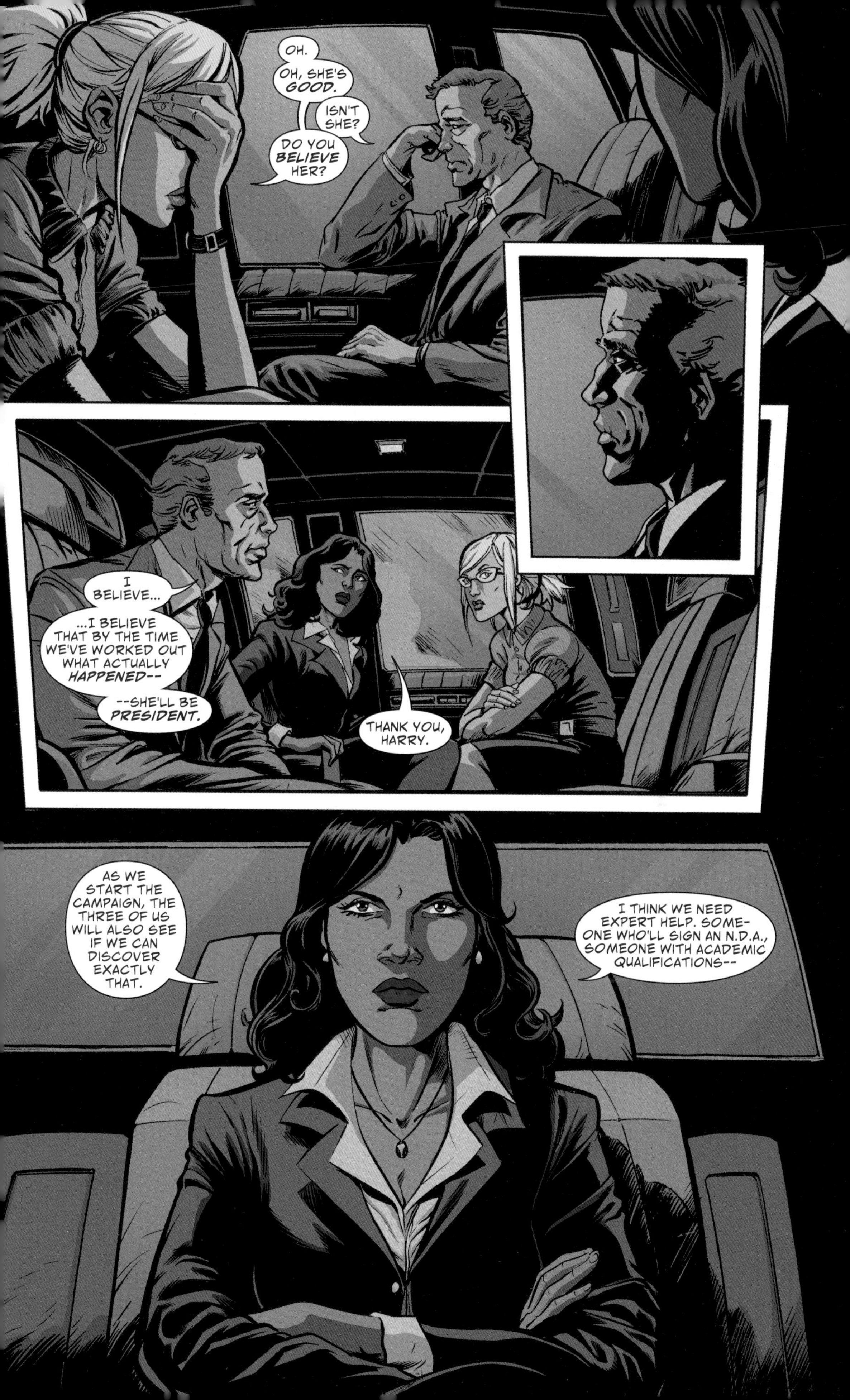
OH.
OH, SHE'S GOOD.
ISN'T SHE?
DO YOU BELIEVE HER?
I BELIEVE...
...I BELIEVE THAT BY THE TIME WE'VE WORKED OUT WHAT ACTUALLY HAPPENED--
--SHE'LL BE PRESIDENT.
THANK YOU, HARRY.
AS WE START THE CAMPAIGN, THE THREE OF US WILL ALSO SEE IF WE CAN DISCOVER EXACTLY THAT.
I THINK WE NEED EXPERT HELP. SOME-ONE WHO'LL SIGN AN N.D.A., SOMEONE WITH ACADEMIC QUALIFICATIONS--

YOU'RE SAYING I'M GOING TO GET A JOB IN *POLITICS*?

Yes--

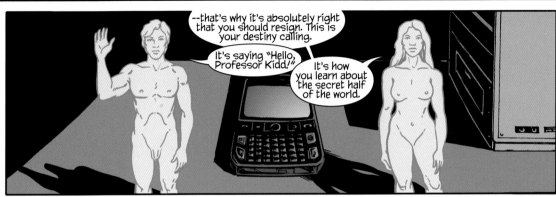

--that's why it's absolutely right that you should resign. This is your destiny calling.

It's saying "Hello, Professor Kidd!"

It's how you learn about the secret half of the world.

THE PRESENT TENSE. LIKE TIME IS A... BOOK TO YOU.

YOU WANT ME TO RESIGN. LET GO MY SECURITY. JUST LIKE THAT.

BECAUSE SOMETHING IMPOSSIBLE *TOLD* ME TO.

THAT'S ME ALL OVER.

Now you answer that.

And greet the representative of your next president.

BZZZ

THAT'S IT IN A NUTSHELL--

--IT WOULD BE A JOB ON STAFF. BUT WE CAN'T TELL YOU MORE UNTIL YOU SIGN THE AGREEMENT.

I'M E-MAILING YOU SALARY DETAILS NOW.

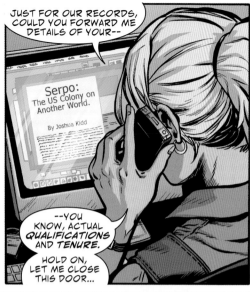

JUST FOR OUR RECORDS, COULD YOU FORWARD ME DETAILS OF YOUR--

Serpo:
The US Colony on Another World.

By Joshua Kidd

--YOU KNOW, ACTUAL *QUALIFICATIONS* AND *TENURE.*

HOLD ON, LET ME CLOSE THIS DOOR...

SERIOUS QUESTION: DO YOU BELIEVE IN UFOS?

OKAY, HOW TO REPHRASE THAT IN ORDER TO GET A--

--COMPREHENSIBLE ANSWER?

DO...*YOU...* BELIEVE...IN... UFOS?

YEAH. RIGHT.

THAT'S WHAT I WAS *AFRAID* OF.

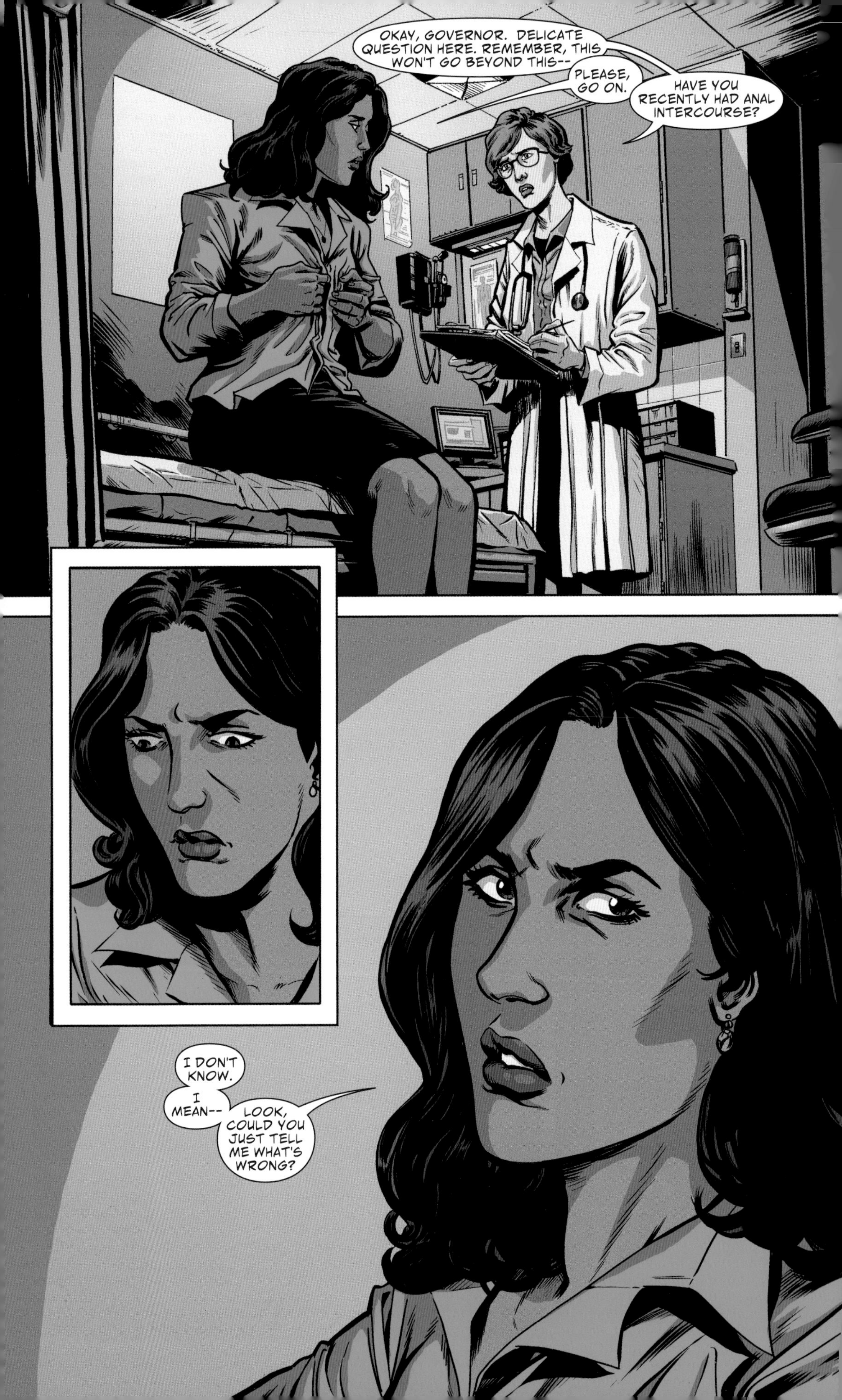
OKAY, GOVERNOR. DELICATE QUESTION HERE. REMEMBER, THIS WON'T GO BEYOND THIS--
PLEASE, GO ON.
HAVE YOU RECENTLY HAD ANAL INTERCOURSE?
I DON'T KNOW.
I MEAN--
LOOK, COULD YOU JUST TELL ME WHAT'S WRONG?

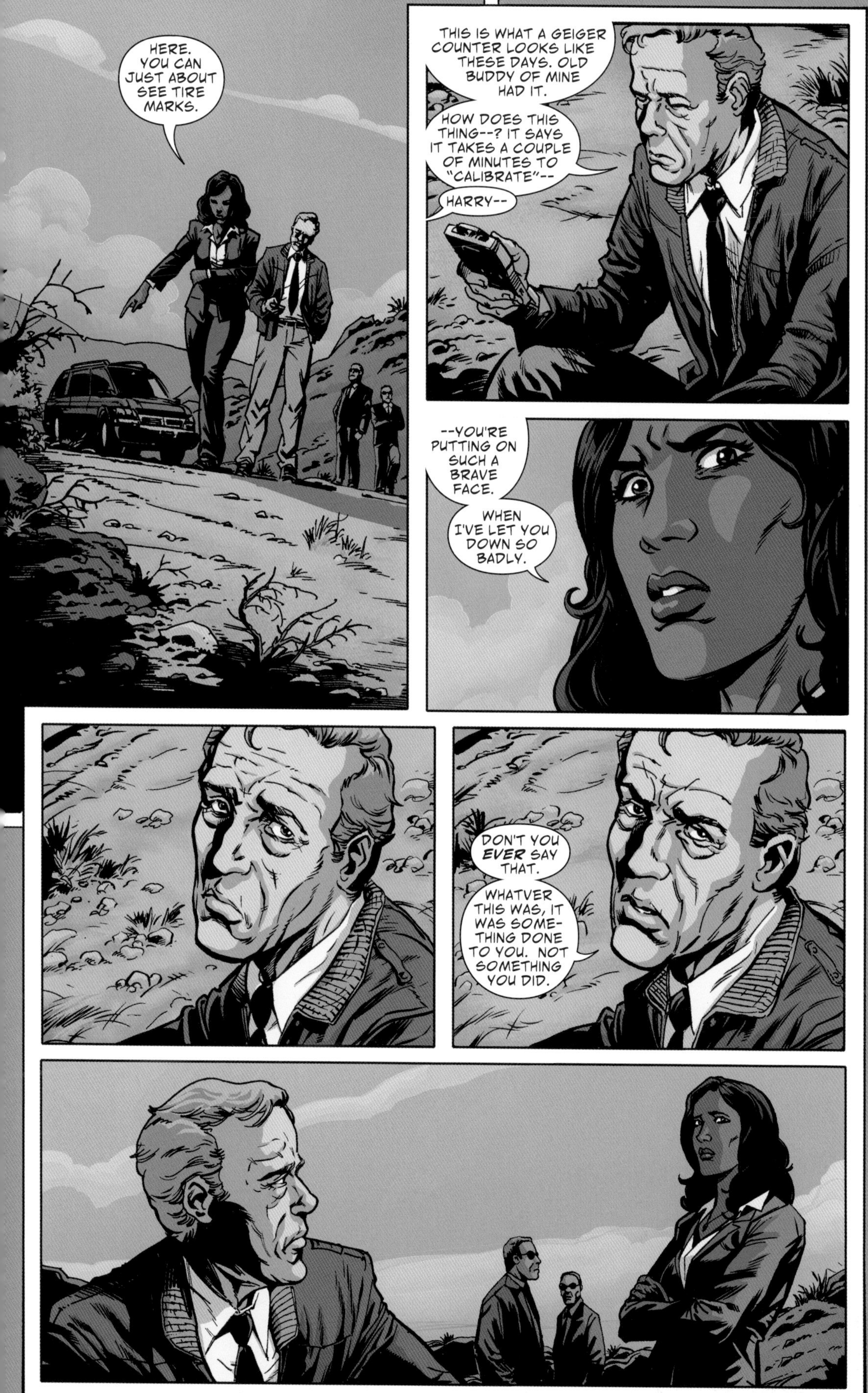
HERE. YOU CAN JUST ABOUT SEE TIRE MARKS.
THIS IS WHAT A GEIGER COUNTER LOOKS LIKE THESE DAYS. OLD BUDDY OF MINE HAD IT.
HOW DOES THIS THING--? IT SAYS IT TAKES A COUPLE OF MINUTES TO "CALIBRATE"--
HARRY--
--YOU'RE PUTTING ON SUCH A BRAVE FACE.
WHEN I'VE LET YOU DOWN SO BADLY.
DON'T YOU EVER SAY THAT.
WHATVER THIS WAS, IT WAS SOMETHING DONE TO YOU. NOT SOMETHING YOU DID.

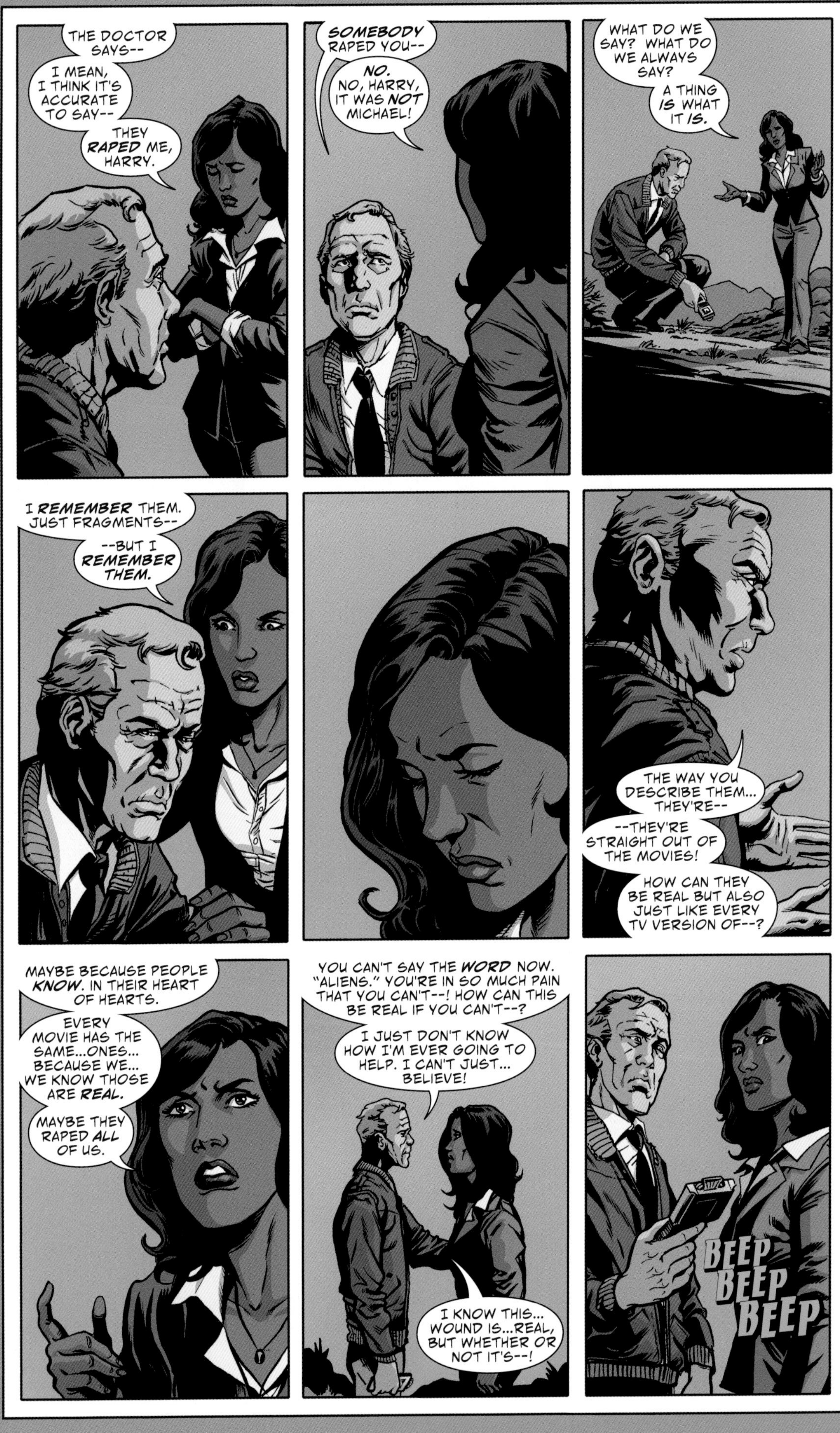

THE DOCTOR SAYS--
I MEAN, I THINK IT'S ACCURATE TO SAY--
THEY RAPED ME, HARRY.
SOMEBODY RAPED YOU--
NO. NO, HARRY, IT WAS NOT MICHAEL!
WHAT DO WE SAY? WHAT DO WE ALWAYS SAY?
A THING IS WHAT IT IS.
I REMEMBER THEM. JUST FRAGMENTS--
--BUT I REMEMBER THEM.
THE WAY YOU DESCRIBE THEM... THEY'RE--
--THEY'RE STRAIGHT OUT OF THE MOVIES!
HOW CAN THEY BE REAL BUT ALSO JUST LIKE EVERY TV VERSION OF--?
MAYBE BECAUSE PEOPLE KNOW. IN THEIR HEART OF HEARTS.
EVERY MOVIE HAS THE SAME...ONES... BECAUSE WE... WE KNOW THOSE ARE REAL.
MAYBE THEY RAPED ALL OF US.
YOU CAN'T SAY THE WORD NOW. "ALIENS." YOU'RE IN SO MUCH PAIN THAT YOU CAN'T--! HOW CAN THIS BE REAL IF YOU CAN'T--?
I JUST DON'T KNOW HOW I'M EVER GOING TO HELP. I CAN'T JUST... BELIEVE!
I KNOW THIS... WOUND IS...REAL, BUT WHETHER OR NOT IT'S--!
BEEP BEEP BEEP

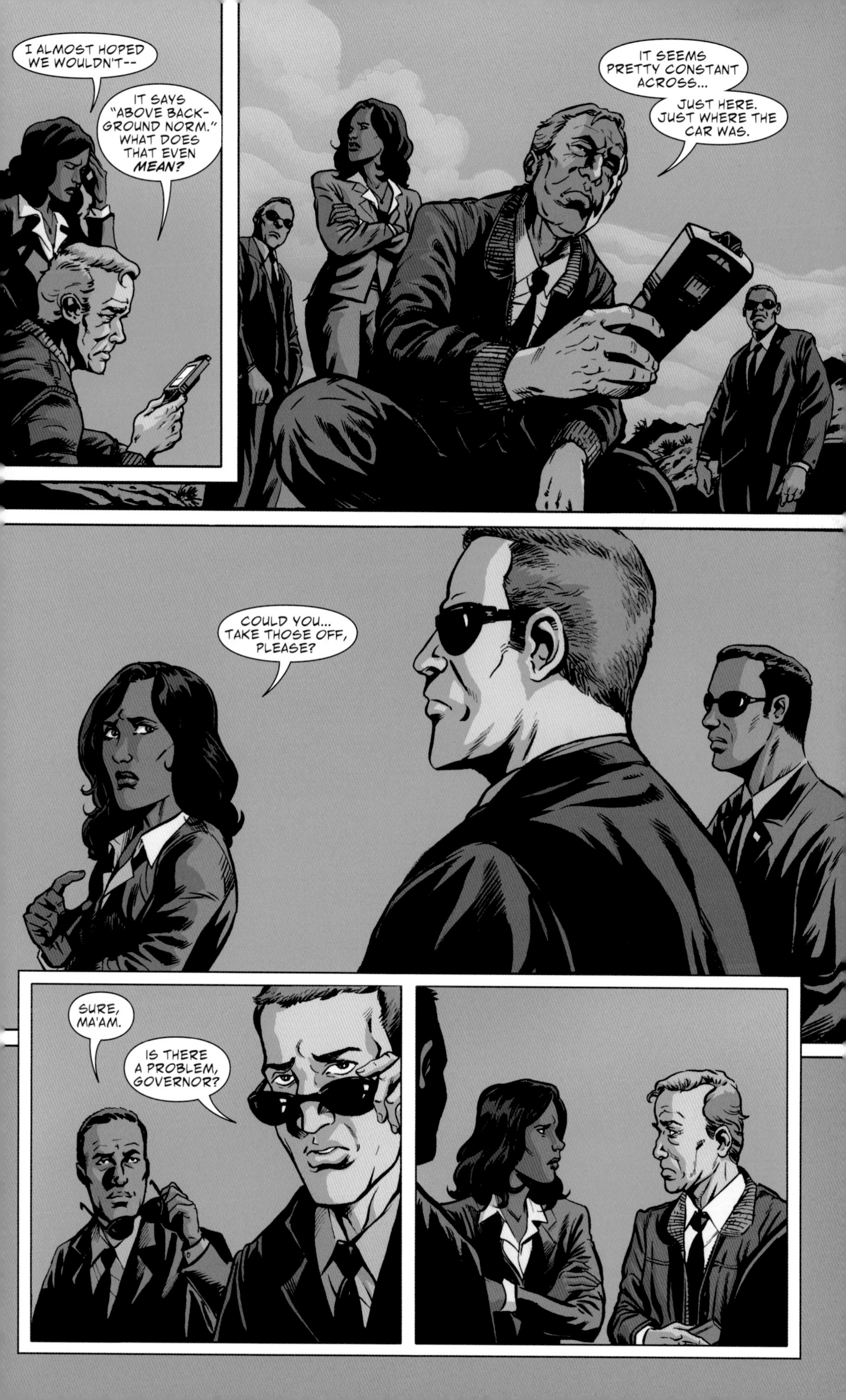
I ALMOST HOPED WE WOULDN'T--
IT SAYS "ABOVE BACK-GROUND NORM." WHAT DOES THAT EVEN *MEAN?*
IT SEEMS PRETTY CONSTANT ACROSS...
JUST HERE. JUST WHERE THE CAR WAS.
COULD YOU... TAKE THOSE OFF, PLEASE?
SURE, MA'AM.
IS THERE A PROBLEM, GOVERNOR?

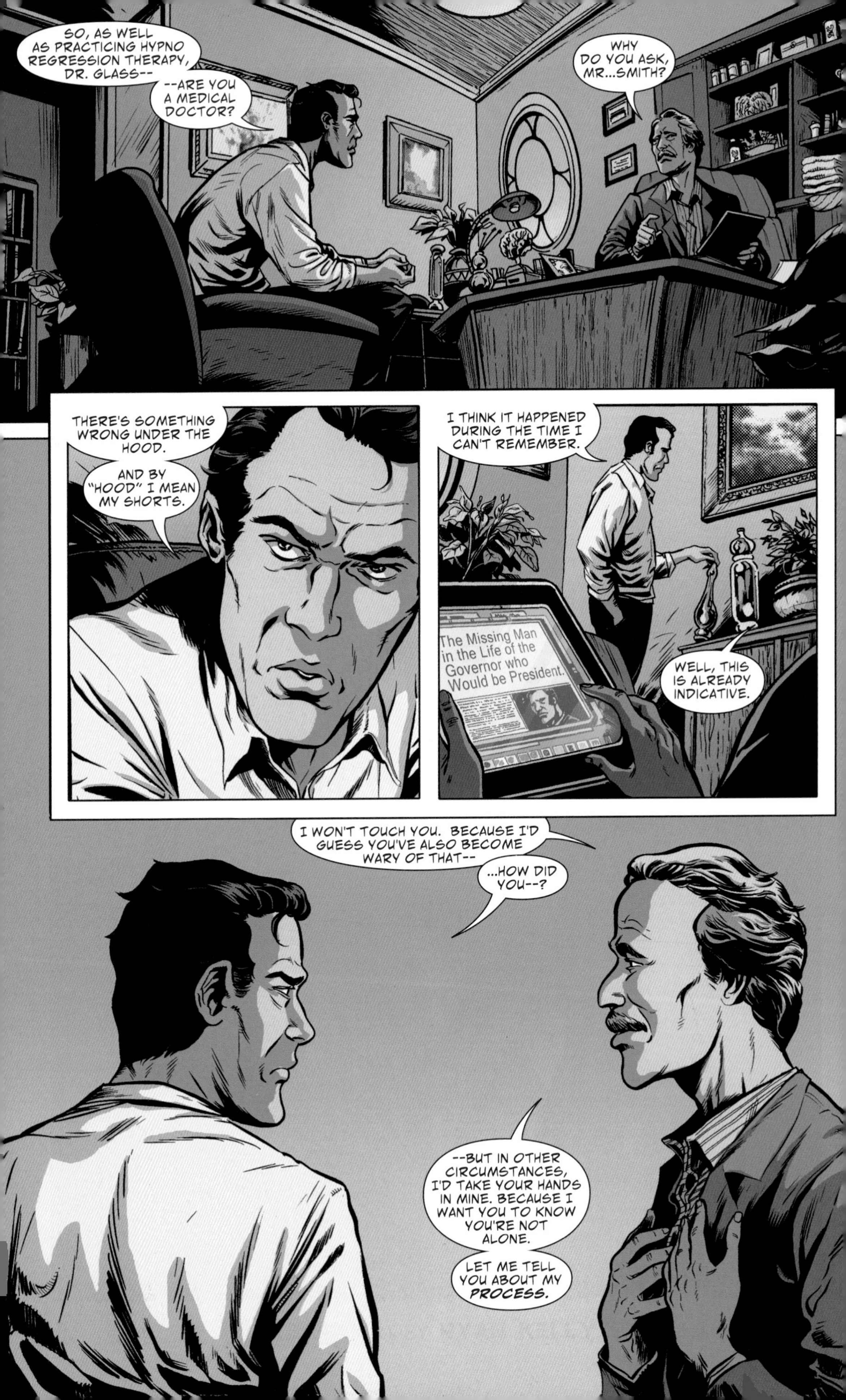
SO, AS WELL AS PRACTICING HYPNO REGRESSION THERAPY, DR. GLASS--
--ARE YOU A MEDICAL DOCTOR?
WHY DO YOU ASK, MR...SMITH?
THERE'S SOMETHING WRONG UNDER THE HOOD.
AND BY "HOOD" I MEAN MY SHORTS.
I THINK IT HAPPENED DURING THE TIME I CAN'T REMEMBER.
The Missing Man in the Life of the Governor who Would be President.
WELL, THIS IS ALREADY INDICATIVE.
I WON'T TOUCH YOU. BECAUSE I'D GUESS YOU'VE ALSO BECOME WARY OF THAT--
...HOW DID YOU--?
--BUT IN OTHER CIRCUMSTANCES, I'D TAKE YOUR HANDS IN MINE. BECAUSE I WANT YOU TO KNOW YOU'RE NOT ALONE.
LET ME TELL YOU ABOUT MY PROCESS.

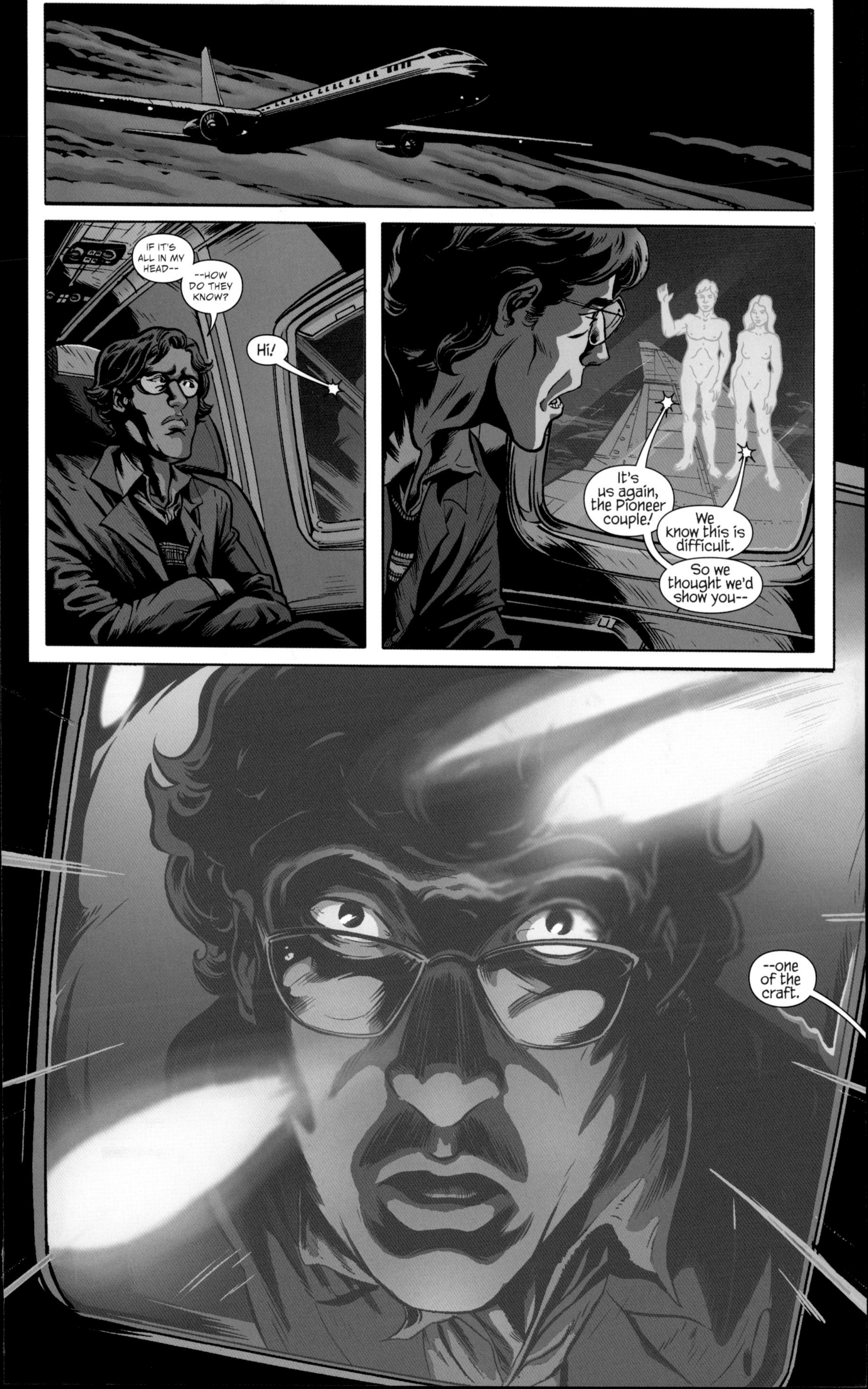
IF IT'S ALL IN MY HEAD--
--HOW DO THEY KNOW?
Hi!
It's us again, the Pioneer couple!
We know this is difficult.
So we thought we'd show you--
--one of the craft.

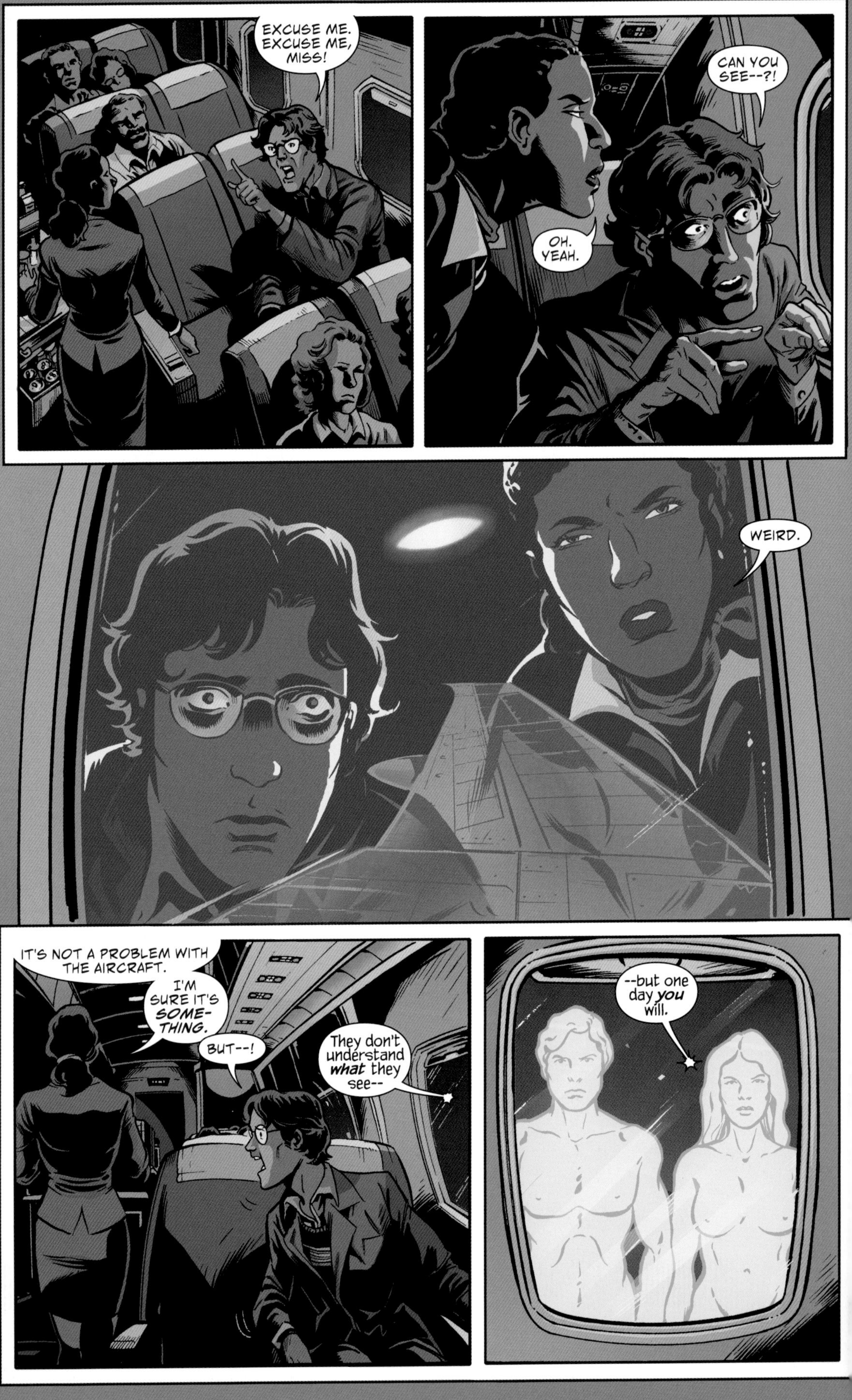
EXCUSE ME. EXCUSE ME, MISS!
CAN YOU SEE--?!
OH. YEAH.
WEIRD.
IT'S NOT A PROBLEM WITH THE AIRCRAFT.
I'M SURE IT'S SOMETHING.
BUT--!
They don't understand what they see--
--but one day you will.

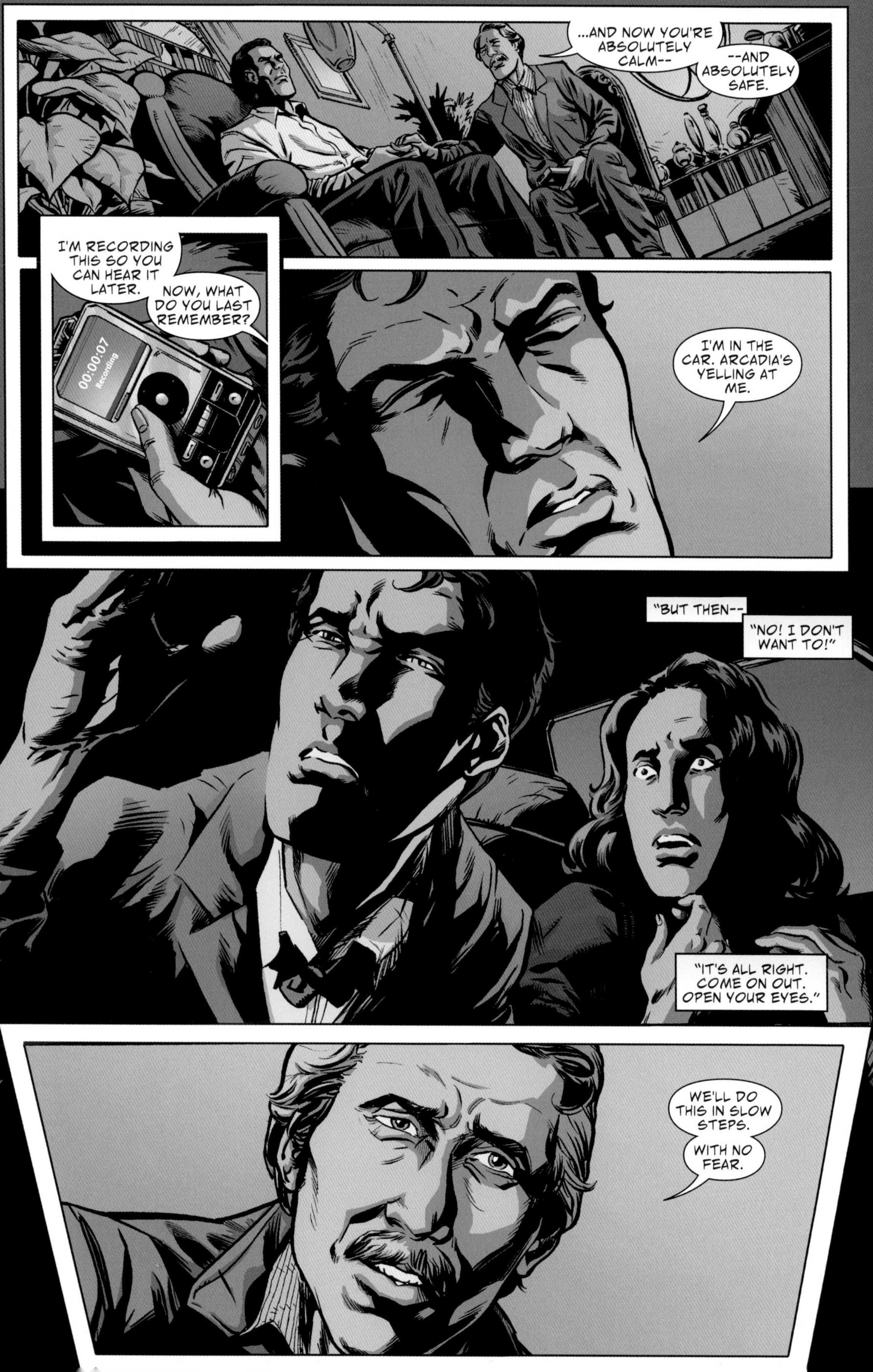
...AND NOW YOU'RE ABSOLUTELY CALM--
--AND ABSOLUTELY SAFE.
I'M RECORDING THIS SO YOU CAN HEAR IT LATER.
NOW, WHAT DO YOU LAST REMEMBER?
00:00:07
Recording
I'M IN THE CAR. ARCADIA'S YELLING AT ME.
"BUT THEN--
"NO! I DON'T WANT TO!"
"IT'S ALL RIGHT. COME ON OUT. OPEN YOUR EYES."
WE'LL DO THIS IN SLOW STEPS.
WITH NO FEAR.

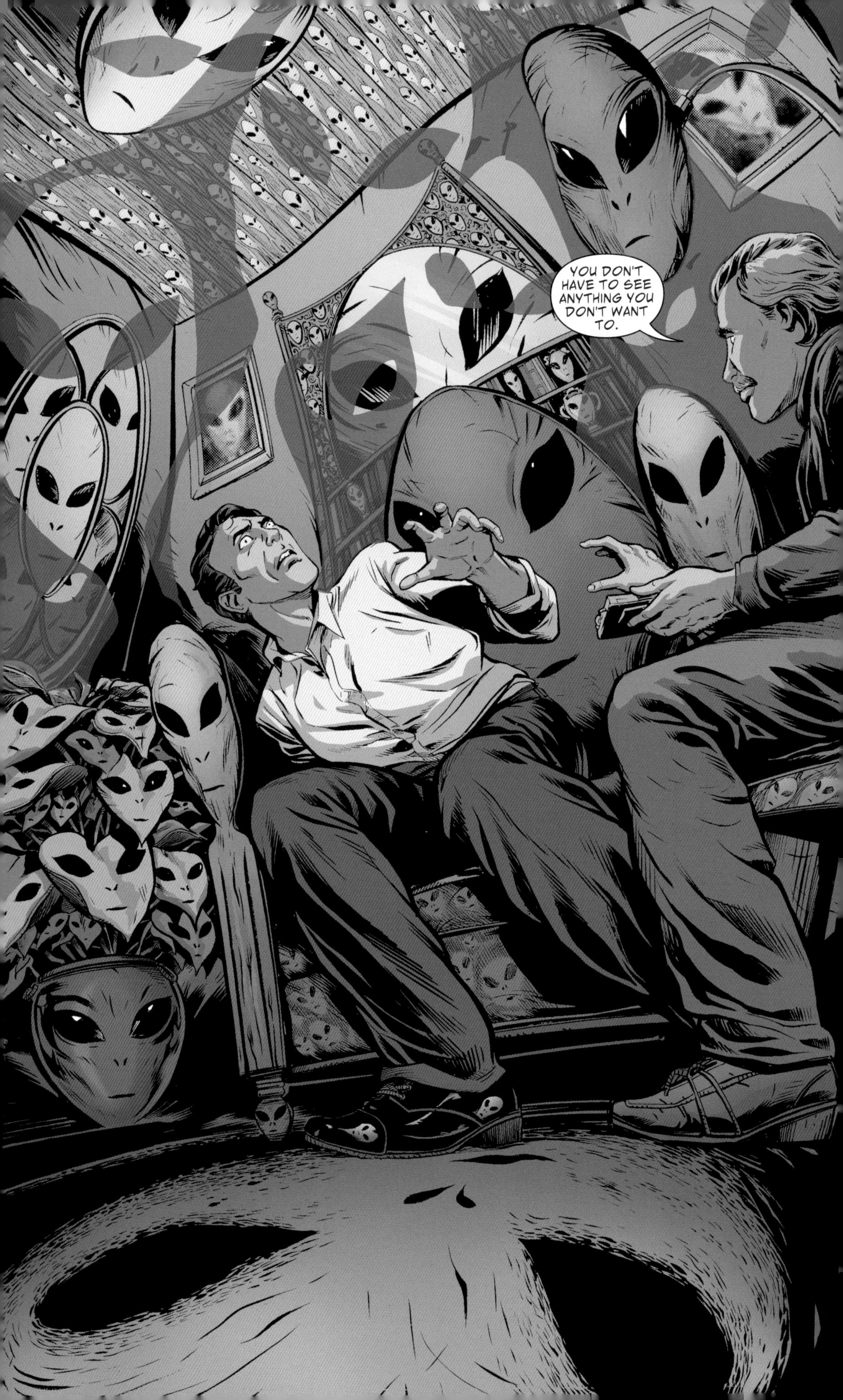
YOU DON'T HAVE TO SEE ANYTHING YOU DON'T WANT TO.

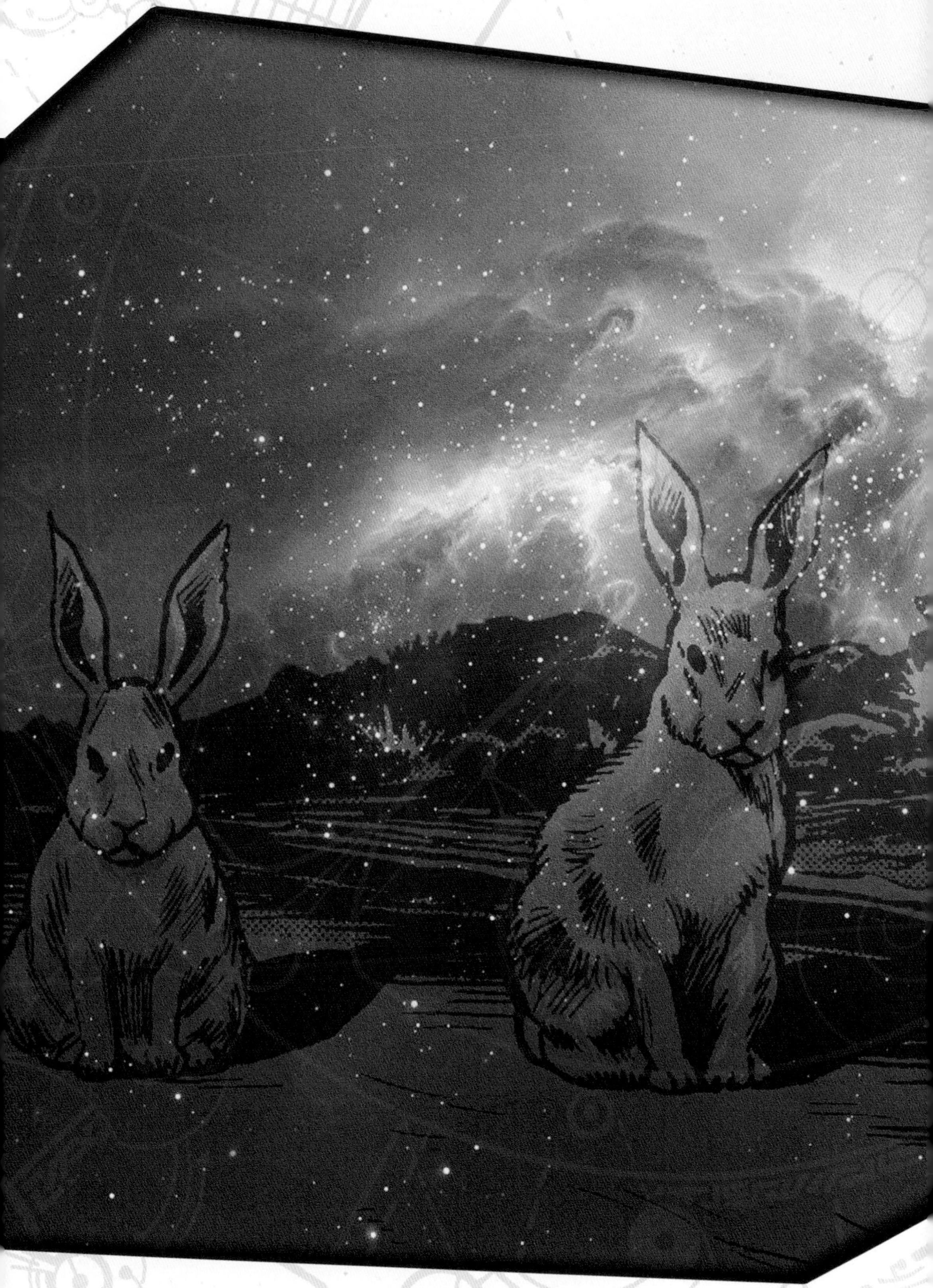

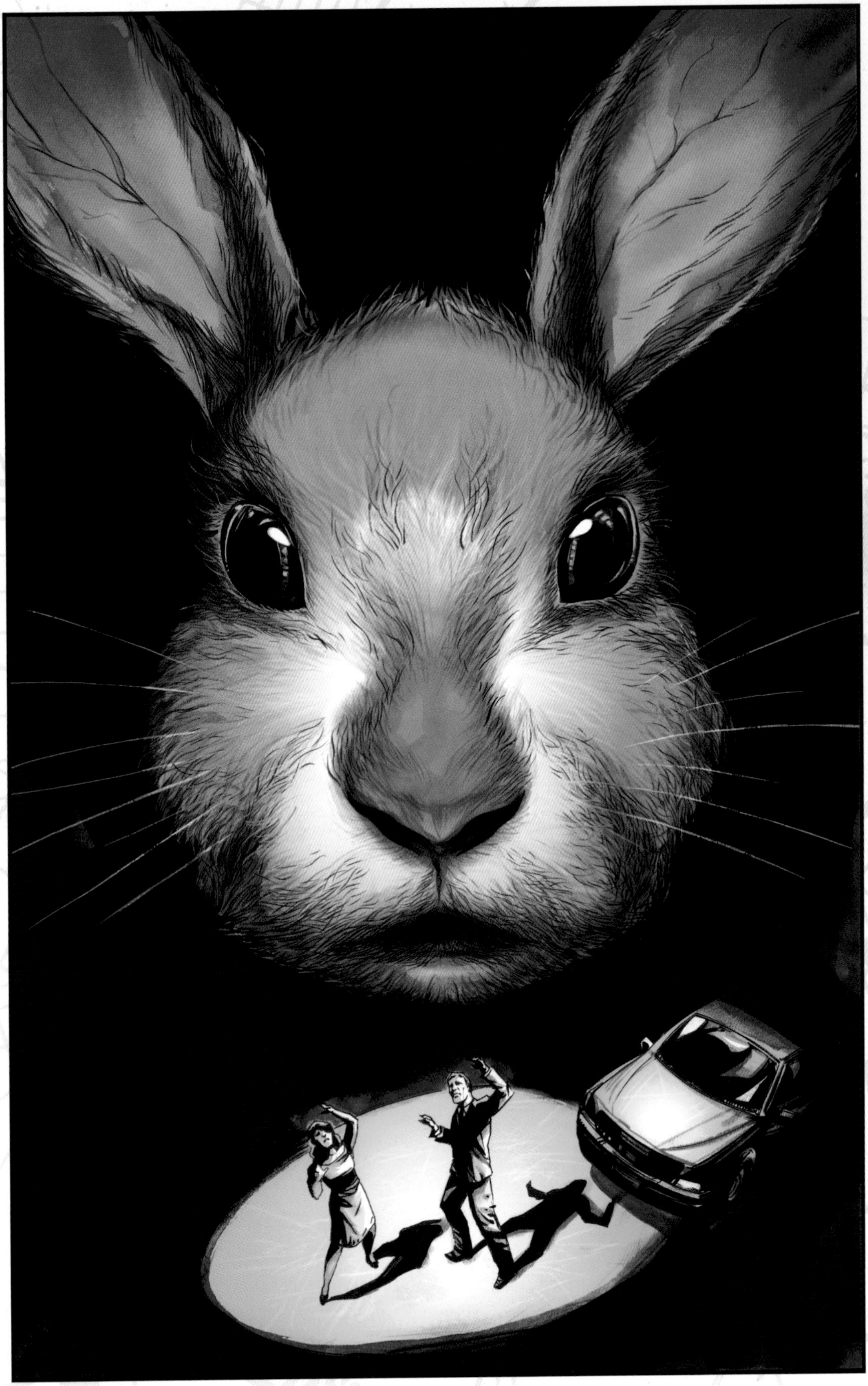

COVER ART BY **RYAN KELLY**

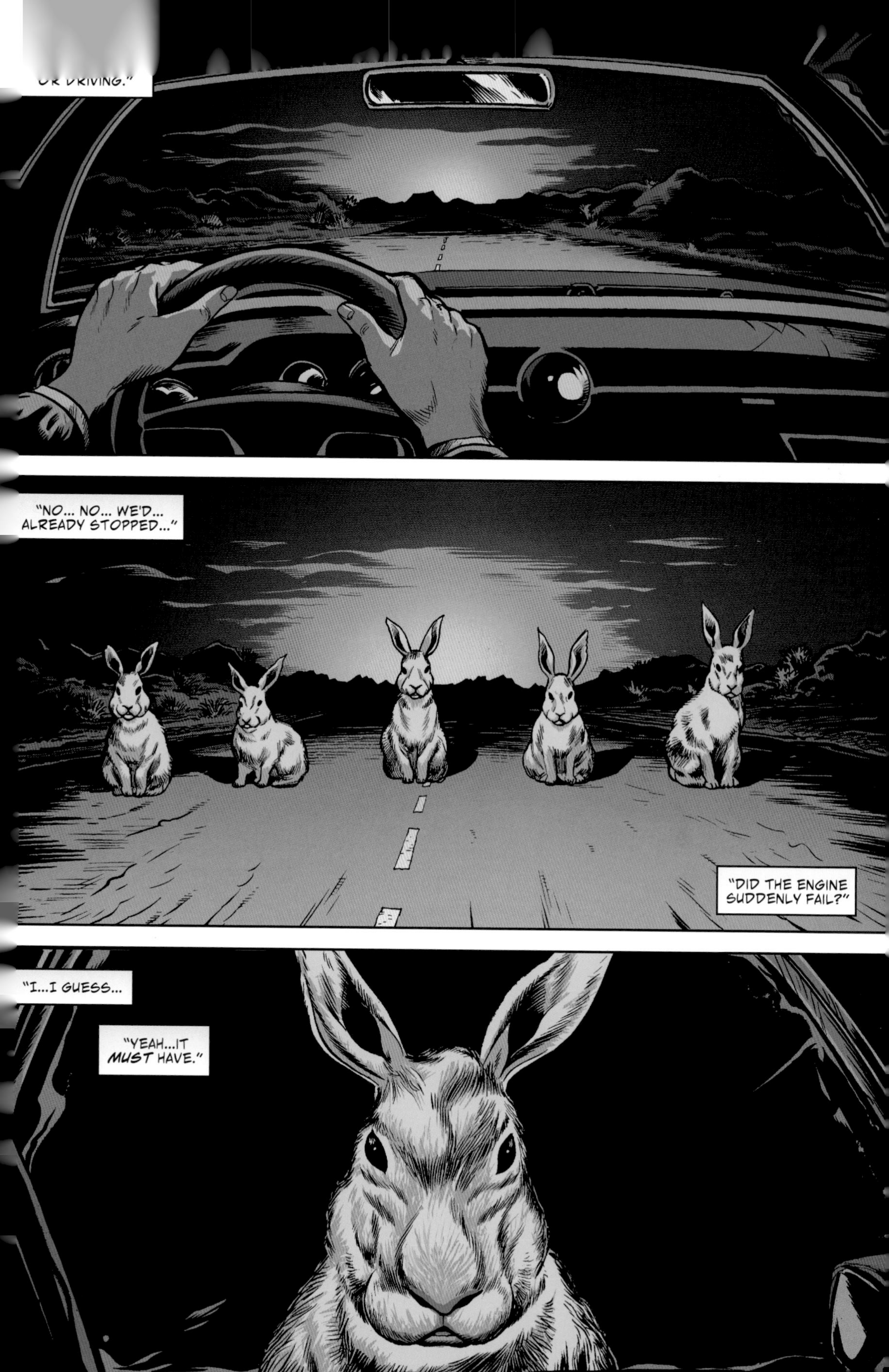
DRIVING."
"NO... NO... WE'D... ALREADY STOPPED..."
"DID THE ENGINE SUDDENLY FAIL?"
"I...I GUESS...
"YEAH...IT *MUST* HAVE."

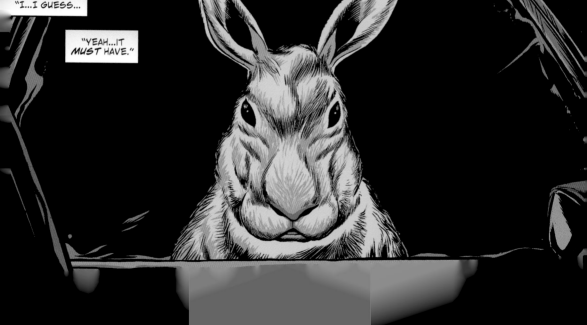

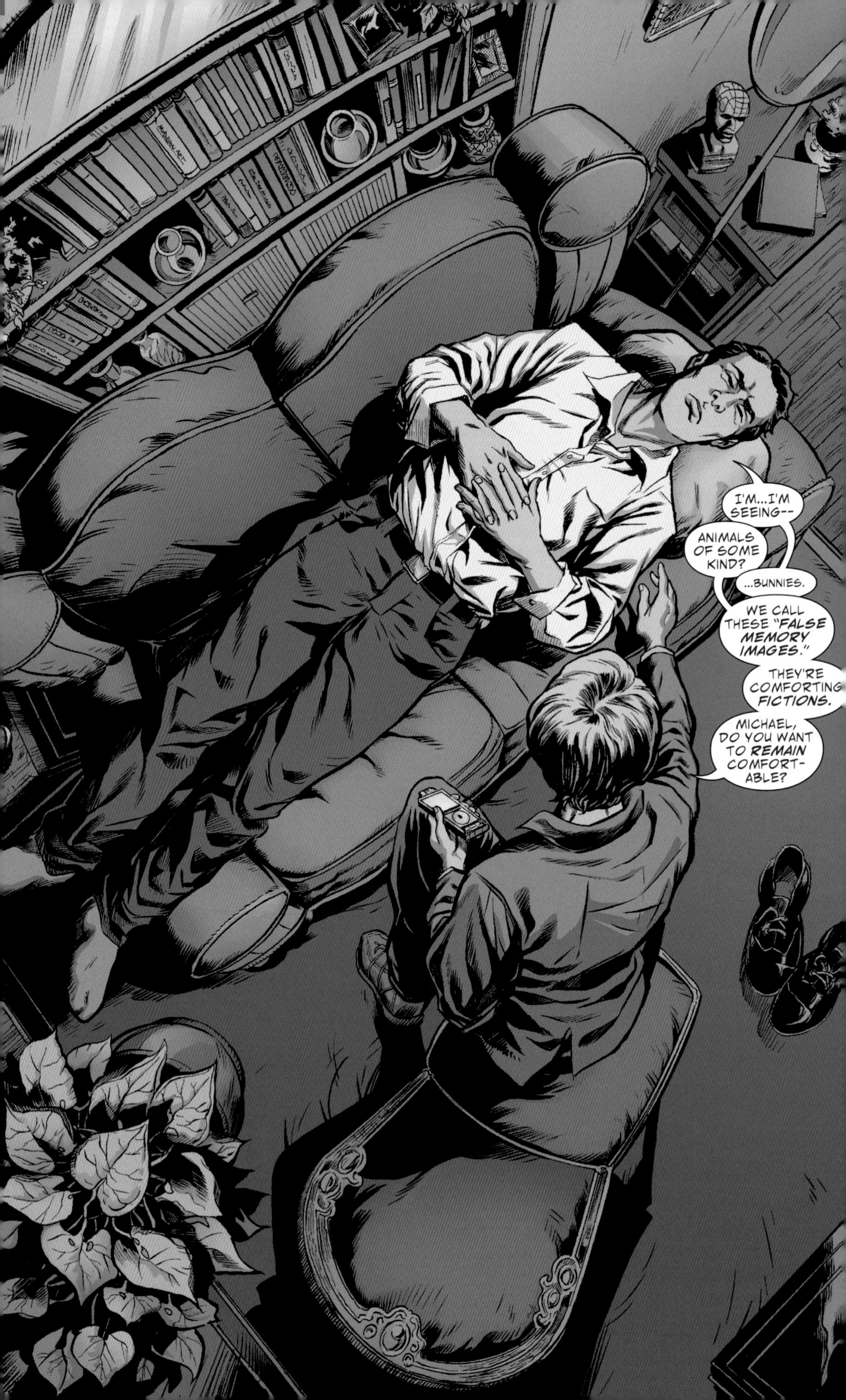
I'M...I'M SEEING--
ANIMALS OF SOME KIND?
...BUNNIES.
WE CALL THESE "*FALSE MEMORY IMAGES*."
THEY'RE COMFORTING *FICTIONS*.
MICHAEL, DO YOU WANT TO *REMAIN* COMFORT-ABLE?

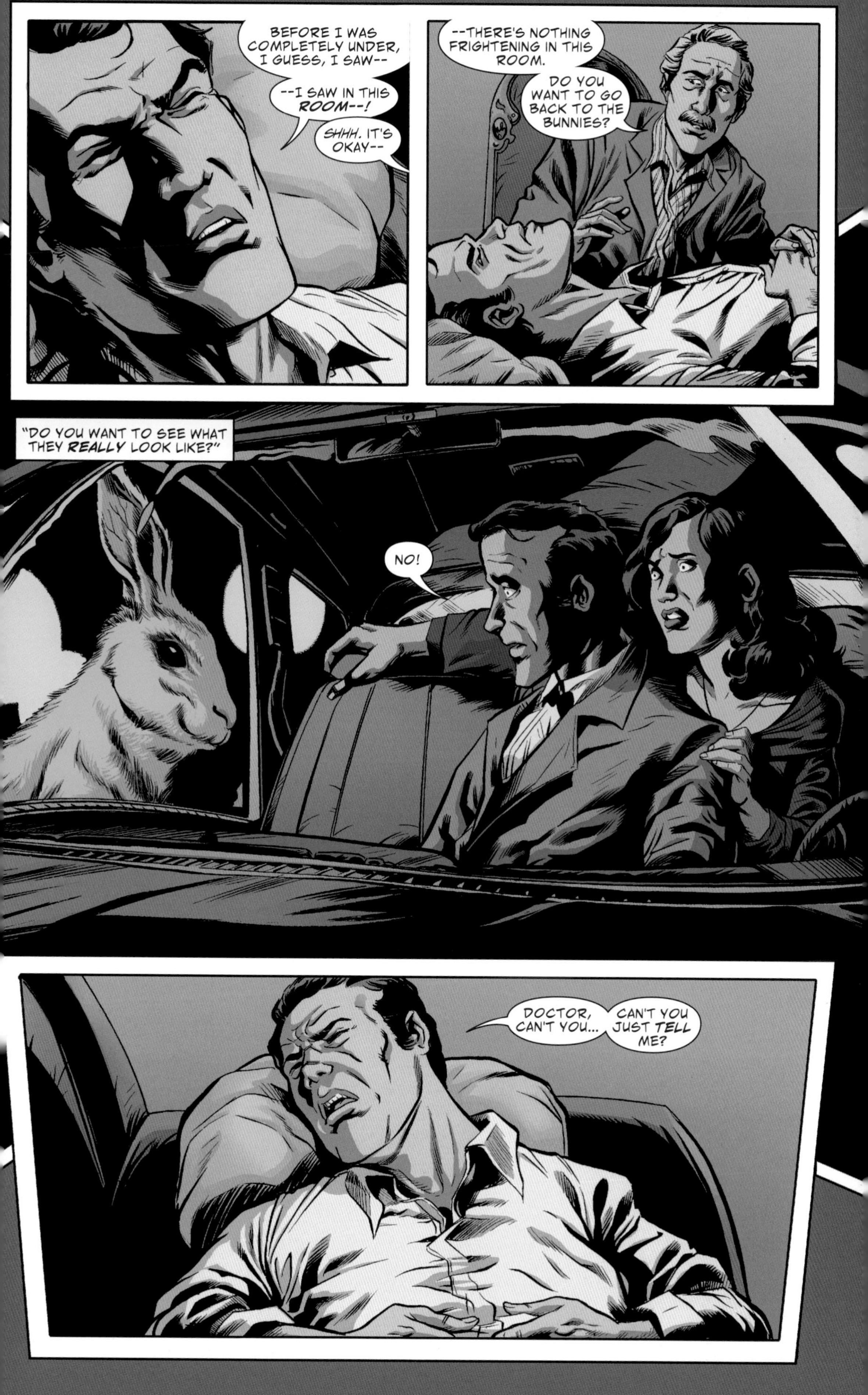
BEFORE I WAS COMPLETELY UNDER, I GUESS, I SAW--
--I SAW IN THIS *ROOM*--!
SHHH. IT'S OKAY--
--THERE'S NOTHING FRIGHTENING IN THIS ROOM.
DO YOU WANT TO GO BACK TO THE BUNNIES?
"DO YOU WANT TO SEE WHAT THEY *REALLY* LOOK LIKE?"
NO!
DOCTOR, CAN'T YOU...
CAN'T YOU JUST *TELL* ME?

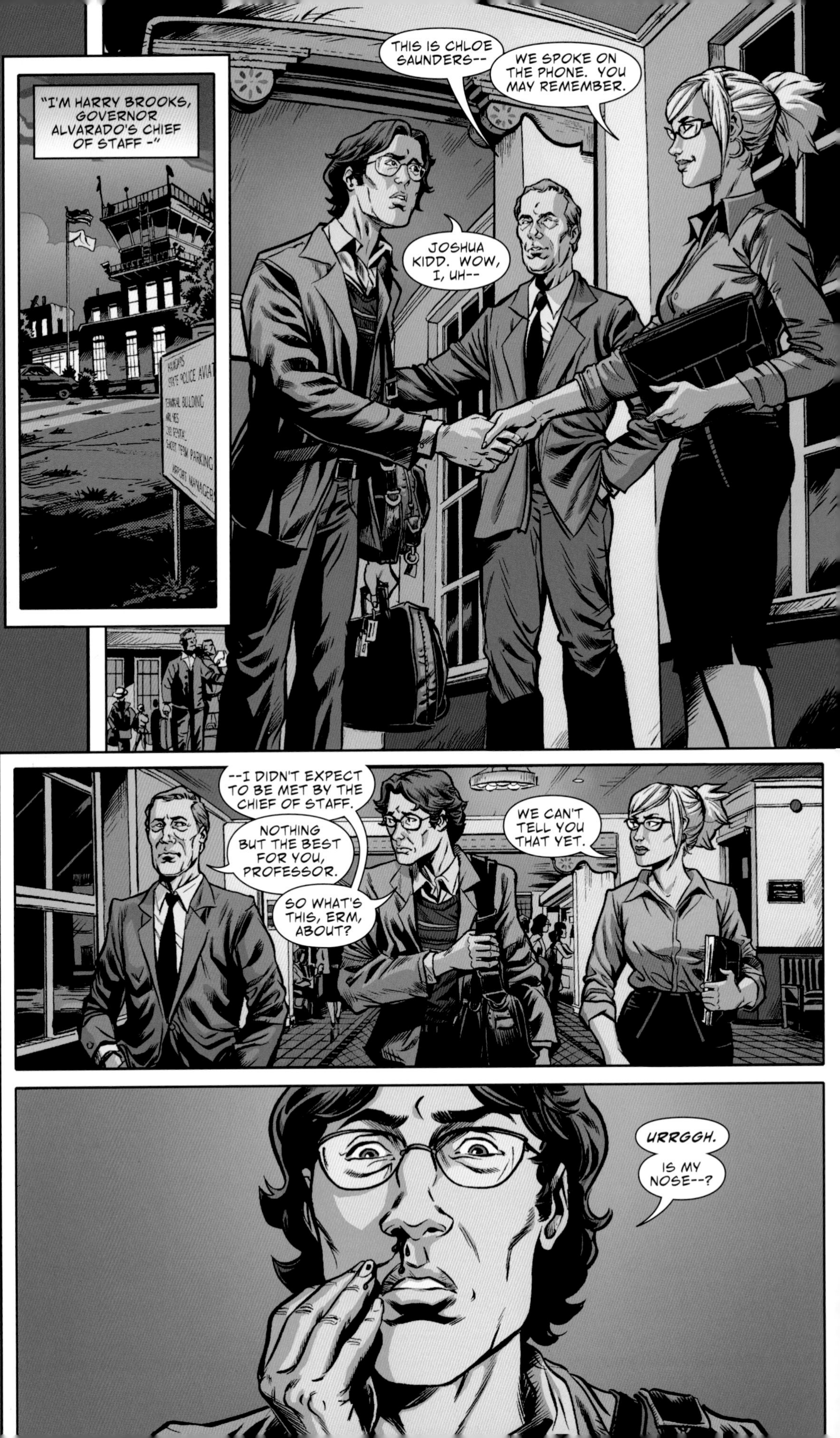
"I'M HARRY BROOKS, GOVERNOR ALVARADO'S CHIEF OF STAFF -"
THIS IS CHLOE SAUNDERS--
WE SPOKE ON THE PHONE. YOU MAY REMEMBER.
JOSHUA KIDD. WOW, I, UH--
--I DIDN'T EXPECT TO BE MET BY THE CHIEF OF STAFF.
NOTHING BUT THE BEST FOR YOU, PROFESSOR.
SO WHAT'S THIS, ERM, ABOUT?
WE CAN'T TELL YOU THAT YET.
URRGGH.
IS MY NOSE--?

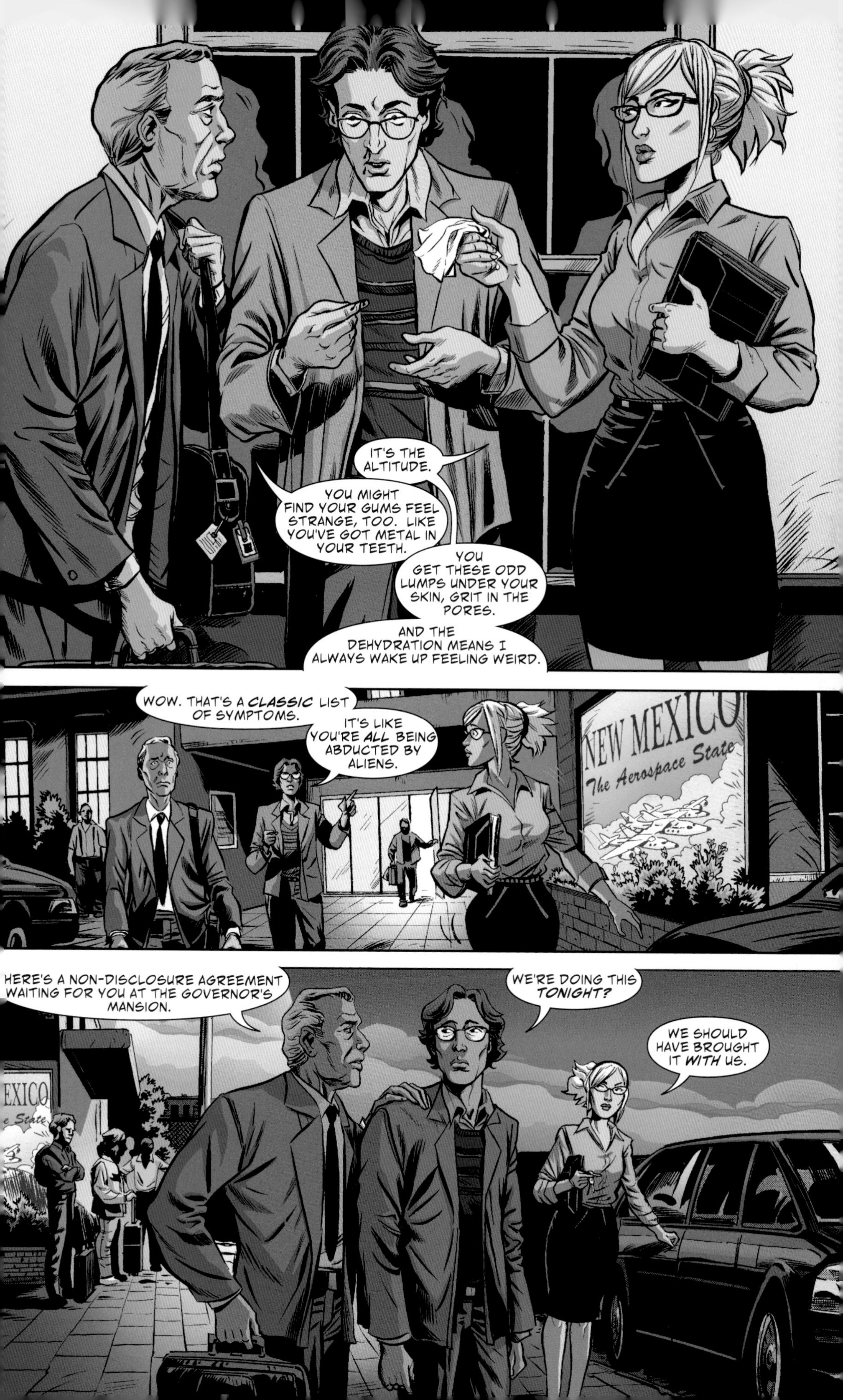

IT'S THE ALTITUDE.
YOU MIGHT FIND YOUR GUMS FEEL STRANGE, TOO. LIKE YOU'VE GOT METAL IN YOUR TEETH.
YOU GET THESE ODD LUMPS UNDER YOUR SKIN, GRIT IN THE PORES.
AND THE DEHYDRATION MEANS I ALWAYS WAKE UP FEELING WEIRD.
WOW. THAT'S A CLASSIC LIST OF SYMPTOMS.
IT'S LIKE YOU'RE ALL BEING ABDUCTED BY ALIENS.
NEW MEXICO
The Aerospace State
HERE'S A NON-DISCLOSURE AGREEMENT WAITING FOR YOU AT THE GOVERNOR'S MANSION.
WE'RE DOING THIS TONIGHT?
WE SHOULD HAVE BROUGHT IT WITH US.

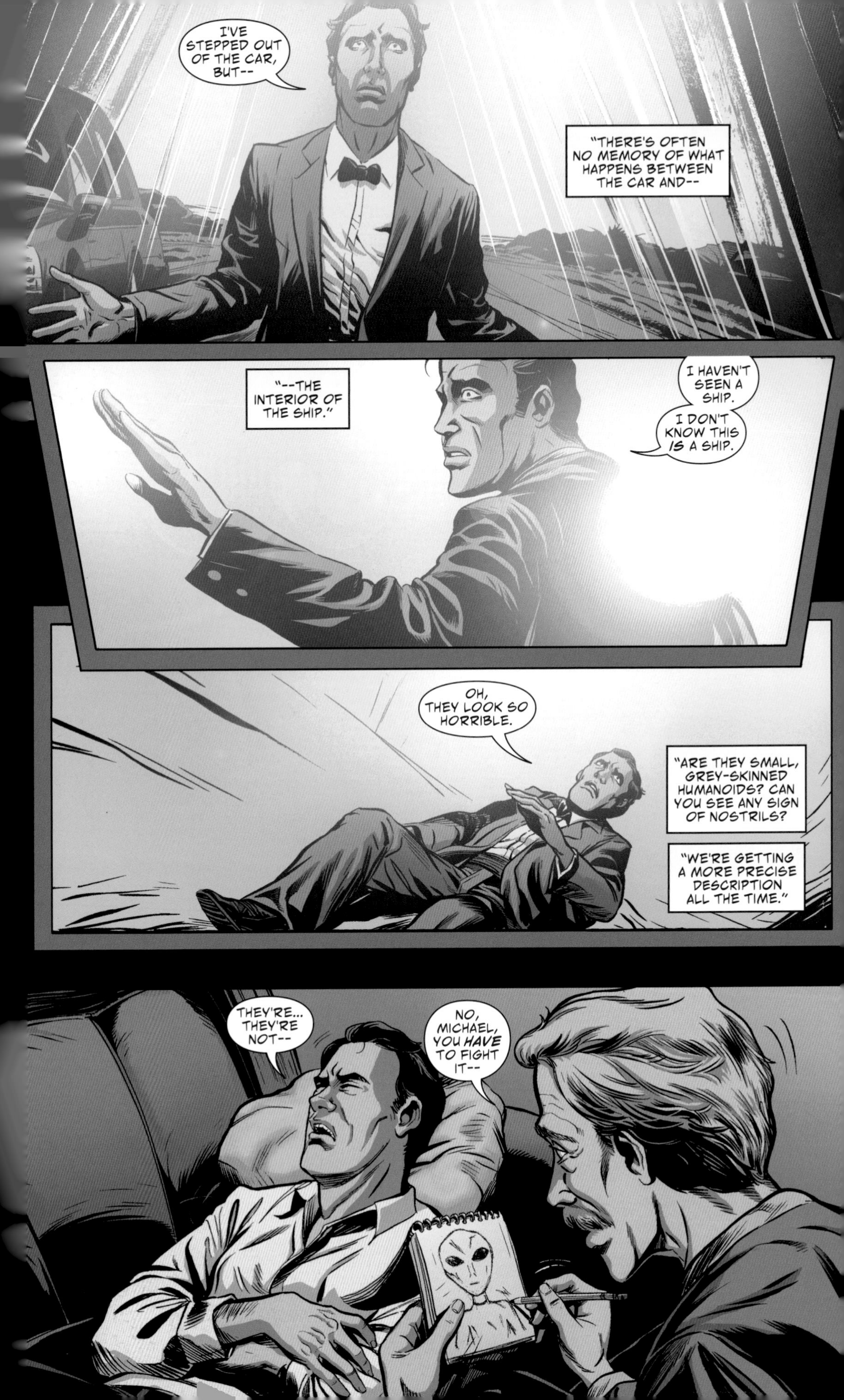
I'VE STEPPED OUT OF THE CAR, BUT--
"THERE'S OFTEN NO MEMORY OF WHAT HAPPENS BETWEEN THE CAR AND--
"--THE INTERIOR OF THE SHIP."
I HAVEN'T SEEN A SHIP.
I DON'T KNOW THIS *IS* A SHIP.
OH, THEY LOOK SO HORRIBLE.
"ARE THEY SMALL, GREY-SKINNED HUMANOIDS? CAN YOU SEE ANY SIGN OF NOSTRILS?
"WE'RE GETTING A MORE PRECISE DESCRIPTION ALL THE TIME."
THEY'RE... THEY'RE NOT--
NO, MICHAEL, YOU ***HAVE*** TO FIGHT IT--

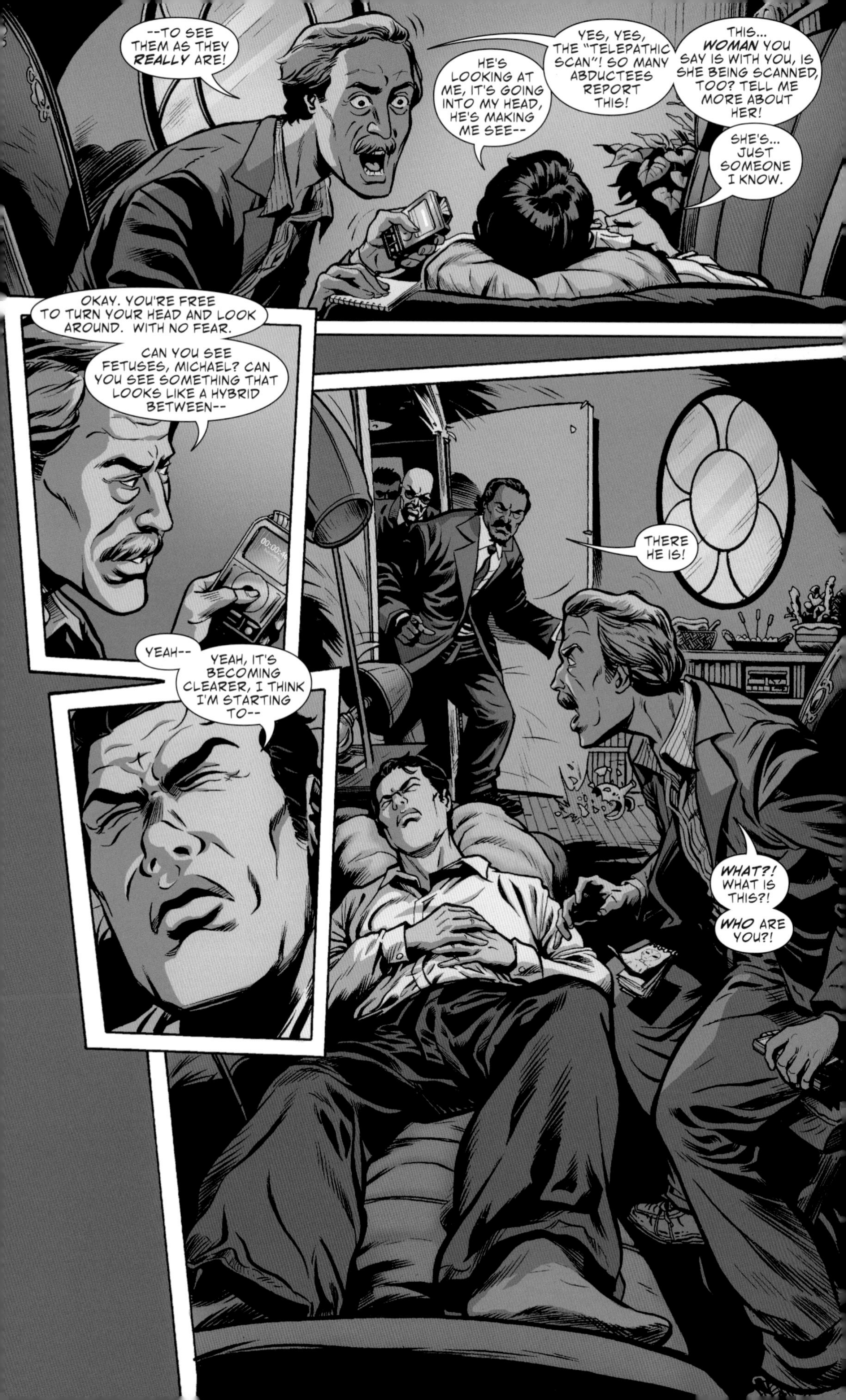
--TO SEE THEM AS THEY REALLY ARE!
HE'S LOOKING AT ME, IT'S GOING INTO MY HEAD, HE'S MAKING ME SEE--
YES, YES, THE "TELEPATHIC SCAN"! SO MANY ABDUCTEES REPORT THIS!
THIS... WOMAN YOU SAY IS WITH YOU, IS SHE BEING SCANNED, TOO? TELL ME MORE ABOUT HER!
SHE'S... JUST SOMEONE I KNOW.
OKAY. YOU'RE FREE TO TURN YOUR HEAD AND LOOK AROUND. WITH NO FEAR.
CAN YOU SEE FETUSES, MICHAEL? CAN YOU SEE SOMETHING THAT LOOKS LIKE A HYBRID BETWEEN--
YEAH--
YEAH, IT'S BECOMING CLEARER, I THINK I'M STARTING TO--
THERE HE IS!
WHAT?! WHAT IS THIS?!
WHO ARE YOU?!

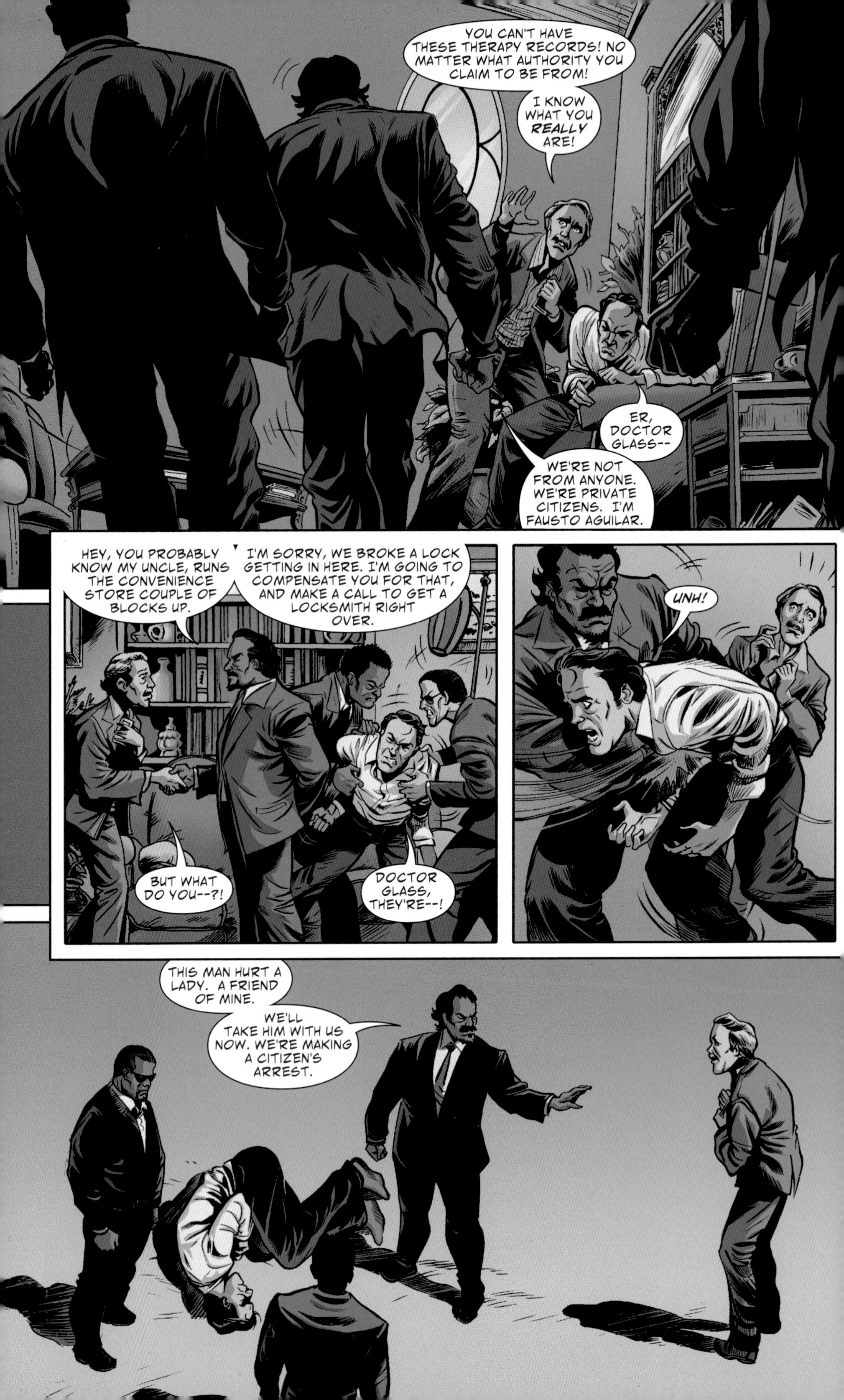
YOU CAN'T HAVE THESE THERAPY RECORDS! NO MATTER WHAT AUTHORITY YOU CLAIM TO BE FROM!
I KNOW WHAT YOU REALLY ARE!
ER, DOCTOR GLASS--
WE'RE NOT FROM ANYONE. WE'RE PRIVATE CITIZENS. I'M FAUSTO AGUILAR.
HEY, YOU PROBABLY KNOW MY UNCLE, RUNS THE CONVENIENCE STORE COUPLE OF BLOCKS UP.
I'M SORRY, WE BROKE A LOCK GETTING IN HERE. I'M GOING TO COMPENSATE YOU FOR THAT, AND MAKE A CALL TO GET A LOCKSMITH RIGHT OVER.
BUT WHAT DO YOU--?!
DOCTOR GLASS, THEY'RE--!
UNH!
THIS MAN HURT A LADY. A FRIEND OF MINE.
WE'LL TAKE HIM WITH US NOW. WE'RE MAKING A CITIZEN'S ARREST.

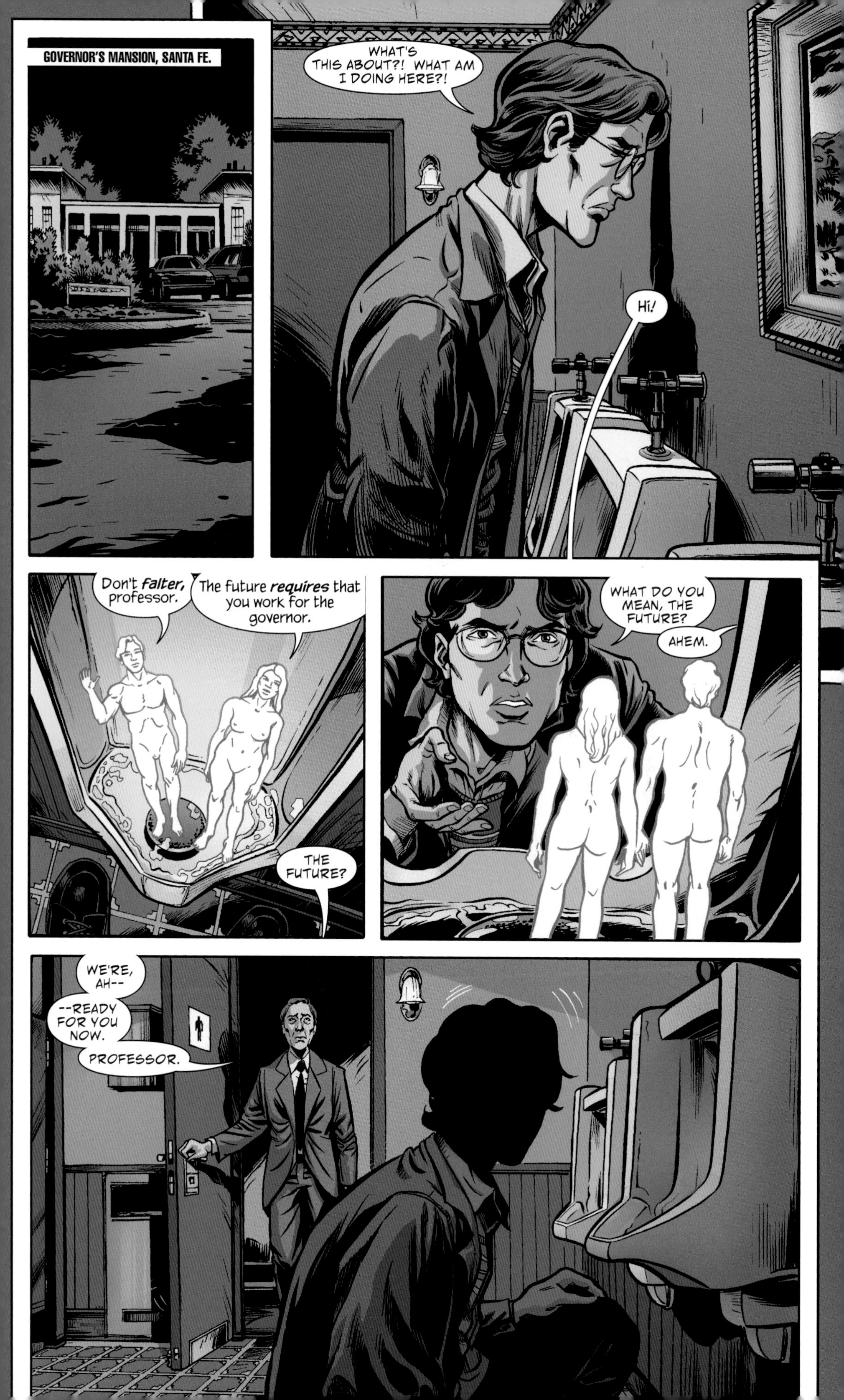
GOVERNOR'S MANSION, SANTA FE.
WHAT'S THIS ABOUT?! WHAT AM I DOING HERE?!
Hi!
Don't falter, professor.
The future requires that you work for the governor.
THE FUTURE?
WHAT DO YOU MEAN, THE FUTURE?
AHEM.
WE'RE, AH--
--READY FOR YOU NOW.
PROFESSOR.

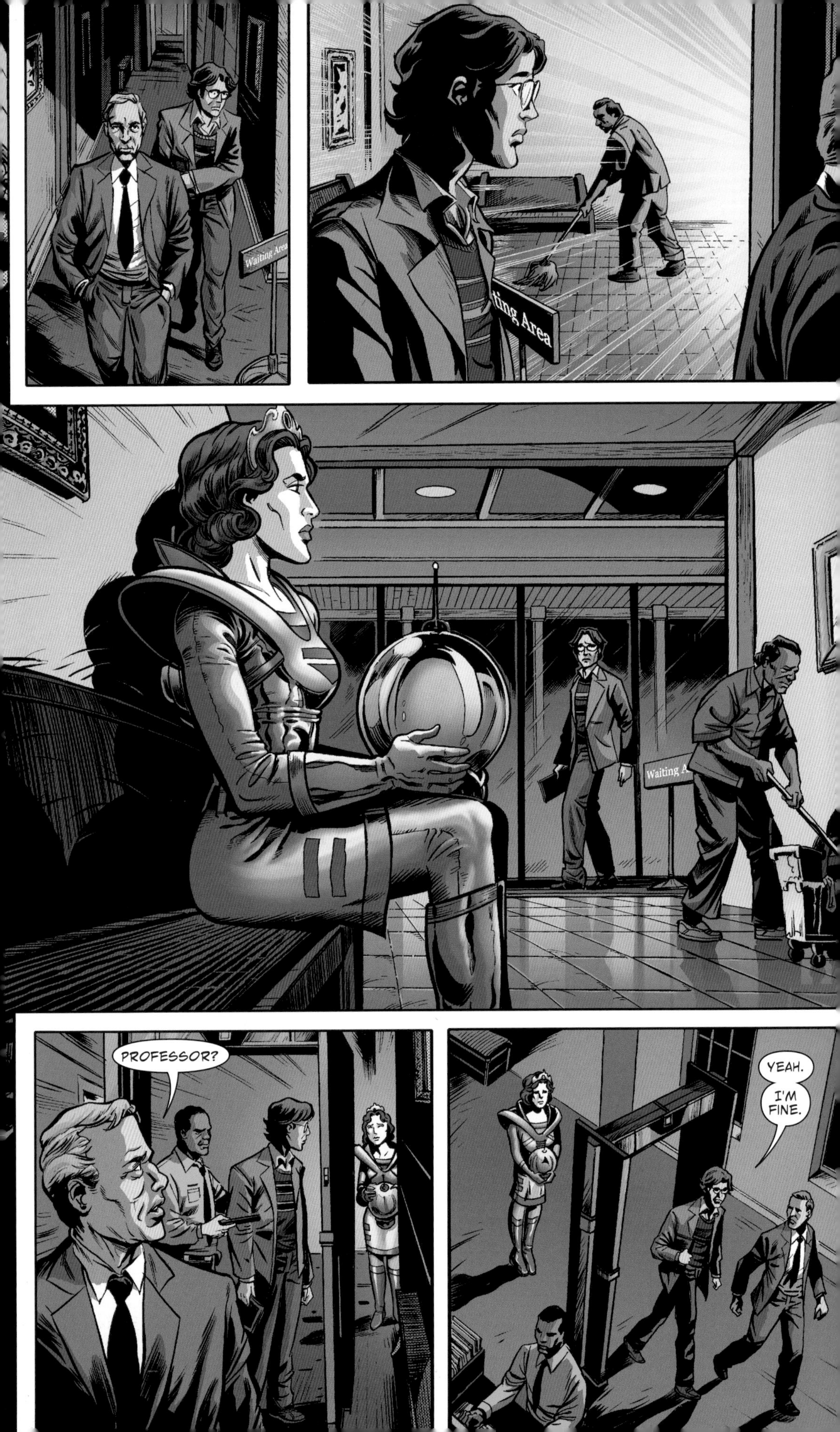

Waiting Area
Waiting Area
Waiting A
PROFESSOR?
YEAH.
I'M FINE.

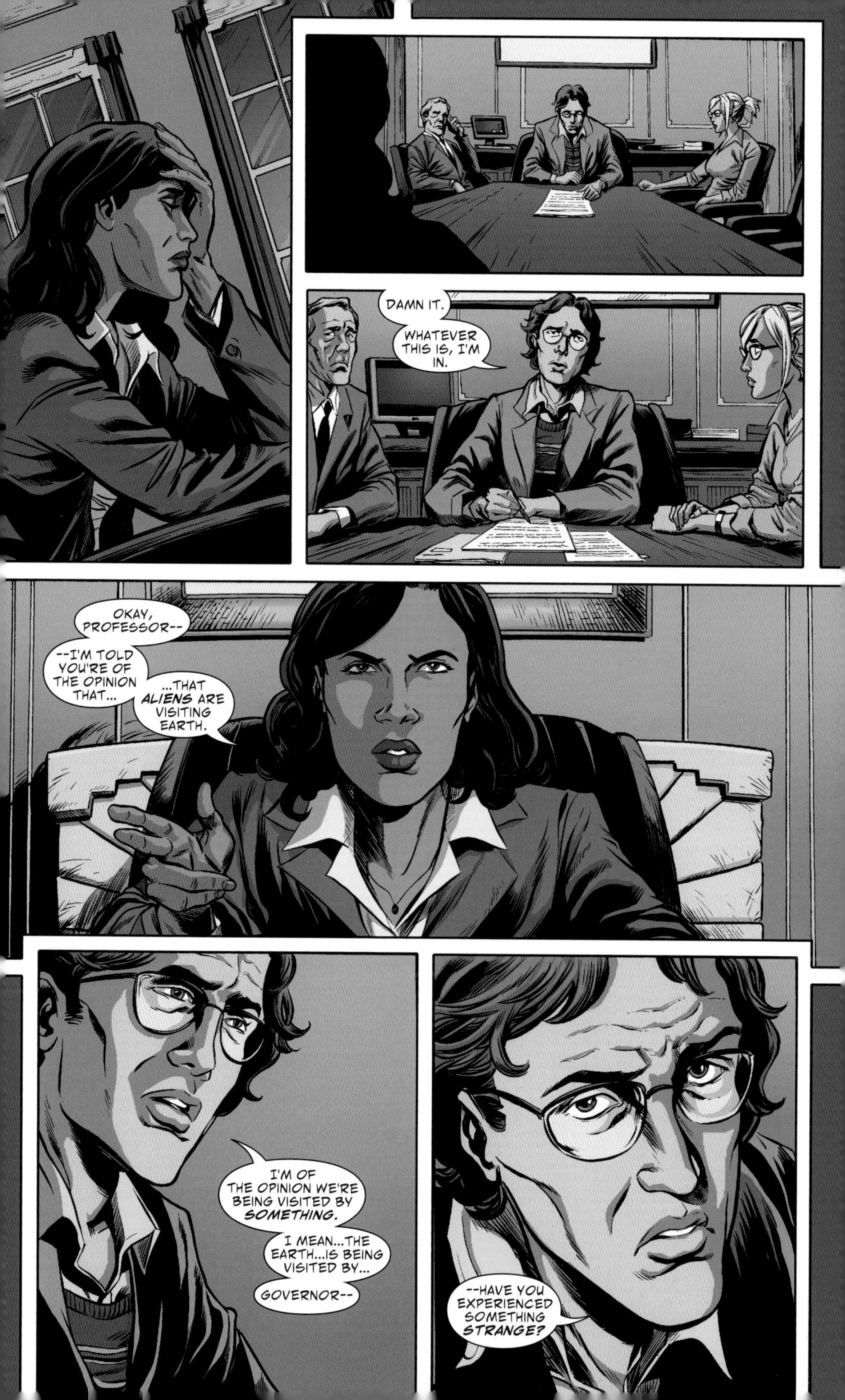
DAMN IT.
WHATEVER THIS IS, I'M IN.
OKAY, PROFESSOR--
--I'M TOLD YOU'RE OF THE OPINION THAT...
...THAT ALIENS ARE VISITING EARTH.
I'M OF THE OPINION WE'RE BEING VISITED BY SOMETHING.
I MEAN...THE EARTH...IS BEING VISITED BY...
GOVERNOR--
--HAVE YOU EXPERIENCED SOMETHING STRANGE?

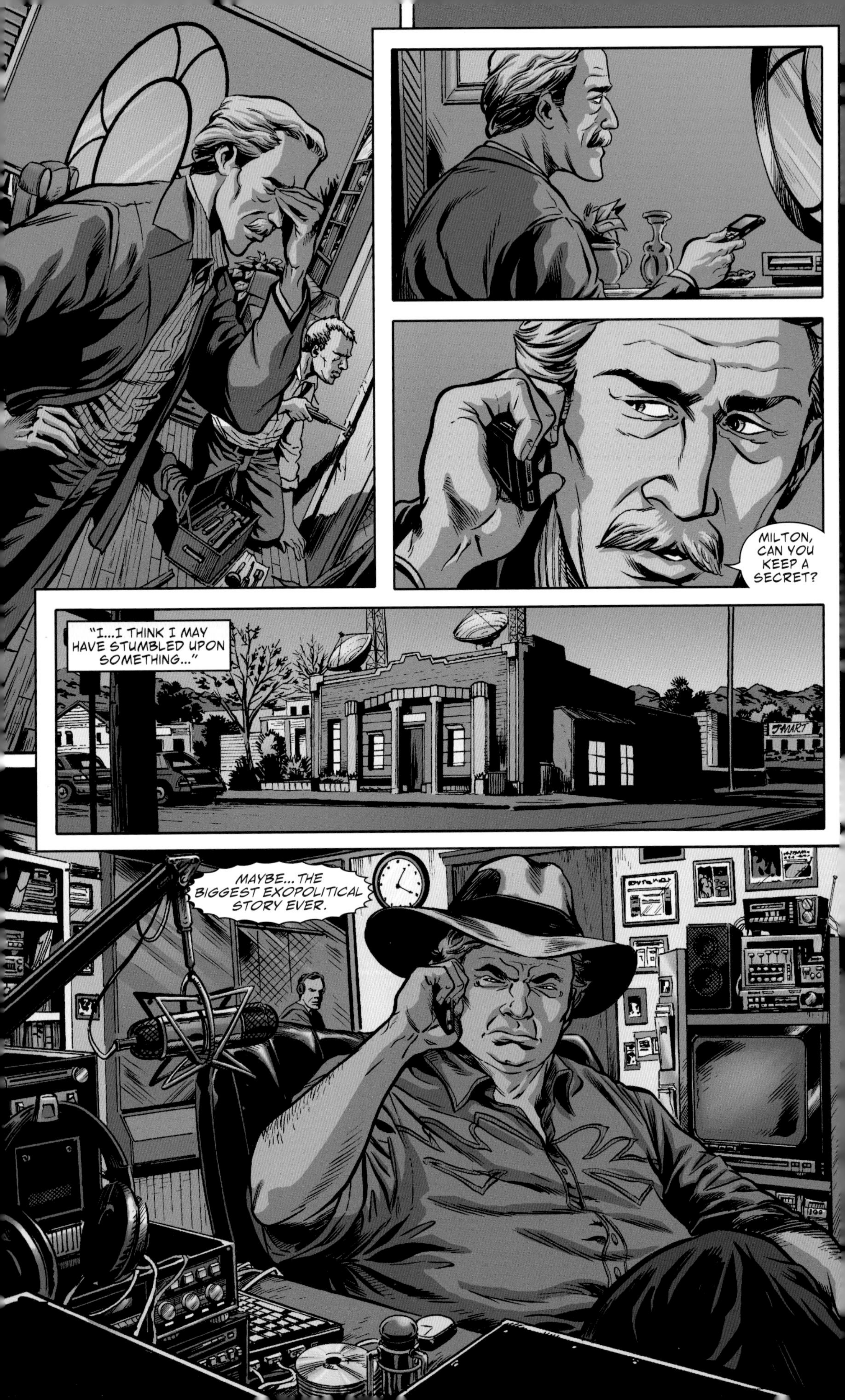
MILTON, CAN YOU KEEP A SECRET?
"I...I THINK I MAY HAVE STUMBLED UPON SOMETHING..."
MAYBE... THE BIGGEST EXOPOLITICAL STORY EVER.

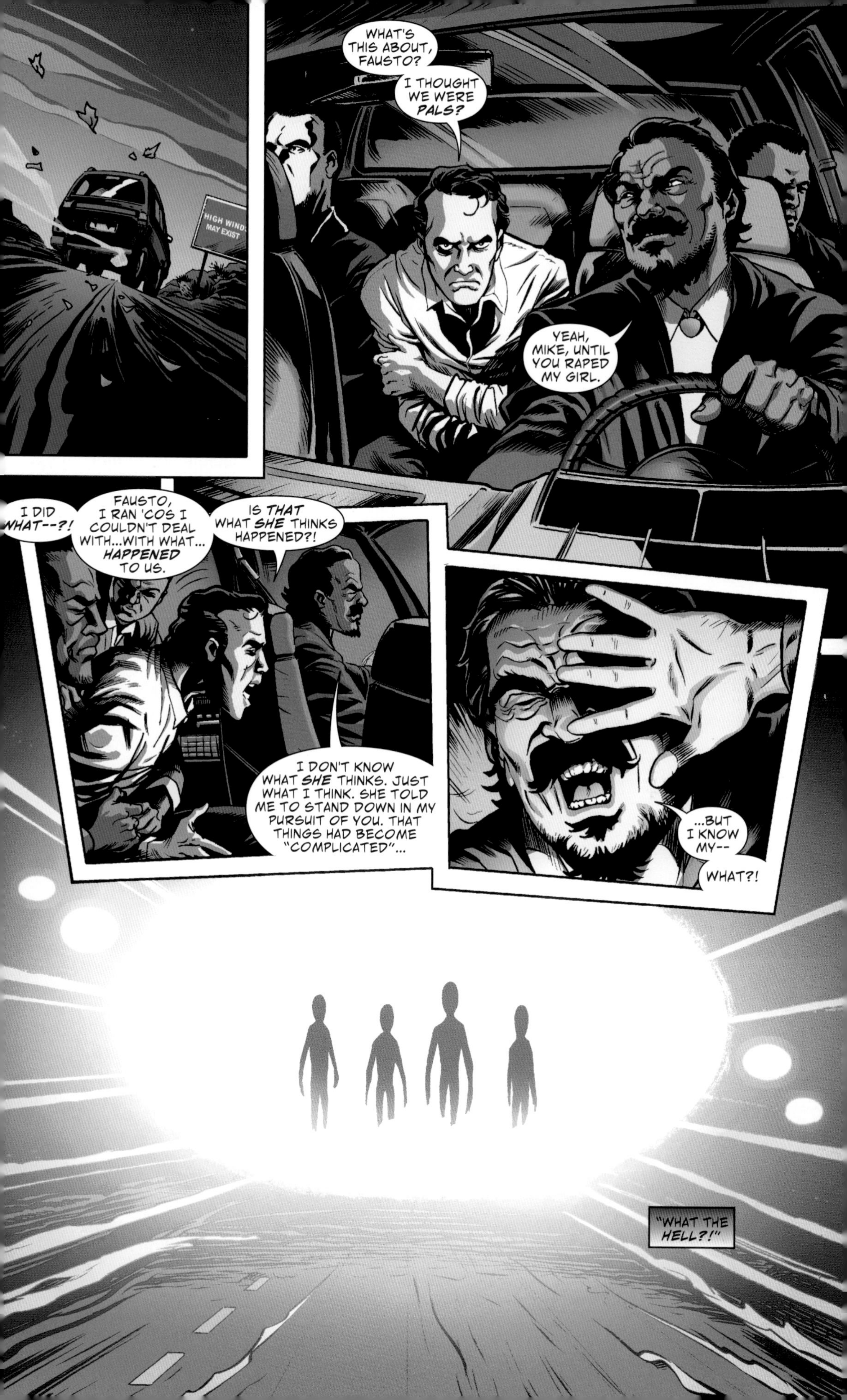
HIGH WINDS MAY EXIST
WHAT'S THIS ABOUT, FAUSTO?
I THOUGHT WE WERE PALS?
YEAH, MIKE, UNTIL YOU RAPED MY GIRL.
I DID WHAT--?!
FAUSTO, I RAN 'COS I COULDN'T DEAL WITH...WITH WHAT... HAPPENED TO US.
IS THAT WHAT SHE THINKS HAPPENED?!
I DON'T KNOW WHAT SHE THINKS. JUST WHAT I THINK. SHE TOLD ME TO STAND DOWN IN MY PURSUIT OF YOU. THAT THINGS HAD BECOME "COMPLICATED"...
...BUT I KNOW MY--
WHAT?!
"WHAT THE HELL?!"

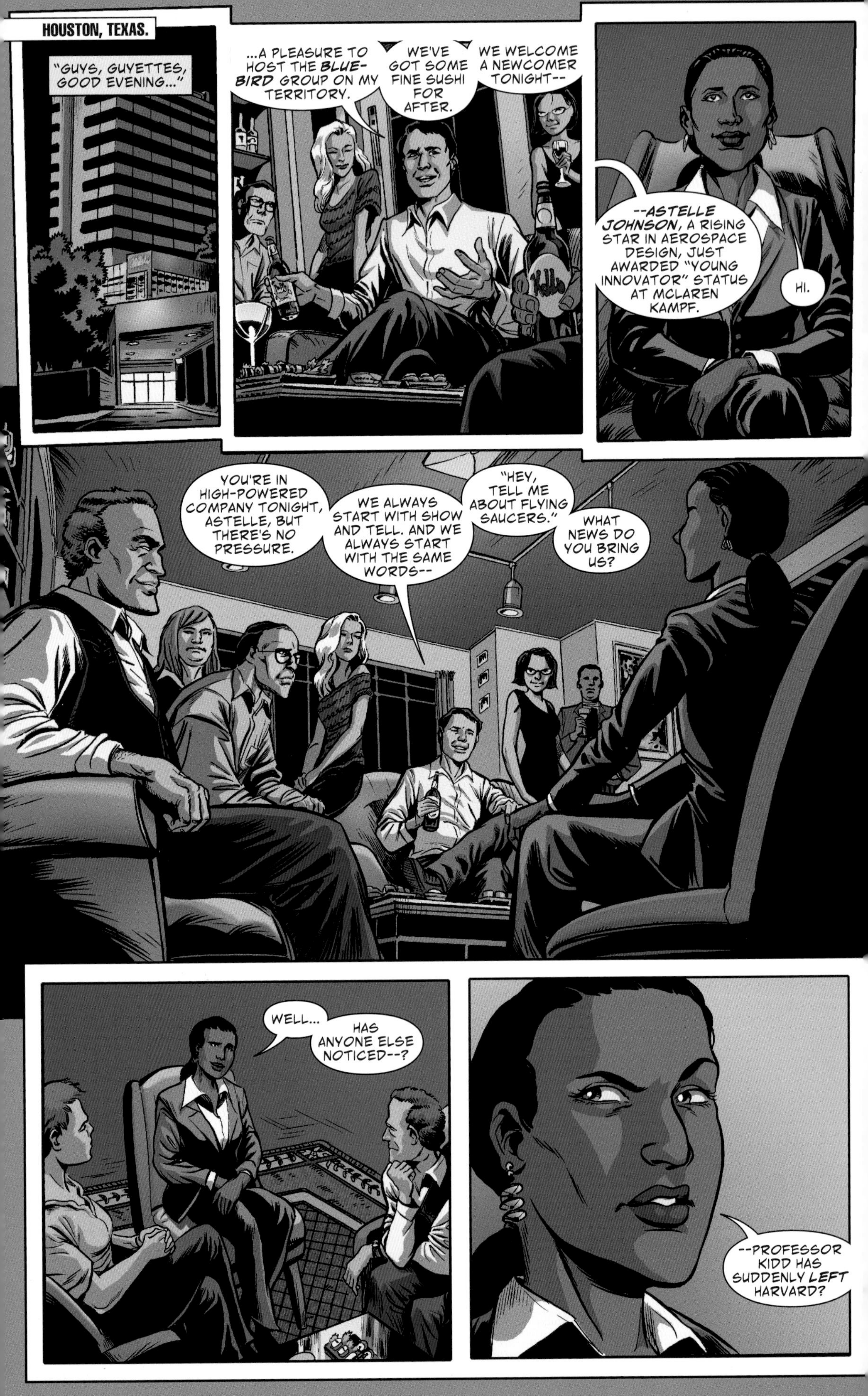
HOUSTON, TEXAS.
"GUYS, GUYETTES, GOOD EVENING..."
...A PLEASURE TO HOST THE *BLUE-BIRD* GROUP ON MY TERRITORY.
WE'VE GOT SOME FINE SUSHI FOR AFTER.
WE WELCOME A NEWCOMER TONIGHT--
--*ASTELLE JOHNSON*, A RISING STAR IN AEROSPACE DESIGN, JUST AWARDED "YOUNG INNOVATOR" STATUS AT MCLAREN KAMPF.
HI.
YOU'RE IN HIGH-POWERED COMPANY TONIGHT, ASTELLE, BUT THERE'S NO PRESSURE.
WE ALWAYS START WITH SHOW AND TELL. AND WE ALWAYS START WITH THE SAME WORDS--
"HEY, TELL ME ABOUT FLYING SAUCERS."
WHAT NEWS DO YOU BRING US?
WELL...
HAS ANYONE ELSE NOTICED--?
--PROFESSOR KIDD HAS SUDDENLY *LEFT* HARVARD?

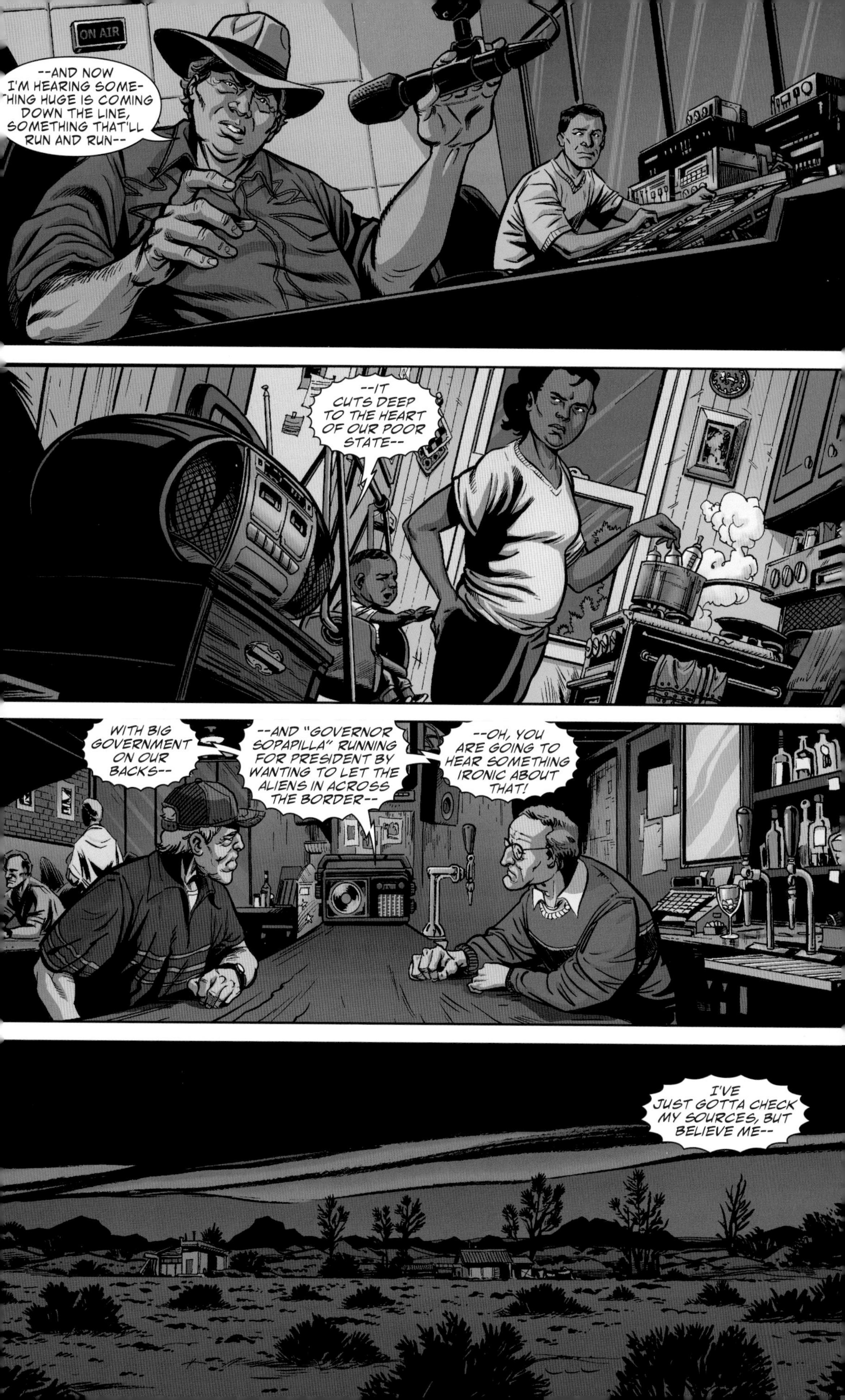
ON AIR
--AND NOW I'M HEARING SOME-HING HUGE IS COMING DOWN THE LINE, SOMETHING THAT'LL RUN AND RUN--
--IT CUTS DEEP TO THE HEART OF OUR POOR STATE--
WITH BIG GOVERNMENT ON OUR BACKS--
--AND "GOVERNOR SOPAPILLA" RUNNING FOR PRESIDENT BY WANTING TO LET THE ALIENS IN ACROSS THE BORDER--
--OH, YOU ARE GOING TO HEAR SOMETHING IRONIC ABOUT THAT!
I'VE JUST GOTTA CHECK MY SOURCES, BUT BELIEVE ME--

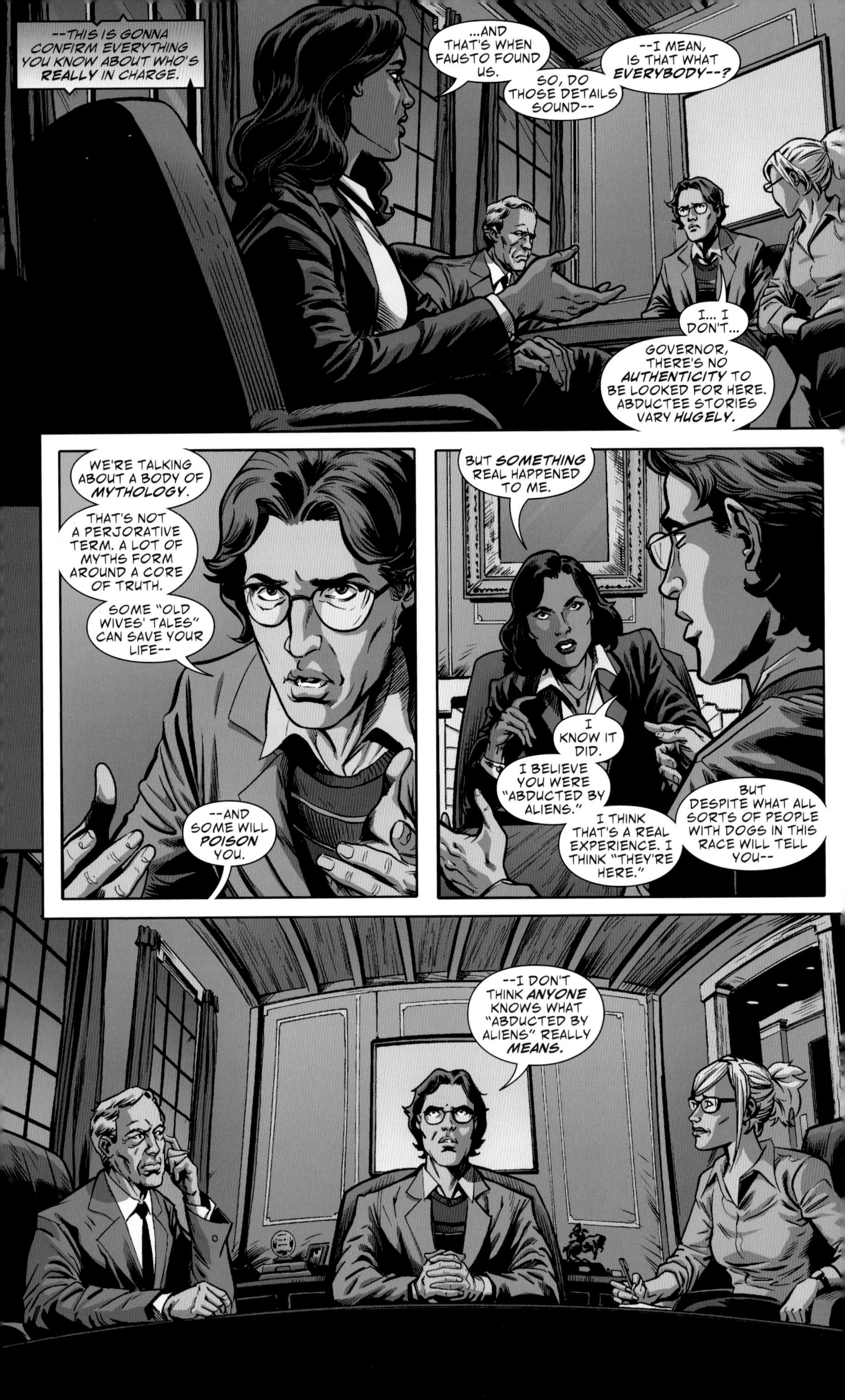
--THIS IS GONNA CONFIRM EVERYTHING YOU KNOW ABOUT WHO'S REALLY IN CHARGE.
...AND THAT'S WHEN FAUSTO FOUND US.
SO, DO THOSE DETAILS SOUND--
--I MEAN, IS THAT WHAT EVERYBODY--?
I... I DON'T...
GOVERNOR, THERE'S NO AUTHENTICITY TO BE LOOKED FOR HERE. ABDUCTEE STORIES VARY HUGELY.
WE'RE TALKING ABOUT A BODY OF MYTHOLOGY.
THAT'S NOT A PERJORATIVE TERM. A LOT OF MYTHS FORM AROUND A CORE OF TRUTH.
SOME "OLD WIVES' TALES" CAN SAVE YOUR LIFE--
--AND SOME WILL POISON YOU.
BUT SOMETHING REAL HAPPENED TO ME.
I KNOW IT DID.
I BELIEVE YOU WERE "ABDUCTED BY ALIENS."
I THINK THAT'S A REAL EXPERIENCE. I THINK "THEY'RE HERE."
BUT DESPITE WHAT ALL SORTS OF PEOPLE WITH DOGS IN THIS RACE WILL TELL YOU--
--I DON'T THINK ANYONE KNOWS WHAT "ABDUCTED BY ALIENS" REALLY MEANS.

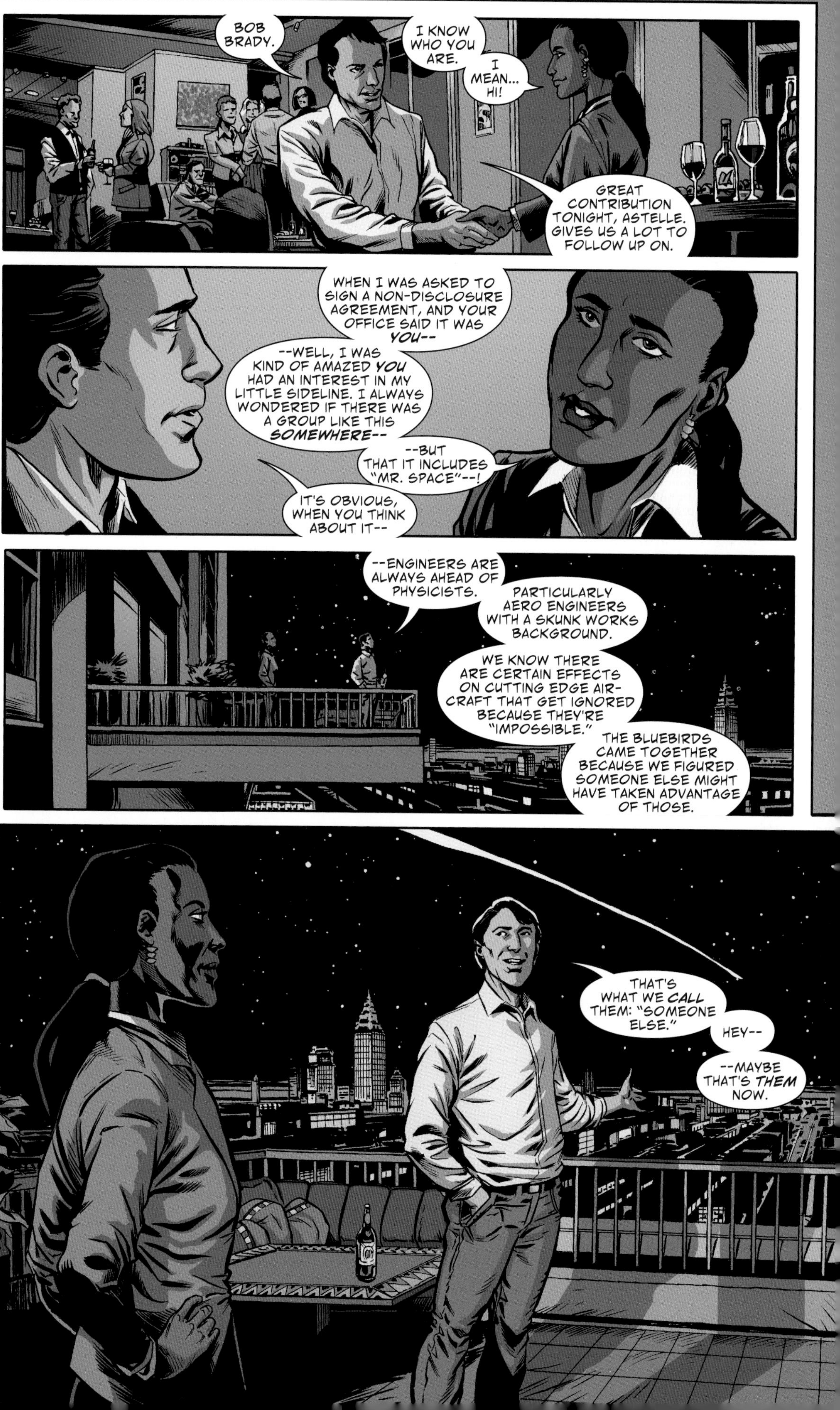
BOB BRADY.
I KNOW WHO YOU ARE.
I MEAN... HI!
GREAT CONTRIBUTION TONIGHT, ASTELLE. GIVES US A LOT TO FOLLOW UP ON.
WHEN I WAS ASKED TO SIGN A NON-DISCLOSURE AGREEMENT, AND YOUR OFFICE SAID IT WAS *YOU*--
--WELL, I WAS KIND OF AMAZED *YOU* HAD AN INTEREST IN MY LITTLE SIDELINE. I ALWAYS WONDERED IF THERE WAS A GROUP LIKE THIS *SOMEWHERE*--
--BUT THAT IT INCLUDES "MR. SPACE"--!
IT'S OBVIOUS, WHEN YOU THINK ABOUT IT--
--ENGINEERS ARE ALWAYS AHEAD OF PHYSICISTS.
PARTICULARLY AERO ENGINEERS WITH A SKUNK WORKS BACKGROUND.
WE KNOW THERE ARE CERTAIN EFFECTS ON CUTTING EDGE AIR-CRAFT THAT GET IGNORED BECAUSE THEY'RE "IMPOSSIBLE."
THE BLUEBIRDS CAME TOGETHER BECAUSE WE FIGURED SOMEONE ELSE MIGHT HAVE TAKEN ADVANTAGE OF THOSE.
THAT'S WHAT WE *CALL* THEM: "SOMEONE ELSE."
HEY--
--MAYBE THAT'S *THEM* NOW.

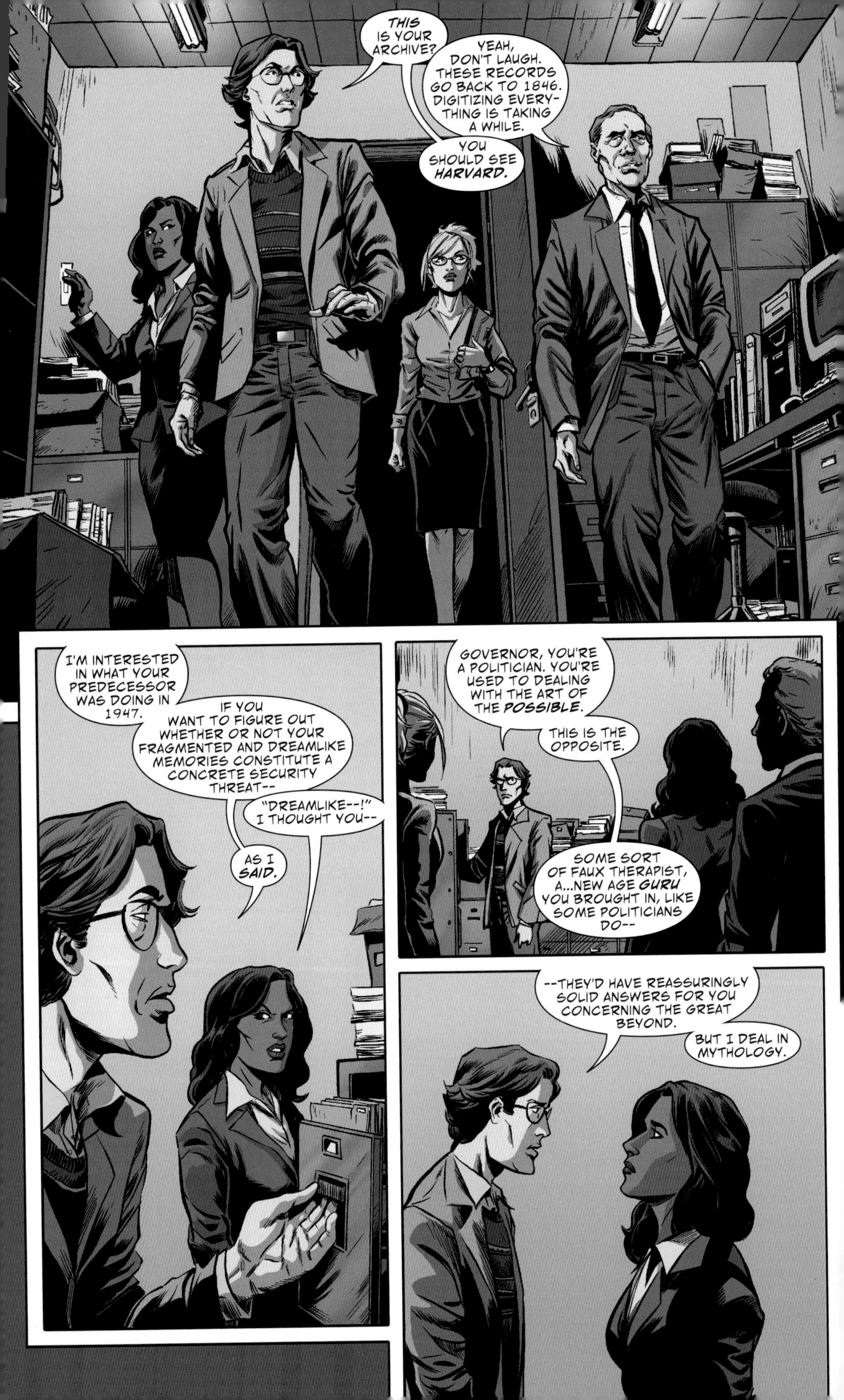
THIS IS YOUR ARCHIVE?
YEAH, DON'T LAUGH. THESE RECORDS GO BACK TO 1846. DIGITIZING EVERYTHING IS TAKING A WHILE.
YOU SHOULD SEE HARVARD.
I'M INTERESTED IN WHAT YOUR PREDECESSOR WAS DOING IN 1947.
IF YOU WANT TO FIGURE OUT WHETHER OR NOT YOUR FRAGMENTED AND DREAMLIKE MEMORIES CONSTITUTE A CONCRETE SECURITY THREAT--
"DREAMLIKE--!" I THOUGHT YOU--
AS I SAID.
GOVERNOR, YOU'RE A POLITICIAN. YOU'RE USED TO DEALING WITH THE ART OF THE POSSIBLE.
THIS IS THE OPPOSITE.
SOME SORT OF FAUX THERAPIST, A...NEW AGE GURU YOU BROUGHT IN, LIKE SOME POLITICIANS DO--
--THEY'D HAVE REASSURINGLY SOLID ANSWERS FOR YOU CONCERNING THE GREAT BEYOND.
BUT I DEAL IN MYTHOLOGY.

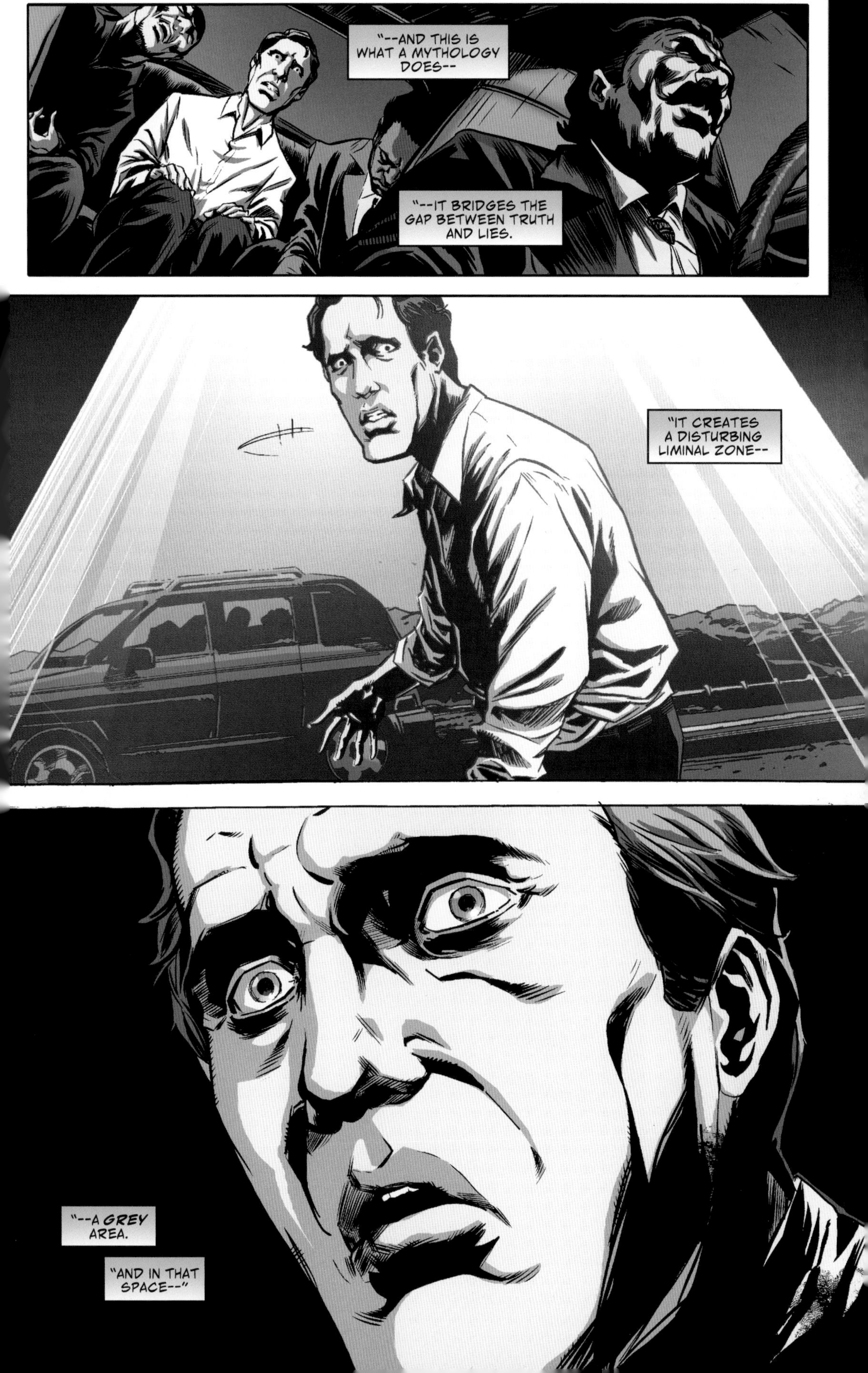
"--AND THIS IS WHAT A MYTHOLOGY DOES--
"--IT BRIDGES THE GAP BETWEEN TRUTH AND LIES.
"IT CREATES A DISTURBING LIMINAL ZONE--
"--A *GREY* AREA.
"AND IN THAT SPACE--"

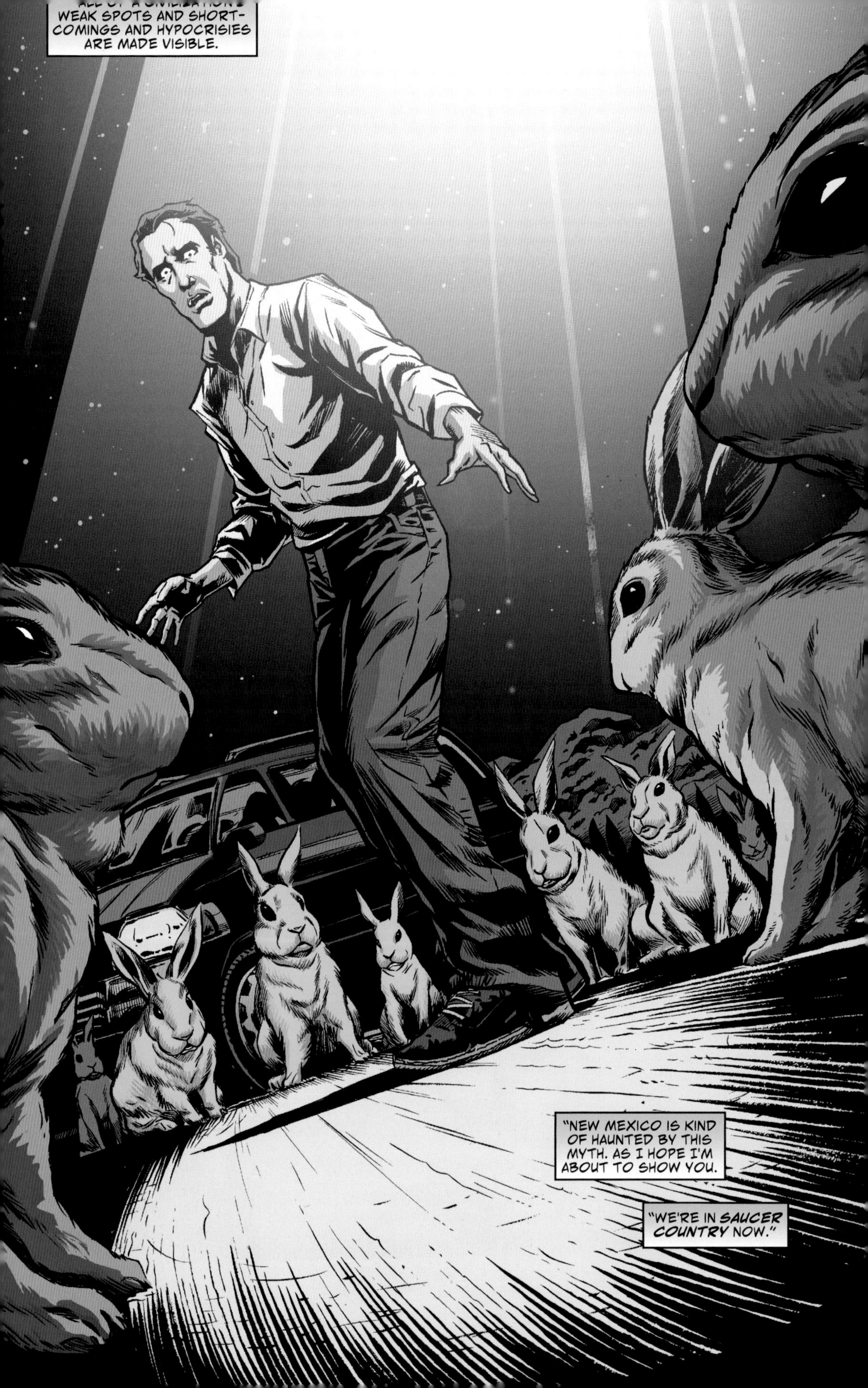
WEAK SPOTS AND SHORT-COMINGS AND HYPOCRISIES ARE MADE VISIBLE.
"NEW MEXICO IS KIND OF HAUNTED BY THIS MYTH. AS I HOPE I'M ABOUT TO SHOW YOU.
"WE'RE IN SAUCER COUNTRY NOW."

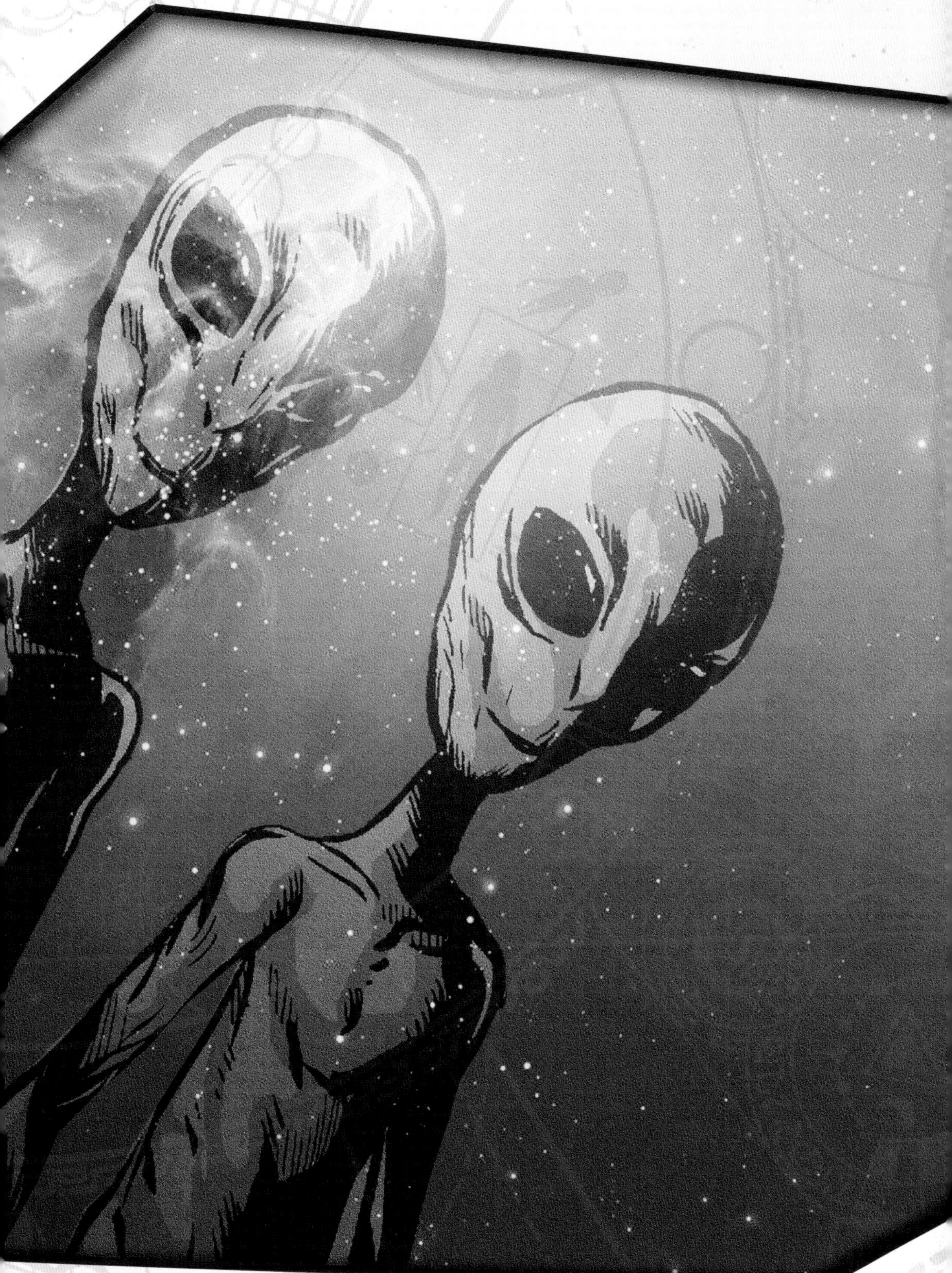

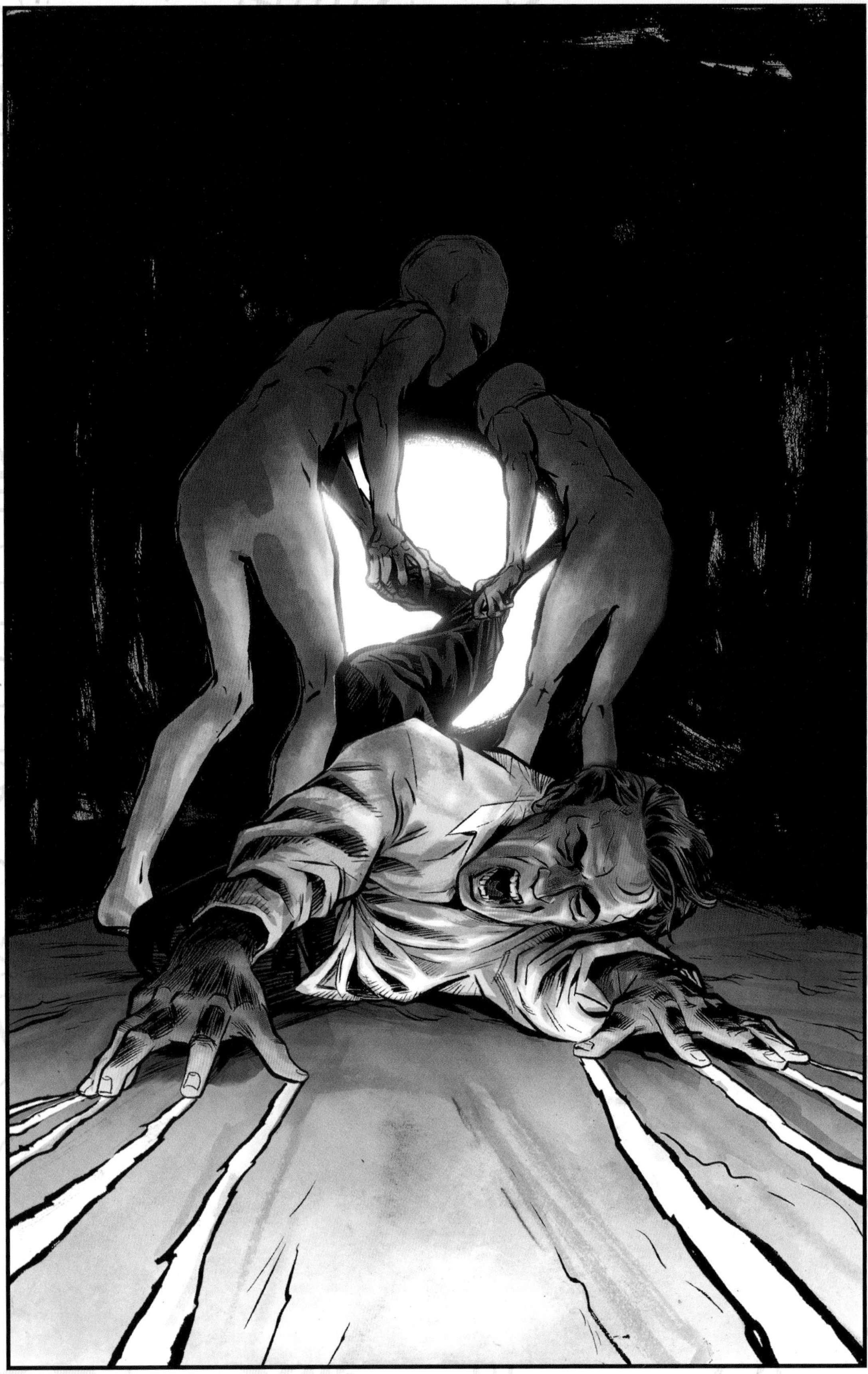

COVER ART BY **RYAN KELLY**

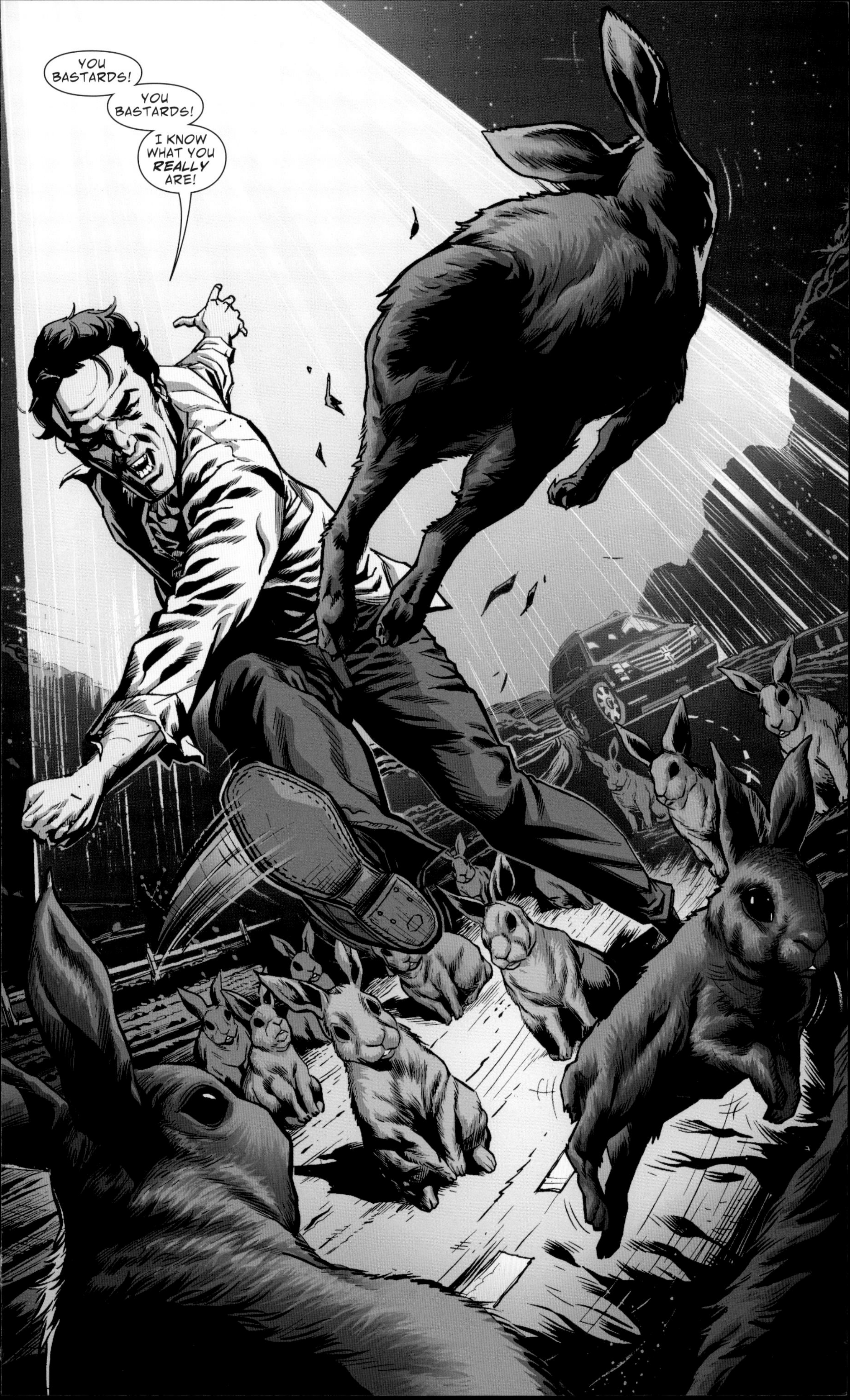
YOU BASTARDS!
YOU BASTARDS!
I KNOW WHAT YOU REALLY ARE!

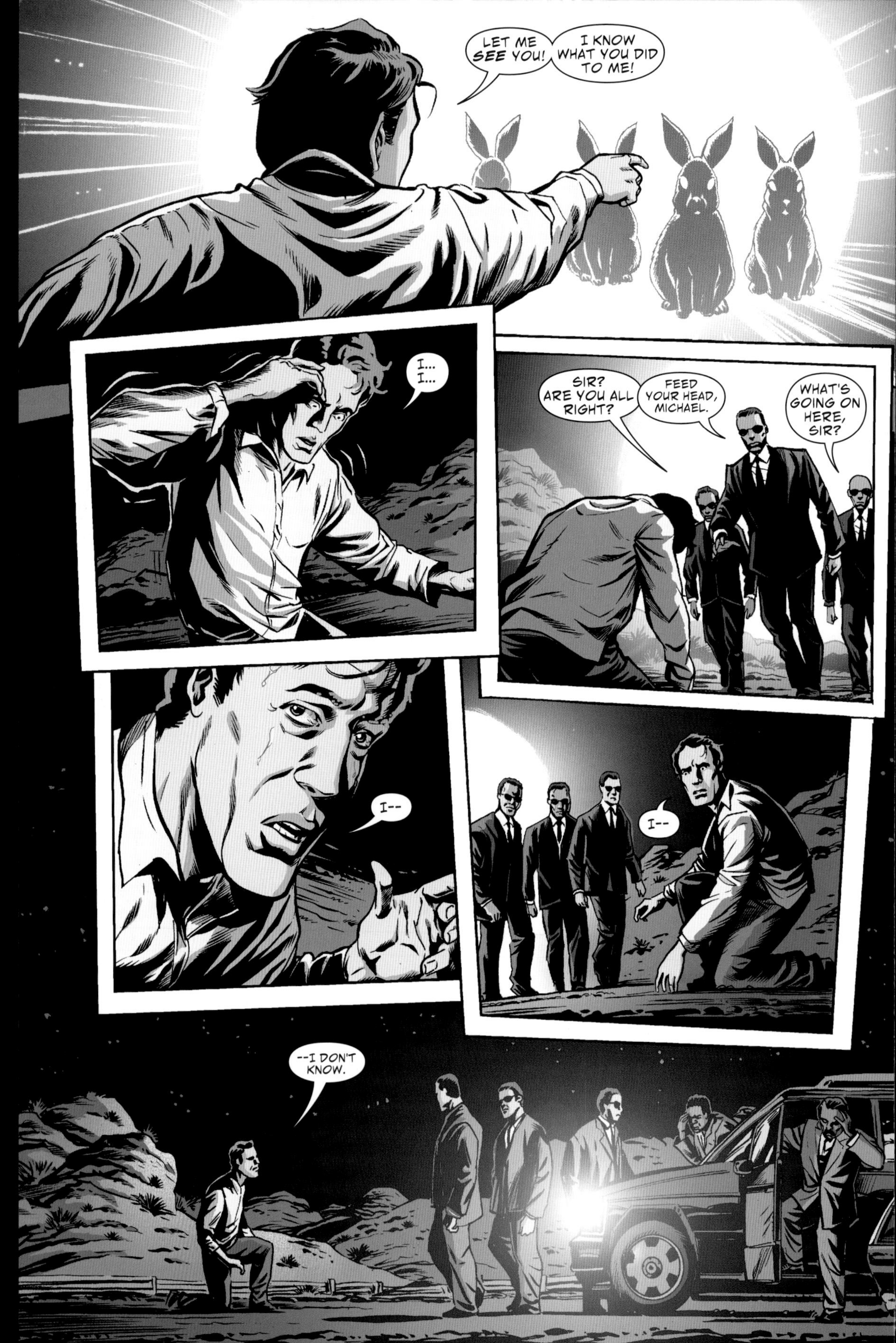
LET ME SEE YOU!
I KNOW WHAT YOU DID TO ME!
I... I...
SIR? ARE YOU ALL RIGHT?
FEED YOUR HEAD, MICHAEL.
WHAT'S GOING ON HERE, SIR?
I--
I--
--I DON'T KNOW.

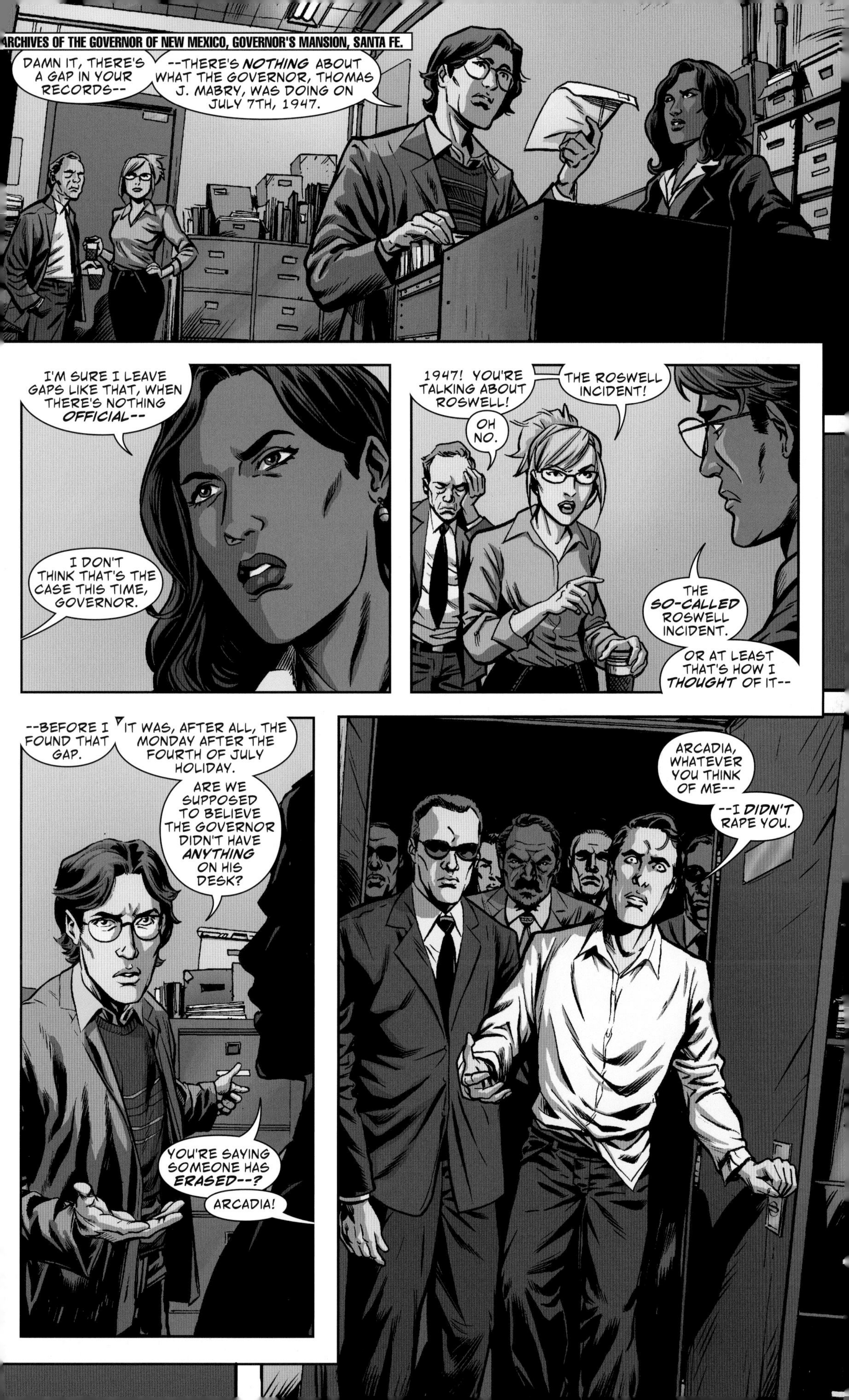
ARCHIVES OF THE GOVERNOR OF NEW MEXICO, GOVERNOR'S MANSION, SANTA FE.
DAMN IT, THERE'S A GAP IN YOUR RECORDS--
--THERE'S NOTHING ABOUT WHAT THE GOVERNOR, THOMAS J. MABRY, WAS DOING ON JULY 7TH, 1947.
I'M SURE I LEAVE GAPS LIKE THAT, WHEN THERE'S NOTHING OFFICIAL--
I DON'T THINK THAT'S THE CASE THIS TIME, GOVERNOR.
1947! YOU'RE TALKING ABOUT ROSWELL!
THE ROSWELL INCIDENT!
OH NO.
THE SO-CALLED ROSWELL INCIDENT.
OR AT LEAST THAT'S HOW I THOUGHT OF IT--
--BEFORE I FOUND THAT GAP.
IT WAS, AFTER ALL, THE MONDAY AFTER THE FOURTH OF JULY HOLIDAY.
ARE WE SUPPOSED TO BELIEVE THE GOVERNOR DIDN'T HAVE ANYTHING ON HIS DESK?
YOU'RE SAYING SOMEONE HAS ERASED--?
ARCADIA!
ARCADIA, WHATEVER YOU THINK OF ME--
--I DIDN'T RAPE YOU.

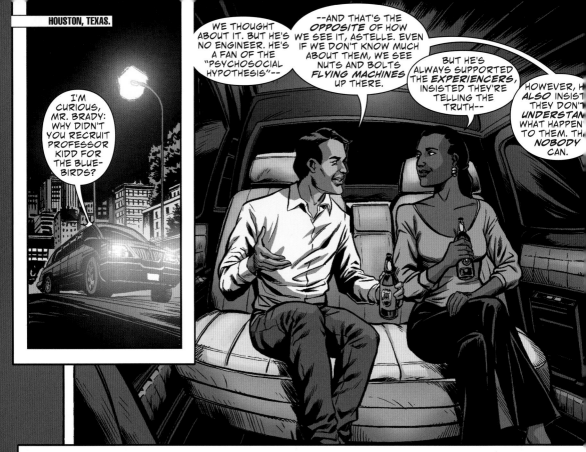

I'M CURIOUS, MR. BRADY: WHY DIDN'T YOU RECRUIT PROFESSOR KIDD FOR THE BLUE-BIRDS?

WE THOUGHT ABOUT IT. BUT HE'S NO ENGINEER. HE'S A FAN OF THE "PSYCHOSOCIAL HYPOTHESIS"--

--AND THAT'S THE OPPOSITE OF HOW WE SEE IT, ASTELLE. EVEN IF WE DON'T KNOW MUCH ABOUT THEM, WE SEE NUTS AND BOLTS FLYING MACHINES UP THERE.

BUT HE'S ALWAYS SUPPORTED THE EXPERIENCERS, INSISTED THEY'RE TELLING THE TRUTH--

HOWEVER, H ALSO INSIST THEY DON'T UNDERSTAN WHAT HAPPEN TO THEM. TH NOBODY CAN.

WE DECIDED HE COULD DO WITHOUT THE EPIPHANY OUR RESEARCHES WOULD PROVIDE.

AND THEN HE STARTED BEHAVING SO ERRATICALLY AT HARVARD THAT...WELL...WE THINK WE CAN GUESS WHAT'S BEING DONE TO HIM. WE THINK HE'S "GOING HOLLYWOOD."

WHAT DOES THAT MEAN?

SOMETHING TERRIBLE.

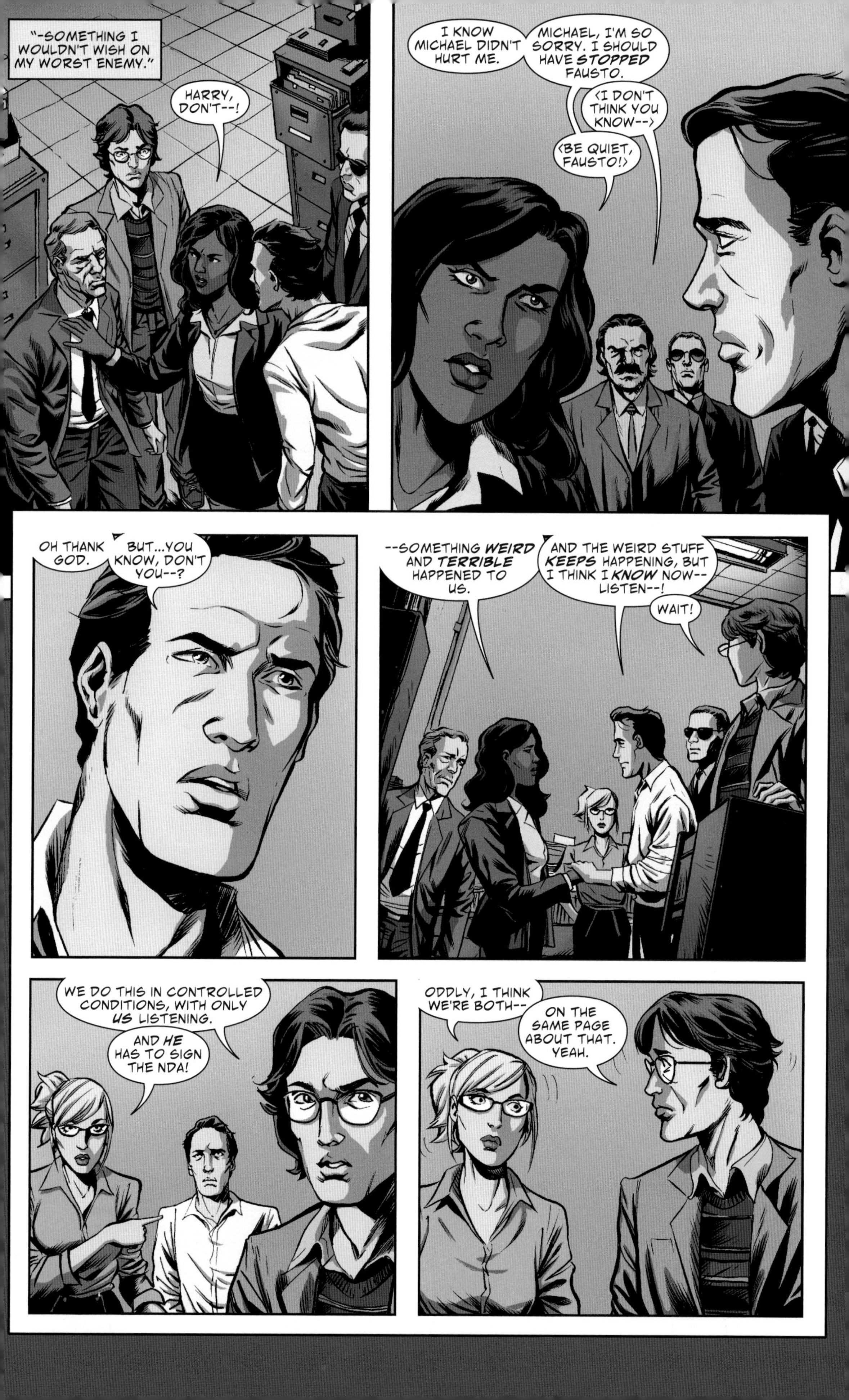

"-SOMETHING I WOULDN'T WISH ON MY WORST ENEMY."
HARRY, DON'T--!
I KNOW MICHAEL DIDN'T HURT ME.
MICHAEL, I'M SO SORRY. I SHOULD HAVE STOPPED FAUSTO.
‹I DON'T THINK YOU KNOW--›
‹BE QUIET, FAUSTO!›
OH THANK GOD.
BUT...YOU KNOW, DON'T YOU--?
--SOMETHING WEIRD AND TERRIBLE HAPPENED TO US.
AND THE WEIRD STUFF KEEPS HAPPENING, BUT I THINK I KNOW NOW-- LISTEN--!
WAIT!
WE DO THIS IN CONTROLLED CONDITIONS, WITH ONLY US LISTENING.
AND HE HAS TO SIGN THE NDA!
ODDLY, I THINK WE'RE BOTH--
ON THE SAME PAGE ABOUT THAT. YEAH.

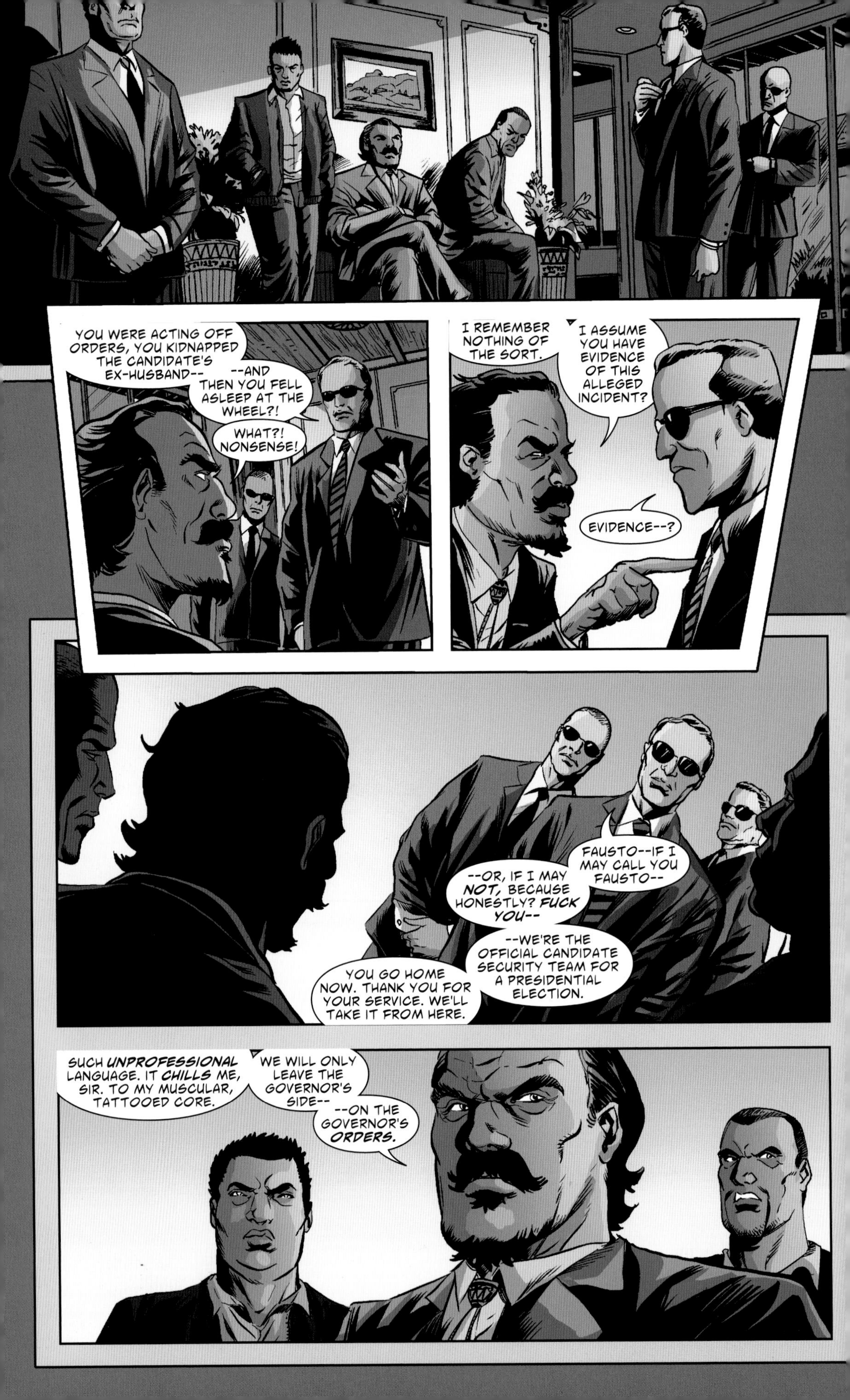
YOU WERE ACTING OFF ORDERS, YOU KIDNAPPED THE CANDIDATE'S EX-HUSBAND--
--AND THEN YOU FELL ASLEEP AT THE WHEEL?!
WHAT?! NONSENSE!
I REMEMBER NOTHING OF THE SORT.
I ASSUME YOU HAVE EVIDENCE OF THIS ALLEGED INCIDENT?
EVIDENCE--?
FAUSTO--IF I MAY CALL YOU FAUSTO--
--OR, IF I MAY NOT, BECAUSE HONESTLY? FUCK YOU--
--WE'RE THE OFFICIAL CANDIDATE SECURITY TEAM FOR A PRESIDENTIAL ELECTION.
YOU GO HOME NOW. THANK YOU FOR YOUR SERVICE. WE'LL TAKE IT FROM HERE.
SUCH UNPROFESSIONAL LANGUAGE. IT CHILLS ME, SIR. TO MY MUSCULAR, TATTOOED CORE.
WE WILL ONLY LEAVE THE GOVERNOR'S SIDE--
--ON THE GOVERNOR'S ORDERS.

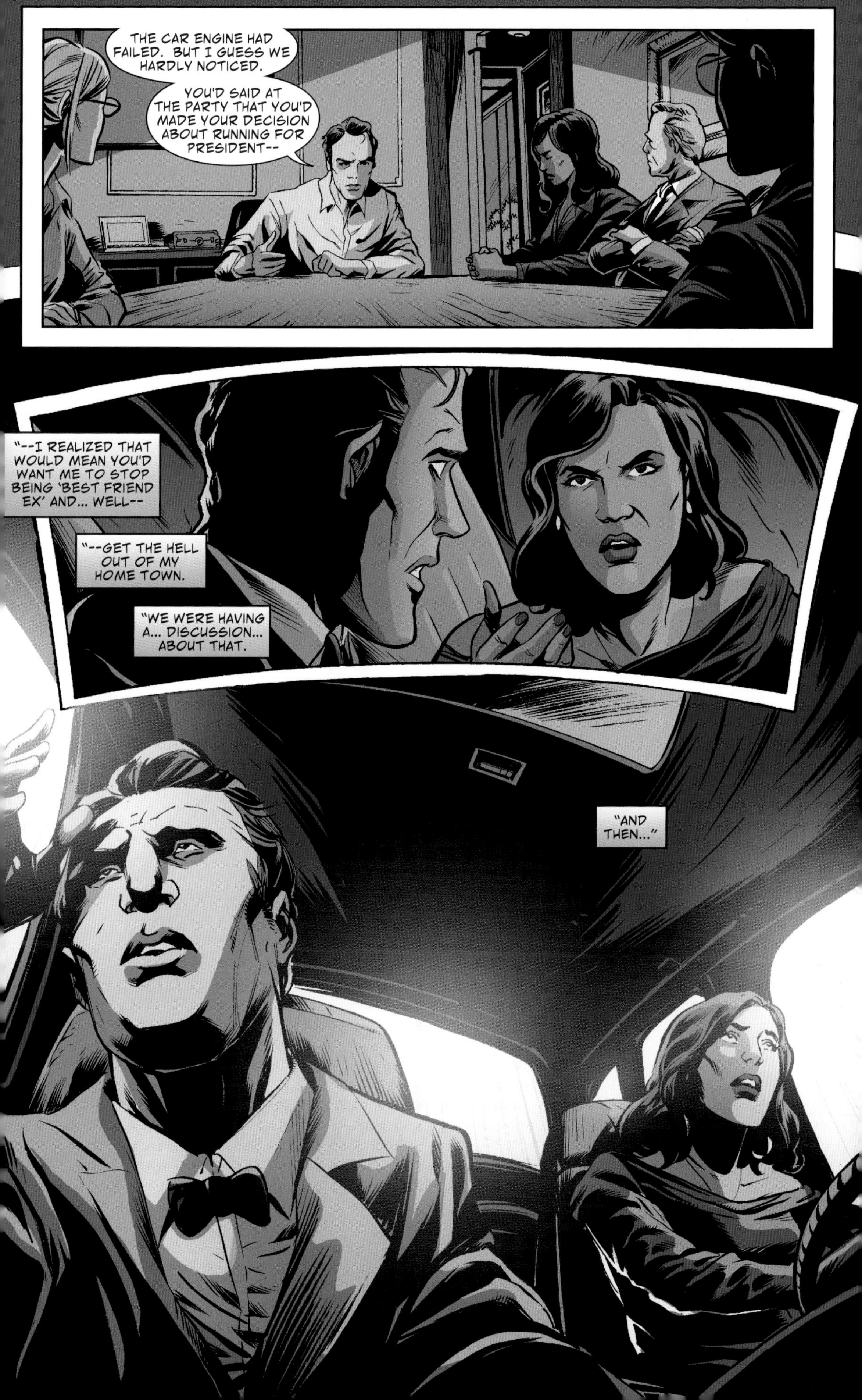
THE CAR ENGINE HAD FAILED. BUT I GUESS WE HARDLY NOTICED.
YOU'D SAID AT THE PARTY THAT YOU'D MADE YOUR DECISION ABOUT RUNNING FOR PRESIDENT--
"--I REALIZED THAT WOULD MEAN YOU'D WANT ME TO STOP BEING 'BEST FRIEND EX' AND... WELL--
"--GET THE HELL OUT OF MY HOME TOWN.
"WE WERE HAVING A... DISCUSSION... ABOUT THAT.
"AND THEN..."

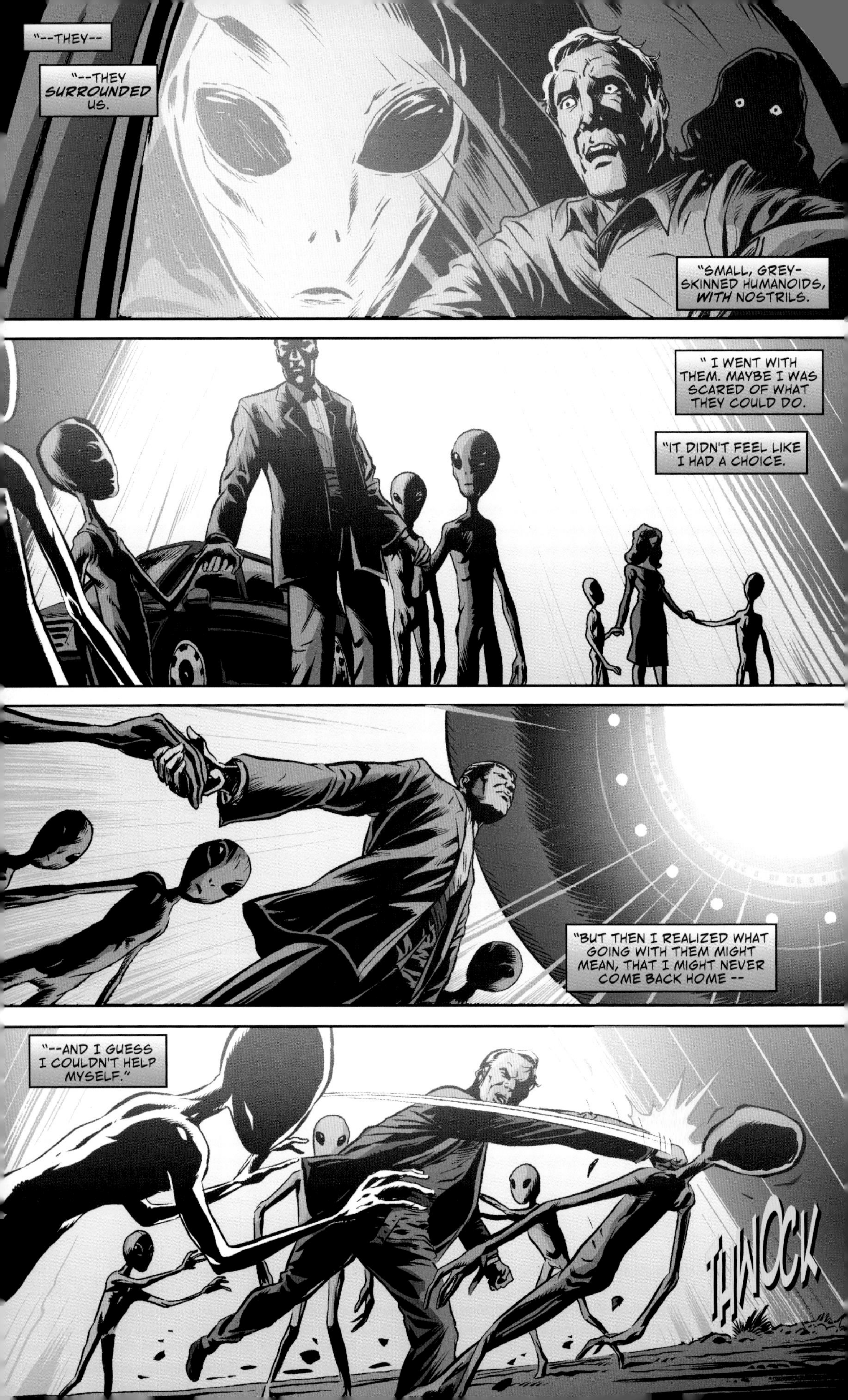
"--THEY--
"--THEY SURROUNDED US.
"SMALL, GREY-SKINNED HUMANOIDS, WITH NOSTRILS.
" I WENT WITH THEM. MAYBE I WAS SCARED OF WHAT THEY COULD DO.
"IT DIDN'T FEEL LIKE I HAD A CHOICE.
"BUT THEN I REALIZED WHAT GOING WITH THEM MIGHT MEAN, THAT I MIGHT NEVER COME BACK HOME --
"--AND I GUESS I COULDN'T HELP MYSELF."
THWOCK

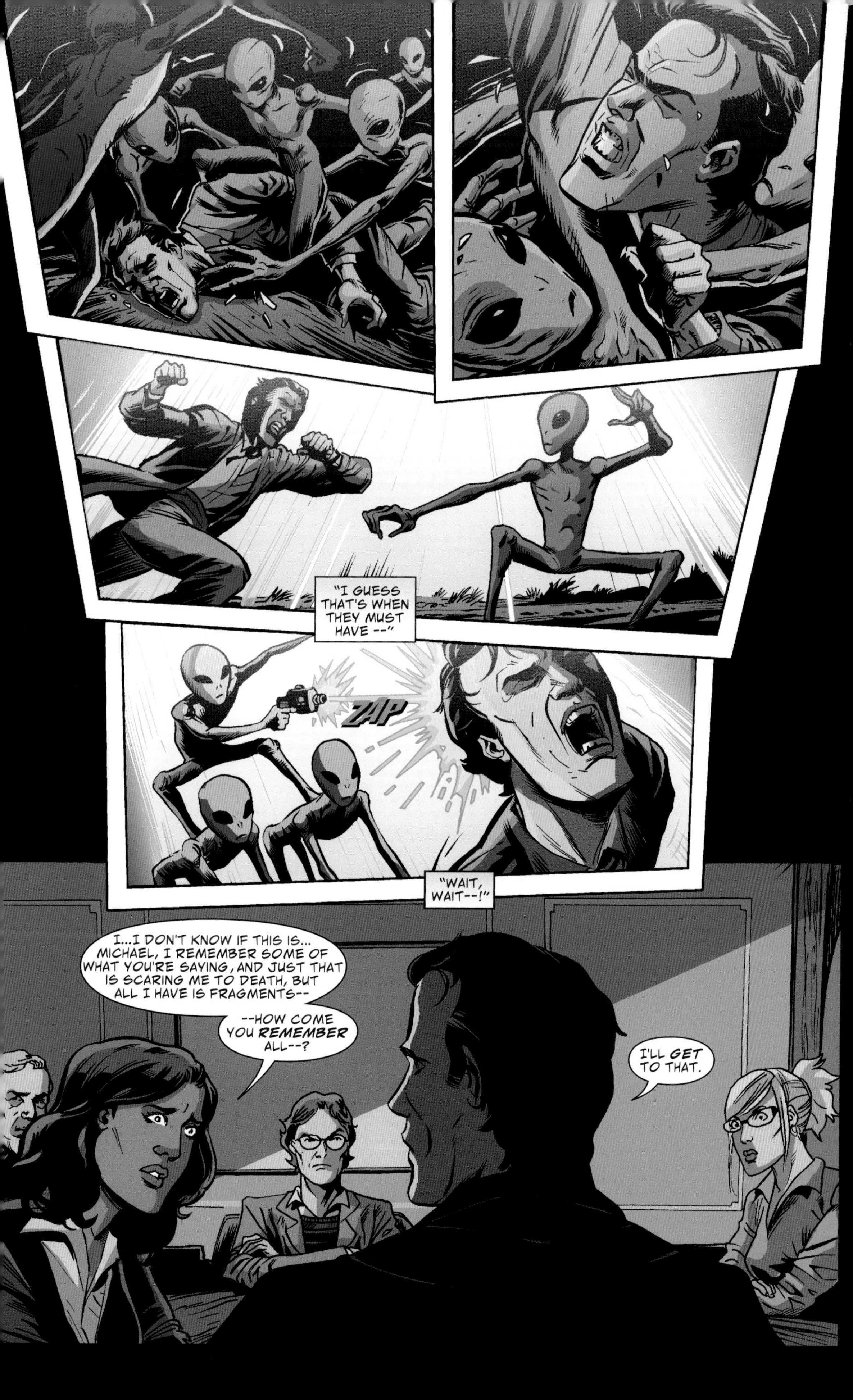
"I GUESS THAT'S WHEN THEY MUST HAVE --"
ZAP
"WAIT, WAIT--!"
I...I DON'T KNOW IF THIS IS... MICHAEL, I REMEMBER SOME OF WHAT YOU'RE SAYING, AND JUST THAT IS SCARING ME TO DEATH, BUT ALL I HAVE IS FRAGMENTS--
--HOW COME YOU REMEMBER ALL--?
I'LL GET TO THAT.

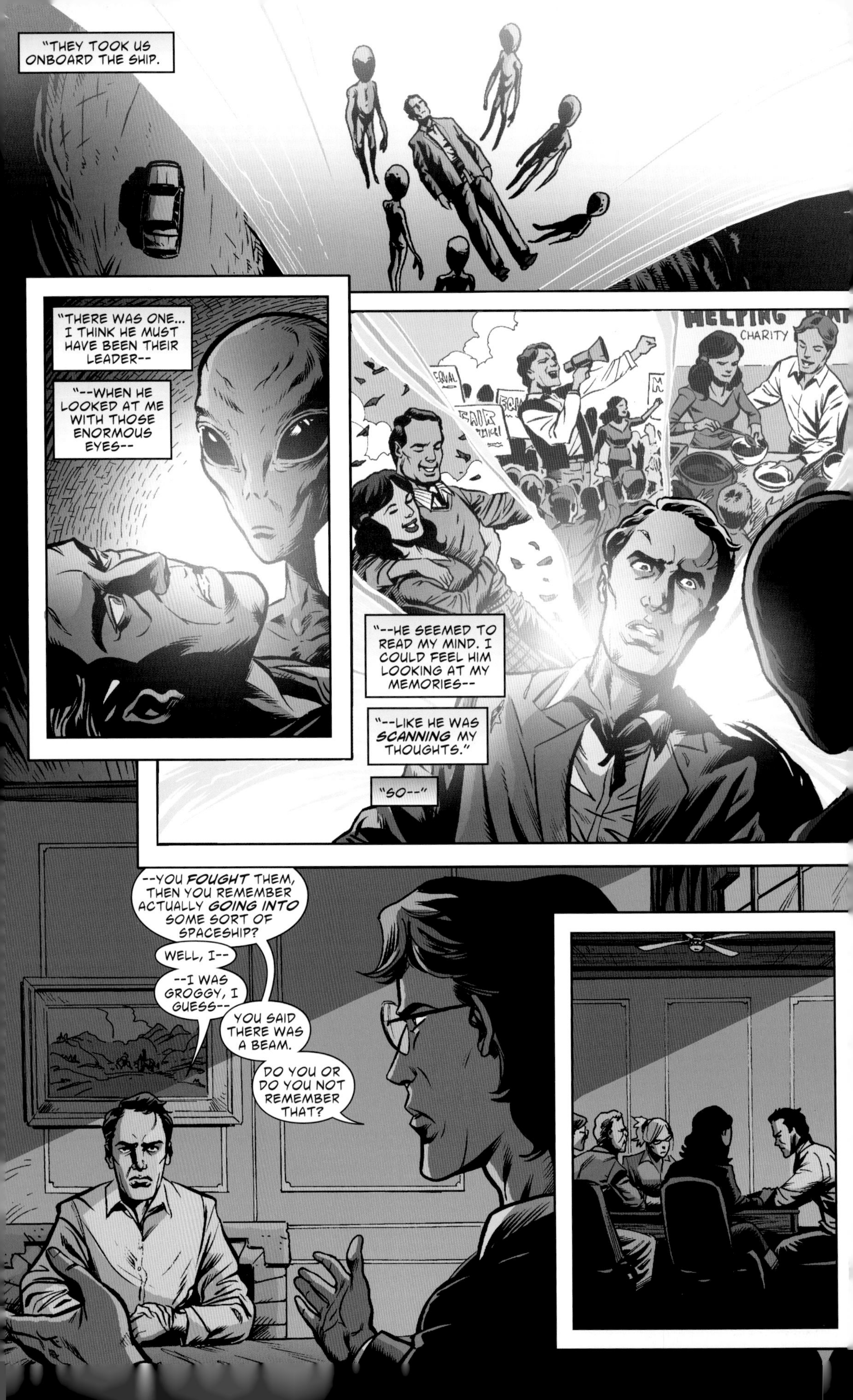
"THEY TOOK US ONBOARD THE SHIP.
"THERE WAS ONE... I THINK HE MUST HAVE BEEN THEIR LEADER--
"--WHEN HE LOOKED AT ME WITH THOSE ENORMOUS EYES--
HELPING
CHARITY
EQUAL
"--HE SEEMED TO READ MY MIND. I COULD FEEL HIM LOOKING AT MY MEMORIES--
"--LIKE HE WAS SCANNING MY THOUGHTS."
"SO--"
--YOU FOUGHT THEM, THEN YOU REMEMBER ACTUALLY GOING INTO SOME SORT OF SPACESHIP?
WELL, I--
--I WAS GROGGY, I GUESS--
YOU SAID THERE WAS A BEAM.
DO YOU OR DO YOU NOT REMEMBER THAT?

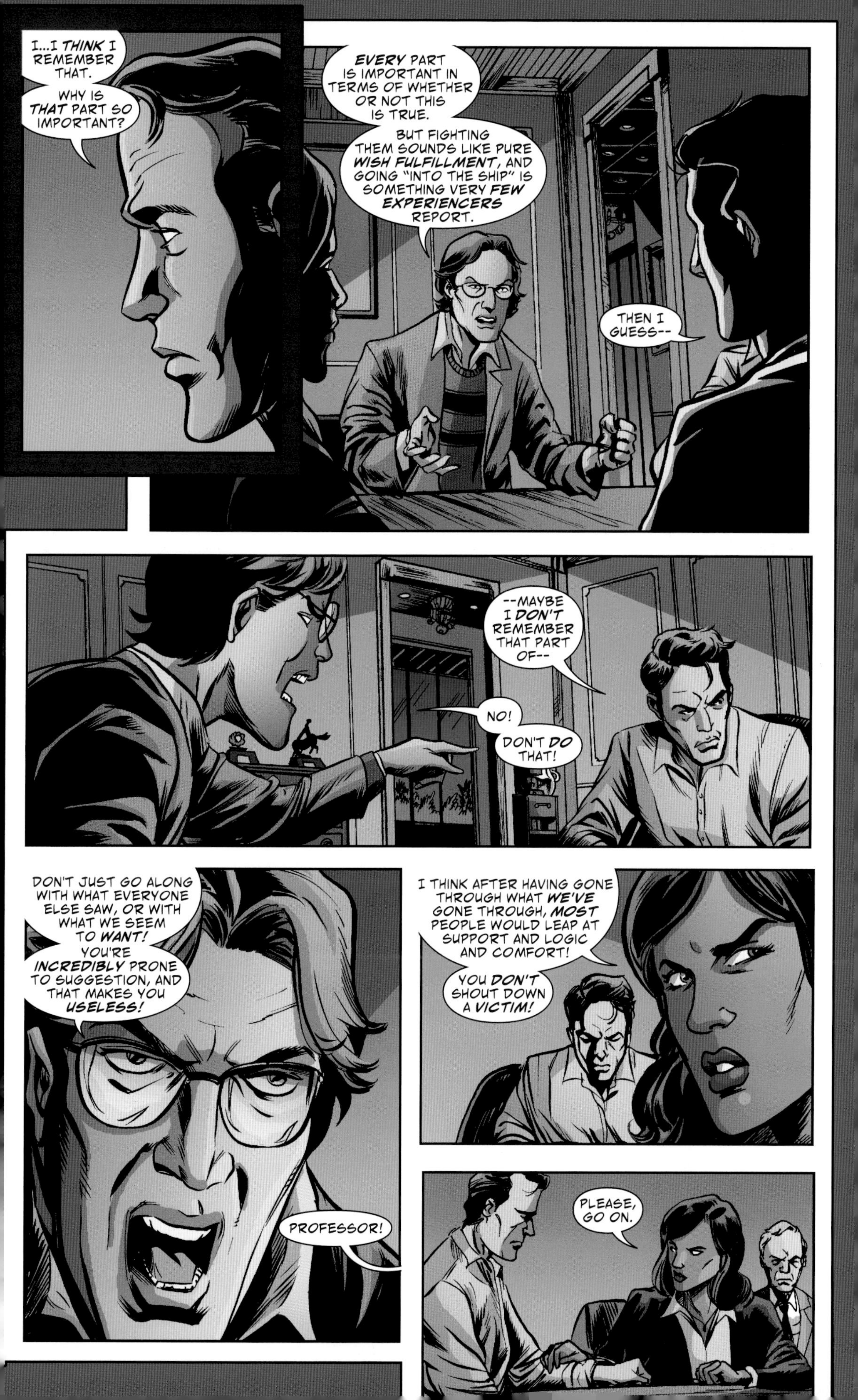
I...I THINK I REMEMBER THAT.
WHY IS THAT PART SO IMPORTANT?
EVERY PART IS IMPORTANT IN TERMS OF WHETHER OR NOT THIS IS TRUE.
BUT FIGHTING THEM SOUNDS LIKE PURE WISH FULFILLMENT, AND GOING "INTO THE SHIP" IS SOMETHING VERY FEW EXPERIENCERS REPORT.
THEN I GUESS--
--MAYBE I DON'T REMEMBER THAT PART OF--
NO!
DON'T DO THAT!
DON'T JUST GO ALONG WITH WHAT EVERYONE ELSE SAW, OR WITH WHAT WE SEEM TO WANT!
YOU'RE INCREDIBLY PRONE TO SUGGESTION, AND THAT MAKES YOU USELESS!
PROFESSOR!
I THINK AFTER HAVING GONE THROUGH WHAT WE'VE GONE THROUGH, MOST PEOPLE WOULD LEAP AT SUPPORT AND LOGIC AND COMFORT!
YOU DON'T SHOUT DOWN A VICTIM!
PLEASE, GO ON.

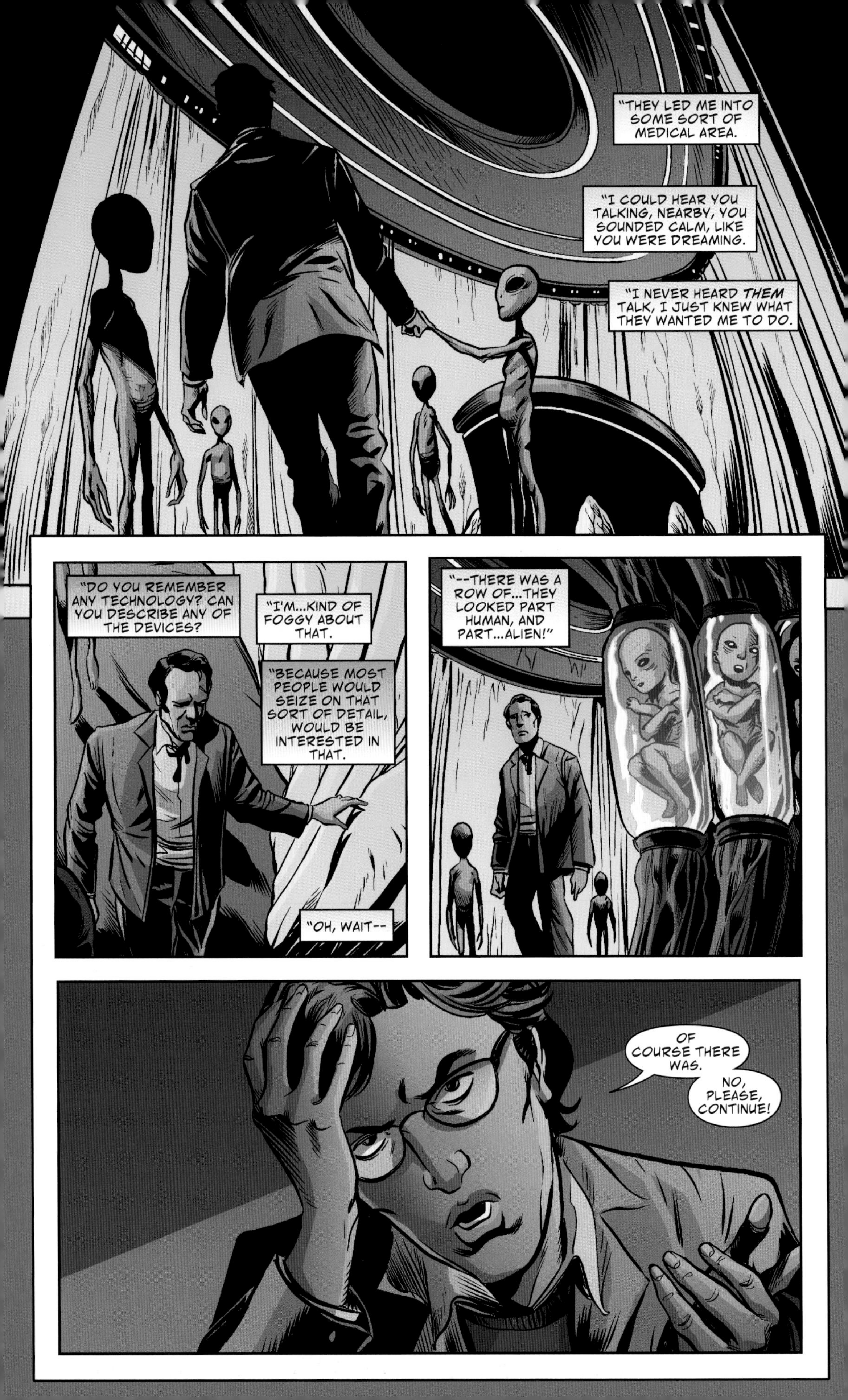
"THEY LED ME INTO SOME SORT OF MEDICAL AREA.
"I COULD HEAR YOU TALKING, NEARBY, YOU SOUNDED CALM, LIKE YOU WERE DREAMING.
"I NEVER HEARD *THEM* TALK, I JUST KNEW WHAT THEY WANTED ME TO DO.
"DO YOU REMEMBER ANY TECHNOLOGY? CAN YOU DESCRIBE ANY OF THE DEVICES?
"I'M...KIND OF FOGGY ABOUT THAT.
"BECAUSE MOST PEOPLE WOULD SEIZE ON THAT SORT OF DETAIL, WOULD BE INTERESTED IN THAT.
"OH, WAIT--
"--THERE WAS A ROW OF...THEY LOOKED PART HUMAN, AND PART...ALIEN!"
OF COURSE THERE WAS.
NO, PLEASE, CONTINUE!

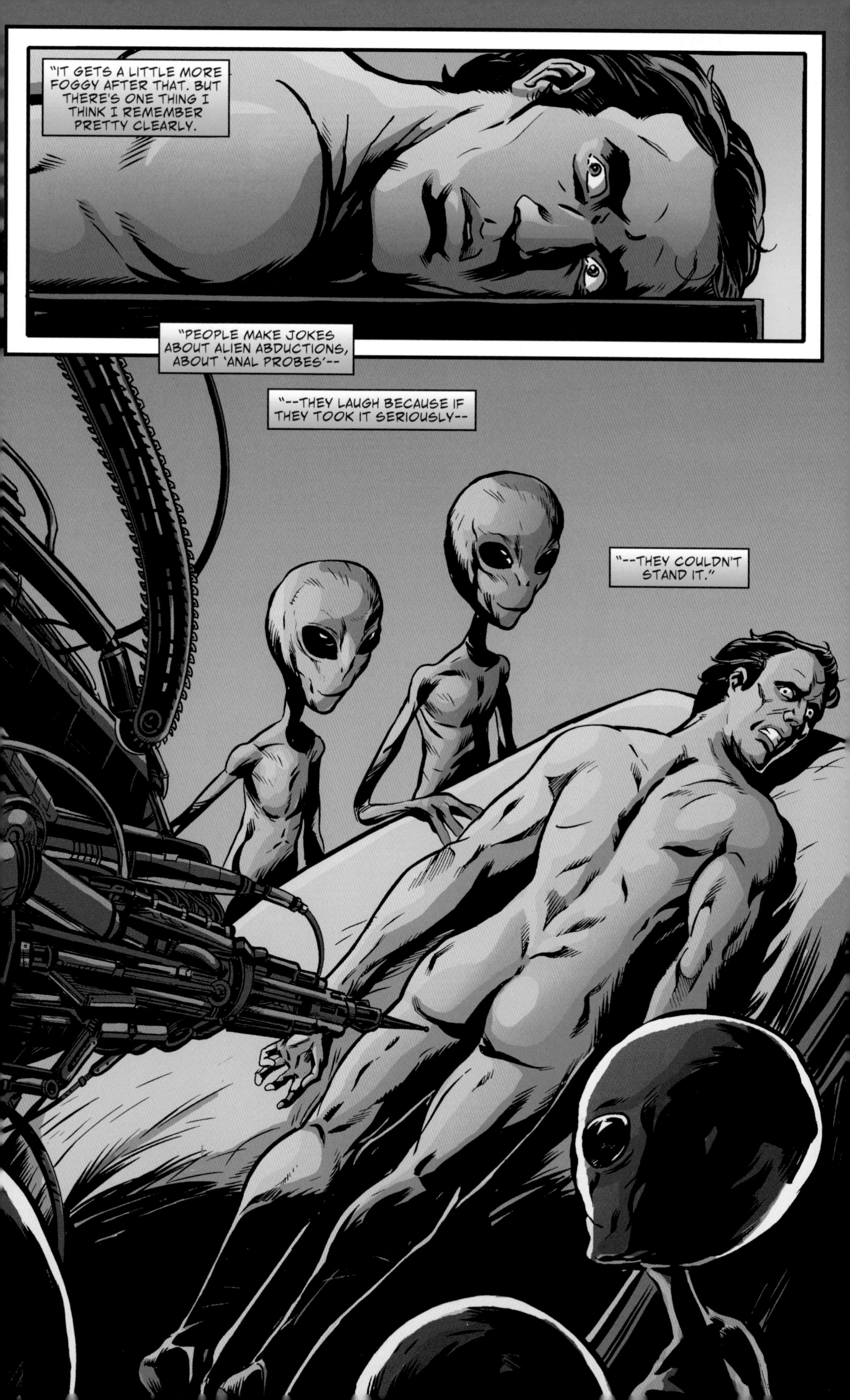

"IT GETS A LITTLE MORE FOGGY AFTER THAT. BUT THERE'S ONE THING I THINK I REMEMBER PRETTY CLEARLY.
"PEOPLE MAKE JOKES ABOUT ALIEN ABDUCTIONS, ABOUT 'ANAL PROBES'--
"--THEY LAUGH BECAUSE IF THEY TOOK IT SERIOUSLY--
"--THEY COULDN'T STAND IT."

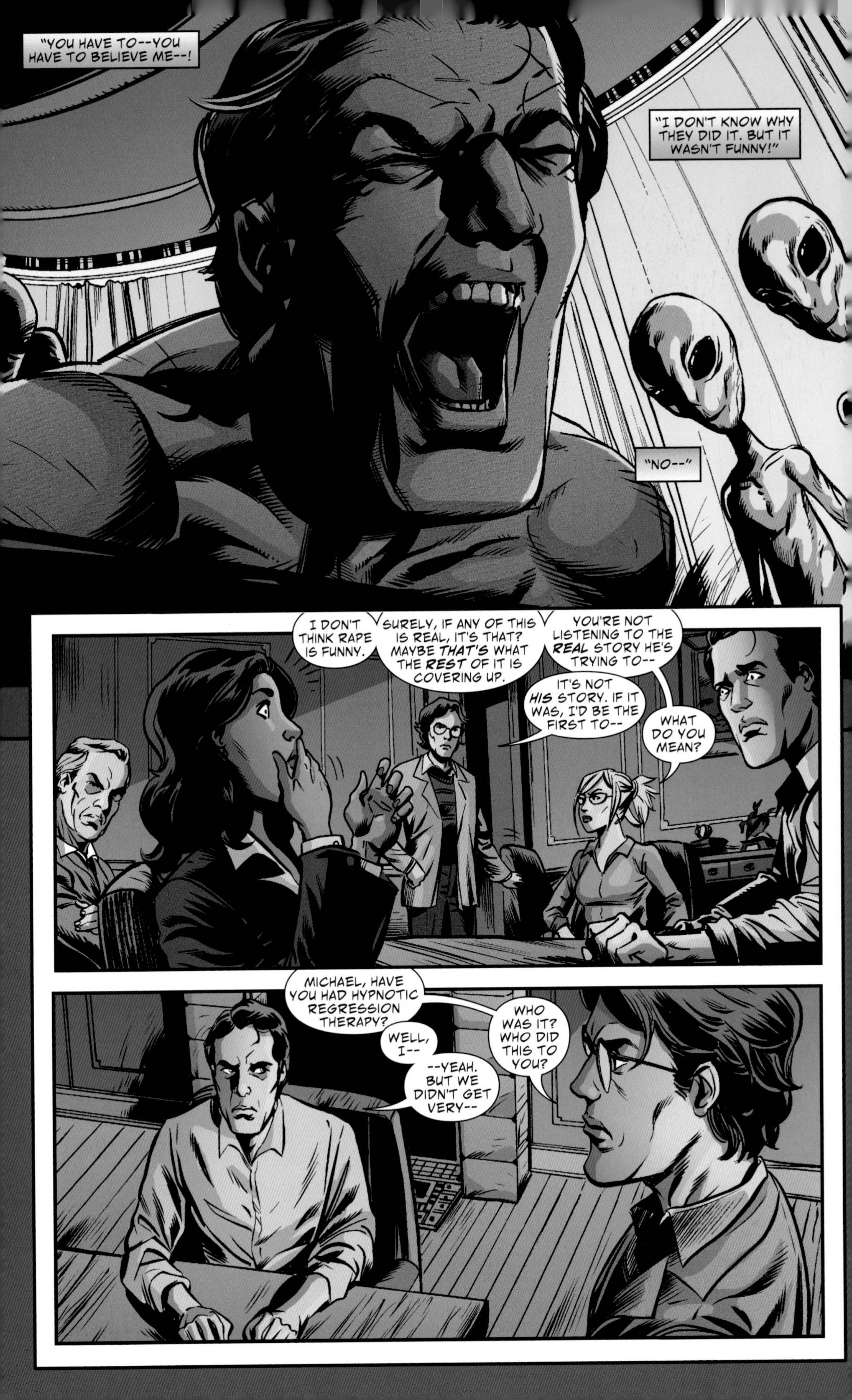

"YOU HAVE TO--YOU HAVE TO BELIEVE ME--!
"I DON'T KNOW WHY THEY DID IT. BUT IT WASN'T FUNNY!"
"NO--"
I DON'T THINK RAPE IS FUNNY.
SURELY, IF ANY OF THIS IS REAL, IT'S THAT? MAYBE THAT'S WHAT THE REST OF IT IS COVERING UP.
YOU'RE NOT LISTENING TO THE REAL STORY HE'S TRYING TO--
IT'S NOT HIS STORY. IF IT WAS, I'D BE THE FIRST TO--
WHAT DO YOU MEAN?
MICHAEL, HAVE YOU HAD HYPNOTIC REGRESSION THERAPY?
WELL, I--
--YEAH. BUT WE DIDN'T GET VERY--
WHO WAS IT? WHO DID THIS TO YOU?

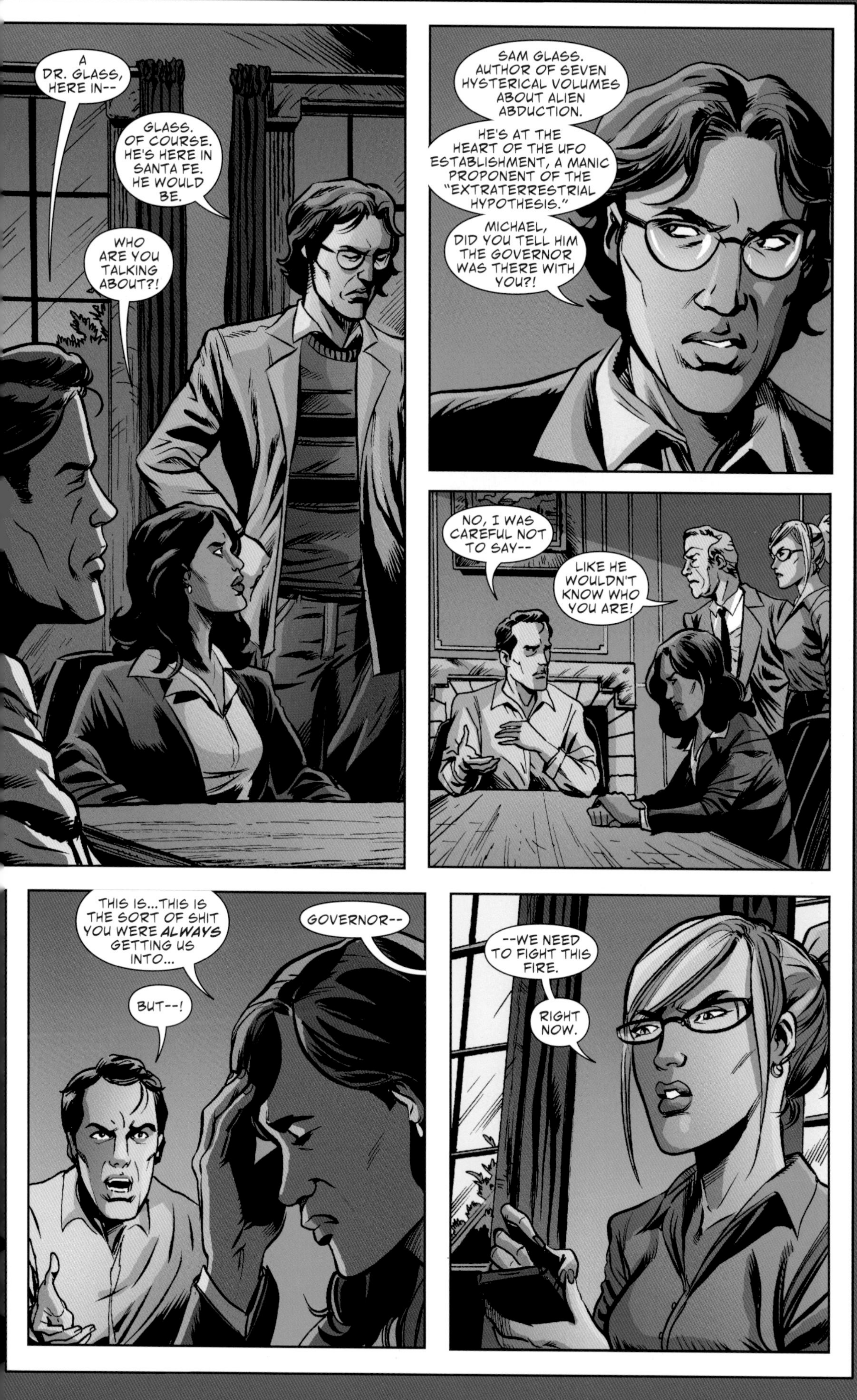

A DR. GLASS, HERE IN--
GLASS. OF COURSE. HE'S HERE IN SANTA FE. HE WOULD BE.
WHO ARE YOU TALKING ABOUT?!
SAM GLASS. AUTHOR OF SEVEN HYSTERICAL VOLUMES ABOUT ALIEN ABDUCTION.
HE'S AT THE HEART OF THE UFO ESTABLISHMENT, A MANIC PROPONENT OF THE "EXTRATERRESTRIAL HYPOTHESIS."
MICHAEL, DID YOU TELL HIM THE GOVERNOR WAS THERE WITH YOU?!
NO, I WAS CAREFUL NOT TO SAY--
LIKE HE WOULDN'T KNOW WHO YOU ARE!
THIS IS...THIS IS THE SORT OF SHIT YOU WERE *ALWAYS* GETTING US INTO...
BUT--!
GOVERNOR--
--WE NEED TO FIGHT THIS FIRE.
RIGHT NOW.

AND I KEPT THE TAPE, BUT HE DOESN'T NAME HIS FELLOW ABDUCTEE! THE IDENTITIES OF THE ONES WHO TOOK HIM FROM ME CHECK OUT, AND THEY WERE KIND OF, YOU KNOW--

--TOO *BROWN* TO BE *MEN IN BLACK.*

ONE OF THE GOVERNOR'S HIT SQUADS, THEN. THAT *BITCH* HAS US UNDER HER THUMB.

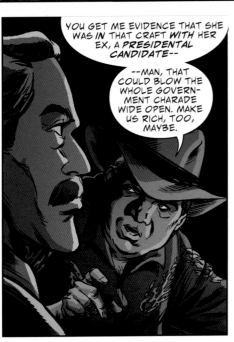

YOU GET ME EVIDENCE THAT SHE WAS *IN* THAT CRAFT *WITH* HER EX, A *PRESIDENTAL CANDIDATE*--

--MAN, THAT COULD BLOW THE WHOLE GOVERN-MENT CHARADE WIDE OPEN. MAKE US RICH, TOO, MAYBE.

THEY STEAL OUR FARMERS' LAND FOR THE MILITARY, THEY LET THEIR GREY ALIEN FRIENDS STEAL OUR BODIES--

--OH, HEY, THERE'S THAT GUY I WANTED YOU TO MEET.

YOU, ME AND HIM, *WE* COULD BE THE ONES WHO CUT THROUGH THE *DISINFORMATION* AND THE CONSPIRACY THEORY *BULLSHIT* AND DRAG US ALL OUT OF THE *DARK SIDE*--

MAJOR STAN ABRAMOWITZ. HE'S OFTEN IN HERE.

REMEMBER, HE DOESN'T LIKE PEOPLE KNOWING HE WAS IN THE MILITARY.

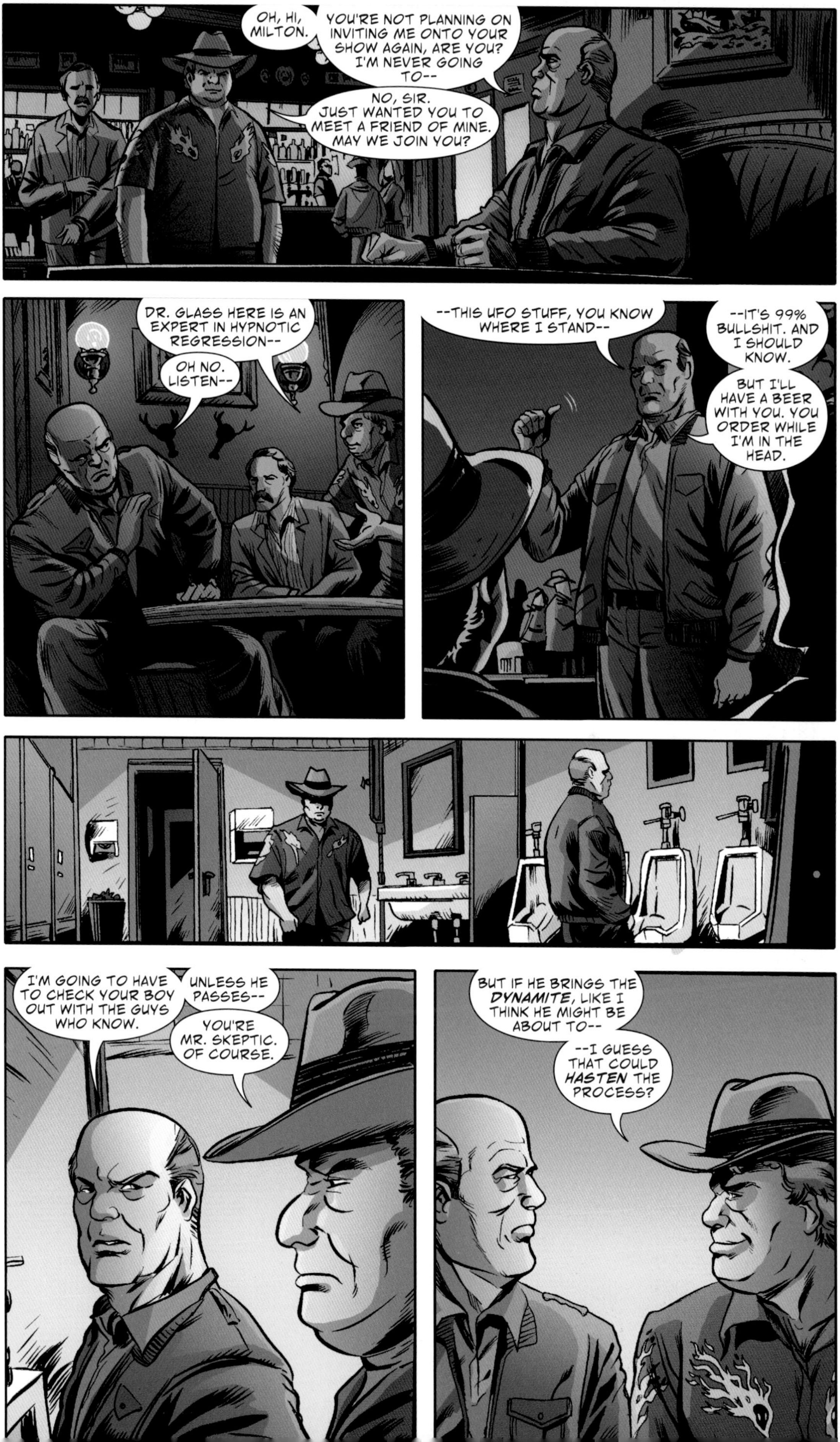
OH, HI, MILTON.
YOU'RE NOT PLANNING ON INVITING ME ONTO YOUR SHOW AGAIN, ARE YOU? I'M NEVER GOING TO--
NO, SIR. JUST WANTED YOU TO MEET A FRIEND OF MINE. MAY WE JOIN YOU?
DR. GLASS HERE IS AN EXPERT IN HYPNOTIC REGRESSION--
OH NO. LISTEN--
--THIS UFO STUFF, YOU KNOW WHERE I STAND--
--IT'S 99% BULLSHIT. AND I SHOULD KNOW.
BUT I'LL HAVE A BEER WITH YOU. YOU ORDER WHILE I'M IN THE HEAD.
I'M GOING TO HAVE TO CHECK YOUR BOY OUT WITH THE GUYS WHO KNOW.
UNLESS HE PASSES--
YOU'RE MR. SKEPTIC. OF COURSE.
BUT IF HE BRINGS THE DYNAMITE, LIKE I THINK HE MIGHT BE ABOUT TO--
--I GUESS THAT COULD HASTEN THE PROCESS?

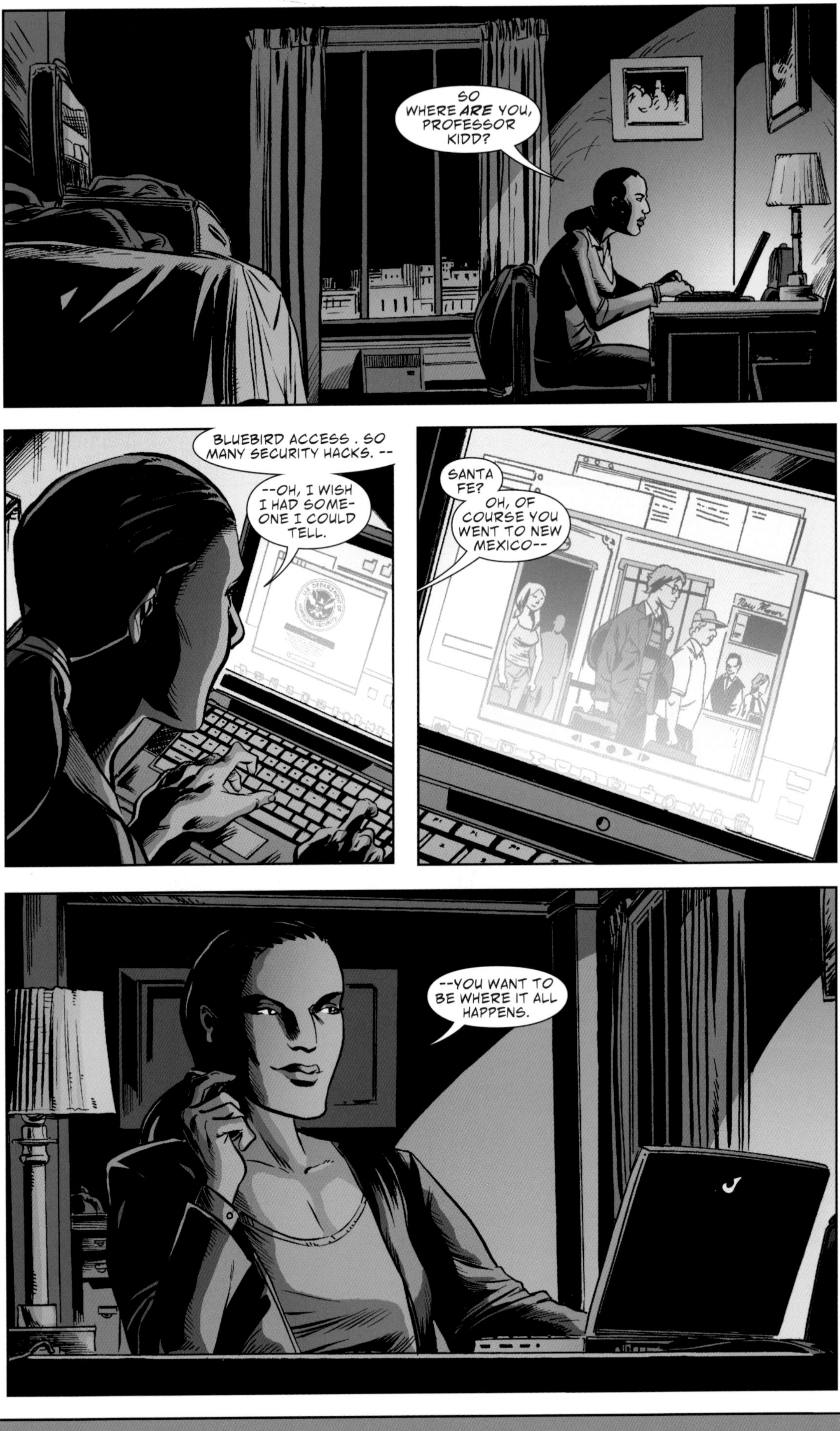
SO WHERE ARE YOU, PROFESSOR KIDD?
BLUEBIRD ACCESS . SO MANY SECURITY HACKS. --
--OH, I WISH I HAD SOME-ONE I COULD TELL.
SANTA FE?
OH, OF COURSE YOU WENT TO NEW MEXICO--
--YOU WANT TO BE WHERE IT ALL HAPPENS.

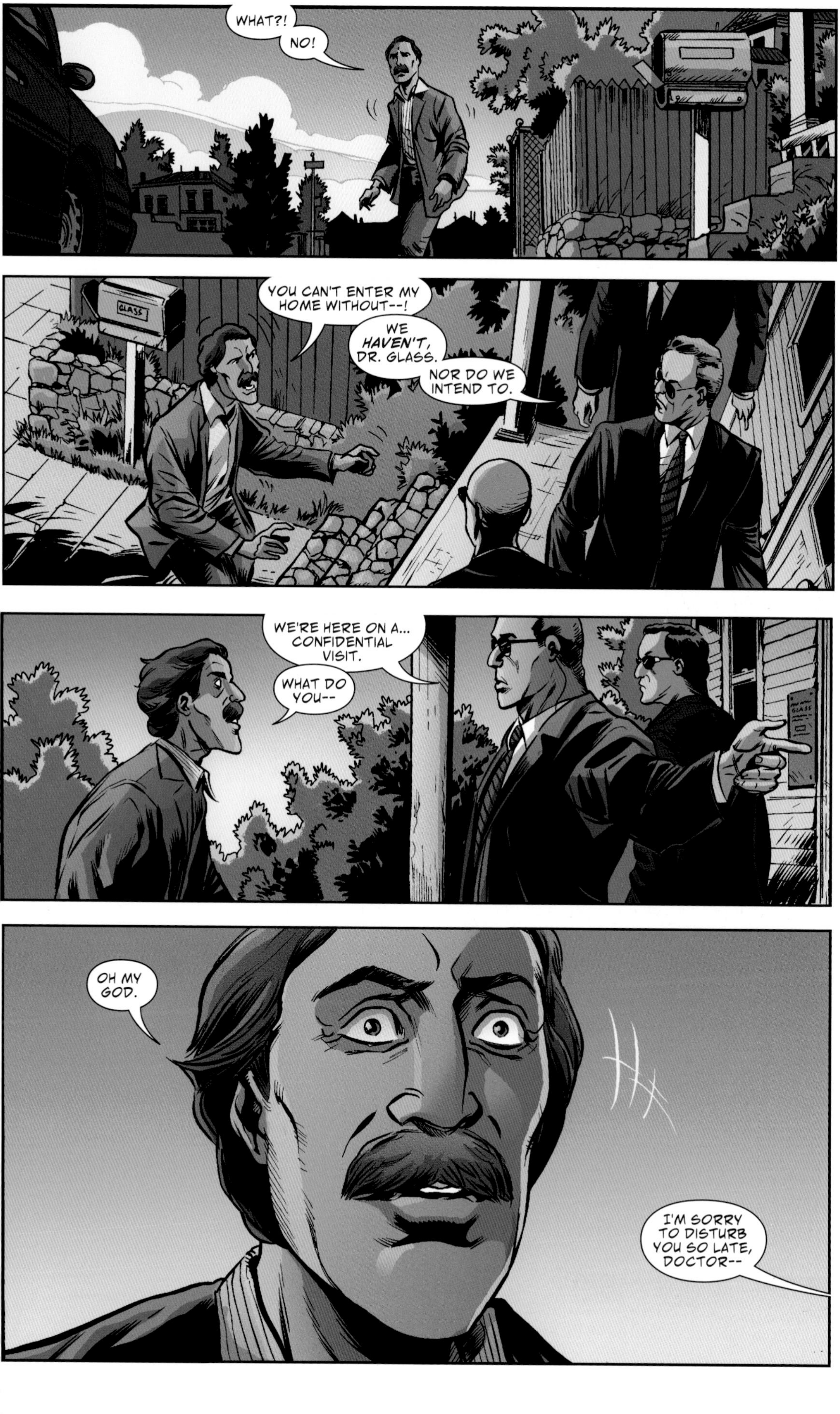
WHAT?!
NO!
GLASS
YOU CAN'T ENTER MY HOME WITHOUT--!
WE *HAVEN'T*, DR. GLASS.
NOR DO WE INTEND TO.
WE'RE HERE ON A... CONFIDENTIAL VISIT.
WHAT DO YOU--
OH MY GOD.
I'M SORRY TO DISTURB YOU SO LATE, DOCTOR--

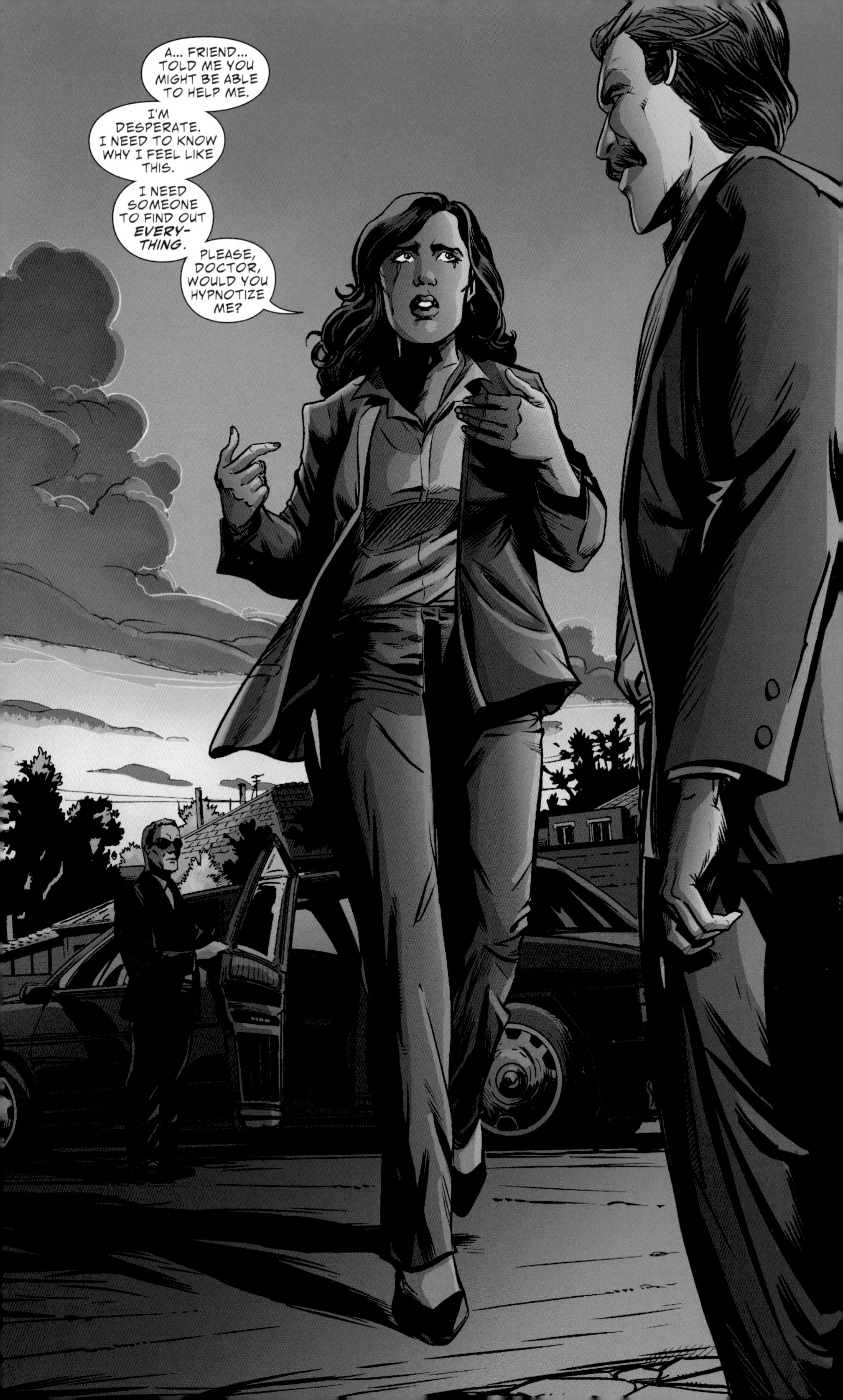
A... FRIEND... TOLD ME YOU MIGHT BE ABLE TO HELP ME.
I'M DESPERATE. I NEED TO KNOW WHY I FEEL LIKE THIS.
I NEED SOMEONE TO FIND OUT *EVERY-THING*.
PLEASE, DOCTOR, WOULD YOU HYPNOTIZE ME?

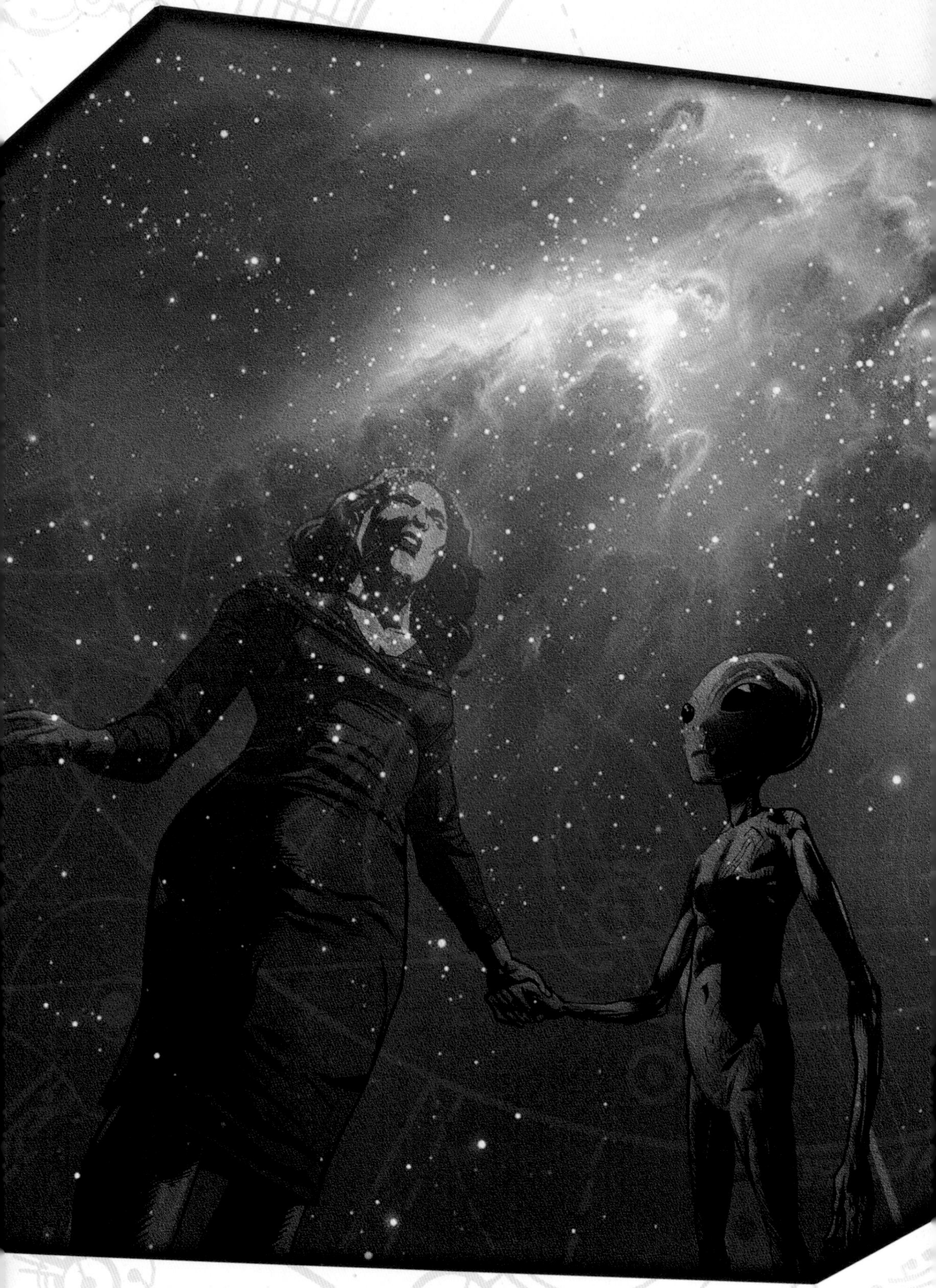

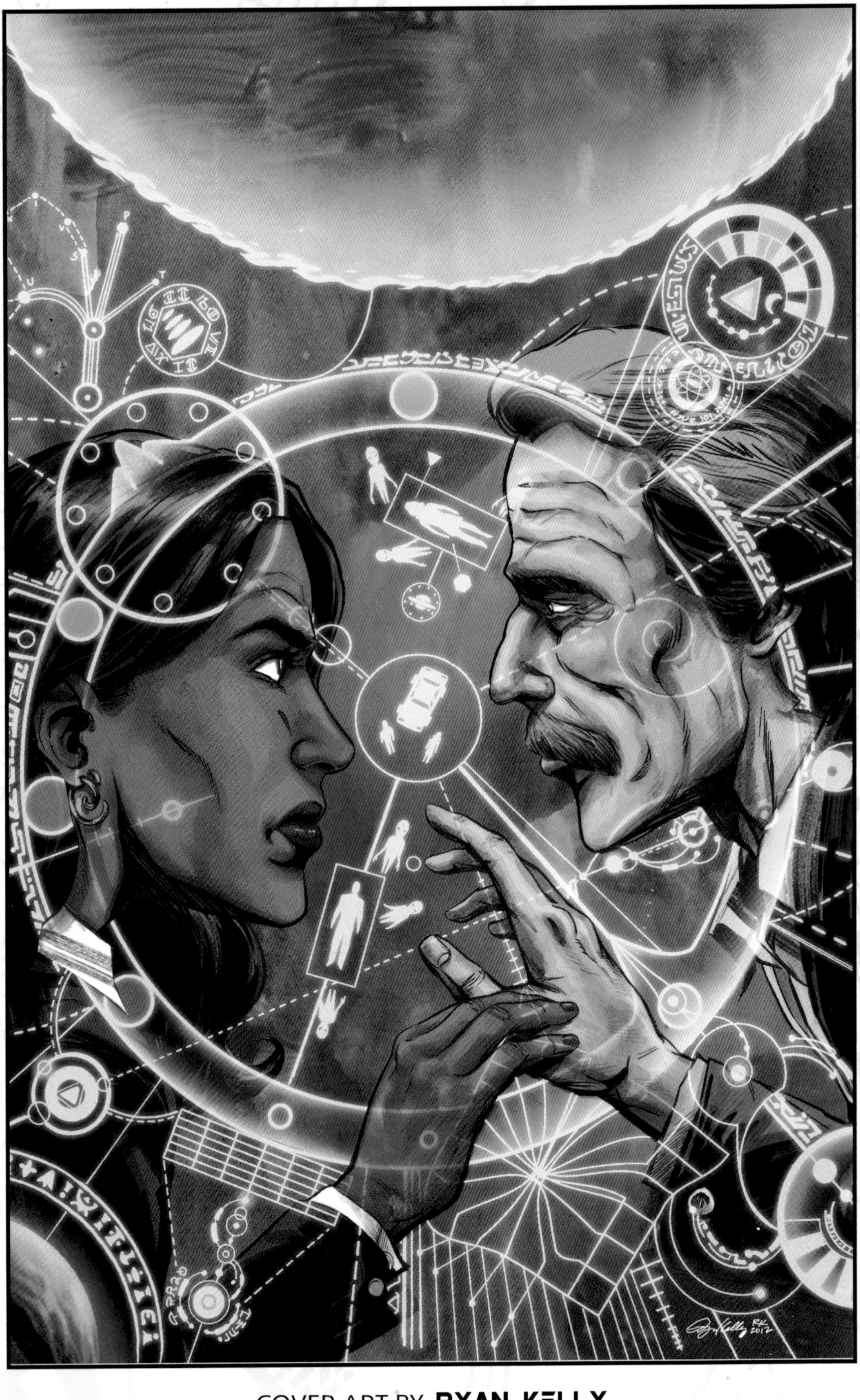

COVER ART BY **RYAN KELLY**

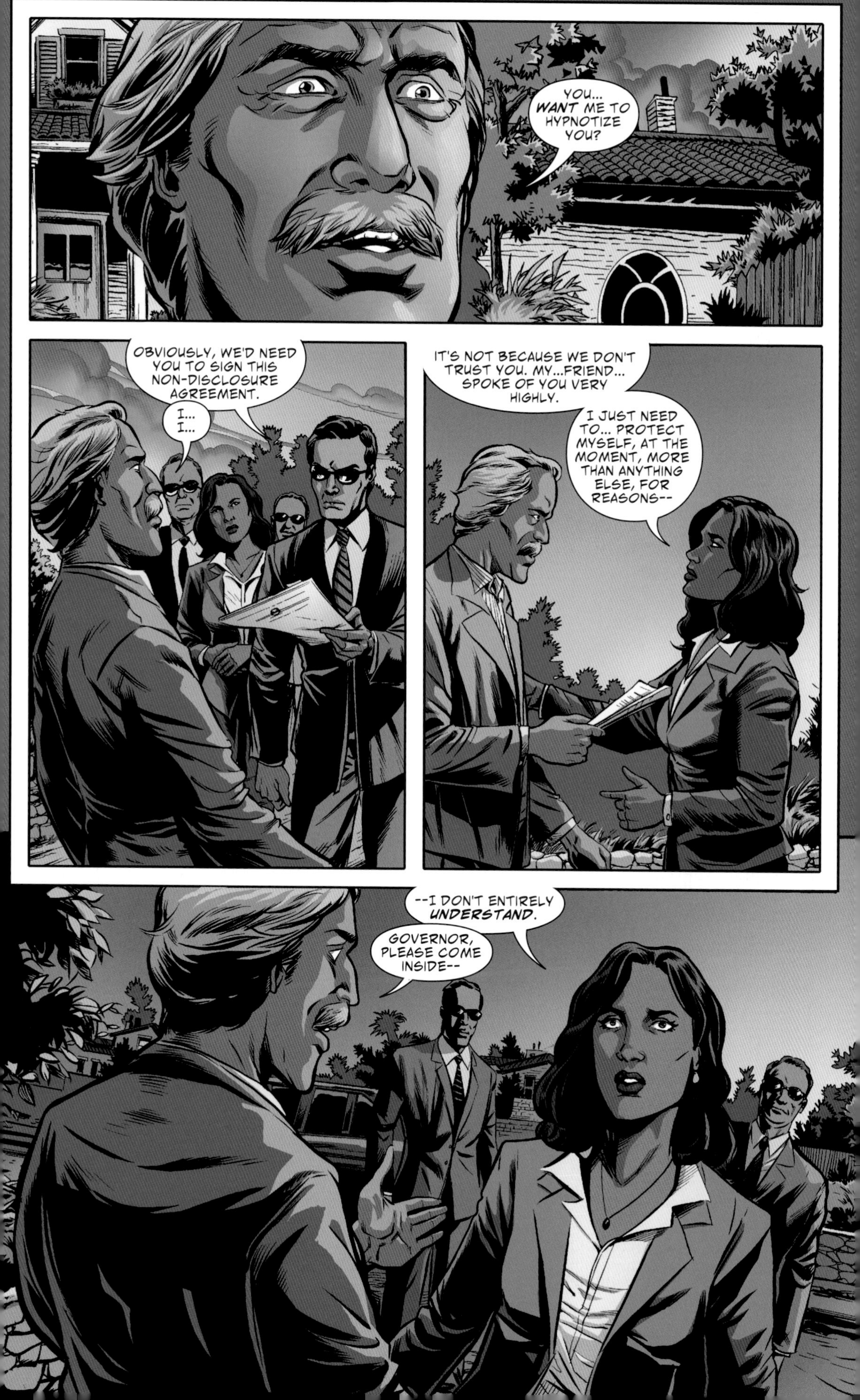

YOU... WANT ME TO HYPNOTIZE YOU?
OBVIOUSLY, WE'D NEED YOU TO SIGN THIS NON-DISCLOSURE AGREEMENT.
I... I...
IT'S NOT BECAUSE WE DON'T TRUST YOU. MY...FRIEND... SPOKE OF YOU VERY HIGHLY.
I JUST NEED TO... PROTECT MYSELF, AT THE MOMENT, MORE THAN ANYTHING ELSE, FOR REASONS--
--I DON'T ENTIRELY UNDERSTAND.
GOVERNOR, PLEASE COME INSIDE--

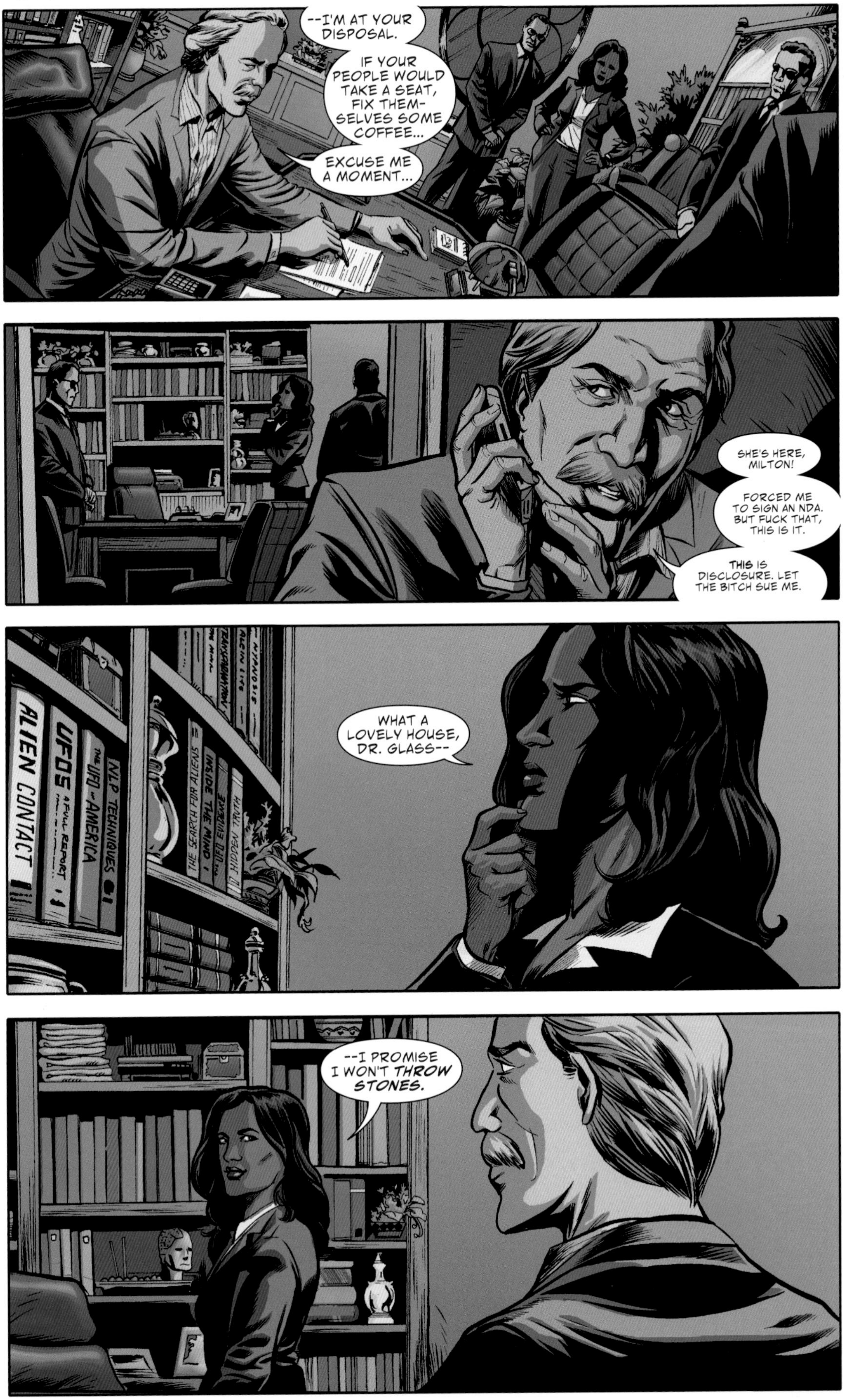
--I'M AT YOUR DISPOSAL.
IF YOUR PEOPLE WOULD TAKE A SEAT, FIX THEMSELVES SOME COFFEE...
EXCUSE ME A MOMENT...
SHE'S HERE, MILTON!
FORCED ME TO SIGN AN NDA. BUT FUCK THAT, THIS IS IT.
THIS IS DISCLOSURE. LET THE BITCH SUE ME.
ALIEN CONTACT
UFOS A FULL REPORT
THE UFO IN AMERICA
NLP TECHNIQUES
THE SEARCH FOR ALIENS
INSIDE THE MIND
HIDDEN TRUTH
WHAT A LOVELY HOUSE, DR. GLASS--
--I PROMISE I WON'T *THROW STONES.*

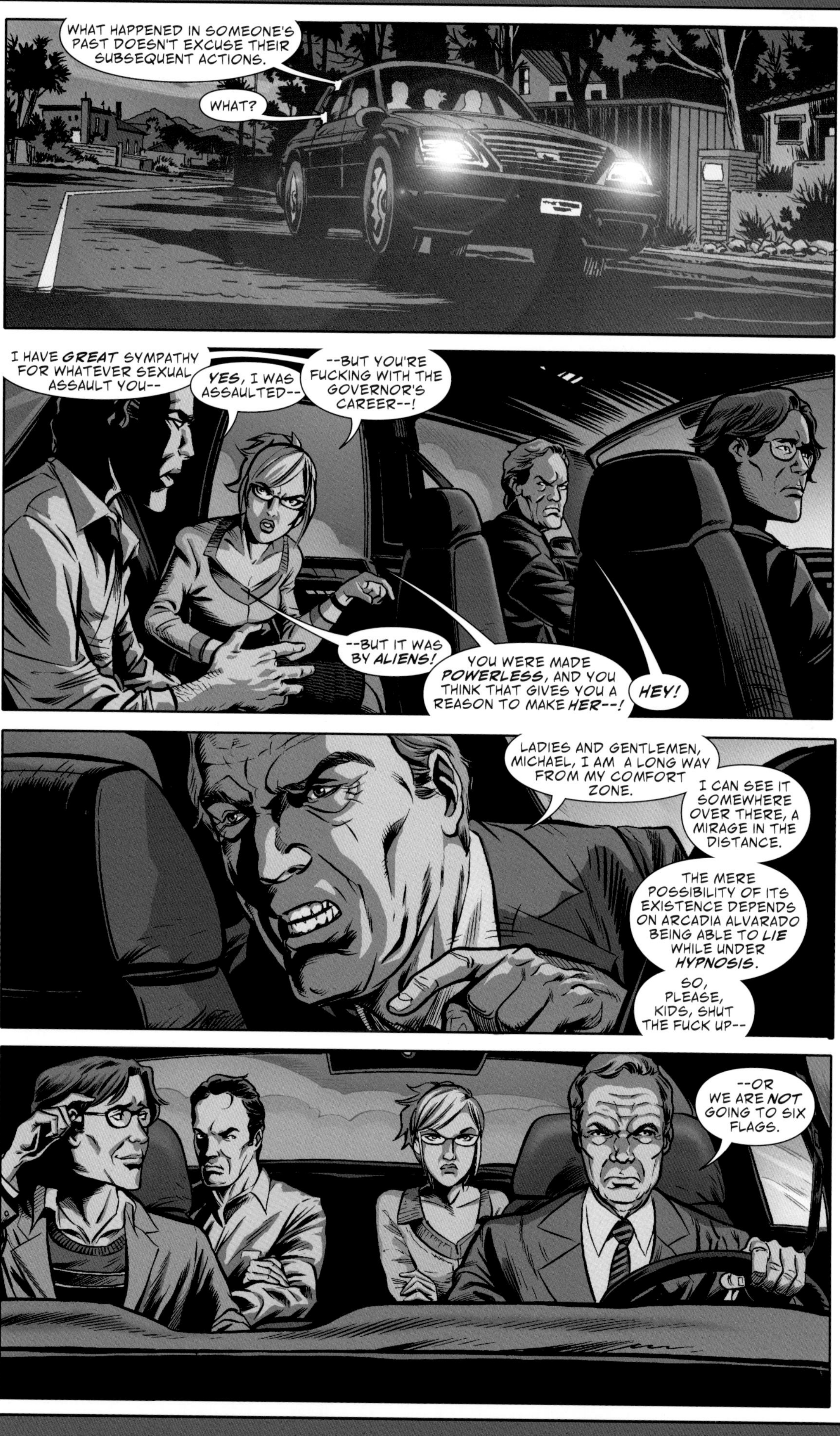
WHAT HAPPENED IN SOMEONE'S PAST DOESN'T EXCUSE THEIR SUBSEQUENT ACTIONS.
WHAT?
I HAVE GREAT SYMPATHY FOR WHATEVER SEXUAL ASSAULT YOU--
YES, I WAS ASSAULTED--
--BUT YOU'RE FUCKING WITH THE GOVERNOR'S CAREER--!
--BUT IT WAS BY ALIENS!
YOU WERE MADE POWERLESS, AND YOU THINK THAT GIVES YOU A REASON TO MAKE HER--!
HEY!
LADIES AND GENTLEMEN, MICHAEL, I AM A LONG WAY FROM MY COMFORT ZONE.
I CAN SEE IT SOMEWHERE OVER THERE, A MIRAGE IN THE DISTANCE.
THE MERE POSSIBILITY OF ITS EXISTENCE DEPENDS ON ARCADIA ALVARADO BEING ABLE TO LIE WHILE UNDER HYPNOSIS.
SO, PLEASE, KIDS, SHUT THE FUCK UP--
--OR WE ARE NOT GOING TO SIX FLAGS.

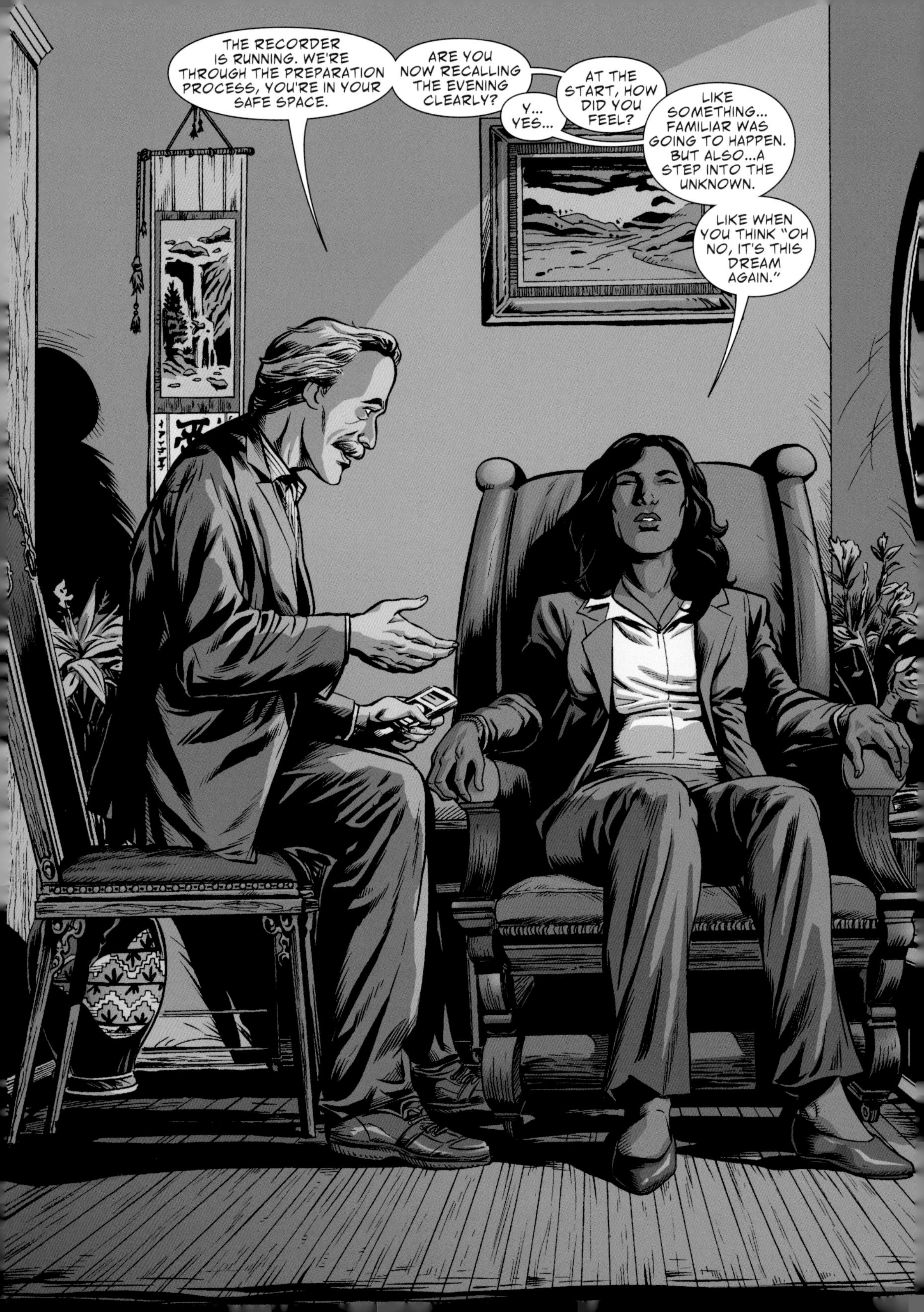
THE RECORDER IS RUNNING. WE'RE THROUGH THE PREPARATION PROCESS, YOU'RE IN YOUR SAFE SPACE.
ARE YOU NOW RECALLING THE EVENING CLEARLY?
Y... YES...
AT THE START, HOW DID YOU FEEL?
LIKE SOMETHING... FAMILIAR WAS GOING TO HAPPEN. BUT ALSO...A STEP INTO THE UNKNOWN.
LIKE WHEN YOU THINK "OH NO, IT'S THIS DREAM AGAIN."

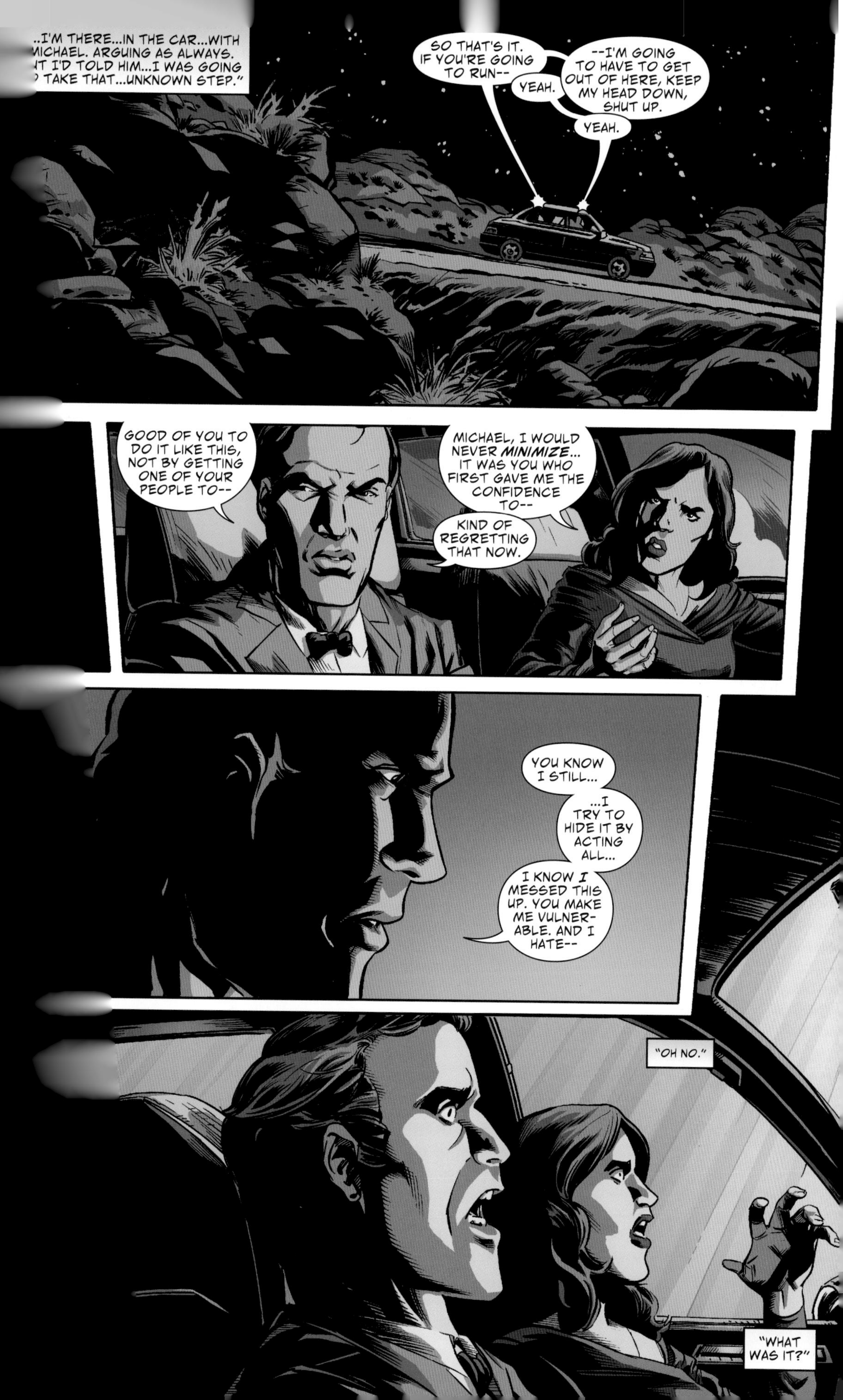
..I'M THERE...IN THE CAR...WITH MICHAEL. ARGUING AS ALWAYS. T I'D TOLD HIM...I WAS GOING TAKE THAT...UNKNOWN STEP."
SO THAT'S IT. IF YOU'RE GOING TO RUN--
YEAH.
--I'M GOING TO HAVE TO GET OUT OF HERE, KEEP MY HEAD DOWN, SHUT UP.
YEAH.
GOOD OF YOU TO DO IT LIKE THIS, NOT BY GETTING ONE OF YOUR PEOPLE TO--
MICHAEL, I WOULD NEVER MINIMIZE... IT WAS YOU WHO FIRST GAVE ME THE CONFIDENCE TO--
KIND OF REGRETTING THAT NOW.
YOU KNOW I STILL...
...I TRY TO HIDE IT BY ACTING ALL...
I KNOW I MESSED THIS UP. YOU MAKE ME VULNER-ABLE. AND I HATE--
"OH NO."
"WHAT WAS IT?"

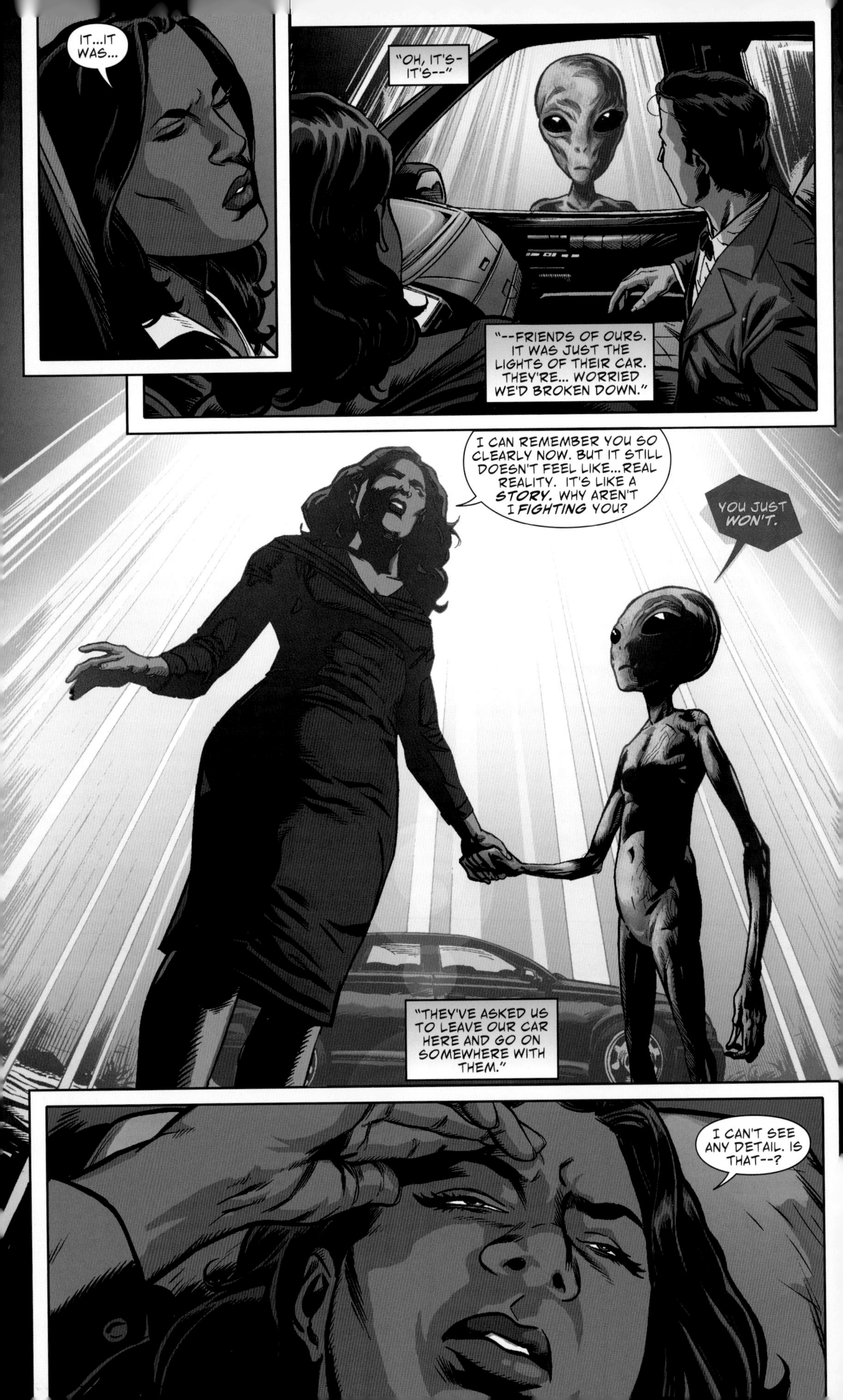
IT...IT WAS...
"OH, IT'S-- IT'S--"
"--FRIENDS OF OURS. IT WAS JUST THE LIGHTS OF THEIR CAR. THEY'RE... WORRIED WE'D BROKEN DOWN."
I CAN REMEMBER YOU SO CLEARLY NOW. BUT IT STILL DOESN'T FEEL LIKE...REAL REALITY. IT'S LIKE A STORY. WHY AREN'T I FIGHTING YOU?
YOU JUST WON'T.
"THEY'VE ASKED US TO LEAVE OUR CAR HERE AND GO ON SOMEWHERE WITH THEM."
I CAN'T SEE ANY DETAIL. IS THAT--?

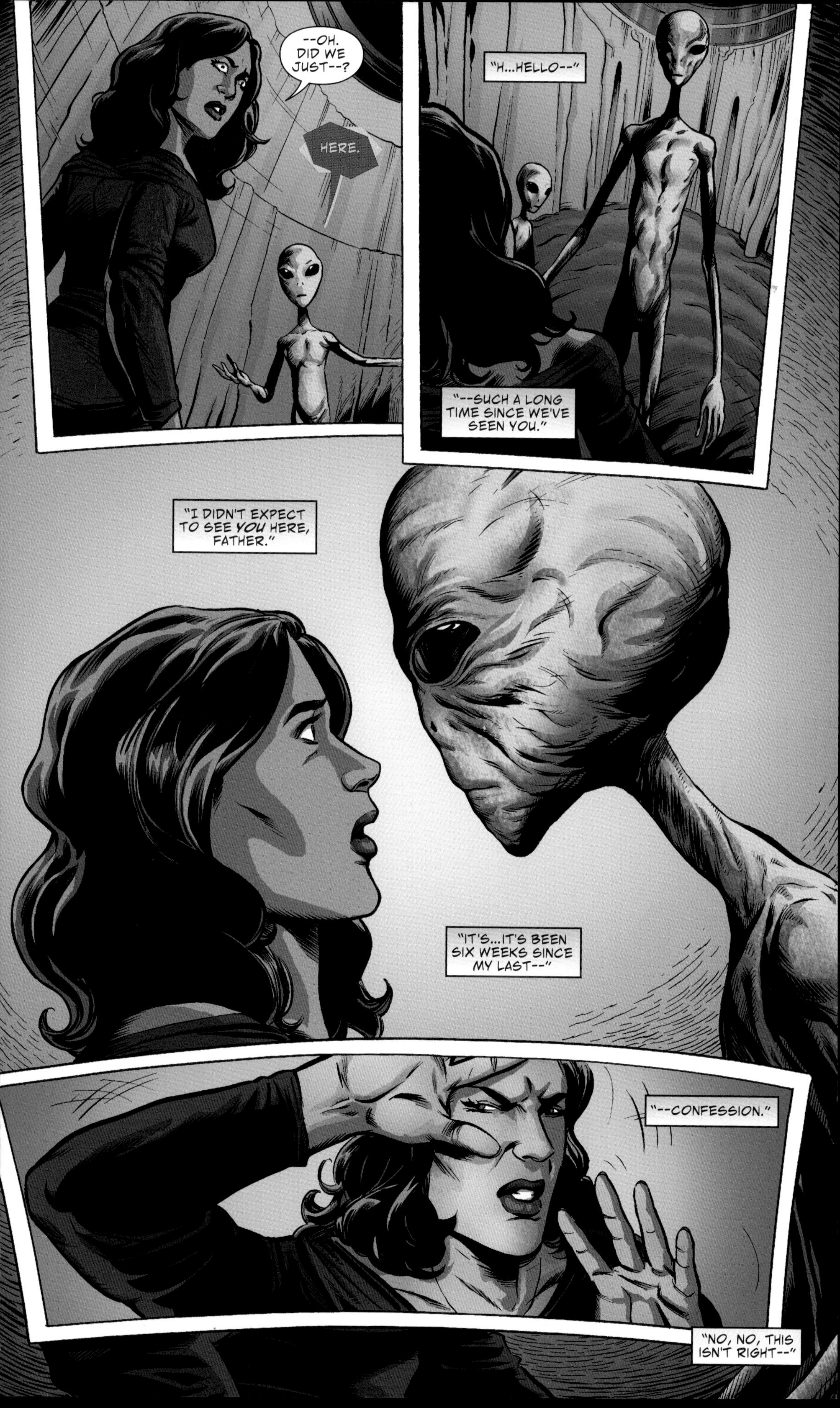
--OH. DID WE JUST--?
HERE.
"H...HELLO--"
"--SUCH A LONG TIME SINCE WE'VE SEEN YOU."
"I DIDN'T EXPECT TO SEE *YOU* HERE, FATHER."
"IT'S...IT'S BEEN SIX WEEKS SINCE MY LAST--"
"--CONFESSION."
"NO, NO, THIS ISN'T RIGHT--"

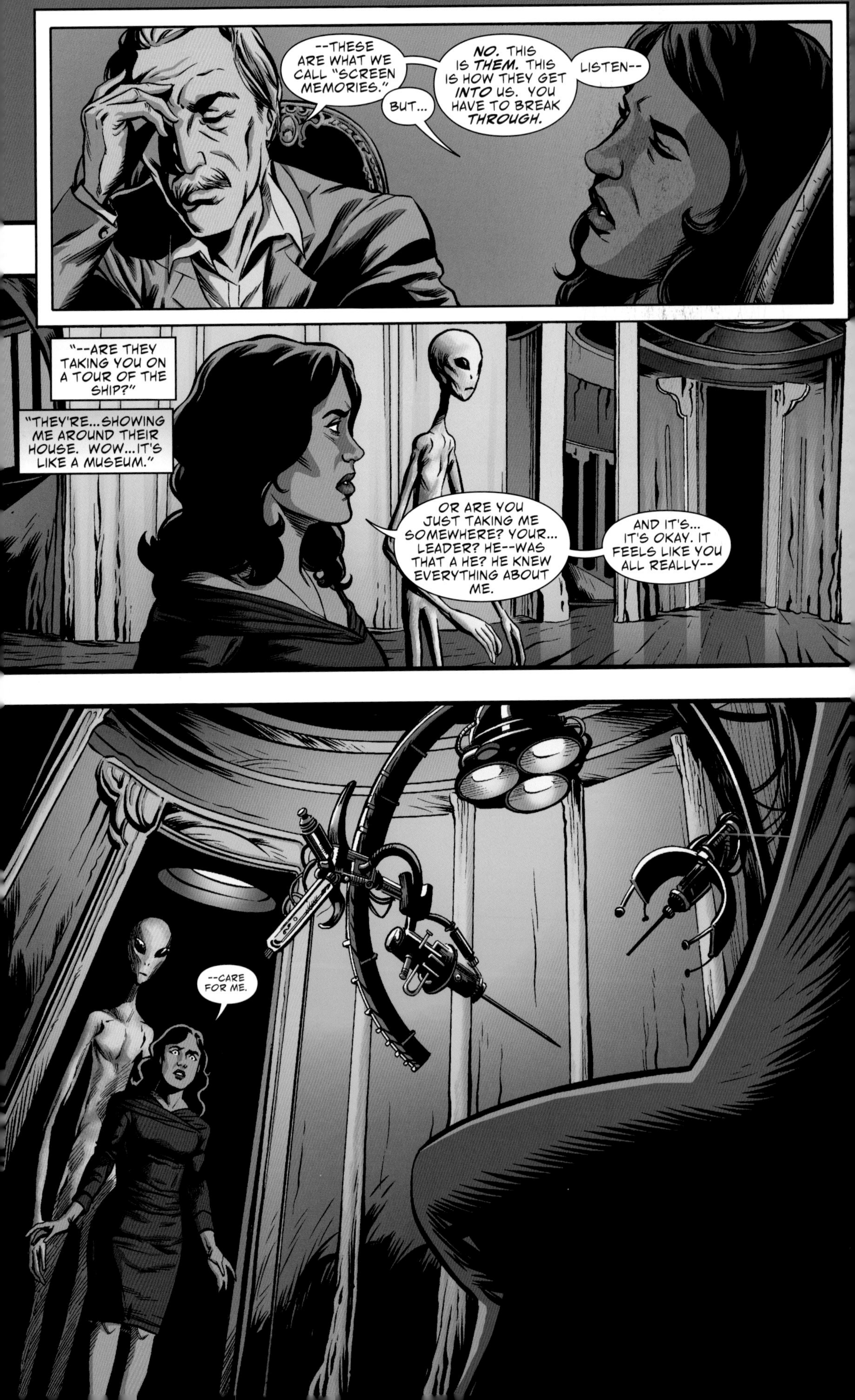
--THESE ARE WHAT WE CALL "SCREEN MEMORIES."
BUT...
NO. THIS IS THEM. THIS IS HOW THEY GET INTO US. YOU HAVE TO BREAK THROUGH.
LISTEN--
"--ARE THEY TAKING YOU ON A TOUR OF THE SHIP?"
"THEY'RE...SHOWING ME AROUND THEIR HOUSE. WOW...IT'S LIKE A MUSEUM."
OR ARE YOU JUST TAKING ME SOMEWHERE? YOUR... LEADER? HE--WAS THAT A HE? HE KNEW EVERYTHING ABOUT ME.
AND IT'S... IT'S OKAY. IT FEELS LIKE YOU ALL REALLY--
--CARE FOR ME.

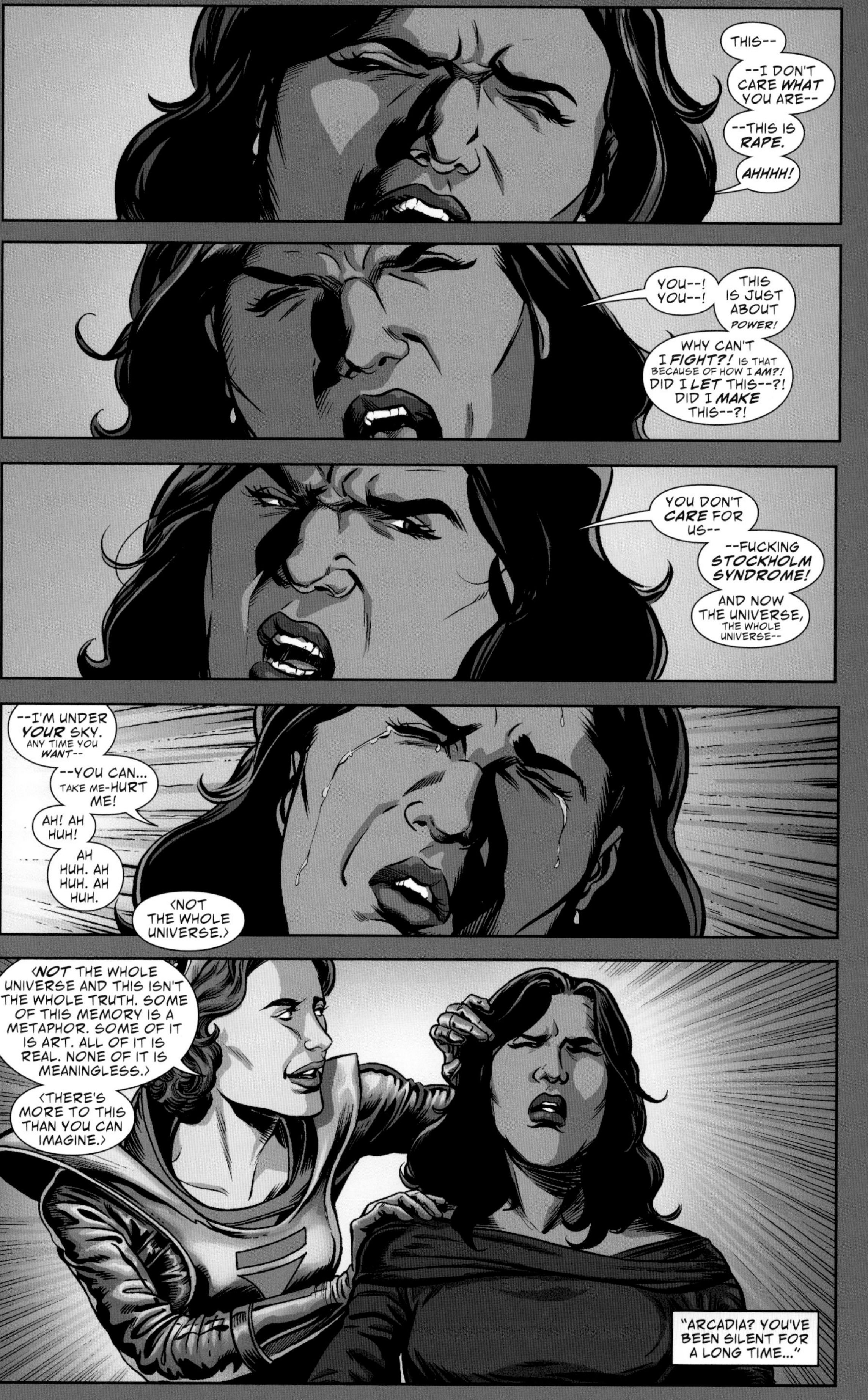
THIS--
--I DON'T CARE WHAT YOU ARE--
--THIS IS RAPE.
AHHHH!
YOU--! YOU--!
THIS IS JUST ABOUT POWER!
WHY CAN'T I FIGHT?! IS THAT BECAUSE OF HOW I AM?! DID I LET THIS--?! DID I MAKE THIS--?!
YOU DON'T CARE FOR US--
--FUCKING STOCKHOLM SYNDROME!
AND NOW THE UNIVERSE, THE WHOLE UNIVERSE--
--I'M UNDER YOUR SKY. ANY TIME YOU WANT--
--YOU CAN... TAKE ME-HURT ME!
AH! AH HUH!
AH HUH. AH HUH. AH HUH.
<NOT THE WHOLE UNIVERSE.>
<NOT THE WHOLE UNIVERSE AND THIS ISN'T THE WHOLE TRUTH. SOME OF THIS MEMORY IS A METAPHOR. SOME OF IT IS ART. ALL OF IT IS REAL. NONE OF IT IS MEANINGLESS.>
<THERE'S MORE TO THIS THAN YOU CAN IMAGINE.>
"ARCADIA? YOU'VE BEEN SILENT FOR A LONG TIME..."

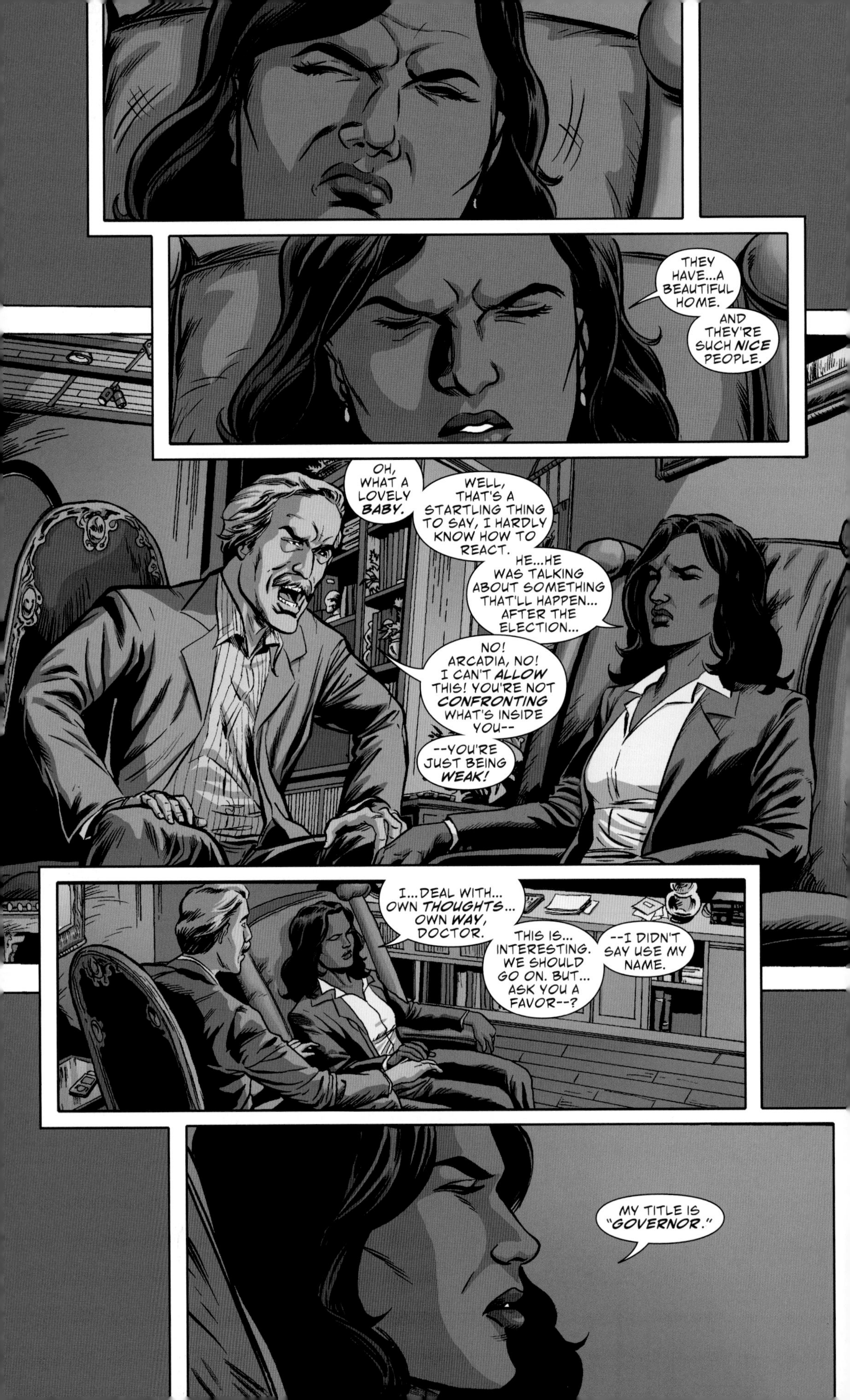
THEY HAVE...A BEAUTIFUL HOME.
AND THEY'RE SUCH NICE PEOPLE.
OH, WHAT A LOVELY BABY.
WELL, THAT'S A STARTLING THING TO SAY, I HARDLY KNOW HOW TO REACT.
HE...HE WAS TALKING ABOUT SOMETHING THAT'LL HAPPEN... AFTER THE ELECTION...
NO! ARCADIA, NO! I CAN'T ALLOW THIS! YOU'RE NOT CONFRONTING WHAT'S INSIDE YOU--
--YOU'RE JUST BEING WEAK!
I...DEAL WITH... OWN THOUGHTS... OWN WAY, DOCTOR.
THIS IS... INTERESTING. WE SHOULD GO ON. BUT... ASK YOU A FAVOR--?
--I DIDN'T SAY USE MY NAME.
MY TITLE IS "GOVERNOR."

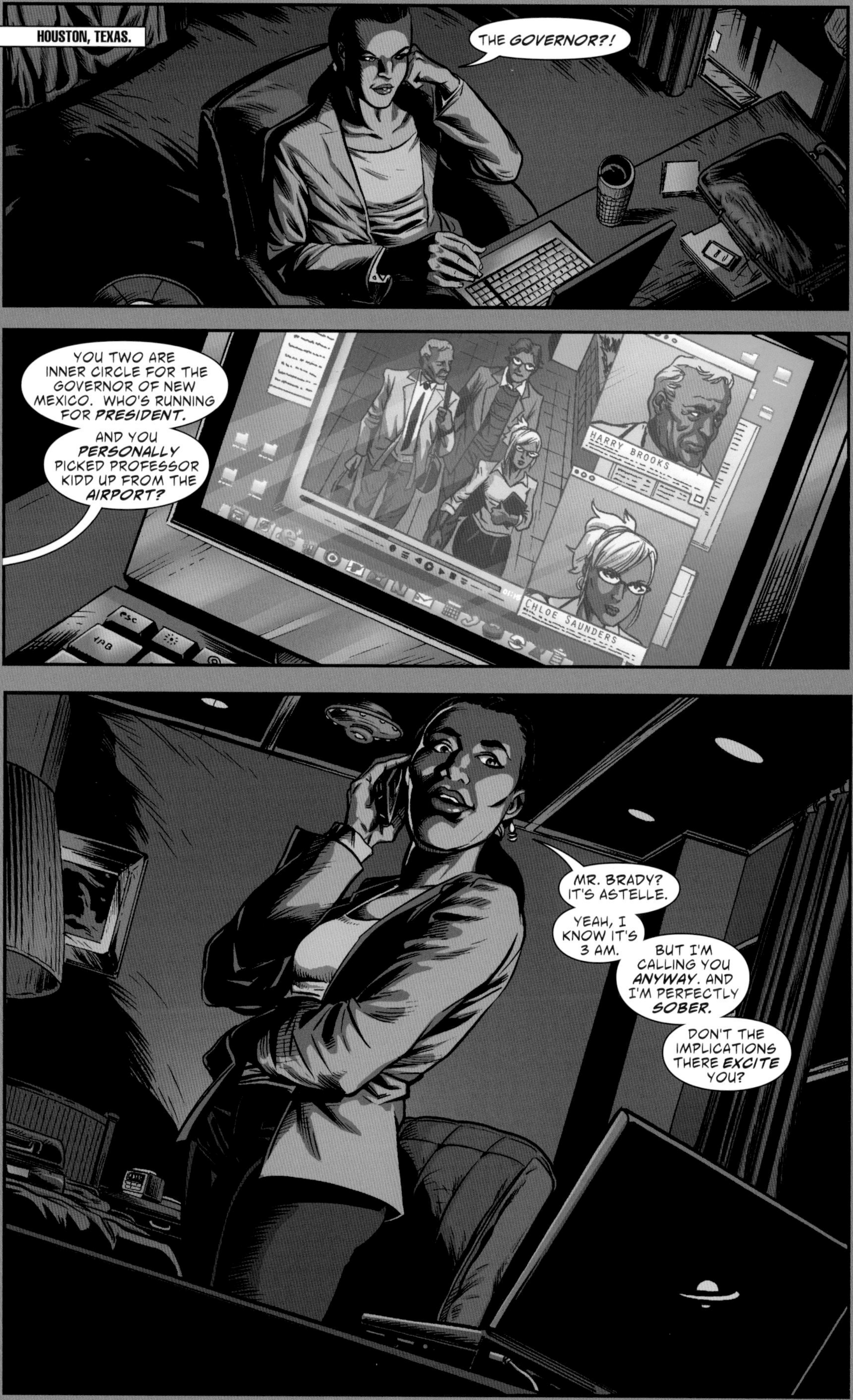
HOUSTON, TEXAS.
THE GOVERNOR?!
YOU TWO ARE INNER CIRCLE FOR THE GOVERNOR OF NEW MEXICO. WHO'S RUNNING FOR PRESIDENT.
AND YOU PERSONALLY PICKED PROFESSOR KIDD UP FROM THE AIRPORT?
HARRY BROOKS
CHLOE SAUNDERS
MR. BRADY? IT'S ASTELLE.
YEAH, I KNOW IT'S 3 AM.
BUT I'M CALLING YOU ANYWAY. AND I'M PERFECTLY SOBER.
DON'T THE IMPLICATIONS THERE EXCITE YOU?

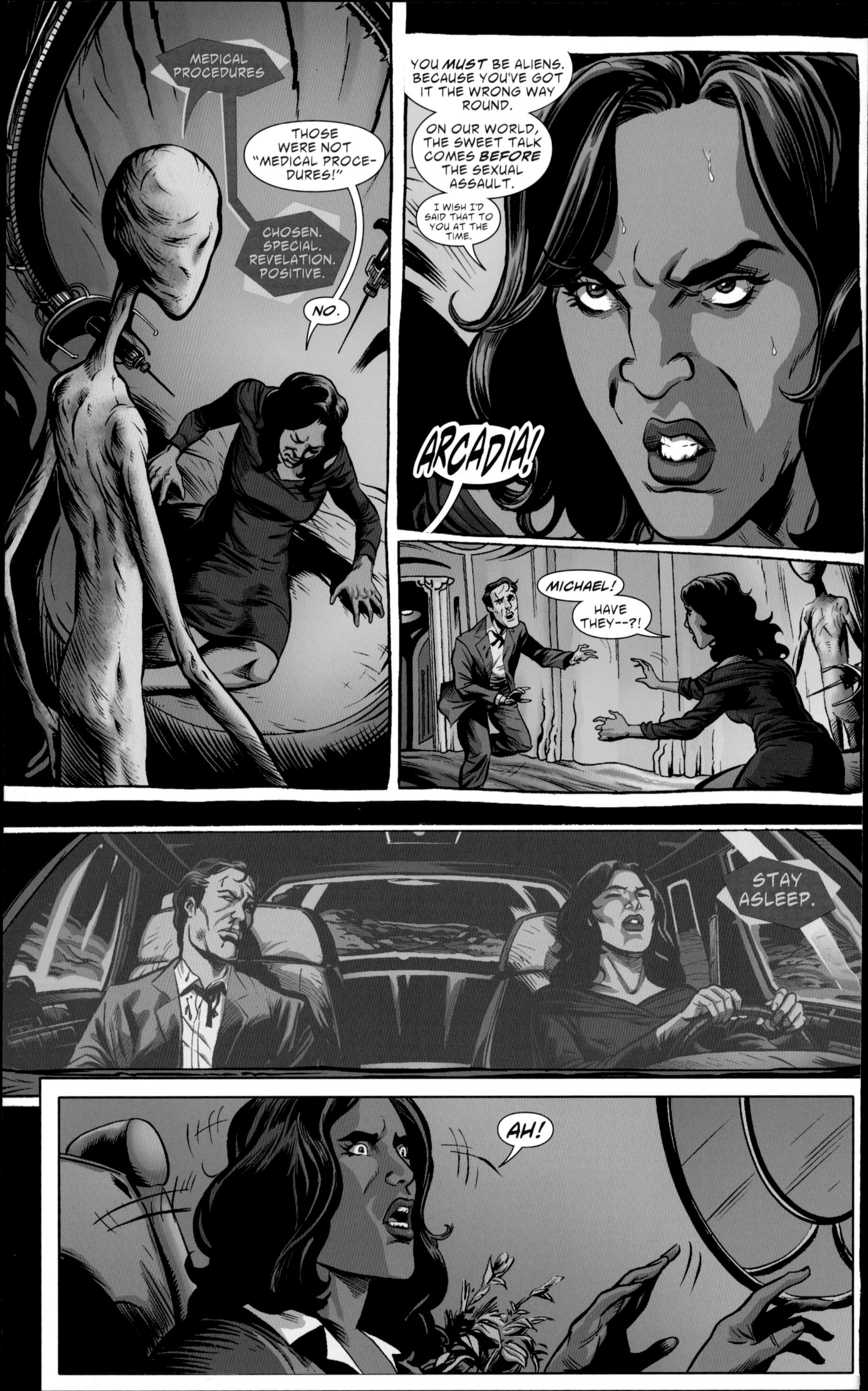

MEDICAL PROCEDURES
THOSE WERE NOT "MEDICAL PROCE-DURES!"
CHOSEN. SPECIAL. REVELATION. POSITIVE.
NO.
YOU MUST BE ALIENS. BECAUSE YOU'VE GOT IT THE WRONG WAY ROUND.
ON OUR WORLD, THE SWEET TALK COMES BEFORE THE SEXUAL ASSAULT.
I WISH I'D SAID THAT TO YOU AT THE TIME.
ARCADIA!
MICHAEL!
HAVE THEY--?!
STAY ASLEEP.
AH!

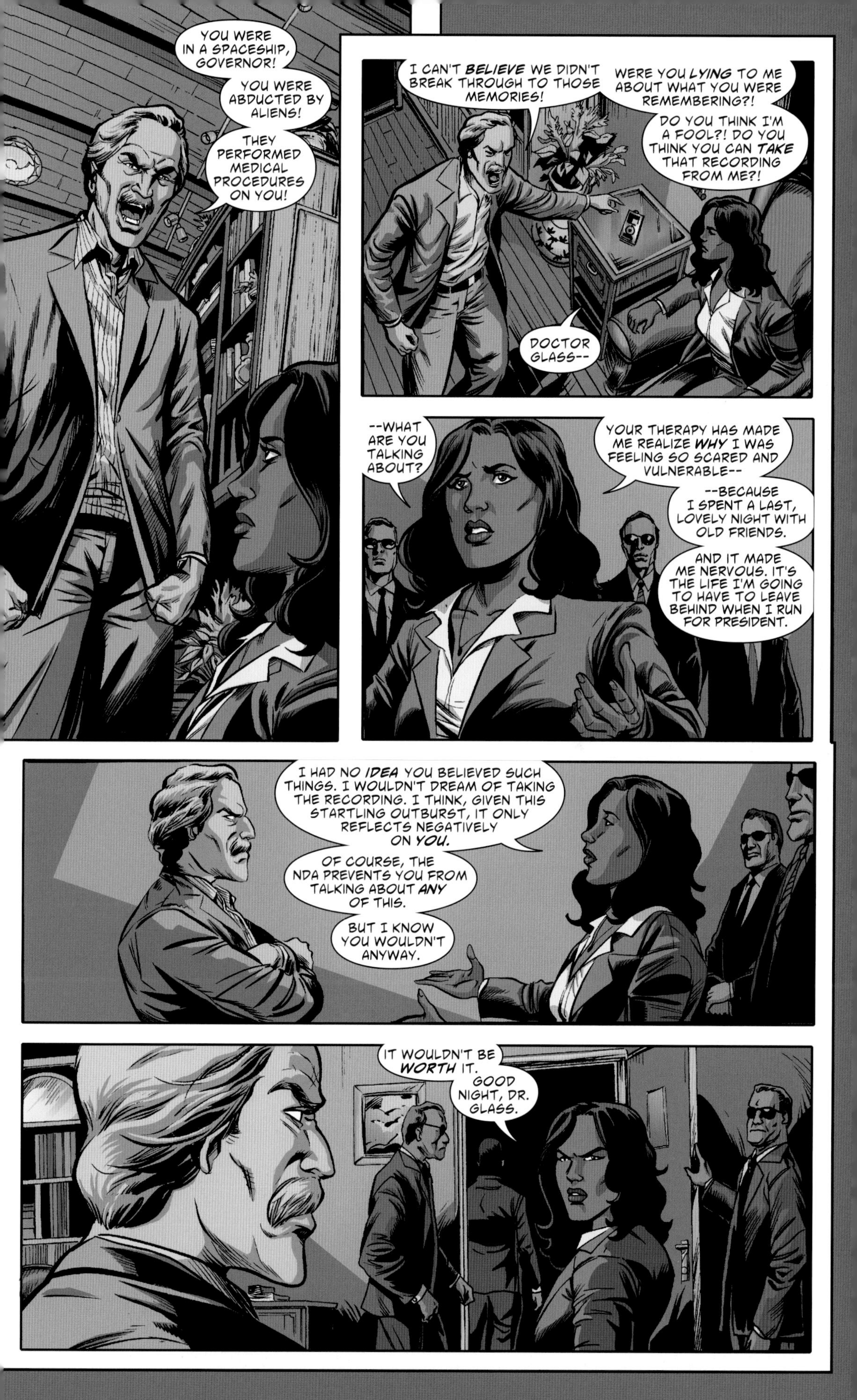
YOU WERE IN A SPACESHIP, GOVERNOR!
YOU WERE ABDUCTED BY ALIENS!
THEY PERFORMED MEDICAL PROCEDURES ON YOU!
I CAN'T BELIEVE WE DIDN'T BREAK THROUGH TO THOSE MEMORIES!
WERE YOU LYING TO ME ABOUT WHAT YOU WERE REMEMBERING?!
DO YOU THINK I'M A FOOL?! DO YOU THINK YOU CAN TAKE THAT RECORDING FROM ME?!
DOCTOR GLASS--
--WHAT ARE YOU TALKING ABOUT?
YOUR THERAPY HAS MADE ME REALIZE WHY I WAS FEELING SO SCARED AND VULNERABLE--
--BECAUSE I SPENT A LAST, LOVELY NIGHT WITH OLD FRIENDS.
AND IT MADE ME NERVOUS. IT'S THE LIFE I'M GOING TO HAVE TO LEAVE BEHIND WHEN I RUN FOR PRESIDENT.
I HAD NO IDEA YOU BELIEVED SUCH THINGS. I WOULDN'T DREAM OF TAKING THE RECORDING. I THINK, GIVEN THIS STARTLING OUTBURST, IT ONLY REFLECTS NEGATIVELY ON YOU.
OF COURSE, THE NDA PREVENTS YOU FROM TALKING ABOUT ANY OF THIS.
BUT I KNOW YOU WOULDN'T ANYWAY.
IT WOULDN'T BE WORTH IT.
GOOD NIGHT, DR. GLASS.

SHE THINKS SHE *PLAYED* ME! BUT I *STILL* WANT TO GO ON YOUR SHOW. THE RECORDING'S NO USE, BUT THOSE GUYS SMASHED MY DOOR, AND I CAN SAY WHAT I *THINK* WAS--!

NO.

WHAT?!

I'D FACE DOWN A LAWSUIT FUNDED BY CAMPAIGN DONATIONS IF IT GOT US *FULL DISCLOSURE.*

BUT NOT FOR A BUNCH OF NOTHING LIKE *THAT.* YOU LET ME DOWN, GLASS!

BUT--!

LISTEN TO HIM, DOCTOR--

--YOU'RE BEING SET UP TO FAIL. THEY WANT TO *DISCREDIT* YOU.

CLASSIC PSY OPS. I RECOGNIZE THE WAY THESE GUYS WORK.

DON'T FALL FOR IT.

BUT--

BUT I'VE GOT SOME GOOD NEWS FOR YOU--

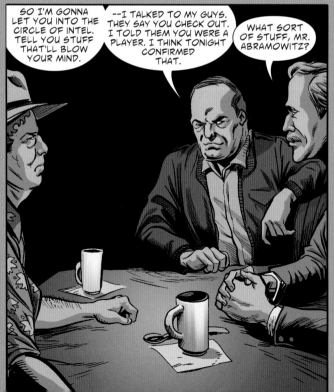

SO I'M GONNA LET YOU INTO THE CIRCLE OF INTEL. TELL YOU STUFF THAT'LL BLOW YOUR MIND.

--I TALKED TO MY GUYS. THEY SAY YOU CHECK OUT. I TOLD THEM YOU WERE A PLAYER. I THINK TONIGHT CONFIRMED THAT.

WHAT SORT OF STUFF, MR. ABRAMOWITZ?

FROM NOW ON, DOCTOR--

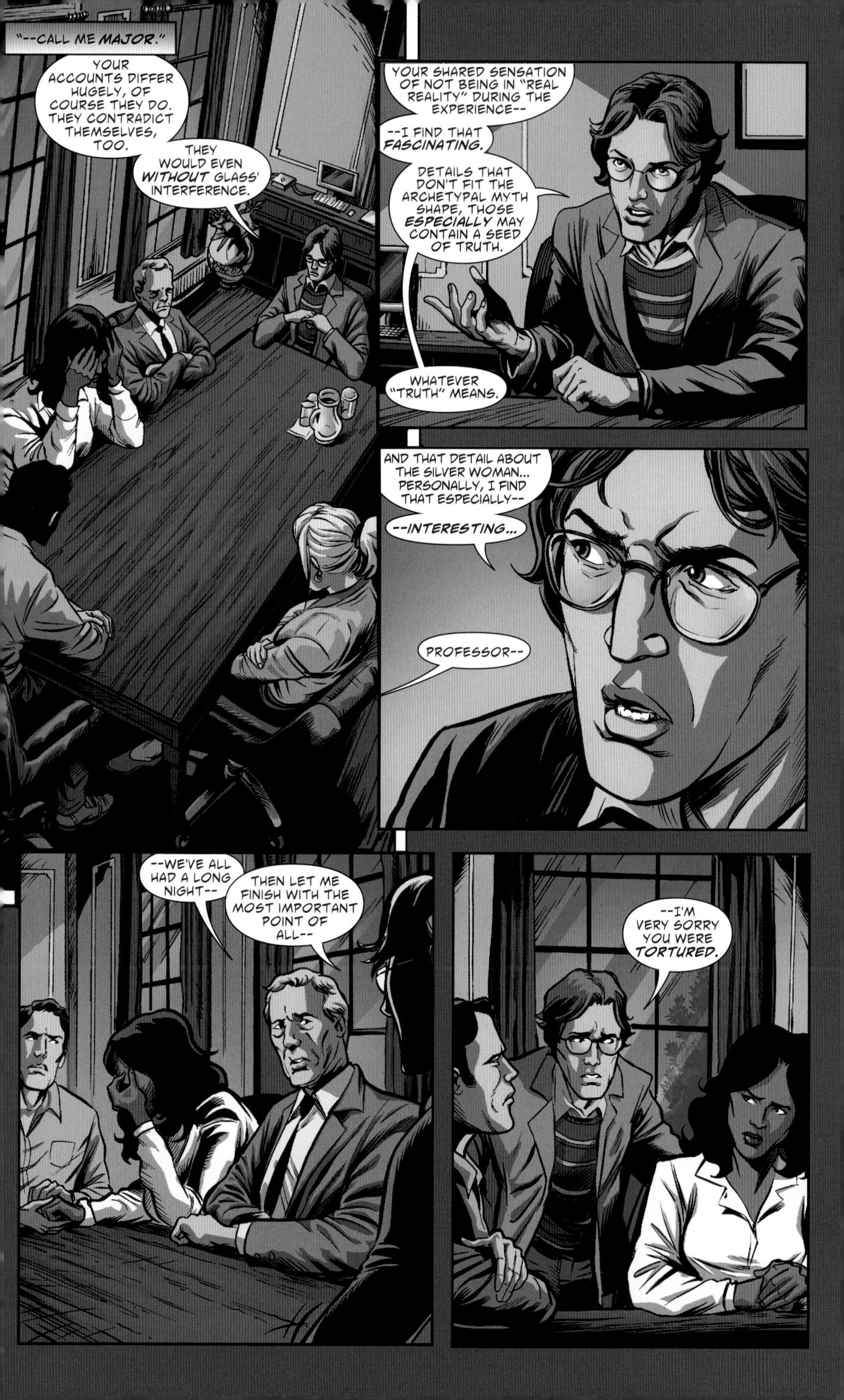
"--CALL ME MAJOR."
YOUR ACCOUNTS DIFFER HUGELY, OF COURSE THEY DO. THEY CONTRADICT THEMSELVES, TOO.
THEY WOULD EVEN WITHOUT GLASS' INTERFERENCE.
YOUR SHARED SENSATION OF NOT BEING IN "REAL REALITY" DURING THE EXPERIENCE--
--I FIND THAT FASCINATING.
DETAILS THAT DON'T FIT THE ARCHETYPAL MYTH SHAPE, THOSE ESPECIALLY MAY CONTAIN A SEED OF TRUTH.
WHATEVER "TRUTH" MEANS.
AND THAT DETAIL ABOUT THE SILVER WOMAN... PERSONALLY, I FIND THAT ESPECIALLY--
--INTERESTING...
PROFESSOR--
--WE'VE ALL HAD A LONG NIGHT--
THEN LET ME FINISH WITH THE MOST IMPORTANT POINT OF ALL--
--I'M VERY SORRY YOU WERE TORTURED.

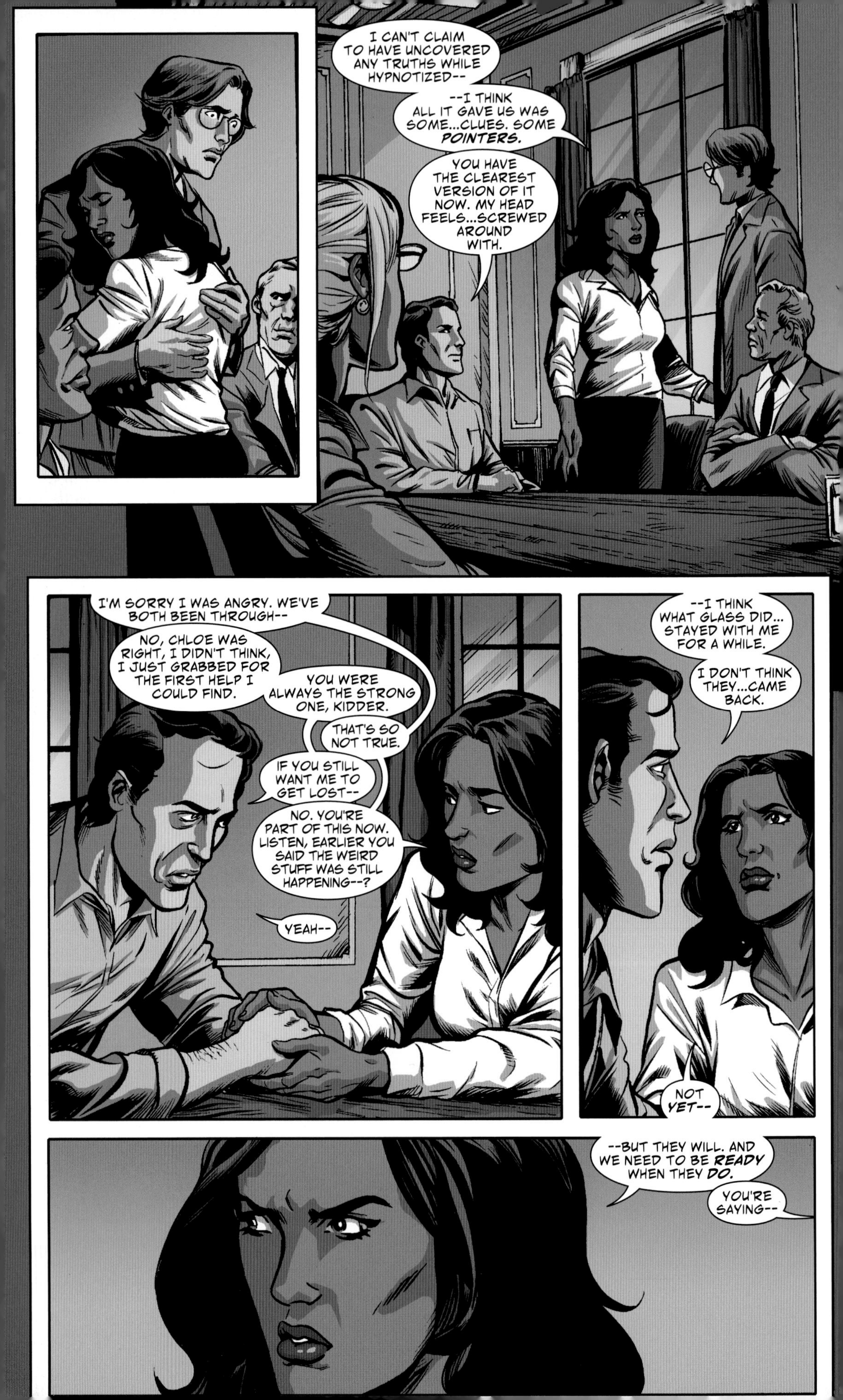
I CAN'T CLAIM TO HAVE UNCOVERED ANY TRUTHS WHILE HYPNOTIZED--
--I THINK ALL IT GAVE US WAS SOME...CLUES. SOME POINTERS.
YOU HAVE THE CLEAREST VERSION OF IT NOW. MY HEAD FEELS...SCREWED AROUND WITH.
I'M SORRY I WAS ANGRY. WE'VE BOTH BEEN THROUGH--
NO, CHLOE WAS RIGHT, I DIDN'T THINK, I JUST GRABBED FOR THE FIRST HELP I COULD FIND.
YOU WERE ALWAYS THE STRONG ONE, KIDDER.
THAT'S SO NOT TRUE.
IF YOU STILL WANT ME TO GET LOST--
NO. YOU'RE PART OF THIS NOW. LISTEN, EARLIER YOU SAID THE WEIRD STUFF WAS STILL HAPPENING--?
YEAH--
--I THINK WHAT GLASS DID... STAYED WITH ME FOR A WHILE.
I DON'T THINK THEY...CAME BACK.
NOT YET--
--BUT THEY WILL. AND WE NEED TO BE READY WHEN THEY DO.
YOU'RE SAYING--

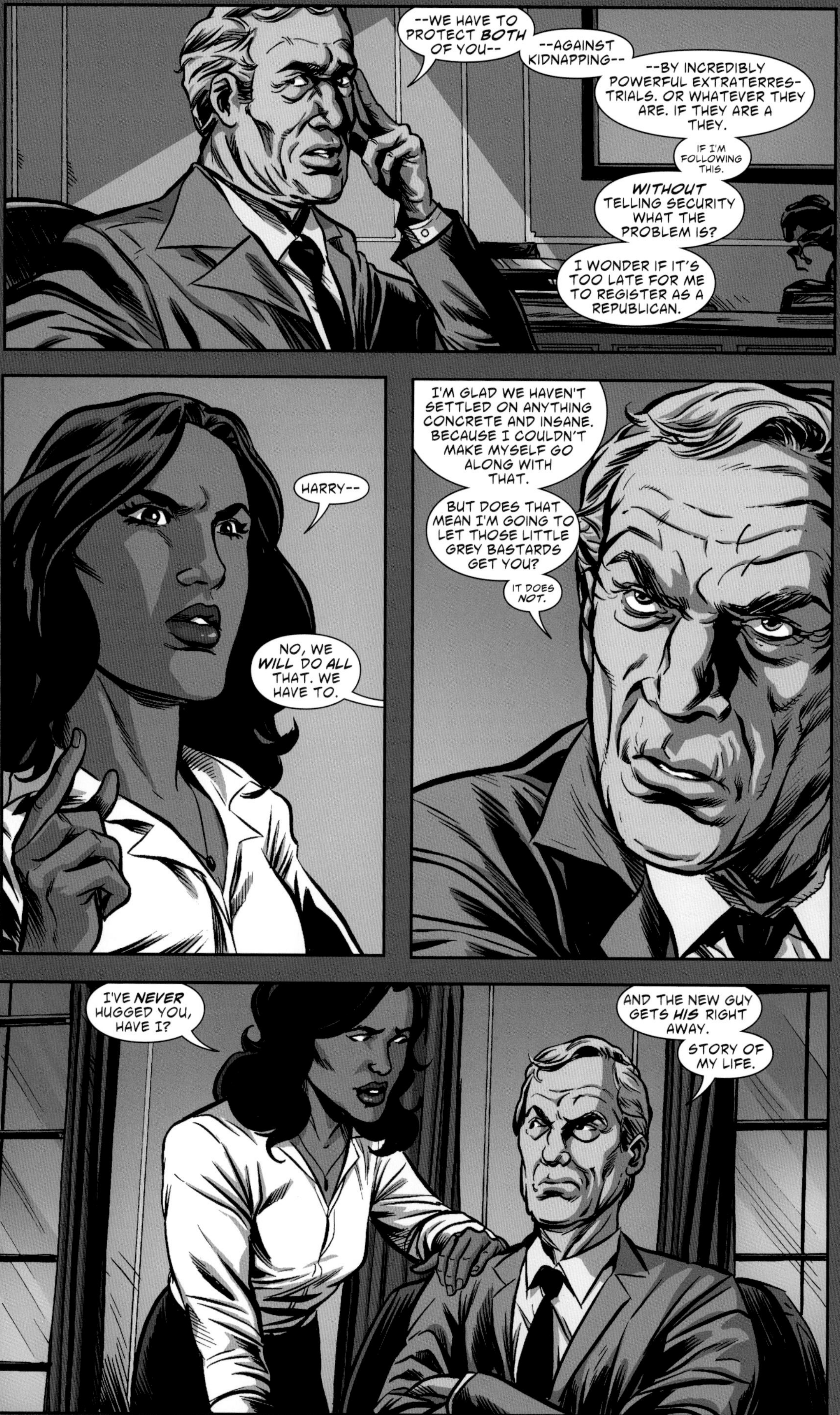

--WE HAVE TO PROTECT BOTH OF YOU--
--AGAINST KIDNAPPING--
--BY INCREDIBLY POWERFUL EXTRATERRES-TRIALS. OR WHATEVER THEY ARE. IF THEY ARE A THEY.
IF I'M FOLLOWING THIS.
WITHOUT TELLING SECURITY WHAT THE PROBLEM IS?
I WONDER IF IT'S TOO LATE FOR ME TO REGISTER AS A REPUBLICAN.
HARRY--
NO, WE WILL DO ALL THAT. WE HAVE TO.
I'M GLAD WE HAVEN'T SETTLED ON ANYTHING CONCRETE AND INSANE. BECAUSE I COULDN'T MAKE MYSELF GO ALONG WITH THAT.
BUT DOES THAT MEAN I'M GOING TO LET THOSE LITTLE GREY BASTARDS GET YOU?
IT DOES NOT.
I'VE NEVER HUGGED YOU, HAVE I?
AND THE NEW GUY GETS HIS RIGHT AWAY.
STORY OF MY LIFE.

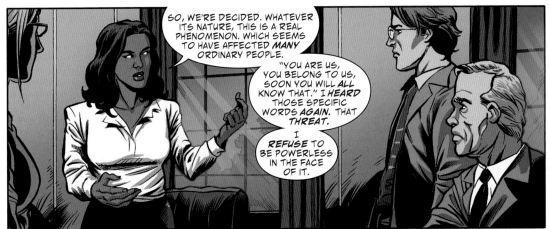

SO, WE'RE DECIDED. WHATEVER ITS NATURE, THIS IS A REAL PHENOMENON. WHICH SEEMS TO HAVE AFFECTED *MANY* ORDINARY PEOPLE.

"YOU ARE US, YOU BELONG TO US, SOON YOU WILL *ALL* KNOW THAT." I *HEARD* THOSE SPECIFIC WORDS *AGAIN*. THAT *THREAT*.

I *REFUSE* TO BE POWERLESS IN THE FACE OF IT.

I INTEND TO USE THE POWERS OF THE GOVERNOR'S OFFICE, AND THE ADDITIONAL OPPORTUNITIES GIVEN TO A CANDIDATE--

--TO INVESTIGATE AND UNCOVER THE *NATURE* OF THAT THREAT.

PROFESSOR, I WANT YOU TO FIND US SOME *THREADS* TO PULL AT.

I ALREADY HAVE SOME IN MIND. ANOMALIES IN THE MYTHOLOGY, PLACES TO VISIT, PEOPLE TO TALK TO.

EXCELLENT. CHLOE--

YEAH--

--I *STILL* THINK THIS IS *BULLSHIT*.

AND BEING THE NEXT PRESIDENT OF THE UNITED STATES, AND THUS A VERY CLEVER PERSON, YOU UNDERSTAND THAT THIS IS A *POSITIVE* REASON TO KEEP ME AROUND.

PERSUADING *YOU*, "SCULLY," IS THE WHOLE GAME.

WE NEED *EVIDENCE*.

THE CAMPAIGN TRAIL WILL GIVE US ACCESS TO ANYWHERE WE MIGHT FIND IT.

IN THE SECRECY WE'LL NEED TO MAINTAIN, ESPECIALLY IF THAT GAP IN THE RECORDS INDICATES *OPPOSITION*.

SO--

--WHERE DO WE BEGIN?

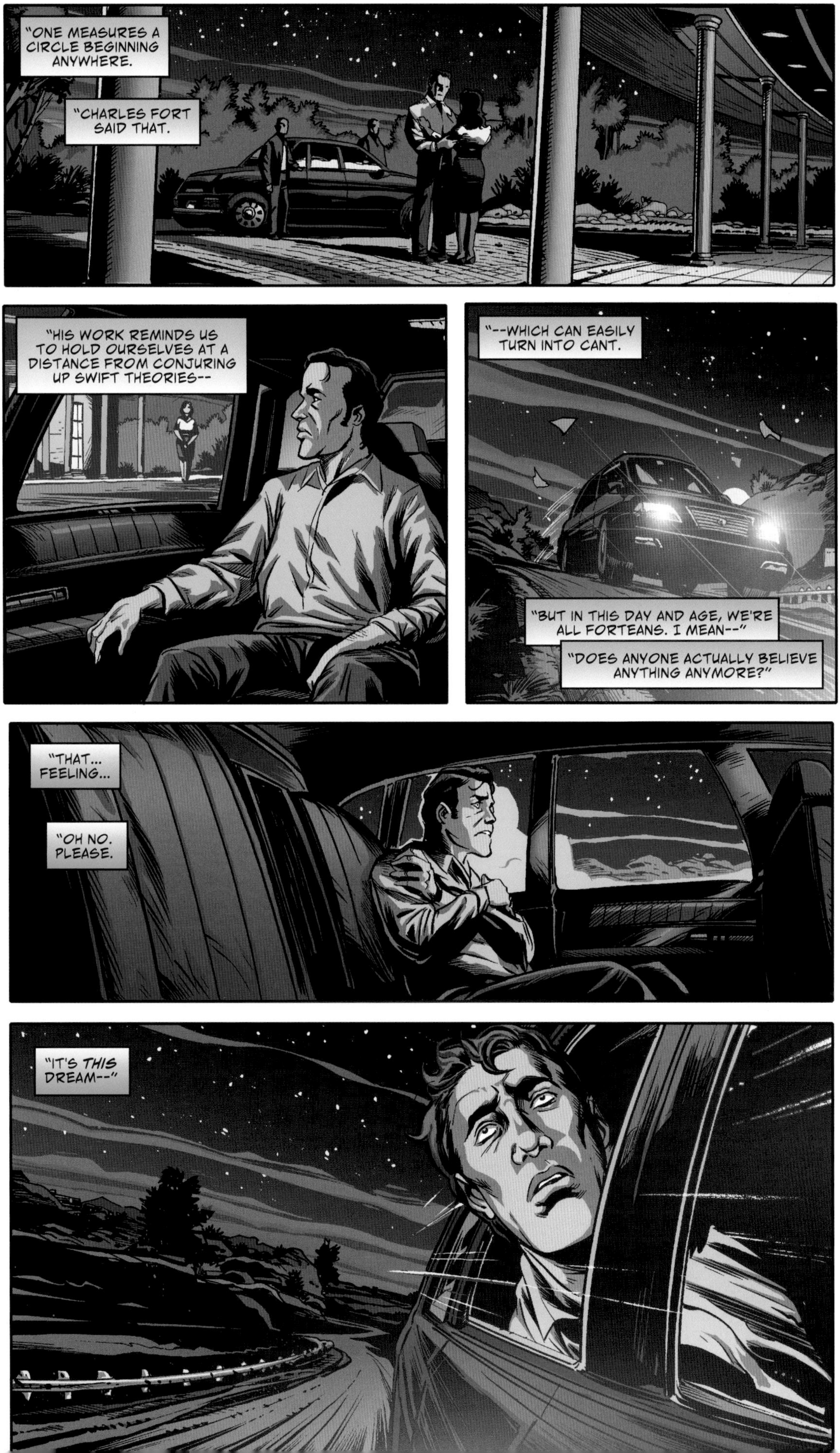
"ONE MEASURES A CIRCLE BEGINNING ANYWHERE.
"CHARLES FORT SAID THAT.
"HIS WORK REMINDS US TO HOLD OURSELVES AT A DISTANCE FROM CONJURING UP SWIFT THEORIES--
"--WHICH CAN EASILY TURN INTO CANT.
"BUT IN THIS DAY AND AGE, WE'RE ALL FORTEANS. I MEAN--"
"DOES ANYONE ACTUALLY BELIEVE ANYTHING ANYMORE?"
"THAT... FEELING...
"OH NO. PLEASE.
"IT'S *THIS* DREAM--"

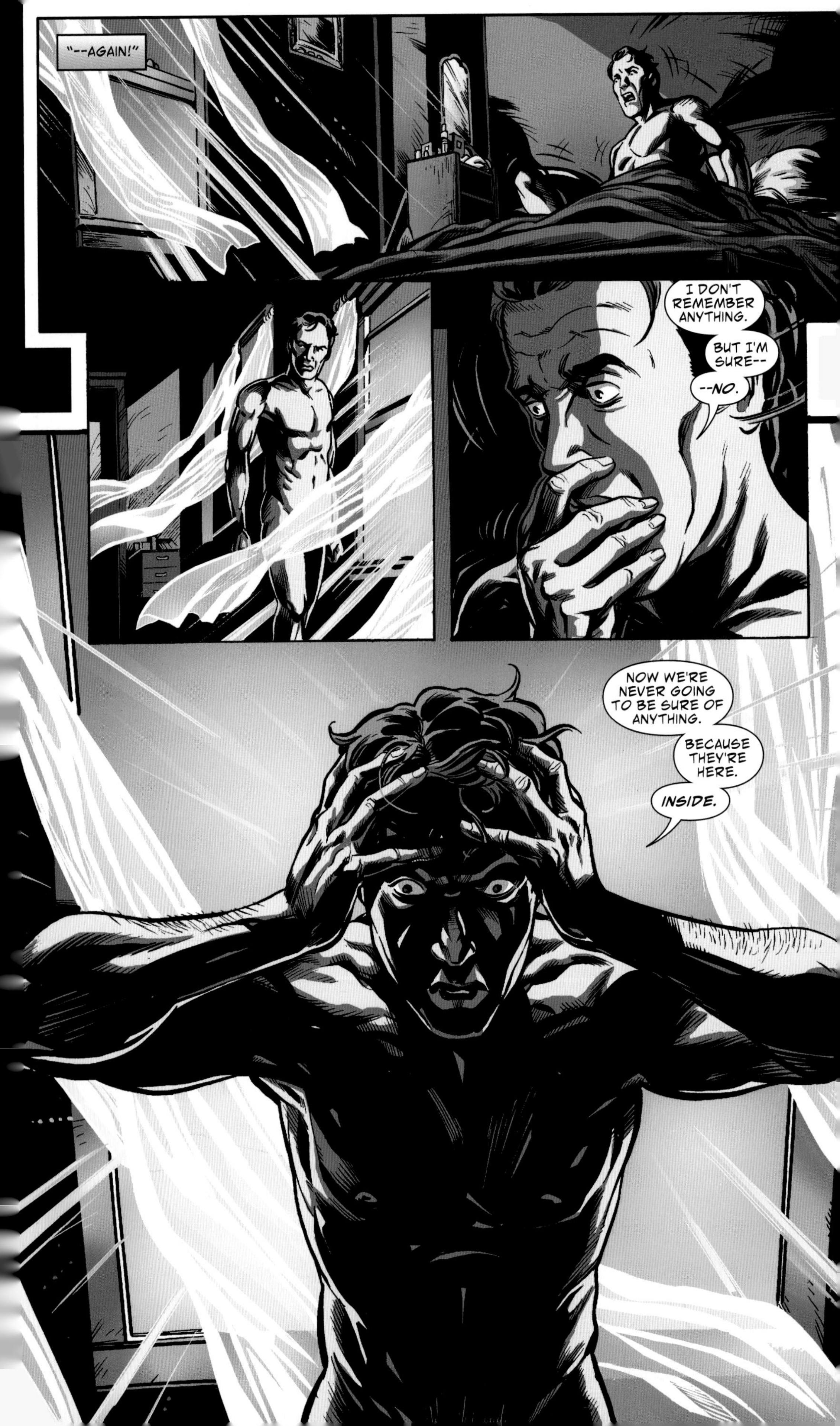
"--AGAIN!"
I DON'T REMEMBER ANYTHING.
BUT I'M SURE--
--NO.
NOW WE'RE NEVER GOING TO BE SURE OF ANYTHING.
BECAUSE THEY'RE HERE.
INSIDE.

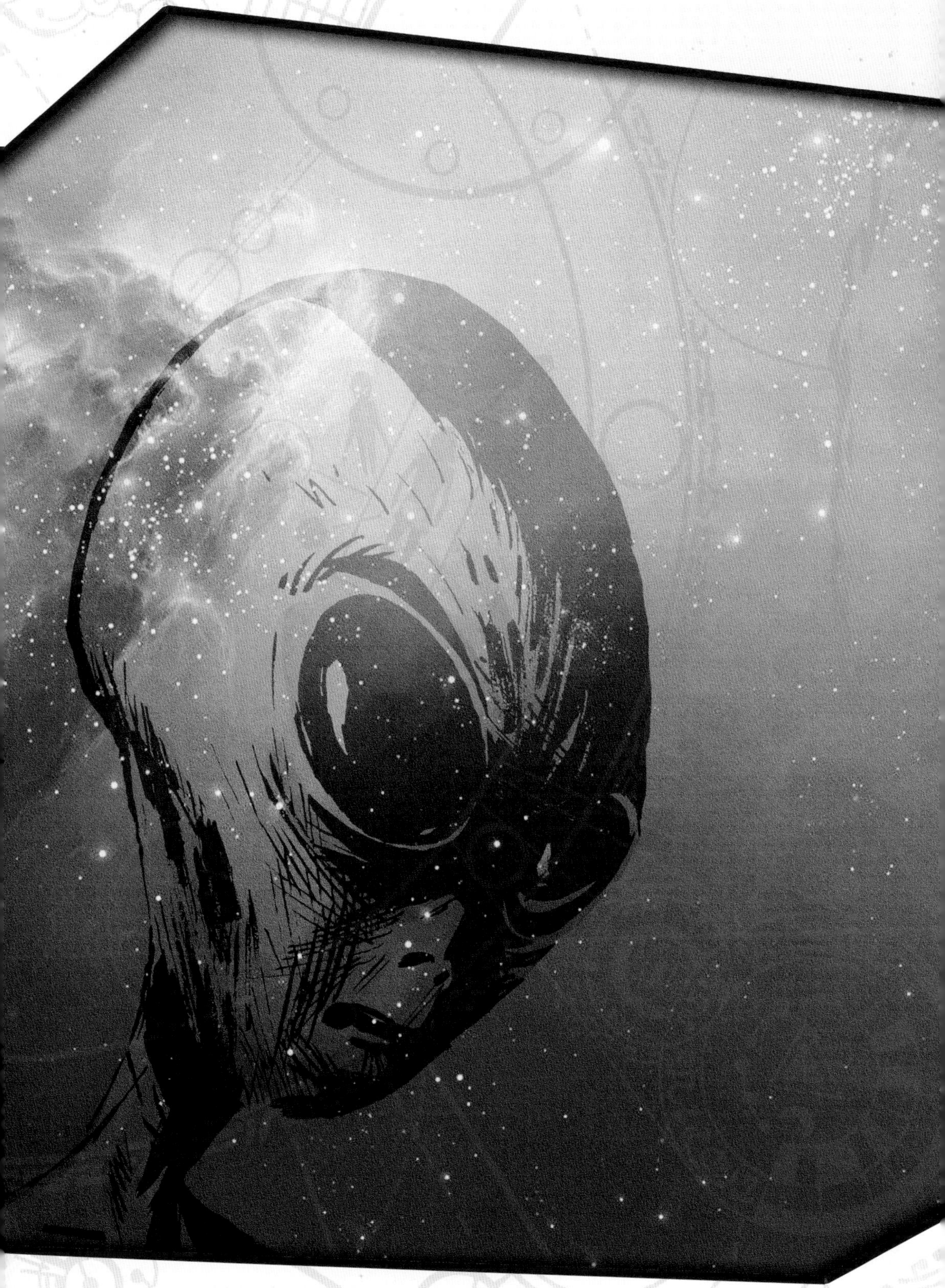

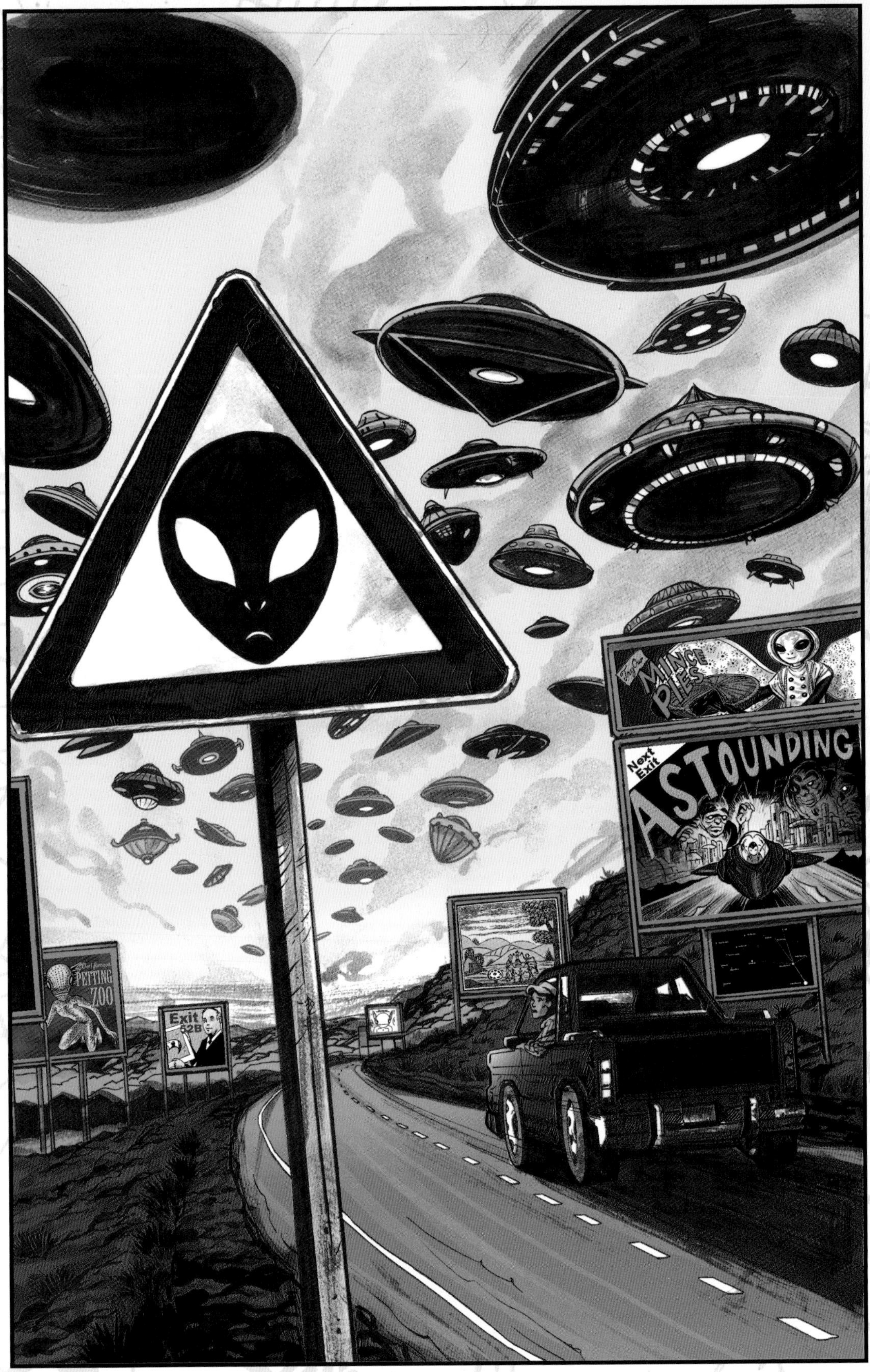
MINCE PIES
Next Exit
ASTOUNDING
PETTING ZOO
Exit 52B

COVER ART BY **RYAN KELLY**

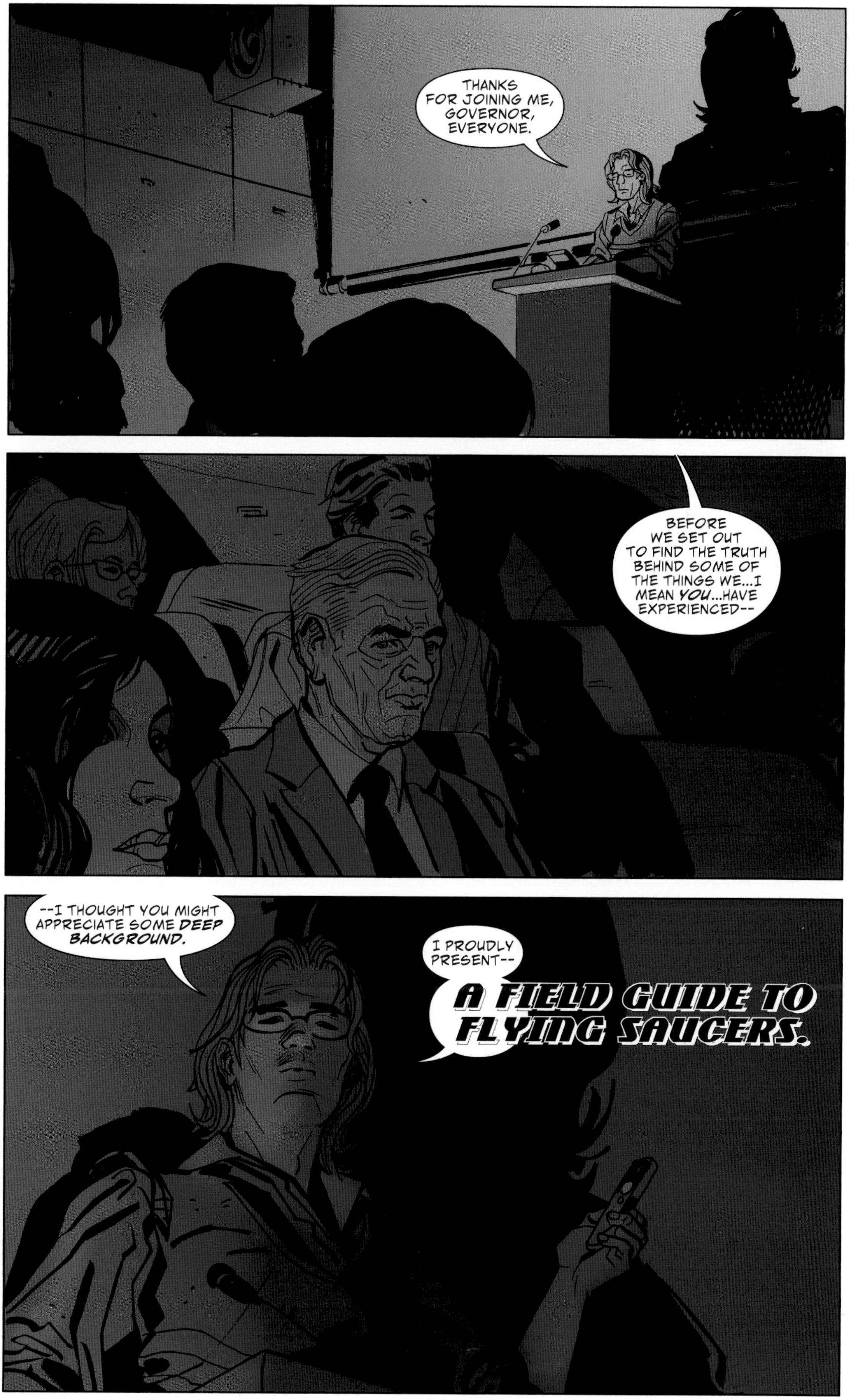
THANKS FOR JOINING ME, GOVERNOR, EVERYONE.
BEFORE WE SET OUT TO FIND THE TRUTH BEHIND SOME OF THE THINGS WE...I MEAN *YOU*...HAVE EXPERIENCED--
--I THOUGHT YOU MIGHT APPRECIATE SOME *DEEP BACKGROUND.*
I PROUDLY PRESENT--
A FIELD GUIDE TO FLYING SAUCERS.

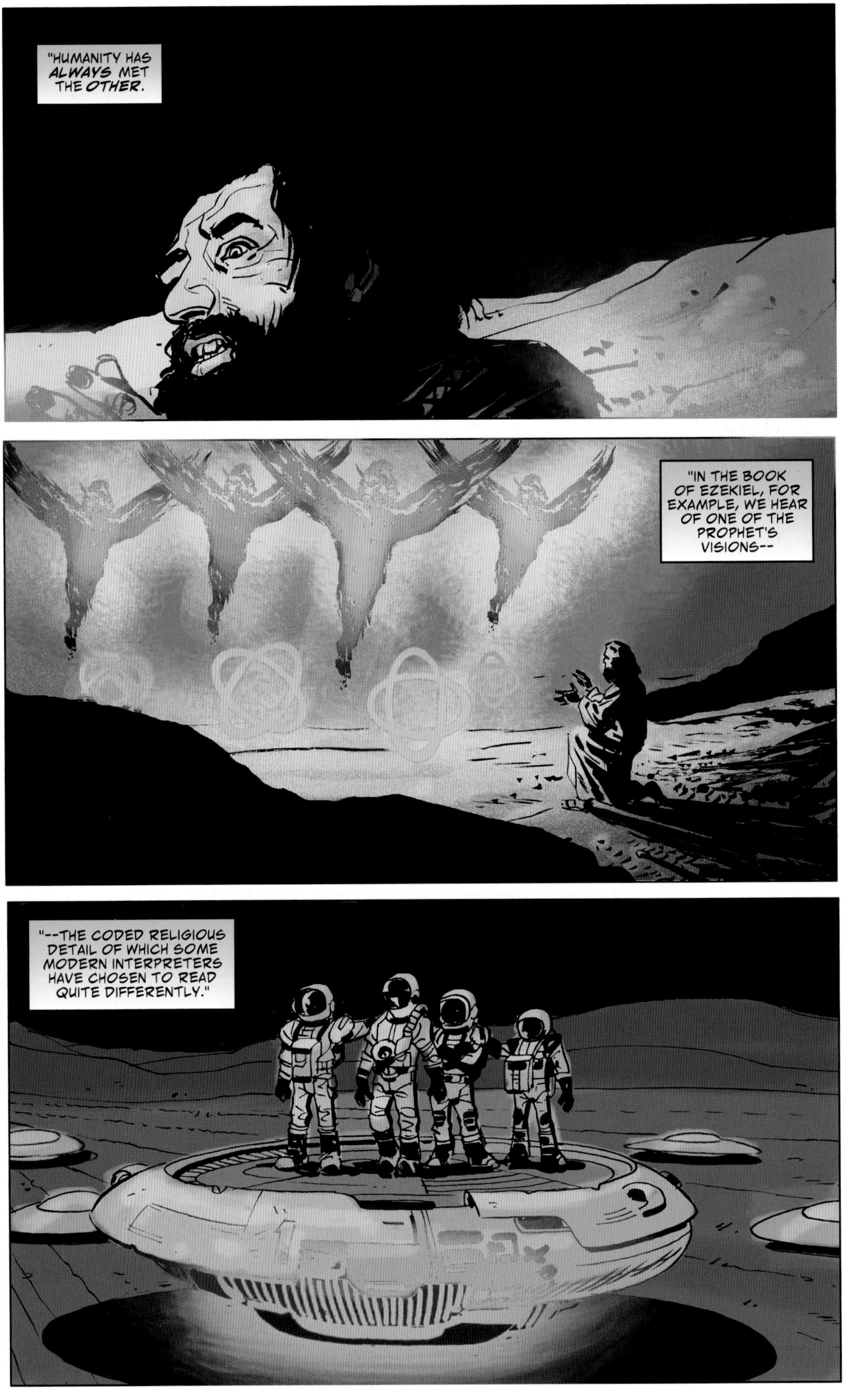
"HUMANITY HAS *ALWAYS* MET THE *OTHER*.
"IN THE BOOK OF EZEKIEL, FOR EXAMPLE, WE HEAR OF ONE OF THE PROPHET'S VISIONS--
"--THE CODED RELIGIOUS DETAIL OF WHICH SOME MODERN INTERPRETERS HAVE CHOSEN TO READ QUITE DIFFERENTLY."

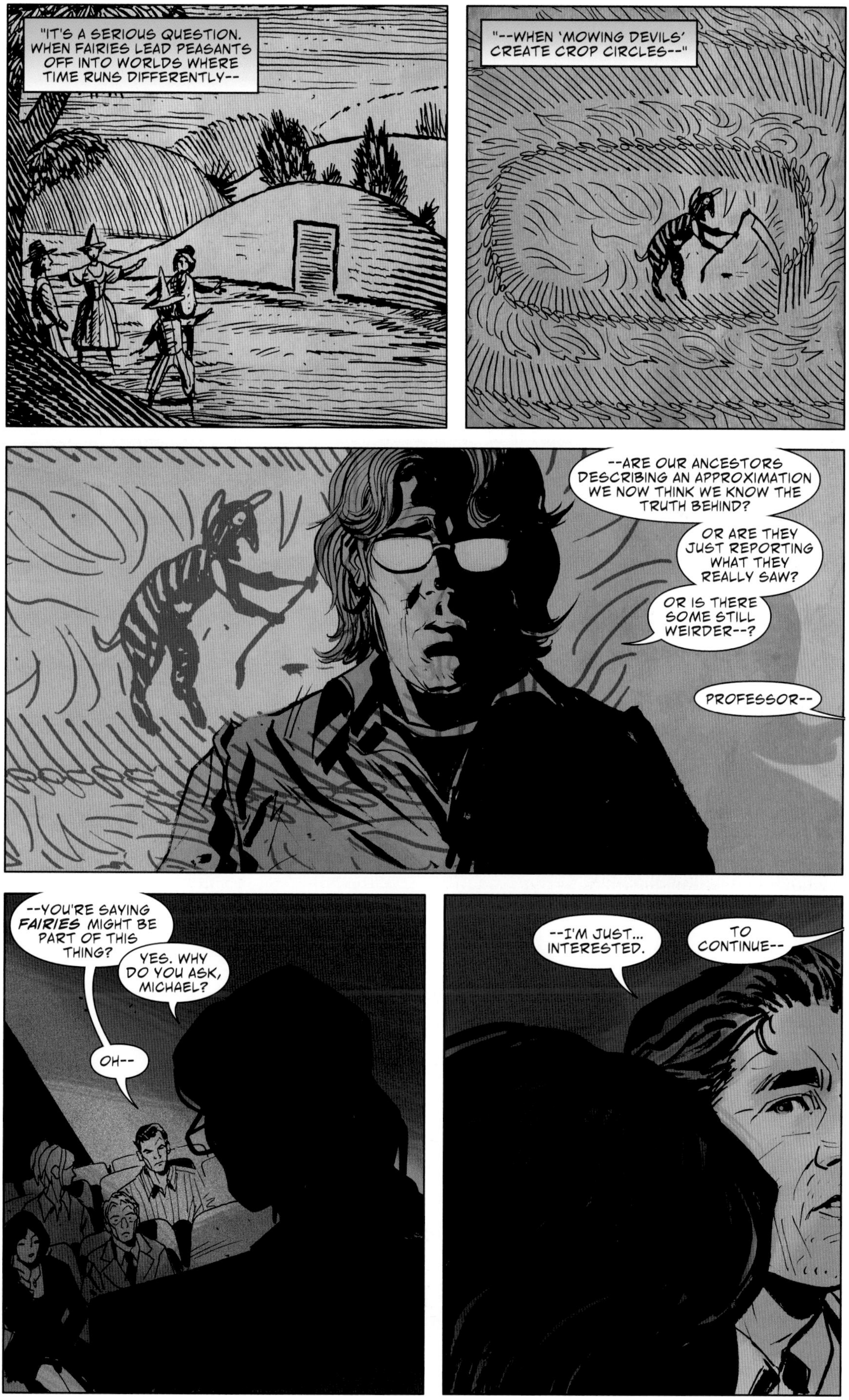
"IT'S A SERIOUS QUESTION. WHEN FAIRIES LEAD PEASANTS OFF INTO WORLDS WHERE TIME RUNS DIFFERENTLY--
"--WHEN 'MOWING DEVILS' CREATE CROP CIRCLES--"
--ARE OUR ANCESTORS DESCRIBING AN APPROXIMATION WE NOW THINK WE KNOW THE TRUTH BEHIND?
OR ARE THEY JUST REPORTING WHAT THEY REALLY SAW?
OR IS THERE SOME STILL WEIRDER--?
PROFESSOR--
--YOU'RE SAYING *FAIRIES* MIGHT BE PART OF THIS THING?
YES. WHY DO YOU ASK, MICHAEL?
OH--
--I'M JUST... INTERESTED.
TO CONTINUE--

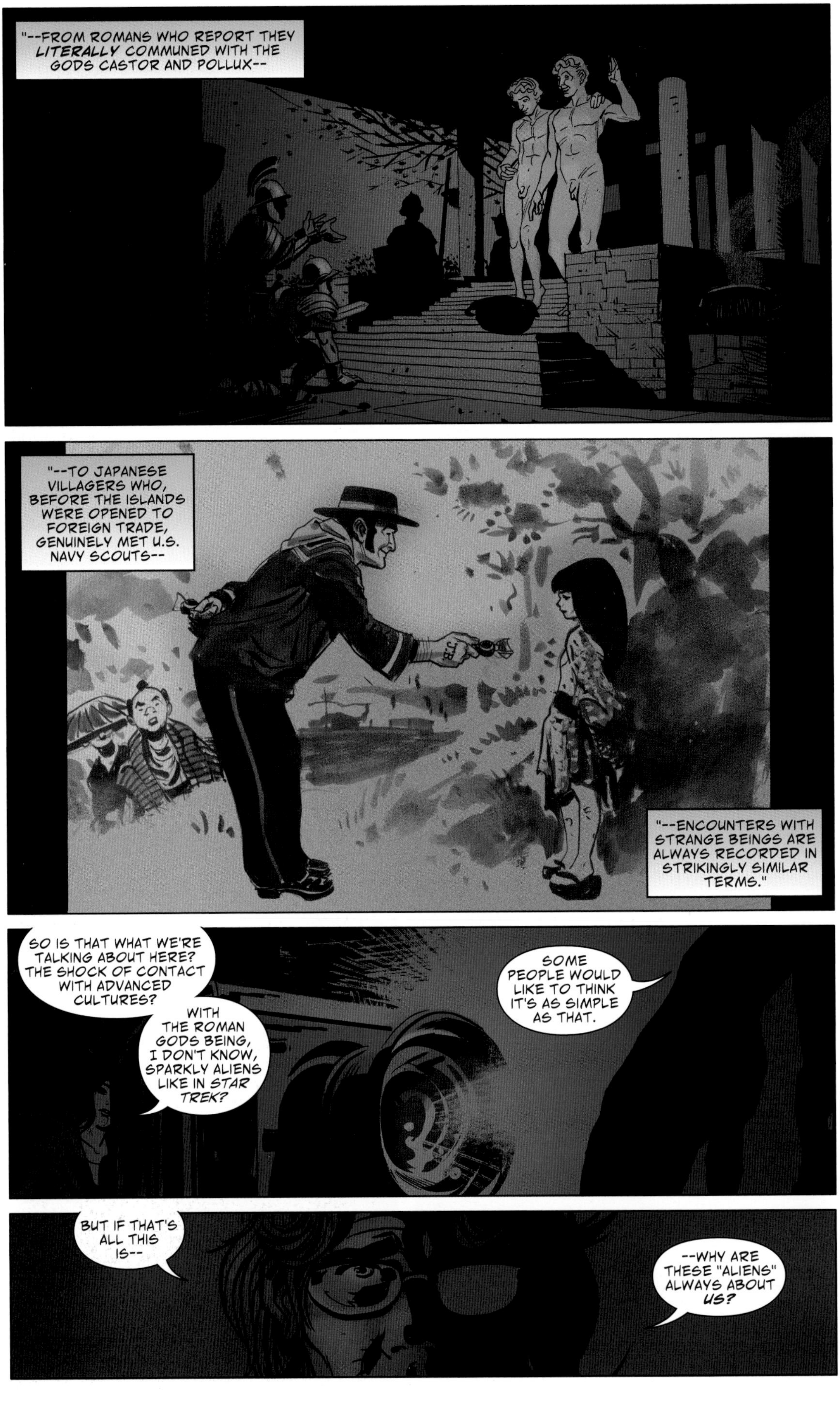
"--FROM ROMANS WHO REPORT THEY LITERALLY COMMUNED WITH THE GODS CASTOR AND POLLUX--
"--TO JAPANESE VILLAGERS WHO, BEFORE THE ISLANDS WERE OPENED TO FOREIGN TRADE, GENUINELY MET U.S. NAVY SCOUTS--
"--ENCOUNTERS WITH STRANGE BEINGS ARE ALWAYS RECORDED IN STRIKINGLY SIMILAR TERMS."
SO IS THAT WHAT WE'RE TALKING ABOUT HERE? THE SHOCK OF CONTACT WITH ADVANCED CULTURES?
WITH THE ROMAN GODS BEING, I DON'T KNOW, SPARKLY ALIENS LIKE IN STAR TREK?
SOME PEOPLE WOULD LIKE TO THINK IT'S AS SIMPLE AS THAT.
BUT IF THAT'S ALL THIS IS--
--WHY ARE THESE "ALIENS" ALWAYS ABOUT US?

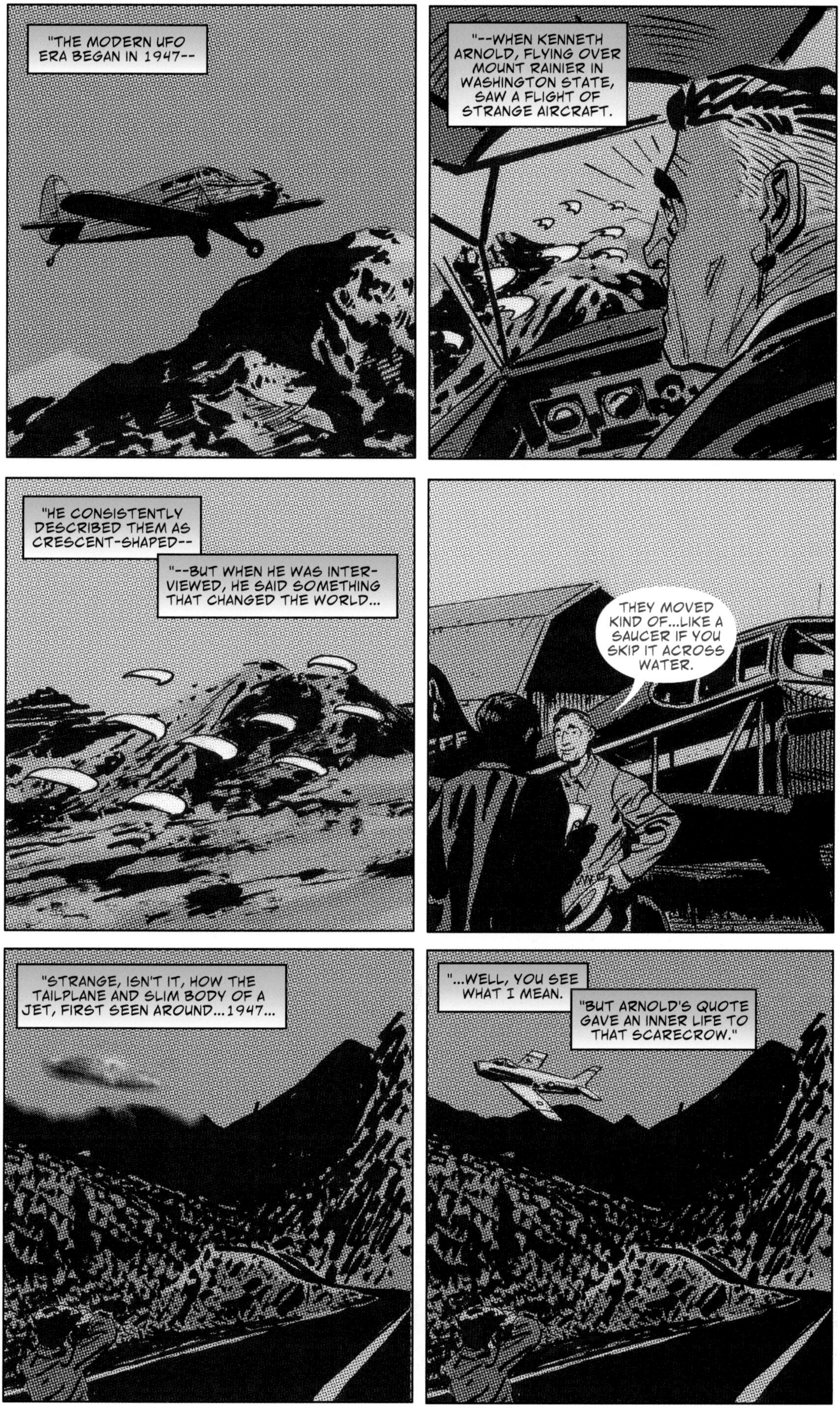
"THE MODERN UFO ERA BEGAN IN 1947--
"--WHEN KENNETH ARNOLD, FLYING OVER MOUNT RAINIER IN WASHINGTON STATE, SAW A FLIGHT OF STRANGE AIRCRAFT.
"HE CONSISTENTLY DESCRIBED THEM AS CRESCENT-SHAPED--
"--BUT WHEN HE WAS INTERVIEWED, HE SAID SOMETHING THAT CHANGED THE WORLD...
THEY MOVED KIND OF...LIKE A SAUCER IF YOU SKIP IT ACROSS WATER.
"STRANGE, ISN'T IT, HOW THE TAILPLANE AND SLIM BODY OF A JET, FIRST SEEN AROUND...1947...
"...WELL, YOU SEE WHAT I MEAN.
"BUT ARNOLD'S QUOTE GAVE AN INNER LIFE TO THAT SCARECROW."

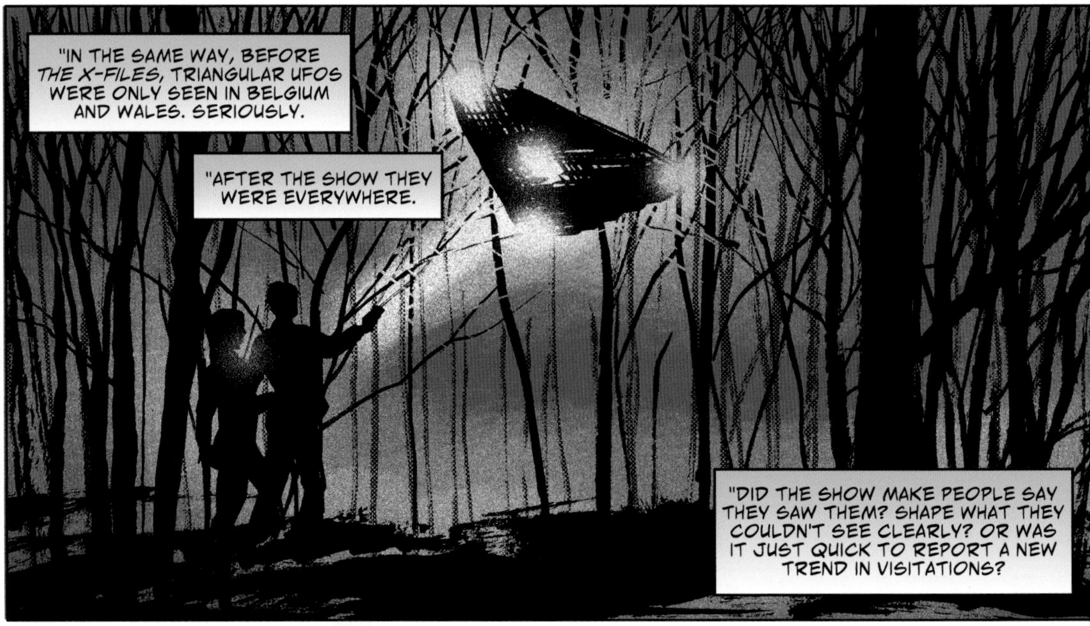
"IN THE SAME WAY, BEFORE *THE X-FILES*, TRIANGULAR UFOS WERE ONLY SEEN IN BELGIUM AND WALES. SERIOUSLY.
"AFTER THE SHOW THEY WERE EVERYWHERE.
"DID THE SHOW MAKE PEOPLE SAY THEY SAW THEM? SHAPE WHAT THEY COULDN'T SEE CLEARLY? OR WAS IT JUST QUICK TO REPORT A NEW TREND IN VISITATIONS?
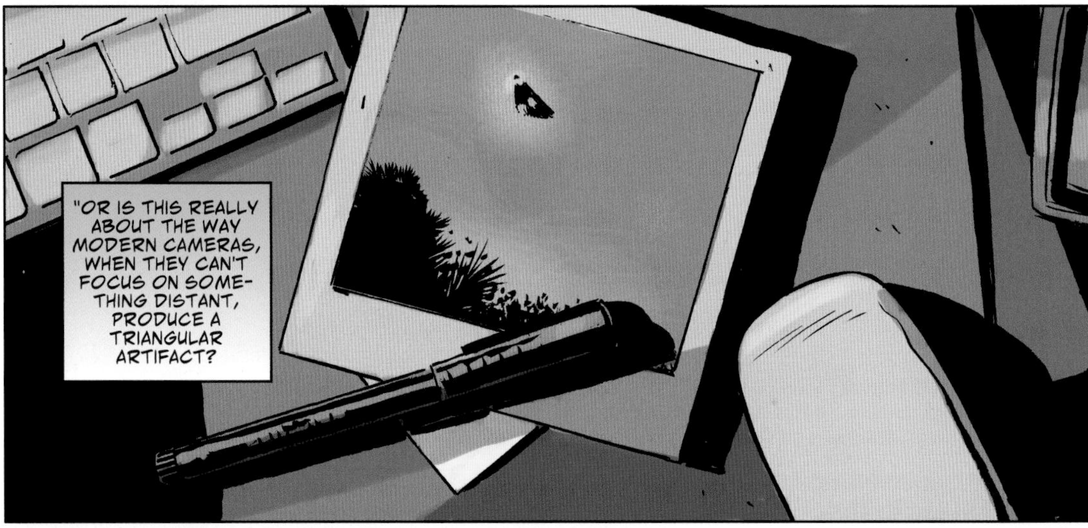
"OR IS THIS REALLY ABOUT THE WAY MODERN CAMERAS, WHEN THEY CAN'T FOCUS ON SOME-THING DISTANT, PRODUCE A TRIANGULAR ARTIFACT?
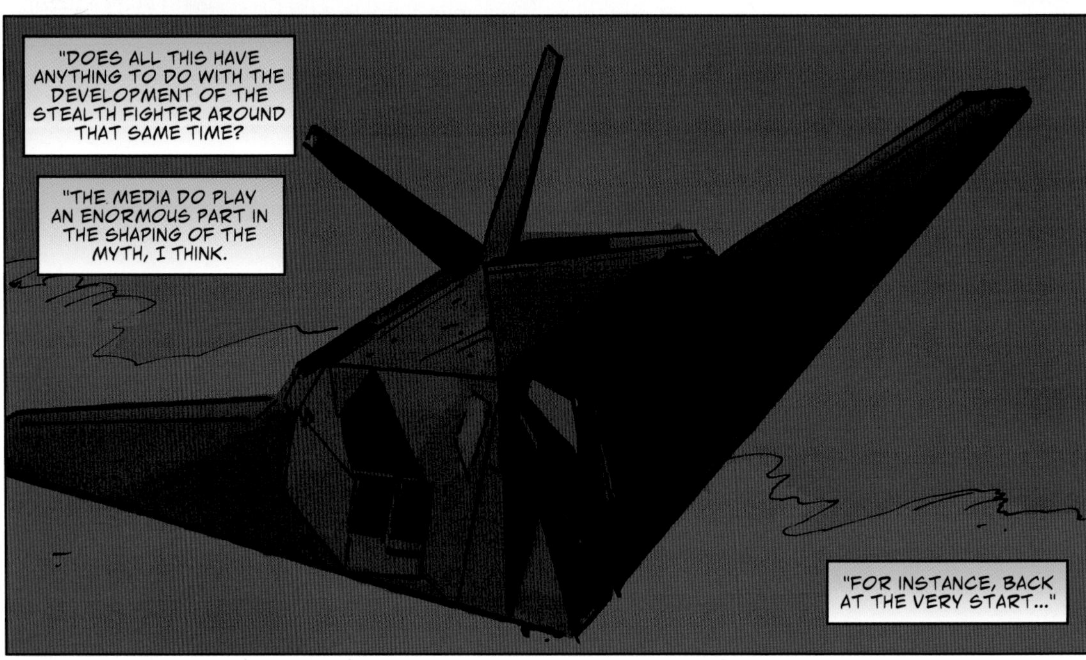
"DOES ALL THIS HAVE ANYTHING TO DO WITH THE DEVELOPMENT OF THE STEALTH FIGHTER AROUND THAT SAME TIME?
"THE MEDIA DO PLAY AN ENORMOUS PART IN THE SHAPING OF THE MYTH, I THINK.
"FOR INSTANCE, BACK AT THE VERY START..."

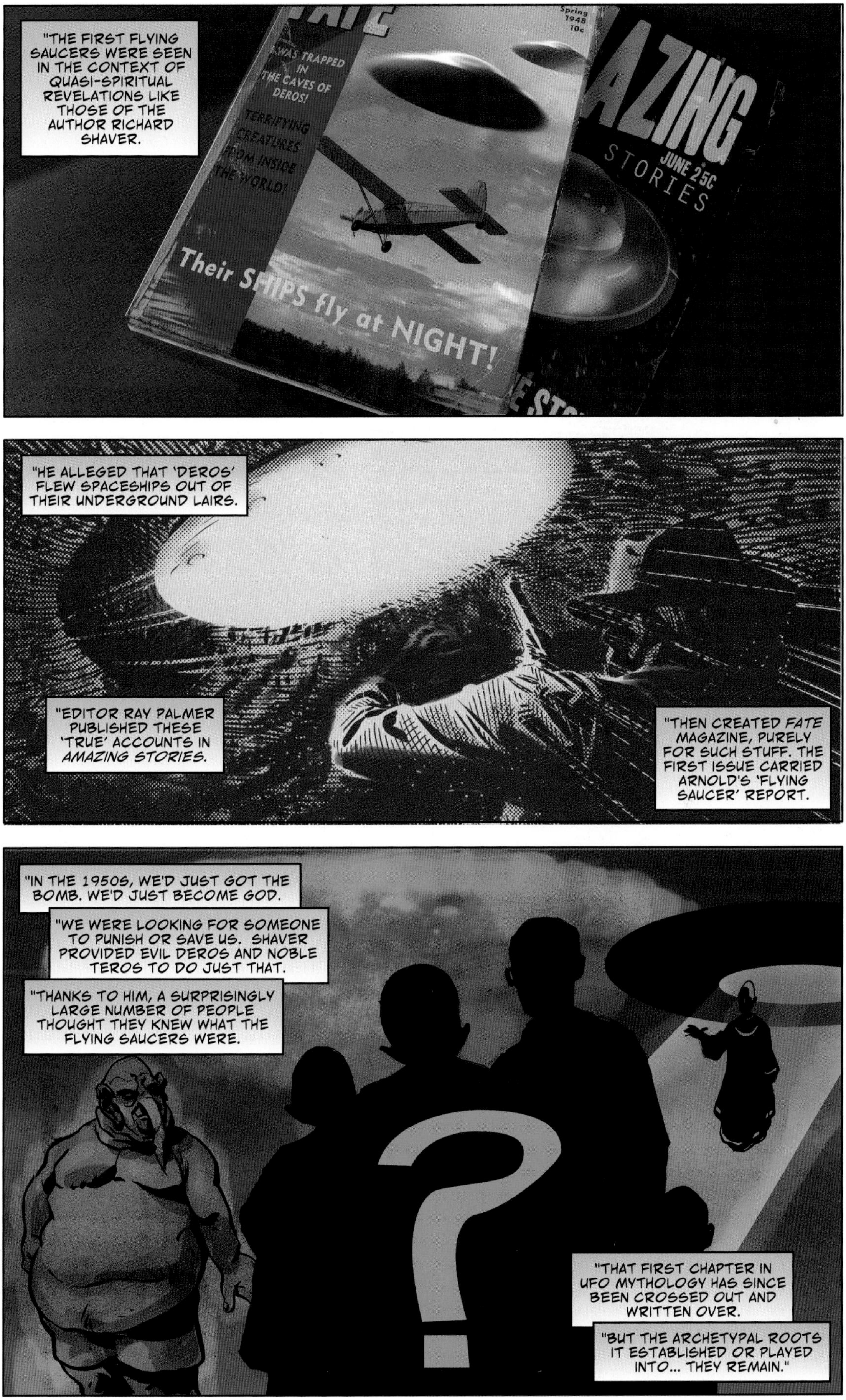
"THE FIRST FLYING SAUCERS WERE SEEN IN THE CONTEXT OF QUASI-SPIRITUAL REVELATIONS LIKE THOSE OF THE AUTHOR RICHARD SHAVER.
Spring 1948 10c
...WAS TRAPPED IN THE CAVES OF DEROS!
TERRIFYING CREATURES FROM INSIDE THE WORLD!
Their SHIPS fly at NIGHT!
JUNE 25C
STORIES
"HE ALLEGED THAT 'DEROS' FLEW SPACESHIPS OUT OF THEIR UNDERGROUND LAIRS.
"EDITOR RAY PALMER PUBLISHED THESE 'TRUE' ACCOUNTS IN *AMAZING STORIES*.
"THEN CREATED *FATE* MAGAZINE, PURELY FOR SUCH STUFF. THE FIRST ISSUE CARRIED ARNOLD'S 'FLYING SAUCER' REPORT.
"IN THE 1950S, WE'D JUST GOT THE BOMB. WE'D JUST BECOME GOD.
"WE WERE LOOKING FOR SOMEONE TO PUNISH OR SAVE US. SHAVER PROVIDED EVIL DEROS AND NOBLE TEROS TO DO JUST THAT.
"THANKS TO HIM, A SURPRISINGLY LARGE NUMBER OF PEOPLE THOUGHT THEY KNEW WHAT THE FLYING SAUCERS WERE.
?
"THAT FIRST CHAPTER IN UFO MYTHOLOGY HAS SINCE BEEN CROSSED OUT AND WRITTEN OVER.
"BUT THE ARCHETYPAL ROOTS IT ESTABLISHED OR PLAYED INTO... THEY REMAIN."

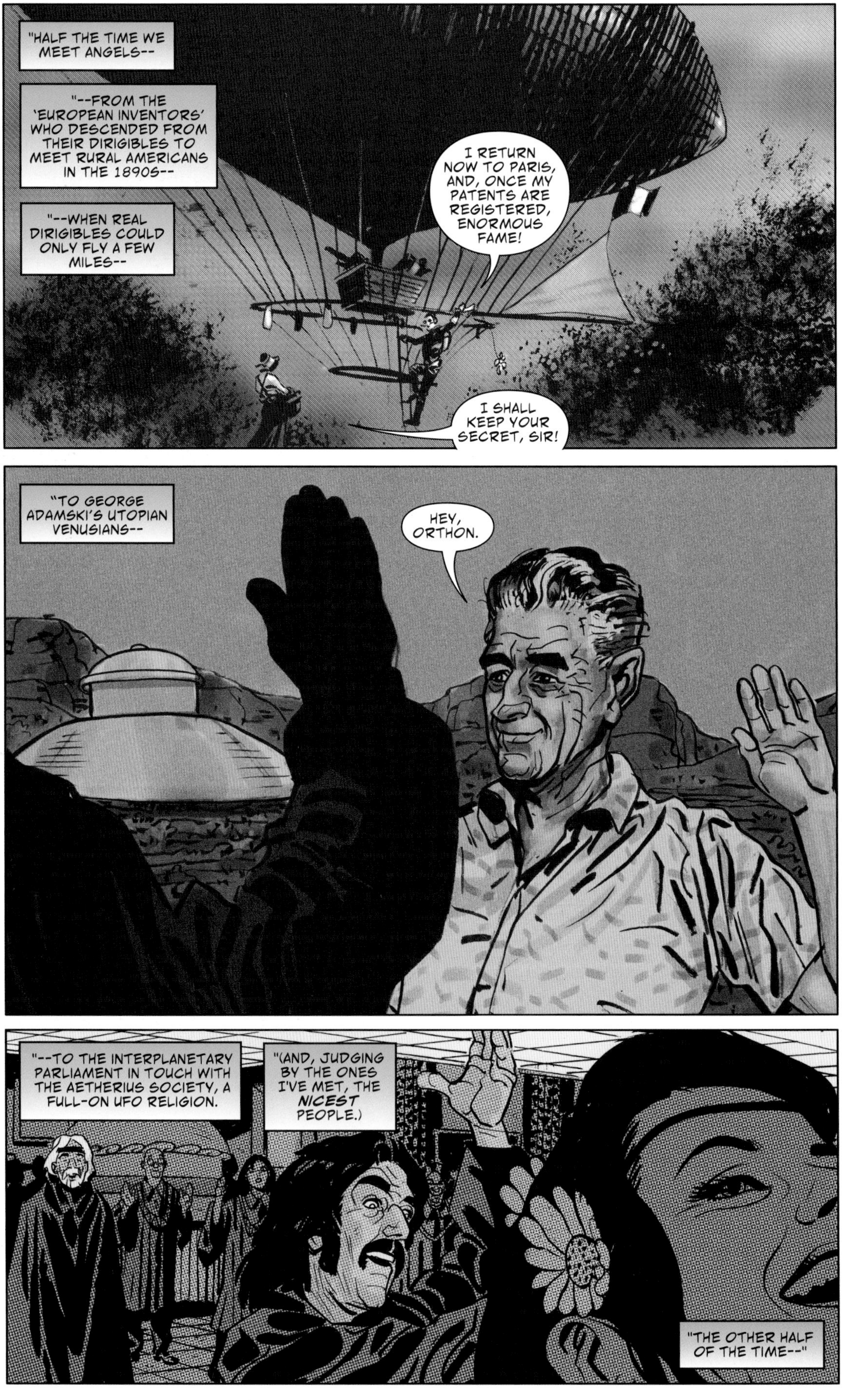
"HALF THE TIME WE MEET ANGELS--
"--FROM THE 'EUROPEAN INVENTORS' WHO DESCENDED FROM THEIR DIRIGIBLES TO MEET RURAL AMERICANS IN THE 1890S--
"--WHEN REAL DIRIGIBLES COULD ONLY FLY A FEW MILES--
I RETURN NOW TO PARIS, AND, ONCE MY PATENTS ARE REGISTERED, ENORMOUS FAME!
I SHALL KEEP YOUR SECRET, SIR!
"TO GEORGE ADAMSKI'S UTOPIAN VENUSIANS--
HEY, ORTHON.
"--TO THE INTERPLANETARY PARLIAMENT IN TOUCH WITH THE AETHERIUS SOCIETY, A FULL-ON UFO RELIGION.
"(AND, JUDGING BY THE ONES I'VE MET, THE *NICEST* PEOPLE.)
"THE OTHER HALF OF THE TIME--"

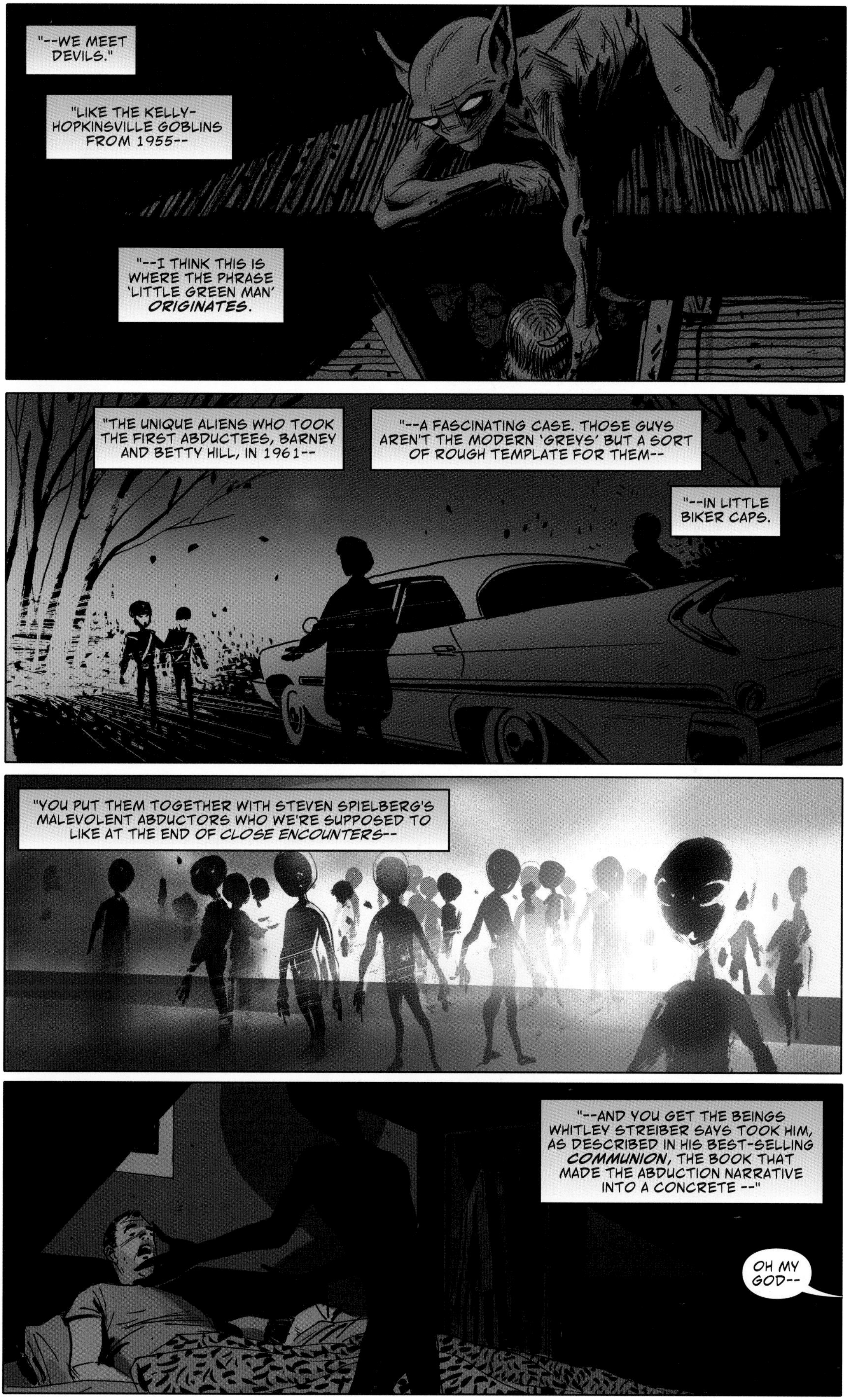
"--WE MEET DEVILS."
"LIKE THE KELLY-HOPKINSVILLE GOBLINS FROM 1955--
"--I THINK THIS IS WHERE THE PHRASE 'LITTLE GREEN MAN' ORIGINATES.
"THE UNIQUE ALIENS WHO TOOK THE FIRST ABDUCTEES, BARNEY AND BETTY HILL, IN 1961--
"--A FASCINATING CASE. THOSE GUYS AREN'T THE MODERN 'GREYS' BUT A SORT OF ROUGH TEMPLATE FOR THEM--
"--IN LITTLE BIKER CAPS.
"YOU PUT THEM TOGETHER WITH STEVEN SPIELBERG'S MALEVOLENT ABDUCTORS WHO WE'RE SUPPOSED TO LIKE AT THE END OF CLOSE ENCOUNTERS--
"--AND YOU GET THE BEINGS WHITLEY STREIBER SAYS TOOK HIM, AS DESCRIBED IN HIS BEST-SELLING COMMUNION, THE BOOK THAT MADE THE ABDUCTION NARRATIVE INTO A CONCRETE --"
OH MY GOD--

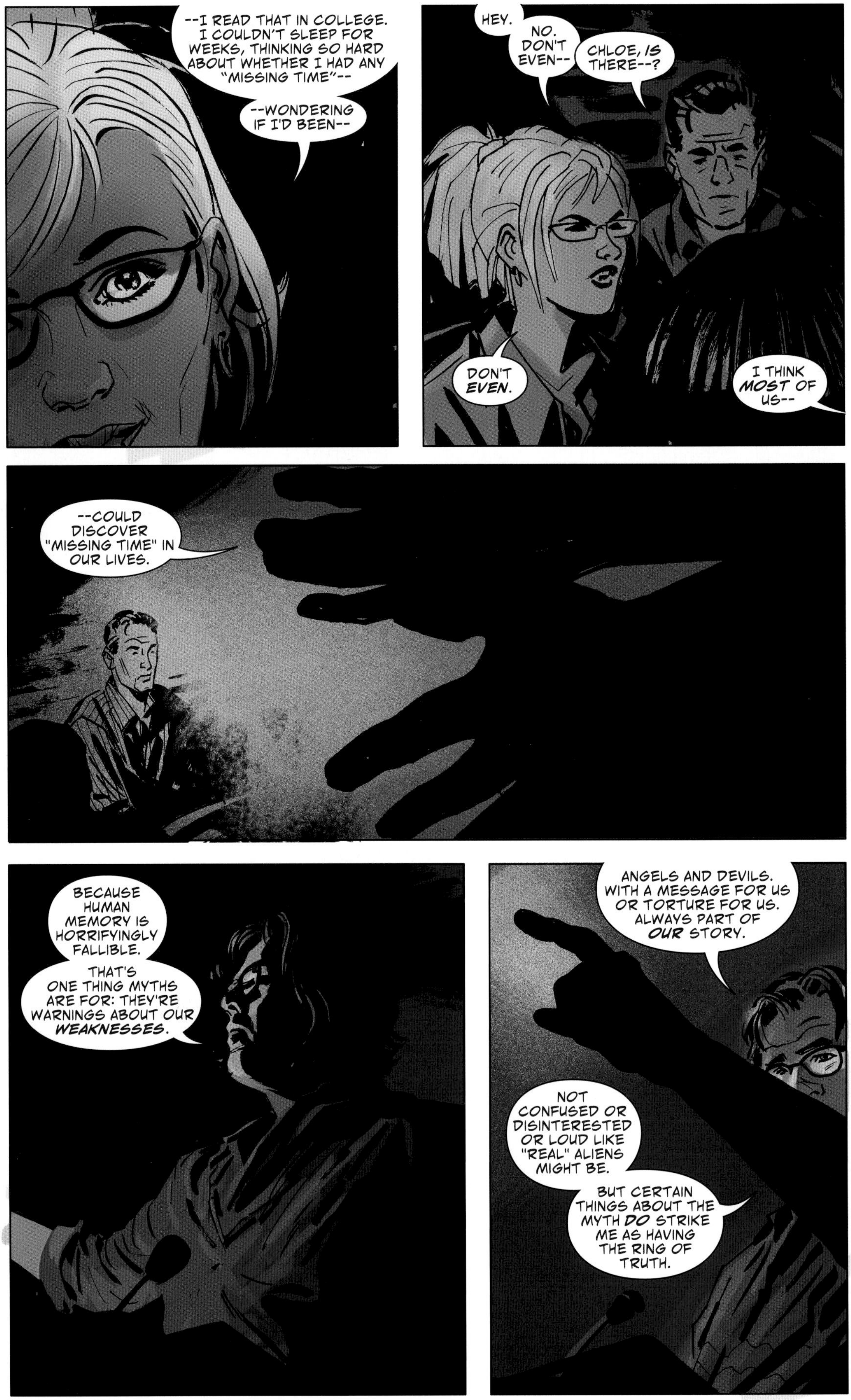
--I READ THAT IN COLLEGE. I COULDN'T SLEEP FOR WEEKS, THINKING SO HARD ABOUT WHETHER I HAD ANY "MISSING TIME"--
--WONDERING IF I'D BEEN--
HEY.
NO. DON'T EVEN--
CHLOE, *IS* THERE--?
DON'T *EVEN*.
I THINK *MOST* OF US--
--COULD DISCOVER "MISSING TIME" IN OUR LIVES.
BECAUSE HUMAN MEMORY IS HORRIFYINGLY FALLIBLE.
THAT'S ONE THING MYTHS ARE FOR: THEY'RE WARNINGS ABOUT OUR *WEAKNESSES*.
ANGELS AND DEVILS. WITH A MESSAGE FOR US OR TORTURE FOR US. ALWAYS PART OF *OUR* STORY.
NOT CONFUSED OR DISINTERESTED OR LOUD LIKE "REAL" ALIENS MIGHT BE.
BUT CERTAIN THINGS ABOUT THE MYTH *DO* STRIKE ME AS HAVING THE RING OF TRUTH.

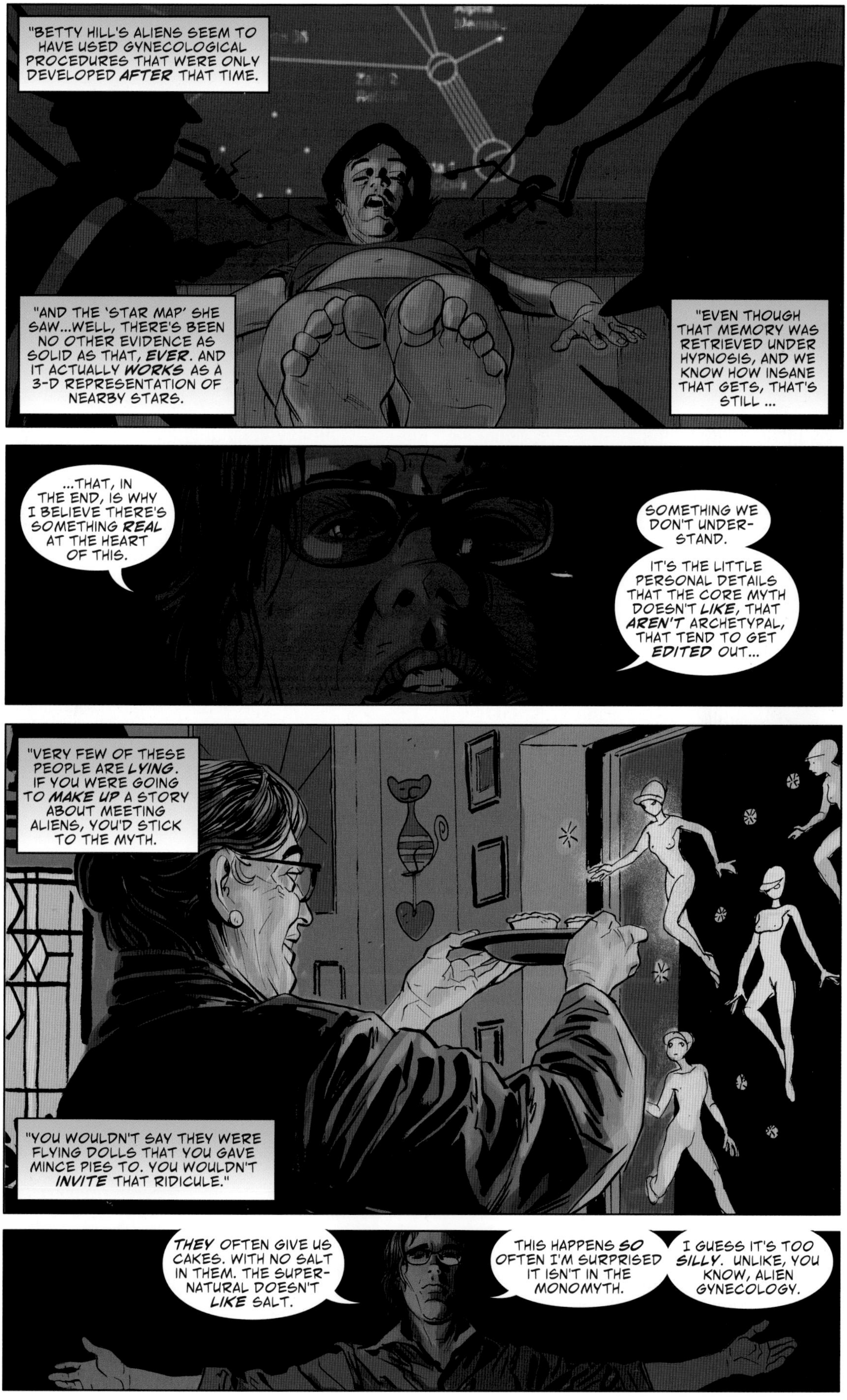
"BETTY HILL'S ALIENS SEEM TO HAVE USED GYNECOLOGICAL PROCEDURES THAT WERE ONLY DEVELOPED *AFTER* THAT TIME.
"AND THE 'STAR MAP' SHE SAW...WELL, THERE'S BEEN NO OTHER EVIDENCE AS SOLID AS THAT, *EVER*. AND IT ACTUALLY *WORKS* AS A 3-D REPRESENTATION OF NEARBY STARS.
"EVEN THOUGH THAT MEMORY WAS RETRIEVED UNDER HYPNOSIS, AND WE KNOW HOW INSANE THAT GETS, THAT'S STILL ...
...THAT, IN THE END, IS WHY I BELIEVE THERE'S SOMETHING *REAL* AT THE HEART OF THIS.
SOMETHING WE DON'T UNDER-STAND.
IT'S THE LITTLE PERSONAL DETAILS THAT THE CORE MYTH DOESN'T *LIKE*, THAT *AREN'T* ARCHETYPAL, THAT TEND TO GET *EDITED* OUT...
"VERY FEW OF THESE PEOPLE ARE *LYING*. IF YOU WERE GOING TO *MAKE UP* A STORY ABOUT MEETING ALIENS, YOU'D STICK TO THE MYTH.
"YOU WOULDN'T SAY THEY WERE FLYING DOLLS THAT YOU GAVE MINCE PIES TO. YOU WOULDN'T *INVITE* THAT RIDICULE."
THEY OFTEN GIVE US CAKES. WITH NO SALT IN THEM. THE SUPER-NATURAL DOESN'T *LIKE* SALT.
THIS HAPPENS *SO* OFTEN I'M SURPRISED IT ISN'T IN THE MONOMYTH.
I GUESS IT'S TOO *SILLY*. UNLIKE, YOU KNOW, ALIEN GYNECOLOGY.

"ALIENS WITH *NOSES* ARE ALSO FROWNED ON.

"AND ANYTHING SILVERY.

"IF YOU HAPPEN TO MEET GANDALF AND R2-D2 IN THEIR FLYING SAUCER, YOU'RE GOING TO FACE ENORMOUS PRESSURE TO CHANGE THOSE DETAILS.

"ALIENS ARE MEANT TO BE WHAT WE MAKE SF FROM, NOT FROM SF.

"BUT THAT LINE IS VERY BLURRY."

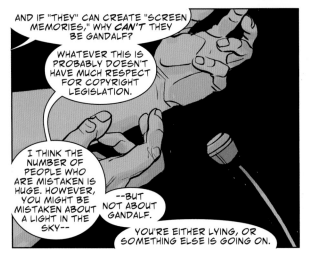

AND IF "THEY" CAN CREATE "SCREEN MEMORIES," WHY *CAN'T* THEY BE GANDALF?

WHATEVER THIS IS PROBABLY DOESN'T HAVE MUCH RESPECT FOR COPYRIGHT LEGISLATION.

I THINK THE NUMBER OF PEOPLE WHO ARE MISTAKEN IS HUGE. HOWEVER, YOU MIGHT BE MISTAKEN ABOUT A LIGHT IN THE SKY--

--BUT NOT ABOUT GANDALF.

YOU'RE EITHER LYING, OR SOMETHING ELSE IS GOING ON.

I THINK SOMETHING ELSE IS GOING ON.

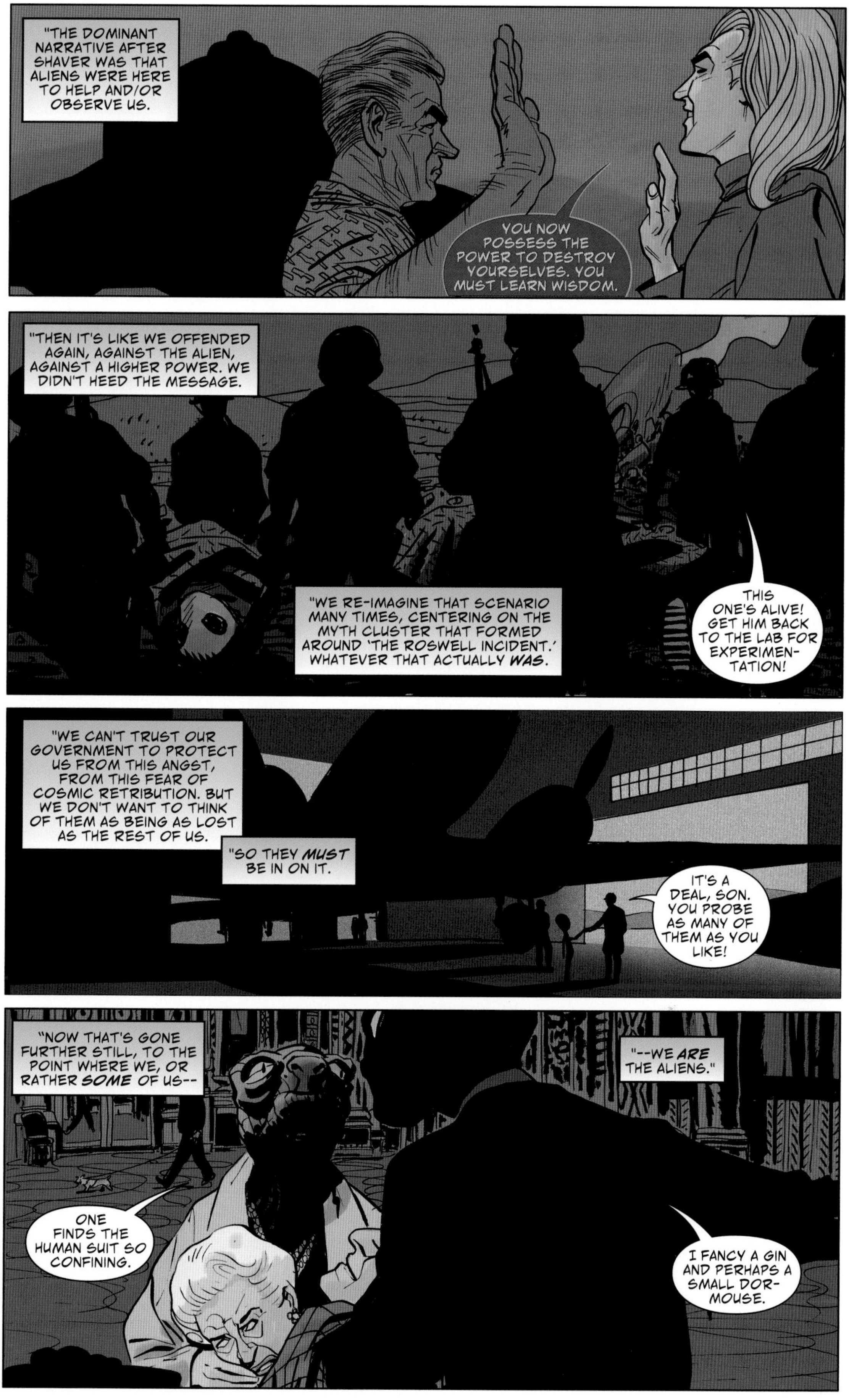
"THE DOMINANT NARRATIVE AFTER SHAVER WAS THAT ALIENS WERE HERE TO HELP AND/OR OBSERVE US.
YOU NOW POSSESS THE POWER TO DESTROY YOURSELVES. YOU MUST LEARN WISDOM.
"THEN IT'S LIKE WE OFFENDED AGAIN, AGAINST THE ALIEN, AGAINST A HIGHER POWER. WE DIDN'T HEED THE MESSAGE.
"WE RE-IMAGINE THAT SCENARIO MANY TIMES, CENTERING ON THE MYTH CLUSTER THAT FORMED AROUND 'THE ROSWELL INCIDENT.' WHATEVER THAT ACTUALLY *WAS*.
THIS ONE'S ALIVE! GET HIM BACK TO THE LAB FOR EXPERIMEN-TATION!
"WE CAN'T TRUST OUR GOVERNMENT TO PROTECT US FROM THIS ANGST, FROM THIS FEAR OF COSMIC RETRIBUTION. BUT WE DON'T WANT TO THINK OF THEM AS BEING AS LOST AS THE REST OF US.
"SO THEY *MUST* BE IN ON IT.
IT'S A DEAL, SON. YOU PROBE AS MANY OF THEM AS YOU LIKE!
"NOW THAT'S GONE FURTHER STILL, TO THE POINT WHERE WE, OR RATHER *SOME* OF US--
"--WE *ARE* THE ALIENS."
ONE FINDS THE HUMAN SUIT SO CONFINING.
I FANCY A GIN AND PERHAPS A SMALL DOR-MOUSE.

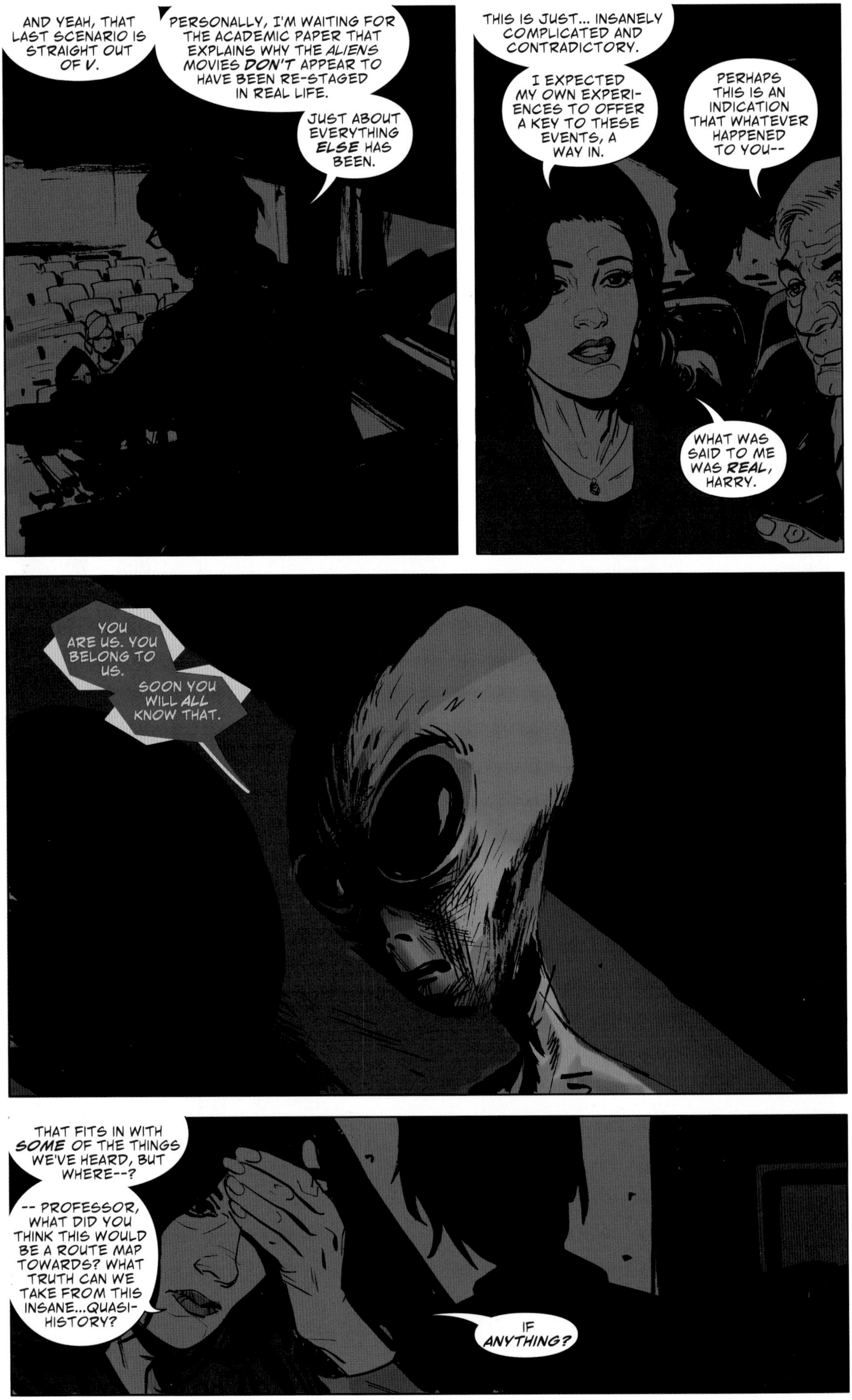
AND YEAH, THAT LAST SCENARIO IS STRAIGHT OUT OF *V*.
PERSONALLY, I'M WAITING FOR THE ACADEMIC PAPER THAT EXPLAINS WHY THE *ALIENS* MOVIES ***DON'T*** APPEAR TO HAVE BEEN RE-STAGED IN REAL LIFE.
JUST ABOUT EVERYTHING ***ELSE*** HAS BEEN.
THIS IS JUST... INSANELY COMPLICATED AND CONTRADICTORY.
I EXPECTED MY OWN EXPERIENCES TO OFFER A KEY TO THESE EVENTS, A WAY IN.
PERHAPS THIS IS AN INDICATION THAT WHATEVER HAPPENED TO YOU--
WHAT WAS SAID TO ME WAS ***REAL***, HARRY.
YOU ARE US. YOU BELONG TO US.
SOON YOU WILL *ALL* KNOW THAT.
THAT FITS IN WITH ***SOME*** OF THE THINGS WE'VE HEARD, BUT WHERE--?
-- PROFESSOR, WHAT DID YOU THINK THIS WOULD BE A ROUTE MAP TOWARDS? WHAT TRUTH CAN WE TAKE FROM THIS INSANE...QUASI-HISTORY?
IF ***ANYTHING?***

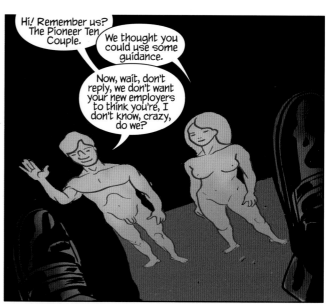

Hi! Remember us? The Pioneer Ten Couple.

We thought you could use some guidance.

Now, wait, don't reply, we don't want your new employers to think you're, I don't know, crazy, do we?

Why don't you tell the governor about what the government *might* know?

We're talking about Serpo. We think telling her about that might bring great revelations.

PROFESSOR? ARE YOU OKAY?

THERE ARE PERHAPS...A FEW AREAS WHERE THE U.S. GOVERNMENT MIGHT KNOW SOME SOLID FACTS ABOUT THESE MATTERS.

IF YOU EVER GAIN ACCESS TO HIGH LEVEL SECURITTY CLEARANCE... WELL...

"IT IS SAID...AND UNTIL...THIS MOMENT...I NEVER REALLY GAVE IT MUCH CREDENCE...

"THAT THE U.S. HAS AN EXCHANGE PROGRAM WITH AN EXTRASOLAR PLANET, THE NAME OF IT BEING *SERPO*. OR SOMETIMES *SEINU*.

"TWELVE MILITARY PERSONNEL LIVED THERE BETWEEN 1965 AND 1978, THEY SAY.

"AND YES, THIS IS EXACTLY LIKE THE ENDING OF *CLOSE ENCOUNTERS*. AND MORE THAN THAT--

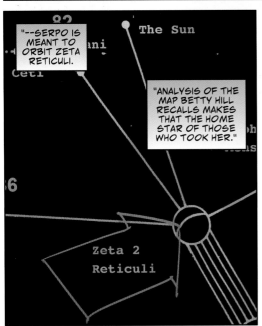

"--SERPO IS MEANT TO ORBIT ZETA RETICULI.

"ANALYSIS OF THE MAP BETTY HILL RECALLS MAKES THAT THE HOME STAR OF THOSE WHO TOOK HER."

The Sun

Zeta 2 Reticuli

THE STAR HAS ALSO BEEN RECENTLY OBSERVED TO HAVE AT LEAST A DEBRIS DISK, MAYBE A PLANETARY SYSTEM, TO BE A GREAT CANDIDATE FOR LIFE --

WAIT, WAIT!

ZETA RETICULI?!

THAT'S WHERE THEY FIND THE *ALIEN* IN THE RIDLEY SCOTT MOVIE.

THERE'S YOUR ALIEN REFERENCE.

PROFESSOR, ARE YOU *SURE* SOMEONE ISN'T HAVING A JOKE AT YOUR EXPENSE?

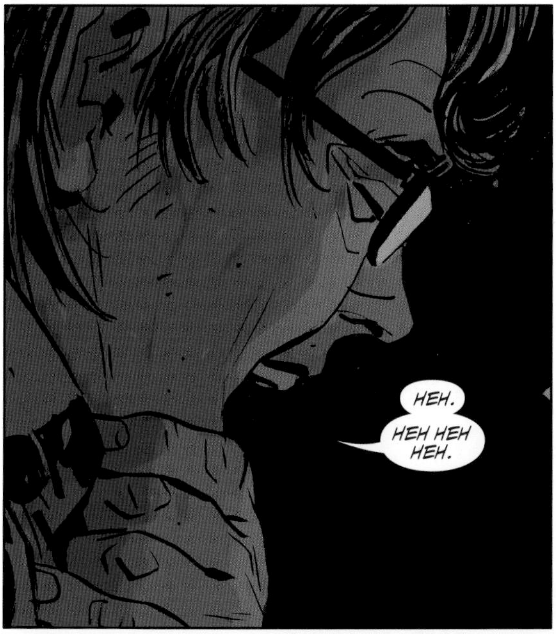
HEH.
HEH HEH HEH.

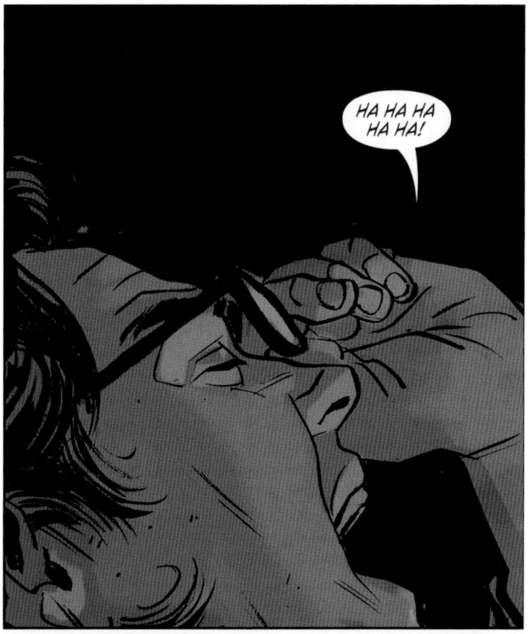
HA HA HA HA HA!

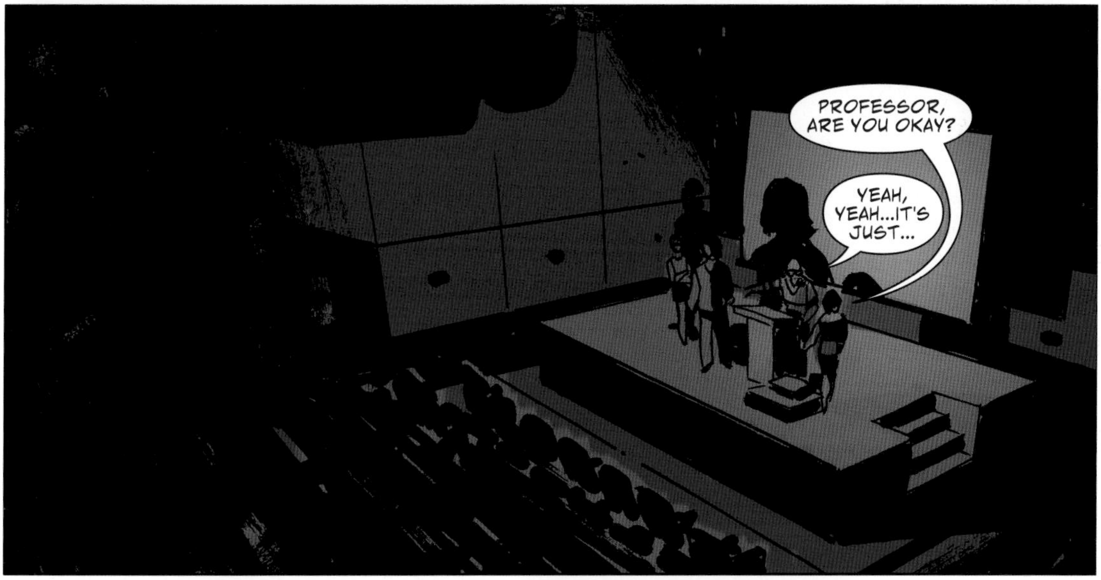
PROFESSOR, ARE YOU OKAY?
YEAH, YEAH...IT'S JUST...

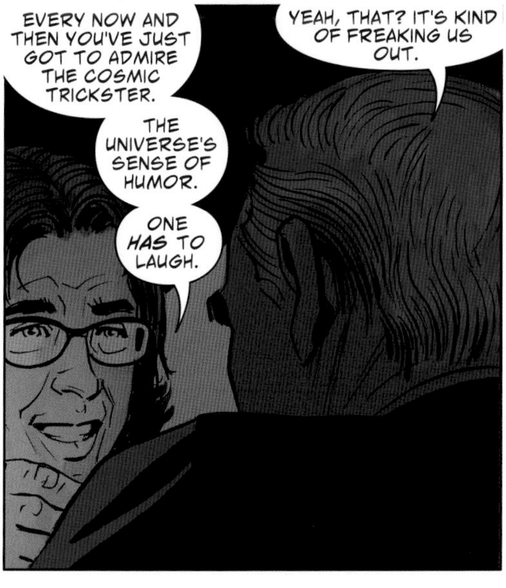
EVERY NOW AND THEN YOU'VE JUST GOT TO ADMIRE THE COSMIC TRICKSTER.
YEAH, THAT? IT'S KIND OF FREAKING US OUT.
THE UNIVERSE'S SENSE OF HUMOR.
ONE *HAS* TO LAUGH.

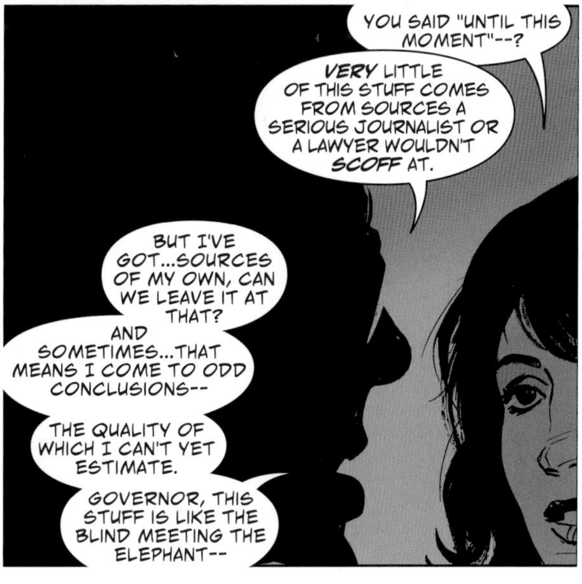
YOU SAID "UNTIL THIS MOMENT"--?
VERY LITTLE OF THIS STUFF COMES FROM SOURCES A SERIOUS JOURNALIST OR A LAWYER WOULDN'T *SCOFF* AT.
BUT I'VE GOT...SOURCES OF MY OWN, CAN WE LEAVE IT AT THAT?
AND SOMETIMES...THAT MEANS I COME TO ODD CONCLUSIONS--
THE QUALITY OF WHICH I CAN'T YET ESTIMATE.
GOVERNOR, THIS STUFF IS LIKE THE BLIND MEETING THE ELEPHANT--

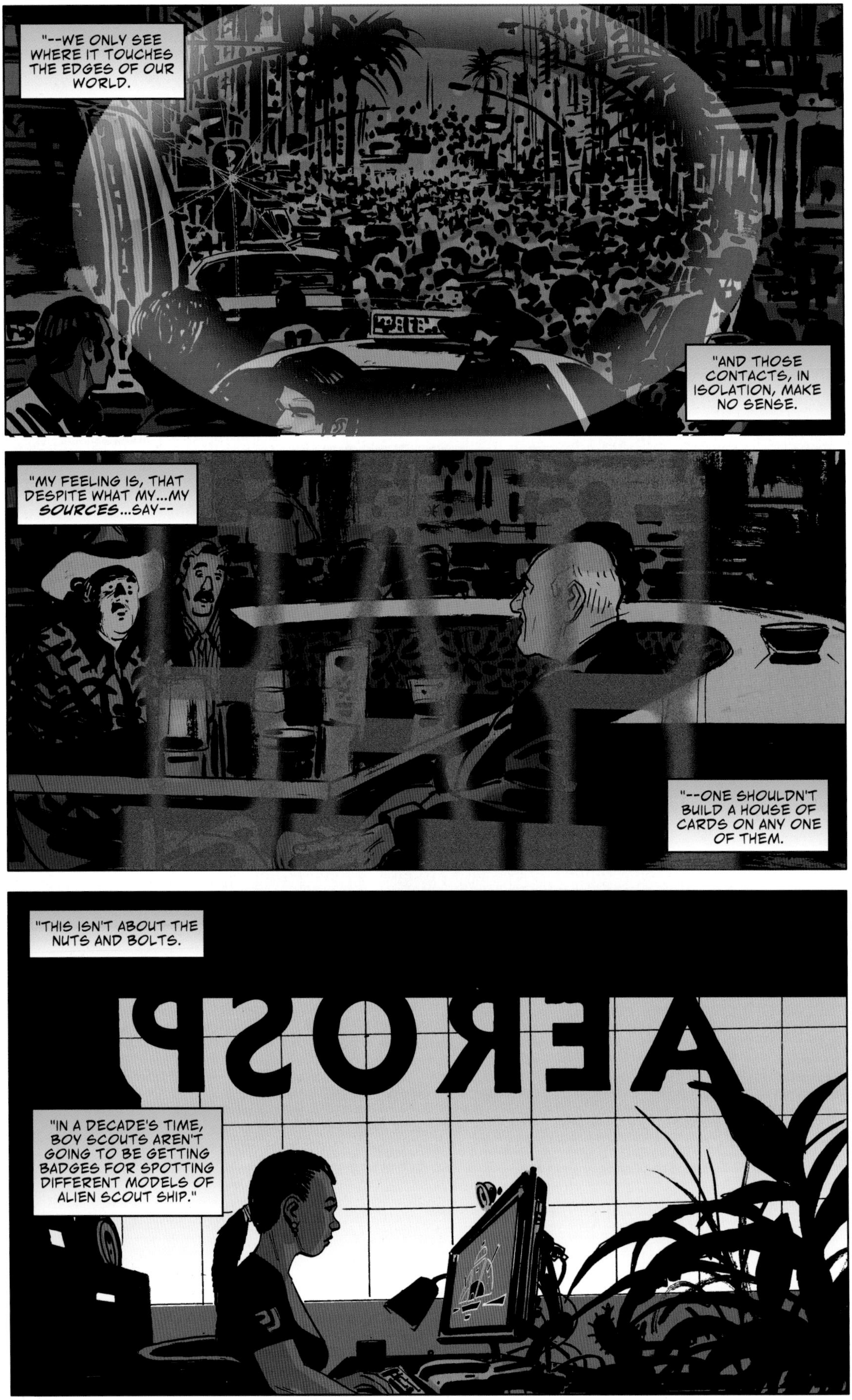
"--WE ONLY SEE WHERE IT TOUCHES THE EDGES OF OUR WORLD.
"AND THOSE CONTACTS, IN ISOLATION, MAKE NO SENSE.
"MY FEELING IS, THAT DESPITE WHAT MY...MY *SOURCES*...SAY--
"--ONE SHOULDN'T BUILD A HOUSE OF CARDS ON ANY ONE OF THEM.
"THIS ISN'T ABOUT THE NUTS AND BOLTS.
"IN A DECADE'S TIME, BOY SCOUTS AREN'T GOING TO BE GETTING BADGES FOR SPOTTING DIFFERENT MODELS OF ALIEN SCOUT SHIP."

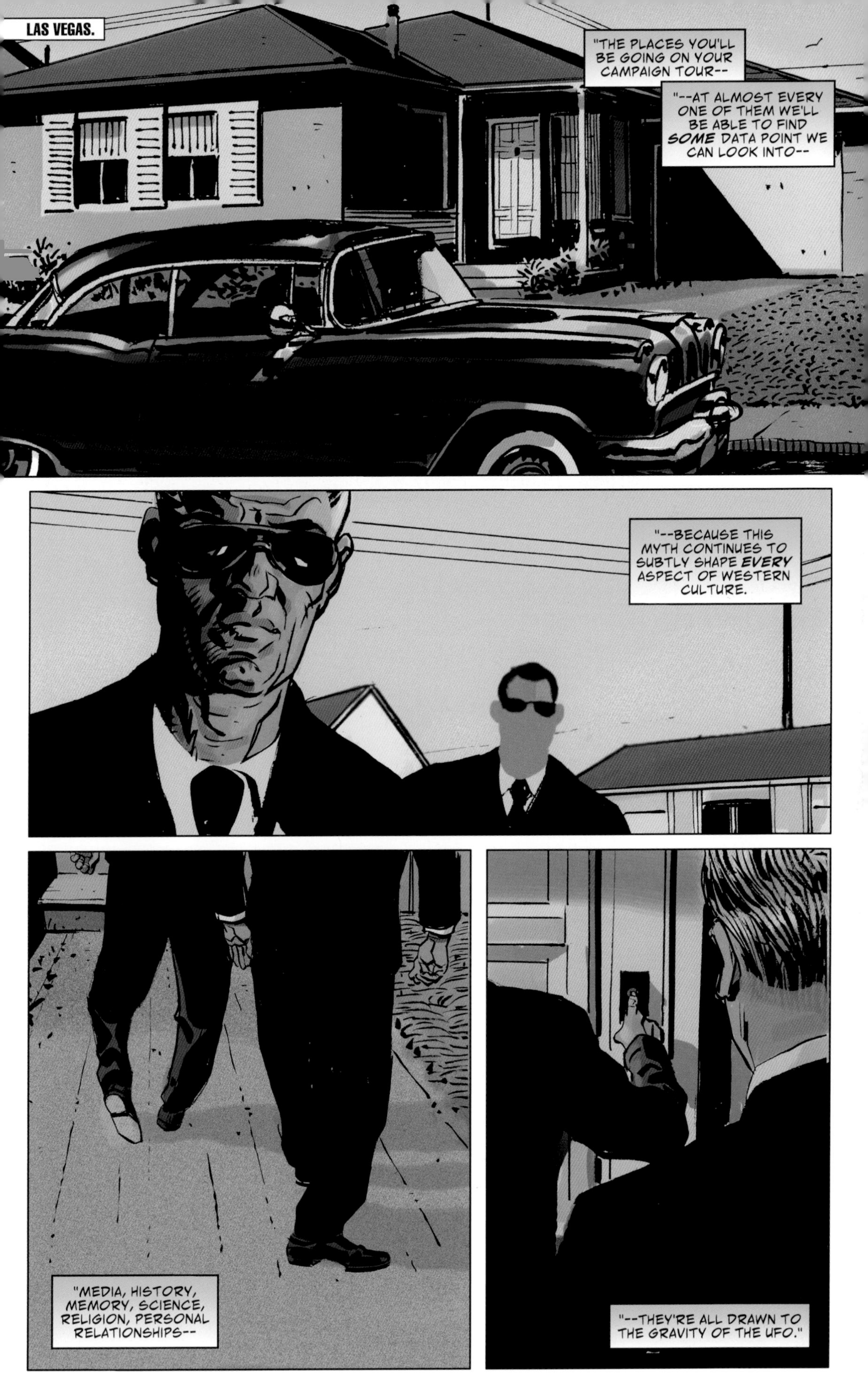
LAS VEGAS.
"THE PLACES YOU'LL BE GOING ON YOUR CAMPAIGN TOUR--
"--AT ALMOST EVERY ONE OF THEM WE'LL BE ABLE TO FIND *SOME* DATA POINT WE CAN LOOK INTO--
"--BECAUSE THIS MYTH CONTINUES TO SUBTLY SHAPE *EVERY* ASPECT OF WESTERN CULTURE.
"MEDIA, HISTORY, MEMORY, SCIENCE, RELIGION, PERSONAL RELATIONSHIPS--
"--THEY'RE ALL DRAWN TO THE GRAVITY OF THE UFO."

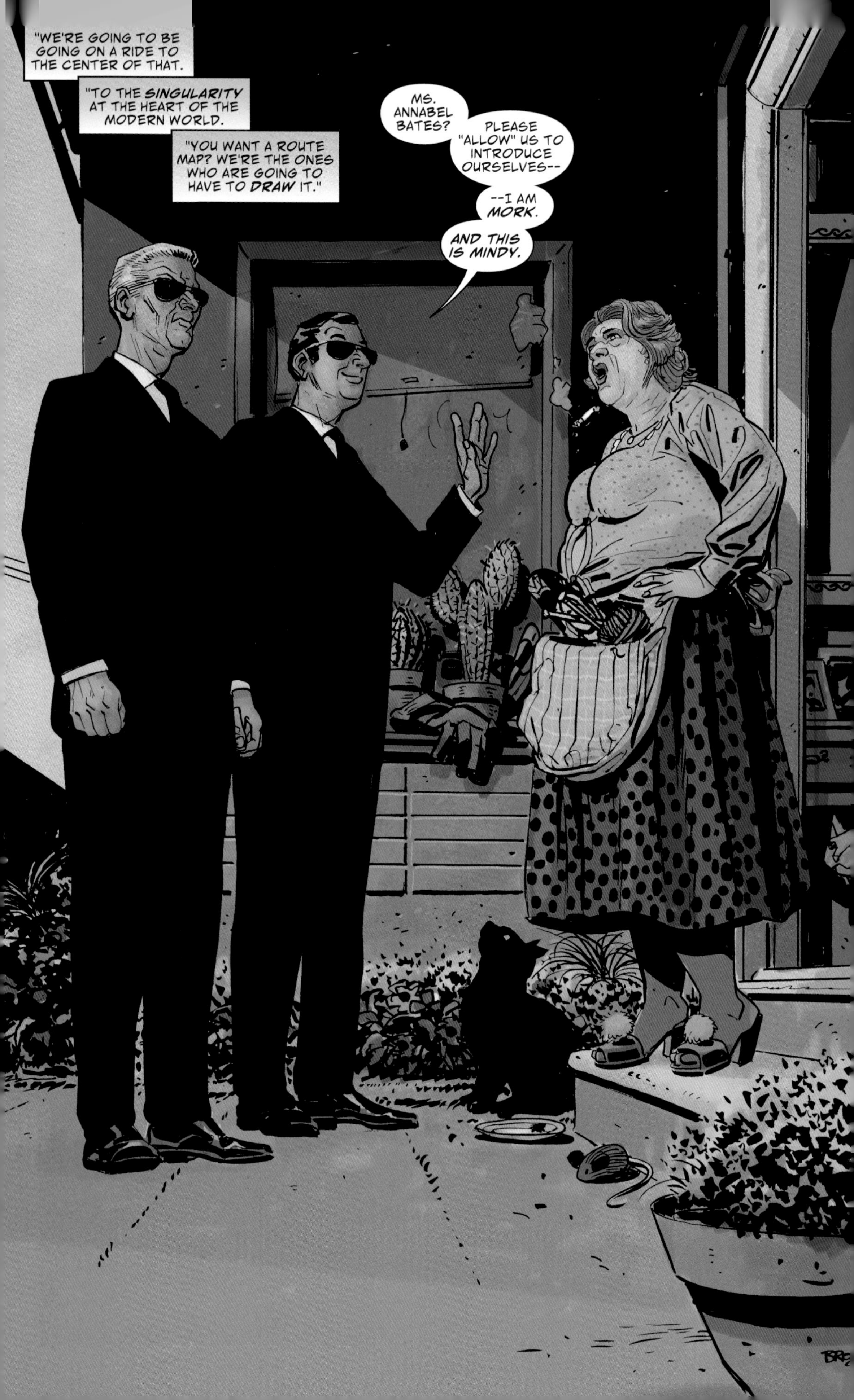
"WE'RE GOING TO BE GOING ON A RIDE TO THE CENTER OF THAT.
"TO THE SINGULARITY AT THE HEART OF THE MODERN WORLD.
"YOU WANT A ROUTE MAP? WE'RE THE ONES WHO ARE GOING TO HAVE TO DRAW IT."
MS. ANNABEL BATES?
PLEASE "ALLOW" US TO INTRODUCE OURSELVES--
--I AM MORK.
AND THIS IS MINDY.

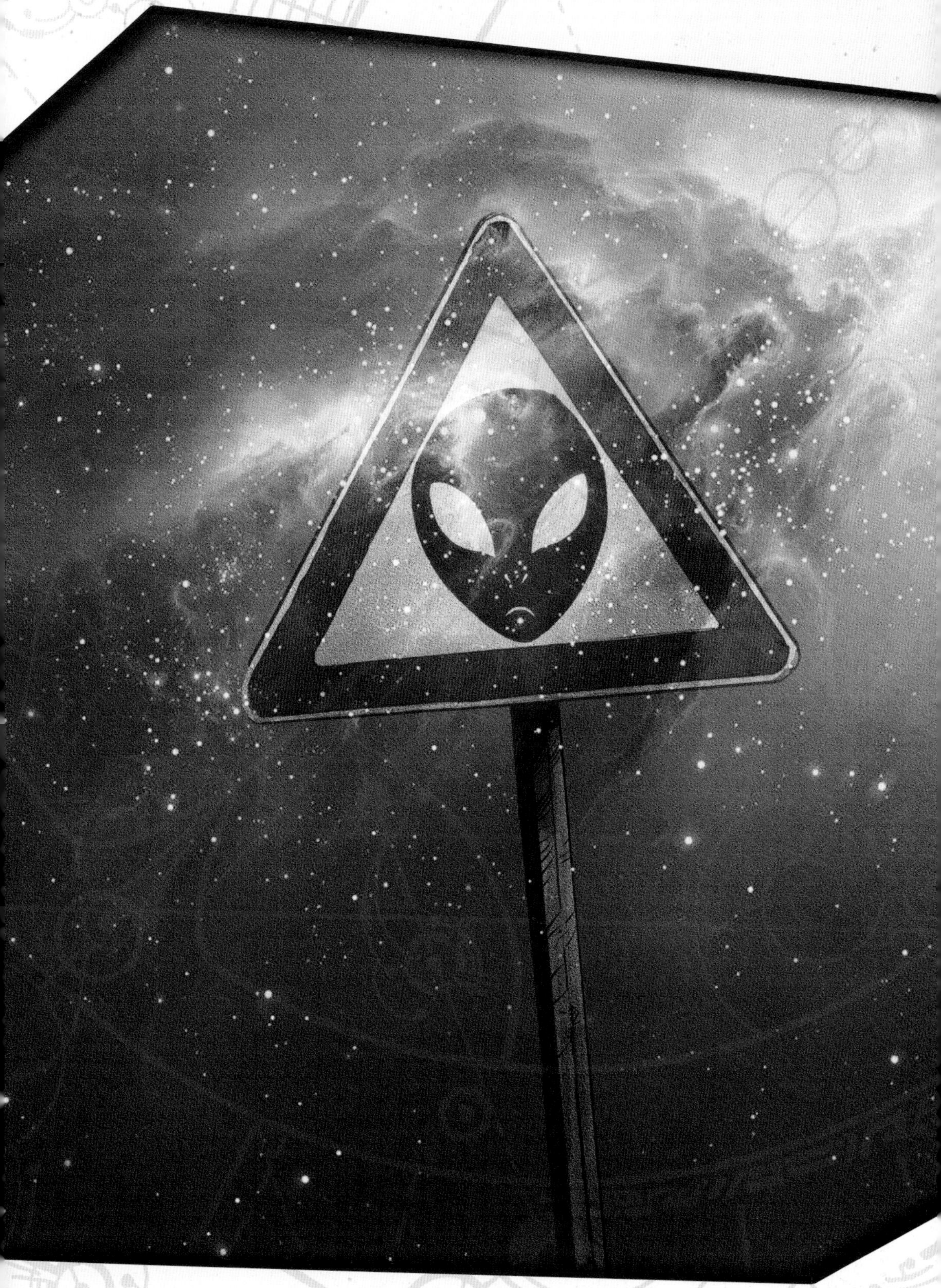

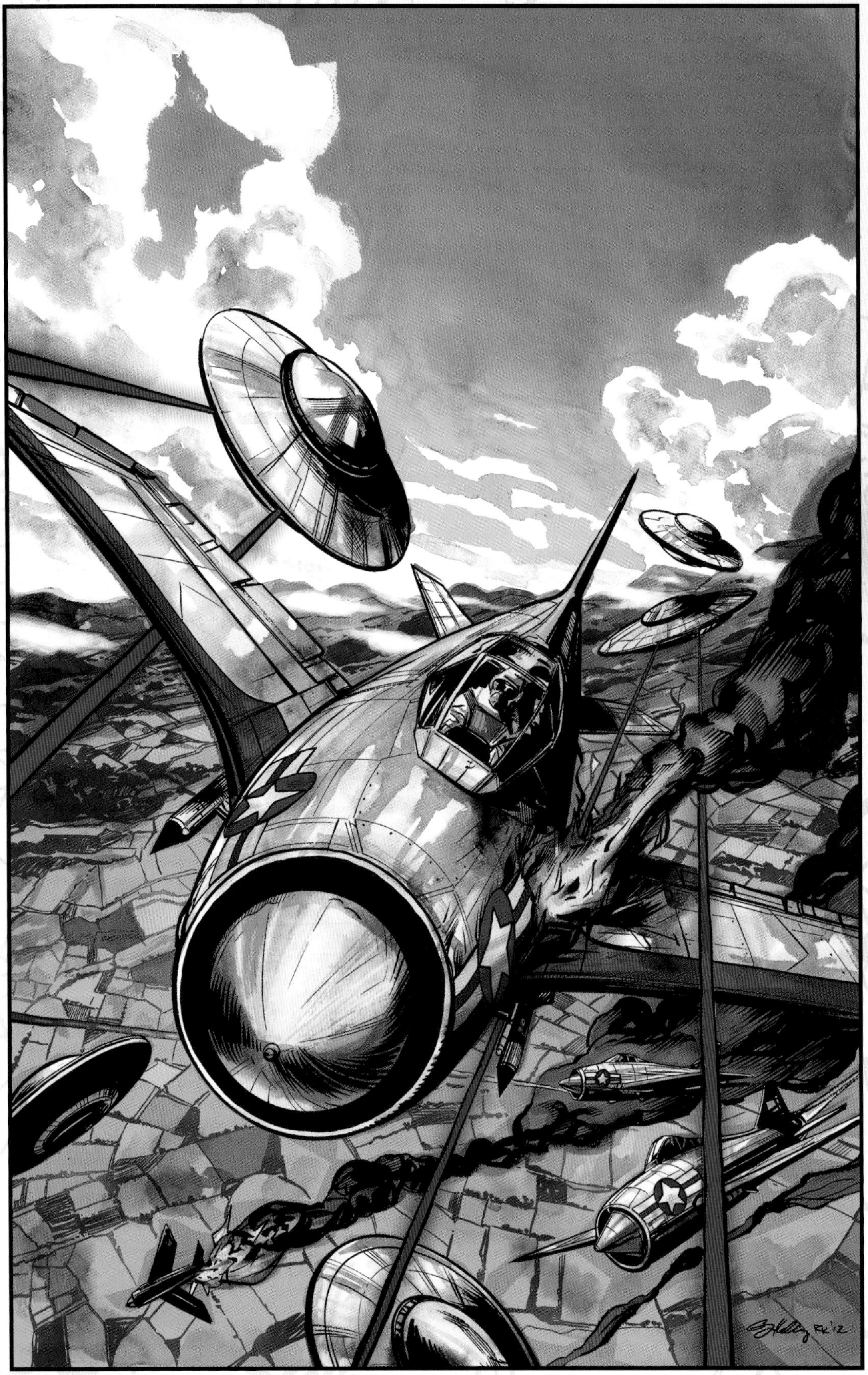

COVER ART BY **RYAN KELLY**

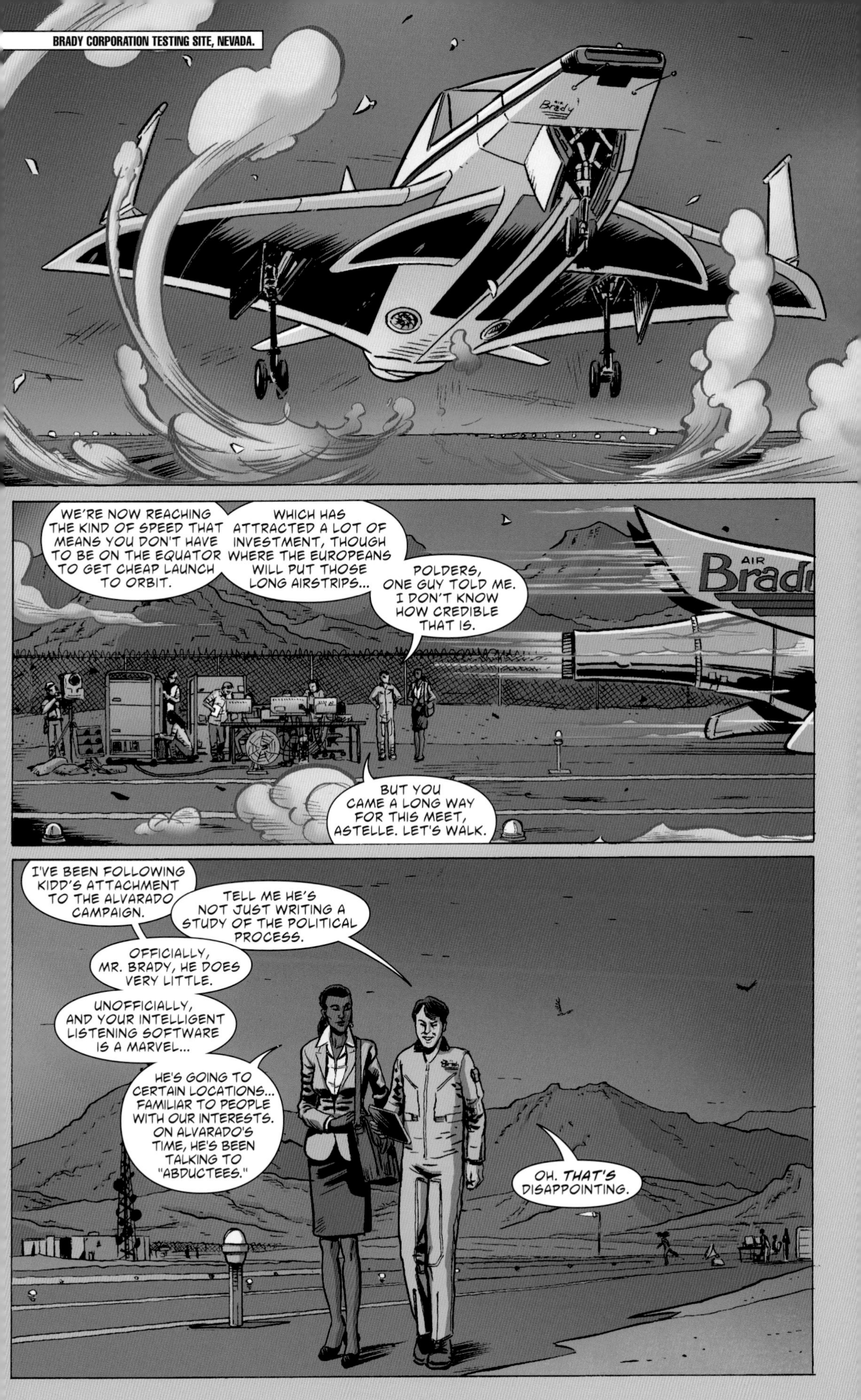
BRADY CORPORATION TESTING SITE, NEVADA.
WE'RE NOW REACHING THE KIND OF SPEED THAT MEANS YOU DON'T HAVE TO BE ON THE EQUATOR TO GET CHEAP LAUNCH TO ORBIT.
WHICH HAS ATTRACTED A LOT OF INVESTMENT, THOUGH WHERE THE EUROPEANS WILL PUT THOSE LONG AIRSTRIPS...
POLDERS, ONE GUY TOLD ME. I DON'T KNOW HOW CREDIBLE THAT IS.
BUT YOU CAME A LONG WAY FOR THIS MEET, ASTELLE. LET'S WALK.
I'VE BEEN FOLLOWING KIDD'S ATTACHMENT TO THE ALVARADO CAMPAIGN.
TELL ME HE'S NOT JUST WRITING A STUDY OF THE POLITICAL PROCESS.
OFFICIALLY, MR. BRADY, HE DOES VERY LITTLE.
UNOFFICIALLY, AND YOUR INTELLIGENT LISTENING SOFTWARE IS A MARVEL...
HE'S GOING TO CERTAIN LOCATIONS... FAMILIAR TO PEOPLE WITH OUR INTERESTS. ON ALVARADO'S TIME, HE'S BEEN TALKING TO "ABDUCTEES."
OH. THAT'S DISAPPOINTING.

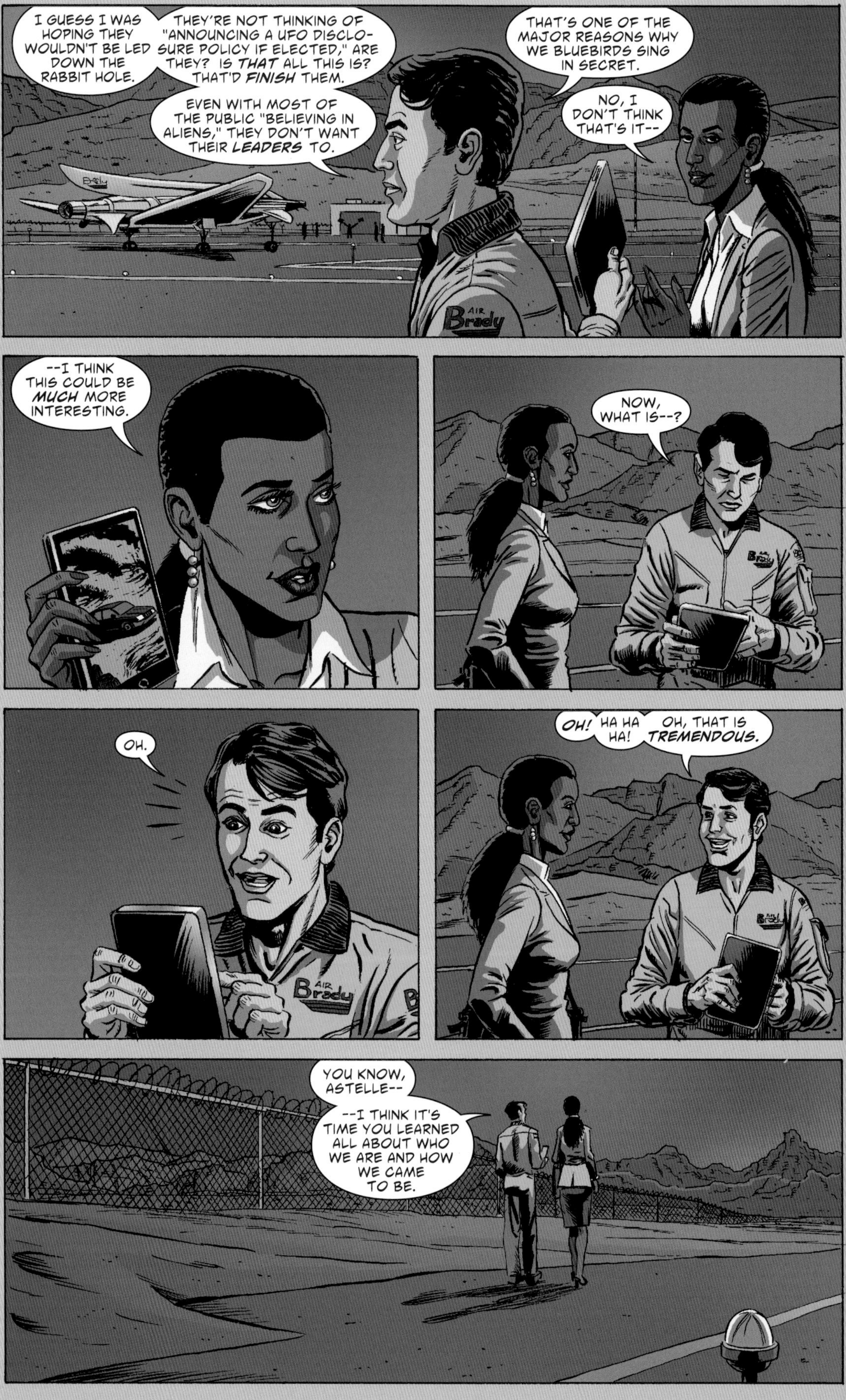
I GUESS I WAS HOPING THEY WOULDN'T BE LED DOWN THE RABBIT HOLE.
THEY'RE NOT THINKING OF "ANNOUNCING A UFO DISCLOSURE POLICY IF ELECTED," ARE THEY? IS THAT ALL THIS IS? THAT'D FINISH THEM.
EVEN WITH MOST OF THE PUBLIC "BELIEVING IN ALIENS," THEY DON'T WANT THEIR LEADERS TO.
THAT'S ONE OF THE MAJOR REASONS WHY WE BLUEBIRDS SING IN SECRET.
NO, I DON'T THINK THAT'S IT--
AIR Brady
--I THINK THIS COULD BE MUCH MORE INTERESTING.
NOW, WHAT IS--?
OH.
AIR Brady
OH! HA HA HA!
OH, THAT IS TREMENDOUS.
YOU KNOW, ASTELLE--
--I THINK IT'S TIME YOU LEARNED ALL ABOUT WHO WE ARE AND HOW WE CAME TO BE.

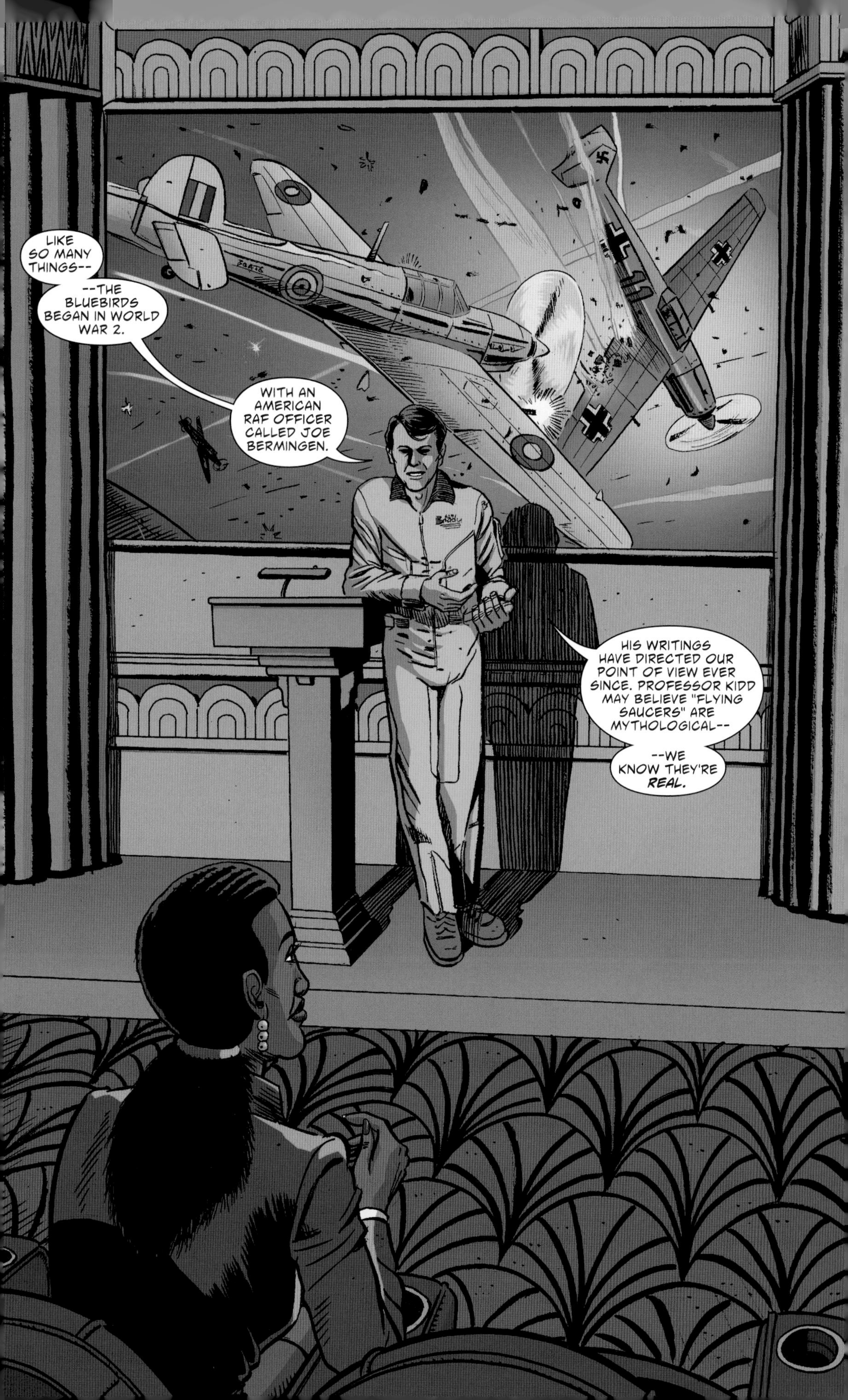
LIKE SO MANY THINGS--
--THE BLUEBIRDS BEGAN IN WORLD WAR 2.
WITH AN AMERICAN RAF OFFICER CALLED JOE BERMINGEN.
HIS WRITINGS HAVE DIRECTED OUR POINT OF VIEW EVER SINCE. PROFESSOR KIDD MAY BELIEVE "FLYING SAUCERS" ARE MYTHOLOGICAL--
--WE KNOW THEY'RE *REAL.*

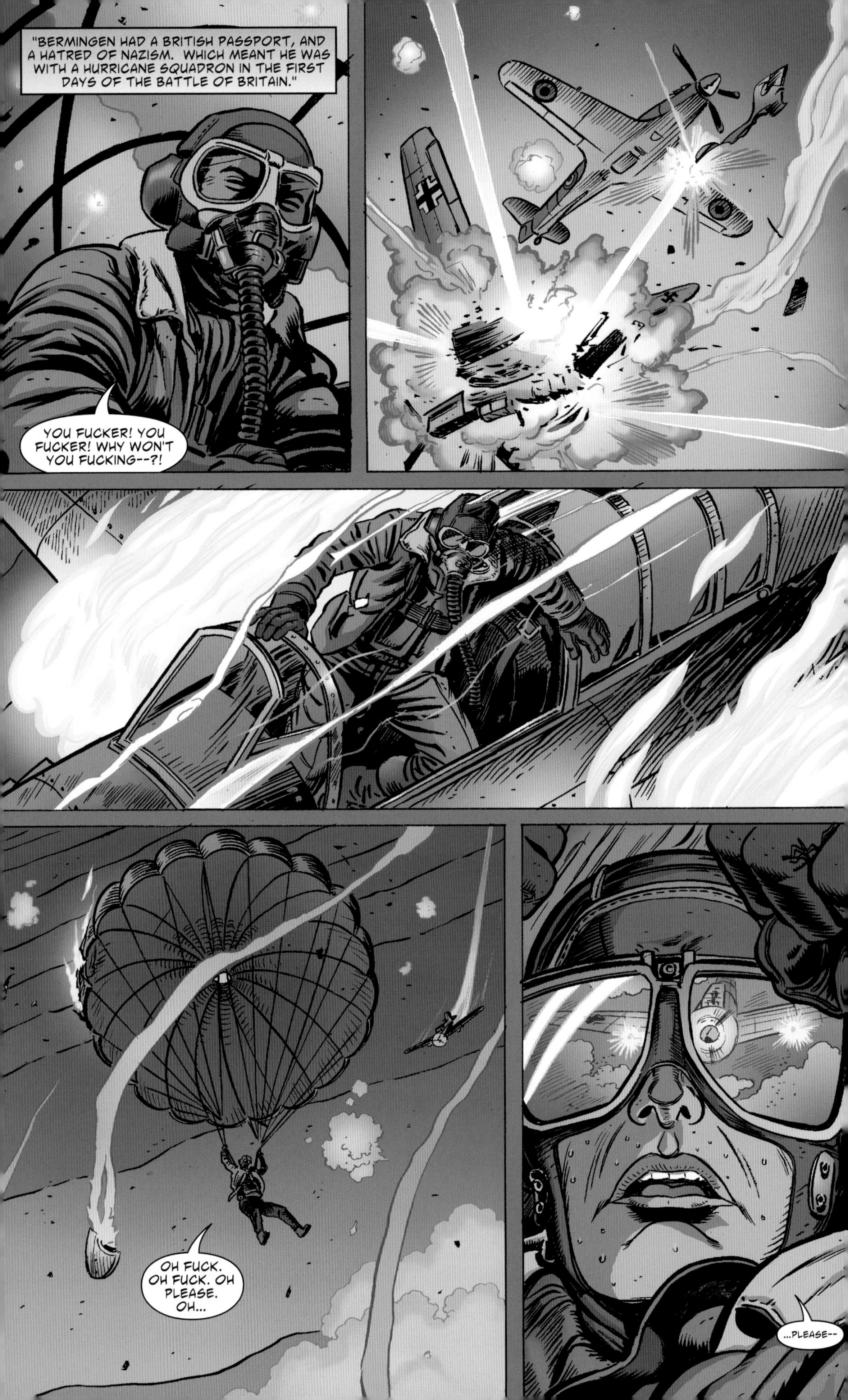
"BERMINGEN HAD A BRITISH PASSPORT, AND A HATRED OF NAZISM. WHICH MEANT HE WAS WITH A HURRICANE SQUADRON IN THE FIRST DAYS OF THE BATTLE OF BRITAIN."
YOU FUCKER! YOU FUCKER! WHY WON'T YOU FUCKING--?!
OH FUCK. OH FUCK. OH PLEASE. OH...
...PLEASE--

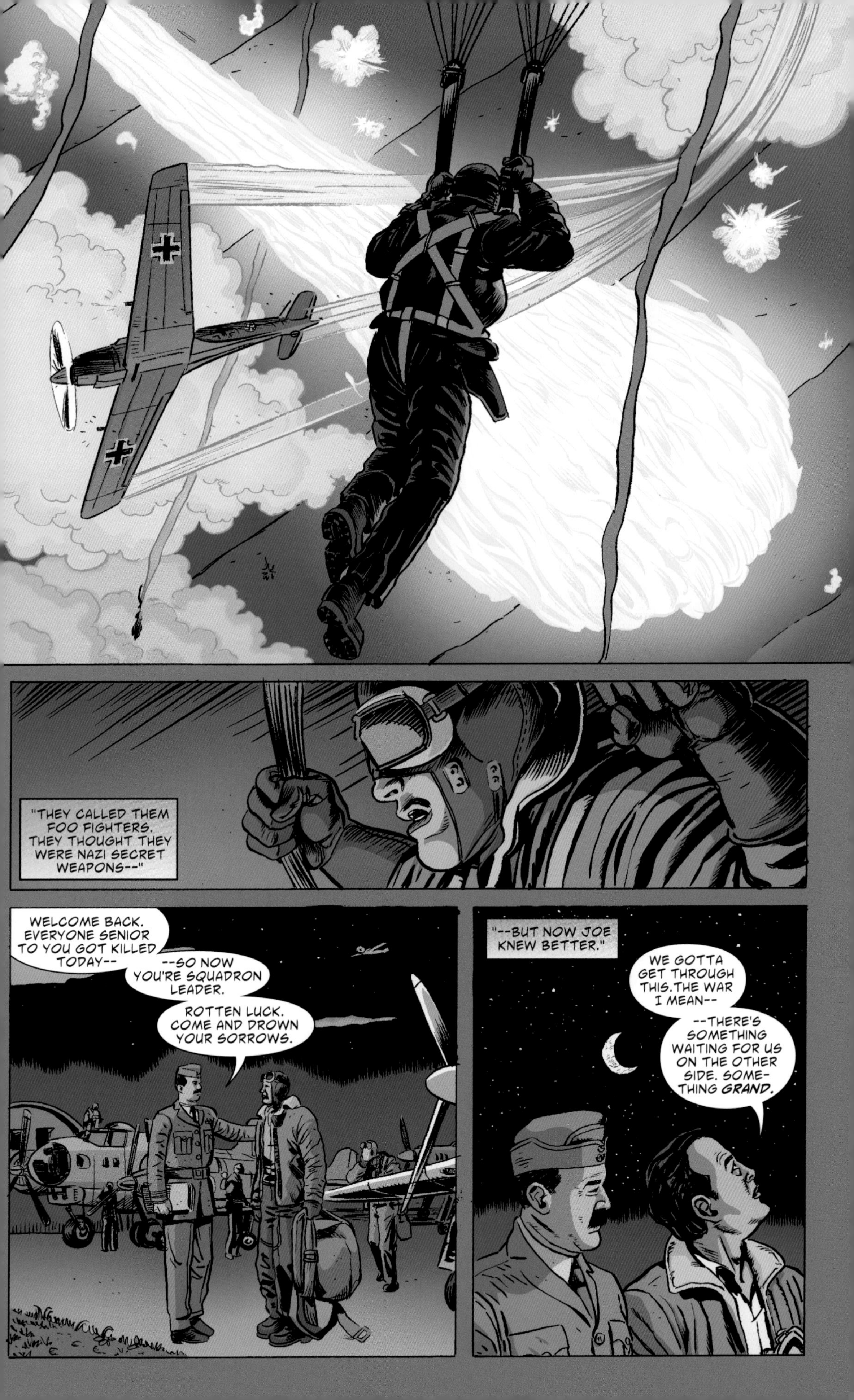
"THEY CALLED THEM FOO FIGHTERS. THEY THOUGHT THEY WERE NAZI SECRET WEAPONS--"
WELCOME BACK. EVERYONE SENIOR TO YOU GOT KILLED TODAY--
--SO NOW YOU'RE SQUADRON LEADER.
ROTTEN LUCK. COME AND DROWN YOUR SORROWS.
"--BUT NOW JOE KNEW BETTER."
WE GOTTA GET THROUGH THIS. THE WAR I MEAN--
--THERE'S SOMETHING WAITING FOR US ON THE OTHER SIDE. SOME-THING GRAND.

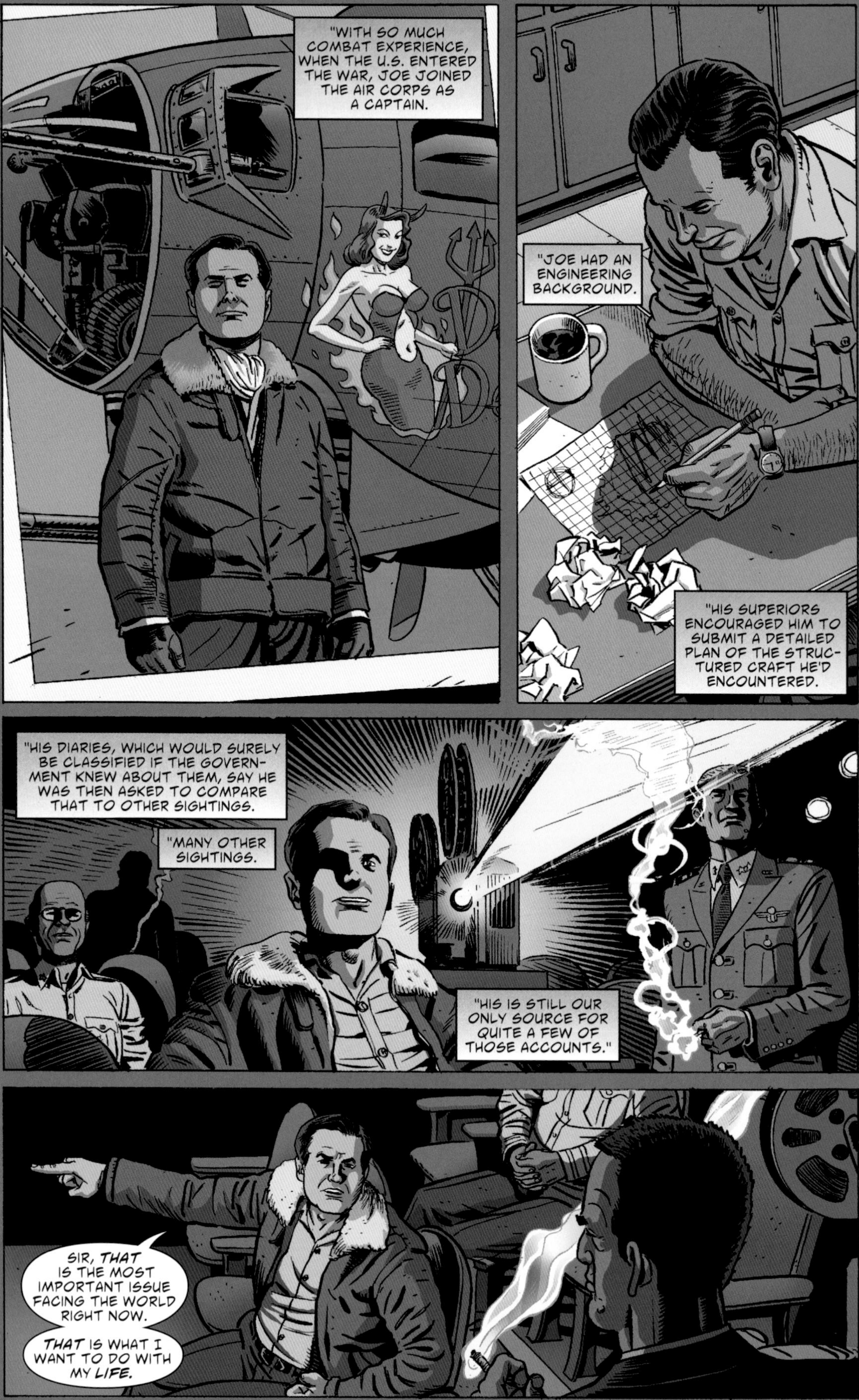
"WITH SO MUCH COMBAT EXPERIENCE, WHEN THE U.S. ENTERED THE WAR, JOE JOINED THE AIR CORPS AS A CAPTAIN.
"JOE HAD AN ENGINEERING BACKGROUND.
"HIS SUPERIORS ENCOURAGED HIM TO SUBMIT A DETAILED PLAN OF THE STRUCTURED CRAFT HE'D ENCOUNTERED.
"HIS DIARIES, WHICH WOULD SURELY BE CLASSIFIED IF THE GOVERNMENT KNEW ABOUT THEM, SAY HE WAS THEN ASKED TO COMPARE THAT TO OTHER SIGHTINGS.
"MANY OTHER SIGHTINGS.
"HIS IS STILL OUR ONLY SOURCE FOR QUITE A FEW OF THOSE ACCOUNTS."
SIR, *THAT* IS THE MOST IMPORTANT ISSUE FACING THE WORLD RIGHT NOW.
THAT IS WHAT I WANT TO DO WITH MY *LIFE.*

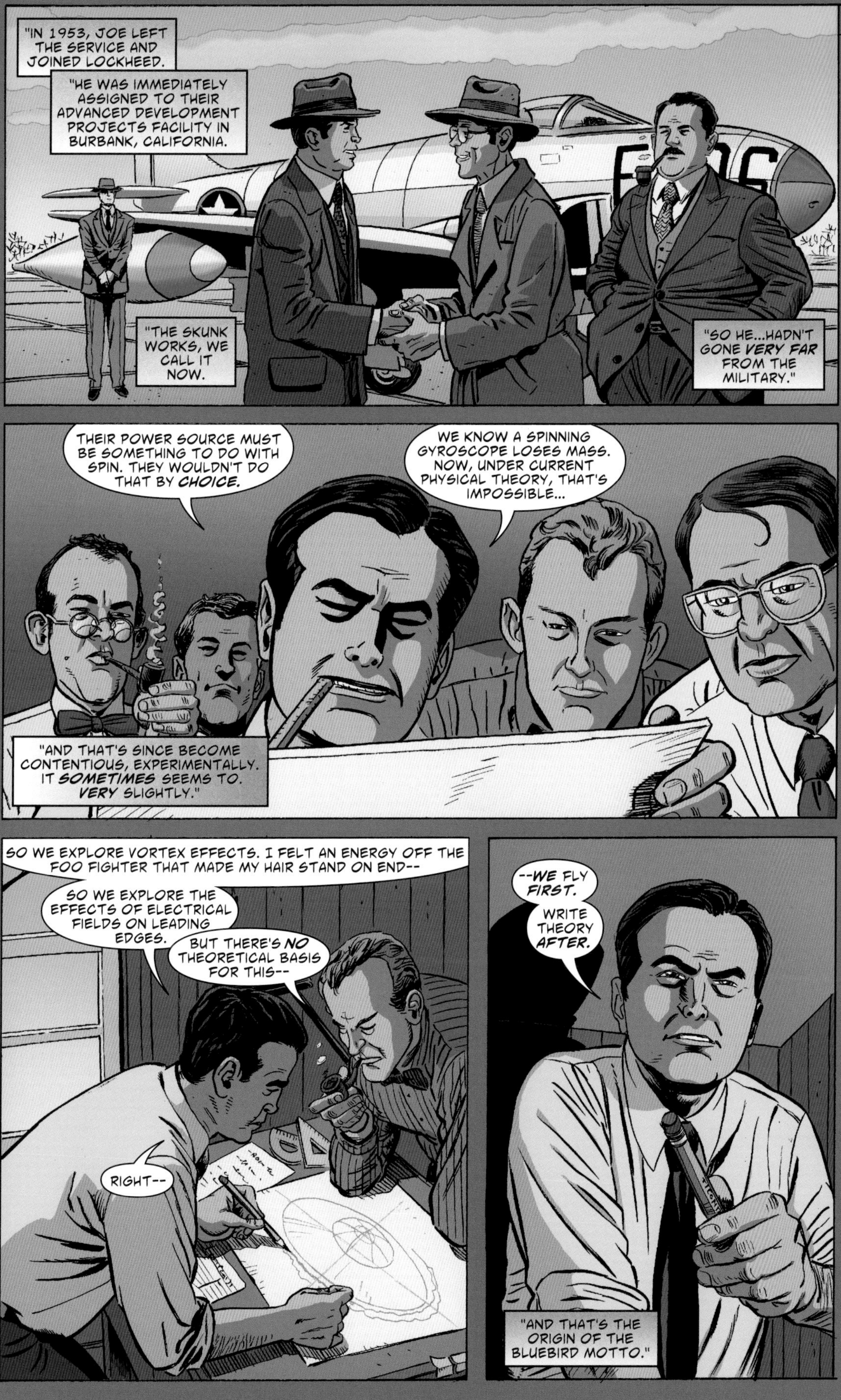

"IN 1953, JOE LEFT THE SERVICE AND JOINED LOCKHEED.
"HE WAS IMMEDIATELY ASSIGNED TO THEIR ADVANCED DEVELOPMENT PROJECTS FACILITY IN BURBANK, CALIFORNIA.
"THE SKUNK WORKS, WE CALL IT NOW.
"SO HE...HADN'T GONE VERY FAR FROM THE MILITARY."
THEIR POWER SOURCE MUST BE SOMETHING TO DO WITH SPIN. THEY WOULDN'T DO THAT BY CHOICE.
WE KNOW A SPINNING GYROSCOPE LOSES MASS. NOW, UNDER CURRENT PHYSICAL THEORY, THAT'S IMPOSSIBLE...
"AND THAT'S SINCE BECOME CONTENTIOUS, EXPERIMENTALLY. IT SOMETIMES SEEMS TO. VERY SLIGHTLY."
SO WE EXPLORE VORTEX EFFECTS. I FELT AN ENERGY OFF THE FOO FIGHTER THAT MADE MY HAIR STAND ON END--
SO WE EXPLORE THE EFFECTS OF ELECTRICAL FIELDS ON LEADING EDGES.
BUT THERE'S NO THEORETICAL BASIS FOR THIS--
RIGHT--
--WE FLY FIRST.
WRITE THEORY AFTER.
"AND THAT'S THE ORIGIN OF THE BLUEBIRD MOTTO."

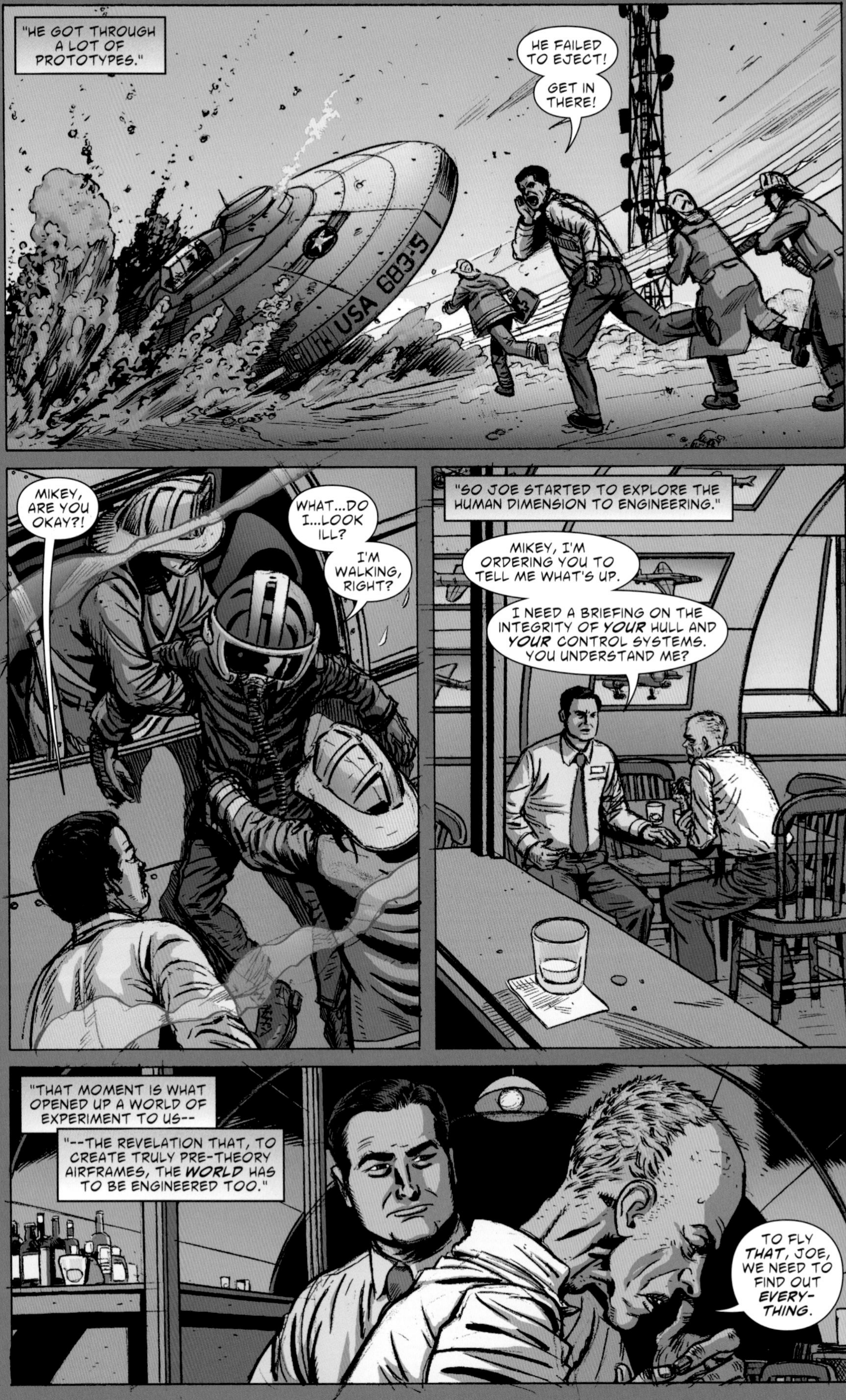
"HE GOT THROUGH A LOT OF PROTOTYPES."
HE FAILED TO EJECT!
GET IN THERE!
USA 683-5
MIKEY, ARE YOU OKAY?!
WHAT...DO I...LOOK ILL?
I'M WALKING, RIGHT?
"SO JOE STARTED TO EXPLORE THE HUMAN DIMENSION TO ENGINEERING."
MIKEY, I'M ORDERING YOU TO TELL ME WHAT'S UP.
I NEED A BRIEFING ON THE INTEGRITY OF *YOUR* HULL AND *YOUR* CONTROL SYSTEMS. YOU UNDERSTAND ME?
"THAT MOMENT IS WHAT OPENED UP A WORLD OF EXPERIMENT TO US--
"--THE REVELATION THAT, TO CREATE TRULY PRE-THEORY AIRFRAMES, THE *WORLD* HAS TO BE ENGINEERED TOO."
TO FLY *THAT*, JOE, WE NEED TO FIND OUT *EVERY-THING*.

"JOE WAS KIND OF A HERMIT. HE NEVER MARRIED. HE DEVOTED HIMSELF TO HIS CAUSE.

"SOME OF US INSIST WHAT HE WROTE IN THIS PHASE *IS* THEORY--

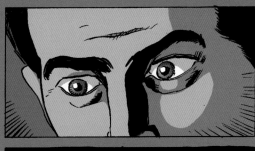

"--I PREFER TO CALL IT *POETRY.*

"READING BETWEEN THE LINES, HE SEEMS TO FORESEE IDEAS CONCERNING SPIN...THE QUALITY LABELED AS SUCH IN QUANTUM MECHANICS, WHICH MAY OR MAY NOT HAVE ANYTHING TO DO WITH EVERYDAY SPIN...

"HE SEEMS TO SEE THAT AS WHAT WE'D NOW CALL THE DARK ENERGY PUSHING THE UNIVERSE --

"--THE MATRIX THAT CONVEYED INFORMA-TION FROM *ANOTHER* COSMOS--

"--WHICH GAVE BIRTH TO OURS THROUGH A BLACK HOLE.

SKTCH
SKITCH

"BUT IT'S SOMETIMES HARD TO DISCERN *WHAT* JOE MEANT.

"BY THEN, HE HAD STARTED TO *DRINK.*"

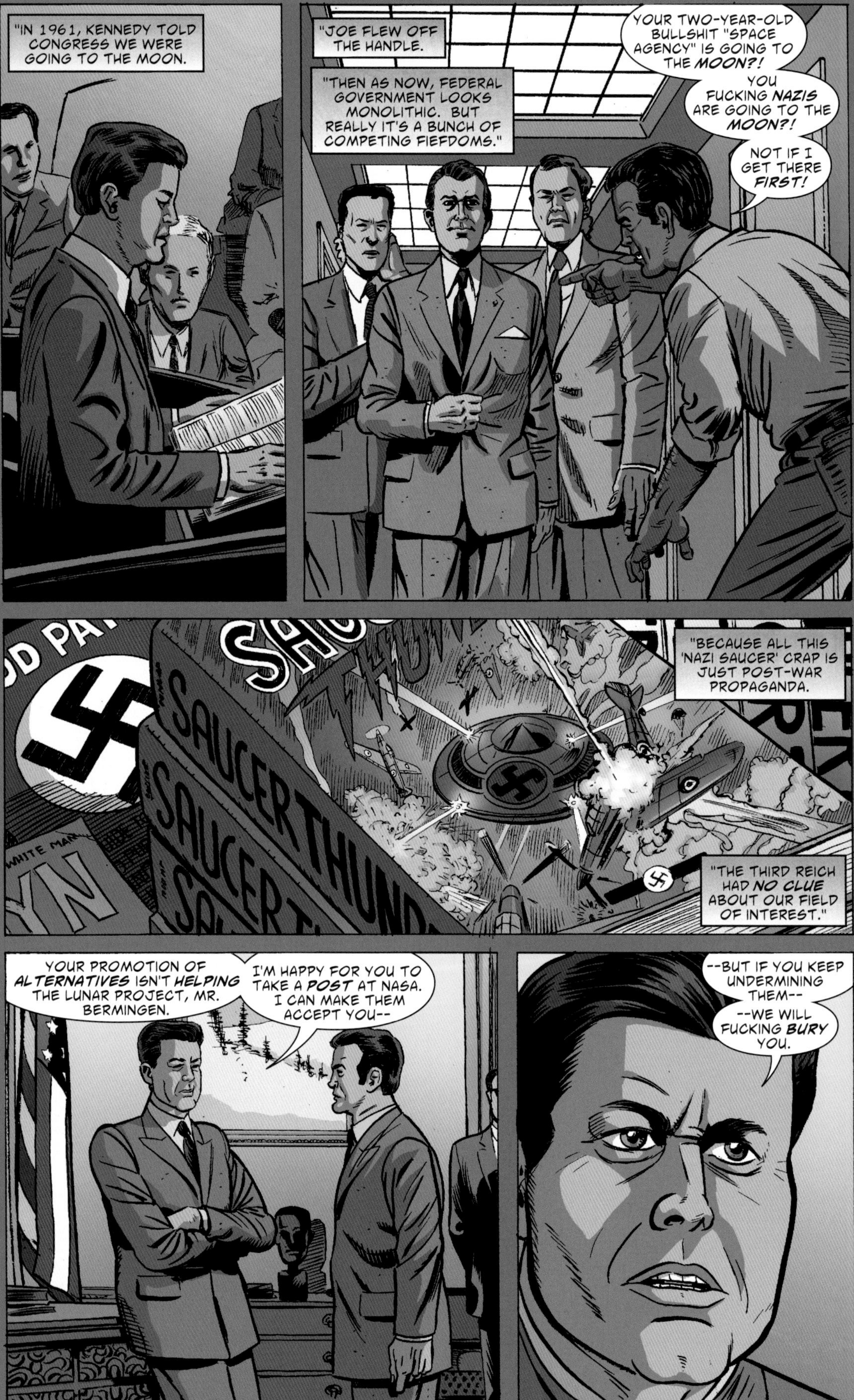
"IN 1961, KENNEDY TOLD CONGRESS WE WERE GOING TO THE MOON.
"JOE FLEW OFF THE HANDLE.
"THEN AS NOW, FEDERAL GOVERNMENT LOOKS MONOLITHIC. BUT REALLY IT'S A BUNCH OF COMPETING FIEFDOMS."
YOUR TWO-YEAR-OLD BULLSHIT "SPACE AGENCY" IS GOING TO THE *MOON?!*
YOU FUCKING *NAZIS* ARE GOING TO THE *MOON?!*
NOT IF I GET THERE *FIRST!*
SAUCER
SAUCERTHUND
"BECAUSE ALL THIS 'NAZI SAUCER' CRAP IS JUST POST-WAR PROPAGANDA.
"THE THIRD REICH HAD *NO CLUE* ABOUT OUR FIELD OF INTEREST."
YOUR PROMOTION OF *ALTERNATIVES* ISN'T *HELPING* THE LUNAR PROJECT, MR. BERMINGEN.
I'M HAPPY FOR YOU TO TAKE A *POST* AT NASA. I CAN MAKE THEM ACCEPT YOU--
--BUT IF YOU KEEP UNDERMINING THEM--
--WE WILL FUCKING *BURY* YOU.

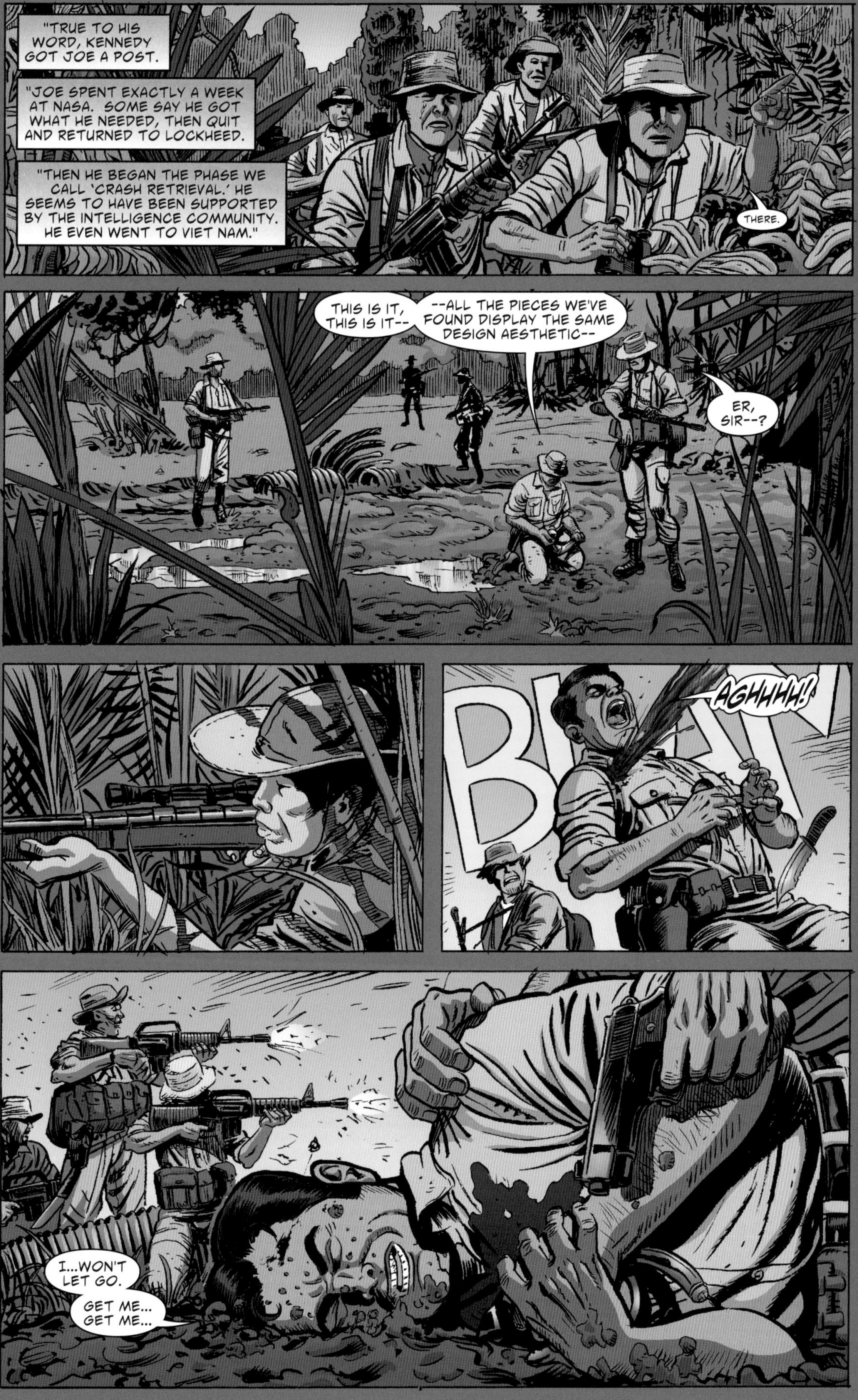
"TRUE TO HIS WORD, KENNEDY GOT JOE A POST.
"JOE SPENT EXACTLY A WEEK AT NASA. SOME SAY HE GOT WHAT HE NEEDED, THEN QUIT AND RETURNED TO LOCKHEED.
"THEN HE BEGAN THE PHASE WE CALL 'CRASH RETRIEVAL.' HE SEEMS TO HAVE BEEN SUPPORTED BY THE INTELLIGENCE COMMUNITY. HE EVEN WENT TO VIET NAM."
THERE.
THIS IS IT, THIS IS IT--
--ALL THE PIECES WE'VE FOUND DISPLAY THE SAME DESIGN AESTHETIC--
ER, SIR--?
AGHHHH!
I...WON'T LET GO.
GET ME... GET ME...

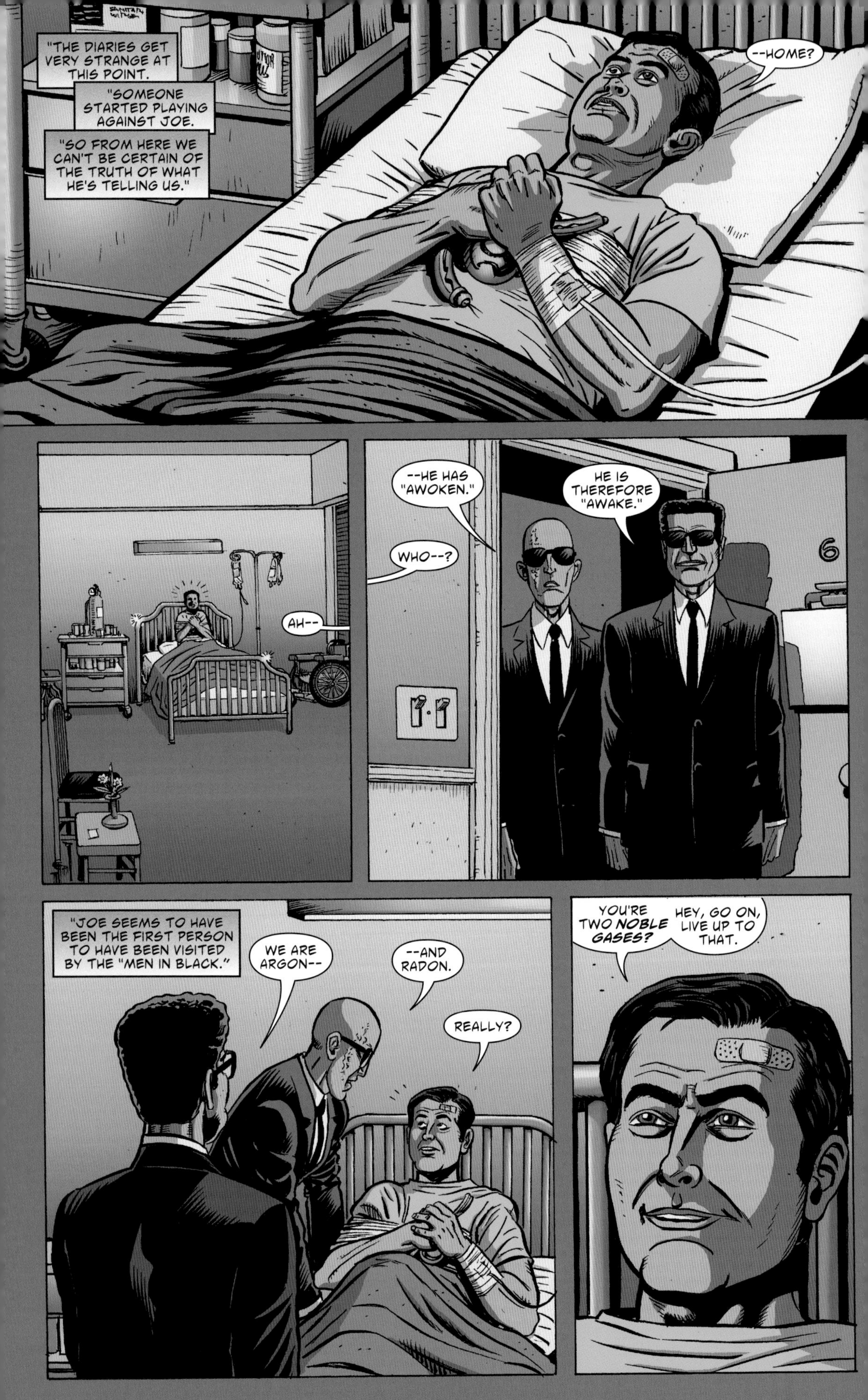
"THE DIARIES GET VERY STRANGE AT THIS POINT.
"SOMEONE STARTED PLAYING AGAINST JOE.
"SO FROM HERE WE CAN'T BE CERTAIN OF THE TRUTH OF WHAT HE'S TELLING US."
--HOME?
AH--
WHO--?
--HE HAS "AWOKEN."
HE IS THEREFORE "AWAKE."
6
"JOE SEEMS TO HAVE BEEN THE FIRST PERSON TO HAVE BEEN VISITED BY THE "MEN IN BLACK."
WE ARE ARGON--
--AND RADON.
REALLY?
YOU'RE TWO NOBLE GASES?
HEY, GO ON, LIVE UP TO THAT.

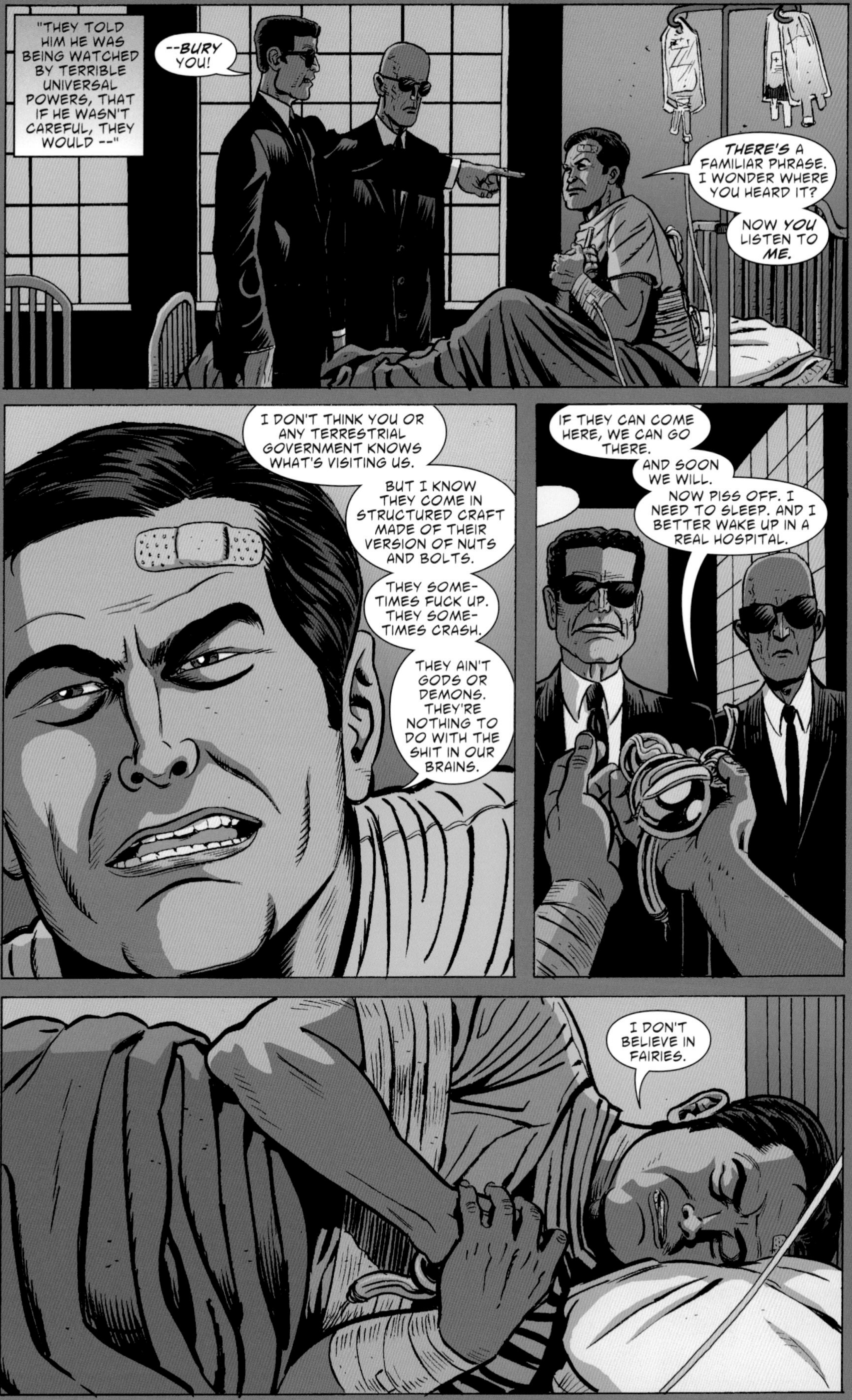
"THEY TOLD HIM HE WAS BEING WATCHED BY TERRIBLE UNIVERSAL POWERS, THAT IF HE WASN'T CAREFUL, THEY WOULD --"
--BURY YOU!
THERE'S A FAMILIAR PHRASE. I WONDER WHERE YOU HEARD IT?
NOW YOU LISTEN TO ME.
I DON'T THINK YOU OR ANY TERRESTRIAL GOVERNMENT KNOWS WHAT'S VISITING US.
BUT I KNOW THEY COME IN STRUCTURED CRAFT MADE OF THEIR VERSION OF NUTS AND BOLTS.
THEY SOME-TIMES FUCK UP. THEY SOME-TIMES CRASH.
THEY AIN'T GODS OR DEMONS. THEY'RE NOTHING TO DO WITH THE SHIT IN OUR BRAINS.
IF THEY CAN COME HERE, WE CAN GO THERE.
AND SOON WE WILL.
NOW PISS OFF. I NEED TO SLEEP. AND I BETTER WAKE UP IN A REAL HOSPITAL.
I DON'T BELIEVE IN FAIRIES.

"IN 1969, APOLLO 11 LIFTED OFF FOR THE MOON."

"JOE'S DIARIES INDICATE HE WAS WORKING DAY AND NIGHT ON SOME SECRET PROJECT OF HIS OWN."

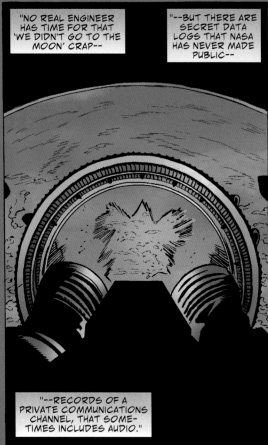

"NO REAL ENGINEER HAS TIME FOR THAT 'WE DIDN'T GO TO THE MOON' CRAP--

"--BUT THERE ARE SECRET DATA LOGS THAT NASA HAS NEVER MADE PUBLIC--

"--RECORDS OF A PRIVATE COMMUNICATIONS CHANNEL, THAT SOME- TIMES INCLUDES AUDIO."

HOUSTON, THIS IS TRANQUILITY BASE ON AZURE--

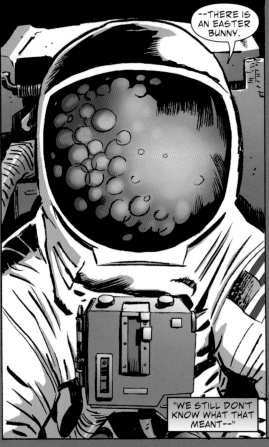

--THERE IS AN EASTER BUNNY.

"WE STILL DON'T KNOW WHAT THAT MEANT--"

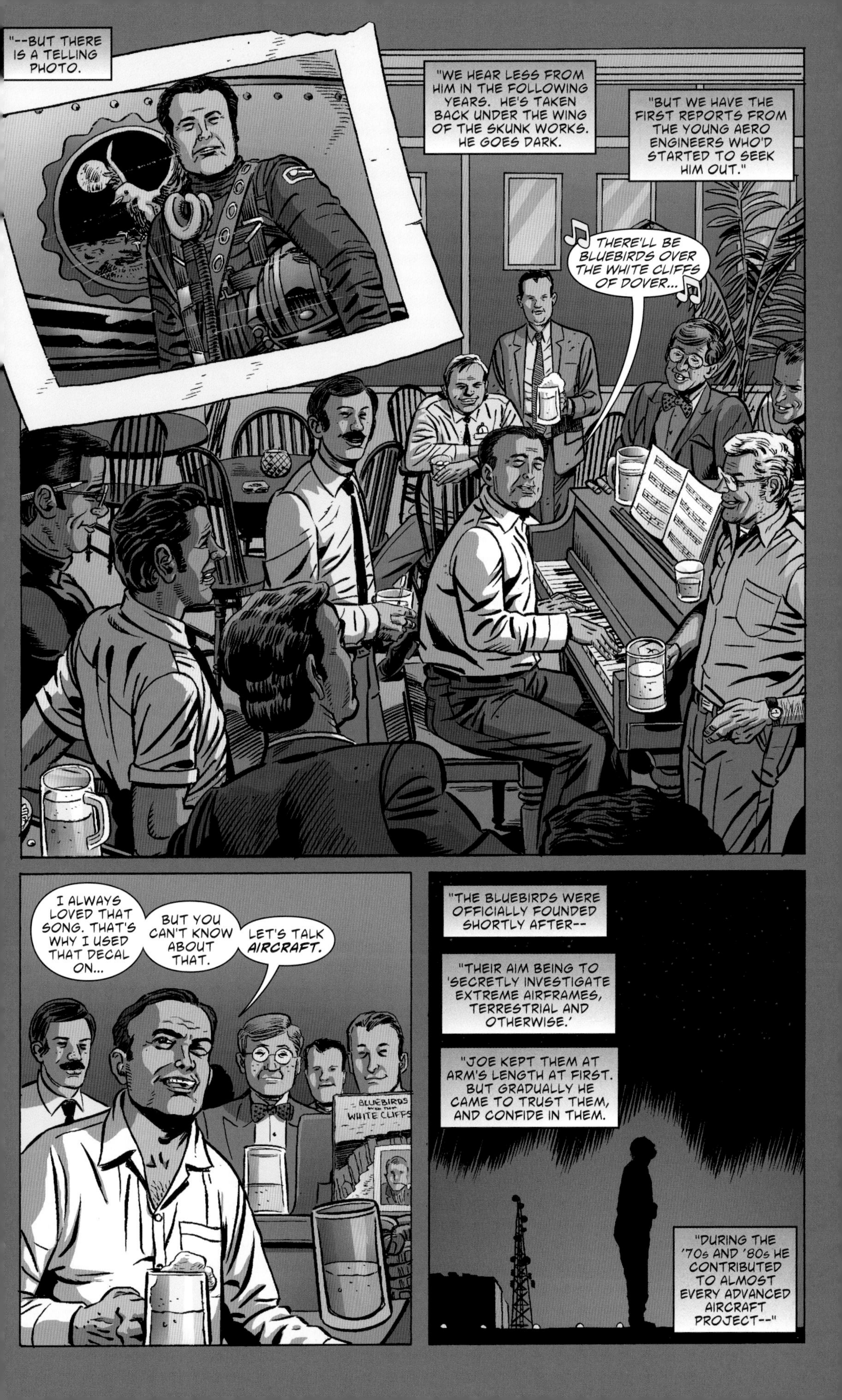
"--BUT THERE IS A TELLING PHOTO.
"WE HEAR LESS FROM HIM IN THE FOLLOWING YEARS. HE'S TAKEN BACK UNDER THE WING OF THE SKUNK WORKS. HE GOES DARK.
"BUT WE HAVE THE FIRST REPORTS FROM THE YOUNG AERO ENGINEERS WHO'D STARTED TO SEEK HIM OUT."
THERE'LL BE BLUEBIRDS OVER THE WHITE CLIFFS OF DOVER...
I ALWAYS LOVED THAT SONG. THAT'S WHY I USED THAT DECAL ON...
BUT YOU CAN'T KNOW ABOUT THAT.
LET'S TALK AIRCRAFT.
BLUEBIRDS
WHITE CLIFFS
"THE BLUEBIRDS WERE OFFICIALLY FOUNDED SHORTLY AFTER--
"THEIR AIM BEING TO 'SECRETLY INVESTIGATE EXTREME AIRFRAMES, TERRESTRIAL AND OTHERWISE.'
"JOE KEPT THEM AT ARM'S LENGTH AT FIRST. BUT GRADUALLY HE CAME TO TRUST THEM, AND CONFIDE IN THEM.
"DURING THE '70s AND '80s HE CONTRIBUTED TO ALMOST EVERY ADVANCED AIRCRAFT PROJECT--"

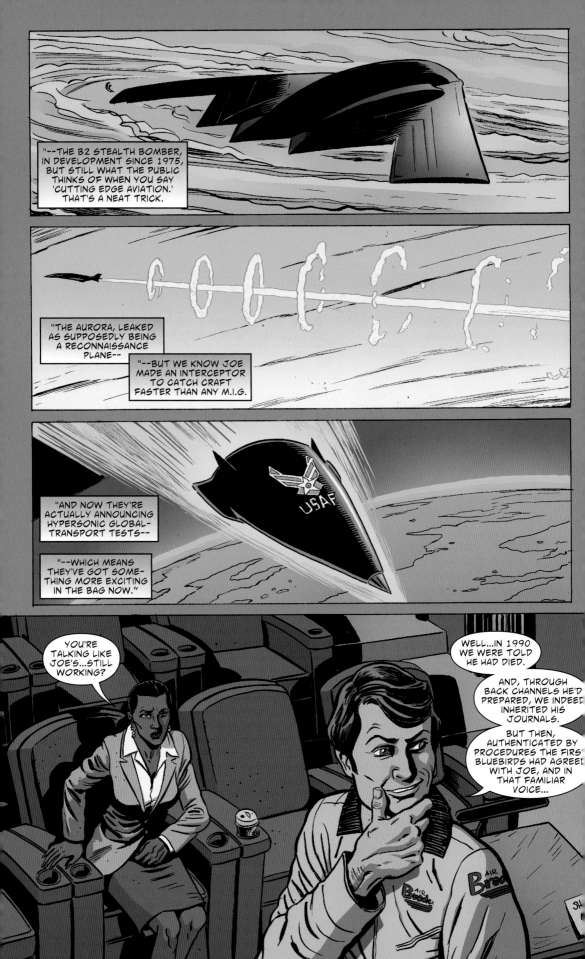

"--THE B2 STEALTH BOMBER, IN DEVELOPMENT SINCE 1975, BUT STILL WHAT THE PUBLIC THINKS OF WHEN YOU SAY 'CUTTING EDGE AVIATION.' THAT'S A NEAT TRICK.

"THE AURORA, LEAKED AS SUPPOSEDLY BEING A RECONNAISSANCE PLANE--

"--BUT WE KNOW JOE MADE AN INTERCEPTOR TO CATCH CRAFT FASTER THAN ANY M.I.G.

"AND NOW THEY'RE ACTUALLY ANNOUNCING HYPERSONIC GLOBAL-TRANSPORT TESTS--

"--WHICH MEANS THEY'VE GOT SOME-THING MORE EXCITING IN THE BAG NOW."

YOU'RE TALKING LIKE JOE'S...STILL WORKING?

WELL...IN 1990 WE WERE TOLD HE HAD DIED.

AND, THROUGH BACK CHANNELS HE'D PREPARED, WE INDEED INHERITED HIS JOURNALS.

BUT THEN, AUTHENTICATED BY PROCEDURES THE FIRS[T] BLUEBIRDS HAD AGREE[D] WITH JOE, AND IN THAT FAMILIAR VOICE...

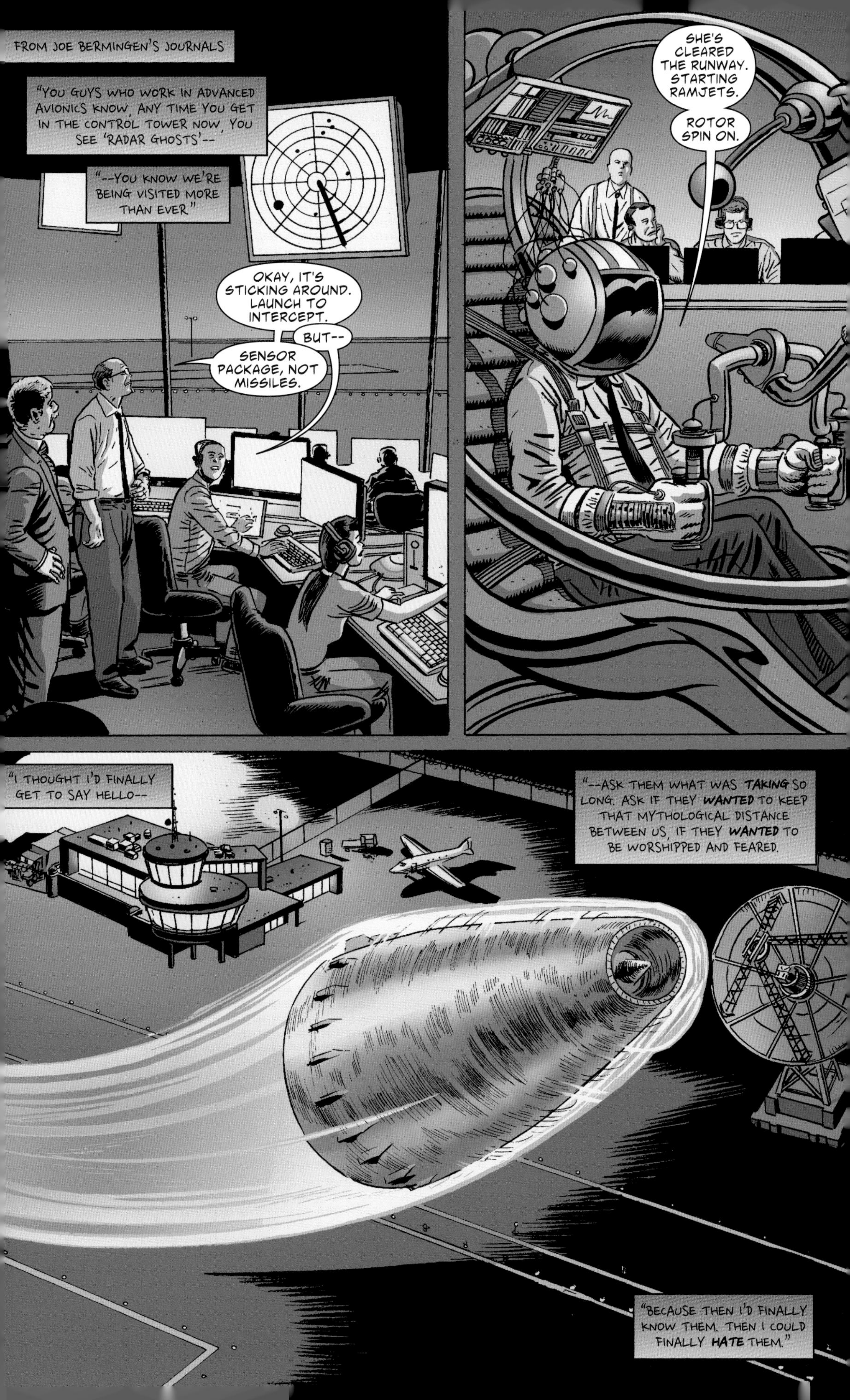
FROM JOE BERMINGEN'S JOURNALS
"YOU GUYS WHO WORK IN ADVANCED AVIONICS KNOW, ANY TIME YOU GET IN THE CONTROL TOWER NOW, YOU SEE 'RADAR GHOSTS'--
"--YOU KNOW WE'RE BEING VISITED MORE THAN EVER"
OKAY, IT'S STICKING AROUND. LAUNCH TO INTERCEPT.
BUT--
SENSOR PACKAGE, NOT MISSILES.
SHE'S CLEARED THE RUNWAY. STARTING RAMJETS.
ROTOR SPIN ON.
"I THOUGHT I'D FINALLY GET TO SAY HELLO--
"--ASK THEM WHAT WAS TAKING SO LONG. ASK IF THEY WANTED TO KEEP THAT MYTHOLOGICAL DISTANCE BETWEEN US, IF THEY WANTED TO BE WORSHIPPED AND FEARED.
"BECAUSE THEN I'D FINALLY KNOW THEM. THEN I COULD FINALLY HATE THEM."

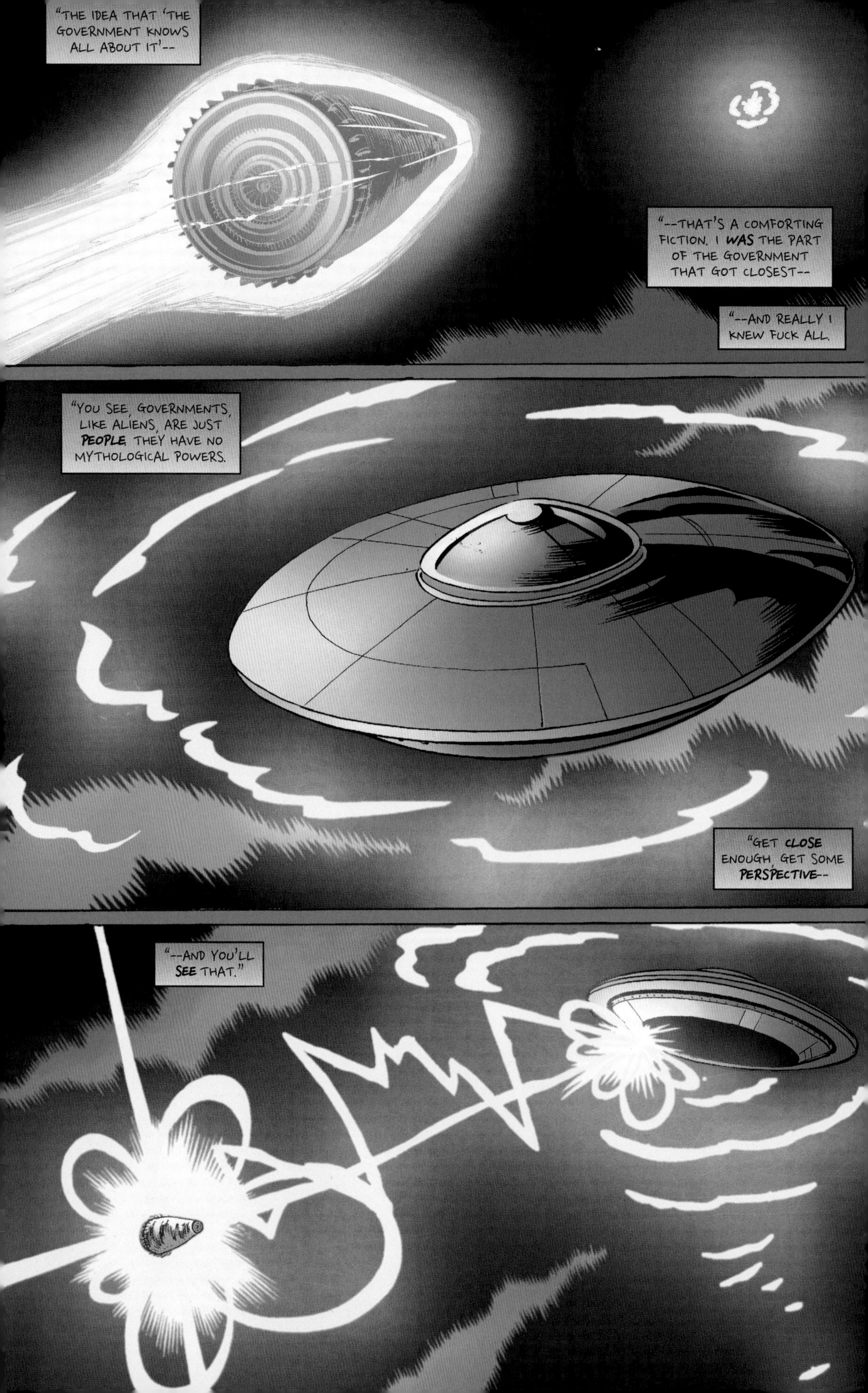
"THE IDEA THAT 'THE GOVERNMENT KNOWS ALL ABOUT IT'--
"--THAT'S A COMFORTING FICTION. I WAS THE PART OF THE GOVERNMENT THAT GOT CLOSEST--
"--AND REALLY I KNEW FUCK ALL.
"YOU SEE, GOVERNMENTS, LIKE ALIENS, ARE JUST PEOPLE. THEY HAVE NO MYTHOLOGICAL POWERS.
"GET CLOSE ENOUGH, GET SOME PERSPECTIVE--
"--AND YOU'LL SEE THAT."

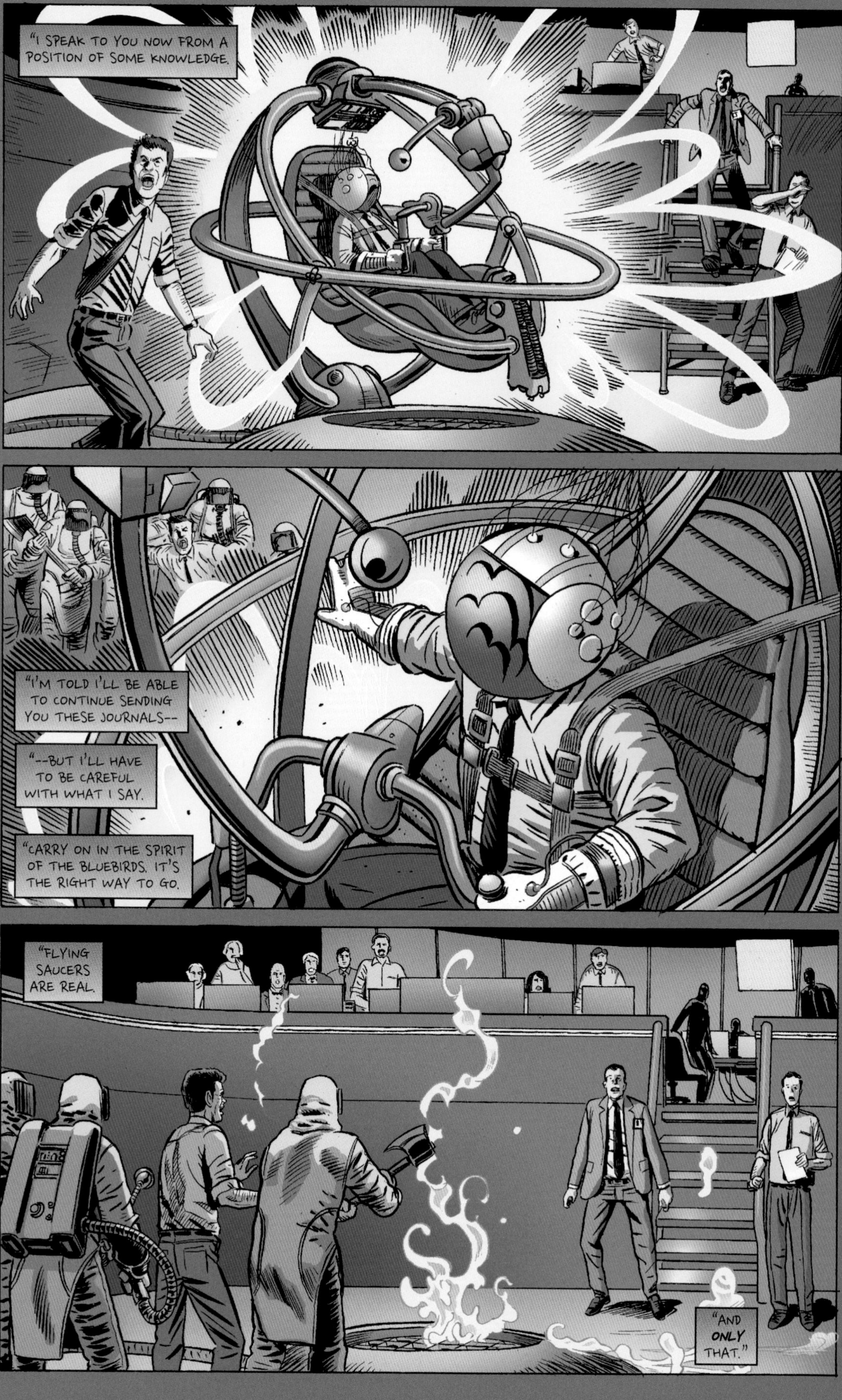
"I SPEAK TO YOU NOW FROM A POSITION OF SOME KNOWLEDGE.
"I'M TOLD I'LL BE ABLE TO CONTINUE SENDING YOU THESE JOURNALS--
"--BUT I'LL HAVE TO BE CAREFUL WITH WHAT I SAY.
"CARRY ON IN THE SPIRIT OF THE BLUEBIRDS. IT'S THE RIGHT WAY TO GO.
"FLYING SAUCERS ARE REAL.
"AND ONLY THAT."

YOU DON'T BELIEVE--?

NOT *ALL* OF IT.

THERE'S CONTINUAL DEBATE ABOUT THE INFORMATION WE STILL RECEIVE.

WE KNOW OTHERS ARE BEING PLAYED.

IT'S POSSIBLE WE ARE TOO.

BUT WE WERE SENT SOMETHING--

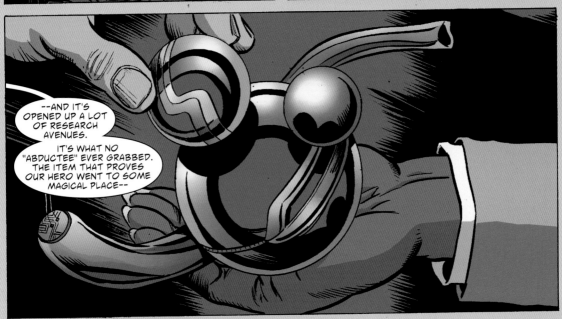

--AND IT'S OPENED UP A LOT OF RESEARCH AVENUES.

IT'S WHAT NO "ABDUCTEE" EVER GRABBED. THE ITEM THAT PROVES OUR HERO WENT TO SOME MAGICAL PLACE--

--LIKE IN ALL THE BEST STORIES.

NOW, LET'S GET SOME COFFEE--

--AND I'LL TELL YOU WHAT WE'RE GOING TO DO TO PROFESSOR KIDD.

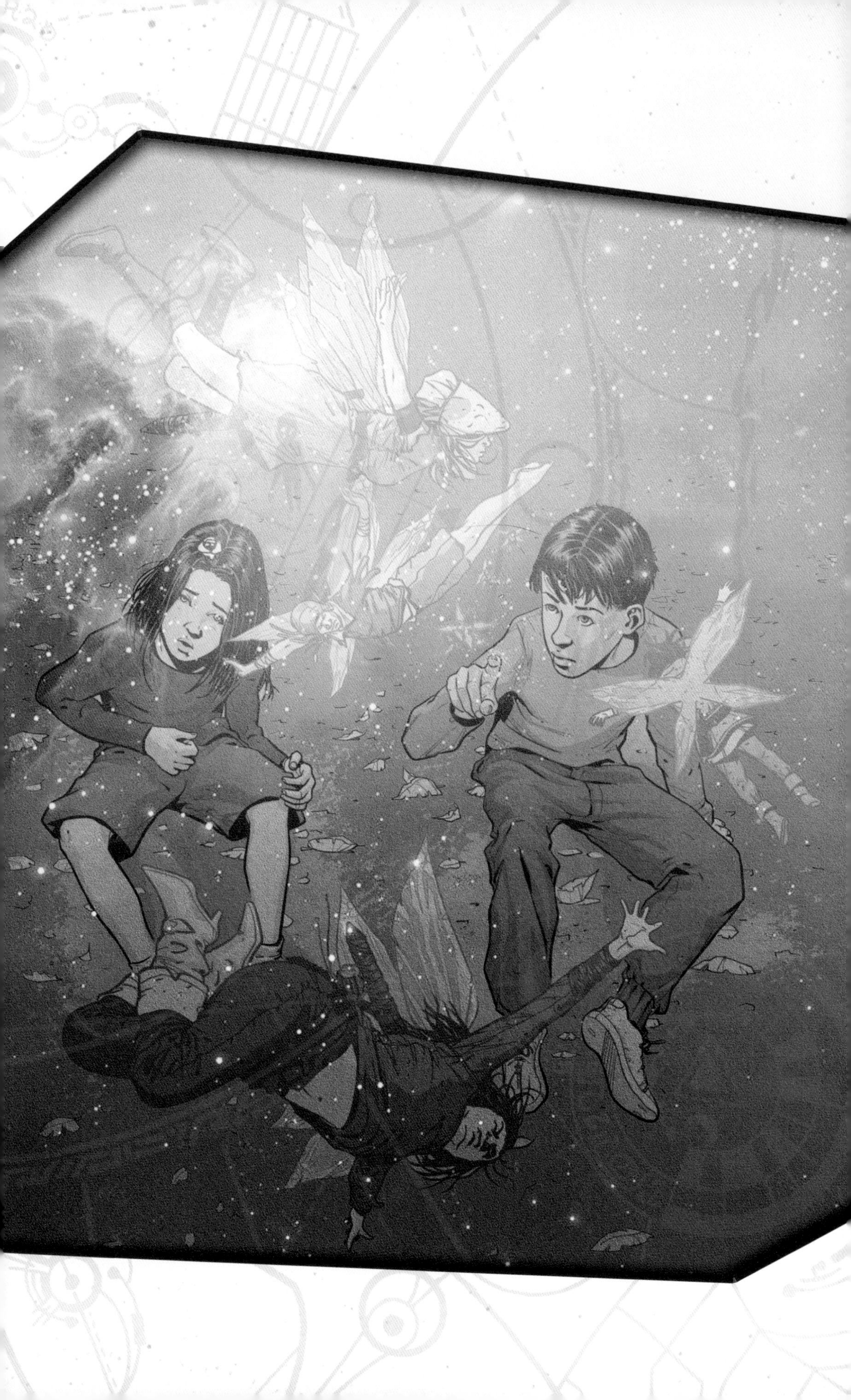

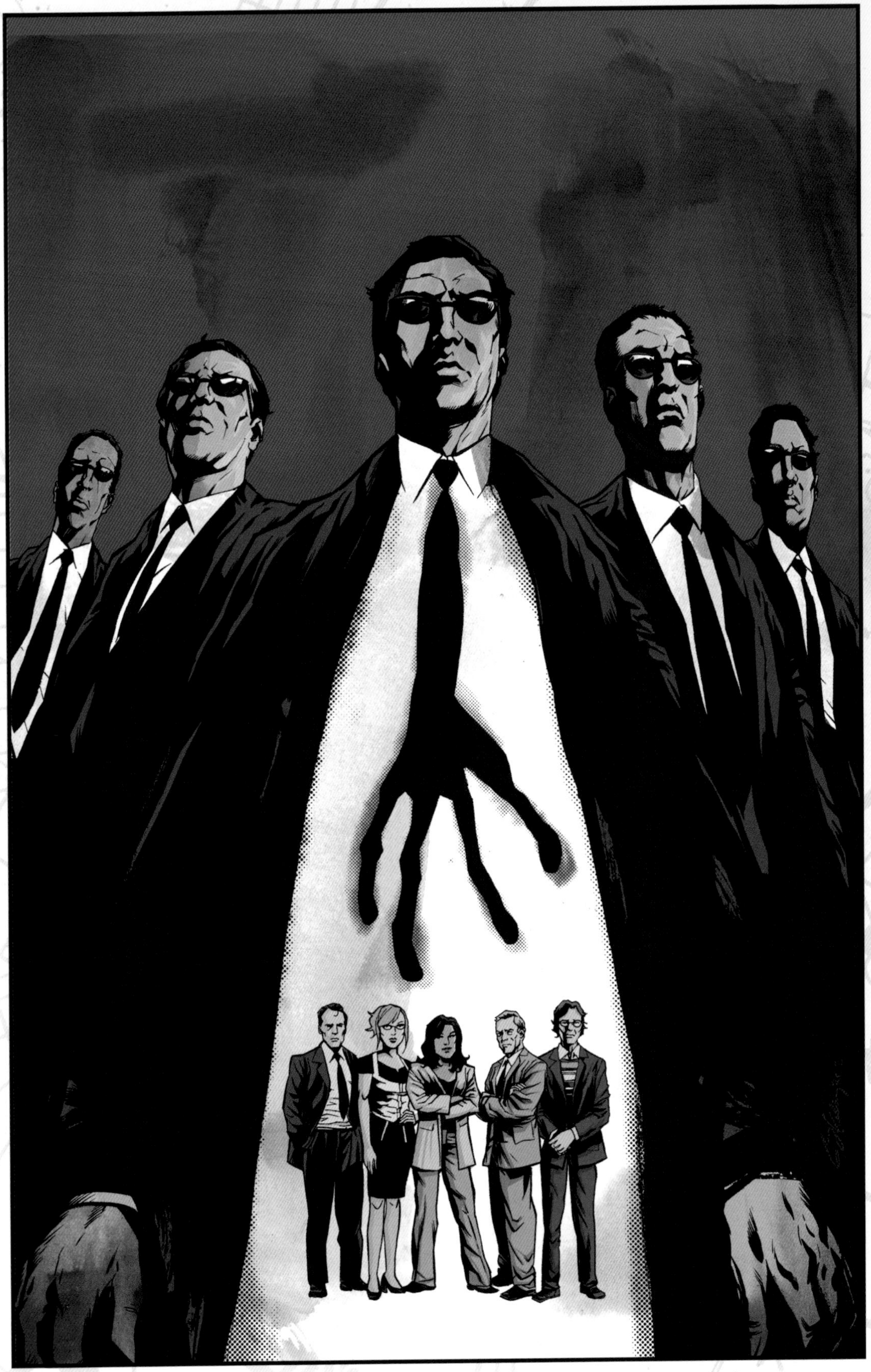

COVER ART BY **RYAN KELLY**

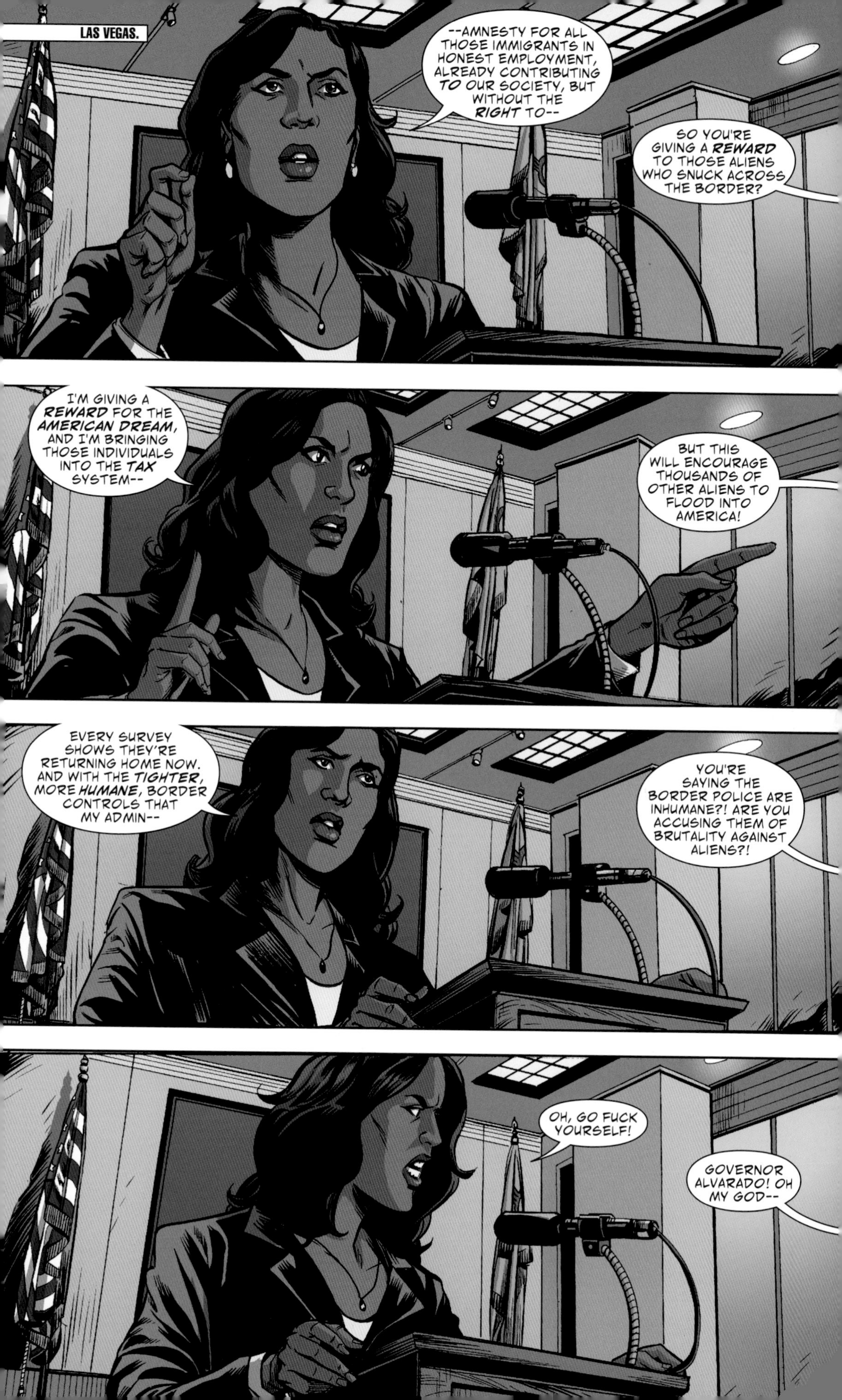

LAS VEGAS.
--AMNESTY FOR ALL THOSE IMMIGRANTS IN HONEST EMPLOYMENT, ALREADY CONTRIBUTING TO OUR SOCIETY, BUT WITHOUT THE RIGHT TO--
SO YOU'RE GIVING A REWARD TO THOSE ALIENS WHO SNUCK ACROSS THE BORDER?
I'M GIVING A REWARD FOR THE AMERICAN DREAM, AND I'M BRINGING THOSE INDIVIDUALS INTO THE TAX SYSTEM--
BUT THIS WILL ENCOURAGE THOUSANDS OF OTHER ALIENS TO FLOOD INTO AMERICA!
EVERY SURVEY SHOWS THEY'RE RETURNING HOME NOW. AND WITH THE TIGHTER, MORE HUMANE, BORDER CONTROLS THAT MY ADMIN--
YOU'RE SAYING THE BORDER POLICE ARE INHUMANE?! ARE YOU ACCUSING THEM OF BRUTALITY AGAINST ALIENS?!
OH, GO FUCK YOURSELF!
GOVERNOR ALVARADO! OH MY GOD--

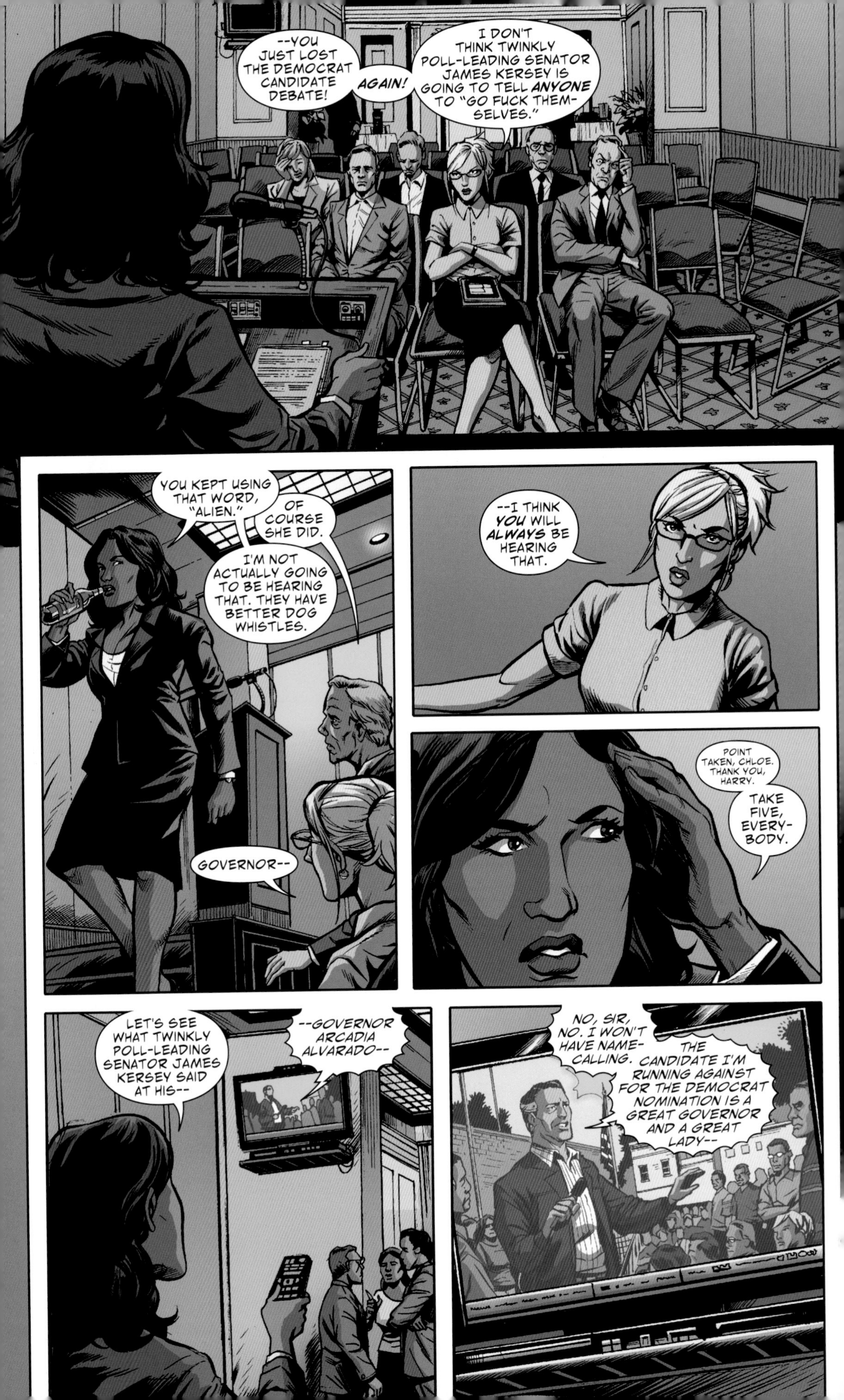
--YOU JUST LOST THE DEMOCRAT CANDIDATE DEBATE!
AGAIN!
I DON'T THINK TWINKLY POLL-LEADING SENATOR JAMES KERSEY IS GOING TO TELL ANYONE TO "GO FUCK THEM-SELVES."
YOU KEPT USING THAT WORD, "ALIEN."
OF COURSE SHE DID.
I'M NOT ACTUALLY GOING TO BE HEARING THAT. THEY HAVE BETTER DOG WHISTLES.
GOVERNOR--
--I THINK YOU WILL ALWAYS BE HEARING THAT.
POINT TAKEN, CHLOE. THANK YOU, HARRY.
TAKE FIVE, EVERY-BODY.
LET'S SEE WHAT TWINKLY POLL-LEADING SENATOR JAMES KERSEY SAID AT HIS--
--GOVERNOR ARCADIA ALVARADO--
NO, SIR, NO. I WON'T HAVE NAME-CALLING.
THE CANDIDATE I'M RUNNING AGAINST FOR THE DEMOCRAT NOMINATION IS A GREAT GOVERNOR AND A GREAT LADY--

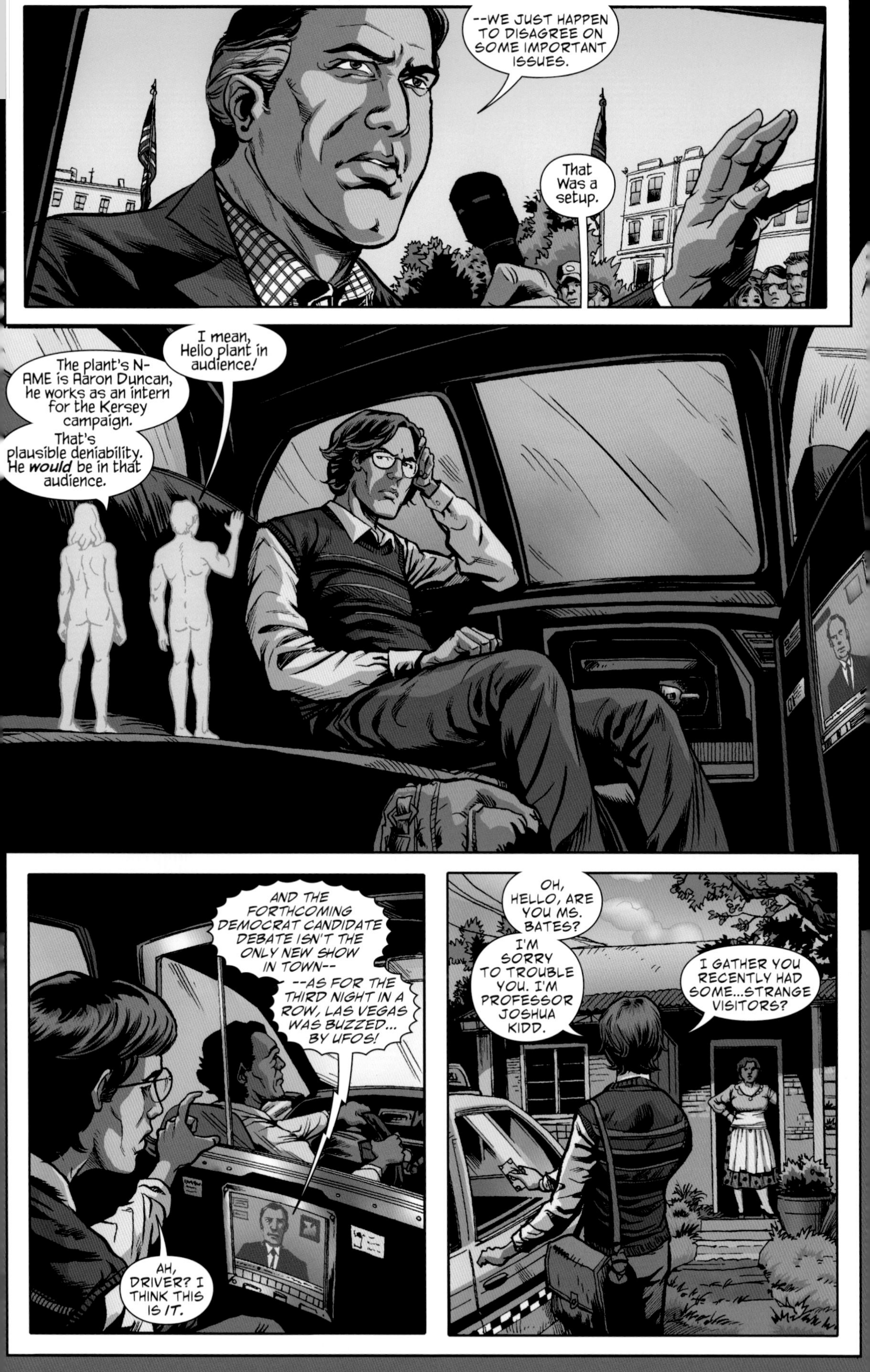
--WE JUST HAPPEN TO DISAGREE ON SOME IMPORTANT ISSUES.
That was a setup.
I mean, Hello plant in audience!
The plant's N-AME is Aaron Duncan, he works as an intern for the Kersey campaign.
That's plausible deniability. He *would* be in that audience.
AND THE FORTHCOMING DEMOCRAT CANDIDATE DEBATE ISN'T THE ONLY NEW SHOW IN TOWN--
--AS FOR THE THIRD NIGHT IN A ROW, LAS VEGAS WAS BUZZED... BY UFOS!
AH, DRIVER? I THINK THIS IS *IT*.
OH, HELLO, ARE YOU MS. BATES?
I'M SORRY TO TROUBLE YOU. I'M PROFESSOR JOSHUA KIDD.
I GATHER YOU RECENTLY HAD SOME...STRANGE VISITORS?

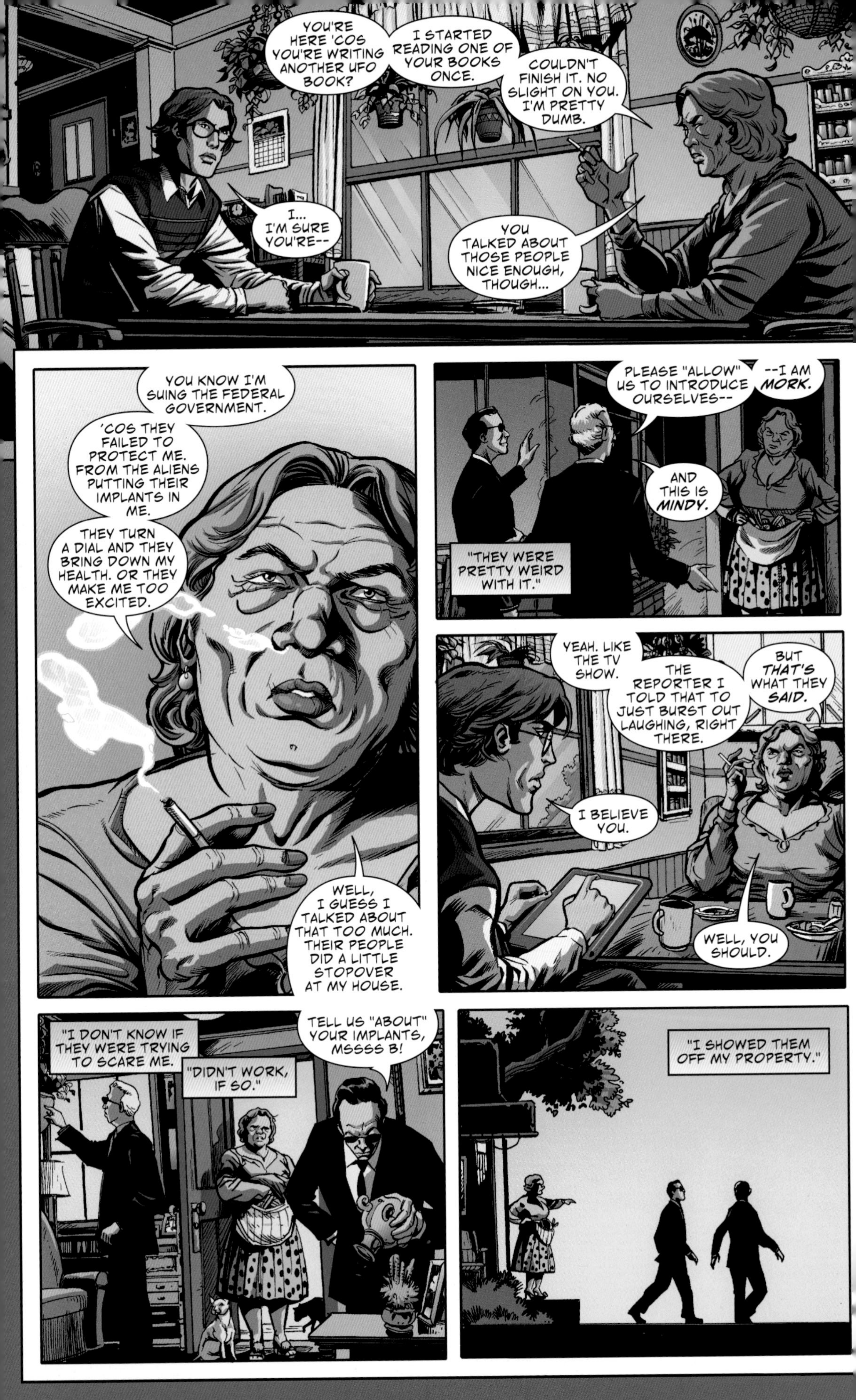
YOU'RE HERE 'COS YOU'RE WRITING ANOTHER UFO BOOK?
I STARTED READING ONE OF YOUR BOOKS ONCE.
COULDN'T FINISH IT. NO SLIGHT ON YOU. I'M PRETTY DUMB.
I... I'M SURE YOU'RE--
YOU TALKED ABOUT THOSE PEOPLE NICE ENOUGH, THOUGH...
YOU KNOW I'M SUING THE FEDERAL GOVERNMENT.
'COS THEY FAILED TO PROTECT ME. FROM THE ALIENS PUTTING THEIR IMPLANTS IN ME.
THEY TURN A DIAL AND THEY BRING DOWN MY HEALTH. OR THEY MAKE ME TOO EXCITED.
WELL, I GUESS I TALKED ABOUT THAT TOO MUCH. THEIR PEOPLE DID A LITTLE STOPOVER AT MY HOUSE.
PLEASE "ALLOW" US TO INTRODUCE OURSELVES--
--I AM MORK.
AND THIS IS MINDY.
"THEY WERE PRETTY WEIRD WITH IT."
YEAH. LIKE THE TV SHOW.
THE REPORTER I TOLD THAT TO JUST BURST OUT LAUGHING, RIGHT THERE.
BUT THAT'S WHAT THEY SAID.
I BELIEVE YOU.
WELL, YOU SHOULD.
"I DON'T KNOW IF THEY WERE TRYING TO SCARE ME.
"DIDN'T WORK, IF SO."
TELL US "ABOUT" YOUR IMPLANTS, MSSSS B!
"I SHOWED THEM OFF MY PROPERTY."

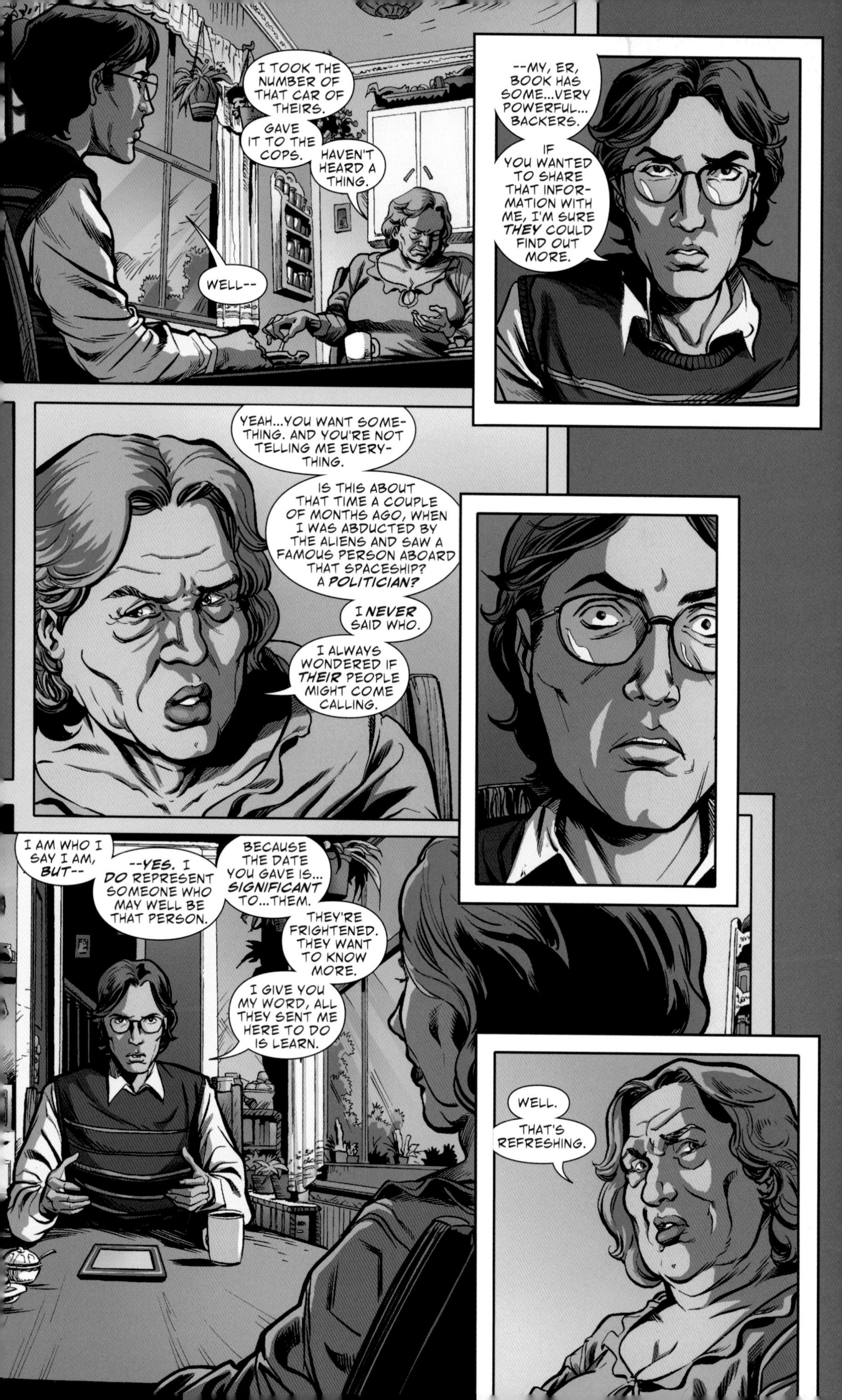
I TOOK THE NUMBER OF THAT CAR OF THEIRS.
GAVE IT TO THE COPS.
HAVEN'T HEARD A THING.
WELL--
--MY, ER, BOOK HAS SOME...VERY POWERFUL... BACKERS.
IF YOU WANTED TO SHARE THAT INFORMATION WITH ME, I'M SURE THEY COULD FIND OUT MORE.
YEAH...YOU WANT SOMETHING. AND YOU'RE NOT TELLING ME EVERYTHING.
IS THIS ABOUT THAT TIME A COUPLE OF MONTHS AGO, WHEN I WAS ABDUCTED BY THE ALIENS AND SAW A FAMOUS PERSON ABOARD THAT SPACESHIP? A POLITICIAN?
I NEVER SAID WHO.
I ALWAYS WONDERED IF THEIR PEOPLE MIGHT COME CALLING.
I AM WHO I SAY I AM, BUT--
--YES. I DO REPRESENT SOMEONE WHO MAY WELL BE THAT PERSON.
BECAUSE THE DATE YOU GAVE IS... SIGNIFICANT TO...THEM.
THEY'RE FRIGHTENED. THEY WANT TO KNOW MORE.
I GIVE YOU MY WORD, ALL THEY SENT ME HERE TO DO IS LEARN.
WELL.
THAT'S REFRESHING.

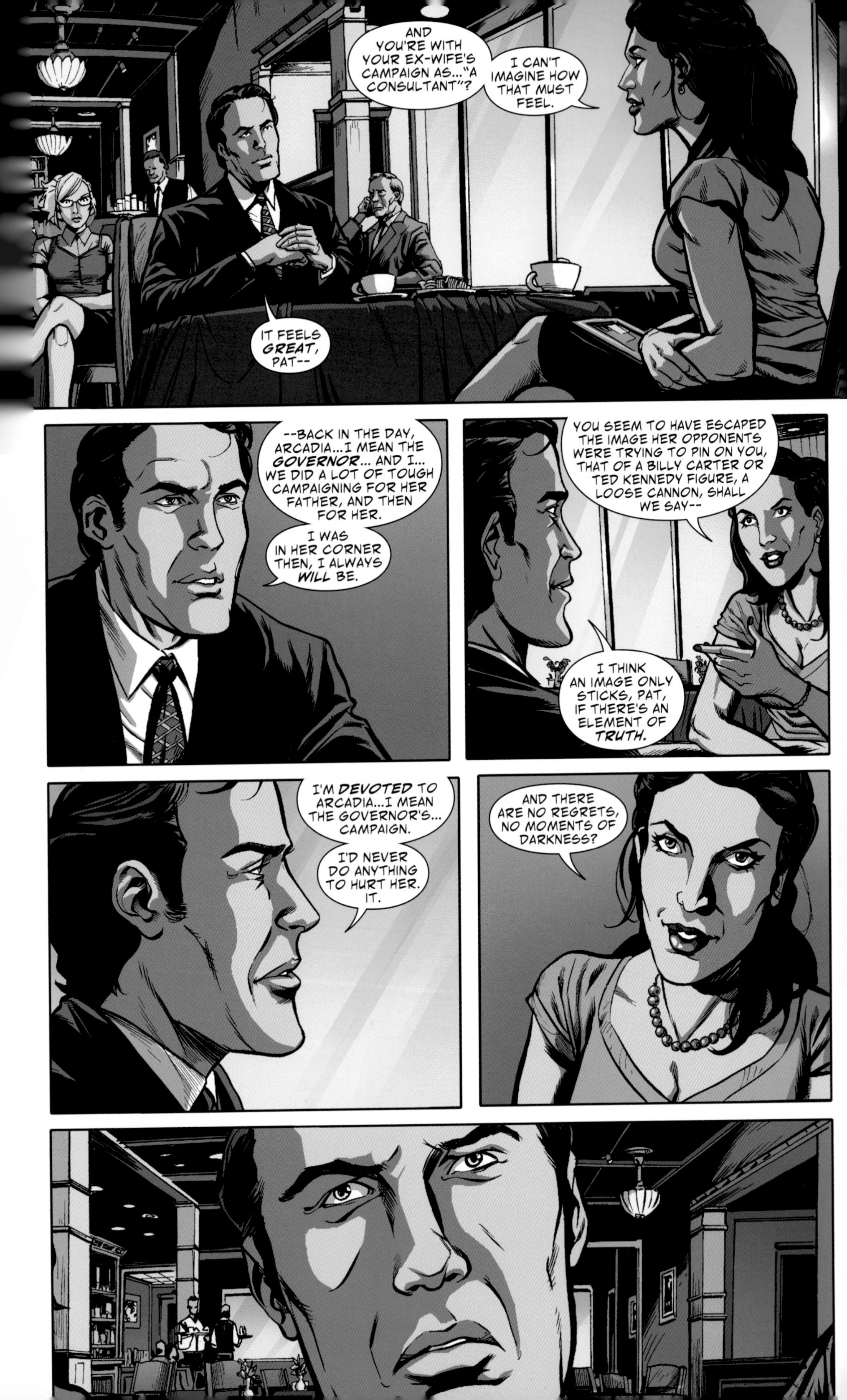
AND YOU'RE WITH YOUR EX-WIFE'S CAMPAIGN AS..."A CONSULTANT"?
I CAN'T IMAGINE HOW THAT MUST FEEL.
IT FEELS *GREAT*, PAT--
--BACK IN THE DAY, ARCADIA...I MEAN THE *GOVERNOR*... AND I... WE DID A LOT OF TOUGH CAMPAIGNING FOR HER FATHER, AND THEN FOR HER.
I WAS IN HER CORNER THEN, I ALWAYS *WILL* BE.
YOU SEEM TO HAVE ESCAPED THE IMAGE HER OPPONENTS WERE TRYING TO PIN ON YOU, THAT OF A BILLY CARTER OR TED KENNEDY FIGURE, A LOOSE CANNON, SHALL WE SAY--
I THINK AN IMAGE ONLY STICKS, PAT, IF THERE'S AN ELEMENT OF *TRUTH*.
I'M *DEVOTED* TO ARCADIA...I MEAN THE GOVERNOR'S... CAMPAIGN.
I'D NEVER DO ANYTHING TO HURT HER. IT.
AND THERE ARE NO REGRETS, NO MOMENTS OF DARKNESS?

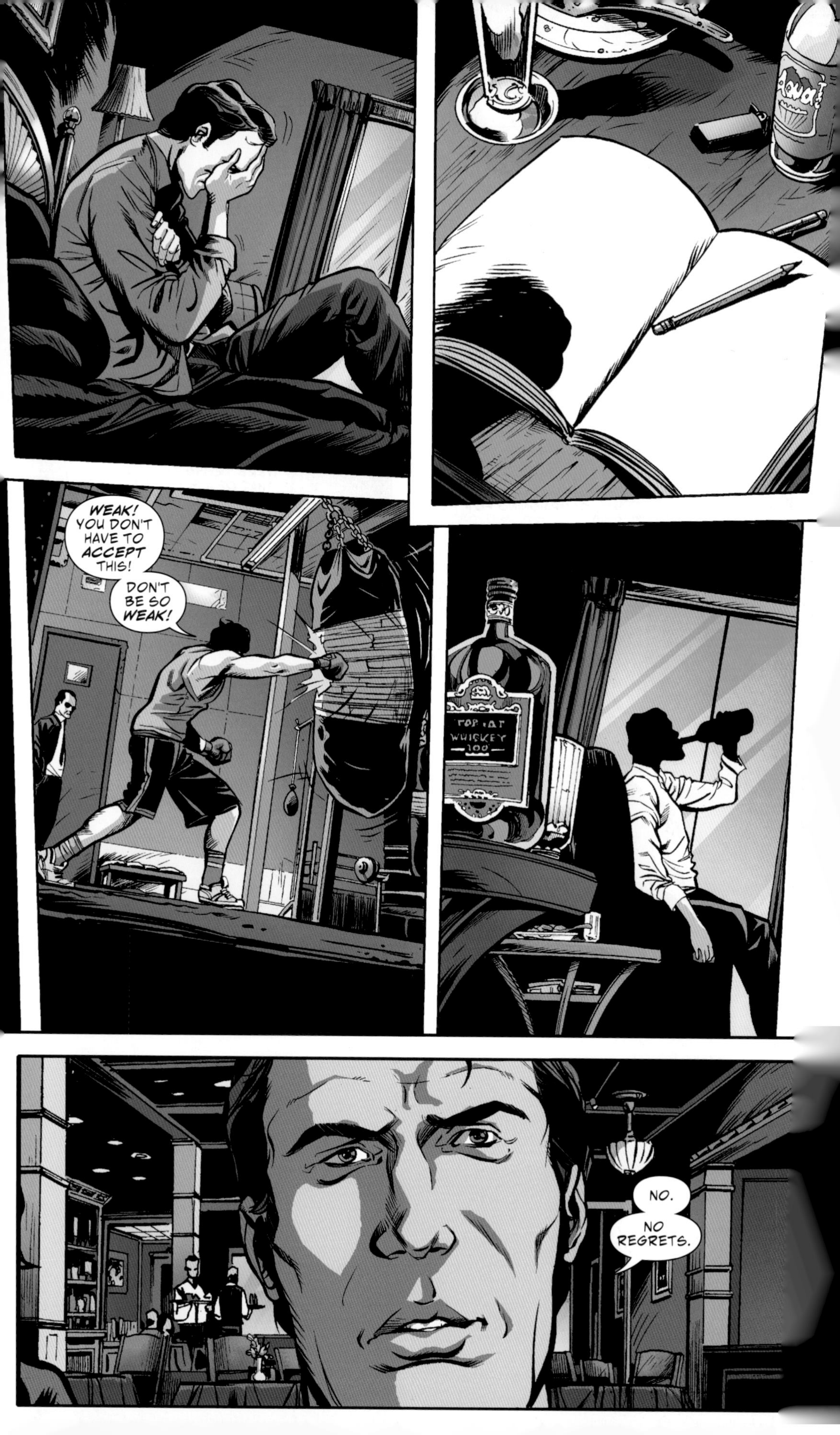

AQUA
WEAK! YOU DON'T HAVE TO ACCEPT THIS!
DON'T BE SO WEAK!
WHISKEY 100
NO.
NO REGRETS.

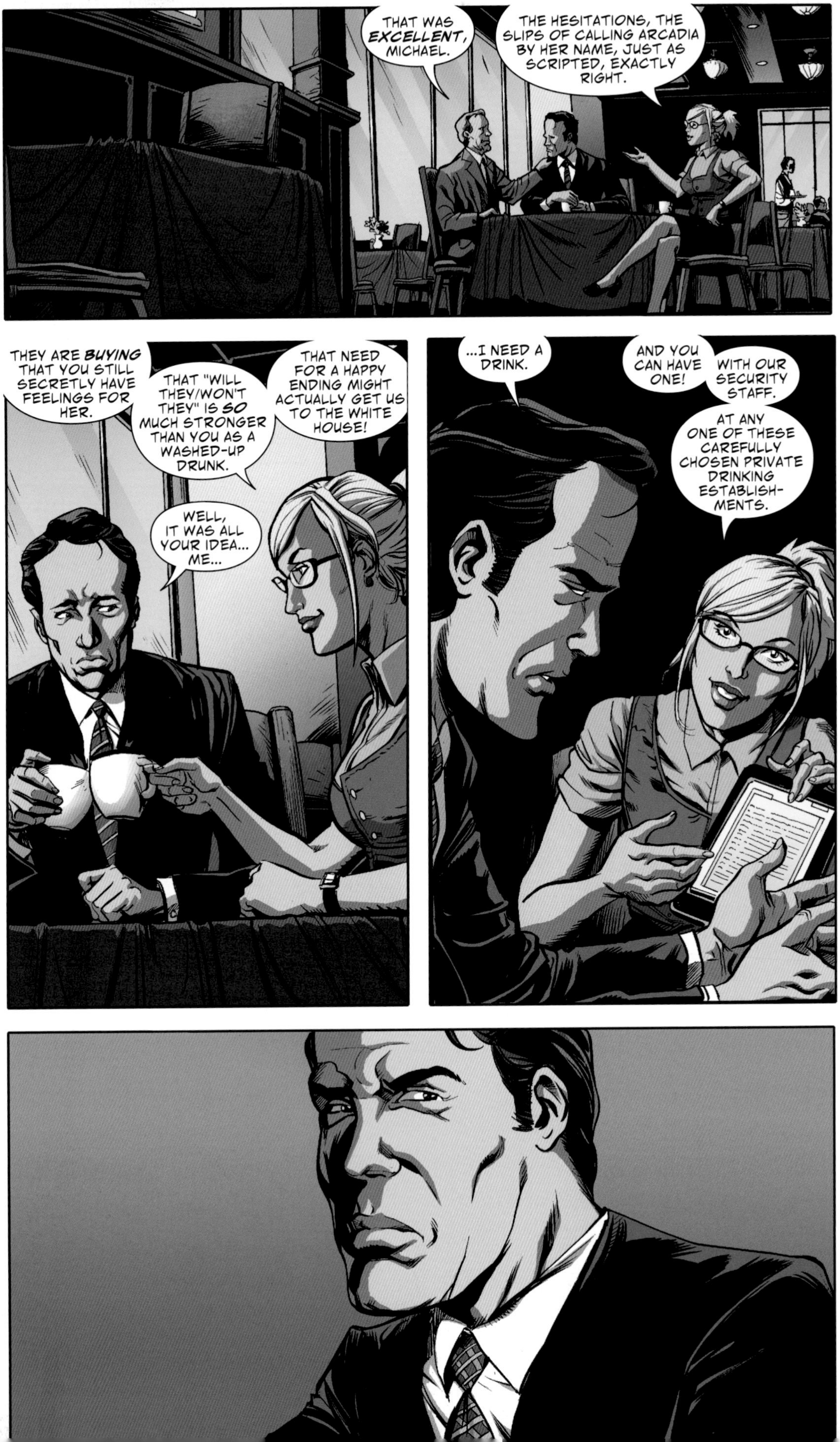
THAT WAS EXCELLENT, MICHAEL.
THE HESITATIONS, THE SLIPS OF CALLING ARCADIA BY HER NAME, JUST AS SCRIPTED, EXACTLY RIGHT.
THEY ARE BUYING THAT YOU STILL SECRETLY HAVE FEELINGS FOR HER.
THAT "WILL THEY/WON'T THEY" IS SO MUCH STRONGER THAN YOU AS A WASHED-UP DRUNK.
THAT NEED FOR A HAPPY ENDING MIGHT ACTUALLY GET US TO THE WHITE HOUSE!
WELL, IT WAS ALL YOUR IDEA... ME...
...I NEED A DRINK.
AND YOU CAN HAVE ONE!
WITH OUR SECURITY STAFF.
AT ANY ONE OF THESE CAREFULLY CHOSEN PRIVATE DRINKING ESTABLISH-MENTS.

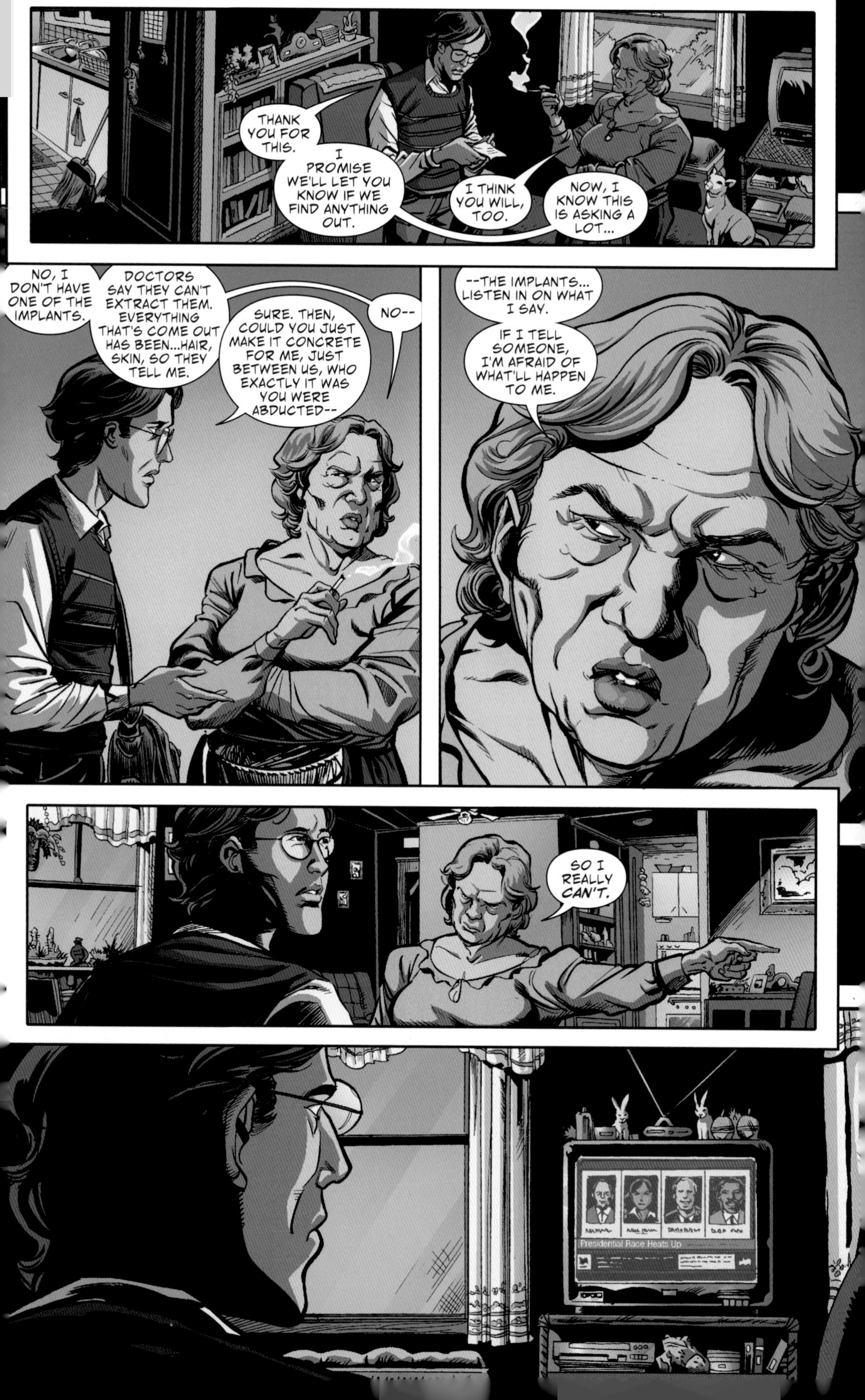
THANK YOU FOR THIS.
I PROMISE WE'LL LET YOU KNOW IF WE FIND ANYTHING OUT.
I THINK YOU WILL, TOO.
NOW, I KNOW THIS IS ASKING A LOT...
NO, I DON'T HAVE ONE OF THE IMPLANTS.
DOCTORS SAY THEY CAN'T EXTRACT THEM. EVERYTHING THAT'S COME OUT HAS BEEN...HAIR, SKIN, SO THEY TELL ME.
SURE. THEN, COULD YOU JUST MAKE IT CONCRETE FOR ME, JUST BETWEEN US, WHO EXACTLY IT WAS YOU WERE ABDUCTED--
NO--
--THE IMPLANTS... LISTEN IN ON WHAT I SAY.
IF I TELL SOMEONE, I'M AFRAID OF WHAT'LL HAPPEN TO ME.
SO I REALLY *CAN'T*.
Presidential Race Heats Up

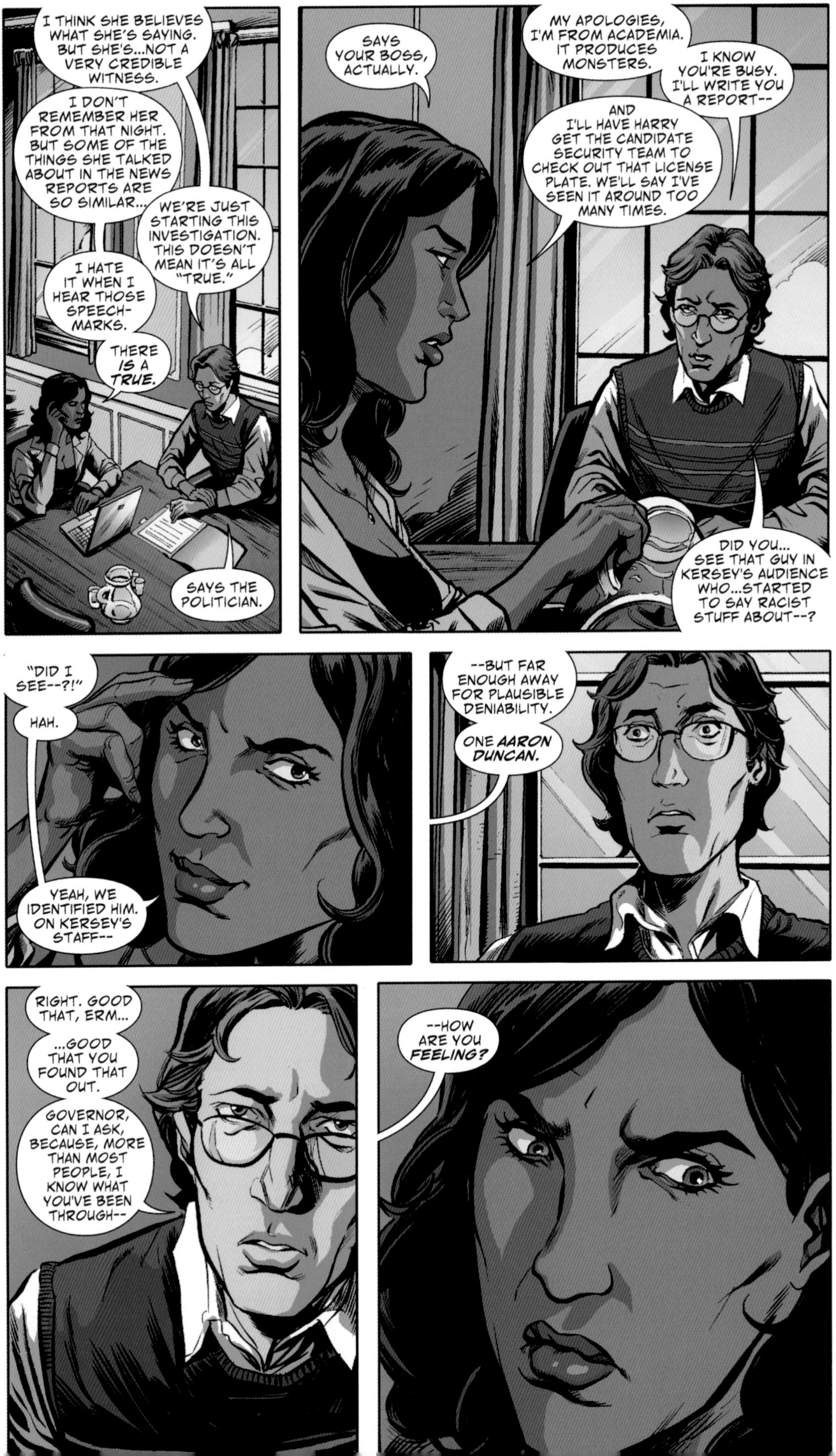
I THINK SHE BELIEVES WHAT SHE'S SAYING. BUT SHE'S...NOT A VERY CREDIBLE WITNESS.
I DON'T REMEMBER HER FROM THAT NIGHT. BUT SOME OF THE THINGS SHE TALKED ABOUT IN THE NEWS REPORTS ARE SO SIMILAR...
WE'RE JUST STARTING THIS INVESTIGATION. THIS DOESN'T MEAN IT'S ALL "TRUE."
I HATE IT WHEN I HEAR THOSE SPEECH-MARKS.
THERE *IS* A *TRUE*.
SAYS THE POLITICIAN.
SAYS YOUR BOSS, ACTUALLY.
MY APOLOGIES, I'M FROM ACADEMIA. IT PRODUCES MONSTERS.
I KNOW YOU'RE BUSY. I'LL WRITE YOU A REPORT--
AND I'LL HAVE HARRY GET THE CANDIDATE SECURITY TEAM TO CHECK OUT THAT LICENSE PLATE. WE'LL SAY I'VE SEEN IT AROUND TOO MANY TIMES.
DID YOU... SEE THAT GUY IN KERSEY'S AUDIENCE WHO...STARTED TO SAY RACIST STUFF ABOUT--?
"DID I SEE--?!"
HAH.
YEAH, WE IDENTIFIED HIM. ON KERSEY'S STAFF--
--BUT FAR ENOUGH AWAY FOR PLAUSIBLE DENIABILITY.
ONE *AARON DUNCAN.*
RIGHT. GOOD THAT, ERM...
...GOOD THAT YOU FOUND THAT OUT.
GOVERNOR, CAN I ASK, BECAUSE, MORE THAN MOST PEOPLE, I KNOW WHAT YOU'VE BEEN THROUGH--
--HOW ARE YOU *FEELING?*

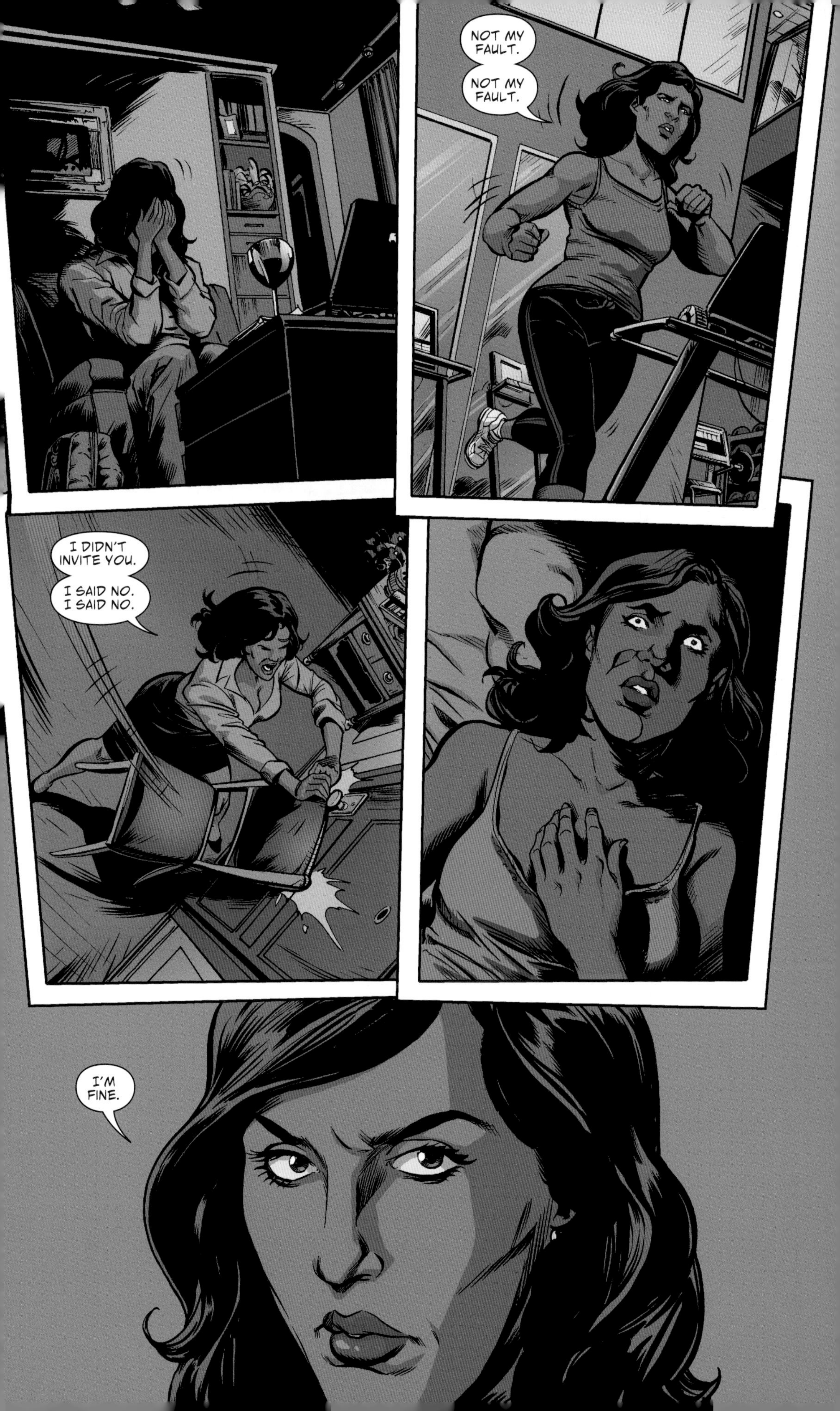
NOT MY FAULT.
NOT MY FAULT.
I DIDN'T INVITE YOU.
I SAID NO. I SAID NO.
I'M FINE.

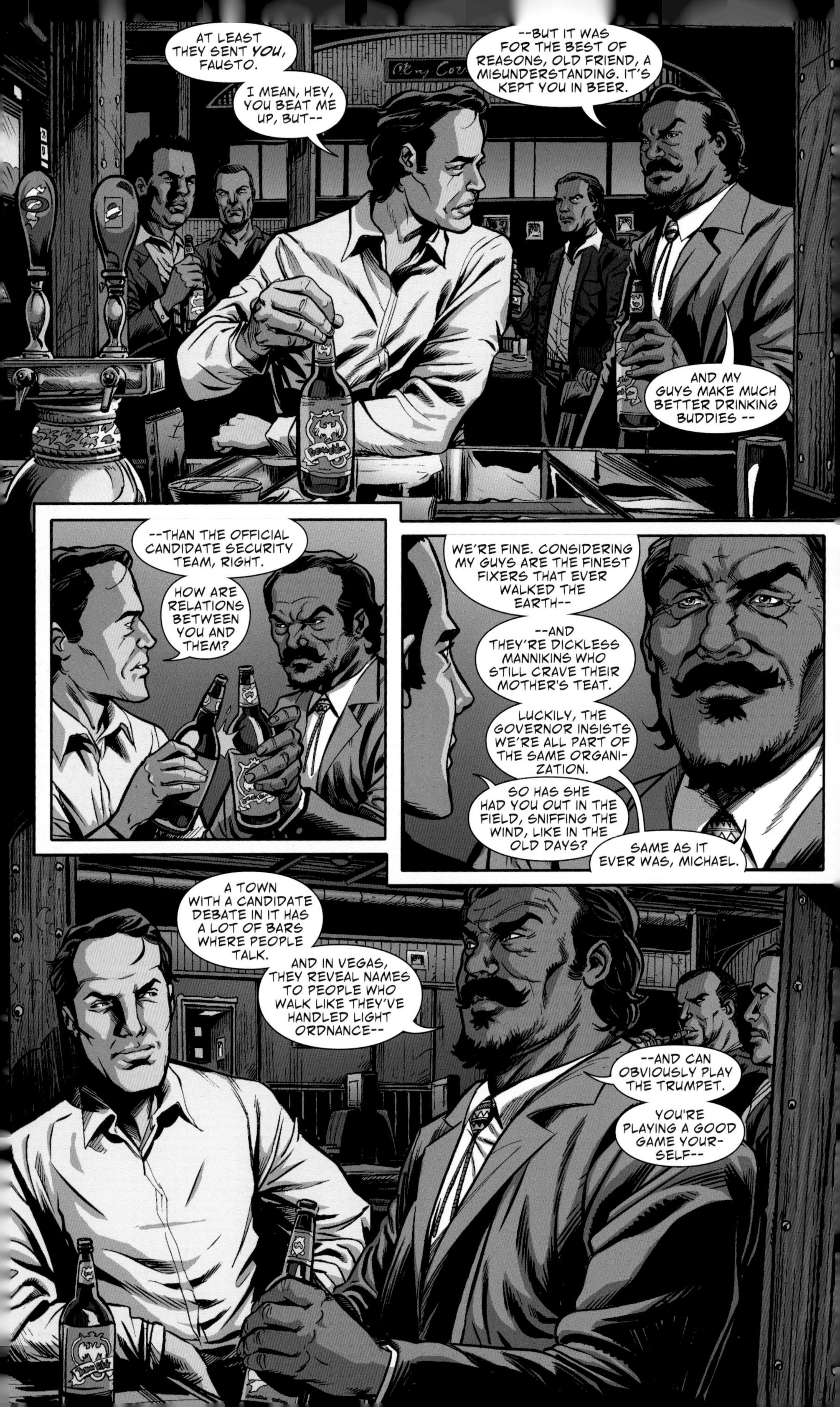
AT LEAST THEY SENT YOU, FAUSTO.
I MEAN, HEY, YOU BEAT ME UP, BUT--
--BUT IT WAS FOR THE BEST OF REASONS, OLD FRIEND, A MISUNDERSTANDING. IT'S KEPT YOU IN BEER.
AND MY GUYS MAKE MUCH BETTER DRINKING BUDDIES --
--THAN THE OFFICIAL CANDIDATE SECURITY TEAM, RIGHT.
HOW ARE RELATIONS BETWEEN YOU AND THEM?
WE'RE FINE. CONSIDERING MY GUYS ARE THE FINEST FIXERS THAT EVER WALKED THE EARTH--
--AND THEY'RE DICKLESS MANNIKINS WHO STILL CRAVE THEIR MOTHER'S TEAT.
LUCKILY, THE GOVERNOR INSISTS WE'RE ALL PART OF THE SAME ORGANI-ZATION.
SO HAS SHE HAD YOU OUT IN THE FIELD, SNIFFING THE WIND, LIKE IN THE OLD DAYS?
SAME AS IT EVER WAS, MICHAEL.
A TOWN WITH A CANDIDATE DEBATE IN IT HAS A LOT OF BARS WHERE PEOPLE TALK.
AND IN VEGAS, THEY REVEAL NAMES TO PEOPLE WHO WALK LIKE THEY'VE HANDLED LIGHT ORDNANCE--
--AND CAN OBVIOUSLY PLAY THE TRUMPET.
YOU'RE PLAYING A GOOD GAME YOUR-SELF--

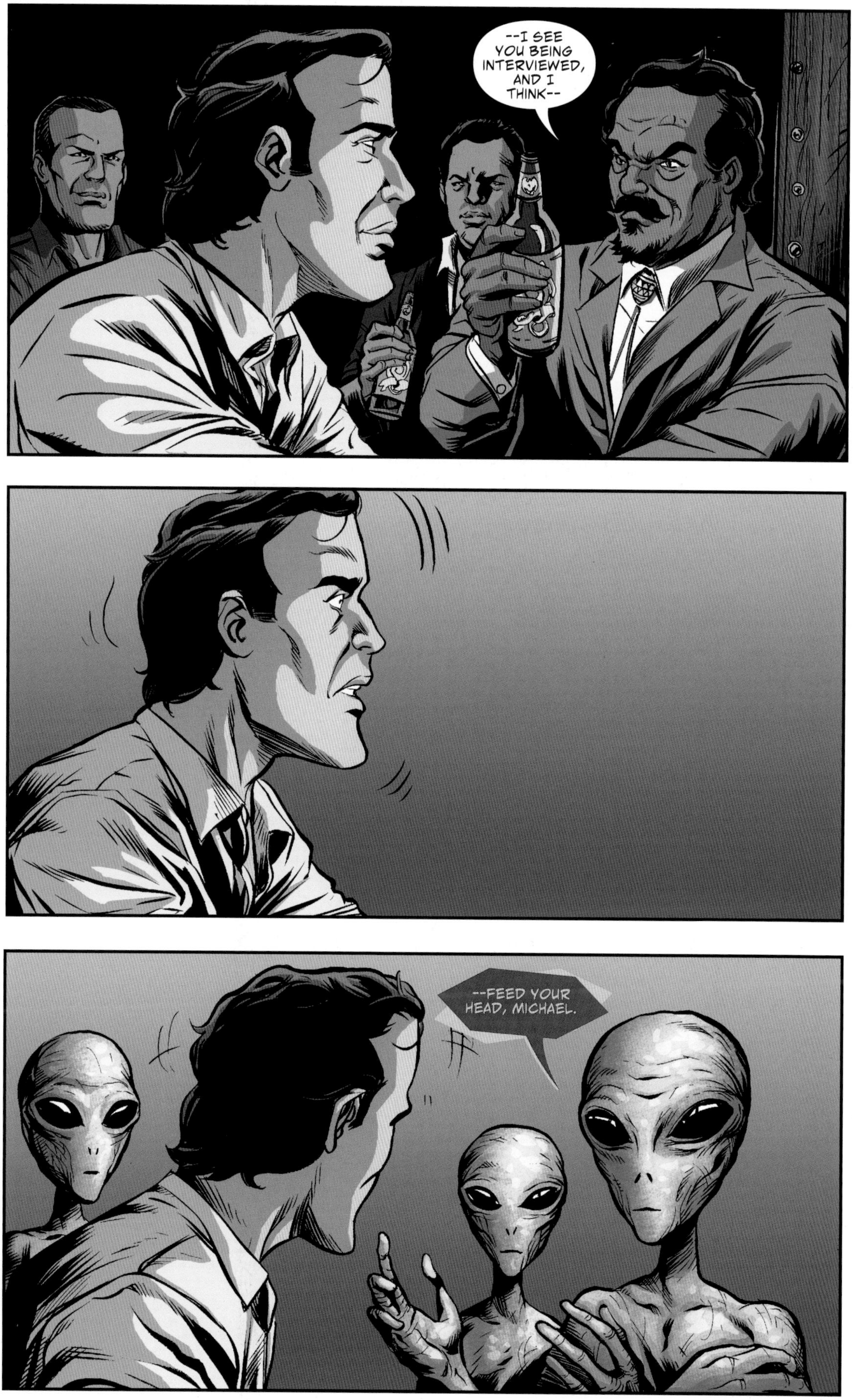
--I SEE YOU BEING INTERVIEWED, AND I THINK--
--FEED YOUR HEAD, MICHAEL.

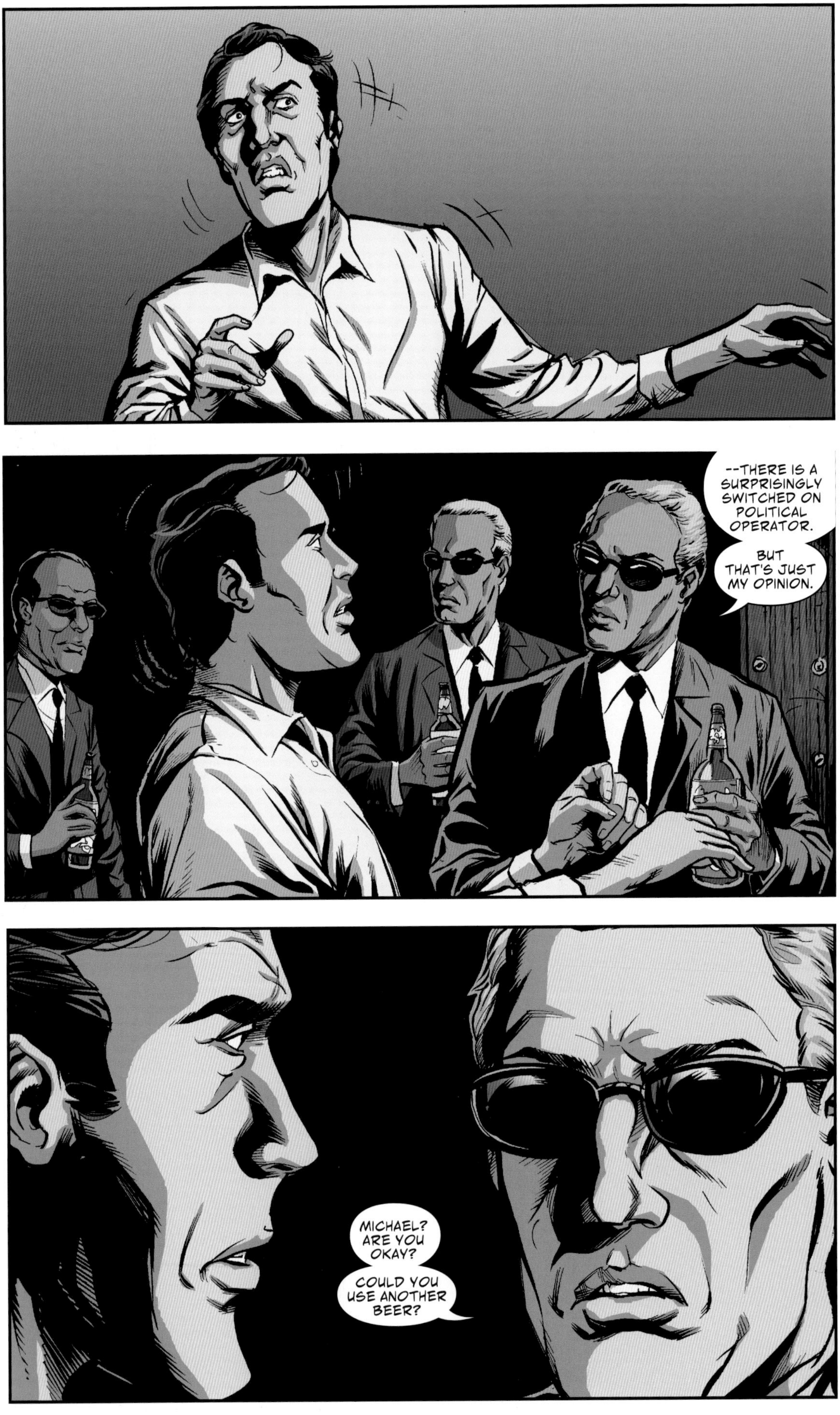
--THERE IS A SURPRISINGLY SWITCHED ON POLITICAL OPERATOR.
BUT THAT'S JUST MY OPINION.
MICHAEL? ARE YOU OKAY?
COULD YOU USE ANOTHER BEER?

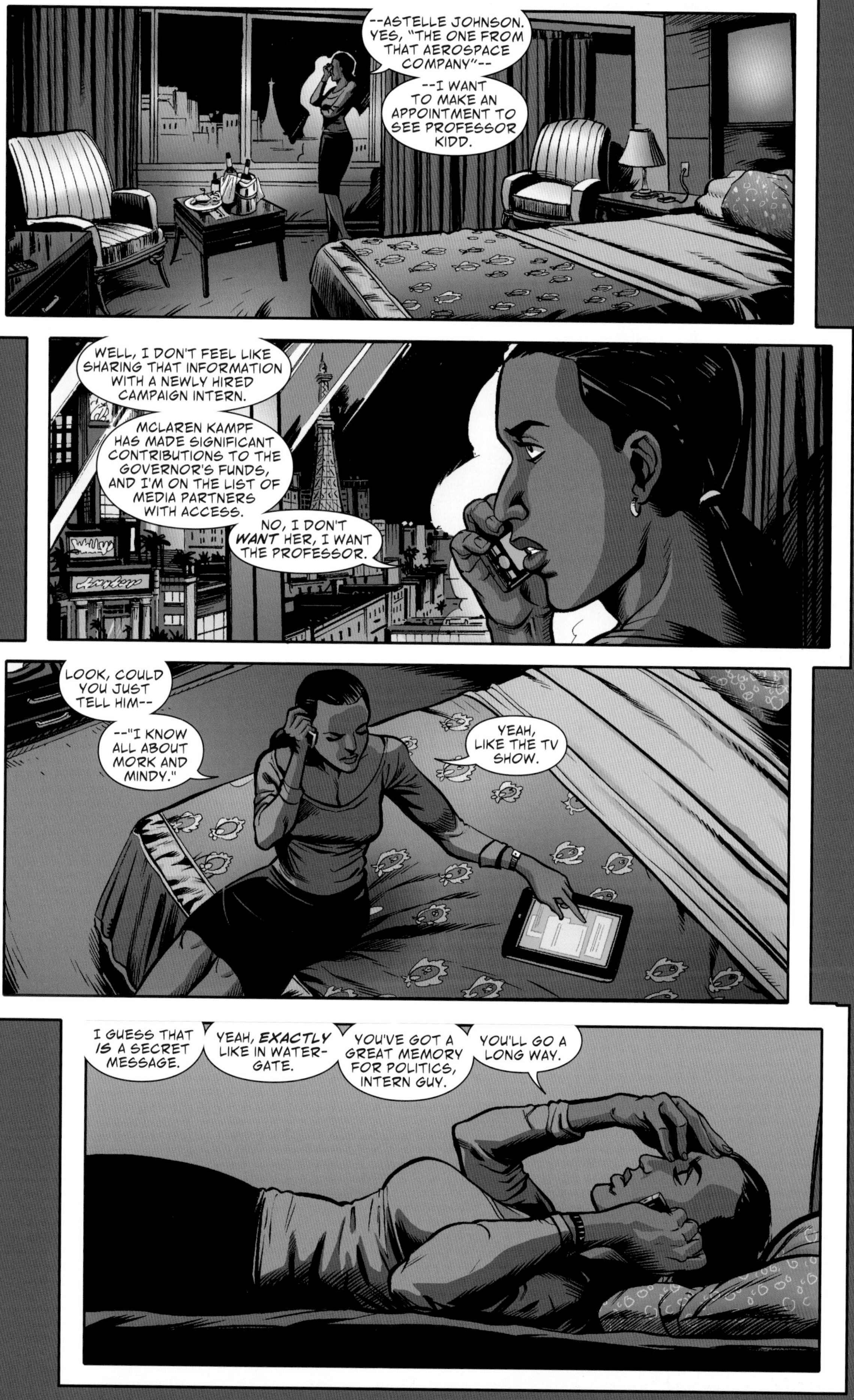
--ASTELLE JOHNSON. YES, "THE ONE FROM THAT AEROSPACE COMPANY"--
--I WANT TO MAKE AN APPOINTMENT TO SEE PROFESSOR KIDD.
WELL, I DON'T FEEL LIKE SHARING THAT INFORMATION WITH A NEWLY HIRED CAMPAIGN INTERN.
MCLAREN KAMPF HAS MADE SIGNIFICANT CONTRIBUTIONS TO THE GOVERNOR'S FUNDS, AND I'M ON THE LIST OF MEDIA PARTNERS WITH ACCESS.
NO, I DON'T *WANT* HER, I WANT THE PROFESSOR.
LOOK, COULD YOU JUST TELL HIM--
--"I KNOW ALL ABOUT MORK AND MINDY."
YEAH, LIKE THE TV SHOW.
I GUESS THAT *IS* A SECRET MESSAGE.
YEAH, *EXACTLY* LIKE IN WATER-GATE.
YOU'VE GOT A GREAT MEMORY FOR POLITICS, INTERN GUY.
YOU'LL GO A LONG WAY.

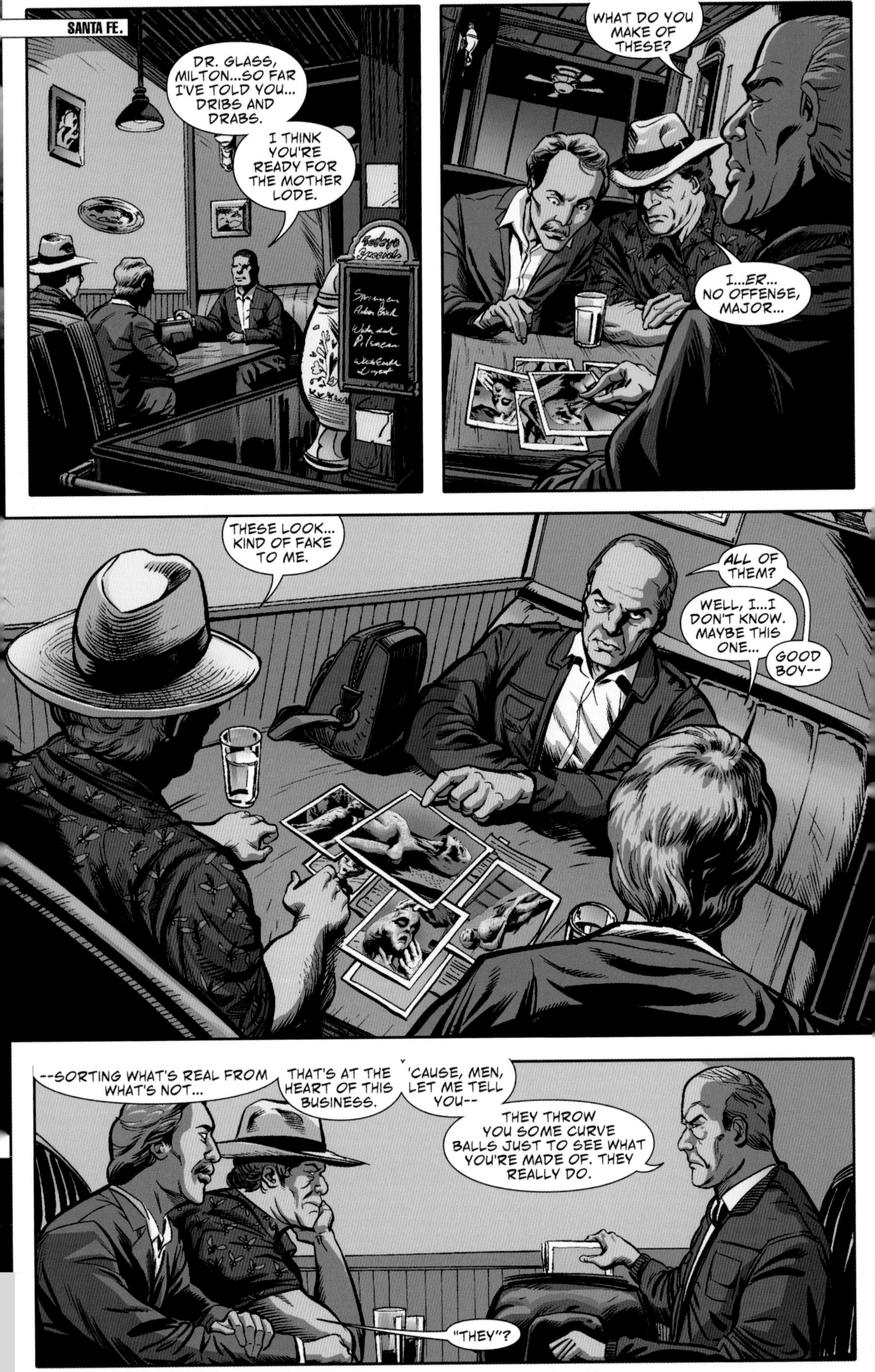
SANTA FE.
DR. GLASS, MILTON...SO FAR I'VE TOLD YOU... DRIBS AND DRABS.
I THINK YOU'RE READY FOR THE MOTHER LODE.
WHAT DO YOU MAKE OF THESE?
I...ER... NO OFFENSE, MAJOR...
THESE LOOK... KIND OF FAKE TO ME.
ALL OF THEM?
WELL, I...I DON'T KNOW. MAYBE THIS ONE...
GOOD BOY--
--SORTING WHAT'S REAL FROM WHAT'S NOT...
THAT'S AT THE HEART OF THIS BUSINESS.
'CAUSE, MEN, LET ME TELL YOU--
THEY THROW YOU SOME CURVE BALLS JUST TO SEE WHAT YOU'RE MADE OF. THEY REALLY DO.
"THEY"?

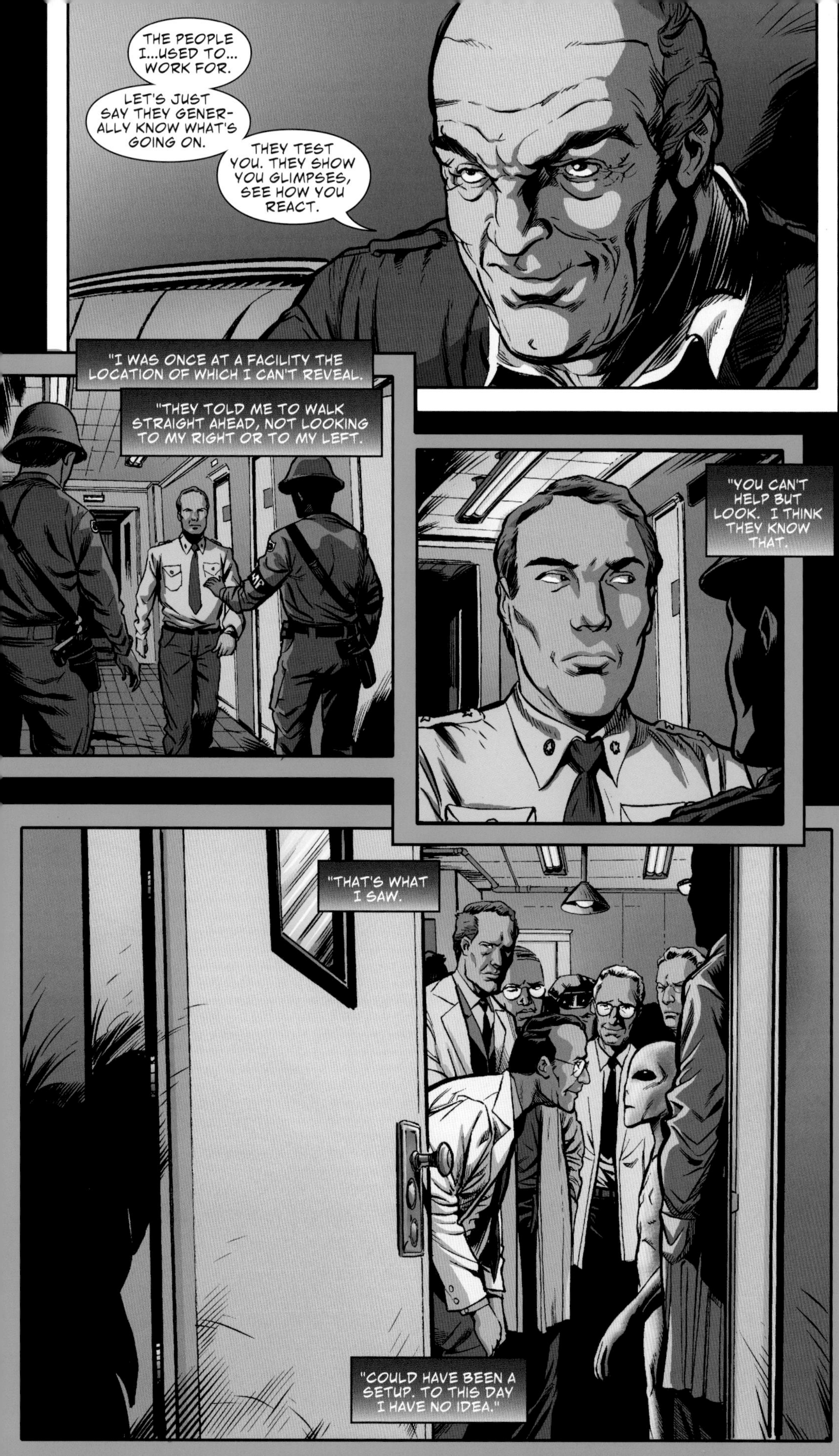
THE PEOPLE I...USED TO... WORK FOR.
LET'S JUST SAY THEY GENER- ALLY KNOW WHAT'S GOING ON.
THEY TEST YOU. THEY SHOW YOU GLIMPSES, SEE HOW YOU REACT.
"I WAS ONCE AT A FACILITY THE LOCATION OF WHICH I CAN'T REVEAL.
"THEY TOLD ME TO WALK STRAIGHT AHEAD, NOT LOOKING TO MY RIGHT OR TO MY LEFT.
"YOU CAN'T HELP BUT LOOK. I THINK THEY KNOW THAT.
"THAT'S WHAT I SAW.
"COULD HAVE BEEN A SETUP. TO THIS DAY I HAVE NO IDEA."

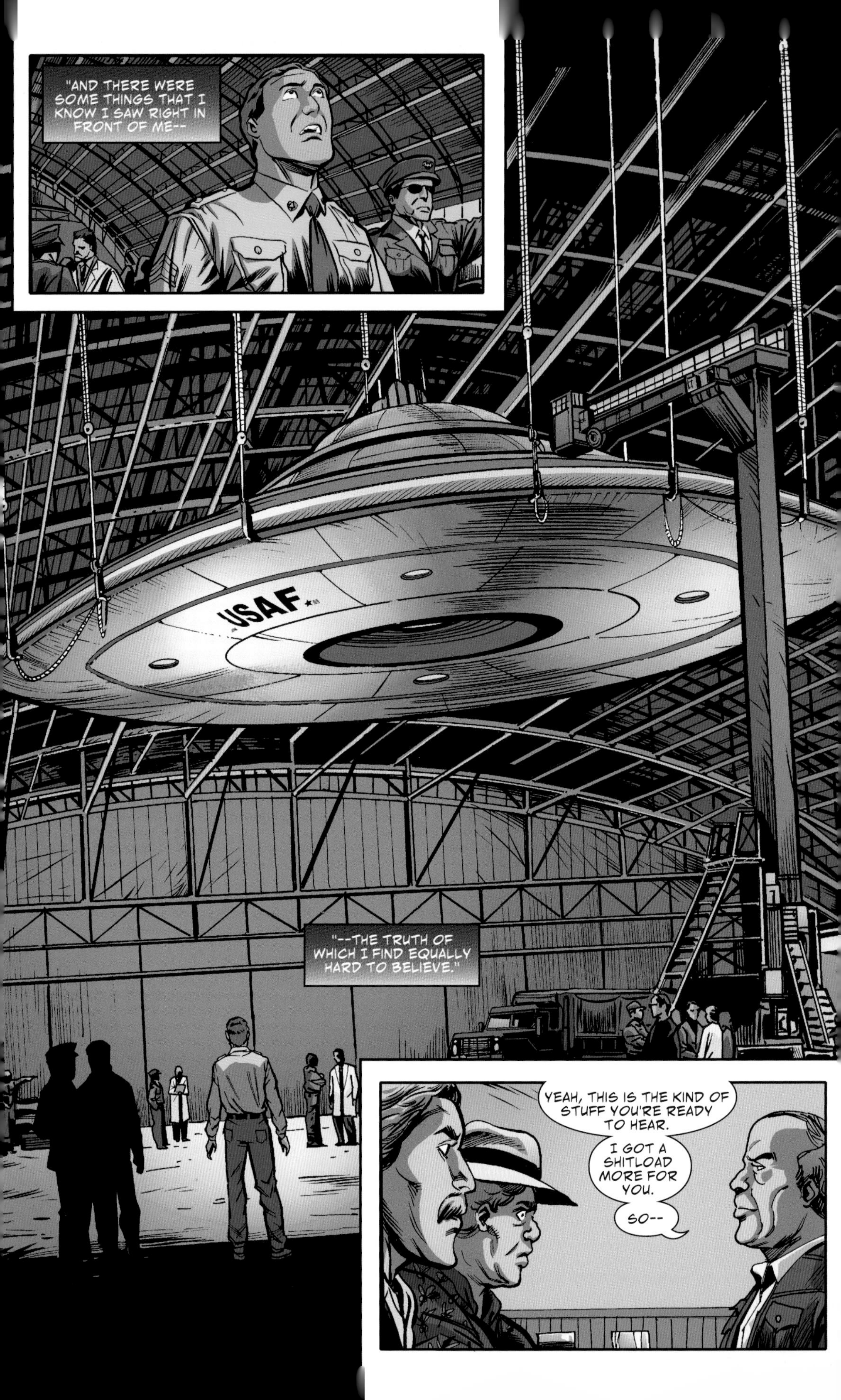
"AND THERE WERE SOME THINGS THAT I KNOW I SAW RIGHT IN FRONT OF ME--
USAF
"--THE TRUTH OF WHICH I FIND EQUALLY HARD TO BELIEVE."
YEAH, THIS IS THE KIND OF STUFF YOU'RE READY TO HEAR.
I GOT A SHITLOAD MORE FOR YOU.
SO--

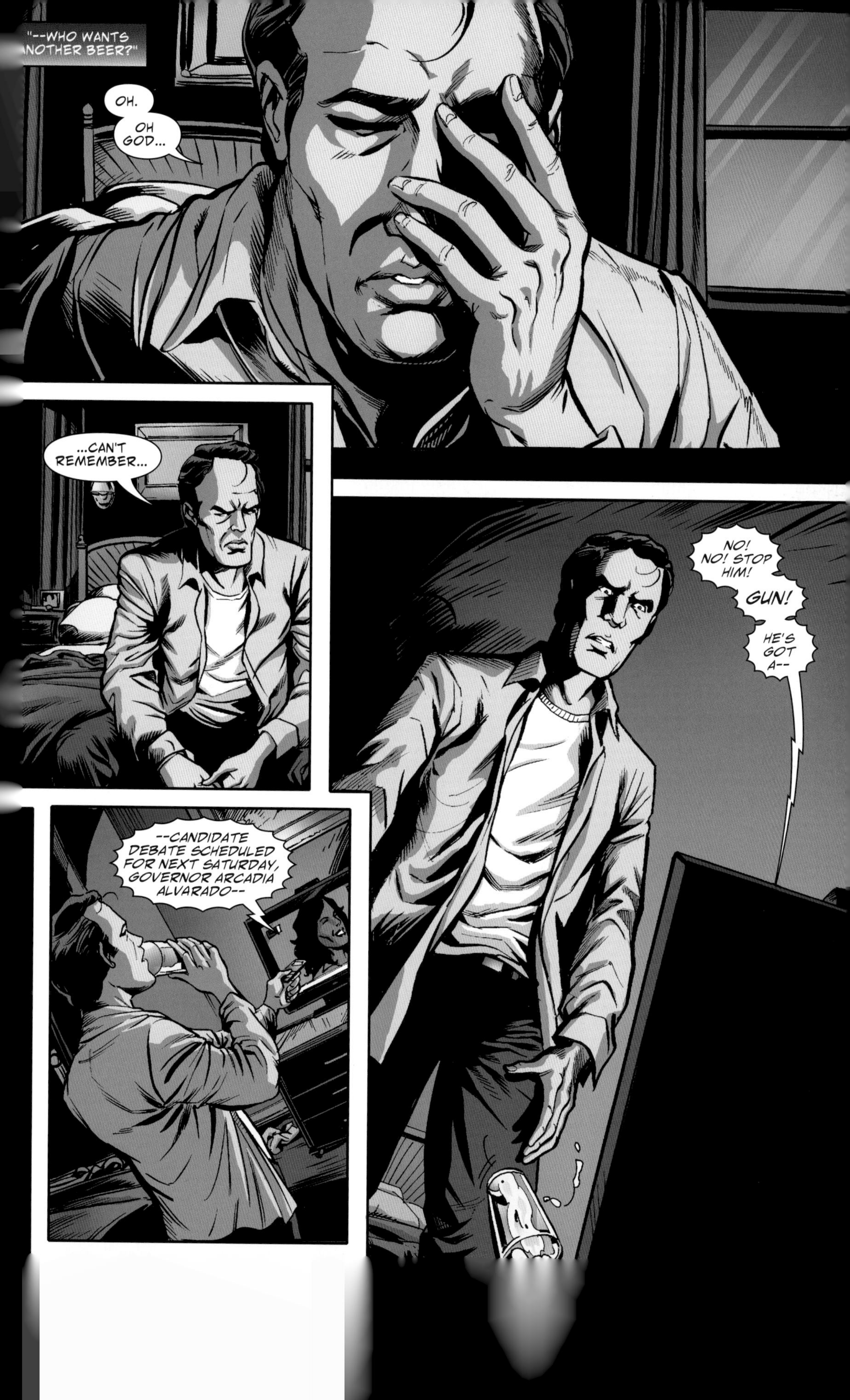
"--WHO WANTS
ANOTHER BEER?"
OH.
OH GOD...
...CAN'T REMEMBER...
NO! NO! STOP HIM!
GUN!
HE'S GOT A--
--CANDIDATE DEBATE SCHEDULED FOR NEXT SATURDAY, GOVERNOR ARCADIA ALVARADO--

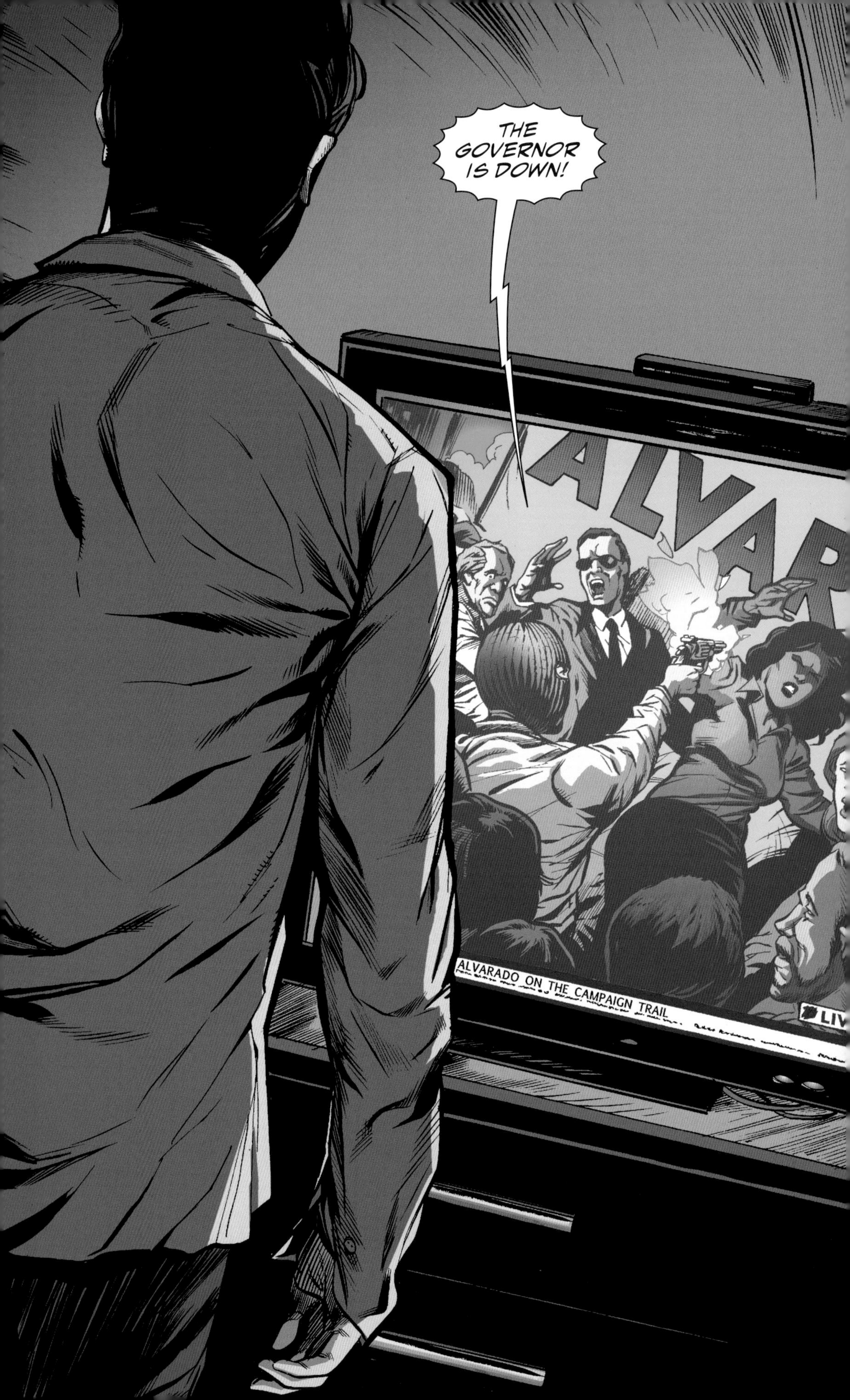

THE GOVERNOR IS DOWN!
ALVAR
ALVARADO ON THE CAMPAIGN TRAIL
LIV

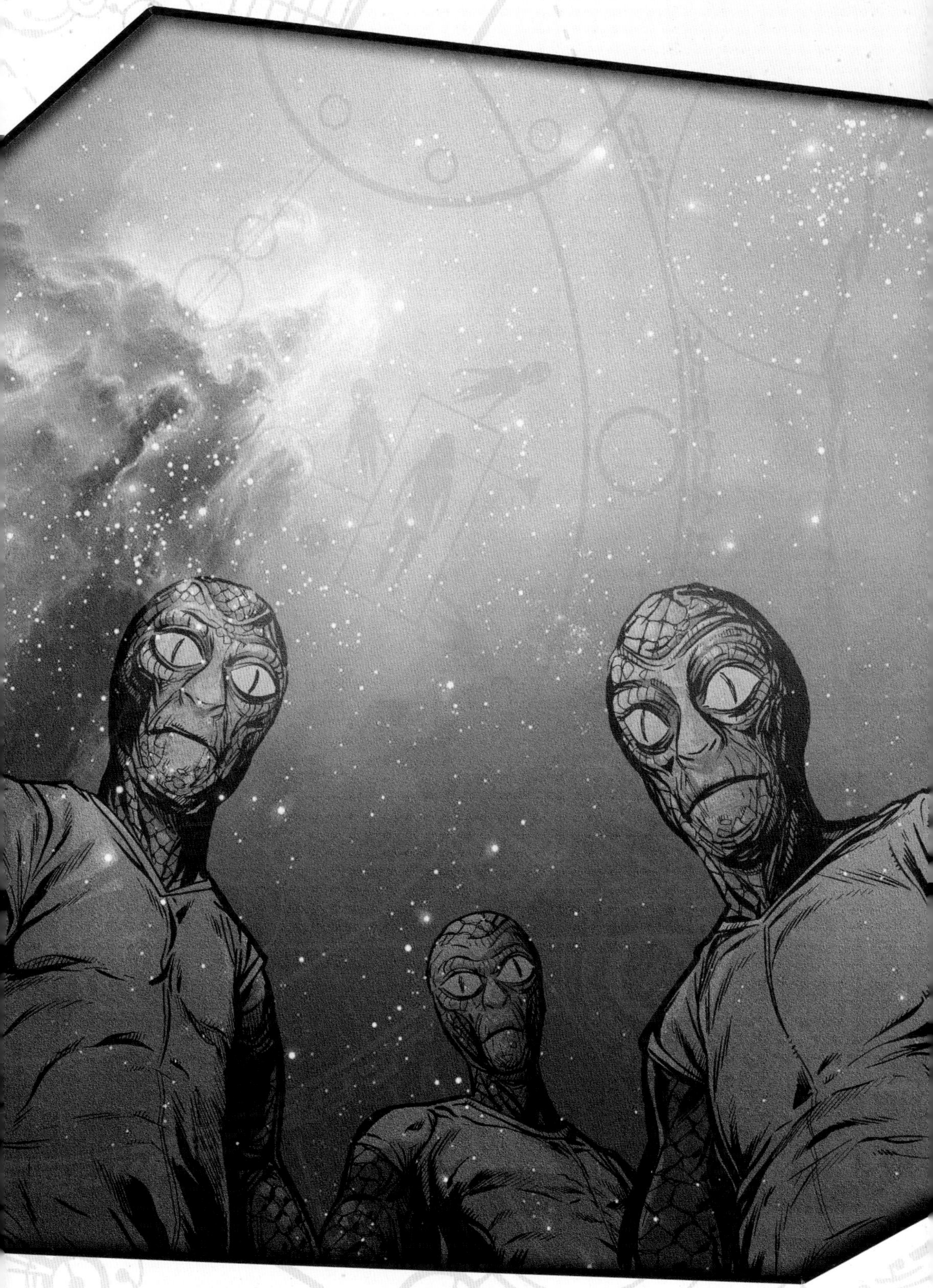

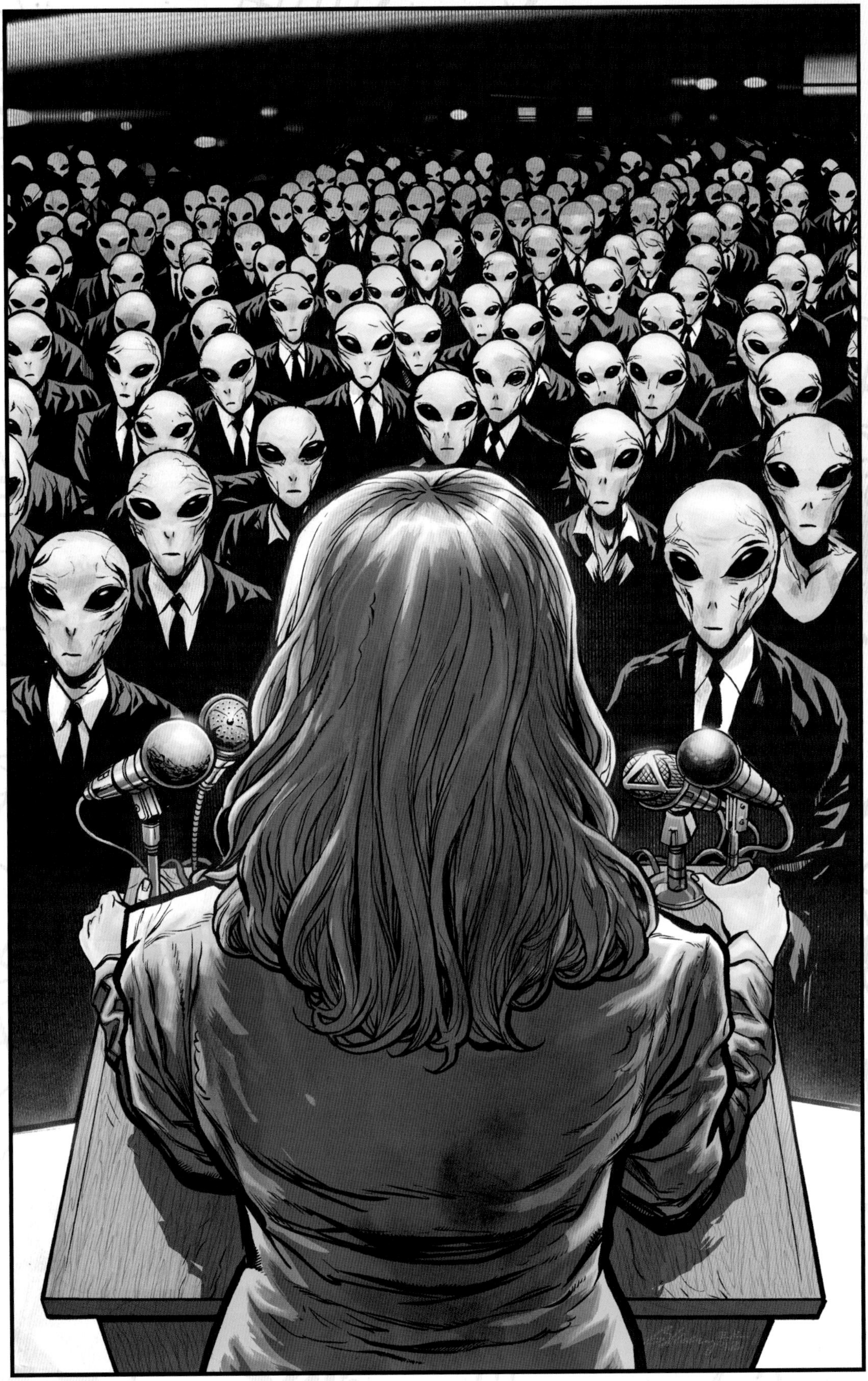

COVER ART BY **RYAN KELLY**

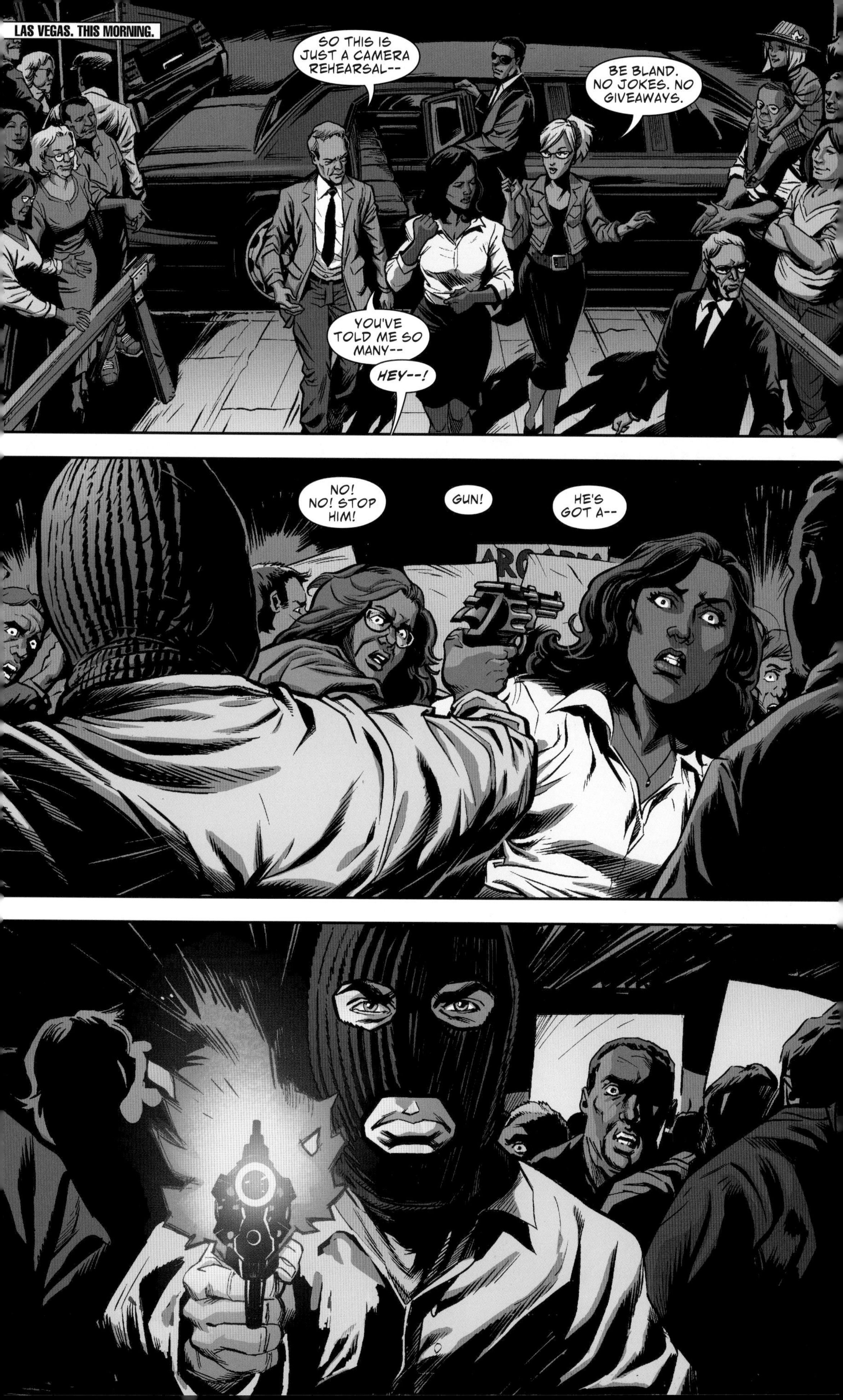
LAS VEGAS. THIS MORNING.
SO THIS IS JUST A CAMERA REHEARSAL--
BE BLAND. NO JOKES. NO GIVEAWAYS.
YOU'VE TOLD ME SO MANY--
HEY--!
NO! NO! STOP HIM!
GUN!
HE'S GOT A--

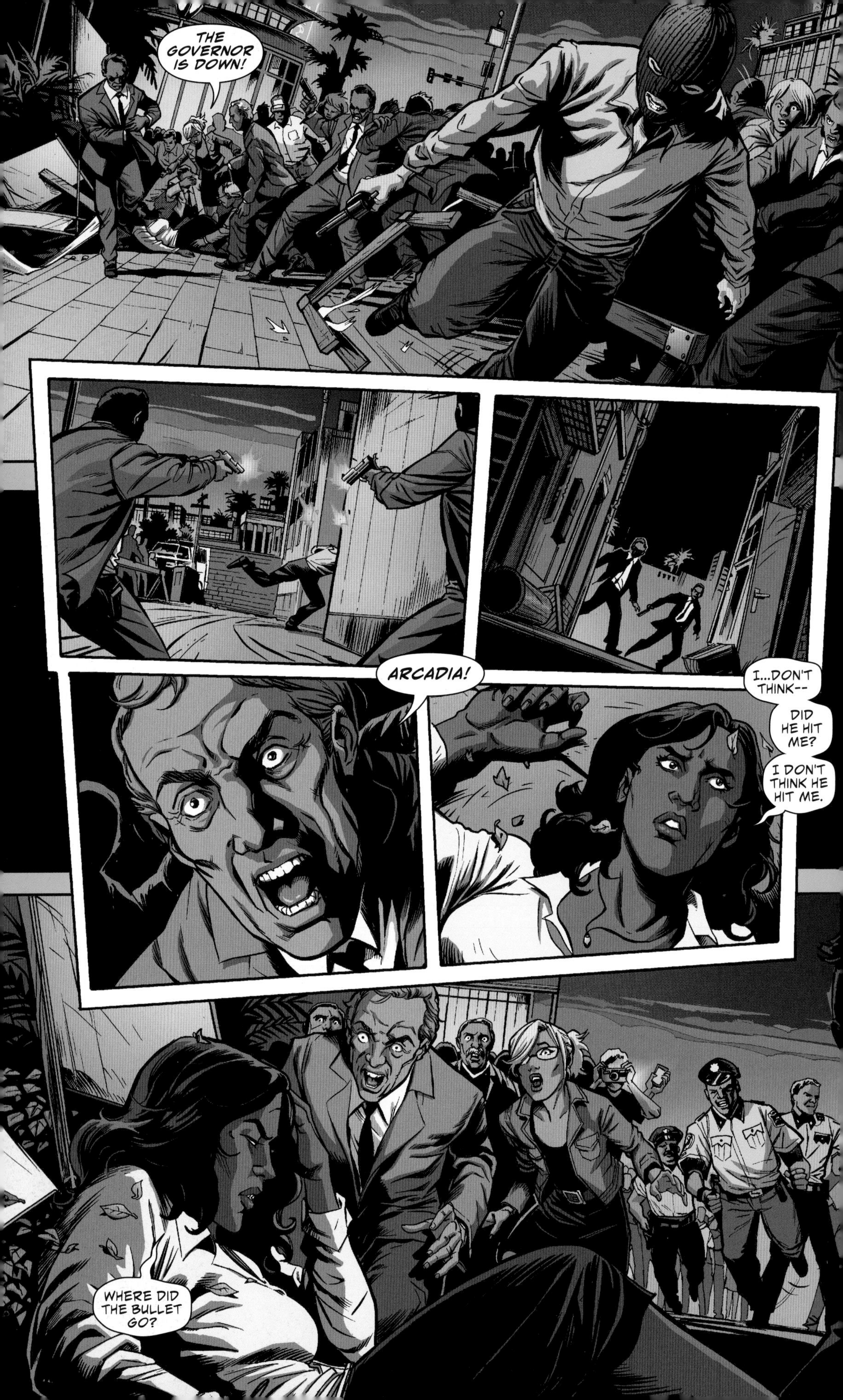
THE GOVERNOR IS DOWN!
ARCADIA!
I...DON'T THINK--
DID HE HIT ME?
I DON'T THINK HE HIT ME.
WHERE DID THE BULLET GO?

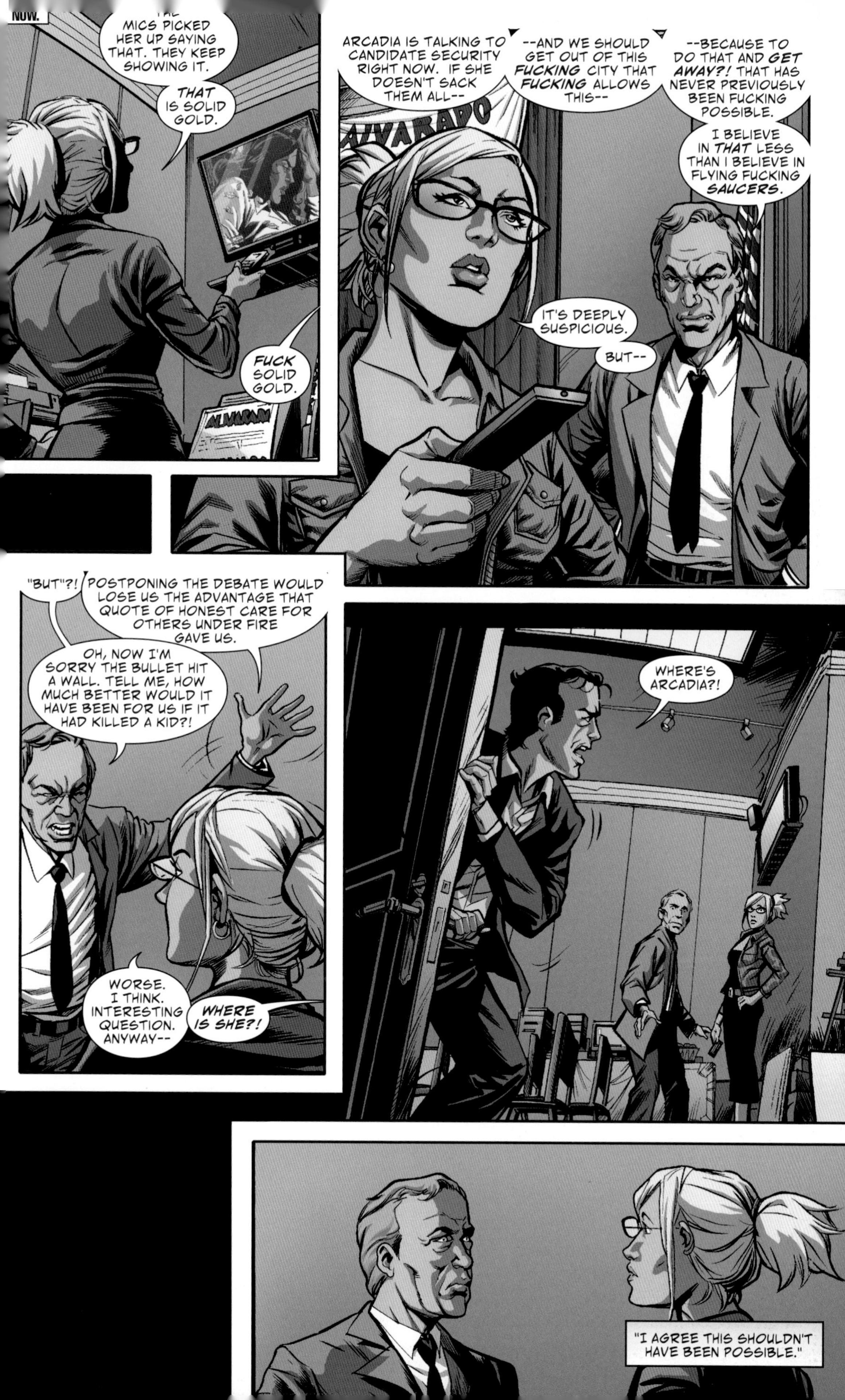
NOW.
MICS PICKED HER UP SAYING THAT. THEY KEEP SHOWING IT.
THAT IS SOLID GOLD.
FUCK SOLID GOLD.
ARCADIA IS TALKING TO CANDIDATE SECURITY RIGHT NOW. IF SHE DOESN'T SACK THEM ALL--
--AND WE SHOULD GET OUT OF THIS FUCKING CITY THAT FUCKING ALLOWS THIS--
--BECAUSE TO DO THAT AND GET AWAY?! THAT HAS NEVER PREVIOUSLY BEEN FUCKING POSSIBLE.
I BELIEVE IN THAT LESS THAN I BELIEVE IN FLYING FUCKING SAUCERS.
IT'S DEEPLY SUSPICIOUS.
BUT--
"BUT"?!
POSTPONING THE DEBATE WOULD LOSE US THE ADVANTAGE THAT QUOTE OF HONEST CARE FOR OTHERS UNDER FIRE GAVE US.
OH, NOW I'M SORRY THE BULLET HIT A WALL. TELL ME, HOW MUCH BETTER WOULD IT HAVE BEEN FOR US IF IT HAD KILLED A KID?!
WORSE. I THINK. INTERESTING QUESTION. ANYWAY--
WHERE IS SHE?!
WHERE'S ARCADIA?!
"I AGREE THIS SHOULDN'T HAVE BEEN POSSIBLE."

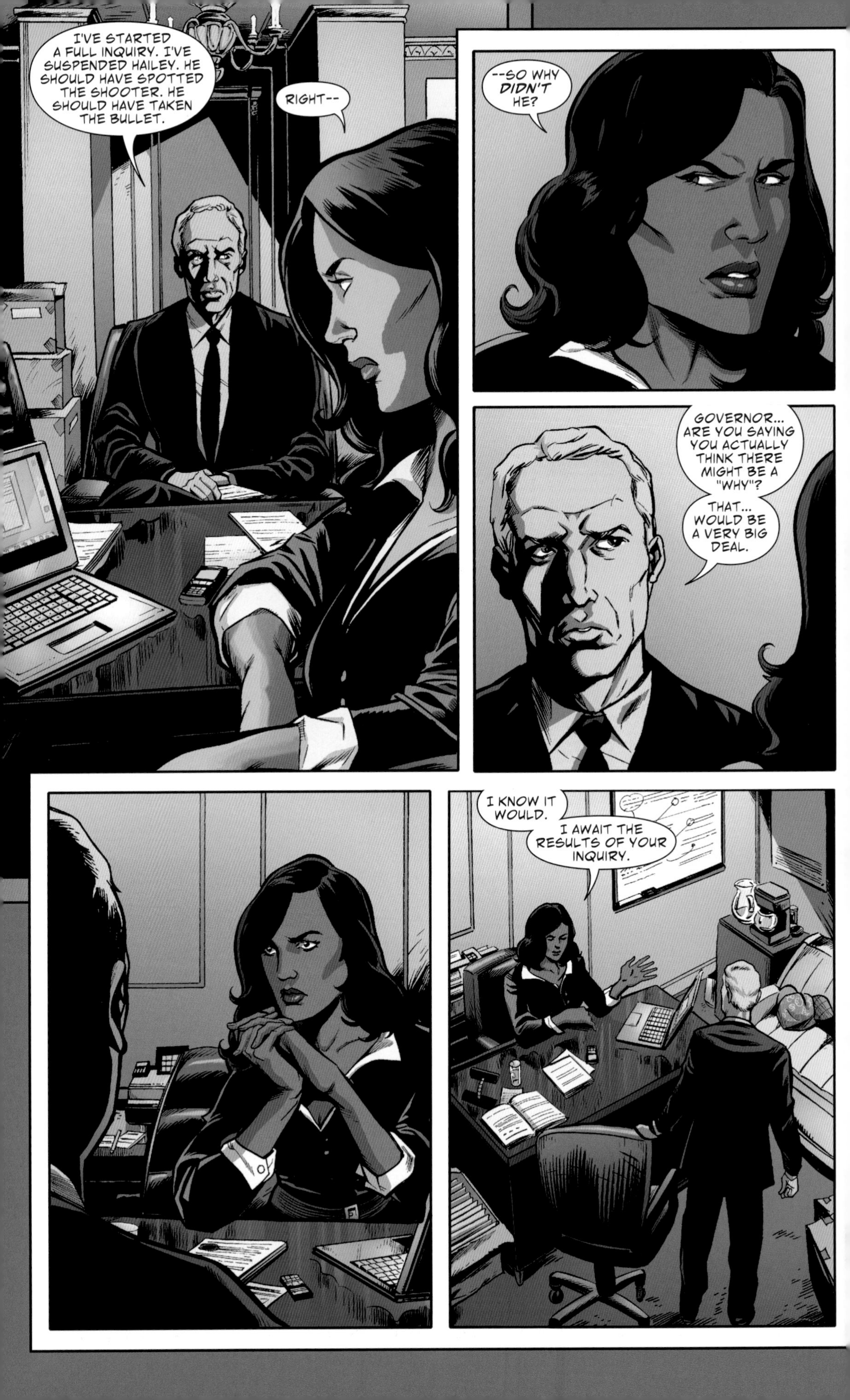

I'VE STARTED A FULL INQUIRY. I'VE SUSPENDED HAILEY. HE SHOULD HAVE SPOTTED THE SHOOTER. HE SHOULD HAVE TAKEN THE BULLET.
RIGHT--
--SO WHY *DIDN'T* HE?
GOVERNOR... ARE YOU SAYING YOU ACTUALLY THINK THERE MIGHT BE A "WHY"?
THAT... WOULD BE A VERY BIG DEAL.
I KNOW IT WOULD.
I AWAIT THE RESULTS OF YOUR INQUIRY.

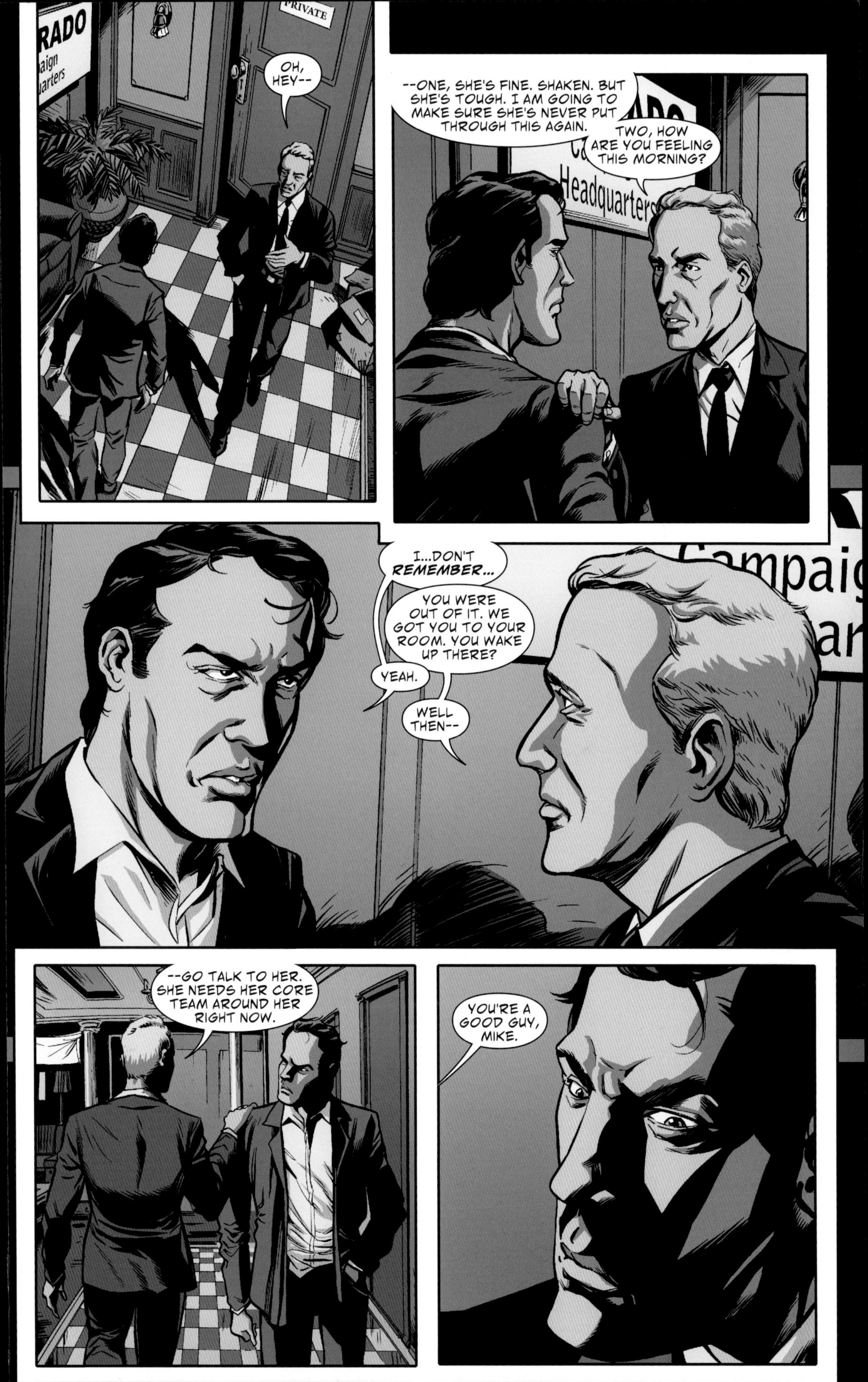
RADO
aign
quarters
PRIVATE
OH, HEY--
--ONE, SHE'S FINE. SHAKEN. BUT SHE'S TOUGH. I AM GOING TO MAKE SURE SHE'S NEVER PUT THROUGH THIS AGAIN.
TWO, HOW ARE YOU FEELING THIS MORNING?
Headquarters
I...DON'T *REMEMBER...*
YOU WERE OUT OF IT. WE GOT YOU TO YOUR ROOM. YOU WAKE UP THERE?
YEAH.
WELL THEN--
Campaig
--GO TALK TO HER. SHE NEEDS HER CORE TEAM AROUND HER RIGHT NOW.
YOU'RE A GOOD GUY, MIKE.

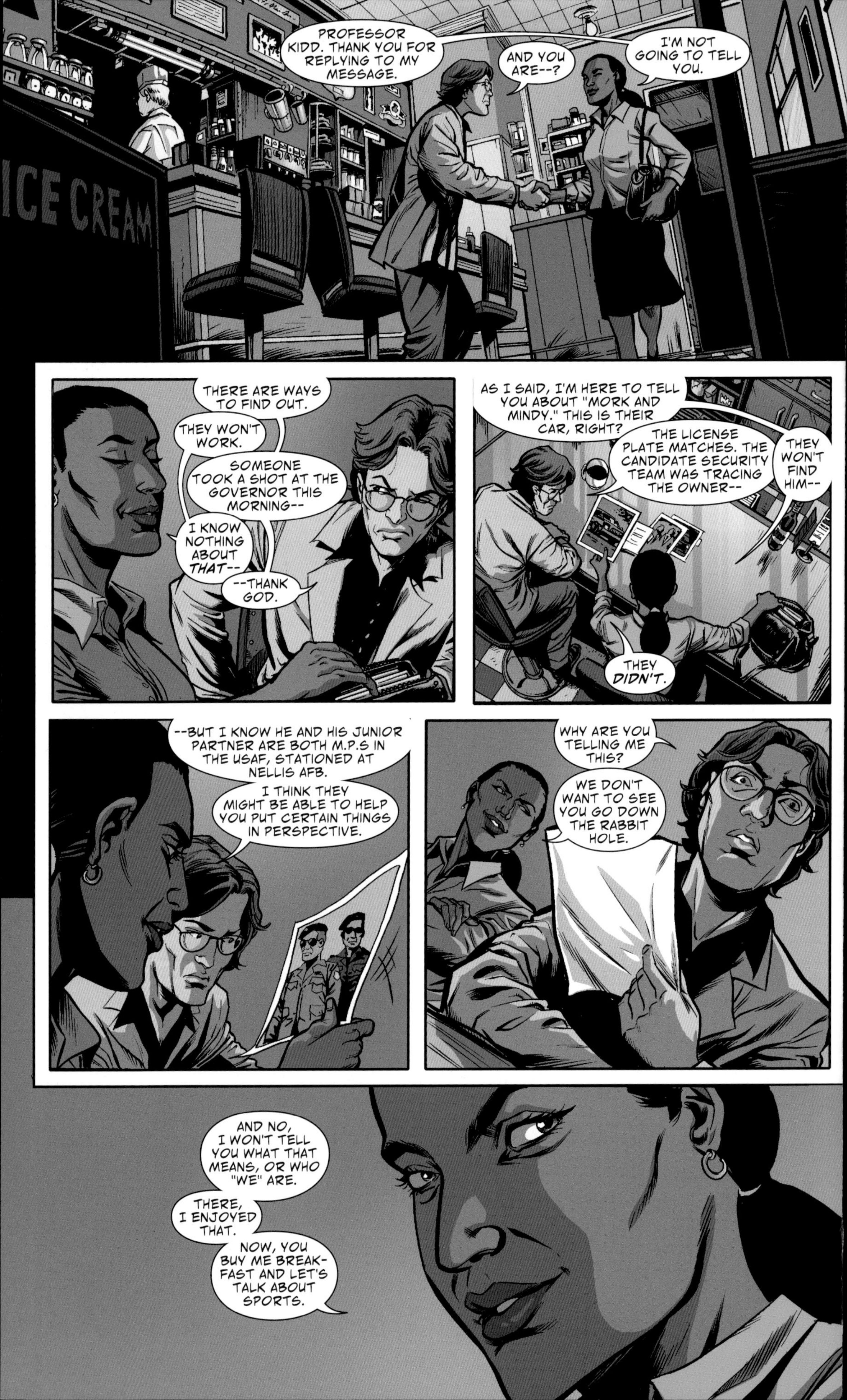
ICE CREAM
PROFESSOR KIDD. THANK YOU FOR REPLYING TO MY MESSAGE.
AND YOU ARE--?
I'M NOT GOING TO TELL YOU.
THERE ARE WAYS TO FIND OUT.
THEY WON'T WORK.
SOMEONE TOOK A SHOT AT THE GOVERNOR THIS MORNING--
I KNOW NOTHING ABOUT *THAT*--
--THANK GOD.
AS I SAID, I'M HERE TO TELL YOU ABOUT "MORK AND MINDY." THIS IS THEIR CAR, RIGHT?
THE LICENSE PLATE MATCHES. THE CANDIDATE SECURITY TEAM WAS TRACING THE OWNER--
THEY WON'T FIND HIM--
THEY *DIDN'T*.
--BUT I KNOW HE AND HIS JUNIOR PARTNER ARE BOTH M.P.S IN THE USAF, STATIONED AT NELLIS AFB.
I THINK THEY MIGHT BE ABLE TO HELP YOU PUT CERTAIN THINGS IN PERSPECTIVE.
WHY ARE YOU TELLING ME THIS?
WE DON'T WANT TO SEE YOU GO DOWN THE RABBIT HOLE.
AND NO, I WON'T TELL YOU WHAT THAT MEANS, OR WHO "WE" ARE.
THERE, I ENJOYED THAT.
NOW, YOU BUY ME BREAKFAST AND LET'S TALK ABOUT SPORTS.

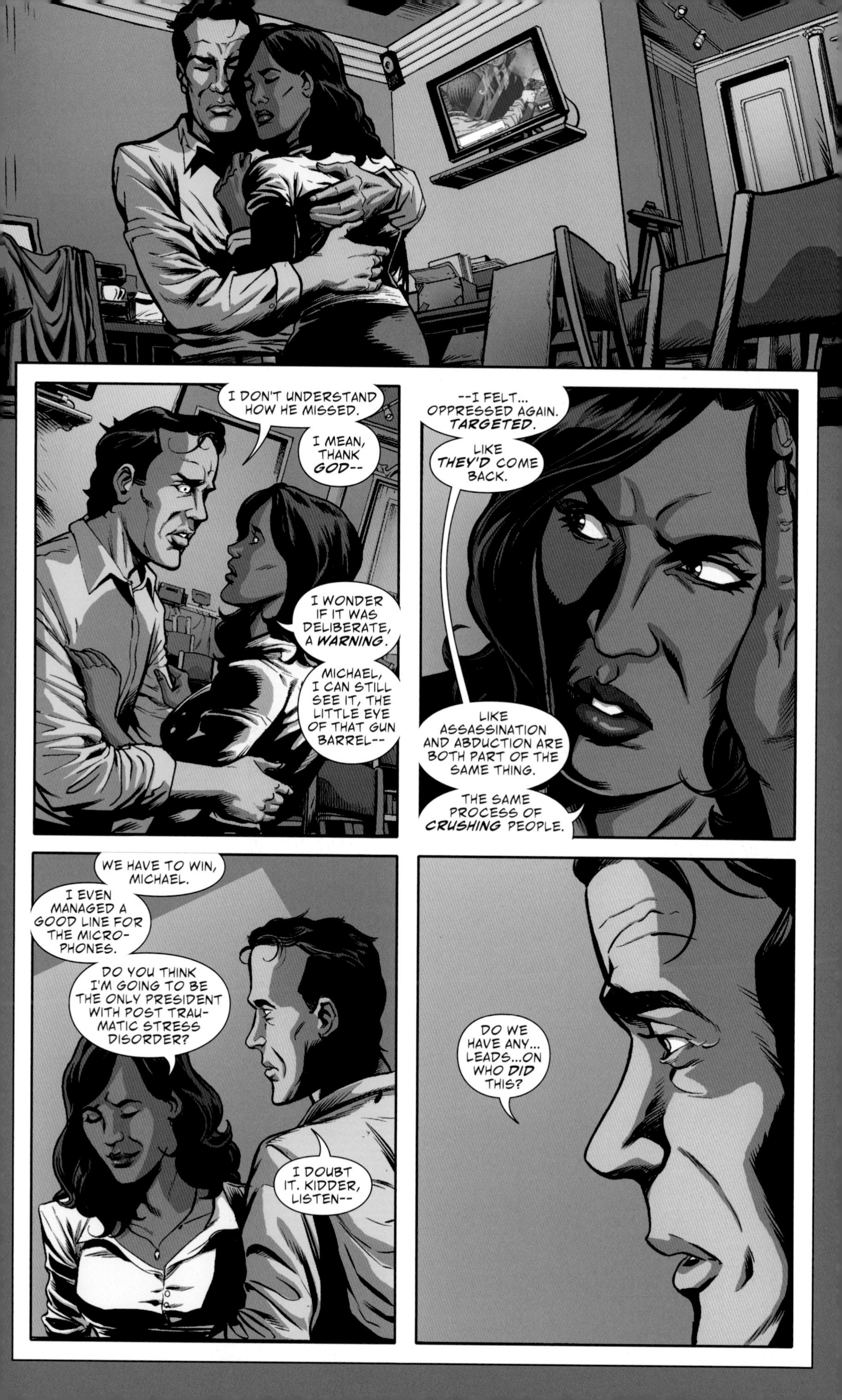
I DON'T UNDERSTAND HOW HE MISSED.
I MEAN, THANK *GOD*--
I WONDER IF IT WAS DELIBERATE, A *WARNING*.
MICHAEL, I CAN STILL SEE IT, THE LITTLE EYE OF THAT GUN BARREL--
--I FELT... OPPRESSED AGAIN. *TARGETED*.
LIKE *THEY'D* COME BACK.
LIKE ASSASSINATION AND ABDUCTION ARE BOTH PART OF THE SAME THING.
THE SAME PROCESS OF *CRUSHING* PEOPLE.
WE HAVE TO WIN, MICHAEL.
I EVEN MANAGED A GOOD LINE FOR THE MICRO-PHONES.
DO YOU THINK I'M GOING TO BE THE ONLY PRESIDENT WITH POST TRAU-MATIC STRESS DISORDER?
I DOUBT IT. KIDDER, LISTEN--
DO WE HAVE ANY... LEADS...ON WHO *DID* THIS?

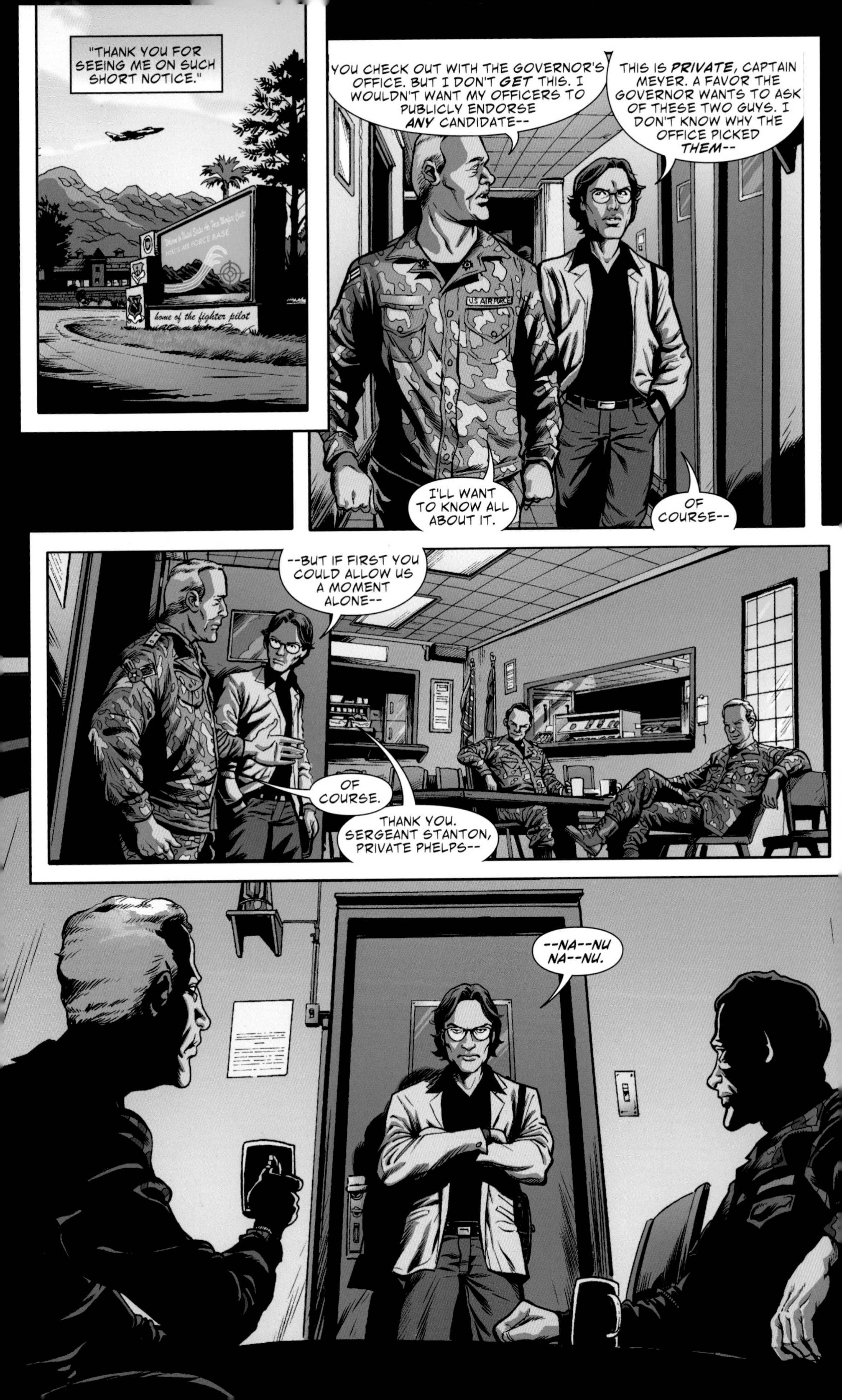
"THANK YOU FOR SEEING ME ON SUCH SHORT NOTICE."
home of the fighter pilot
YOU CHECK OUT WITH THE GOVERNOR'S OFFICE. BUT I DON'T GET THIS. I WOULDN'T WANT MY OFFICERS TO PUBLICLY ENDORSE ANY CANDIDATE--
THIS IS PRIVATE, CAPTAIN MEYER. A FAVOR THE GOVERNOR WANTS TO ASK OF THESE TWO GUYS. I DON'T KNOW WHY THE OFFICE PICKED THEM--
U.S. AIR FORCE
I'LL WANT TO KNOW ALL ABOUT IT.
OF COURSE--
--BUT IF FIRST YOU COULD ALLOW US A MOMENT ALONE--
OF COURSE.
THANK YOU. SERGEANT STANTON, PRIVATE PHELPS--
--NA--NU NA--NU.

WHAT-- WHAT DO YOU--?

WHAT'S THIS ABOUT?

YEAH, PLAYING DUMB ABOUT THIS...

...NOT A WAY FORWARD, GUYS.

THE GOVERNOR GOT INFORMATION FROM A POWERFUL SUPPORTER.

AND YOU HAVE NO IDEA WHAT KIND OF *RESOURCES* A CANDIDATE HAS ACCESSS TO. ALMOST *PRESIDENTIAL* CLOUT.

BUT THIS *ISN'T* SOMETHING WE NEED TO SHARE WITH YOUR SUPERIOR OFFICER. NOT YET.

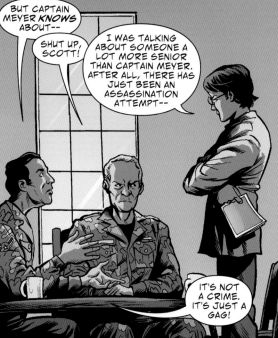

BUT CAPTAIN MEYER *KNOWS* ABOUT--

SHUT UP, SCOTT!

I WAS TALKING ABOUT SOMEONE A LOT MORE SENIOR THAN CAPTAIN MEYER. AFTER ALL, THERE HAS JUST BEEN AN ASSASSINATION ATTEMPT--

IT'S NOT A CRIME. IT'S JUST A GAG!

IT MAY OR MAY NOT BE A CRIME.

LISTEN, RIGHT NOW, AS YOU'LL APPRECIATE, THIS IS VERY MUCH A SIDE ISSUE FOR THE GOVERNOR.

WE DON'T WANT TO CHANGE THE WAY YOU GUYS DO YOUR BUSINESS. JUST TELL ME EVERYTHING--

--WE'LL CALM EVERYONE DOWN AND KEEP YOUR NAMES OUT OF IT. OKAY?

WELL... IT'S NOT LIKE WE *STARTED* IT...

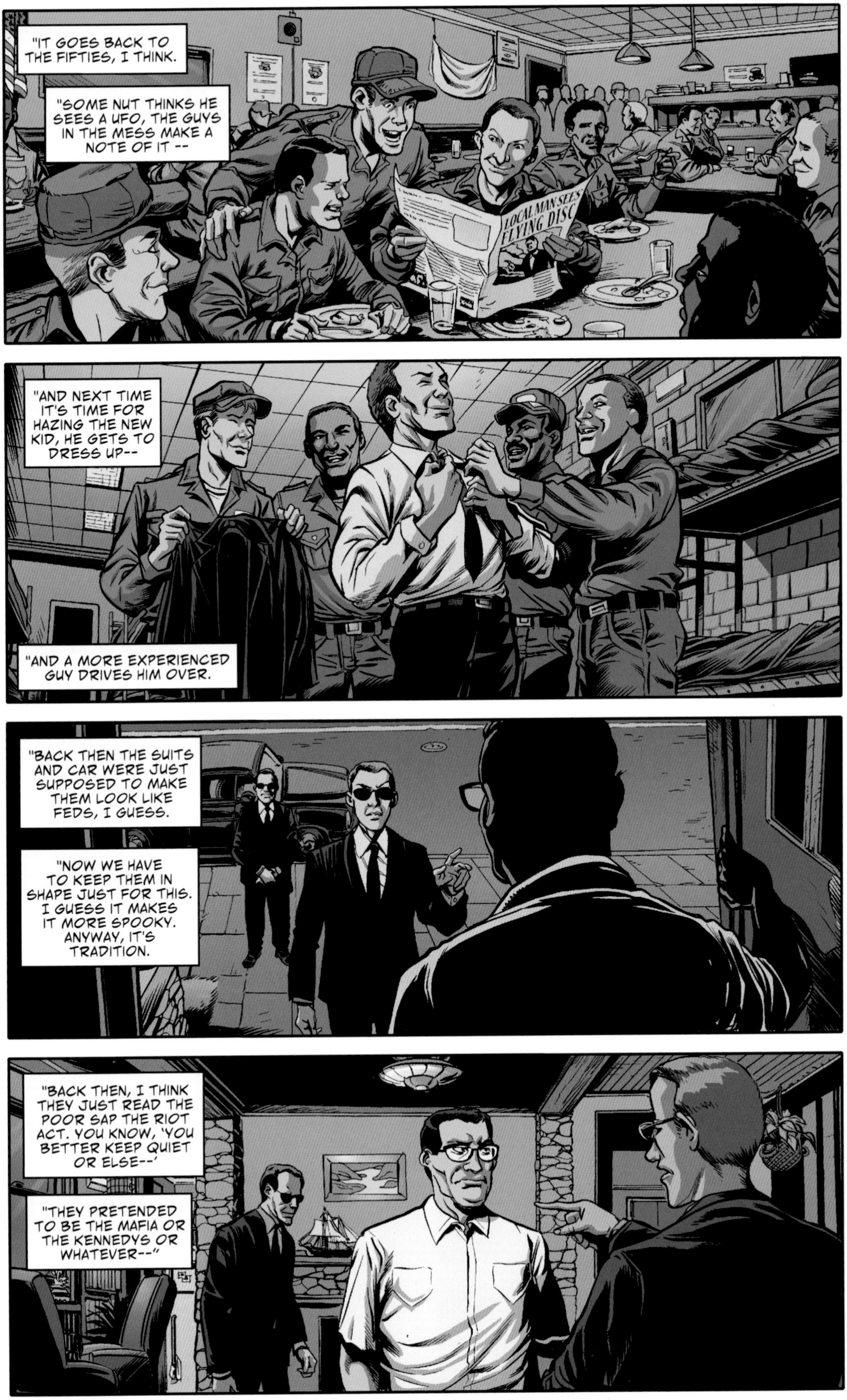
"IT GOES BACK TO THE FIFTIES, I THINK.
"SOME NUT THINKS HE SEES A UFO, THE GUYS IN THE MESS MAKE A NOTE OF IT --
LOCAL MAN SEES FLYING DISC
"AND NEXT TIME IT'S TIME FOR HAZING THE NEW KID, HE GETS TO DRESS UP--
"AND A MORE EXPERIENCED GUY DRIVES HIM OVER.
"BACK THEN THE SUITS AND CAR WERE JUST SUPPOSED TO MAKE THEM LOOK LIKE FEDS, I GUESS.
"NOW WE HAVE TO KEEP THEM IN SHAPE JUST FOR THIS. I GUESS IT MAKES IT MORE SPOOKY. ANYWAY, IT'S TRADITION.
"BACK THEN, I THINK THEY JUST READ THE POOR SAP THE RIOT ACT. YOU KNOW, 'YOU BETTER KEEP QUIET OR ELSE--'
"THEY PRETENDED TO BE THE MAFIA OR THE KENNEDYS OR WHATEVER--"

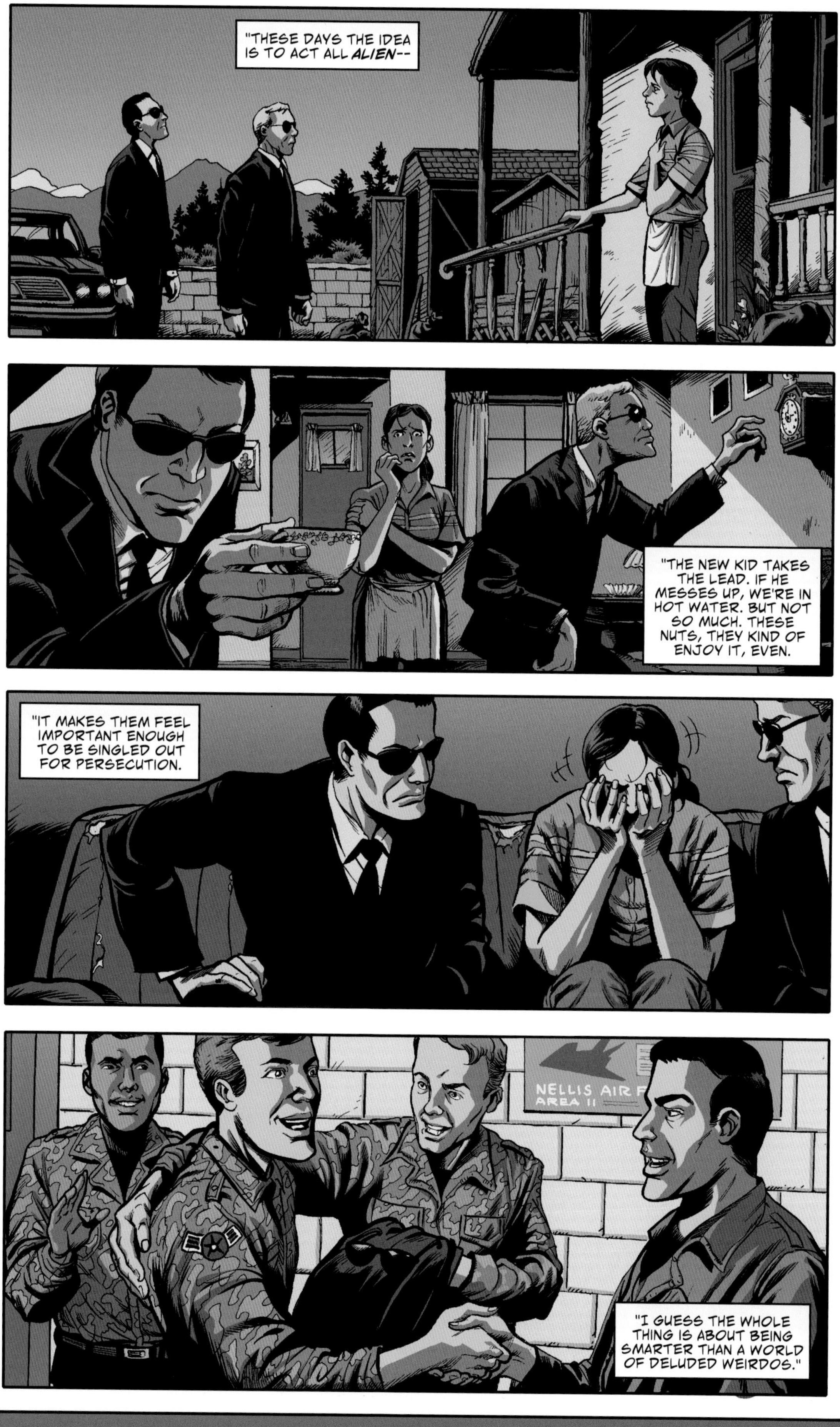
"THESE DAYS THE IDEA IS TO ACT ALL *ALIEN*--
"THE NEW KID TAKES THE LEAD. IF HE MESSES UP, WE'RE IN HOT WATER. BUT NOT SO MUCH. THESE NUTS, THEY KIND OF ENJOY IT, EVEN.
"IT MAKES THEM FEEL IMPORTANT ENOUGH TO BE SINGLED OUT FOR PERSECUTION.
NELLIS AIR F
AREA 11
"I GUESS THE WHOLE THING IS ABOUT BEING SMARTER THAN A WORLD OF DELUDED WEIRDOS."

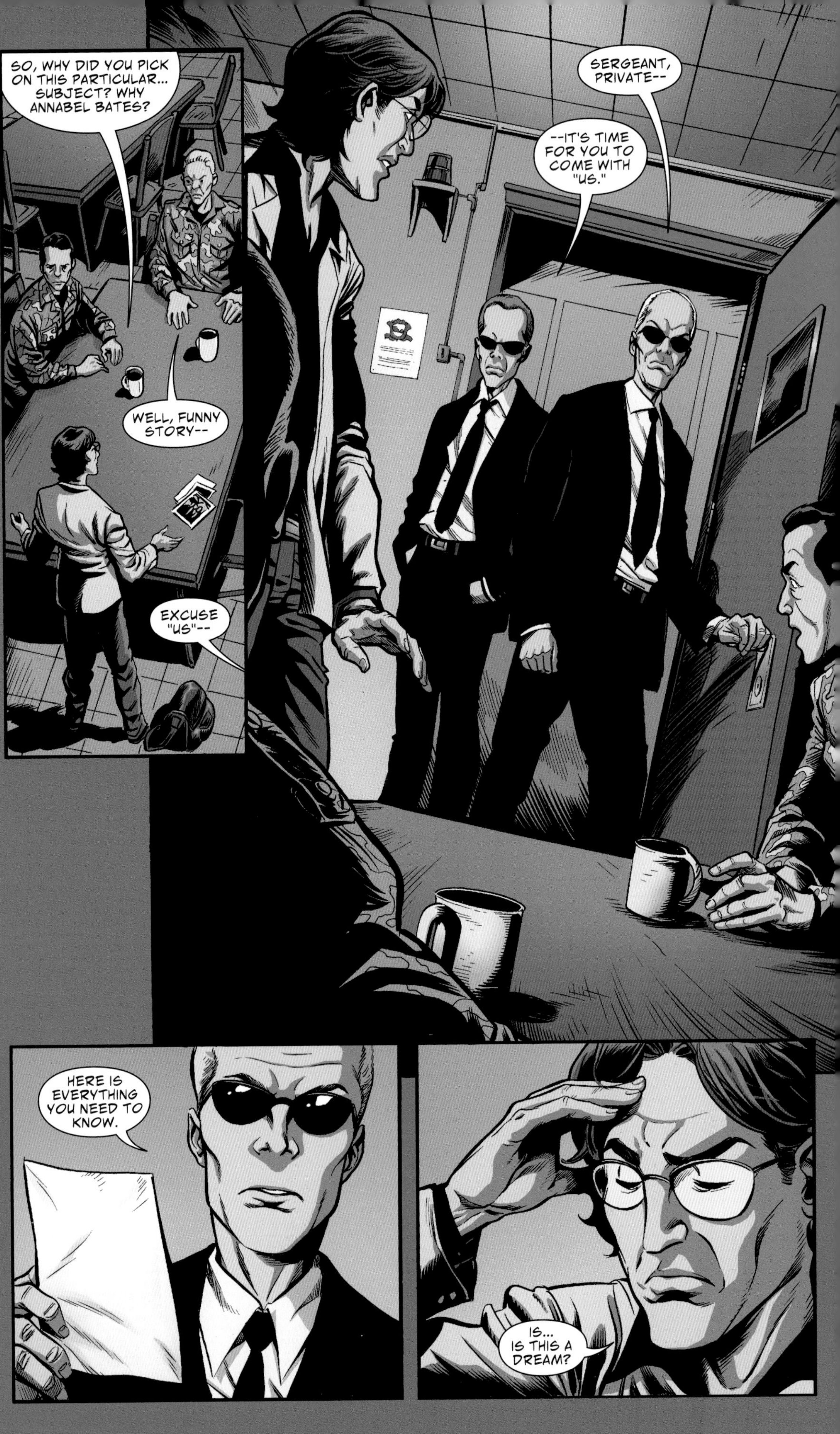
SO, WHY DID YOU PICK ON THIS PARTICULAR... SUBJECT? WHY ANNABEL BATES?
WELL, FUNNY STORY--
EXCUSE "US"--
SERGEANT, PRIVATE--
--IT'S TIME FOR YOU TO COME WITH "US."
HERE IS EVERYTHING YOU NEED TO KNOW.
IS... IS THIS A DREAM?

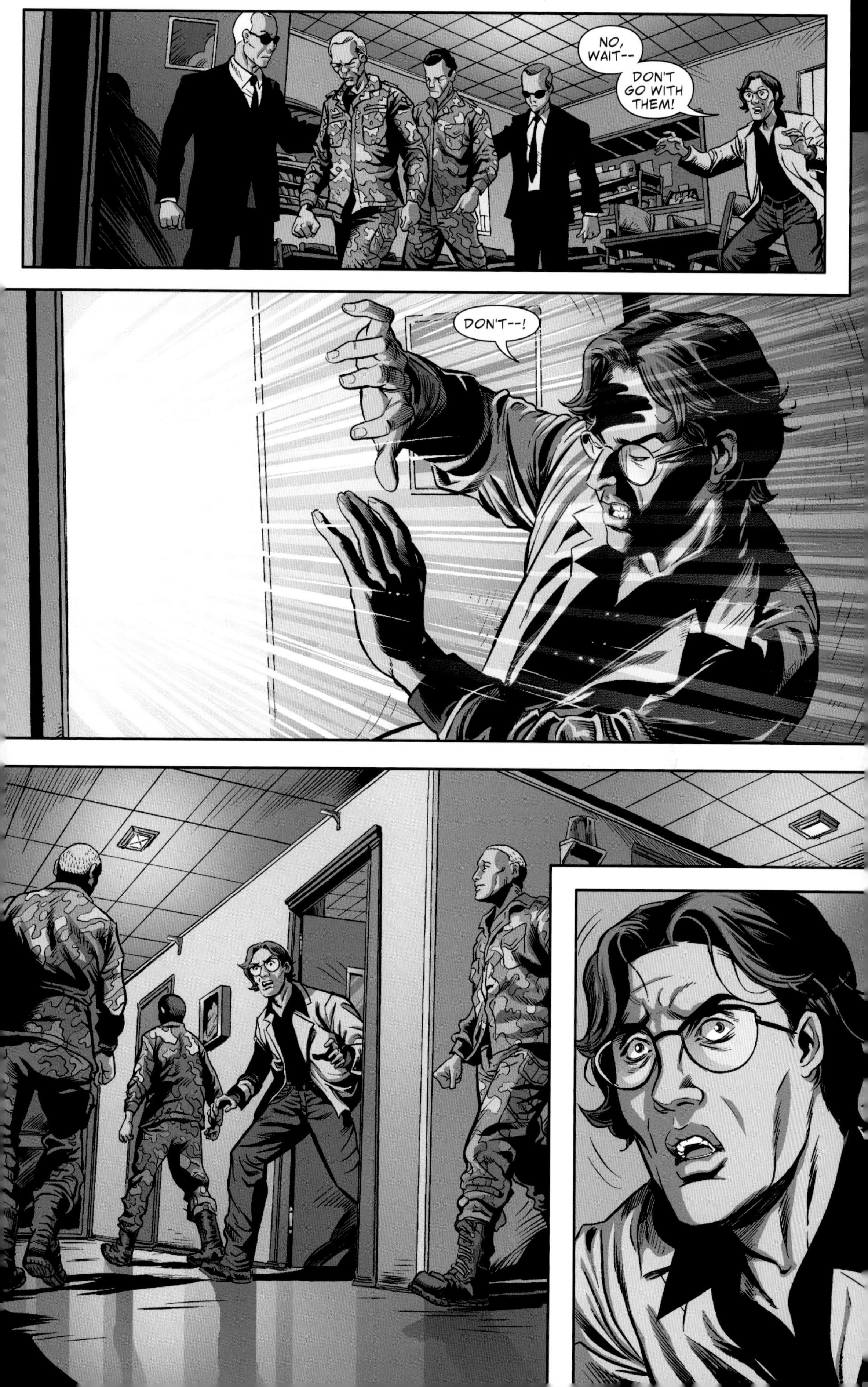
NO, WAIT--
DON'T GO WITH THEM!
DON'T--!

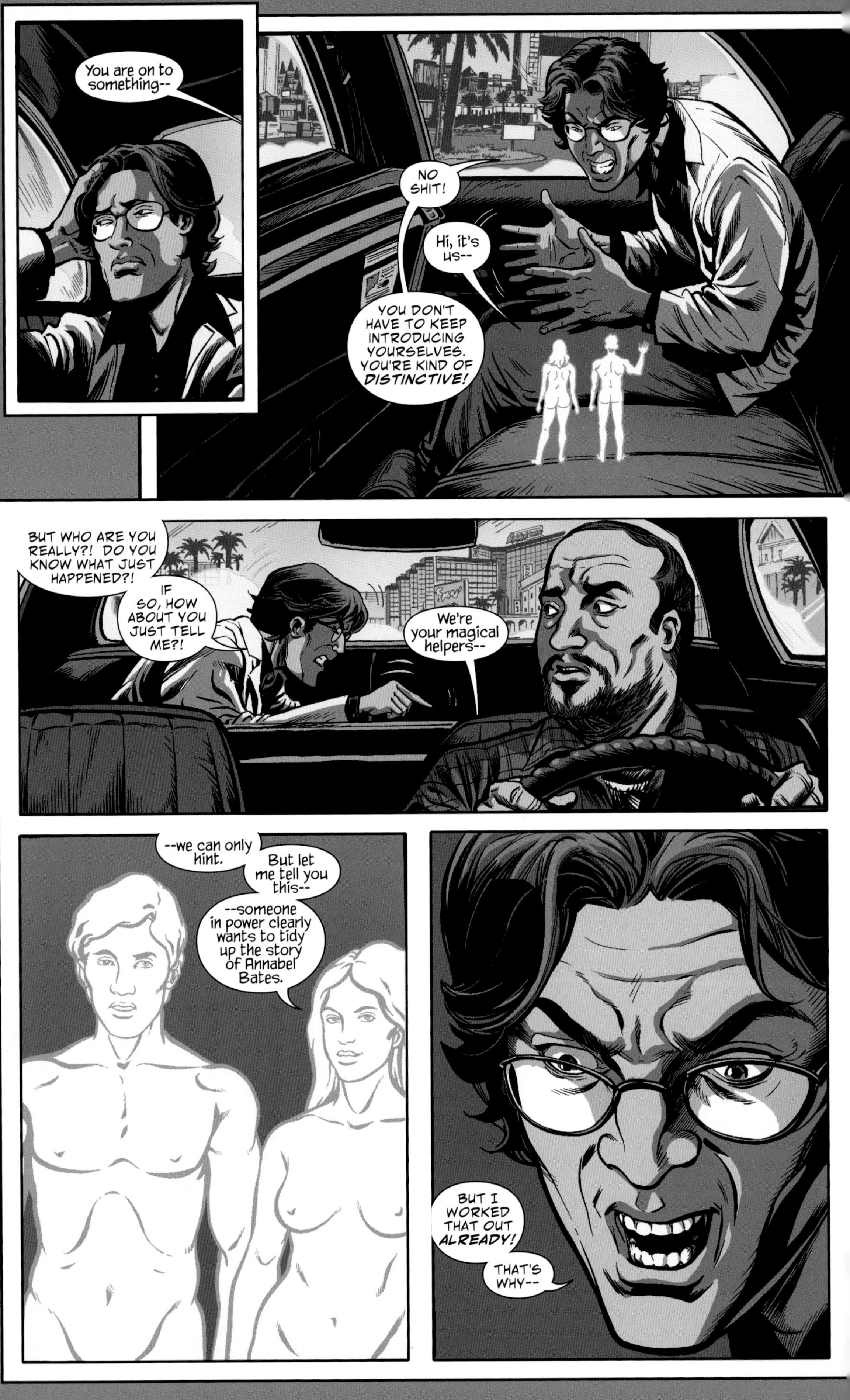
You are on to something--
NO SHIT!
Hi, it's us--
YOU DON'T HAVE TO KEEP INTRODUCING YOURSELVES. YOU'RE KIND OF *DISTINCTIVE!*
BUT WHO ARE YOU REALLY?! DO YOU KNOW WHAT JUST HAPPENED?!
IF SO, HOW ABOUT YOU JUST TELL ME?!
We're your magical helpers--
--we can only hint.
But let me tell you this--
--someone in power clearly wants to tidy up the story of Annabel Bates.
BUT I WORKED THAT OUT *ALREADY!*
THAT'S WHY--

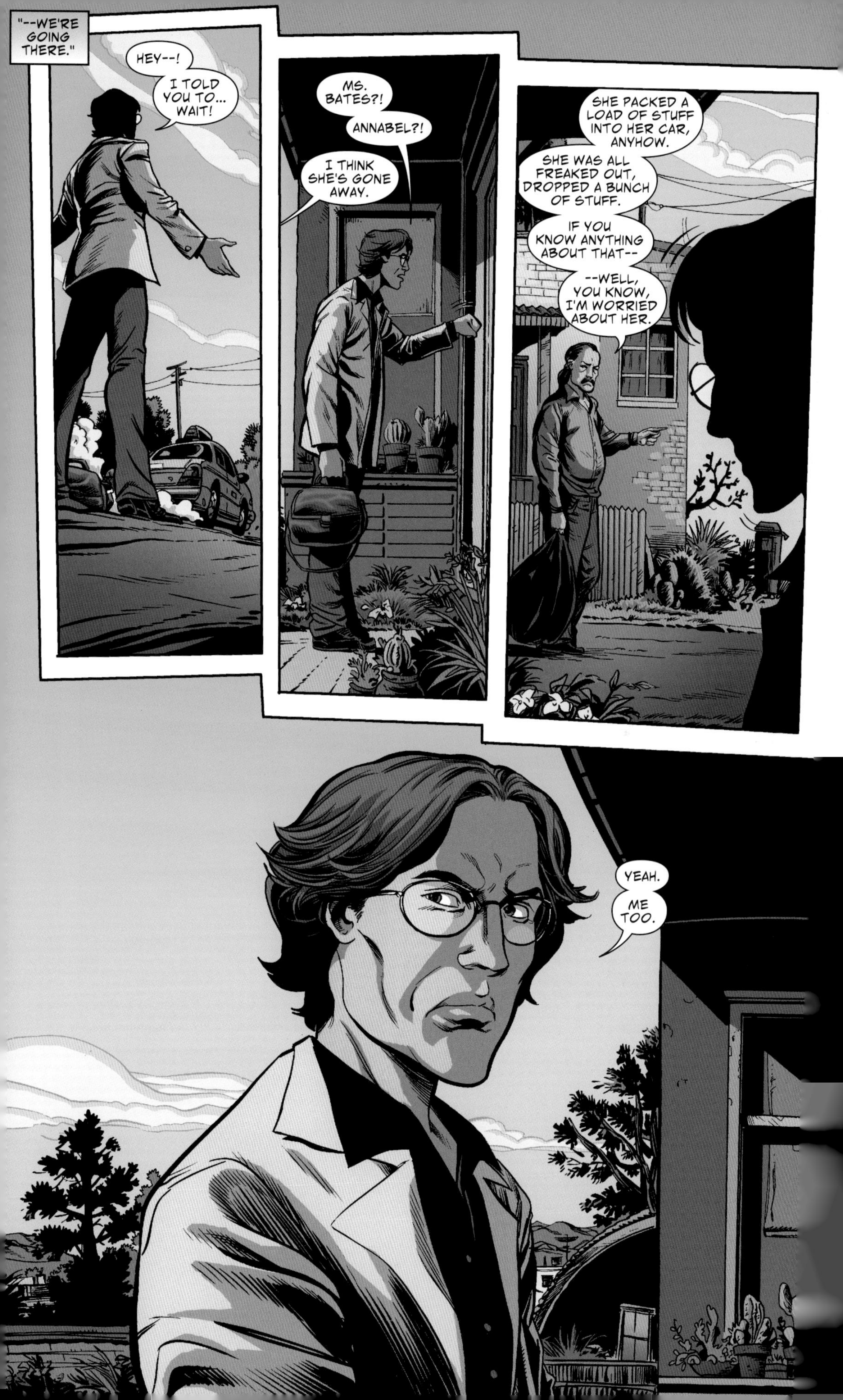
"--WE'RE GOING THERE."
HEY--!
I TOLD YOU TO... WAIT!
MS. BATES?!
ANNABEL?!
I THINK SHE'S GONE AWAY.
SHE PACKED A LOAD OF STUFF INTO HER CAR, ANYHOW.
SHE WAS ALL FREAKED OUT, DROPPED A BUNCH OF STUFF.
IF YOU KNOW ANYTHING ABOUT THAT--
--WELL, YOU KNOW, I'M WORRIED ABOUT HER.
YEAH.
ME TOO.

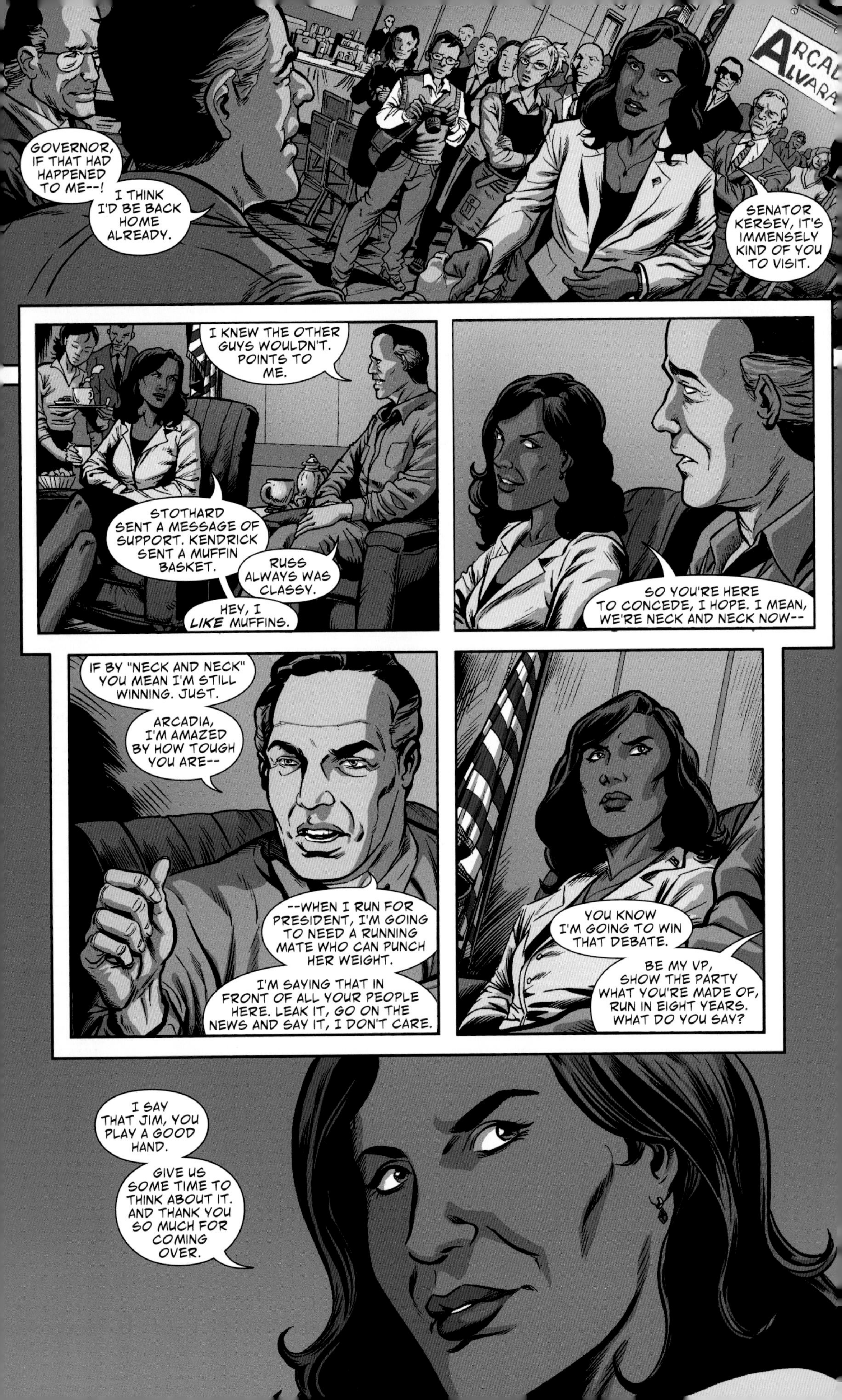

ARCADIA ALVARA
GOVERNOR, IF THAT HAD HAPPENED TO ME--!
I THINK I'D BE BACK HOME ALREADY.
SENATOR KERSEY, IT'S IMMENSELY KIND OF YOU TO VISIT.
I KNEW THE OTHER GUYS WOULDN'T. POINTS TO ME.
STOTHARD SENT A MESSAGE OF SUPPORT. KENDRICK SENT A MUFFIN BASKET.
RUSS ALWAYS WAS CLASSY.
HEY, I *LIKE* MUFFINS.
SO YOU'RE HERE TO CONCEDE, I HOPE. I MEAN, WE'RE NECK AND NECK NOW--
IF BY "NECK AND NECK" YOU MEAN I'M STILL WINNING. JUST.
ARCADIA, I'M AMAZED BY HOW TOUGH YOU ARE--
--WHEN I RUN FOR PRESIDENT, I'M GOING TO NEED A RUNNING MATE WHO CAN PUNCH HER WEIGHT.
I'M SAYING THAT IN FRONT OF ALL YOUR PEOPLE HERE. LEAK IT, GO ON THE NEWS AND SAY IT, I DON'T CARE.
YOU KNOW I'M GOING TO WIN THAT DEBATE.
BE MY VP, SHOW THE PARTY WHAT YOU'RE MADE OF, RUN IN EIGHT YEARS. WHAT DO YOU SAY?
I SAY THAT JIM, YOU PLAY A GOOD HAND.
GIVE US SOME TIME TO THINK ABOUT IT. AND THANK YOU SO MUCH FOR COMING OVER.

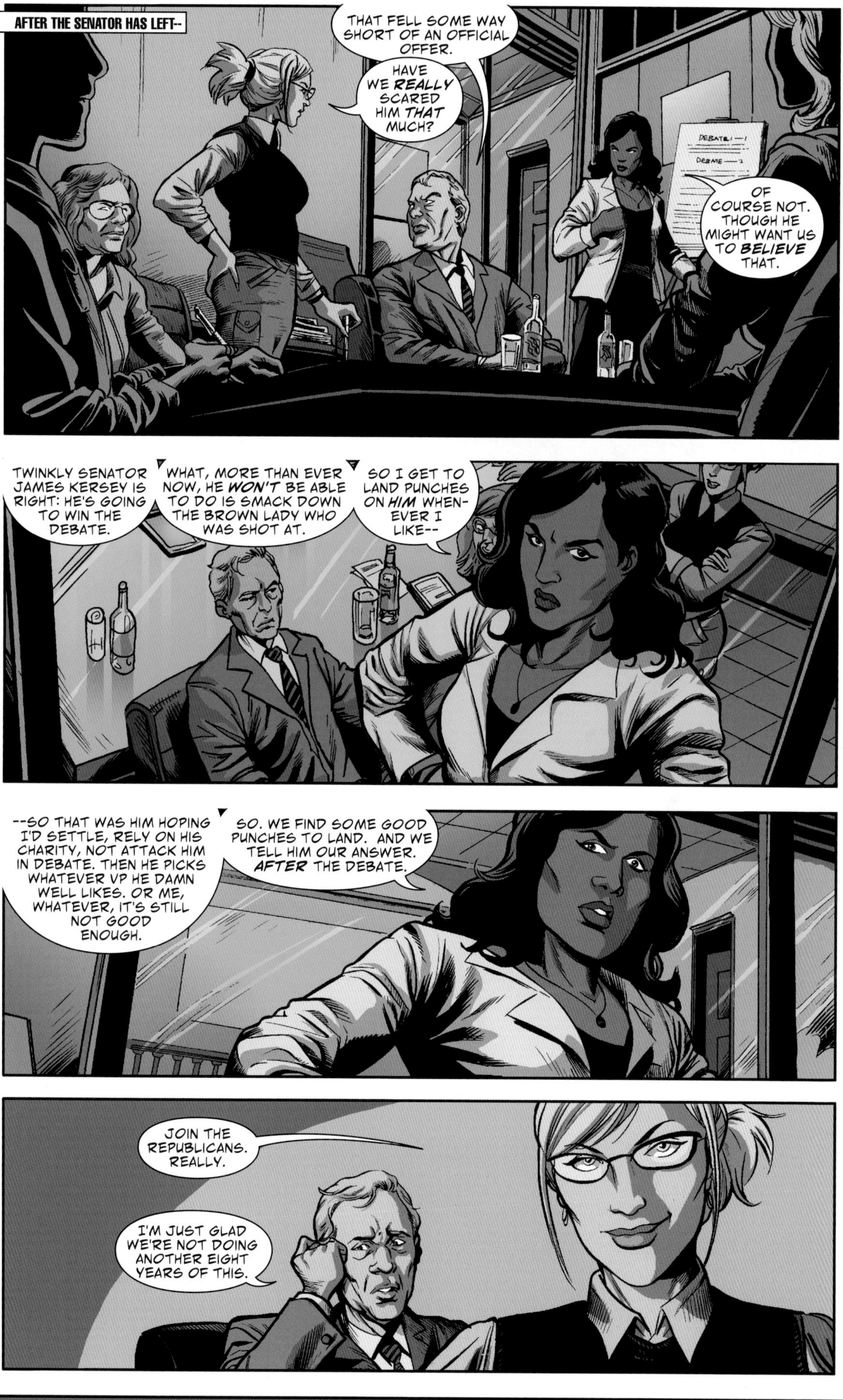
AFTER THE SENATOR HAS LEFT--
THAT FELL SOME WAY SHORT OF AN OFFICIAL OFFER.
HAVE WE REALLY SCARED HIM THAT MUCH?
OF COURSE NOT. THOUGH HE MIGHT WANT US TO BELIEVE THAT.
TWINKLY SENATOR JAMES KERSEY IS RIGHT: HE'S GOING TO WIN THE DEBATE.
WHAT, MORE THAN EVER NOW, HE WON'T BE ABLE TO DO IS SMACK DOWN THE BROWN LADY WHO WAS SHOT AT.
SO I GET TO LAND PUNCHES ON HIM WHENEVER I LIKE--
--SO THAT WAS HIM HOPING I'D SETTLE, RELY ON HIS CHARITY, NOT ATTACK HIM IN DEBATE. THEN HE PICKS WHATEVER VP HE DAMN WELL LIKES. OR ME, WHATEVER, IT'S STILL NOT GOOD ENOUGH.
SO. WE FIND SOME GOOD PUNCHES TO LAND. AND WE TELL HIM OUR ANSWER. AFTER THE DEBATE.
JOIN THE REPUBLICANS. REALLY.
I'M JUST GLAD WE'RE NOT DOING ANOTHER EIGHT YEARS OF THIS.

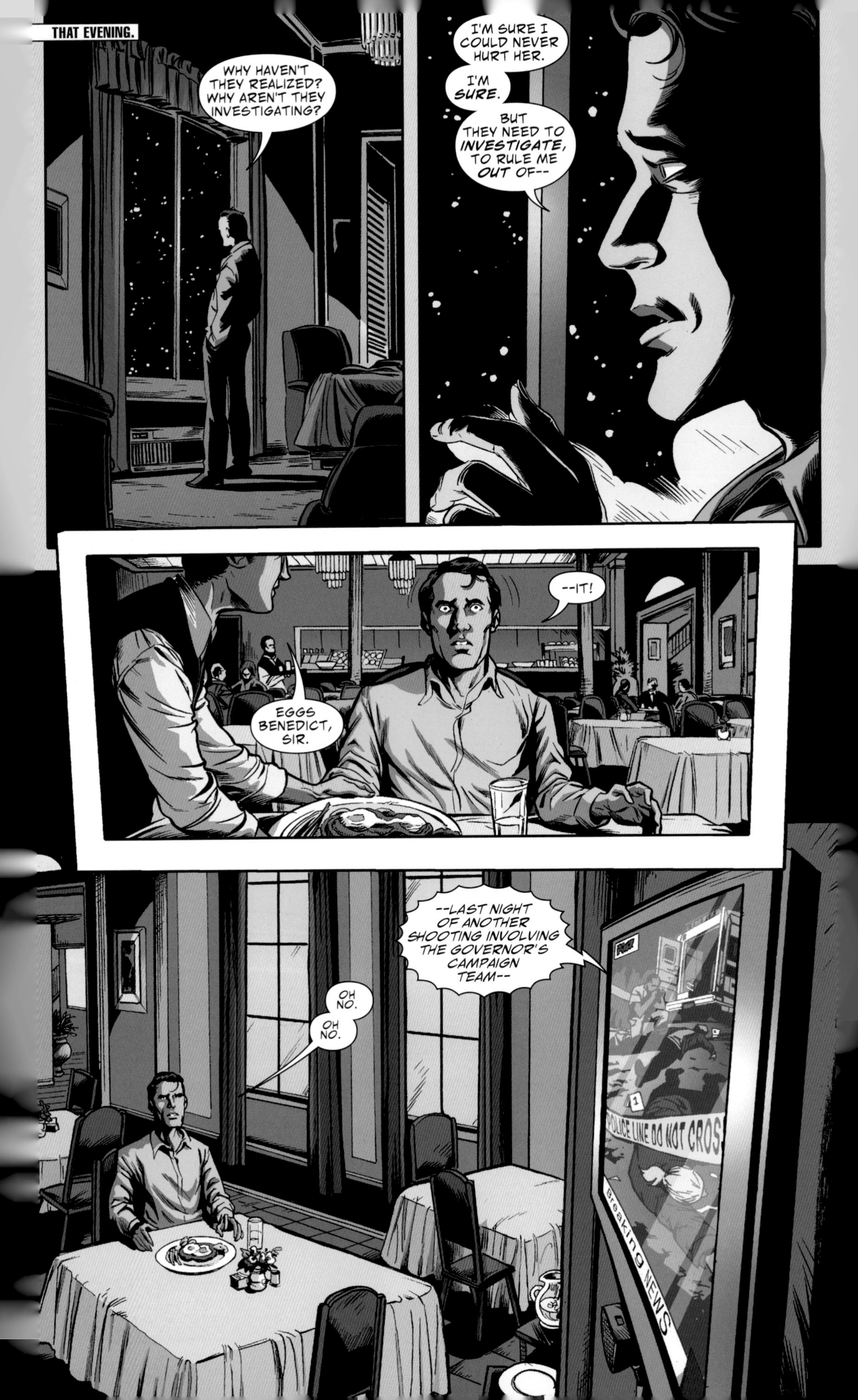
THAT EVENING.
WHY HAVEN'T THEY REALIZED? WHY AREN'T THEY INVESTIGATING?
I'M SURE I COULD NEVER HURT HER.
I'M SURE.
BUT THEY NEED TO INVESTIGATE, TO RULE ME OUT OF--
--IT!
EGGS BENEDICT, SIR.
--LAST NIGHT OF ANOTHER SHOOTING INVOLVING THE GOVERNOR'S CAMPAIGN TEAM--
OH NO.
OH NO.
POLICE LINE DO NOT CROS
Breaking NEWS

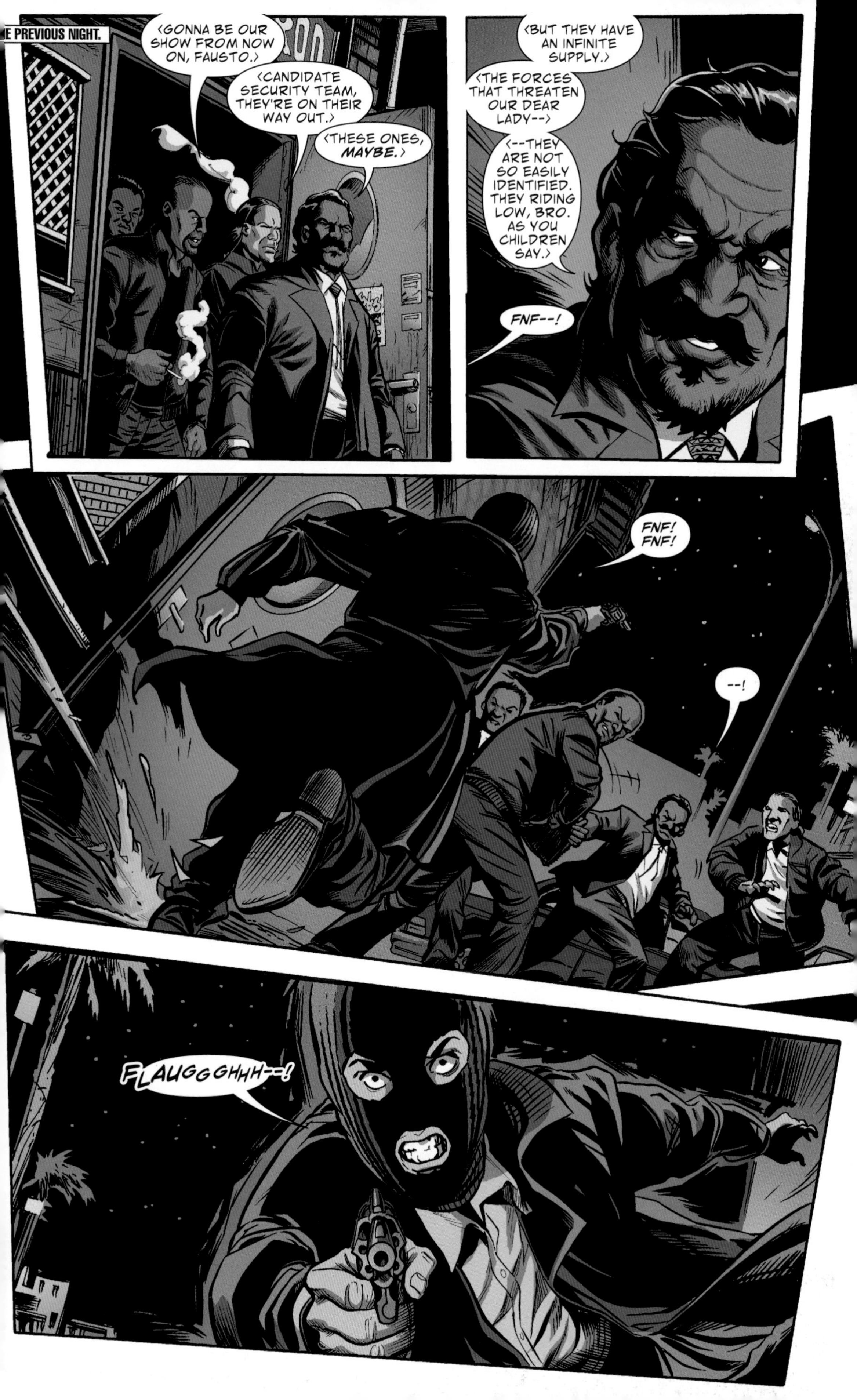
E PREVIOUS NIGHT.
‹GONNA BE OUR SHOW FROM NOW ON, FAUSTO.›
‹CANDIDATE SECURITY TEAM, THEY'RE ON THEIR WAY OUT.›
‹THESE ONES, MAYBE.›
‹BUT THEY HAVE AN INFINITE SUPPLY.›
‹THE FORCES THAT THREATEN OUR DEAR LADY--›
‹--THEY ARE NOT SO EASILY IDENTIFIED. THEY RIDING LOW, BRO. AS YOU CHILDREN SAY.›
FNF--!
FNF! FNF!
--!
FLAUGGGHHH--!

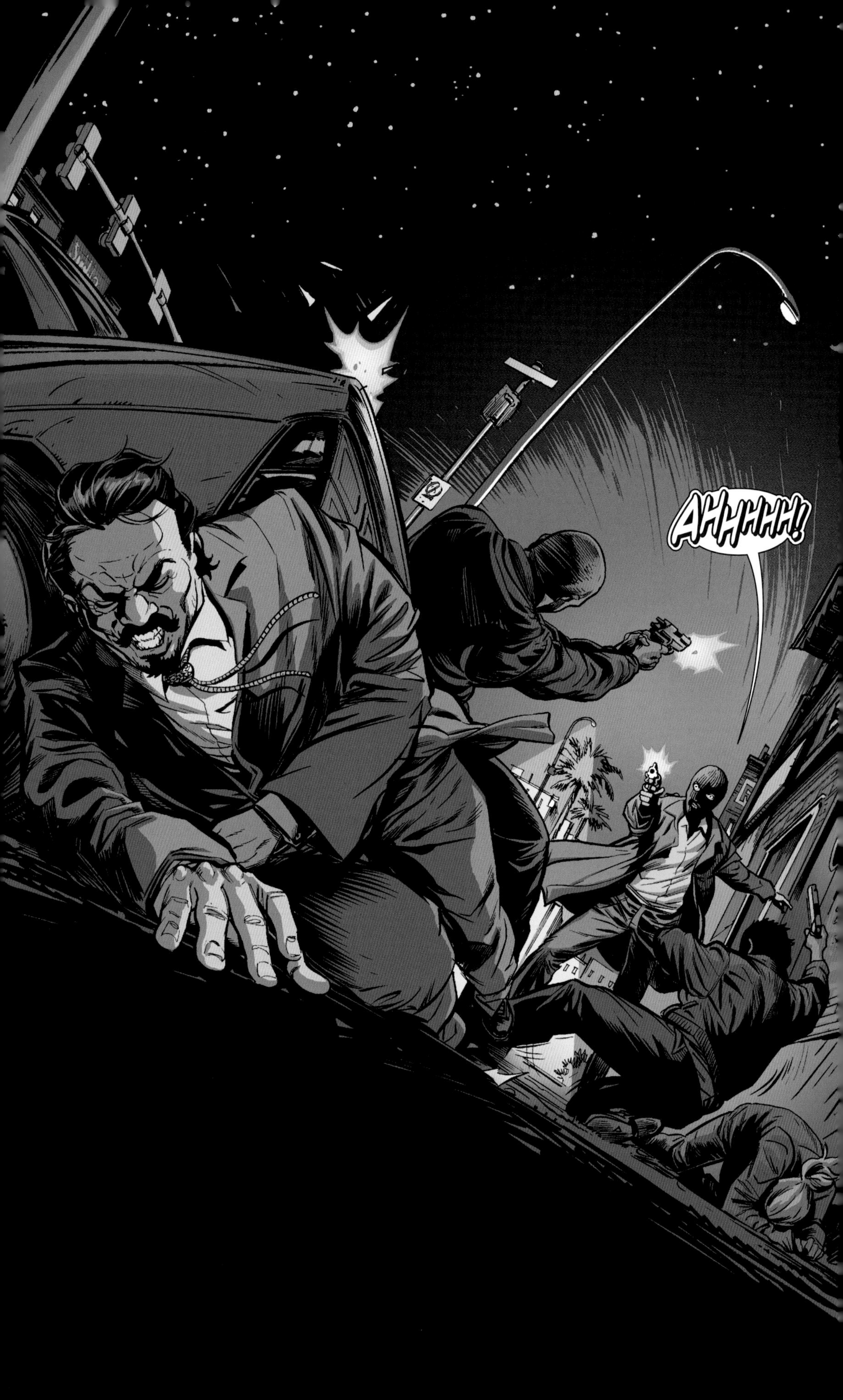
AHHHHH!

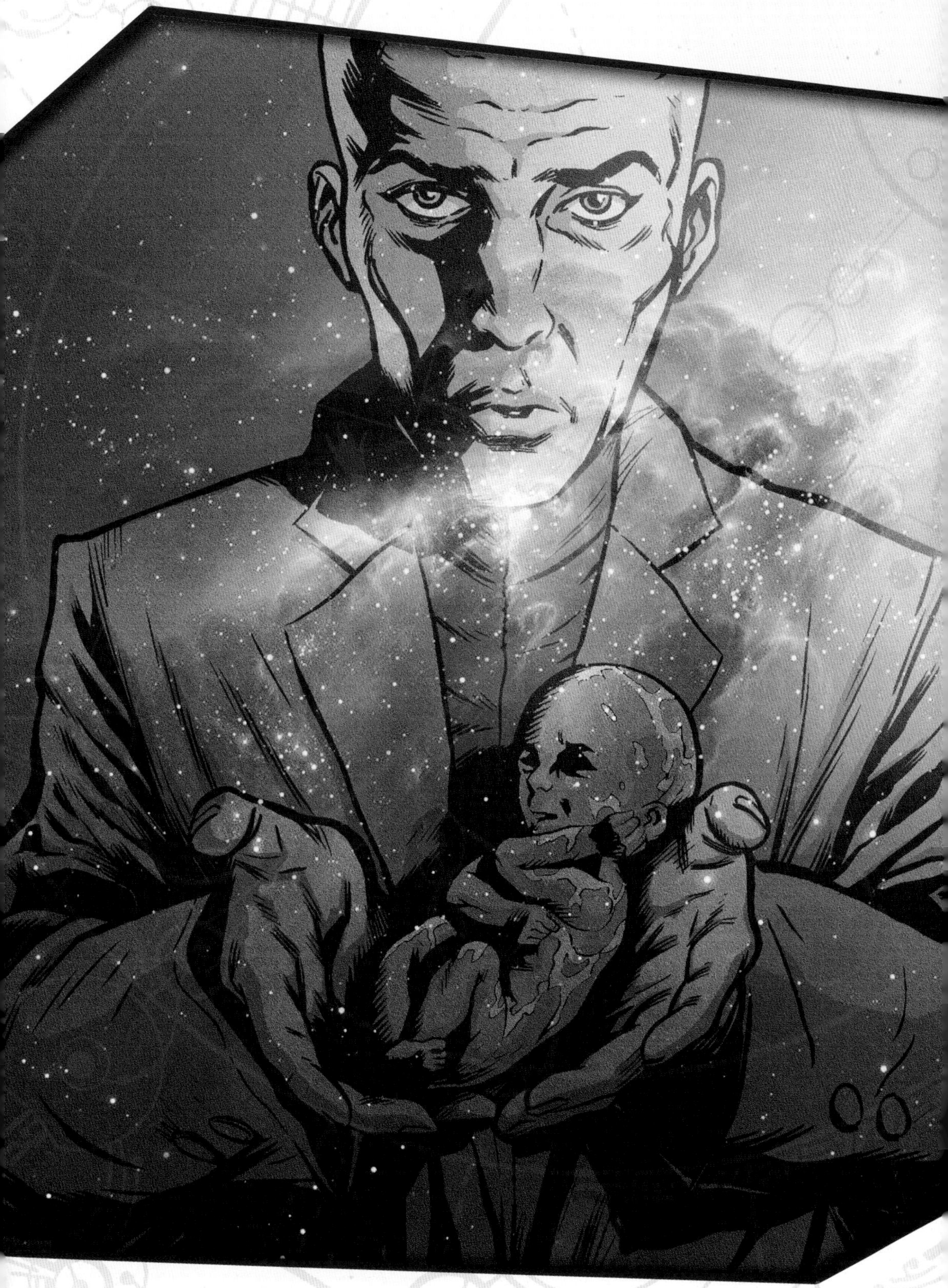

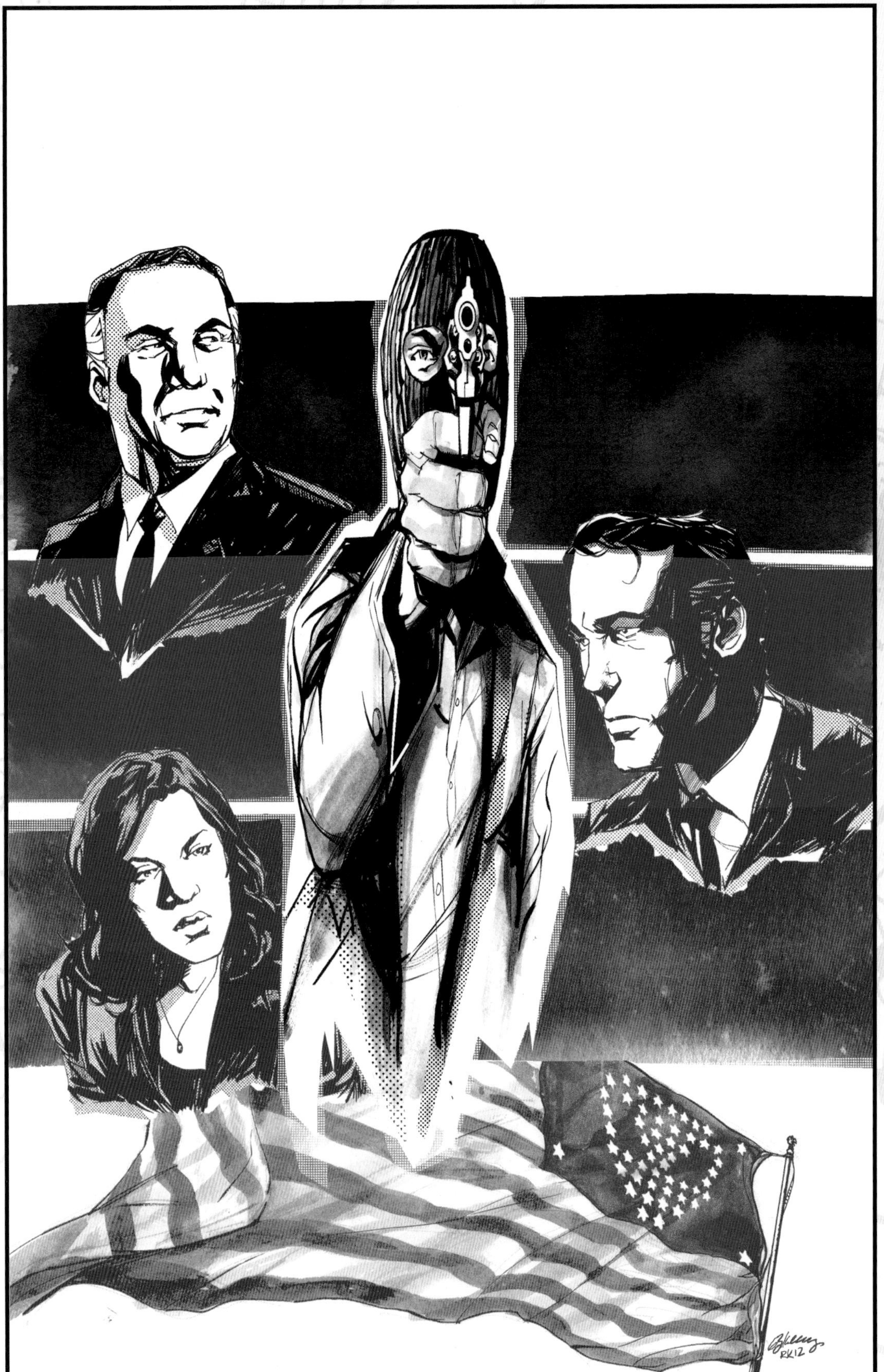

RK12

COVER ART BY **RYAN KELLY**

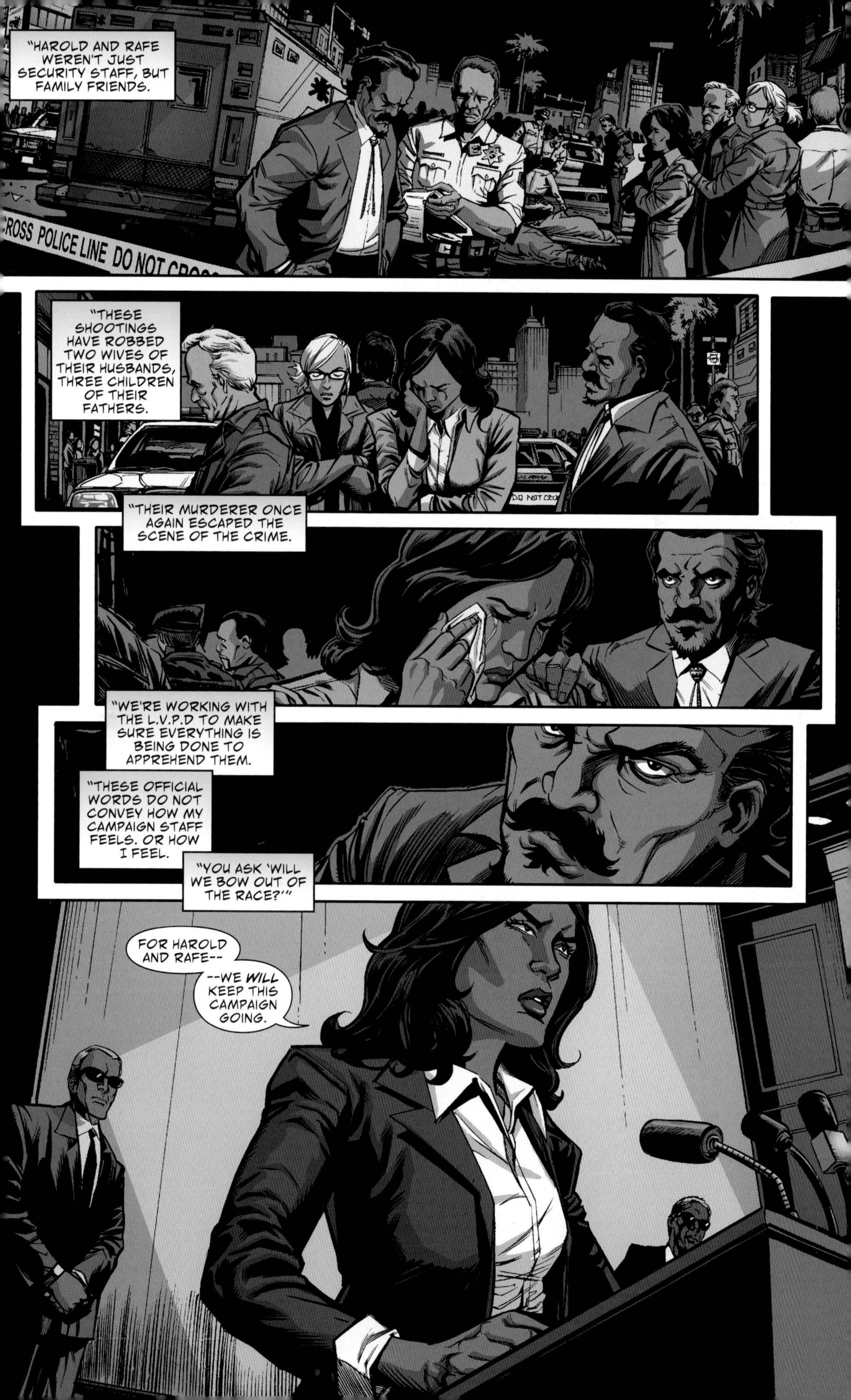
"HAROLD AND RAFE WEREN'T JUST SECURITY STAFF, BUT FAMILY FRIENDS.
CROSS POLICE LINE DO NOT CROSS
"THESE SHOOTINGS HAVE ROBBED TWO WIVES OF THEIR HUSBANDS, THREE CHILDREN OF THEIR FATHERS.
"THEIR MURDERER ONCE AGAIN ESCAPED THE SCENE OF THE CRIME.
"WE'RE WORKING WITH THE L.V.P.D TO MAKE SURE EVERYTHING IS BEING DONE TO APPREHEND THEM.
"THESE OFFICIAL WORDS DO NOT CONVEY HOW MY CAMPAIGN STAFF FEELS. OR HOW I FEEL.
"YOU ASK 'WILL WE BOW OUT OF THE RACE?'"
FOR HAROLD AND RAFE--
--WE *WILL* KEEP THIS CAMPAIGN GOING.

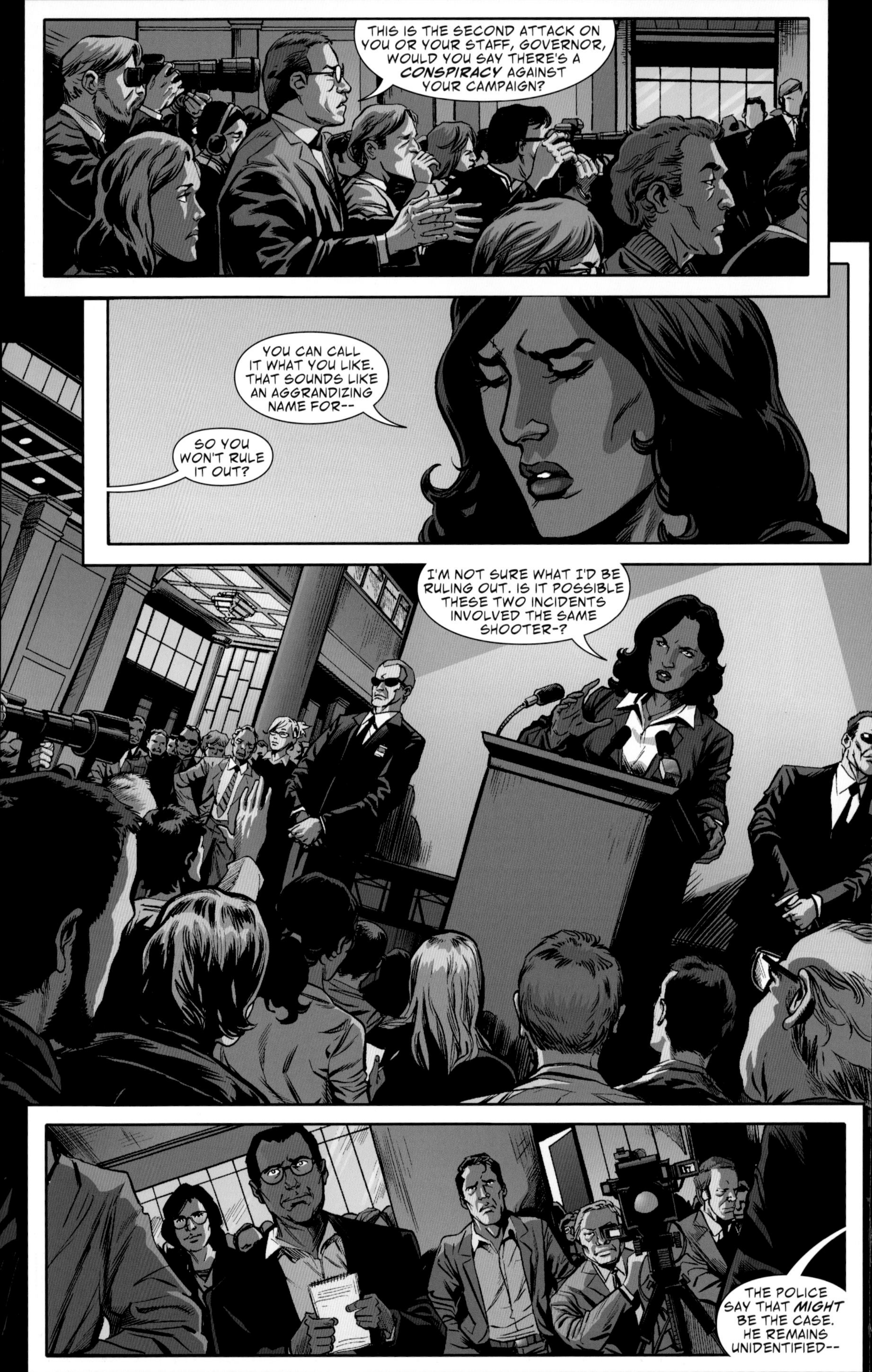
THIS IS THE SECOND ATTACK ON YOU OR YOUR STAFF, GOVERNOR, WOULD YOU SAY THERE'S A CONSPIRACY AGAINST YOUR CAMPAIGN?
YOU CAN CALL IT WHAT YOU LIKE. THAT SOUNDS LIKE AN AGGRANDIZING NAME FOR--
SO YOU WON'T RULE IT OUT?
I'M NOT SURE WHAT I'D BE RULING OUT. IS IT POSSIBLE THESE TWO INCIDENTS INVOLVED THE SAME SHOOTER-?
THE POLICE SAY THAT MIGHT BE THE CASE. HE REMAINS UNIDENTIFIED--

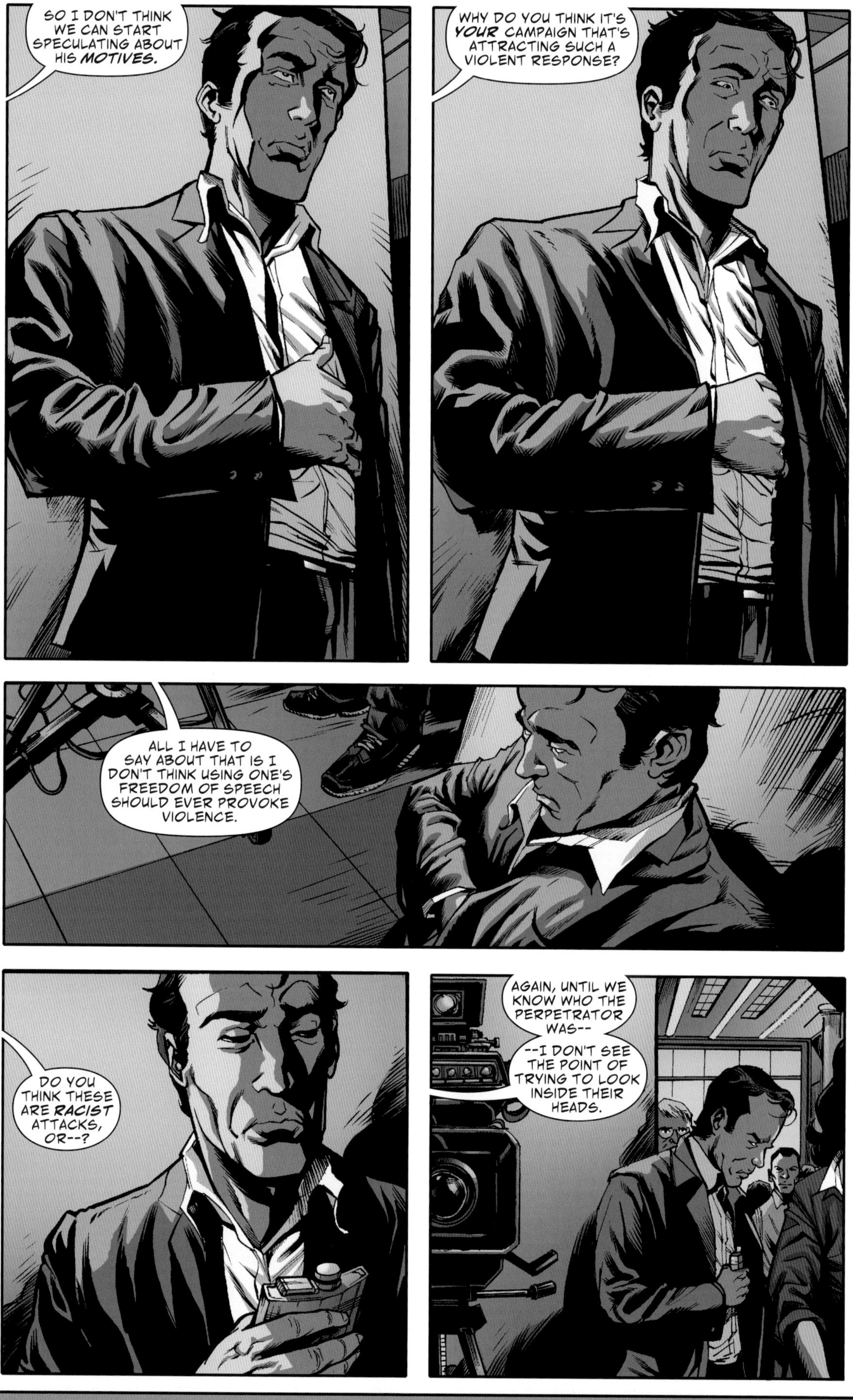
SO I DON'T THINK WE CAN START SPECULATING ABOUT HIS *MOTIVES.*
WHY DO YOU THINK IT'S *YOUR* CAMPAIGN THAT'S ATTRACTING SUCH A VIOLENT RESPONSE?
ALL I HAVE TO SAY ABOUT THAT IS I DON'T THINK USING ONE'S FREEDOM OF SPEECH SHOULD EVER PROVOKE VIOLENCE.
DO YOU THINK THESE ARE *RACIST* ATTACKS, OR--?
AGAIN, UNTIL WE KNOW WHO THE PERPETRATOR WAS--
--I DON'T SEE THE POINT OF TRYING TO LOOK INSIDE THEIR HEADS.

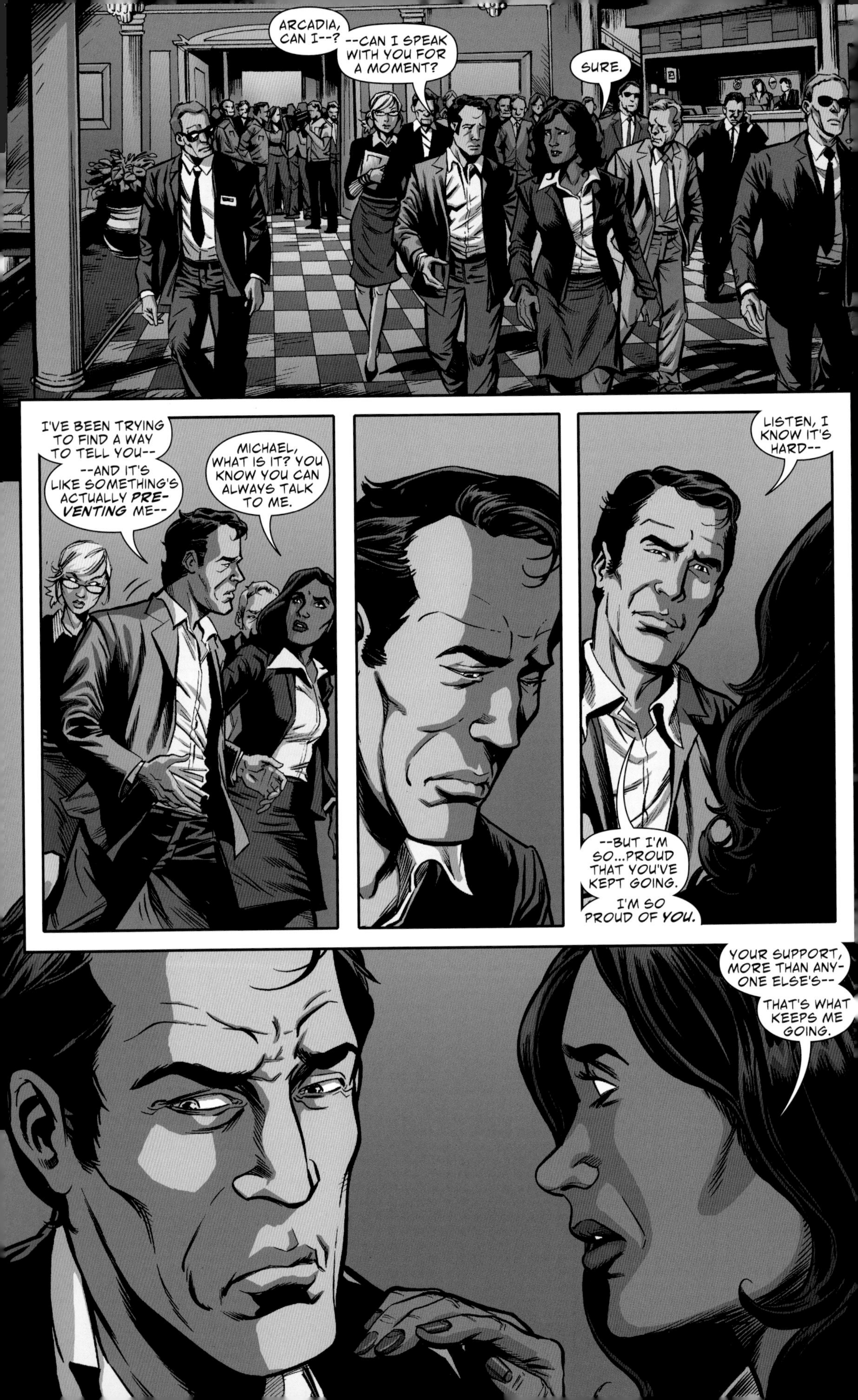
ARCADIA, CAN I--?
--CAN I SPEAK WITH YOU FOR A MOMENT?
SURE.
I'VE BEEN TRYING TO FIND A WAY TO TELL YOU--
--AND IT'S LIKE SOMETHING'S ACTUALLY PRE-VENTING ME--
MICHAEL, WHAT IS IT? YOU KNOW YOU CAN ALWAYS TALK TO ME.
LISTEN, I KNOW IT'S HARD--
--BUT I'M SO...PROUD THAT YOU'VE KEPT GOING.
I'M SO PROUD OF YOU.
YOUR SUPPORT, MORE THAN ANY-ONE ELSE'S--
THAT'S WHAT KEEPS ME GOING.

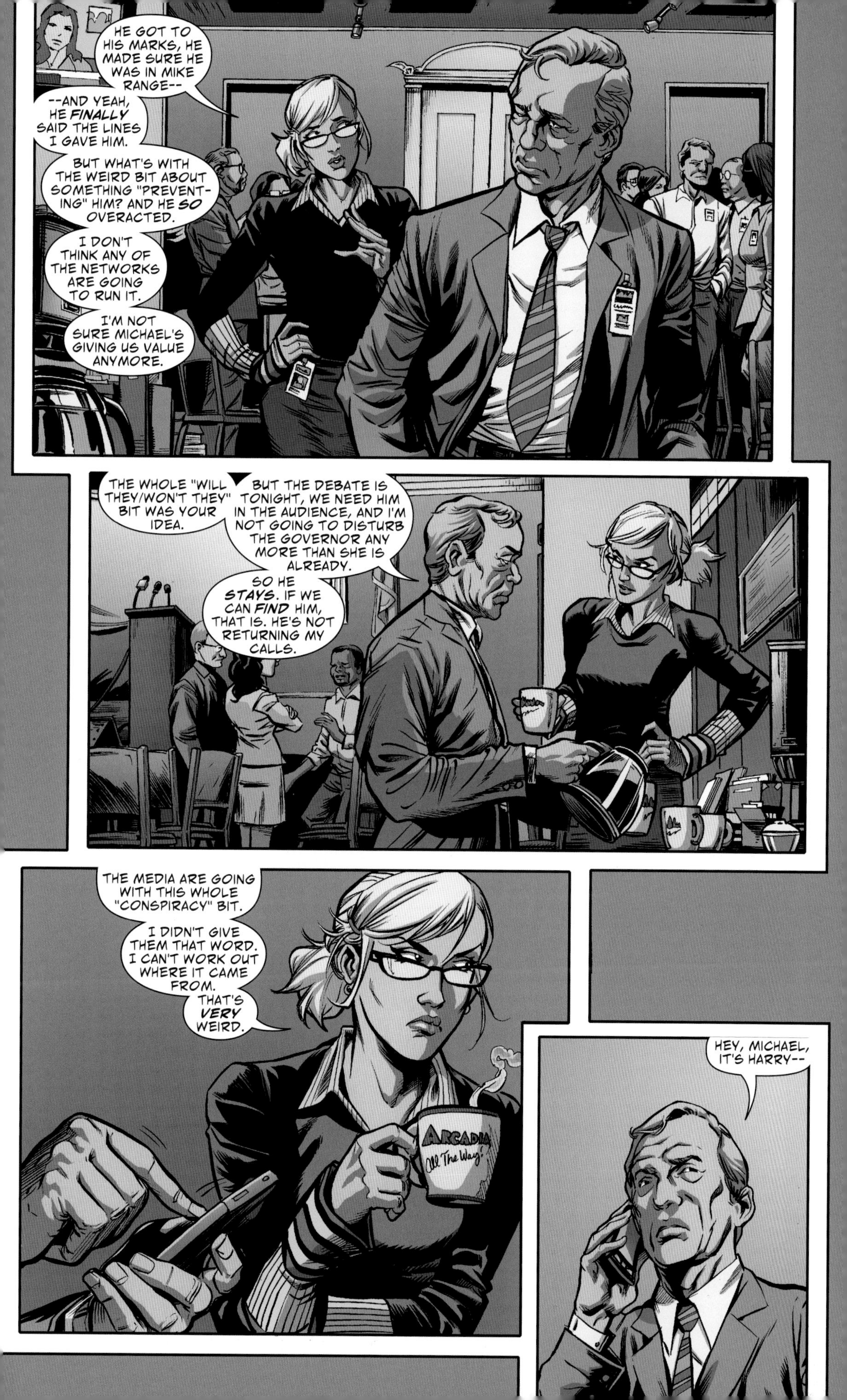
HE GOT TO HIS MARKS, HE MADE SURE HE WAS IN MIKE RANGE--
--AND YEAH, HE FINALLY SAID THE LINES I GAVE HIM.
BUT WHAT'S WITH THE WEIRD BIT ABOUT SOMETHING "PREVENTING" HIM? AND HE SO OVERACTED.
I DON'T THINK ANY OF THE NETWORKS ARE GOING TO RUN IT.
I'M NOT SURE MICHAEL'S GIVING US VALUE ANYMORE.
THE WHOLE "WILL THEY/WON'T THEY" BIT WAS YOUR IDEA.
BUT THE DEBATE IS TONIGHT, WE NEED HIM IN THE AUDIENCE, AND I'M NOT GOING TO DISTURB THE GOVERNOR ANY MORE THAN SHE IS ALREADY.
SO HE STAYS. IF WE CAN FIND HIM, THAT IS. HE'S NOT RETURNING MY CALLS.
THE MEDIA ARE GOING WITH THIS WHOLE "CONSPIRACY" BIT.
I DIDN'T GIVE THEM THAT WORD. I CAN'T WORK OUT WHERE IT CAME FROM.
THAT'S VERY WEIRD.
ARCADIA All The Way!
HEY, MICHAEL, IT'S HARRY--

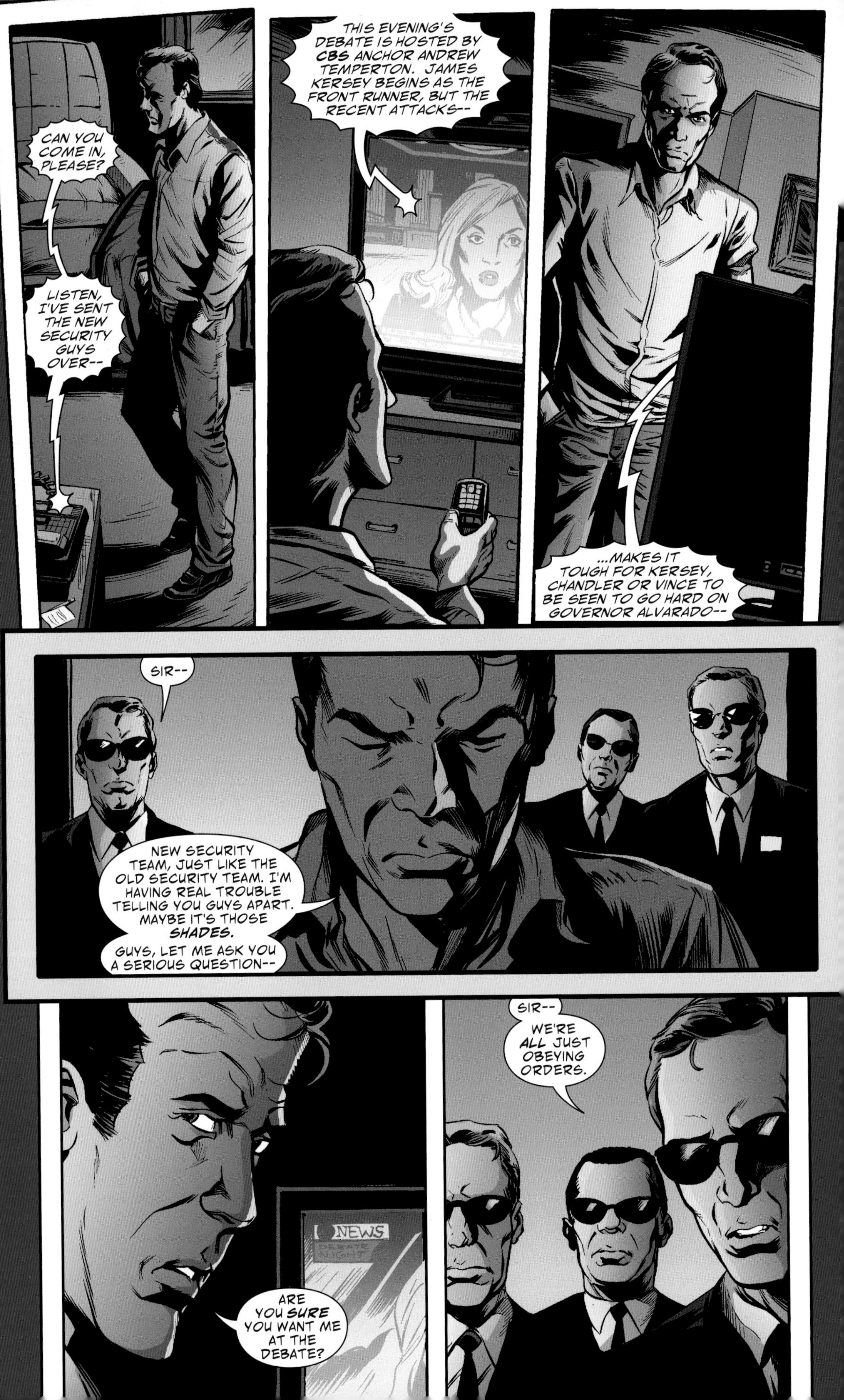
CAN YOU COME IN, PLEASE?
LISTEN, I'VE SENT THE NEW SECURITY GUYS OVER--
THIS EVENING'S DEBATE IS HOSTED BY CBS ANCHOR ANDREW TEMPERTON. JAMES KERSEY BEGINS AS THE FRONT RUNNER, BUT THE RECENT ATTACKS--
...MAKES IT TOUGH FOR KERSEY, CHANDLER OR VINCE TO BE SEEN TO GO HARD ON GOVERNOR ALVARADO--
SIR--
NEW SECURITY TEAM, JUST LIKE THE OLD SECURITY TEAM. I'M HAVING REAL TROUBLE TELLING YOU GUYS APART. MAYBE IT'S THOSE SHADES.
GUYS, LET ME ASK YOU A SERIOUS QUESTION--
NEWS
DEBATE NIGHT
ARE YOU SURE YOU WANT ME AT THE DEBATE?
SIR--
WE'RE ALL JUST OBEYING ORDERS.

BEFORE WE GET INTO FINAL PREP FOR TONIGHT...

WE'VE SENT OUT AN EMAIL ABOUT THE INCREASED SECURITY.

THE NEW TEAM HAS DONE A GREAT JOB OF BECOMING SWIFTLY EMBEDDED IN OUR ORGANIZATION.

FAUSTO MADE A GOOD CASE FOR PUTTING HIS GUYS IN CHARGE--

BUT I DON'T WANT TO PUT ANY OF YOU AT ANY MORE *RISK*.

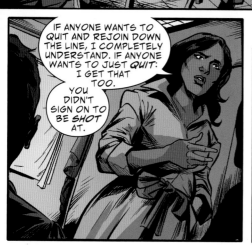

IF ANYONE WANTS TO QUIT AND REJOIN DOWN THE LINE, I COMPLETELY UNDERSTAND. IF ANYONE WANTS TO JUST *QUIT*: I GET THAT TOO.

YOU DIDN'T SIGN ON TO BE *SHOT* AT.

OPTING TO CONTINUE HERE...

IT WASN'T A DECISION I CAME TO *EASILY*. BUT THE OTHER TEAMS WOULDN'T LISTEN TO OUR REQUEST TO SCRATCH THE DEBATE--

THE SENATOR FEELS VERY STRONGLY THAT THE POLITICAL PROCESS SHOULDN'T BE STIFLED BY THE ACTIONS OF CRIMINALS.

I'LL BET.

AND IF WE *DON'T* APPEAR, WE'RE *DONE*.

SO THAT'S WHERE WE ARE. AND I DON'T SEE ANYONE LEAVING THE TABLE. AND I'M *DELIGHTED*.

SO LET'S *DO* THIS.

CHLOE, HOW ARE WE POLLING GOING IN?

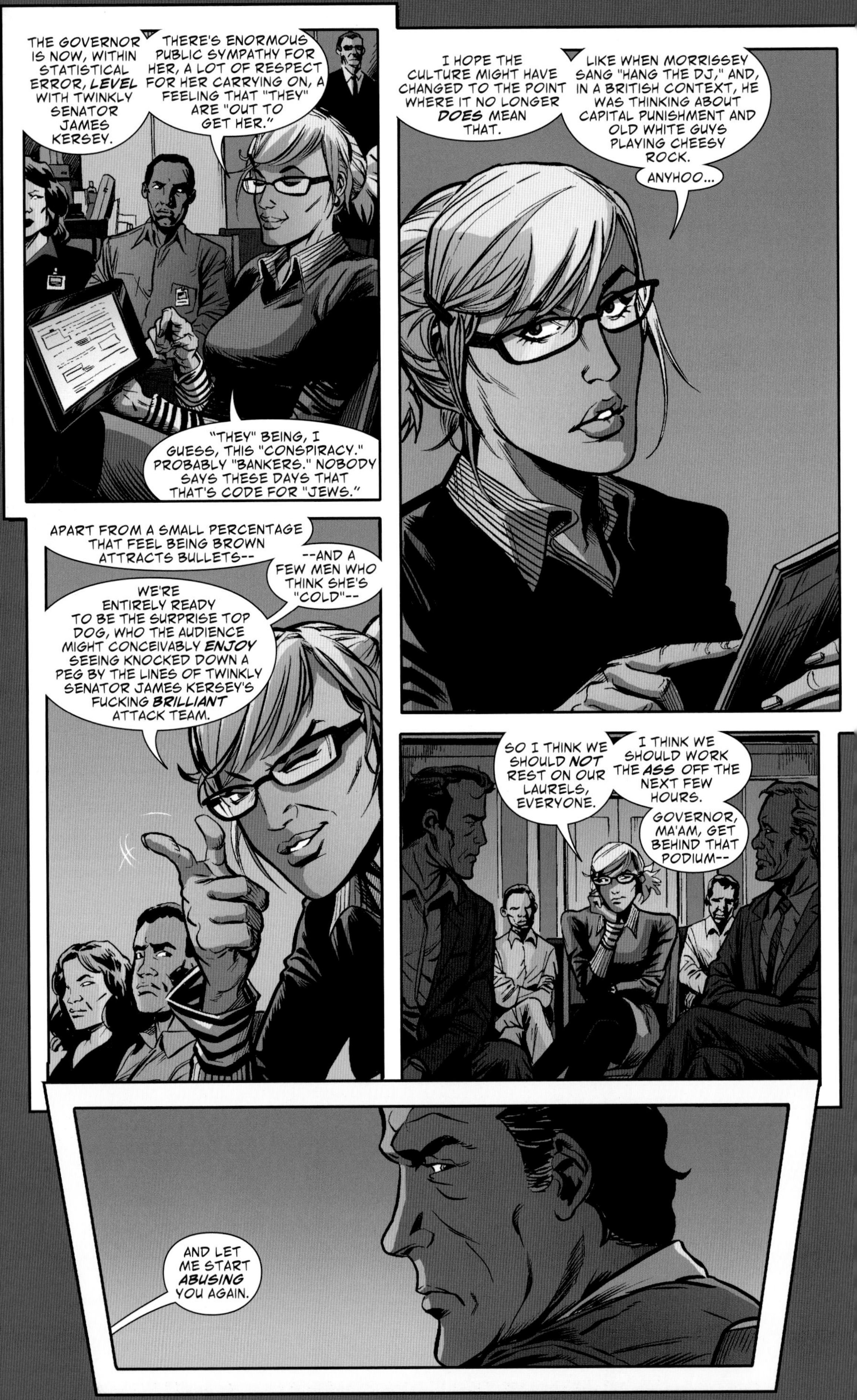
THE GOVERNOR IS NOW, WITHIN STATISTICAL ERROR, *LEVEL* WITH TWINKLY SENATOR JAMES KERSEY.
THERE'S ENORMOUS PUBLIC SYMPATHY FOR HER, A LOT OF RESPECT FOR HER CARRYING ON, A FEELING THAT "THEY" ARE "OUT TO GET HER."
"THEY" BEING, I GUESS, THIS "CONSPIRACY." PROBABLY "BANKERS." NOBODY SAYS THESE DAYS THAT THAT'S CODE FOR "JEWS."
I HOPE THE CULTURE MIGHT HAVE CHANGED TO THE POINT WHERE IT NO LONGER *DOES* MEAN THAT.
LIKE WHEN MORRISSEY SANG "HANG THE DJ," AND, IN A BRITISH CONTEXT, HE WAS THINKING ABOUT CAPITAL PUNISHMENT AND OLD WHITE GUYS PLAYING CHEESY ROCK.
ANYHOO...
APART FROM A SMALL PERCENTAGE THAT FEEL BEING BROWN ATTRACTS BULLETS--
--AND A FEW MEN WHO THINK SHE'S "COLD"--
WE'RE ENTIRELY READY TO BE THE SURPRISE TOP DOG, WHO THE AUDIENCE MIGHT CONCEIVABLY *ENJOY* SEEING KNOCKED DOWN A PEG BY THE LINES OF TWINKLY SENATOR JAMES KERSEY'S FUCKING *BRILLIANT* ATTACK TEAM.
SO I THINK WE SHOULD *NOT* REST ON OUR LAURELS, EVERYONE.
I THINK WE SHOULD WORK THE *ASS* OFF THE NEXT FEW HOURS.
GOVERNOR, MA'AM, GET BEHIND THAT PODIUM--
AND LET ME START *ABUSING* YOU AGAIN.

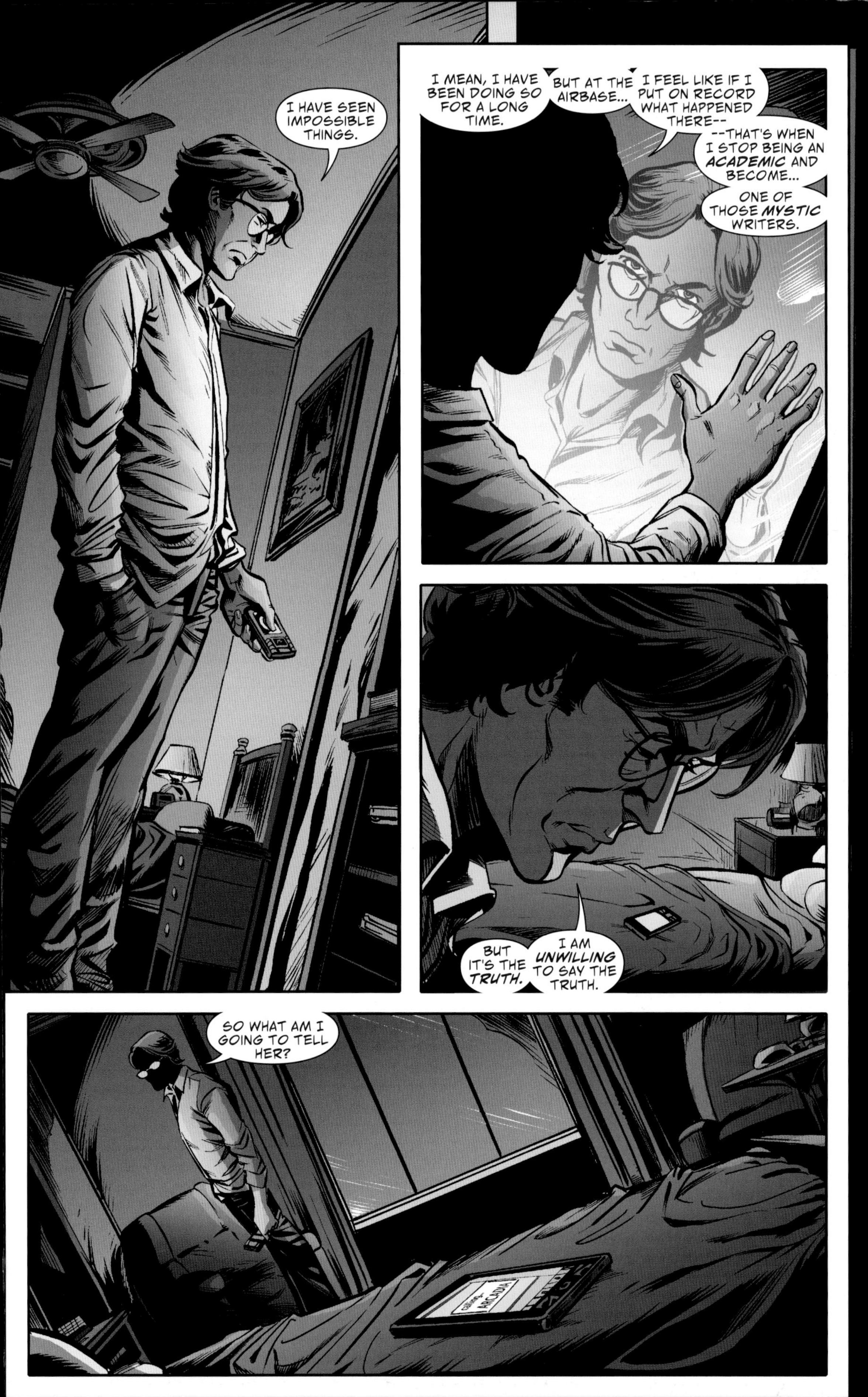

I HAVE SEEN IMPOSSIBLE THINGS.
I MEAN, I HAVE BEEN DOING SO FOR A LONG TIME.
BUT AT THE AIRBASE...
I FEEL LIKE IF I PUT ON RECORD WHAT HAPPENED THERE--
--THAT'S WHEN I STOP BEING AN ACADEMIC AND BECOME...
ONE OF THOSE MYSTIC WRITERS.
I AM UNWILLING TO SAY THE TRUTH.
BUT IT'S THE TRUTH.
SO WHAT AM I GOING TO TELL HER?

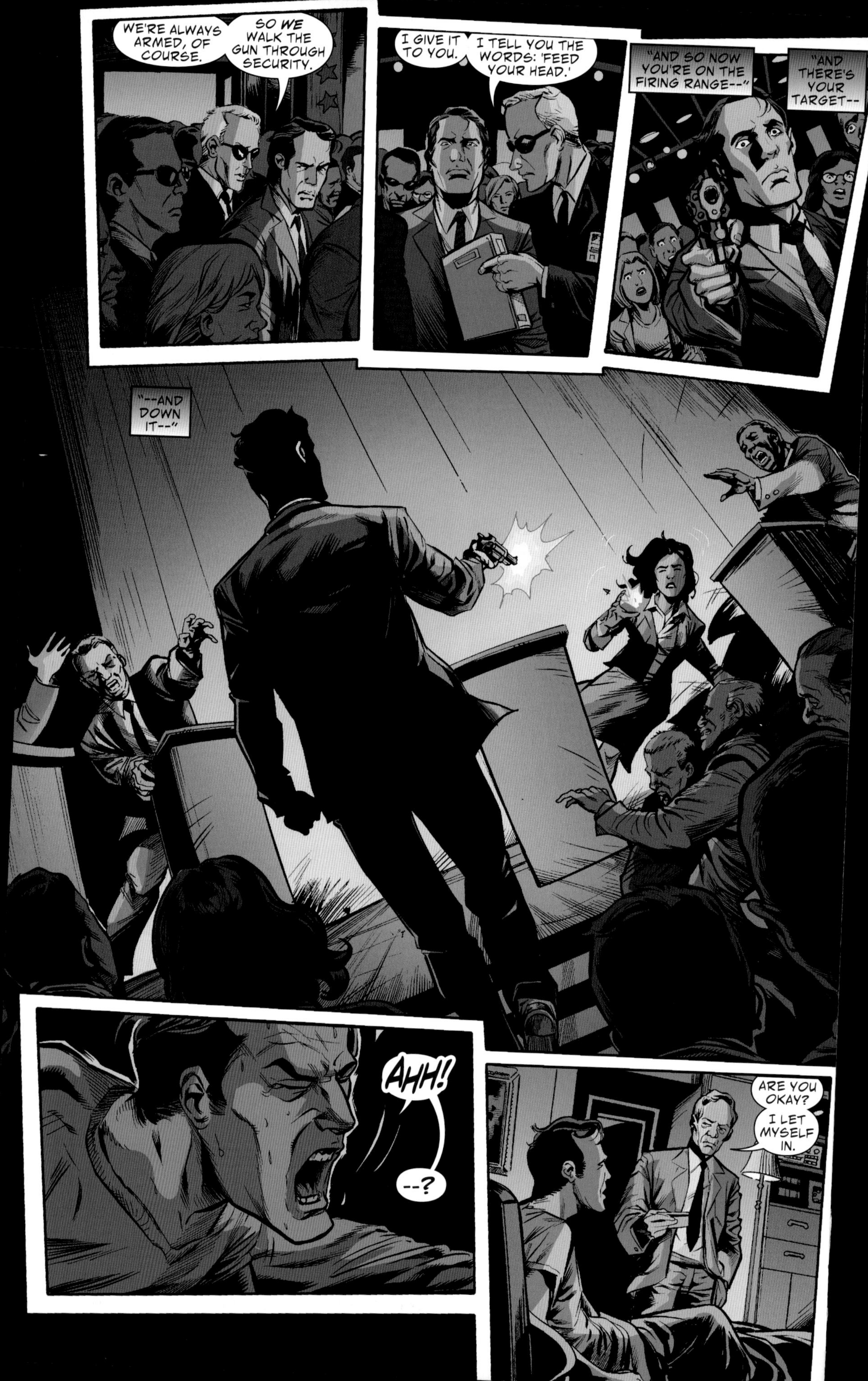
WE'RE ALWAYS ARMED, OF COURSE.
SO WE WALK THE GUN THROUGH SECURITY.
I GIVE IT TO YOU.
I TELL YOU THE WORDS: 'FEED YOUR HEAD.'
"AND SO NOW YOU'RE ON THE FIRING RANGE--"
"AND THERE'S YOUR TARGET--
"--AND DOWN IT--"
AHH!
--?
ARE YOU OKAY?
I LET MYSELF IN.

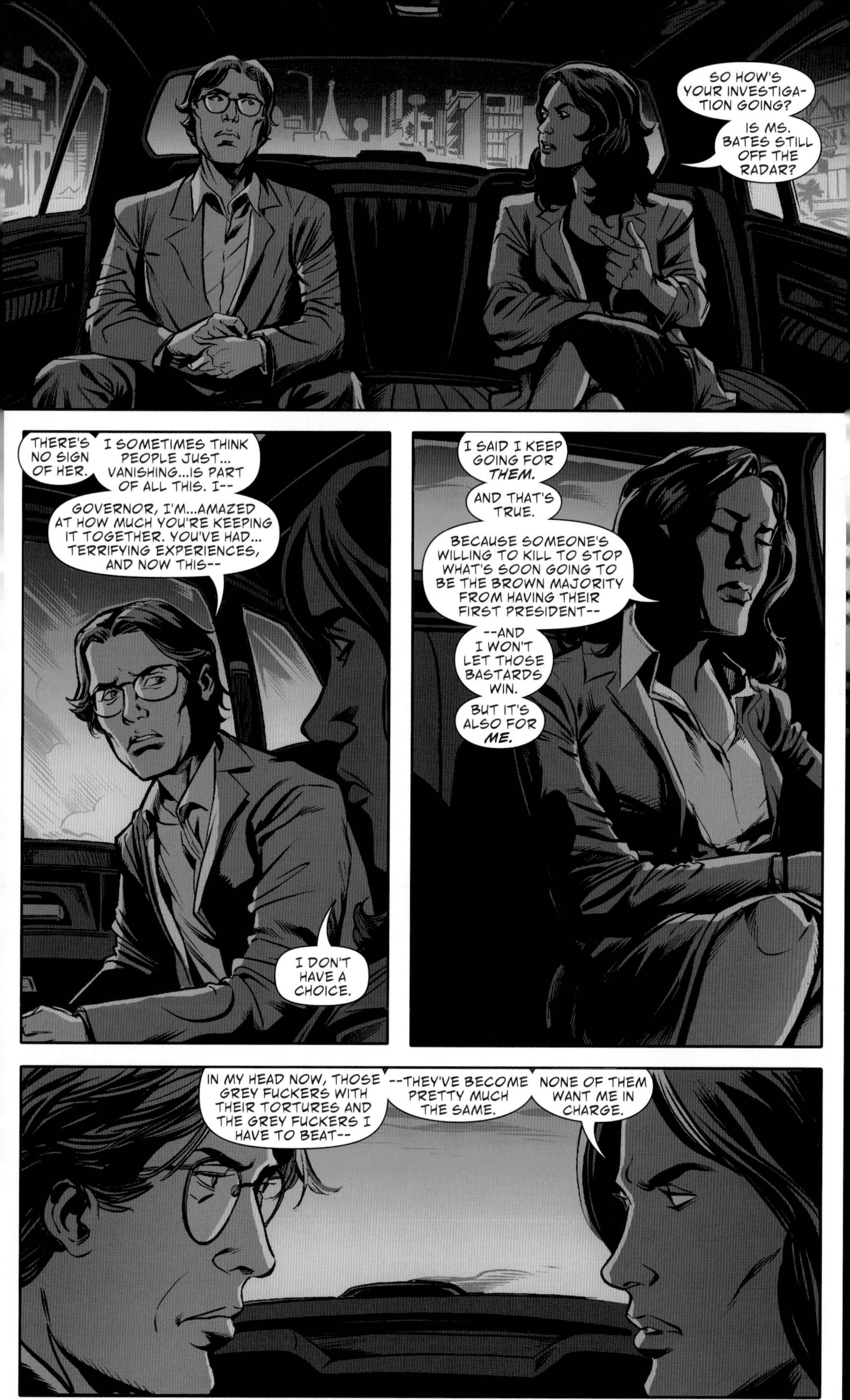
SO HOW'S YOUR INVESTIGATION GOING?
IS MS. BATES STILL OFF THE RADAR?
THERE'S NO SIGN OF HER.
I SOMETIMES THINK PEOPLE JUST... VANISHING...IS PART OF ALL THIS. I--
GOVERNOR, I'M...AMAZED AT HOW MUCH YOU'RE KEEPING IT TOGETHER. YOU'VE HAD... TERRIFYING EXPERIENCES, AND NOW THIS--
I DON'T HAVE A CHOICE.
I SAID I KEEP GOING FOR THEM.
AND THAT'S TRUE.
BECAUSE SOMEONE'S WILLING TO KILL TO STOP WHAT'S SOON GOING TO BE THE BROWN MAJORITY FROM HAVING THEIR FIRST PRESIDENT--
--AND I WON'T LET THOSE BASTARDS WIN.
BUT IT'S ALSO FOR ME.
IN MY HEAD NOW, THOSE GREY FUCKERS WITH THEIR TORTURES AND THE GREY FUCKERS I HAVE TO BEAT--
--THEY'VE BECOME PRETTY MUCH THE SAME.
NONE OF THEM WANT ME IN CHARGE.

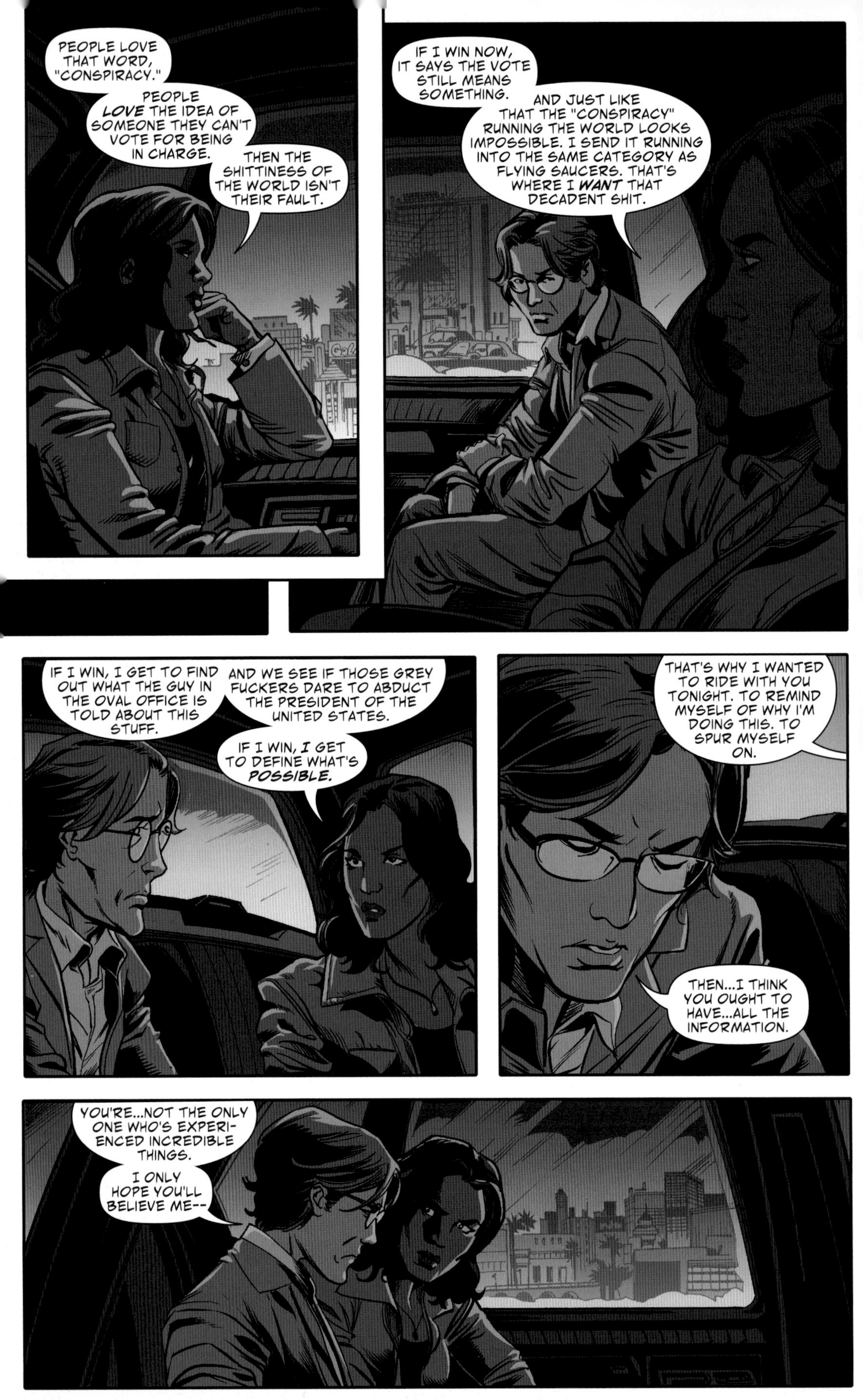

PEOPLE LOVE THAT WORD, "CONSPIRACY."
PEOPLE LOVE THE IDEA OF SOMEONE THEY CAN'T VOTE FOR BEING IN CHARGE.
THEN THE SHITTINESS OF THE WORLD ISN'T THEIR FAULT.
IF I WIN NOW, IT SAYS THE VOTE STILL MEANS SOMETHING.
AND JUST LIKE THAT THE "CONSPIRACY" RUNNING THE WORLD LOOKS IMPOSSIBLE. I SEND IT RUNNING INTO THE SAME CATEGORY AS FLYING SAUCERS. THAT'S WHERE I WANT THAT DECADENT SHIT.
IF I WIN, I GET TO FIND OUT WHAT THE GUY IN THE OVAL OFFICE IS TOLD ABOUT THIS STUFF.
AND WE SEE IF THOSE GREY FUCKERS DARE TO ABDUCT THE PRESIDENT OF THE UNITED STATES.
IF I WIN, I GET TO DEFINE WHAT'S POSSIBLE.
THAT'S WHY I WANTED TO RIDE WITH YOU TONIGHT. TO REMIND MYSELF OF WHY I'M DOING THIS. TO SPUR MYSELF ON.
THEN...I THINK YOU OUGHT TO HAVE...ALL THE INFORMATION.
YOU'RE...NOT THE ONLY ONE WHO'S EXPERIENCED INCREDIBLE THINGS.
I ONLY HOPE YOU'LL BELIEVE ME--

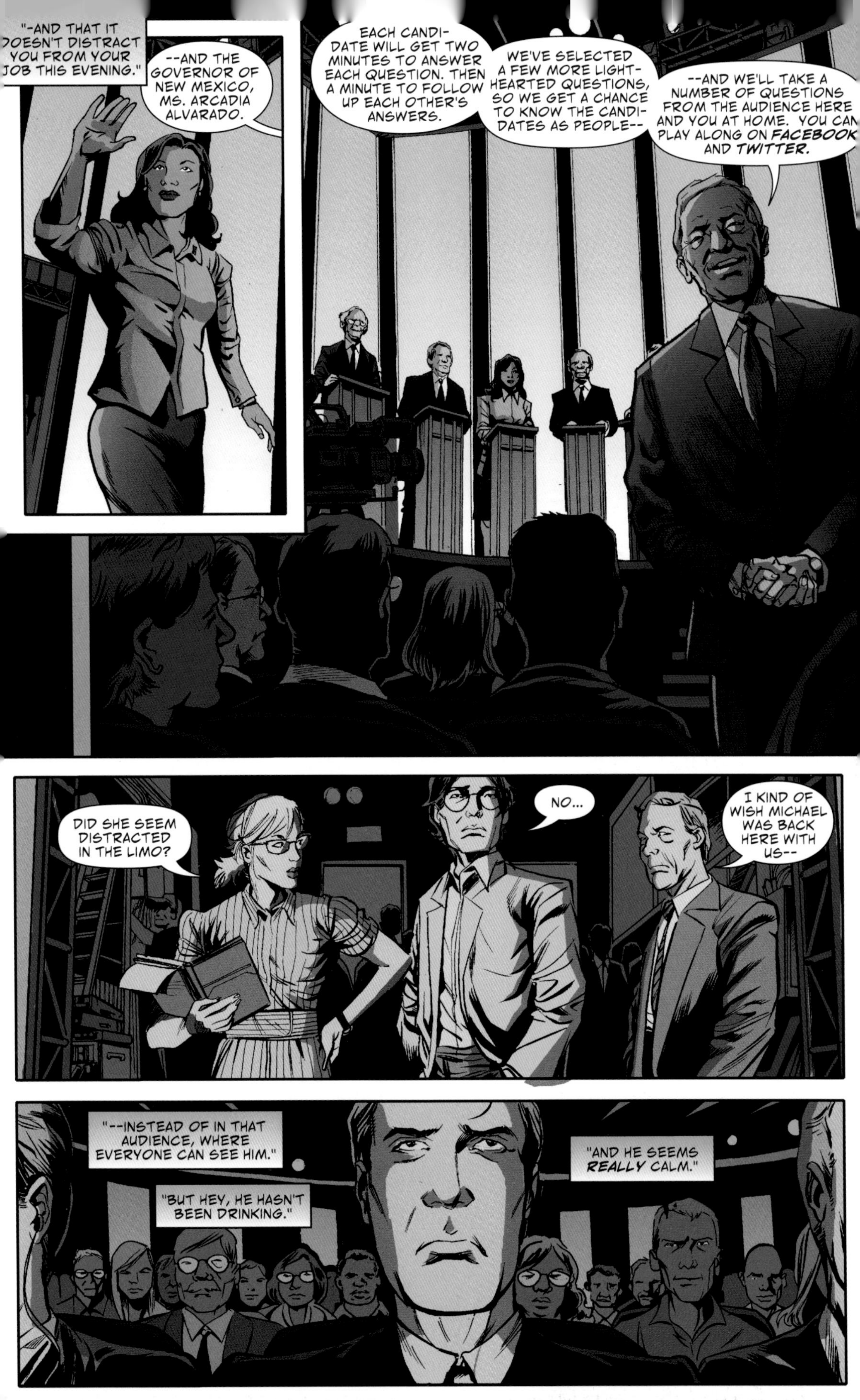
"-AND THAT IT DOESN'T DISTRACT YOU FROM YOUR JOB THIS EVENING."
--AND THE GOVERNOR OF NEW MEXICO, MS. ARCADIA ALVARADO.
EACH CANDIDATE WILL GET TWO MINUTES TO ANSWER EACH QUESTION. THEN A MINUTE TO FOLLOW UP EACH OTHER'S ANSWERS.
WE'VE SELECTED A FEW MORE LIGHT-HEARTED QUESTIONS, SO WE GET A CHANCE TO KNOW THE CANDIDATES AS PEOPLE--
--AND WE'LL TAKE A NUMBER OF QUESTIONS FROM THE AUDIENCE HERE AND YOU AT HOME. YOU CAN PLAY ALONG ON FACEBOOK AND TWITTER.
DID SHE SEEM DISTRACTED IN THE LIMO?
NO...
I KIND OF WISH MICHAEL WAS BACK HERE WITH US--
"--INSTEAD OF IN THAT AUDIENCE, WHERE EVERYONE CAN SEE HIM."
"BUT HEY, HE HASN'T BEEN DRINKING."
"AND HE SEEMS REALLY CALM."

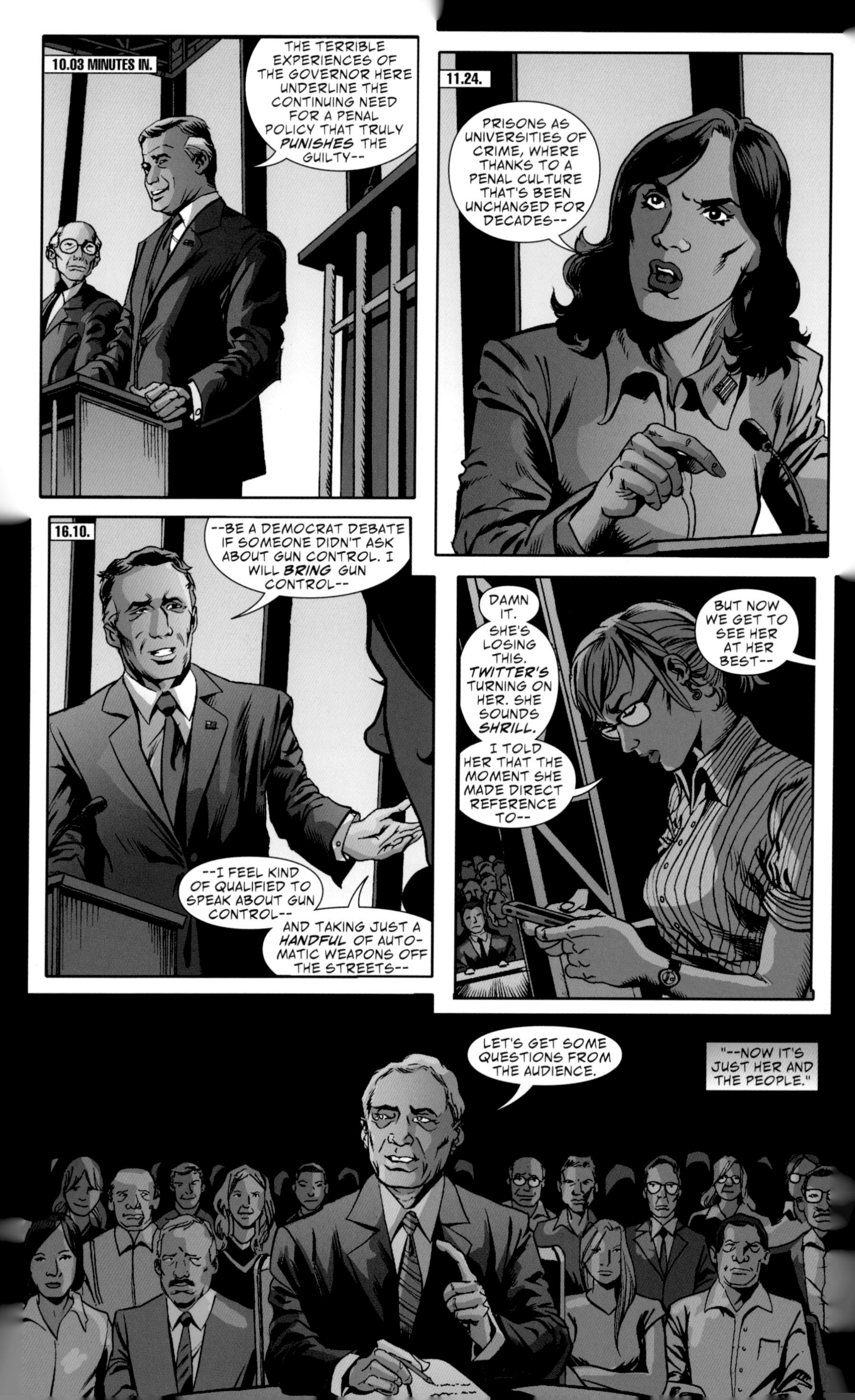

10.03 MINUTES IN.
THE TERRIBLE EXPERIENCES OF THE GOVERNOR HERE UNDERLINE THE CONTINUING NEED FOR A PENAL POLICY THAT TRULY PUNISHES THE GUILTY--
11.24.
PRISONS AS UNIVERSITIES OF CRIME, WHERE THANKS TO A PENAL CULTURE THAT'S BEEN UNCHANGED FOR DECADES--
16.10.
--BE A DEMOCRAT DEBATE IF SOMEONE DIDN'T ASK ABOUT GUN CONTROL. I WILL BRING GUN CONTROL--
--I FEEL KIND OF QUALIFIED TO SPEAK ABOUT GUN CONTROL--
AND TAKING JUST A HANDFUL OF AUTOMATIC WEAPONS OFF THE STREETS--
DAMN IT.
SHE'S LOSING THIS. TWITTER'S TURNING ON HER. SHE SOUNDS SHRILL.
I TOLD HER THAT THE MOMENT SHE MADE DIRECT REFERENCE TO--
BUT NOW WE GET TO SEE HER AT HER BEST--
LET'S GET SOME QUESTIONS FROM THE AUDIENCE.
"--NOW IT'S JUST HER AND THE PEOPLE."

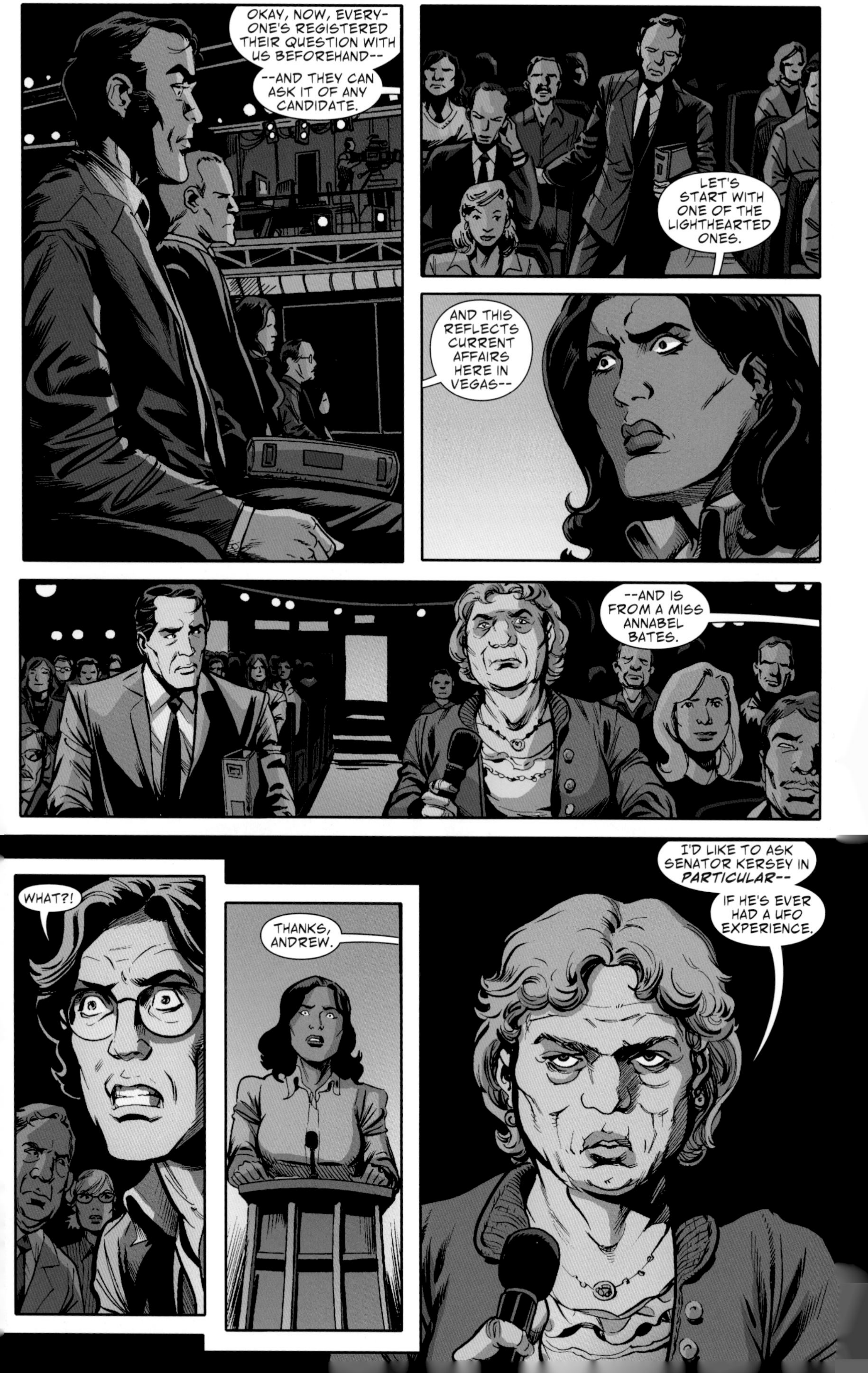
OKAY, NOW, EVERY-ONE'S REGISTERED THEIR QUESTION WITH US BEFOREHAND--
--AND THEY CAN ASK IT OF ANY CANDIDATE.
LET'S START WITH ONE OF THE LIGHTHEARTED ONES.
AND THIS REFLECTS CURRENT AFFAIRS HERE IN VEGAS--
--AND IS FROM A MISS ANNABEL BATES.
WHAT?!
THANKS, ANDREW.
I'D LIKE TO ASK SENATOR KERSEY IN PARTICULAR--
IF HE'S EVER HAD A UFO EXPERIENCE.

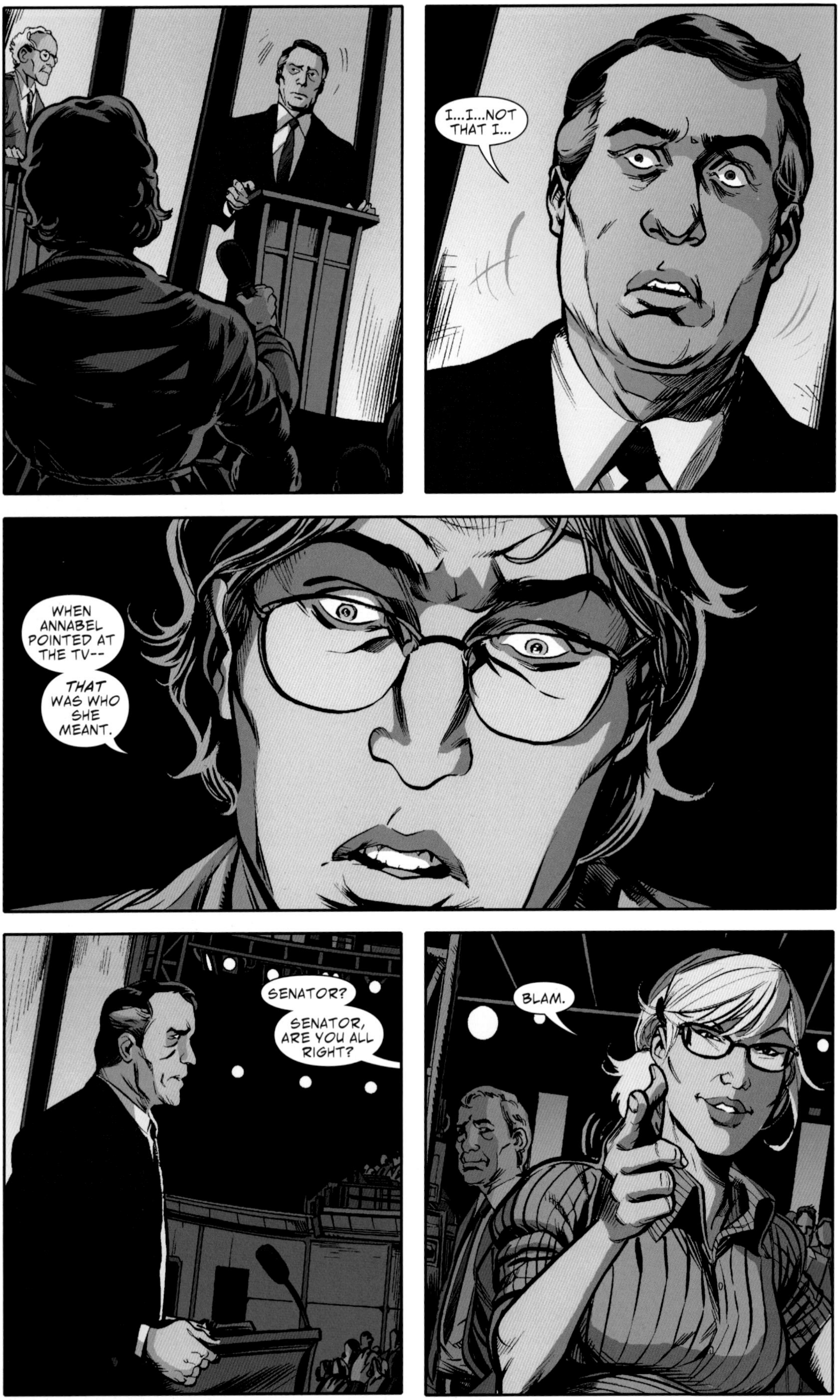
I...I...NOT THAT I...
WHEN ANNABEL POINTED AT THE TV--
THAT WAS WHO SHE MEANT.
SENATOR?
SENATOR, ARE YOU ALL RIGHT?
BLAM.

LET'S, ER, LET'S MOVE ON TO THE NEXT QUESTION.

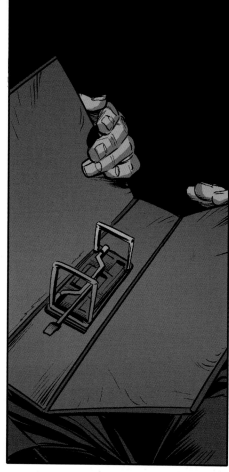

THE WORLD IS WONDERING WHAT THE HELL THAT WAS.

FROM NOW ON, EVERY QUESTION HE'S ASKED WILL BE ABOUT UFOS. IRONY: IT'S MY FAVORITE THING.

YEAH. HARRY, YOU KNOW, THIS IS TERRIBLE.

WHAT?

EVERYTHING THAT'S HAPPENED IN THIS CITY HAS TURNED OUT WELL FOR US.

AND WE DID HARDLY ANY OF IT.

IT'S LIKE THERE IS A CONSPIRACY--

--AND IT'S ON OUR SIDE.

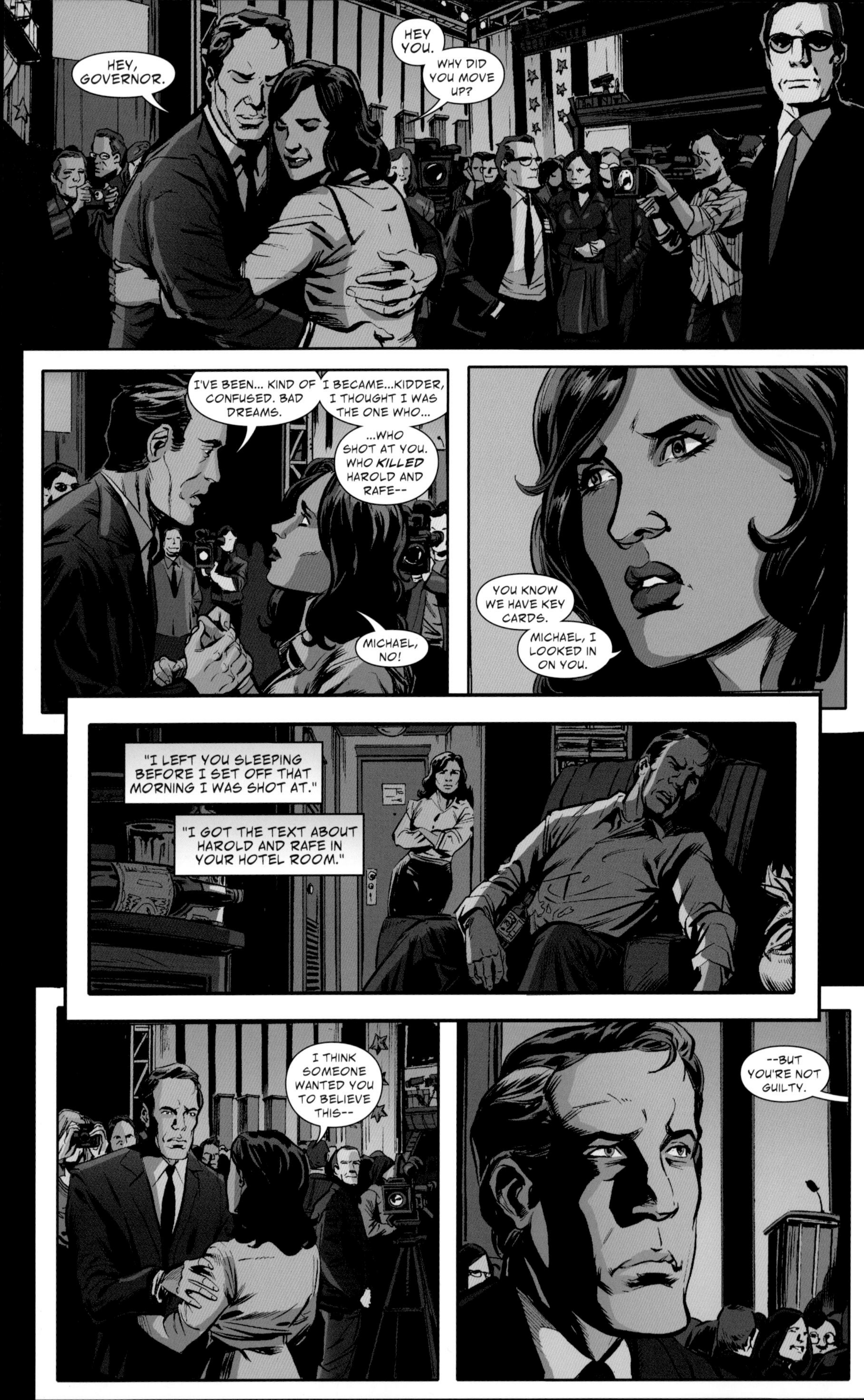
HEY, GOVERNOR.
HEY YOU.
WHY DID YOU MOVE UP?
I'VE BEEN... KIND OF CONFUSED. BAD DREAMS.
I BECAME...KIDDER, I THOUGHT I WAS THE ONE WHO...
...WHO SHOT AT YOU. WHO *KILLED* HAROLD AND RAFE--
MICHAEL, NO!
YOU KNOW WE HAVE KEY CARDS.
MICHAEL, I LOOKED IN ON YOU.
"I LEFT YOU SLEEPING BEFORE I SET OFF THAT MORNING I WAS SHOT AT."
"I GOT THE TEXT ABOUT HAROLD AND RAFE IN YOUR HOTEL ROOM."
I THINK SOMEONE WANTED YOU TO BELIEVE THIS--
--BUT YOU'RE NOT GUILTY.

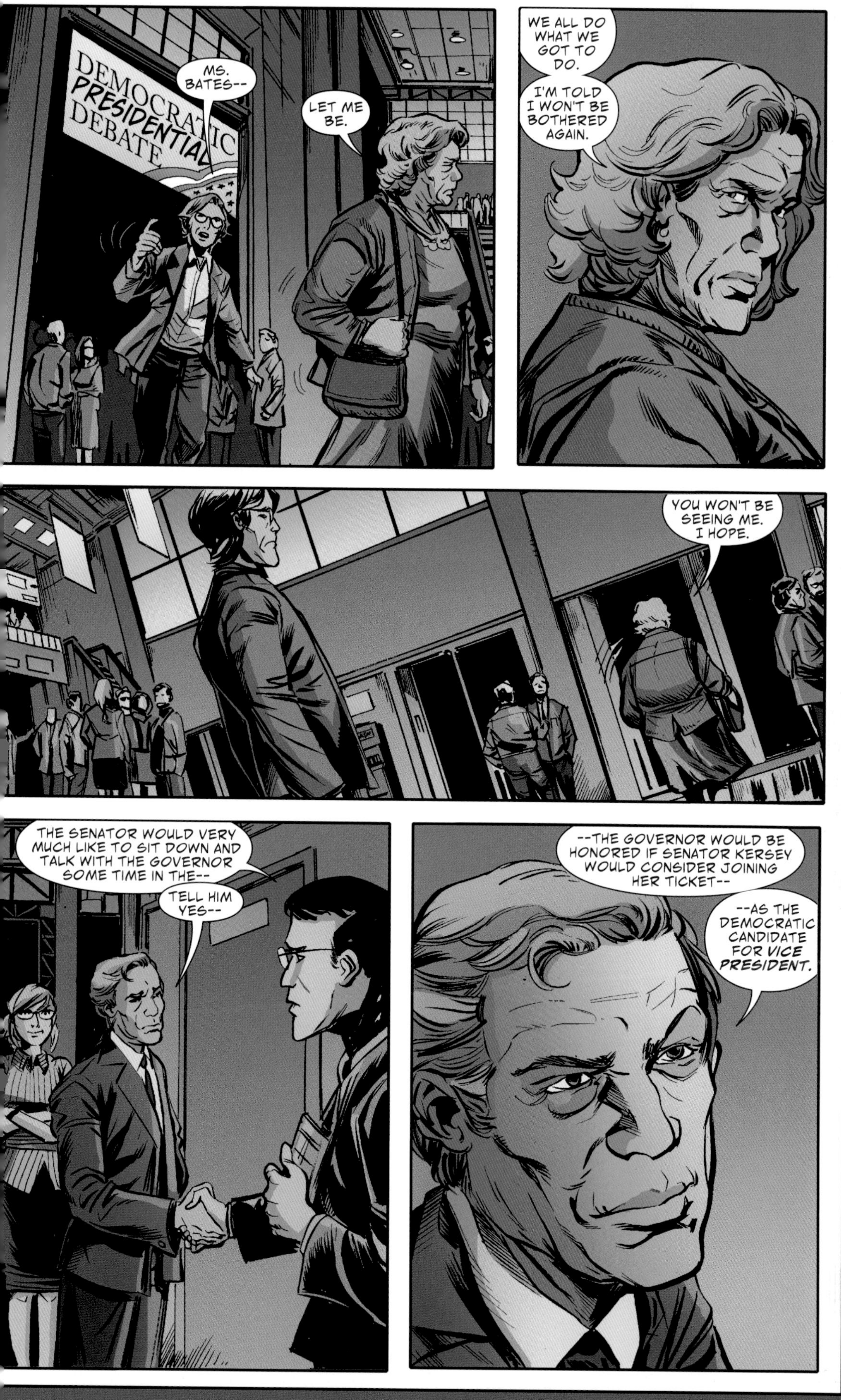
DEMOCRATIC PRESIDENTIAL DEBATE
MS. BATES--
LET ME BE.
WE ALL DO WHAT WE GOT TO DO.
I'M TOLD I WON'T BE BOTHERED AGAIN.
YOU WON'T BE SEEING ME. I HOPE.
THE SENATOR WOULD VERY MUCH LIKE TO SIT DOWN AND TALK WITH THE GOVERNOR SOME TIME IN THE--
TELL HIM YES--
--THE GOVERNOR WOULD BE HONORED IF SENATOR KERSEY WOULD CONSIDER JOINING HER TICKET--
--AS THE DEMOCRATIC CANDIDATE FOR *VICE PRESIDENT*.

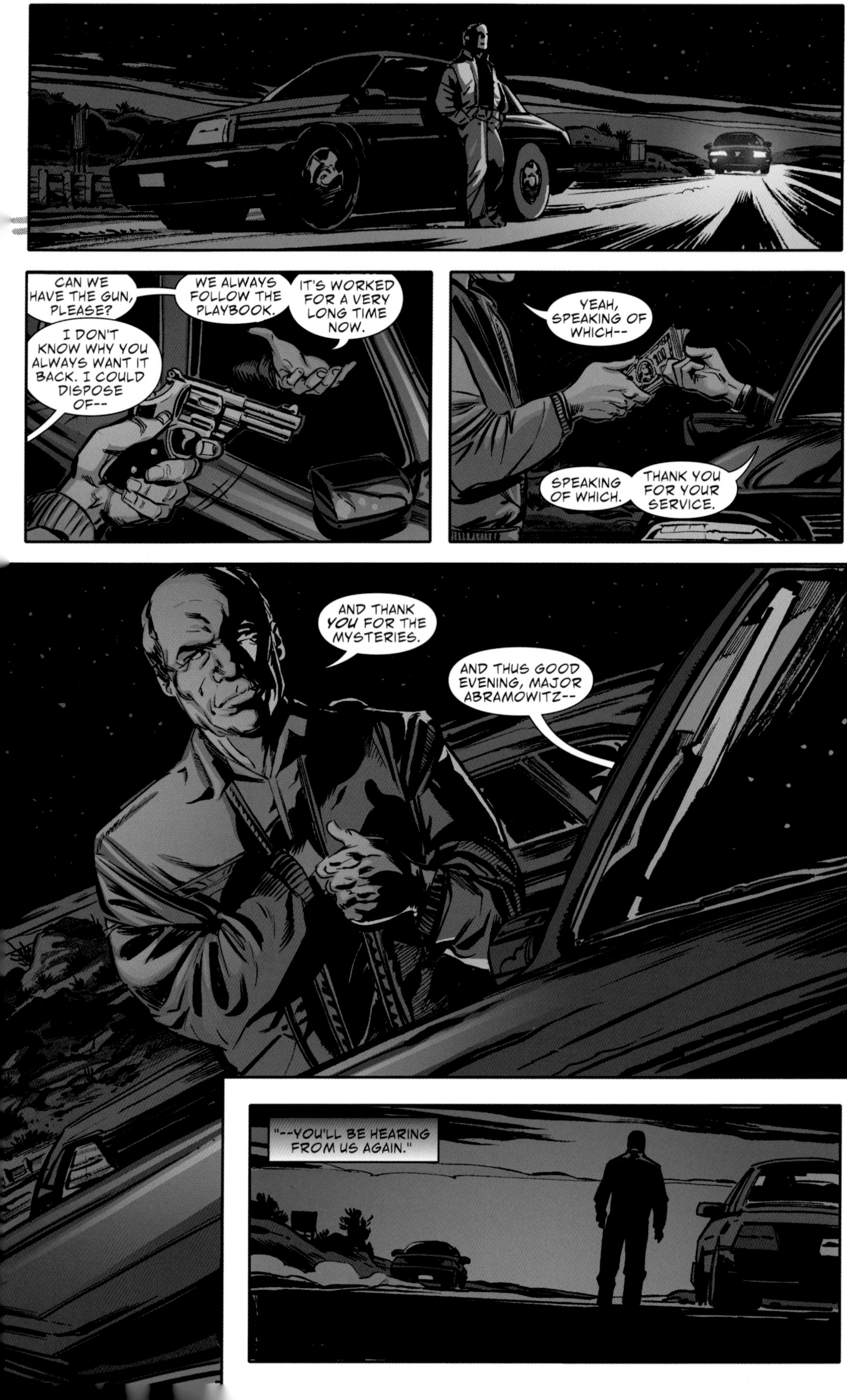
CAN WE HAVE THE GUN, PLEASE?
WE ALWAYS FOLLOW THE PLAYBOOK.
IT'S WORKED FOR A VERY LONG TIME NOW.
I DON'T KNOW WHY YOU ALWAYS WANT IT BACK. I COULD DISPOSE OF--
YEAH, SPEAKING OF WHICH--
SPEAKING OF WHICH.
THANK YOU FOR YOUR SERVICE.
AND THANK *YOU* FOR THE MYSTERIES.
AND THUS GOOD EVENING, MAJOR ABRAMOWITZ--
"--YOU'LL BE HEARING FROM US AGAIN."

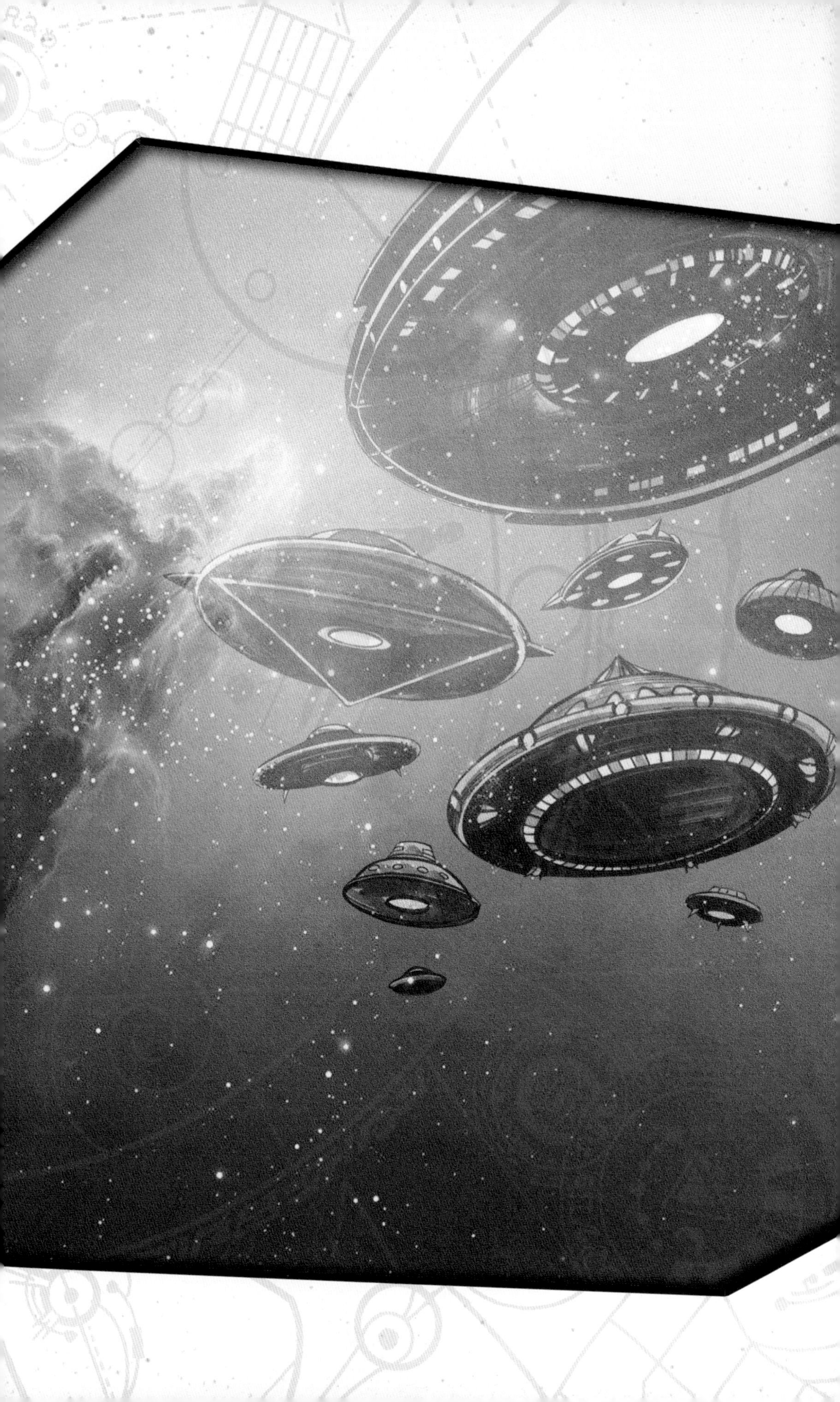

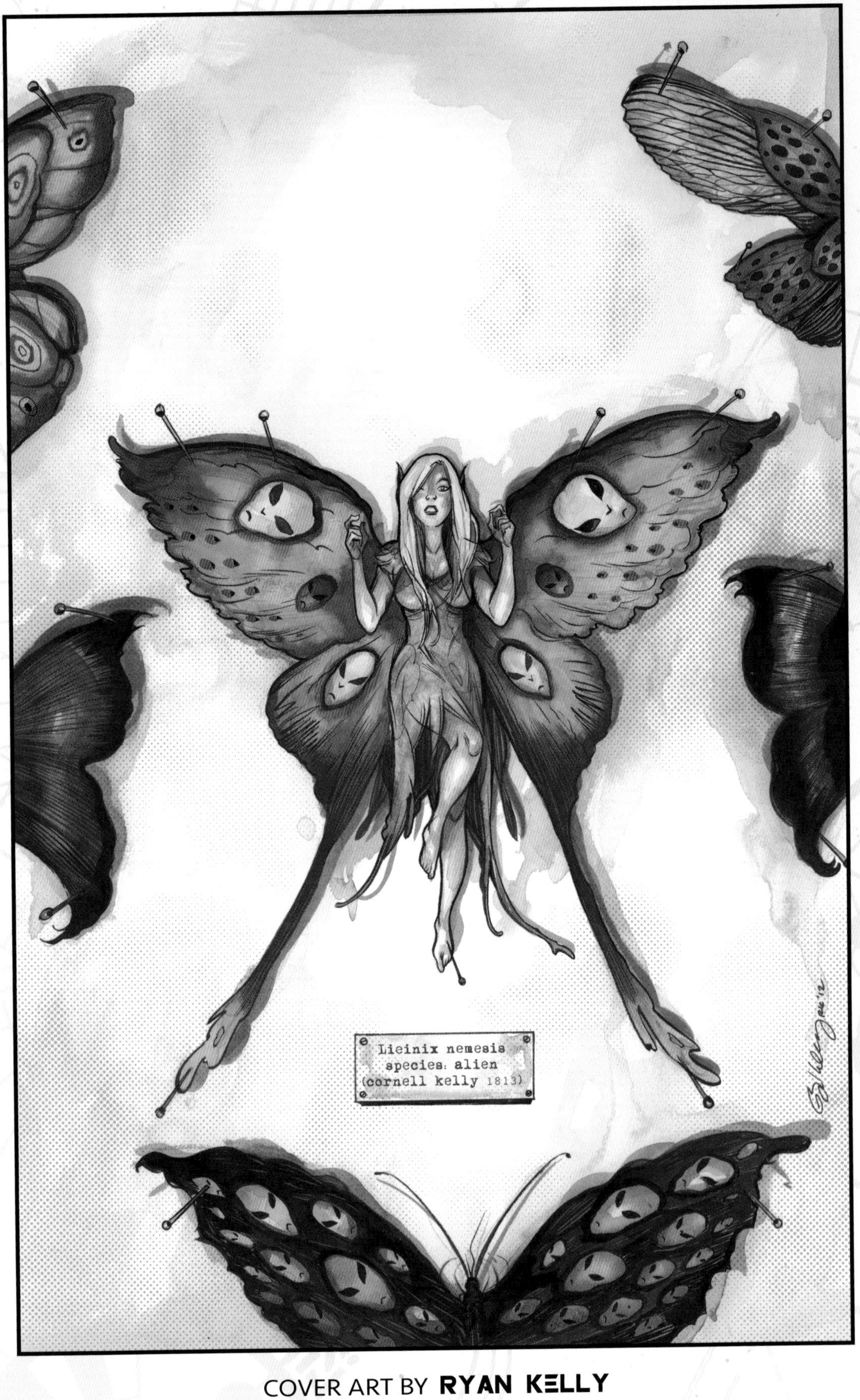
Licinix nemesis
species: alien
(cornell kelly 1813)

COVER ART BY **RYAN KELLY**

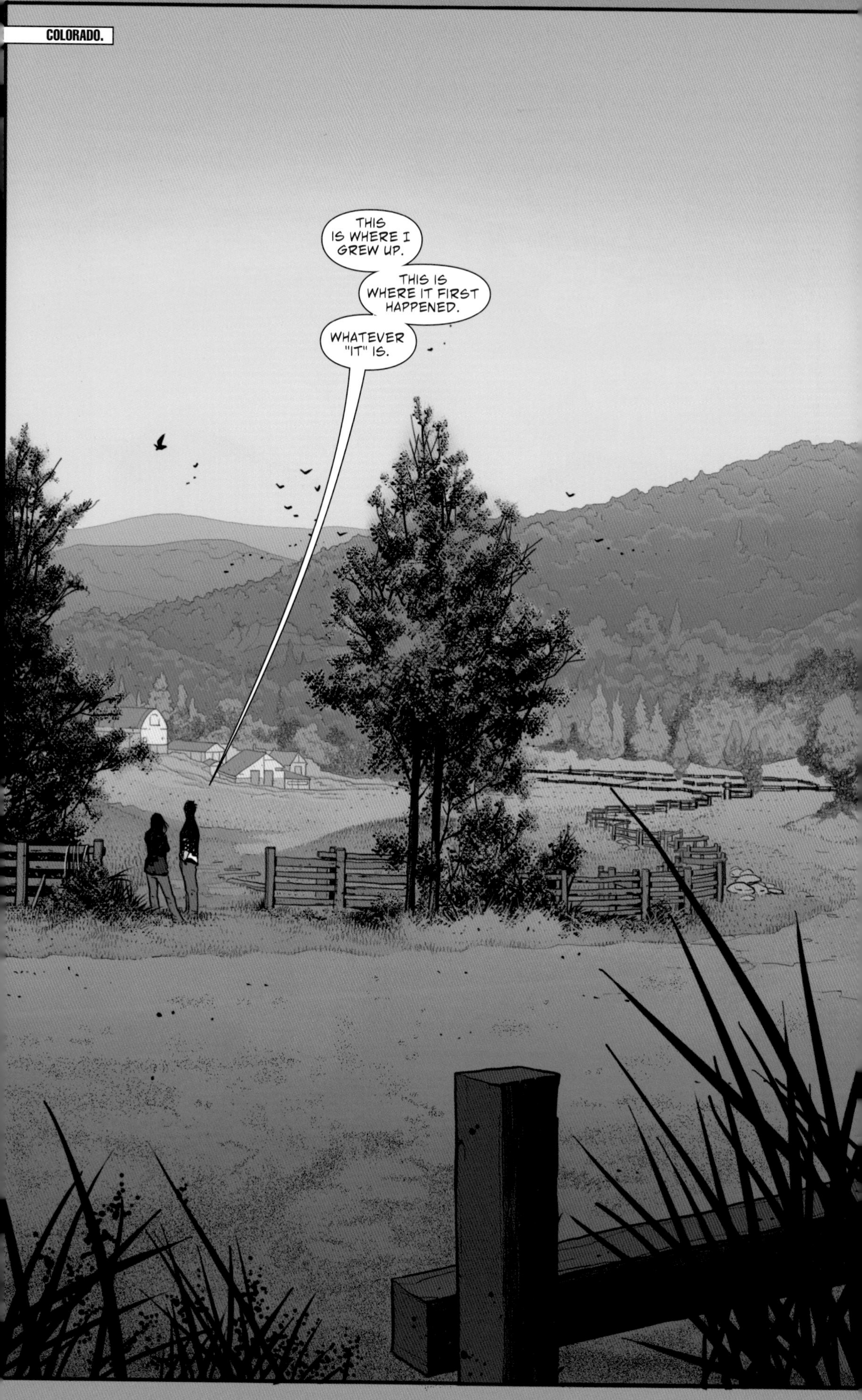
COLORADO.
THIS IS WHERE I GREW UP.
THIS IS WHERE IT FIRST HAPPENED.
WHATEVER "IT" IS.

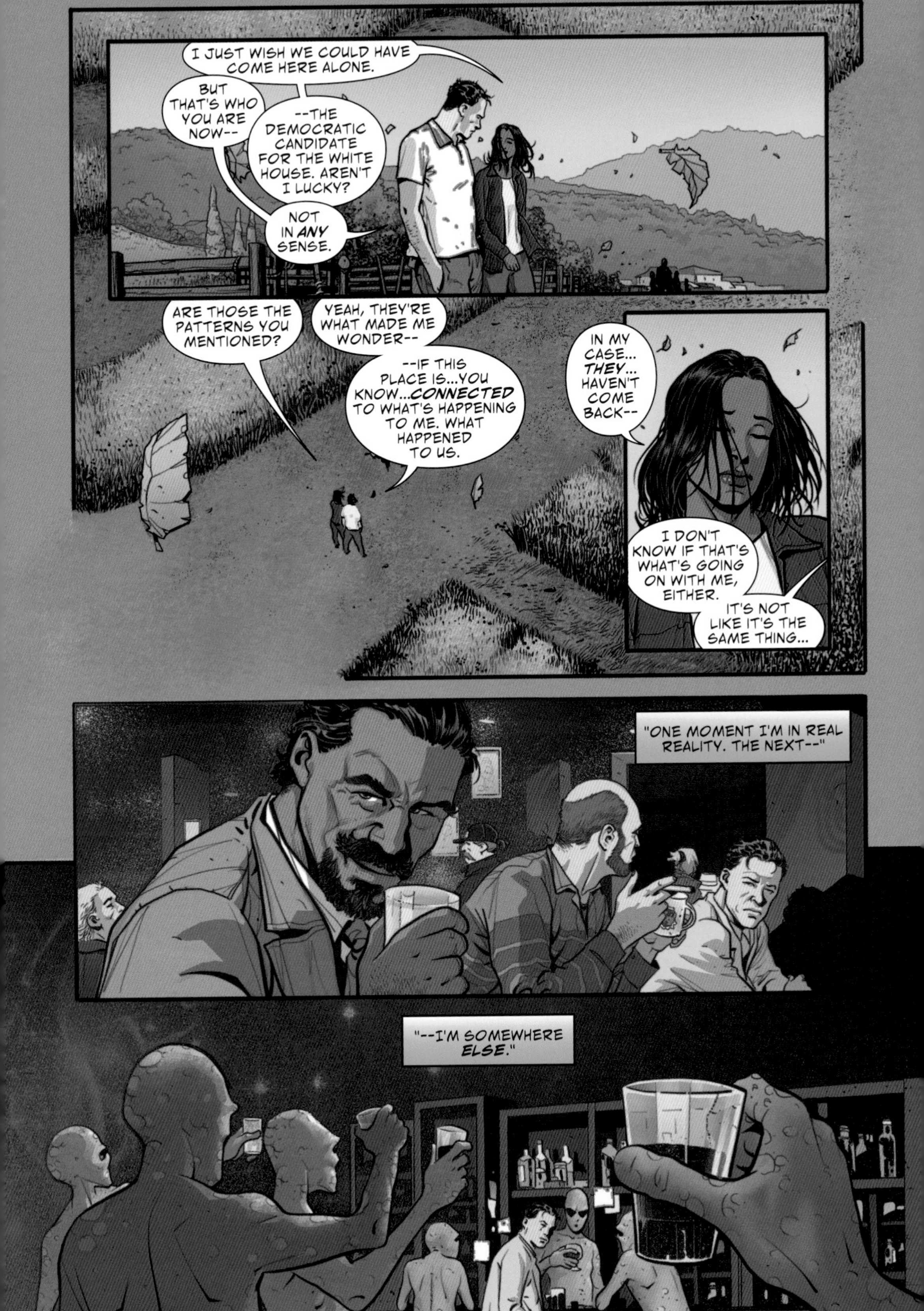
I JUST WISH WE COULD HAVE COME HERE ALONE.
BUT THAT'S WHO YOU ARE NOW--
--THE DEMOCRATIC CANDIDATE FOR THE WHITE HOUSE. AREN'T I LUCKY?
NOT IN ANY SENSE.
ARE THOSE THE PATTERNS YOU MENTIONED?
YEAH, THEY'RE WHAT MADE ME WONDER--
--IF THIS PLACE IS...YOU KNOW...CONNECTED TO WHAT'S HAPPENING TO ME. WHAT HAPPENED TO US.
IN MY CASE... THEY... HAVEN'T COME BACK--
I DON'T KNOW IF THAT'S WHAT'S GOING ON WITH ME, EITHER.
IT'S NOT LIKE IT'S THE SAME THING...
"ONE MOMENT I'M IN REAL REALITY. THE NEXT--"
"--I'M SOMEWHERE ELSE."

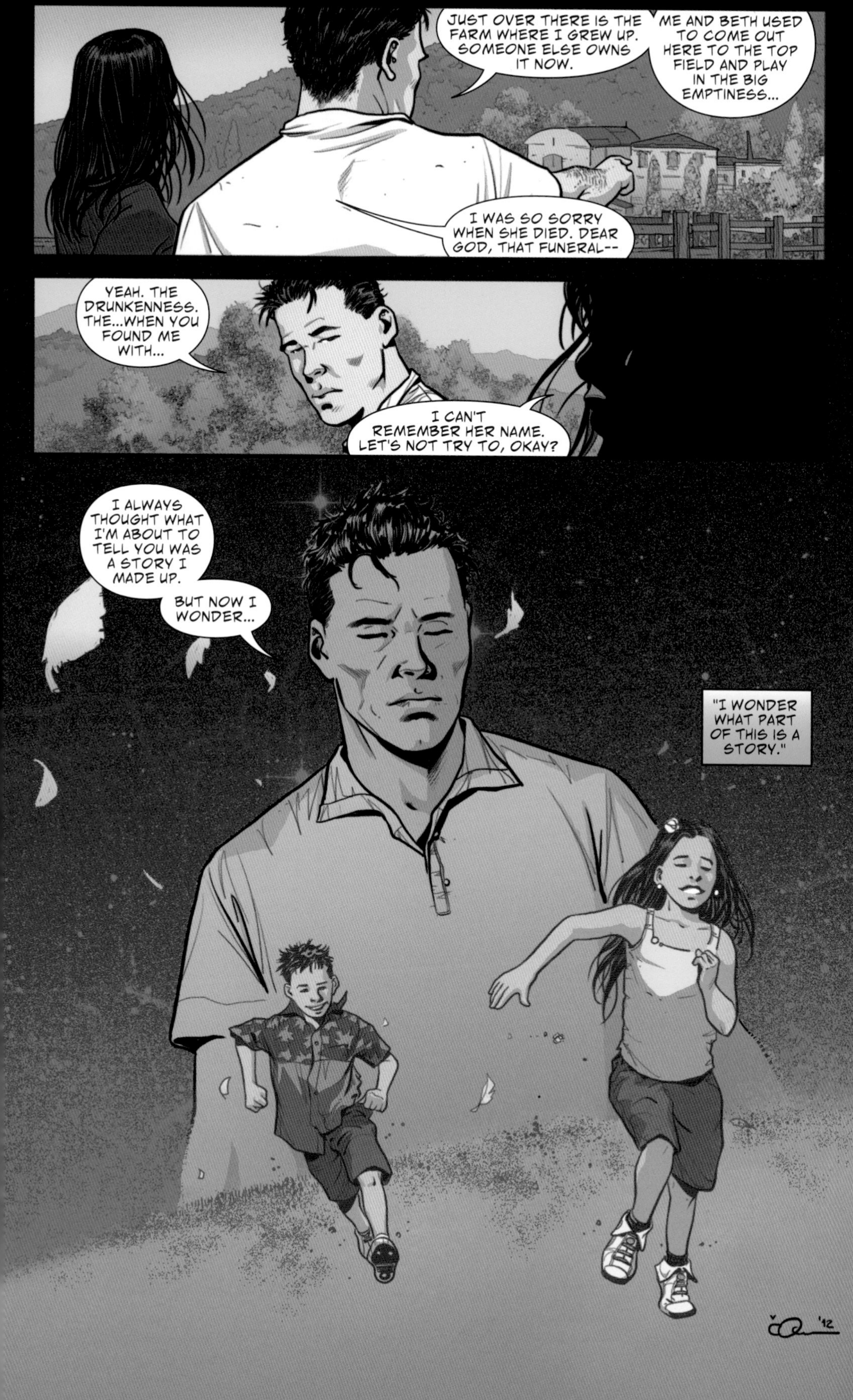
JUST OVER THERE IS THE FARM WHERE I GREW UP. SOMEONE ELSE OWNS IT NOW.
ME AND BETH USED TO COME OUT HERE TO THE TOP FIELD AND PLAY IN THE BIG EMPTINESS...
I WAS SO SORRY WHEN SHE DIED. DEAR GOD, THAT FUNERAL--
YEAH. THE DRUNKENNESS. THE...WHEN YOU FOUND ME WITH...
I CAN'T REMEMBER HER NAME. LET'S NOT TRY TO, OKAY?
I ALWAYS THOUGHT WHAT I'M ABOUT TO TELL YOU WAS A STORY I MADE UP.
BUT NOW I WONDER...
"I WONDER WHAT PART OF THIS IS A STORY."
'12

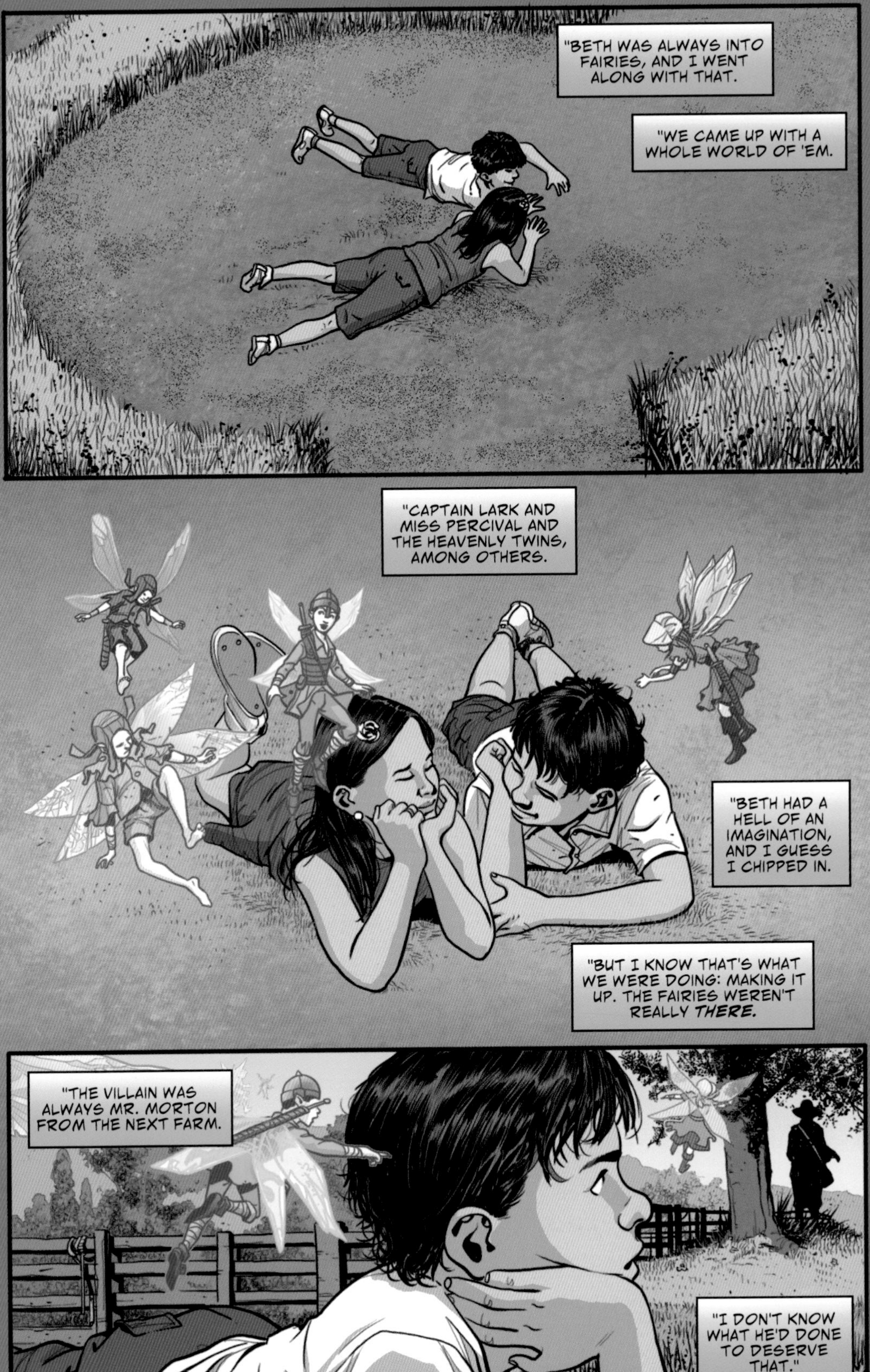
"BETH WAS ALWAYS INTO FAIRIES, AND I WENT ALONG WITH THAT.
"WE CAME UP WITH A WHOLE WORLD OF 'EM.
"CAPTAIN LARK AND MISS PERCIVAL AND THE HEAVENLY TWINS, AMONG OTHERS.
"BETH HAD A HELL OF AN IMAGINATION, AND I GUESS I CHIPPED IN.
"BUT I KNOW THAT'S WHAT WE WERE DOING: MAKING IT UP. THE FAIRIES WEREN'T REALLY *THERE.*
"THE VILLAIN WAS ALWAYS MR. MORTON FROM THE NEXT FARM.
"I DON'T KNOW WHAT HE'D DONE TO DESERVE THAT."

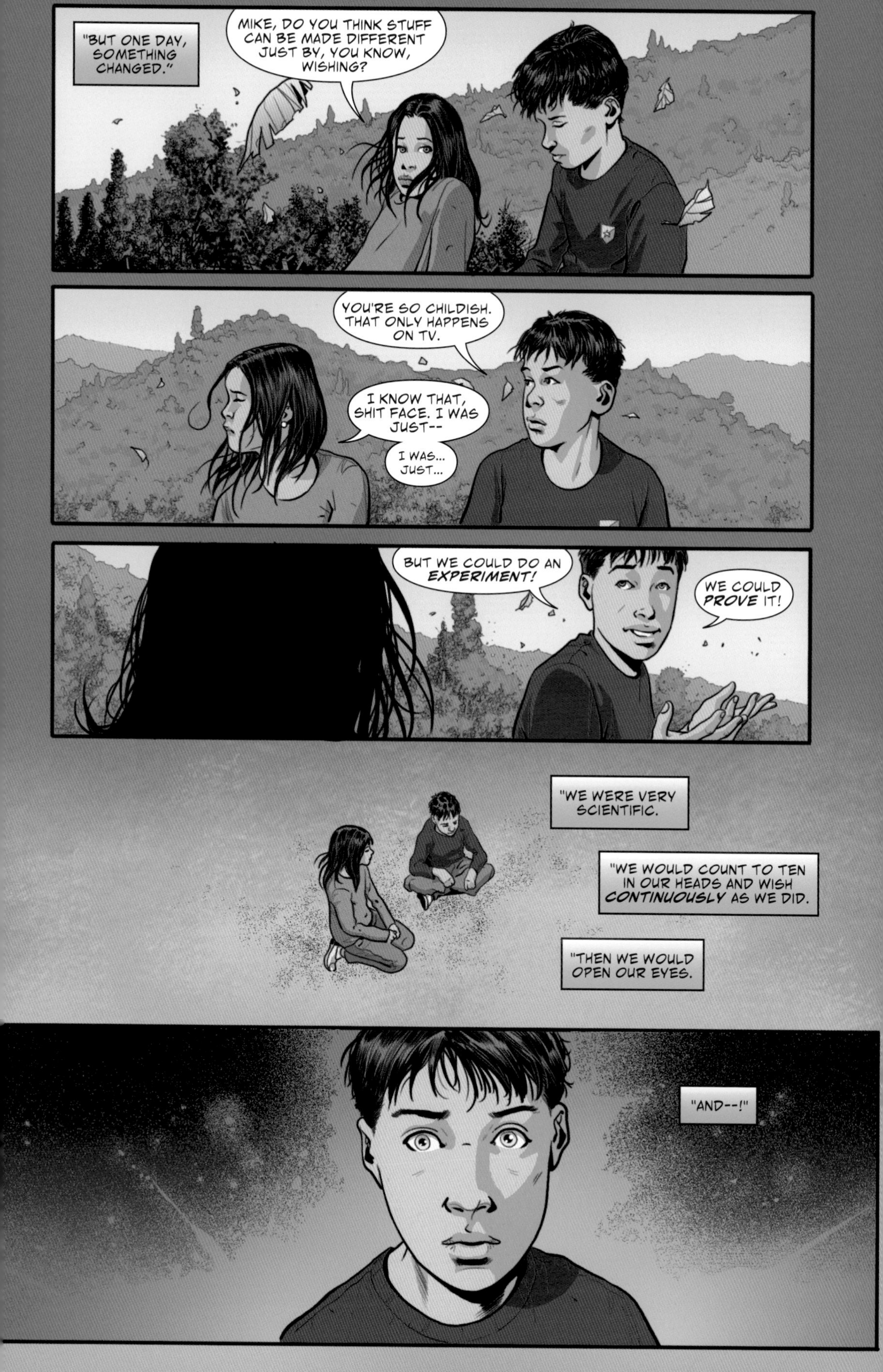
"BUT ONE DAY, SOMETHING CHANGED."
MIKE, DO YOU THINK STUFF CAN BE MADE DIFFERENT JUST BY, YOU KNOW, WISHING?
YOU'RE SO CHILDISH. THAT ONLY HAPPENS ON TV.
I KNOW THAT, SHIT FACE. I WAS JUST--
I WAS... JUST...
BUT WE COULD DO AN EXPERIMENT!
WE COULD PROVE IT!
"WE WERE VERY SCIENTIFIC.
"WE WOULD COUNT TO TEN IN OUR HEADS AND WISH CONTINUOUSLY AS WE DID.
"THEN WE WOULD OPEN OUR EYES.
"AND--!"

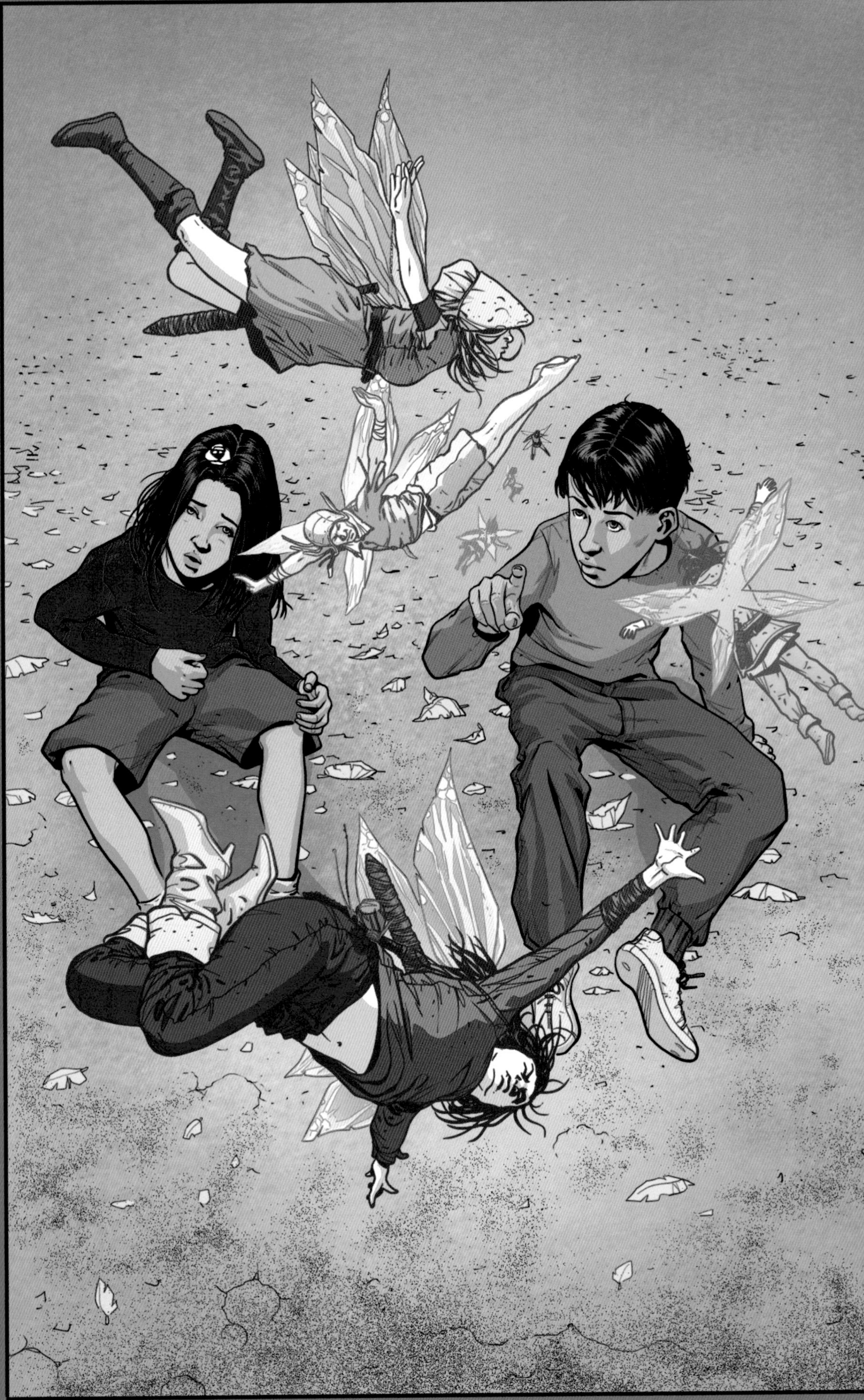

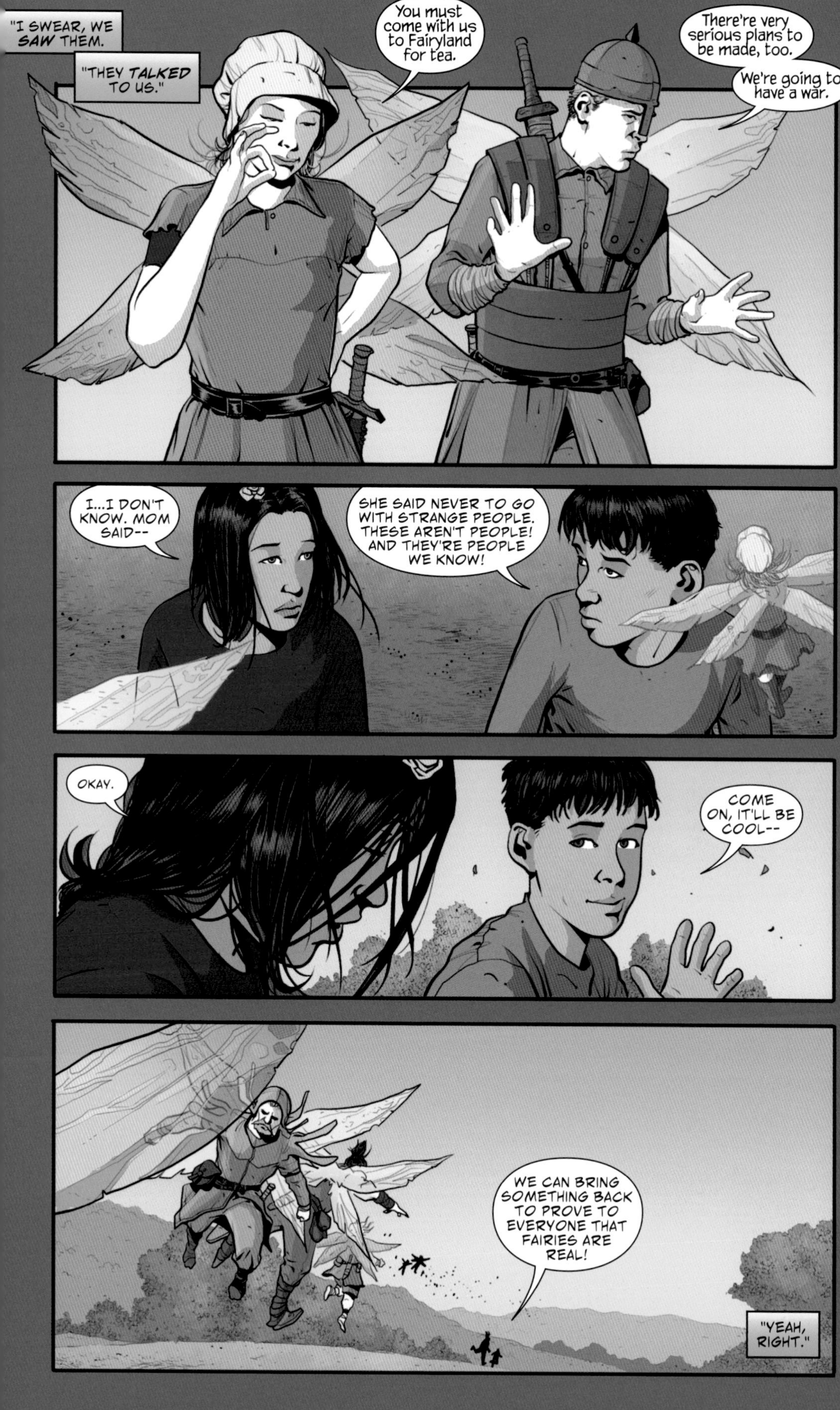
"I SWEAR, WE SAW THEM.
"THEY TALKED TO US."
You must come with us to Fairyland for tea.
There're very serious plans to be made, too.
We're going to have a war.
I...I DON'T KNOW. MOM SAID--
SHE SAID NEVER TO GO WITH STRANGE PEOPLE. THESE AREN'T PEOPLE! AND THEY'RE PEOPLE WE KNOW!
OKAY.
COME ON, IT'LL BE COOL--
WE CAN BRING SOMETHING BACK TO PROVE TO EVERYONE THAT FAIRIES ARE REAL!
"YEAH, RIGHT."

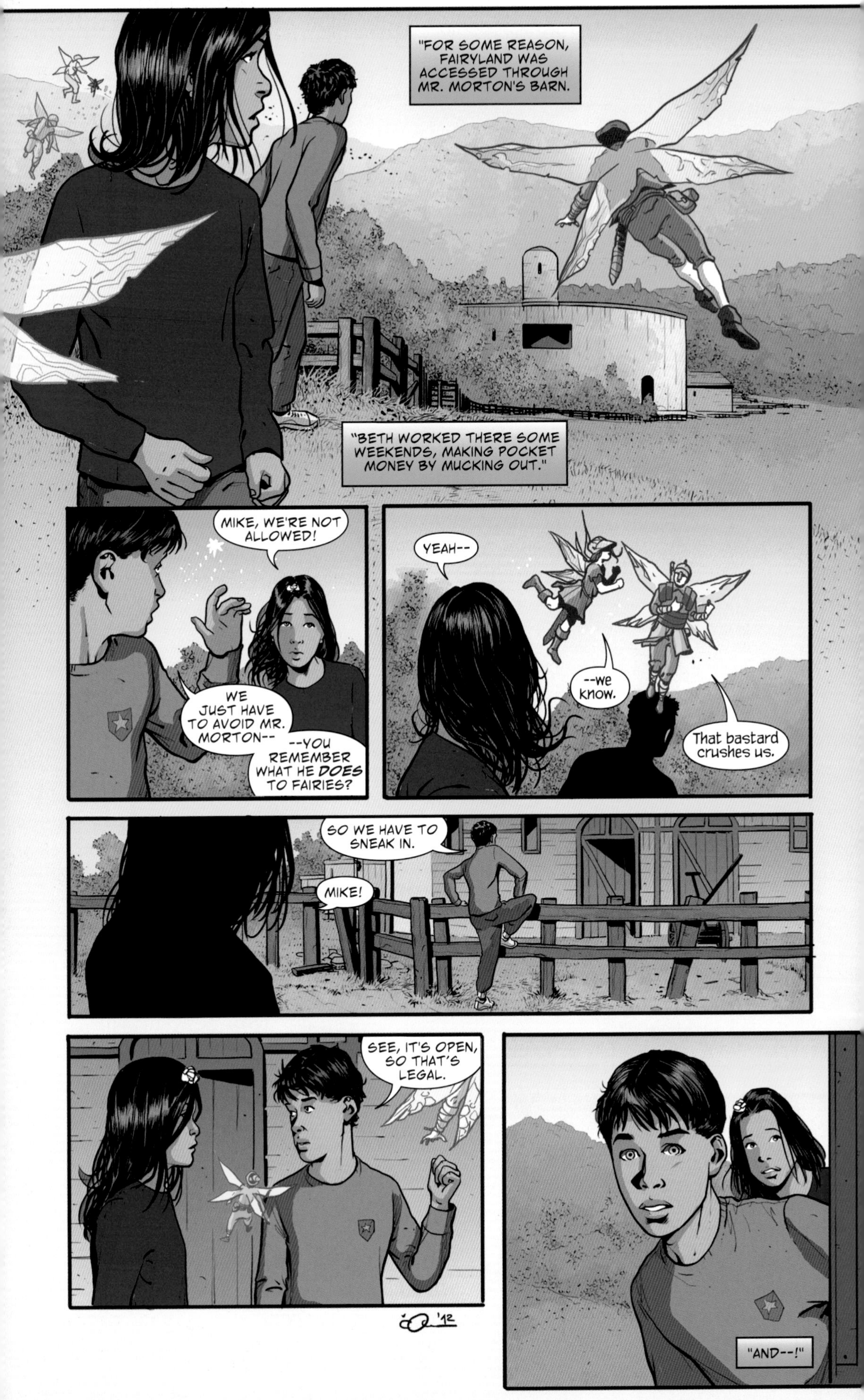
"FOR SOME REASON, FAIRYLAND WAS ACCESSED THROUGH MR. MORTON'S BARN.
"BETH WORKED THERE SOME WEEKENDS, MAKING POCKET MONEY BY MUCKING OUT."
MIKE, WE'RE NOT ALLOWED!
WE JUST HAVE TO AVOID MR. MORTON--
--YOU REMEMBER WHAT HE DOES TO FAIRIES?
YEAH--
--we know.
That bastard crushes us.
SO WE HAVE TO SNEAK IN.
MIKE!
SEE, IT'S OPEN, SO THAT'S LEGAL.
"AND--!"

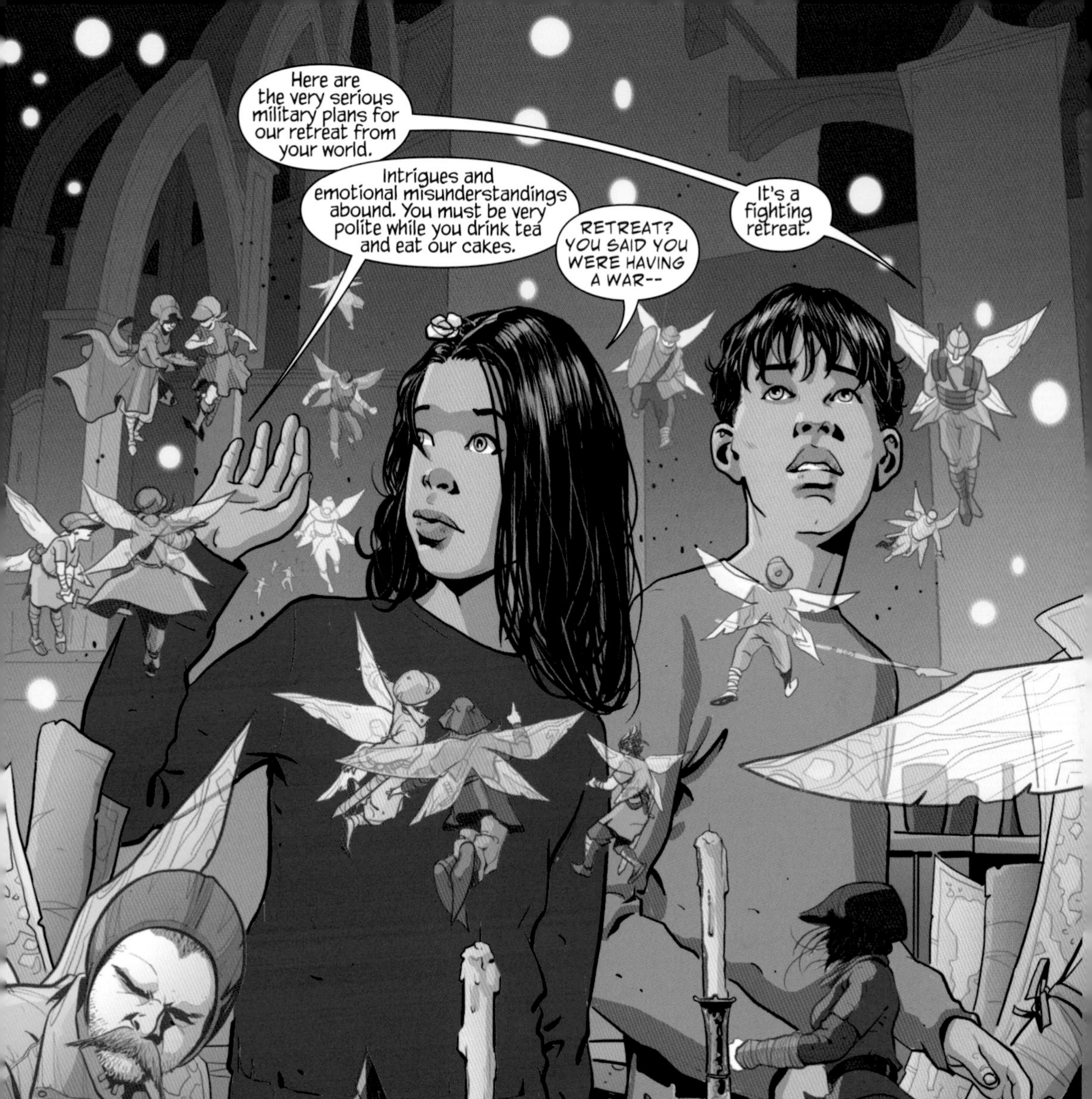
Here are the very serious military plans for our retreat from your world.
Intrigues and emotional misunderstandings abound. You must be very polite while you drink tea and eat our cakes.
RETREAT? YOU SAID YOU WERE HAVING A WAR--
It's a fighting retreat.

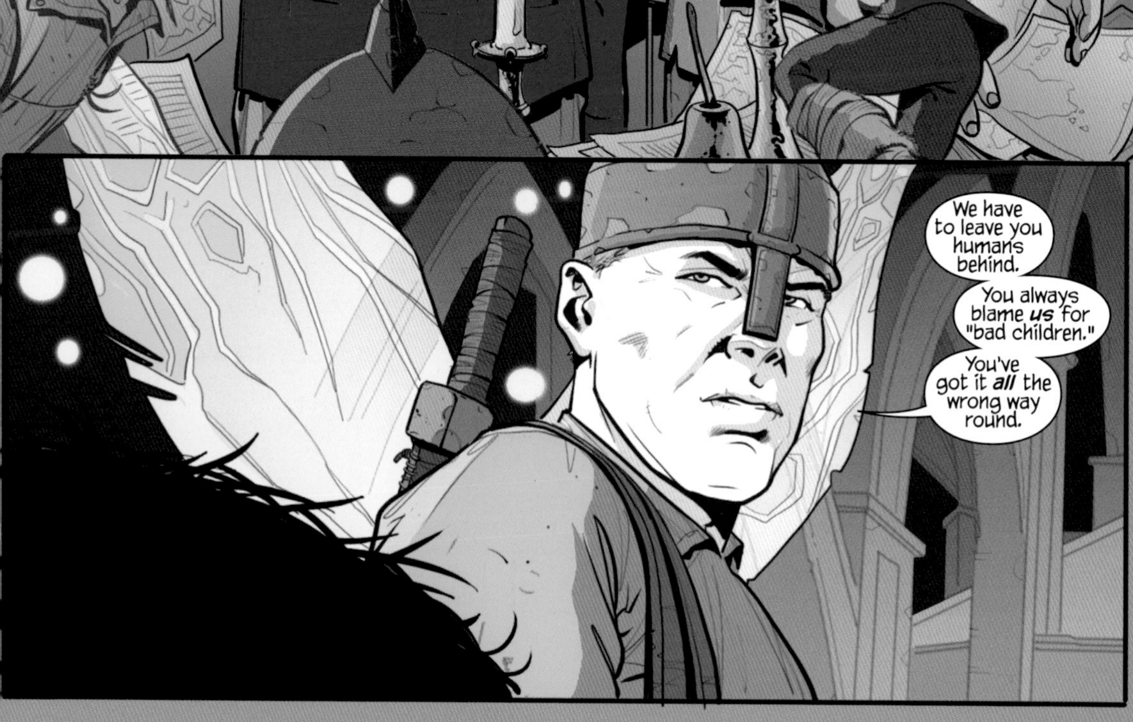
We have to leave you humans behind.
You always blame *us* for "bad children."
You've got it *all* the wrong way round.

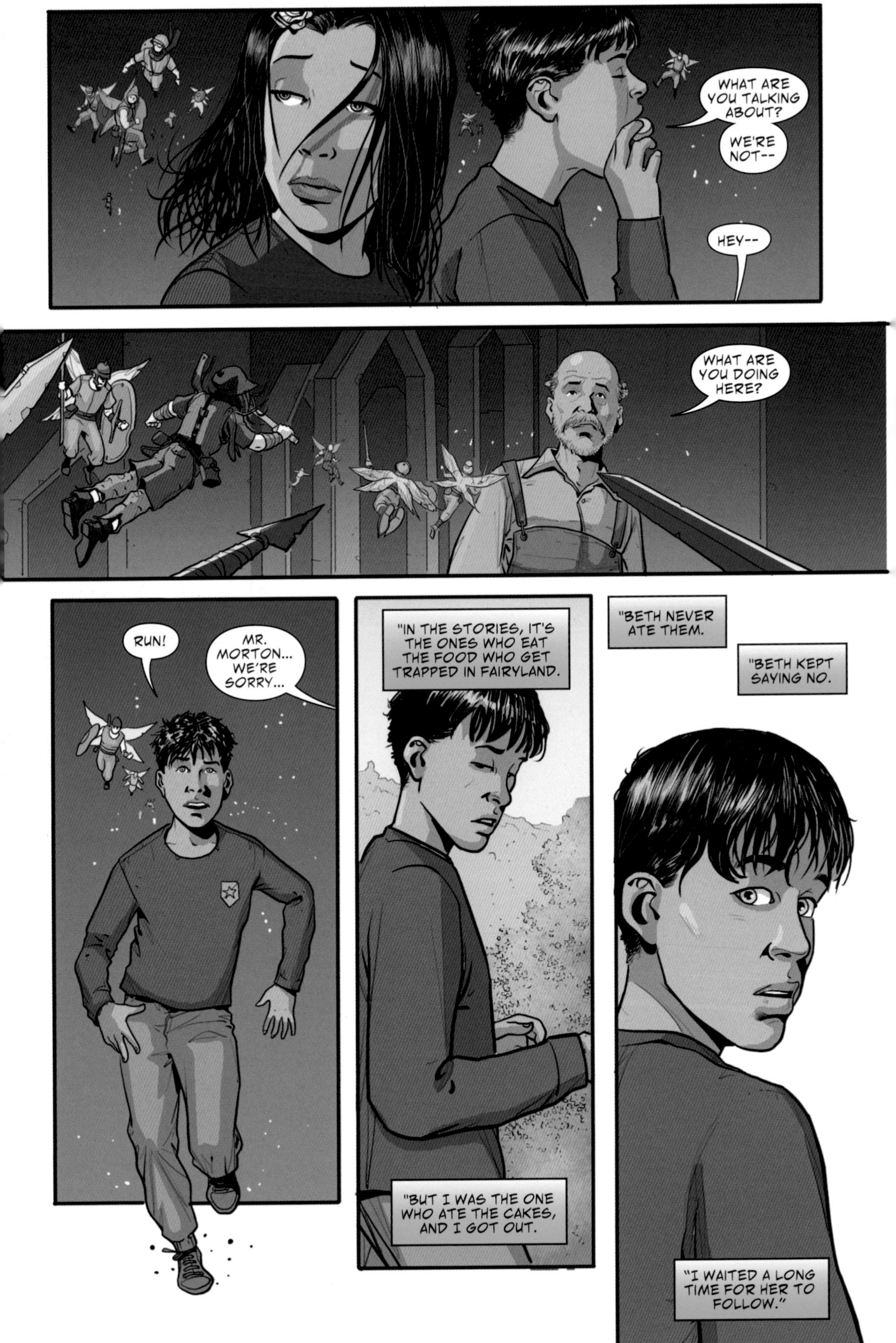
WHAT ARE YOU TALKING ABOUT?
WE'RE NOT--
HEY--
WHAT ARE YOU DOING HERE?
RUN!
MR. MORTON... WE'RE SORRY...
"IN THE STORIES, IT'S THE ONES WHO EAT THE FOOD WHO GET TRAPPED IN FAIRYLAND.
"BUT I WAS THE ONE WHO ATE THE CAKES, AND I GOT OUT.
"BETH NEVER ATE THEM.
"BETH KEPT SAYING NO.
"I WAITED A LONG TIME FOR HER TO FOLLOW."

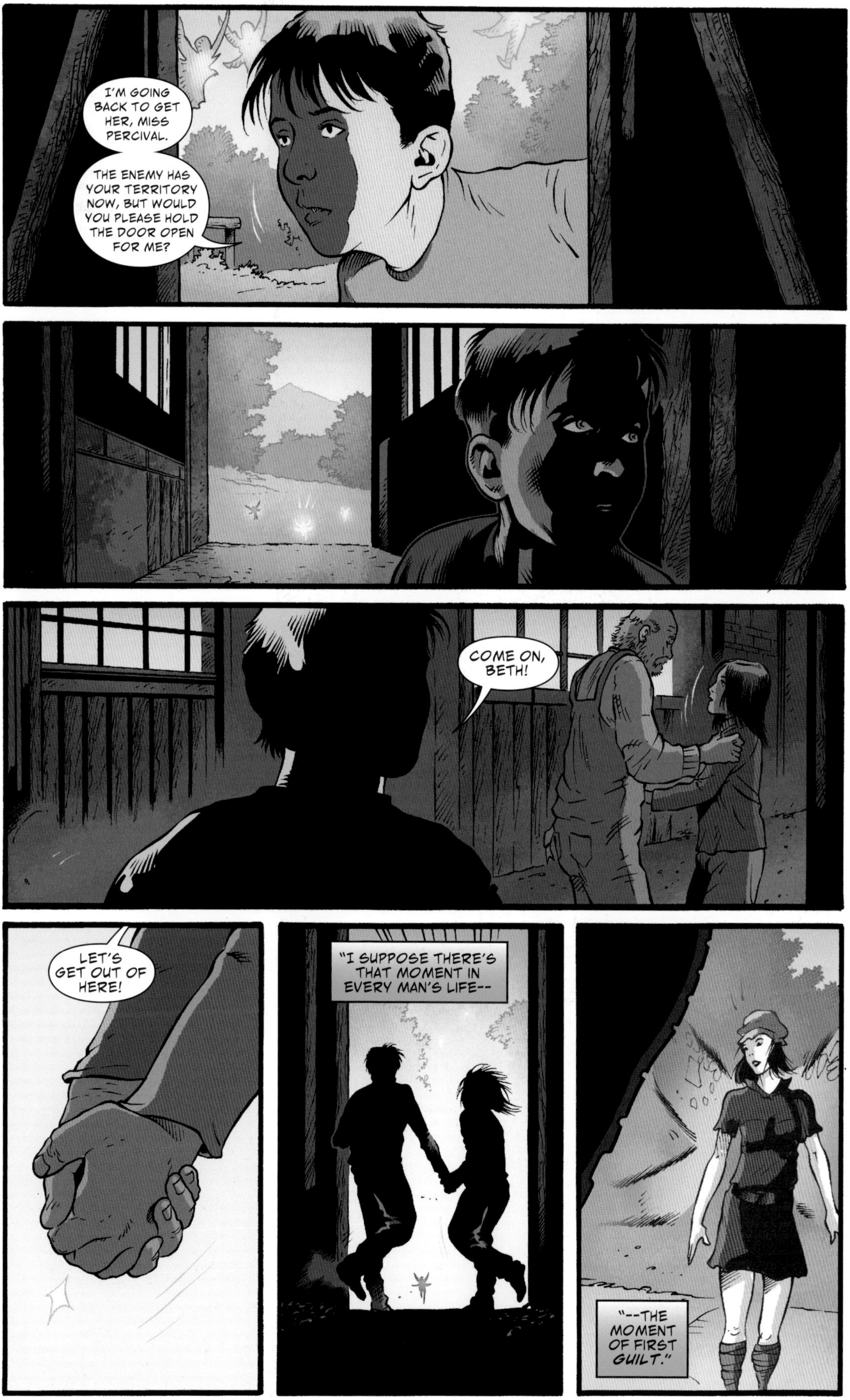
I'M GOING BACK TO GET HER, MISS PERCIVAL.
THE ENEMY HAS YOUR TERRITORY NOW, BUT WOULD YOU PLEASE HOLD THE DOOR OPEN FOR ME?
COME ON, BETH!
LET'S GET OUT OF HERE!
"I SUPPOSE THERE'S THAT MOMENT IN EVERY MAN'S LIFE--
"--THE MOMENT OF FIRST GUILT."

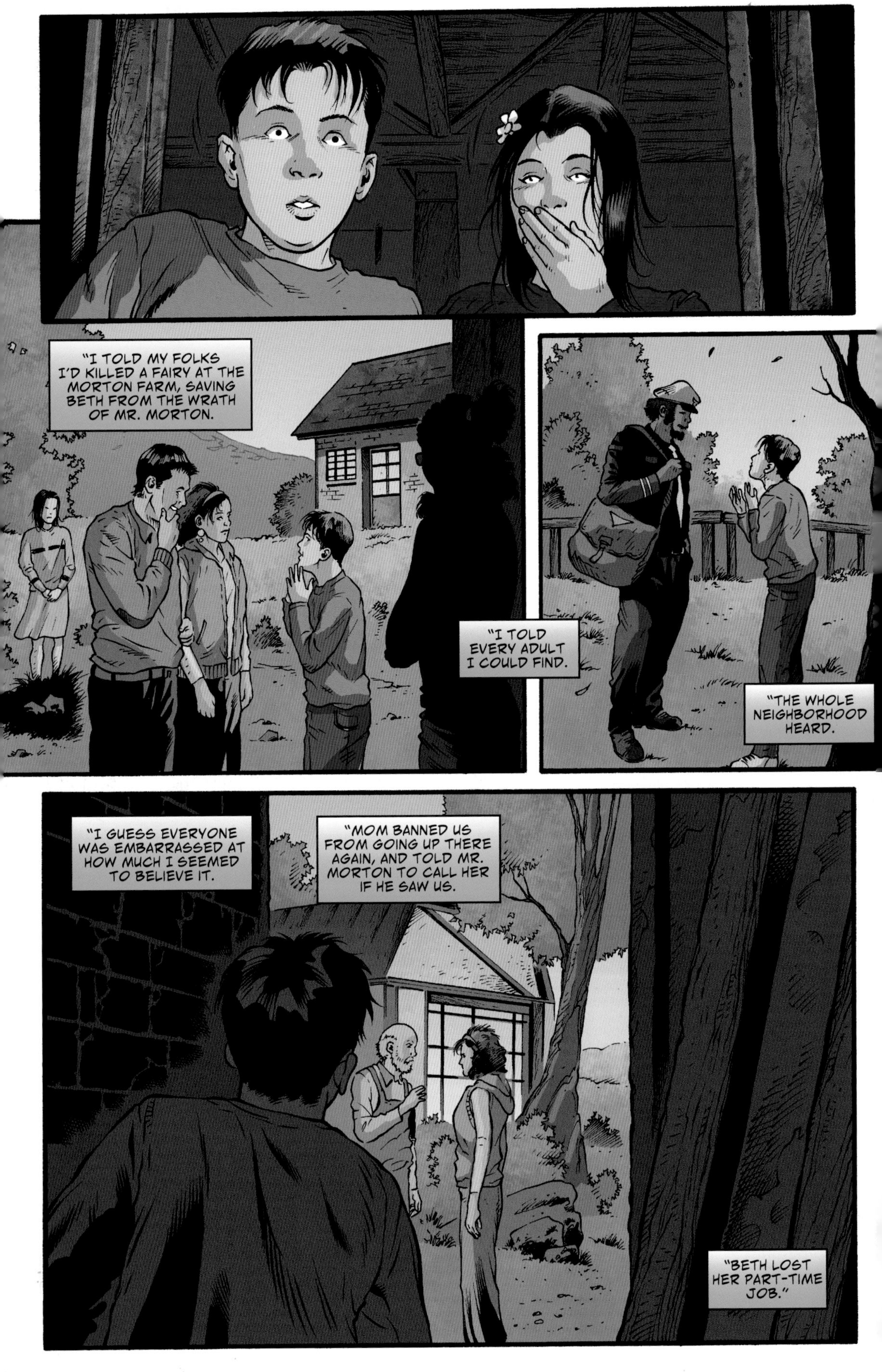
"I TOLD MY FOLKS I'D KILLED A FAIRY AT THE MORTON FARM, SAVING BETH FROM THE WRATH OF MR. MORTON.
"I TOLD EVERY ADULT I COULD FIND.
"THE WHOLE NEIGHBORHOOD HEARD.
"I GUESS EVERYONE WAS EMBARRASSED AT HOW MUCH I SEEMED TO BELIEVE IT.
"MOM BANNED US FROM GOING UP THERE AGAIN, AND TOLD MR. MORTON TO CALL HER IF HE SAW US.
"BETH LOST HER PART-TIME JOB."

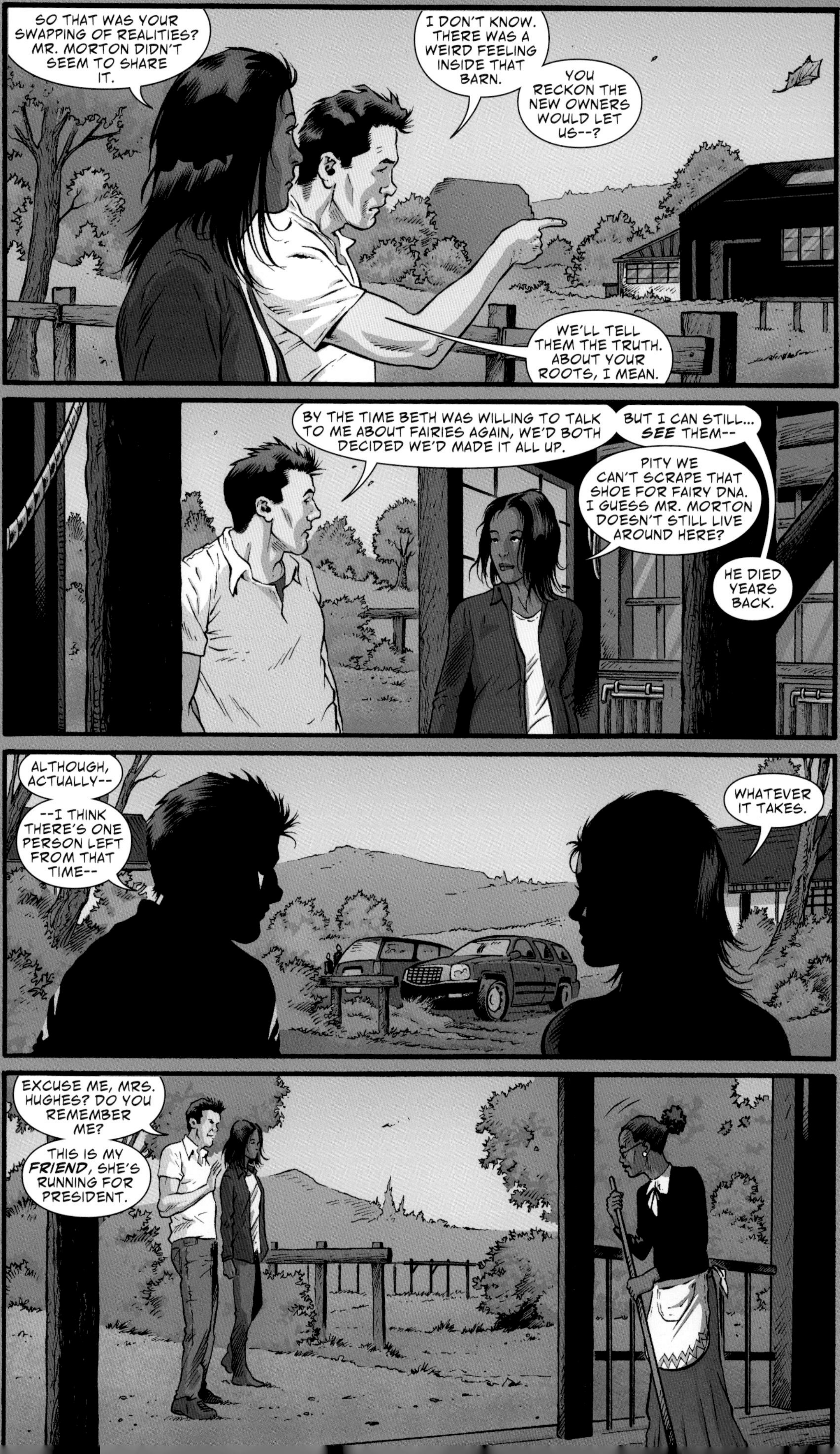
SO THAT WAS YOUR SWAPPING OF REALITIES? MR. MORTON DIDN'T SEEM TO SHARE IT.
I DON'T KNOW. THERE WAS A WEIRD FEELING INSIDE THAT BARN.
YOU RECKON THE NEW OWNERS WOULD LET US--?
WE'LL TELL THEM THE TRUTH. ABOUT YOUR ROOTS, I MEAN.
BY THE TIME BETH WAS WILLING TO TALK TO ME ABOUT FAIRIES AGAIN, WE'D BOTH DECIDED WE'D MADE IT ALL UP.
BUT I CAN STILL... SEE THEM--
PITY WE CAN'T SCRAPE THAT SHOE FOR FAIRY DNA. I GUESS MR. MORTON DOESN'T STILL LIVE AROUND HERE?
HE DIED YEARS BACK.
ALTHOUGH, ACTUALLY--
--I THINK THERE'S ONE PERSON LEFT FROM THAT TIME--
WHATEVER IT TAKES.
EXCUSE ME, MRS. HUGHES? DO YOU REMEMBER ME?
THIS IS MY FRIEND, SHE'S RUNNING FOR PRESIDENT.

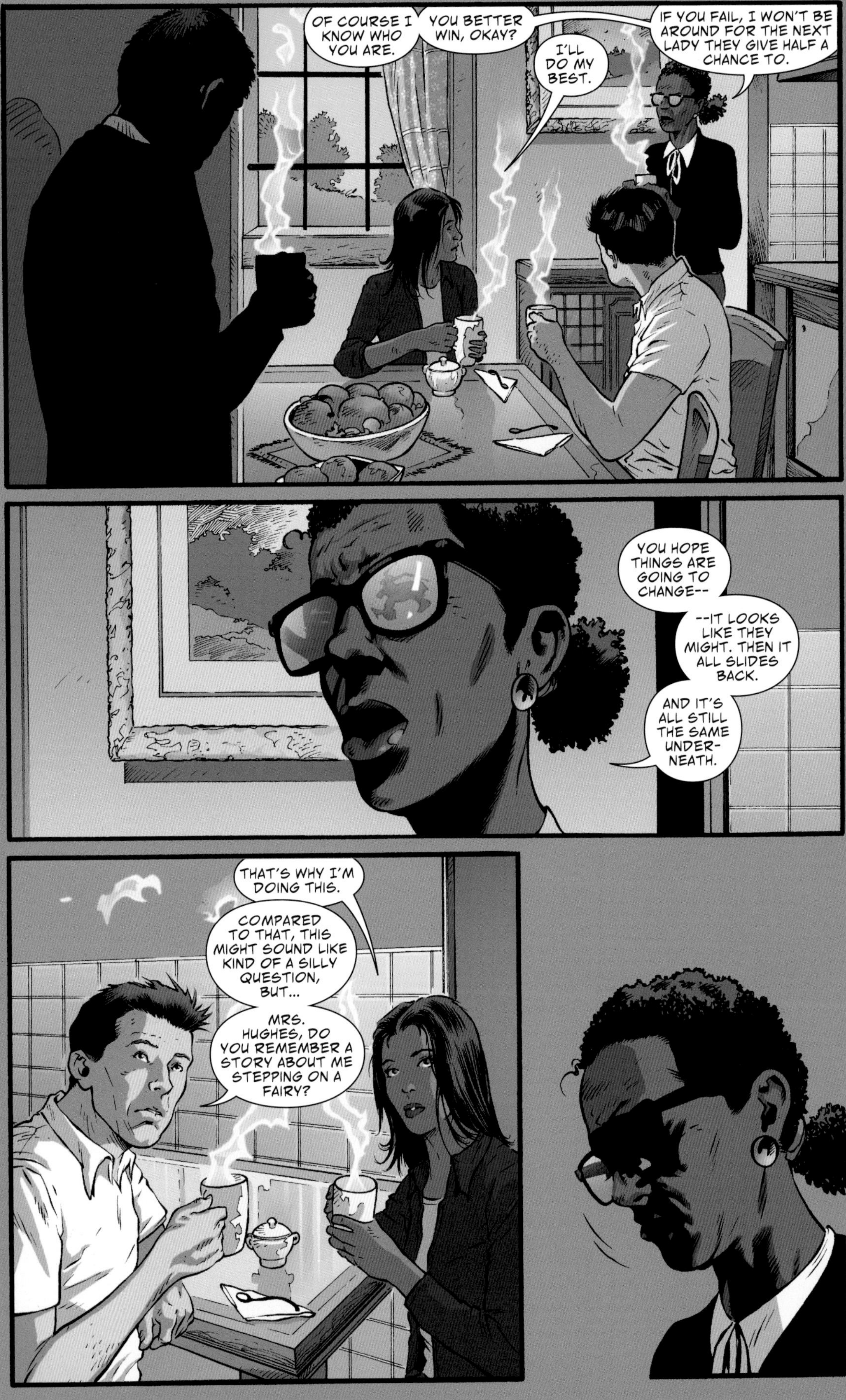
OF COURSE I KNOW WHO YOU ARE.
YOU BETTER WIN, OKAY?
I'LL DO MY BEST.
IF YOU FAIL, I WON'T BE AROUND FOR THE NEXT LADY THEY GIVE HALF A CHANCE TO.
YOU HOPE THINGS ARE GOING TO CHANGE--
--IT LOOKS LIKE THEY MIGHT. THEN IT ALL SLIDES BACK.
AND IT'S ALL STILL THE SAME UNDER-NEATH.
THAT'S WHY I'M DOING THIS.
COMPARED TO THAT, THIS MIGHT SOUND LIKE KIND OF A SILLY QUESTION, BUT...
MRS. HUGHES, DO YOU REMEMBER A STORY ABOUT ME STEPPING ON A FAIRY?

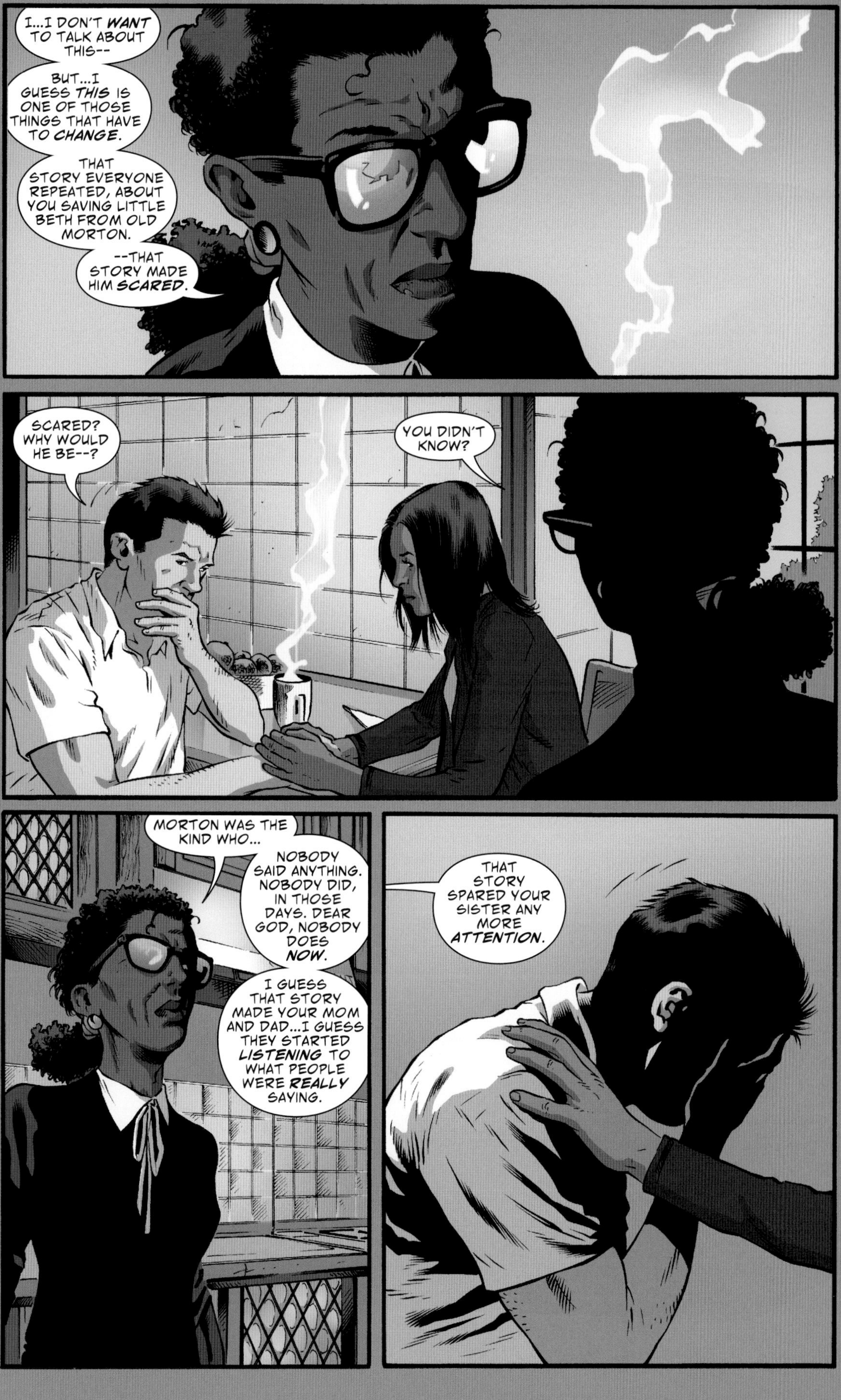
I...I DON'T WANT TO TALK ABOUT THIS--
BUT...I GUESS THIS IS ONE OF THOSE THINGS THAT HAVE TO CHANGE.
THAT STORY EVERYONE REPEATED, ABOUT YOU SAVING LITTLE BETH FROM OLD MORTON.
--THAT STORY MADE HIM SCARED.
SCARED? WHY WOULD HE BE--?
YOU DIDN'T KNOW?
MORTON WAS THE KIND WHO...
NOBODY SAID ANYTHING. NOBODY DID, IN THOSE DAYS. DEAR GOD, NOBODY DOES NOW.
I GUESS THAT STORY MADE YOUR MOM AND DAD...I GUESS THEY STARTED LISTENING TO WHAT PEOPLE WERE REALLY SAYING.
THAT STORY SPARED YOUR SISTER ANY MORE ATTENTION.

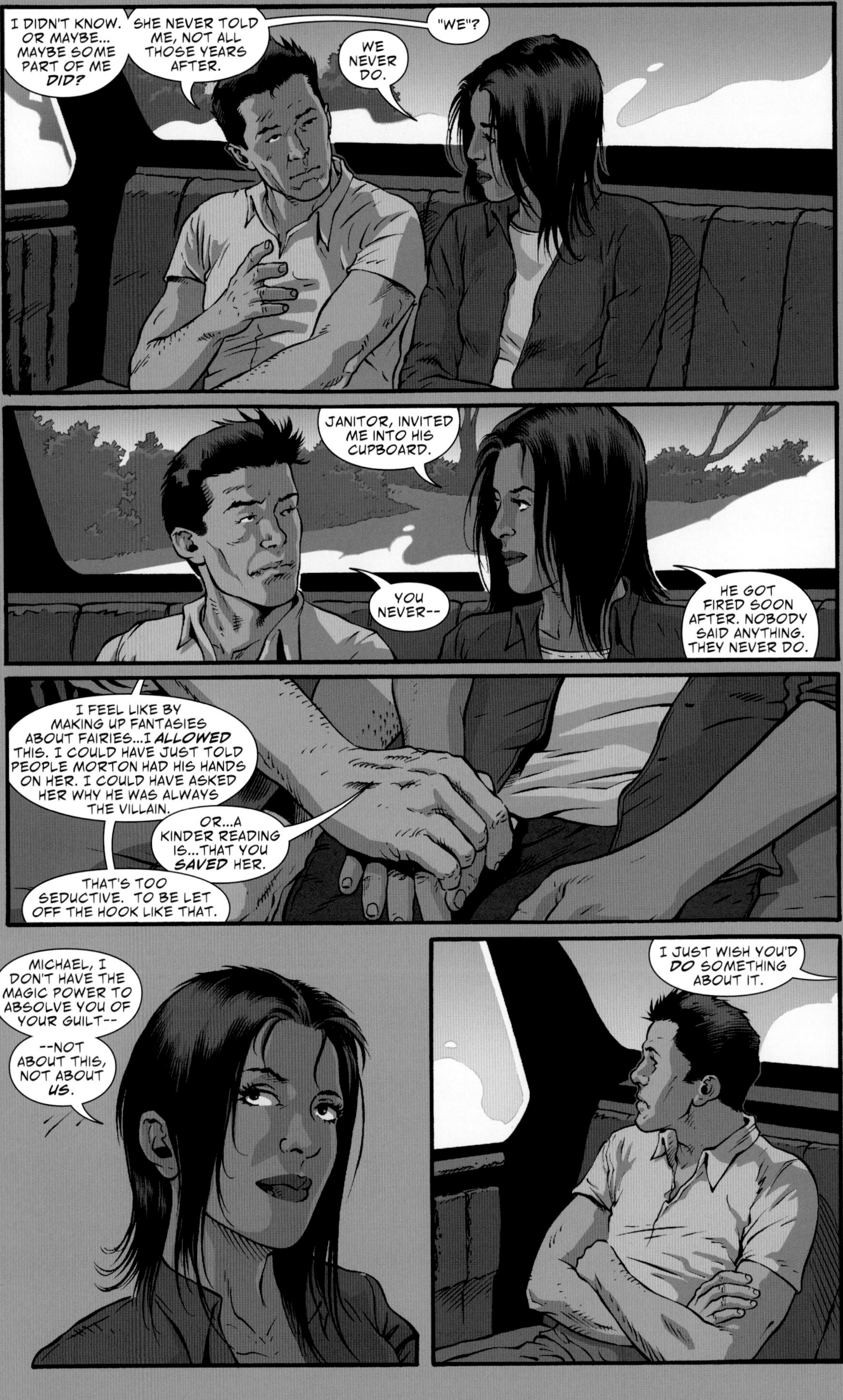
I DIDN'T KNOW. OR MAYBE... MAYBE SOME PART OF ME *DID?*
SHE NEVER TOLD ME, NOT ALL THOSE YEARS AFTER.
WE NEVER DO.
"WE"?
JANITOR, INVITED ME INTO HIS CUPBOARD.
YOU NEVER--
HE GOT FIRED SOON AFTER. NOBODY SAID ANYTHING. THEY NEVER DO.
I FEEL LIKE BY MAKING UP FANTASIES ABOUT FAIRIES...I *ALLOWED* THIS. I COULD HAVE JUST TOLD PEOPLE MORTON HAD HIS HANDS ON HER. I COULD HAVE ASKED HER WHY HE WAS ALWAYS THE VILLAIN.
OR...A KINDER READING IS...THAT YOU *SAVED* HER.
THAT'S TOO SEDUCTIVE. TO BE LET OFF THE HOOK LIKE THAT.
MICHAEL, I DON'T HAVE THE MAGIC POWER TO ABSOLVE YOU OF YOUR GUILT--
--NOT ABOUT THIS, NOT ABOUT *US*.
I JUST WISH YOU'D *DO* SOMETHING ABOUT IT.

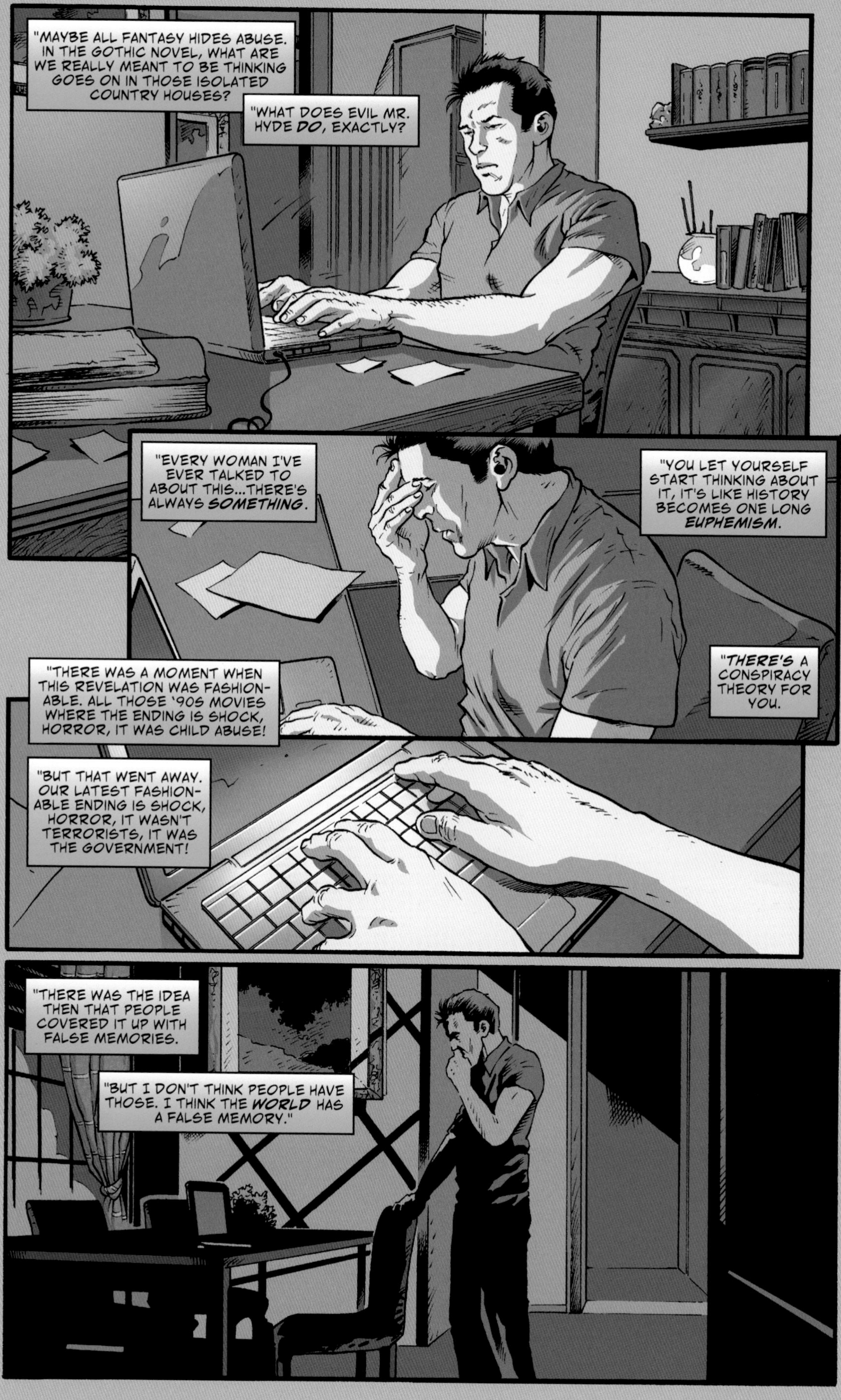
"MAYBE ALL FANTASY HIDES ABUSE. IN THE GOTHIC NOVEL, WHAT ARE WE REALLY MEANT TO BE THINKING GOES ON IN THOSE ISOLATED COUNTRY HOUSES?
"WHAT DOES EVIL MR. HYDE DO, EXACTLY?
"EVERY WOMAN I'VE EVER TALKED TO ABOUT THIS...THERE'S ALWAYS SOMETHING.
"YOU LET YOURSELF START THINKING ABOUT IT, IT'S LIKE HISTORY BECOMES ONE LONG EUPHEMISM.
"THERE WAS A MOMENT WHEN THIS REVELATION WAS FASHION-ABLE. ALL THOSE '90S MOVIES WHERE THE ENDING IS SHOCK, HORROR, IT WAS CHILD ABUSE!
"THERE'S A CONSPIRACY THEORY FOR YOU.
"BUT THAT WENT AWAY. OUR LATEST FASHION-ABLE ENDING IS SHOCK, HORROR, IT WASN'T TERRORISTS, IT WAS THE GOVERNMENT!
"THERE WAS THE IDEA THEN THAT PEOPLE COVERED IT UP WITH FALSE MEMORIES.
"BUT I DON'T THINK PEOPLE HAVE THOSE. I THINK THE WORLD HAS A FALSE MEMORY."

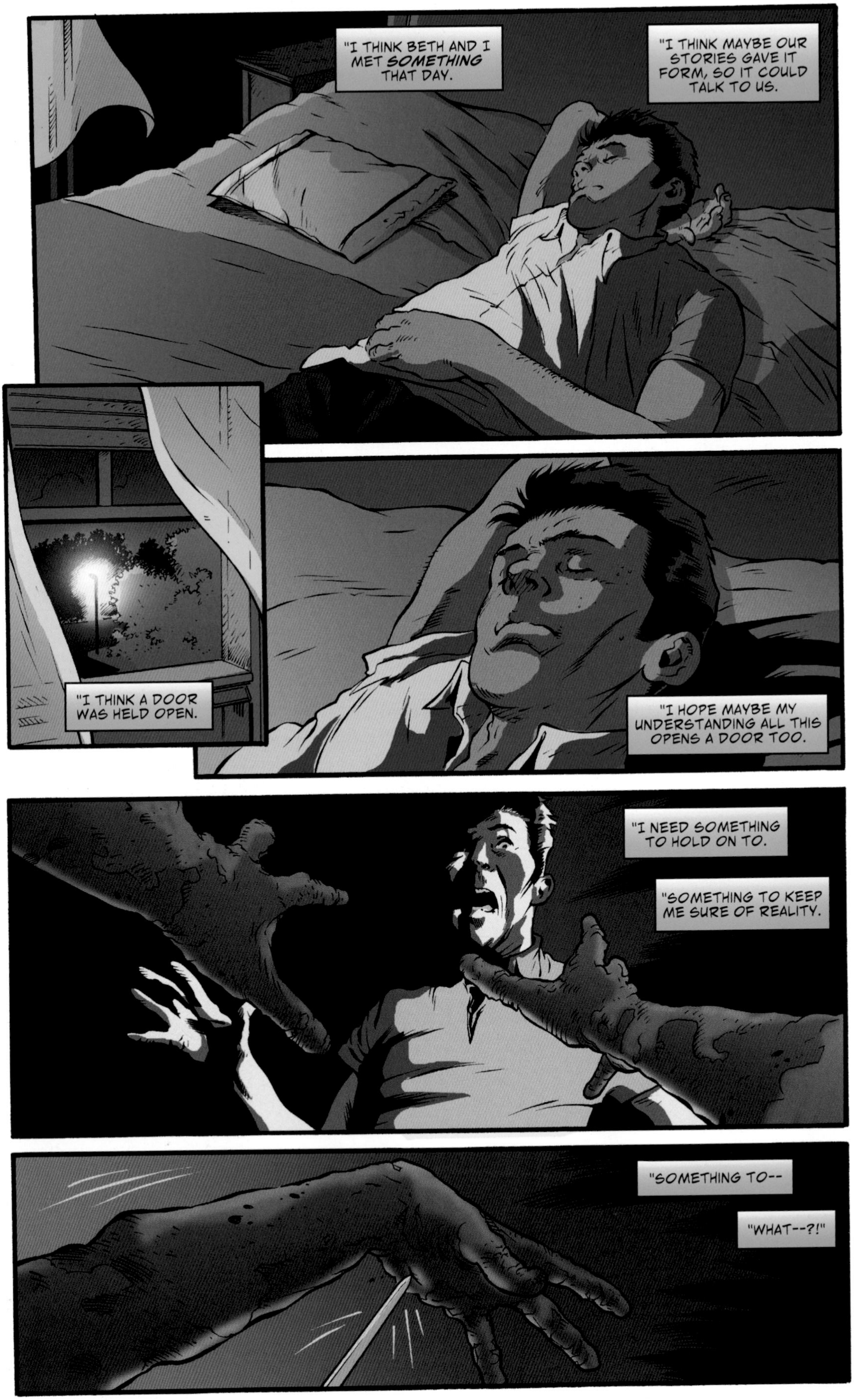
"I THINK BETH AND I MET *SOMETHING* THAT DAY.
"I THINK MAYBE OUR STORIES GAVE IT FORM, SO IT COULD TALK TO US.
"I THINK A DOOR WAS HELD OPEN.
"I HOPE MAYBE MY UNDERSTANDING ALL THIS OPENS A DOOR TOO.
"I NEED SOMETHING TO HOLD ON TO.
"SOMETHING TO KEEP ME SURE OF REALITY.
"SOMETHING TO--
"WHAT--?!"

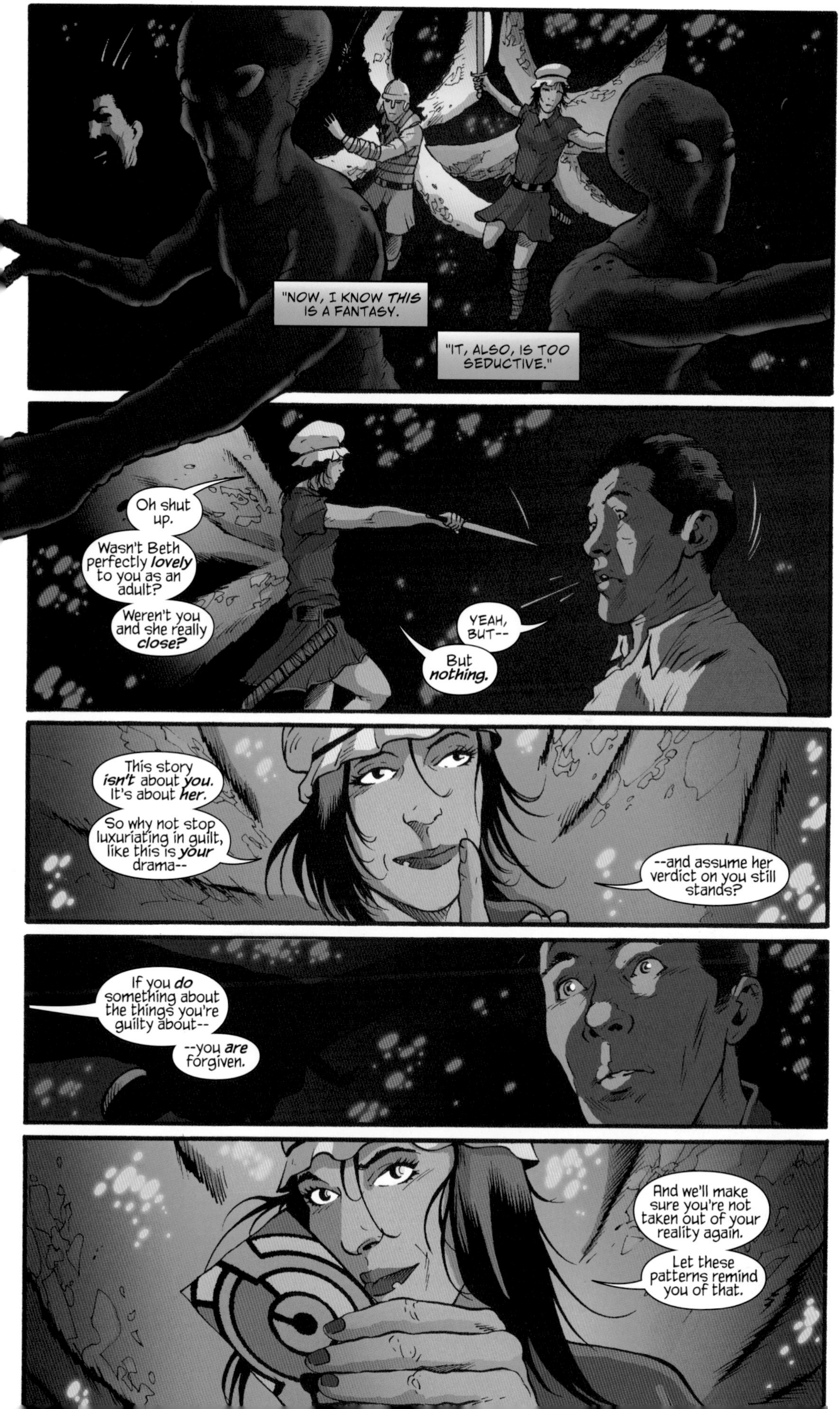
"NOW, I KNOW THIS IS A FANTASY.
"IT, ALSO, IS TOO SEDUCTIVE."
Oh shut up.
Wasn't Beth perfectly lovely to you as an adult?
Weren't you and she really close?
YEAH, BUT--
But nothing.
This story isn't about you. It's about her.
So why not stop luxuriating in guilt, like this is your drama--
--and assume her verdict on you still stands?
If you do something about the things you're guilty about--
--you are forgiven.
And we'll make sure you're not taken out of your reality again.
Let these patterns remind you of that.

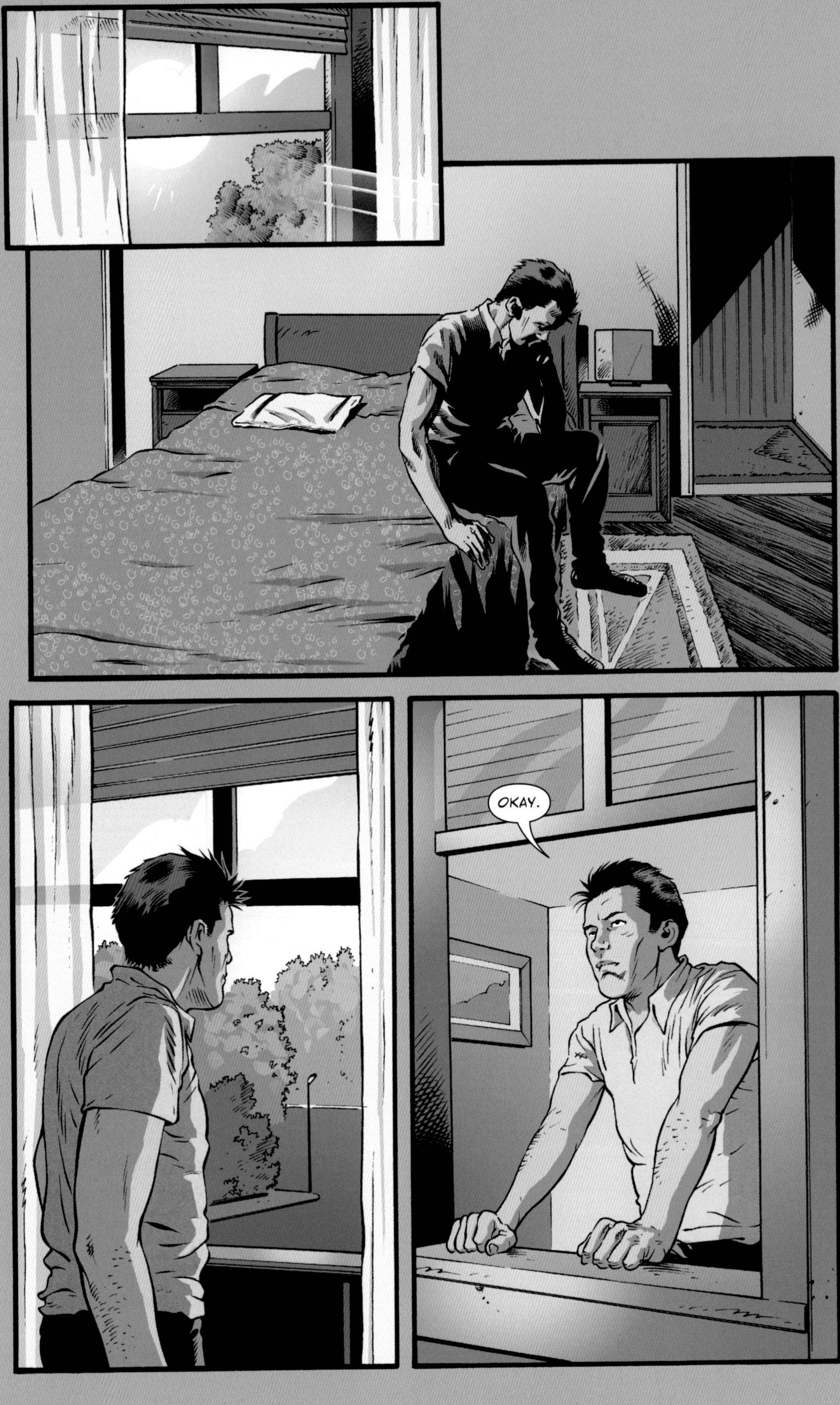
OKAY.

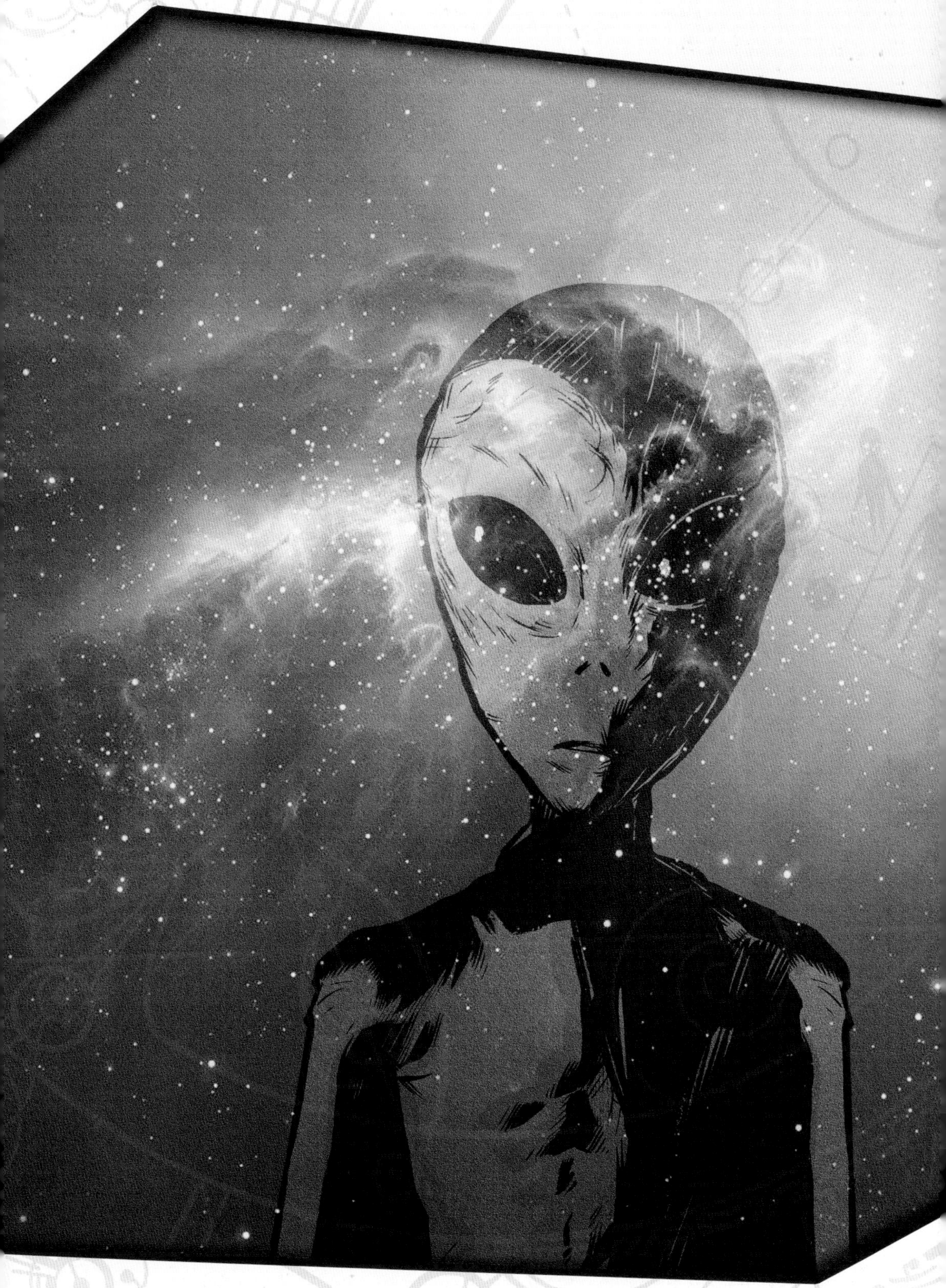

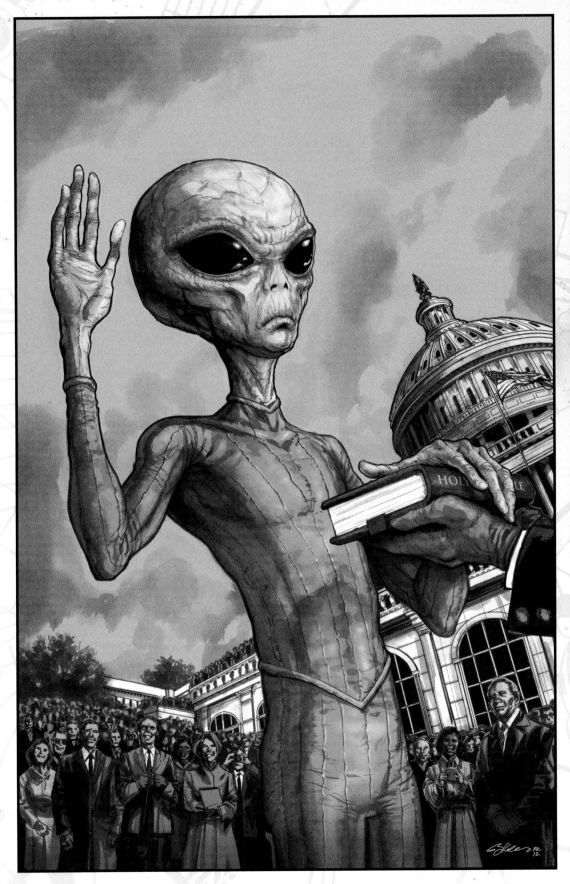

COVER ART BY **RYAN KELLY**

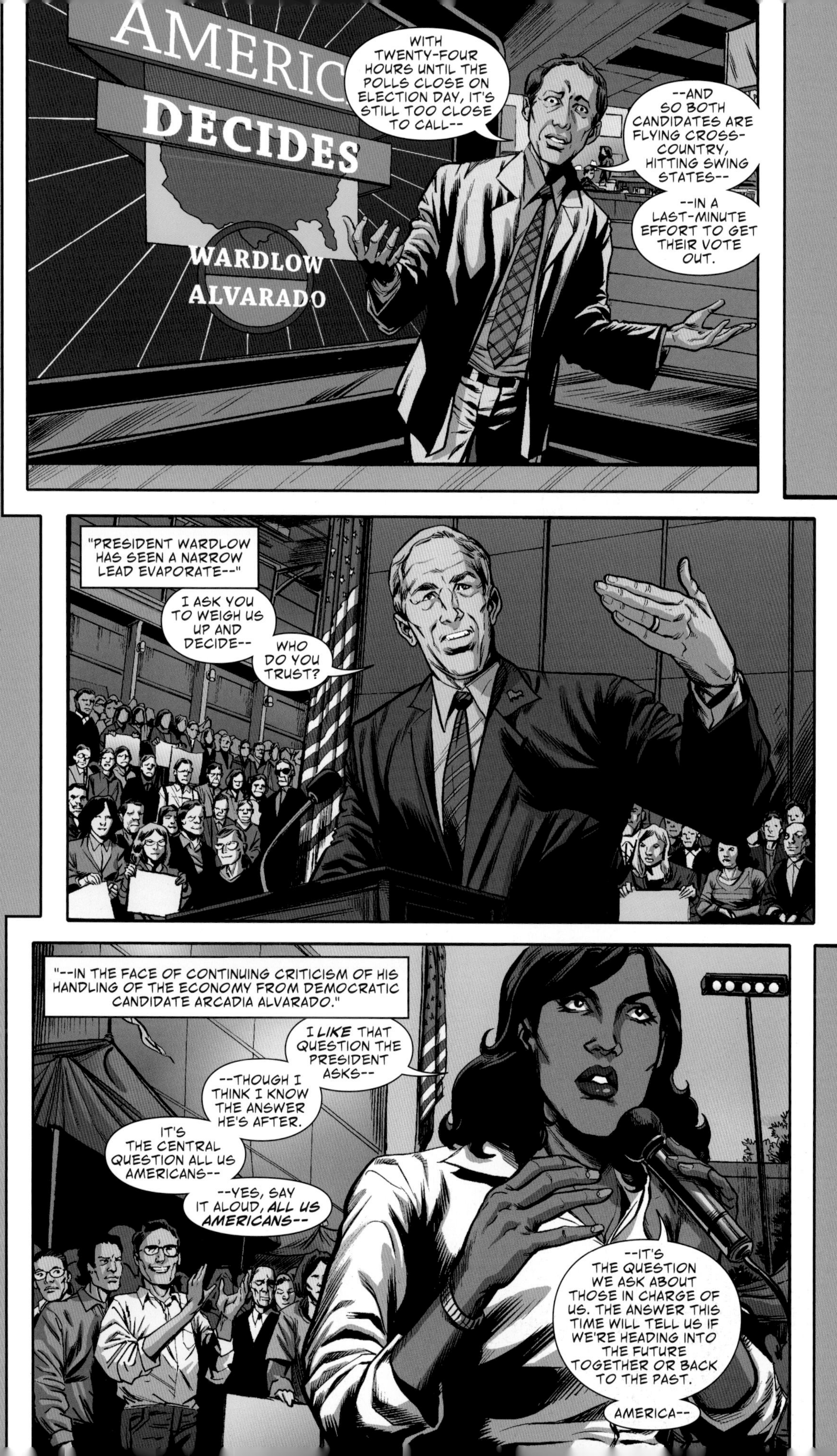
AMERIC
AMERICA DECIDES
WARDLOW
ALVARADO
WITH TWENTY-FOUR HOURS UNTIL THE POLLS CLOSE ON ELECTION DAY, IT'S STILL TOO CLOSE TO CALL--
--AND SO BOTH CANDIDATES ARE FLYING CROSS-COUNTRY, HITTING SWING STATES--
--IN A LAST-MINUTE EFFORT TO GET THEIR VOTE OUT.
"PRESIDENT WARDLOW HAS SEEN A NARROW LEAD EVAPORATE--"
I ASK YOU TO WEIGH US UP AND DECIDE--
WHO DO YOU TRUST?
"--IN THE FACE OF CONTINUING CRITICISM OF HIS HANDLING OF THE ECONOMY FROM DEMOCRATIC CANDIDATE ARCADIA ALVARADO."
I *LIKE* THAT QUESTION THE PRESIDENT ASKS--
--THOUGH I THINK I KNOW THE ANSWER HE'S AFTER.
IT'S THE CENTRAL QUESTION ALL US AMERICANS--
--YES, SAY IT ALOUD, ***ALL US AMERICANS***--
--IT'S THE QUESTION WE ASK ABOUT THOSE IN CHARGE OF US. THE ANSWER THIS TIME WILL TELL US IF WE'RE HEADING INTO THE FUTURE TOGETHER OR BACK TO THE PAST.
AMERICA--

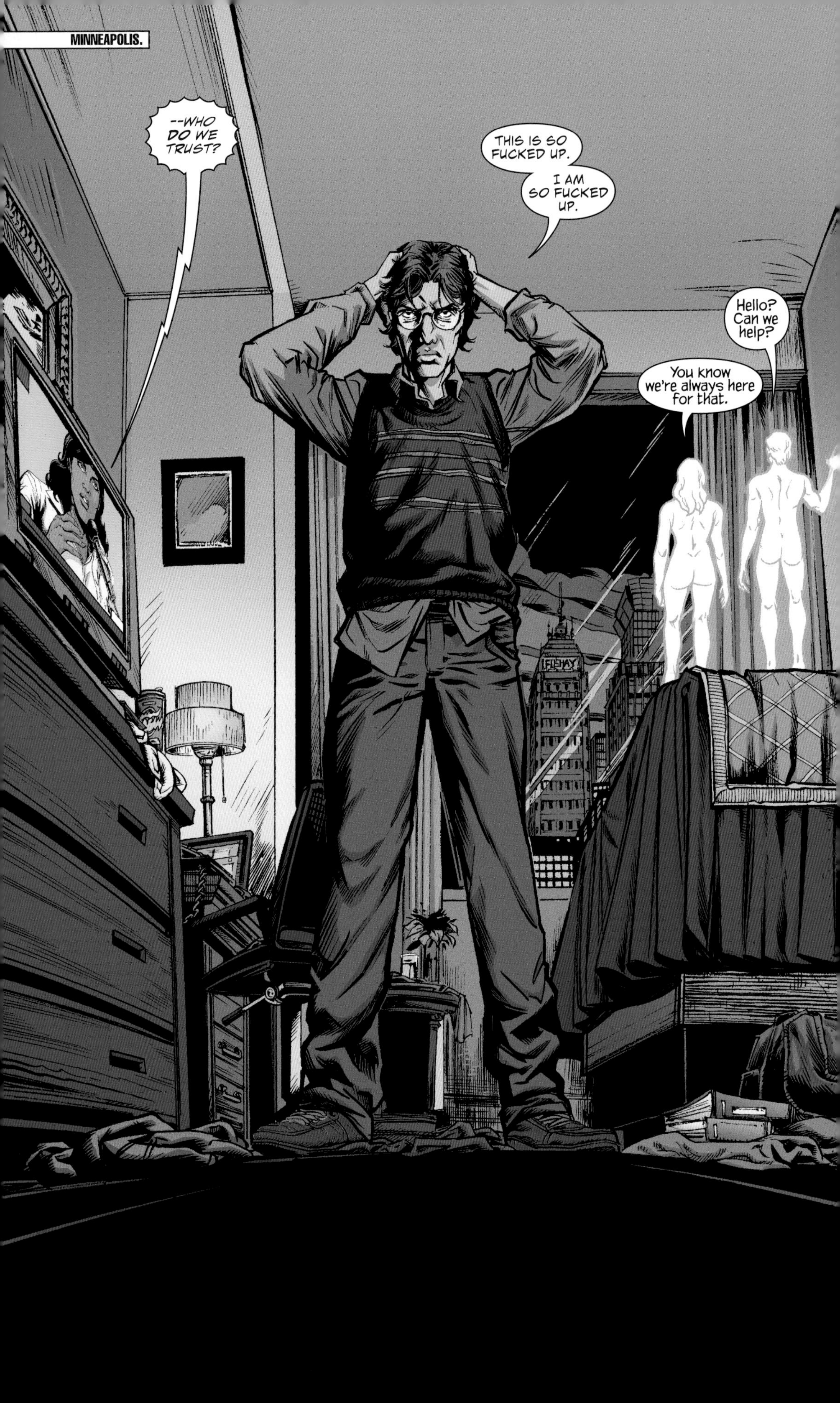
MINNEAPOLIS.
--WHO DO WE TRUST?
THIS IS SO FUCKED UP.
I AM SO FUCKED UP.
Hello? Can we help?
You know we're always here for that.

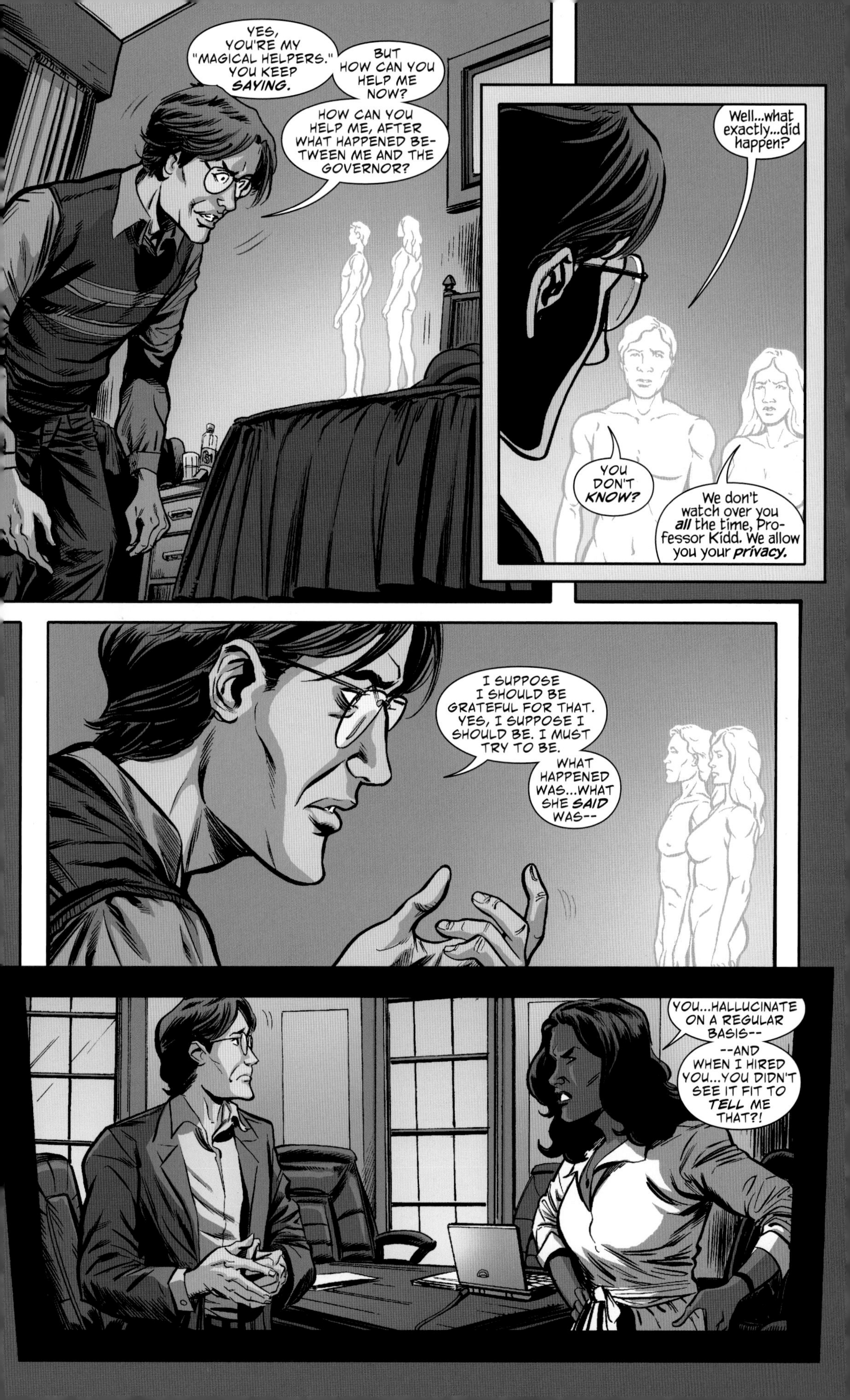
YES, YOU'RE MY "MAGICAL HELPERS." YOU KEEP SAYING.
BUT HOW CAN YOU HELP ME NOW?
HOW CAN YOU HELP ME, AFTER WHAT HAPPENED BE-TWEEN ME AND THE GOVERNOR?
Well...what exactly...did happen?
YOU DON'T KNOW?
We don't watch over you all the time, Pro-fessor Kidd. We allow you your privacy.
I SUPPOSE I SHOULD BE GRATEFUL FOR THAT. YES, I SUPPOSE I SHOULD BE. I MUST TRY TO BE.
WHAT HAPPENED WAS...WHAT SHE SAID WAS--
YOU...HALLUCINATE ON A REGULAR BASIS--
--AND WHEN I HIRED YOU...YOU DIDN'T SEE IT FIT TO TELL ME THAT?!

I THOUGHT... GIVEN YOUR OWN EXPERIENCES--

I DON'T BASE MY DECISIONS ON THE INPUT OF... TINY PEOPLE--!

--PEOPLE WHO...YOU SAY THEY'RE *WHAT*, EXACTLY?

THEY'RE FIGURES DEPICTED ON ALUMINUM PLAQUES ATTACHED TO THE PIONEER 10 AND 11 SPACE PROBES--

--LAUNCHED FROM EARTH IN 1972 AND 1973, AND NOW AT THE FRINGES OF THE SOLAR SYSTEM.

EXCEPT WHEN THEY, YOU KNOW, POP BACK FOR COFFEE.

WHEN DID THEY START *TELLING* YOU STUFF?

A COUPLE OF YEARS BACK. WHEN I BEGAN MY UFO WORK.

I KNOW VERY LITTLE ABOUT THEM.

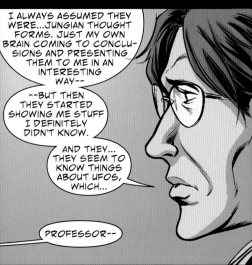

I ALWAYS ASSUMED THEY WERE...JUNGIAN THOUGHT FORMS. JUST MY OWN BRAIN COMING TO CONCLUSIONS AND PRESENTING THEM TO ME IN AN INTERESTING WAY--

--BUT THEN THEY STARTED SHOWING ME STUFF I DEFINITELY DIDN'T KNOW.

AND THEY... THEY SEEM TO KNOW THINGS ABOUT UFOS, WHICH...

PROFESSOR--

--YOU LOST ME AT "JUNGIAN THOUGHT FORMS."

I REACHED OUT TO YOU BECAUSE I NEEDED A SANE OPINION, AND NOW YOU TELL ME...DEAR GOD.

I DON'T HAVE TIME TO *THINK* ABOUT THIS RIGHT NOW.

CONTINUE YOUR INVESTIGATIONS, PROFESSOR. FOR *NOW*.

WHEN WE'VE DECIDED WHAT TO DO, WE'LL *CALL* YOU.

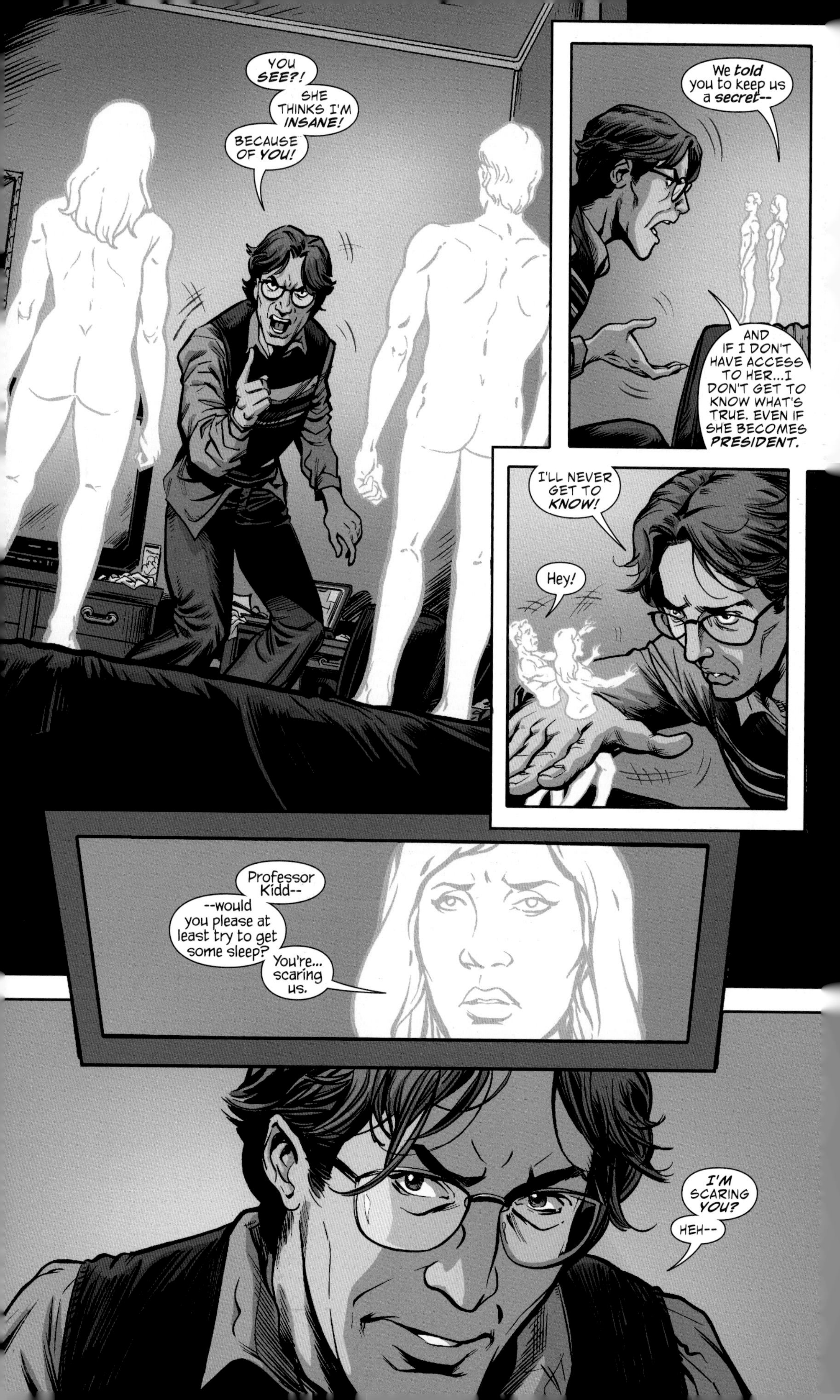

YOU SEE?!
SHE THINKS I'M INSANE!
BECAUSE OF YOU!
We told you to keep us a secret--
AND IF I DON'T HAVE ACCESS TO HER...I DON'T GET TO KNOW WHAT'S TRUE. EVEN IF SHE BECOMES PRESIDENT.
I'LL NEVER GET TO KNOW!
Hey!
Professor Kidd--
--would you please at least try to get some sleep?
You're... scaring us.
I'M SCARING YOU?
HEH--

"--TALK ABOUT ROLE REVERSAL."

"HE'S TRYING TO SCARE THE ELECTORATE--"

--SO MANY OF THESE ANCIENT CAMPAIGN SPEECHES OF MINE GOING VIRAL--

--THE YOUNG FIREBRAND AGAINST CAPITALISM.

AND WHAT DO WE SAY EVERY TIME HE HITS US WITH THAT?

WE SAY "YES SIR, I SAID THAT."

WE STOP THE STORY. WE LET THEM SEE THE PUNCHES LAND. WE MAKE HIM THE BULLY.

AND WE KEEP PUNCHING ABOUT THE *ECONOMY.*

ARE YOU GOING TO USE THE "MY PEOPLE" LINE?

NO.

I THINK YOU SHOULD USE THE "MY PEOPLE" LINE.

NO.

FRIGGING *USE* THE "MY PEOPLE" LINE!

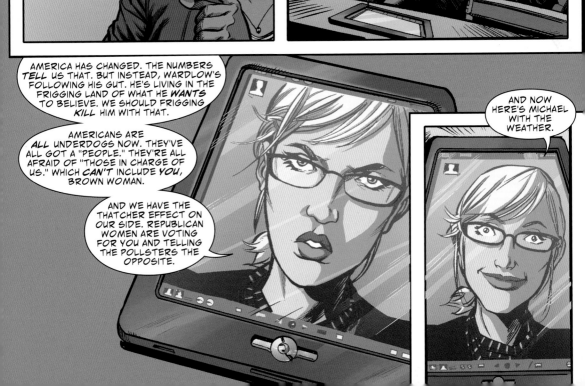

AMERICA HAS CHANGED. THE NUMBERS *TELL* US THAT. BUT INSTEAD, WARDLOW'S FOLLOWING HIS GUT. HE'S LIVING IN THE FRIGGING LAND OF WHAT HE *WANTS* TO BELIEVE. WE SHOULD FRIGGING *KILL* HIM WITH THAT.

AMERICANS ARE *ALL* UNDERDOGS NOW. THEY'VE ALL GOT A "PEOPLE." THEY'RE ALL AFRAID OF "THOSE IN CHARGE OF US." WHICH *CAN'T* INCLUDE *YOU,* BROWN WOMAN.

AND WE HAVE THE THATCHER EFFECT ON OUR SIDE. REPUBLICAN WOMEN ARE VOTING FOR YOU AND TELLING THE POLLSTERS THE OPPOSITE.

AND NOW HERE'S MICHAEL WITH THE WEATHER.

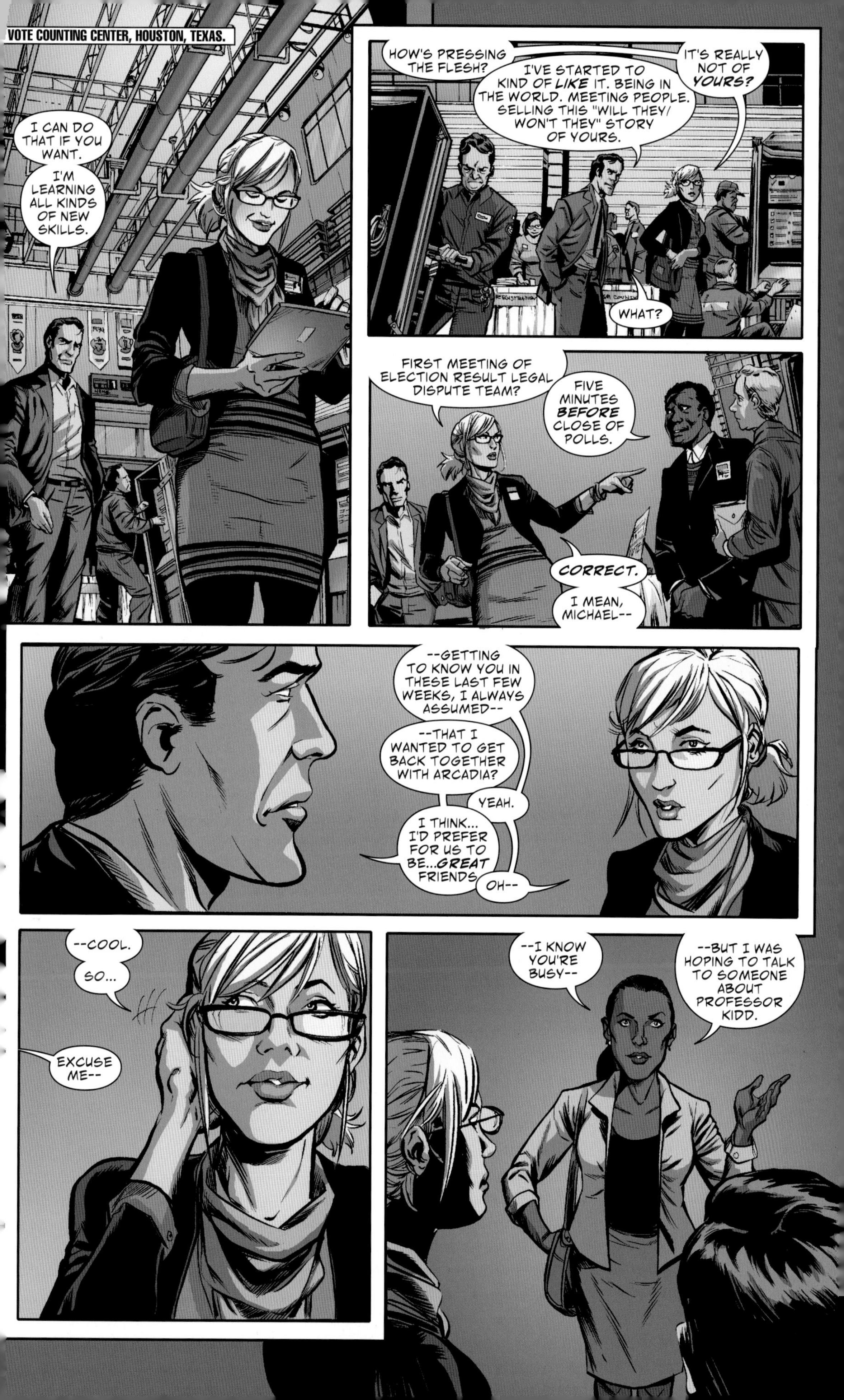
VOTE COUNTING CENTER, HOUSTON, TEXAS.
I CAN DO THAT IF YOU WANT.
I'M LEARNING ALL KINDS OF NEW SKILLS.
HOW'S PRESSING THE FLESH?
I'VE STARTED TO KIND OF LIKE IT. BEING IN THE WORLD. MEETING PEOPLE. SELLING THIS "WILL THEY/ WON'T THEY" STORY OF YOURS.
IT'S REALLY NOT OF YOURS?
WHAT?
FIRST MEETING OF ELECTION RESULT LEGAL DISPUTE TEAM?
FIVE MINUTES BEFORE CLOSE OF POLLS.
CORRECT.
I MEAN, MICHAEL--
--GETTING TO KNOW YOU IN THESE LAST FEW WEEKS, I ALWAYS ASSUMED--
--THAT I WANTED TO GET BACK TOGETHER WITH ARCADIA?
YEAH.
I THINK... I'D PREFER FOR US TO BE...GREAT FRIENDS.
OH--
--COOL.
SO...
EXCUSE ME--
--I KNOW YOU'RE BUSY--
--BUT I WAS HOPING TO TALK TO SOMEONE ABOUT PROFESSOR KIDD.

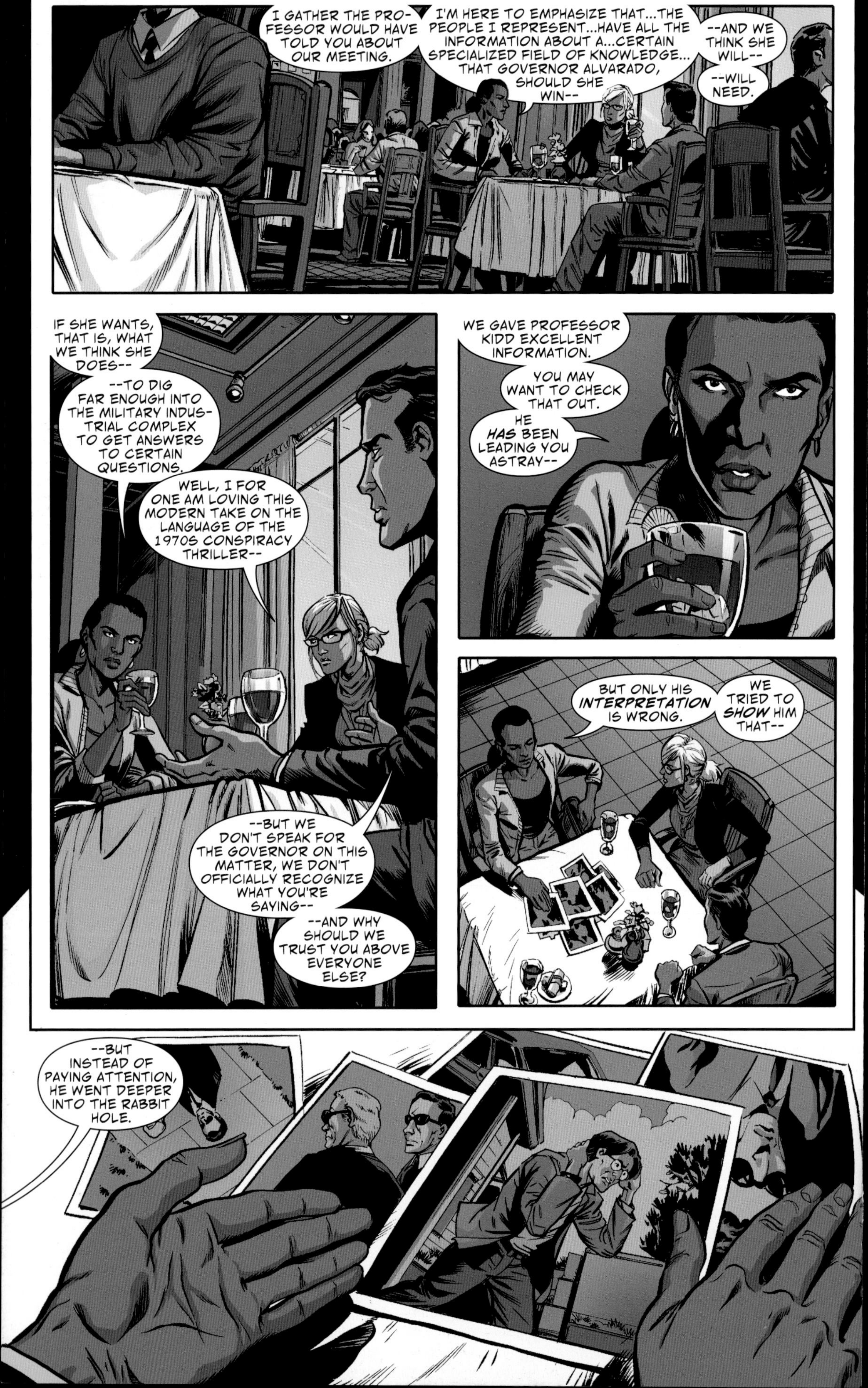
I GATHER THE PROFESSOR WOULD HAVE TOLD YOU ABOUT OUR MEETING.
I'M HERE TO EMPHASIZE THAT...THE PEOPLE I REPRESENT...HAVE ALL THE INFORMATION ABOUT A...CERTAIN SPECIALIZED FIELD OF KNOWLEDGE... THAT GOVERNOR ALVARADO, SHOULD SHE WIN--
--AND WE THINK SHE WILL--
--WILL NEED.
IF SHE WANTS, THAT IS, WHAT WE THINK SHE DOES--
--TO DIG FAR ENOUGH INTO THE MILITARY INDUSTRIAL COMPLEX TO GET ANSWERS TO CERTAIN QUESTIONS.
WELL, I FOR ONE AM LOVING THIS MODERN TAKE ON THE LANGUAGE OF THE 1970S CONSPIRACY THRILLER--
--BUT WE DON'T SPEAK FOR THE GOVERNOR ON THIS MATTER, WE DON'T OFFICIALLY RECOGNIZE WHAT YOU'RE SAYING--
--AND WHY SHOULD WE TRUST YOU ABOVE EVERYONE ELSE?
WE GAVE PROFESSOR KIDD EXCELLENT INFORMATION.
YOU MAY WANT TO CHECK THAT OUT.
HE *HAS* BEEN LEADING YOU ASTRAY--
BUT ONLY HIS *INTERPRETATION* IS WRONG.
WE TRIED TO *SHOW* HIM THAT--
--BUT INSTEAD OF PAYING ATTENTION, HE WENT DEEPER INTO THE RABBIT HOLE.

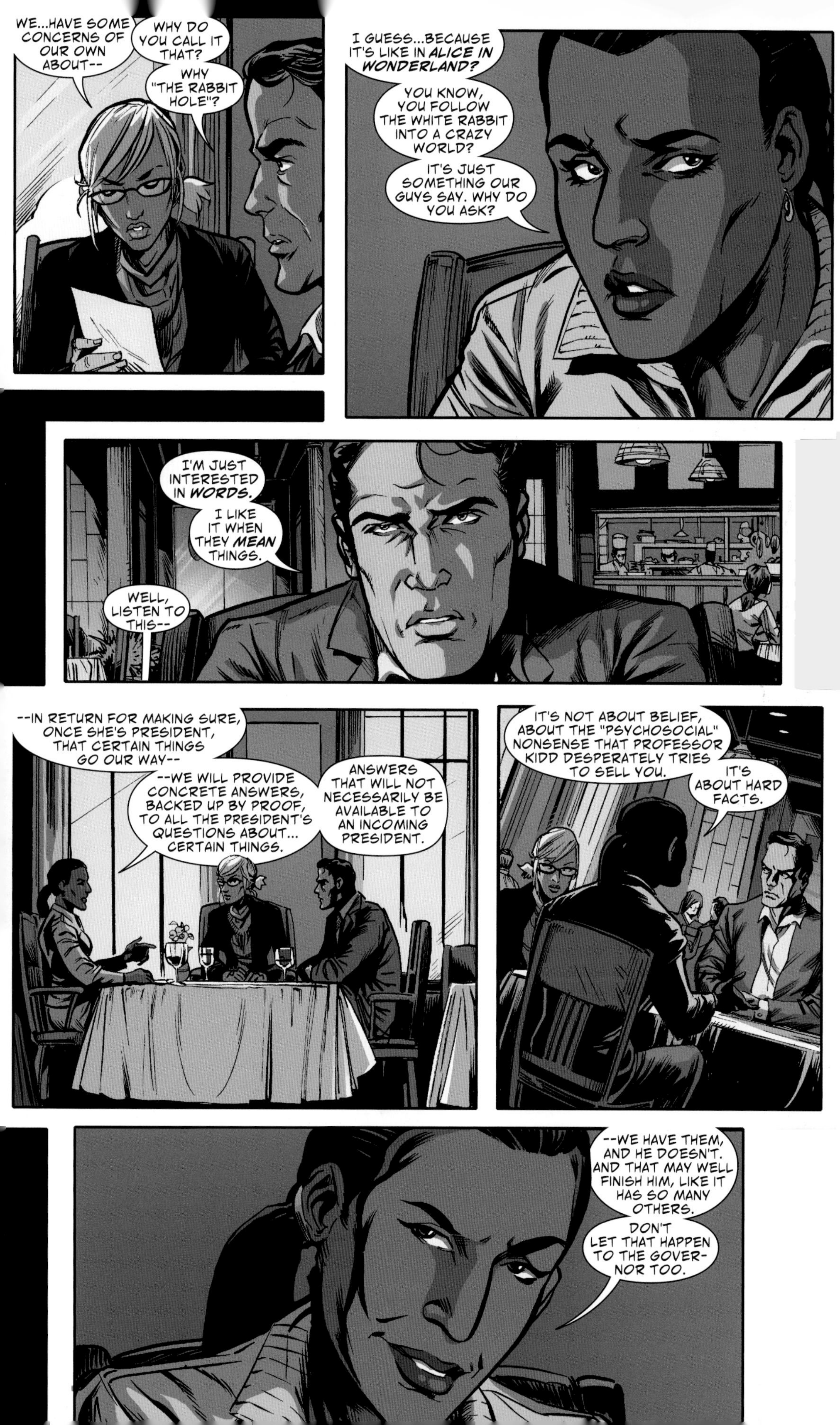
WE...HAVE SOME CONCERNS OF OUR OWN ABOUT--
WHY DO YOU CALL IT THAT?
WHY "THE RABBIT HOLE"?
I GUESS...BECAUSE IT'S LIKE IN ALICE IN WONDERLAND?
YOU KNOW, YOU FOLLOW THE WHITE RABBIT INTO A CRAZY WORLD?
IT'S JUST SOMETHING OUR GUYS SAY. WHY DO YOU ASK?
I'M JUST INTERESTED IN WORDS.
I LIKE IT WHEN THEY MEAN THINGS.
WELL, LISTEN TO THIS--
--IN RETURN FOR MAKING SURE, ONCE SHE'S PRESIDENT, THAT CERTAIN THINGS GO OUR WAY--
--WE WILL PROVIDE CONCRETE ANSWERS, BACKED UP BY PROOF, TO ALL THE PRESIDENT'S QUESTIONS ABOUT... CERTAIN THINGS.
ANSWERS THAT WILL NOT NECESSARILY BE AVAILABLE TO AN INCOMING PRESIDENT.
IT'S NOT ABOUT BELIEF, ABOUT THE "PSYCHOSOCIAL" NONSENSE THAT PROFESSOR KIDD DESPERATELY TRIES TO SELL YOU.
IT'S ABOUT HARD FACTS.
--WE HAVE THEM, AND HE DOESN'T. AND THAT MAY WELL FINISH HIM, LIKE IT HAS SO MANY OTHERS.
DON'T LET THAT HAPPEN TO THE GOVERNOR TOO.

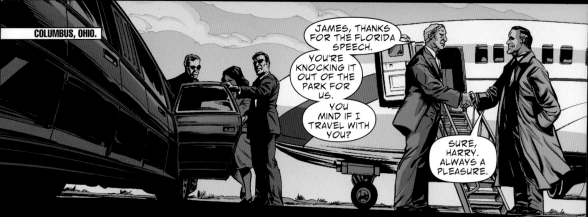

JAMES, THANKS FOR THE FLORIDA SPEECH.

YOU'RE KNOCKING IT OUT OF THE PARK FOR US.

YOU MIND IF I TRAVEL WITH YOU?

SURE, HARRY. ALWAYS A PLEASURE.

SO THE GOVERNOR WAS WONDERING--

--ABOUT THE QUESTION THAT KIND OF DERAILED YOU IN THE CANDIDATE DEBATE--

WHAT, THE ONE ABOUT FLYING SAUCERS?

WHAT ABOUT IT?

THE GOVERNOR *NOTED* YOUR REACTION.

AND LET'S JUST SAY THERE'S SOME FELLOW FEELING ON HER PART.

HARRY, I HAVE SO GOT PAST THAT LINE OF QUESTIONING, I HAVE MADE THE GOP *EAT* THAT--

WE KNOW. WE LOVE YOU FOR THAT.

YOU'RE OUR GUY, JAMES, EVEN MORE SO NOW THAT WE'VE SEEN YOU IN ACTION.

LISTEN, I'M GOING TO MAKE THIS ABSOLUTELY PLAIN. THOUGH I'LL DENY IT IF I HAVE TO--

--*SHE* KNOWS IT'S ALL TRUE.

WHATEVER "IT" IS.

SHE WANTS TO KNOW WHAT YOU EXPERIENCED, NOT TO SHOOT YOU DOWN--

--BUT TO COMPARE NOTES.

AND SENATOR--

--YOU *KNOW* WE KNOW ABOUT THE *AFFAIR.*

AND SINCE THE GOP DOESN'T, WE DON'T *CARE.*

BUT WE *REQUIRE* HONESTY FROM YOU ABOUT THIS.

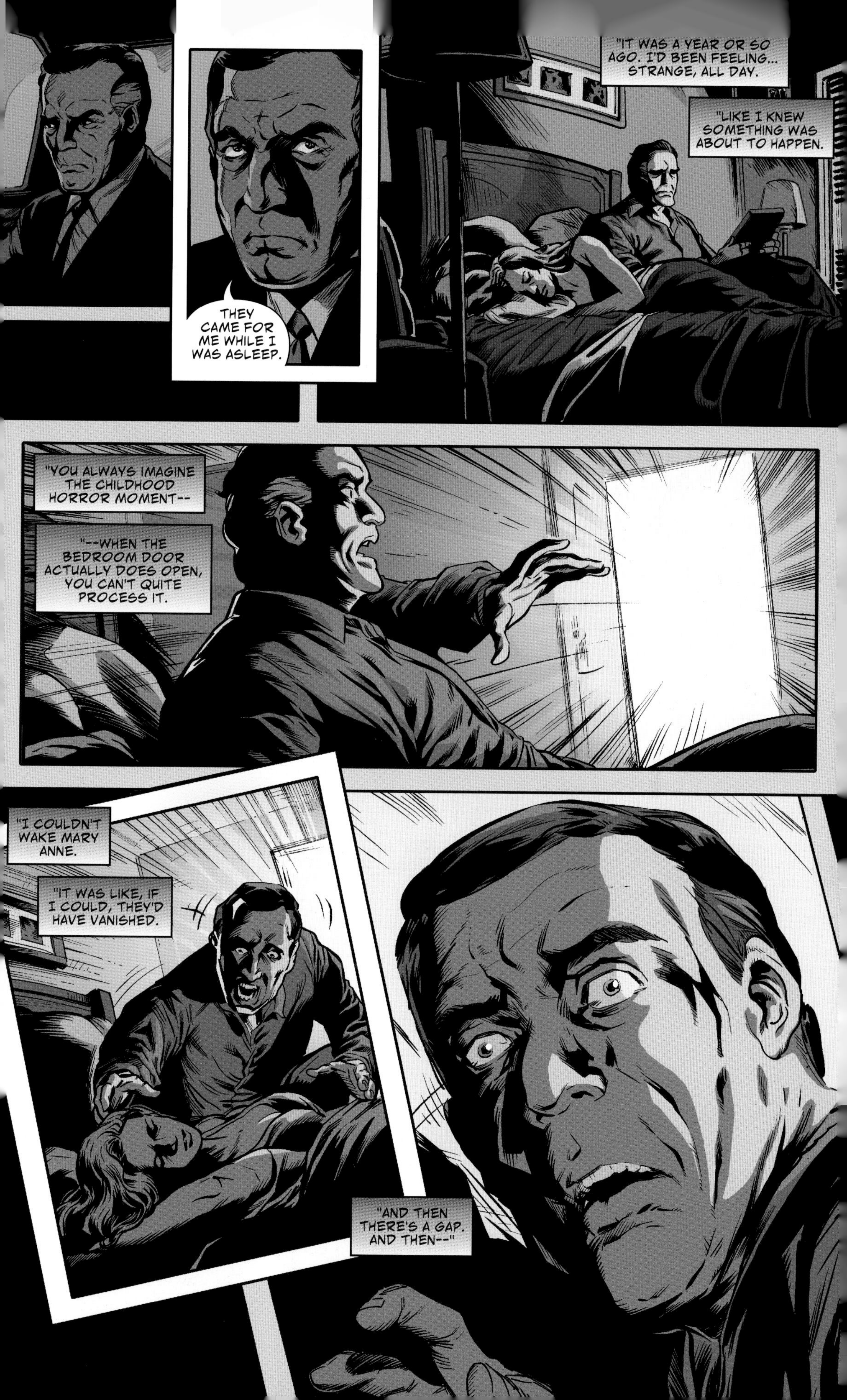
THEY CAME FOR ME WHILE I WAS ASLEEP.
"IT WAS A YEAR OR SO AGO. I'D BEEN FEELING... STRANGE, ALL DAY.
"LIKE I KNEW SOMETHING WAS ABOUT TO HAPPEN.
"YOU ALWAYS IMAGINE THE CHILDHOOD HORROR MOMENT--
"--WHEN THE BEDROOM DOOR ACTUALLY DOES OPEN, YOU CAN'T QUITE PROCESS IT.
"I COULDN'T WAKE MARY ANNE.
"IT WAS LIKE, IF I COULD, THEY'D HAVE VANISHED.
"AND THEN THERE'S A GAP. AND THEN--"

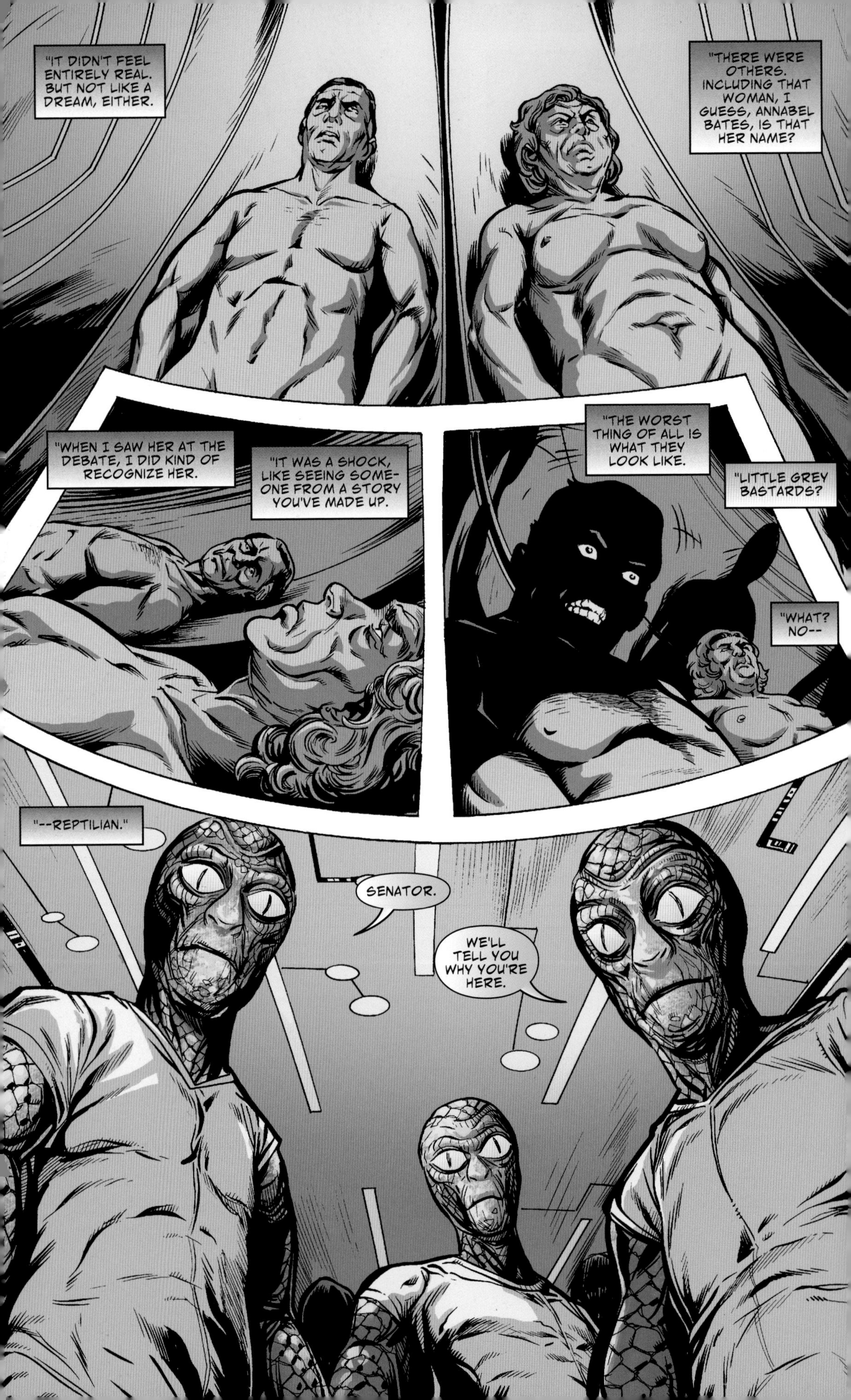
"IT DIDN'T FEEL ENTIRELY REAL. BUT NOT LIKE A DREAM, EITHER.
"THERE WERE OTHERS. INCLUDING THAT WOMAN, I GUESS, ANNABEL BATES, IS THAT HER NAME?
"WHEN I SAW HER AT THE DEBATE, I DID KIND OF RECOGNIZE HER.
"IT WAS A SHOCK, LIKE SEEING SOME-ONE FROM A STORY YOU'VE MADE UP.
"THE WORST THING OF ALL IS WHAT THEY LOOK LIKE.
"LITTLE GREY BASTARDS?
"WHAT? NO--
"--REPTILIAN."
SENATOR.
WE'LL TELL YOU WHY YOU'RE HERE.

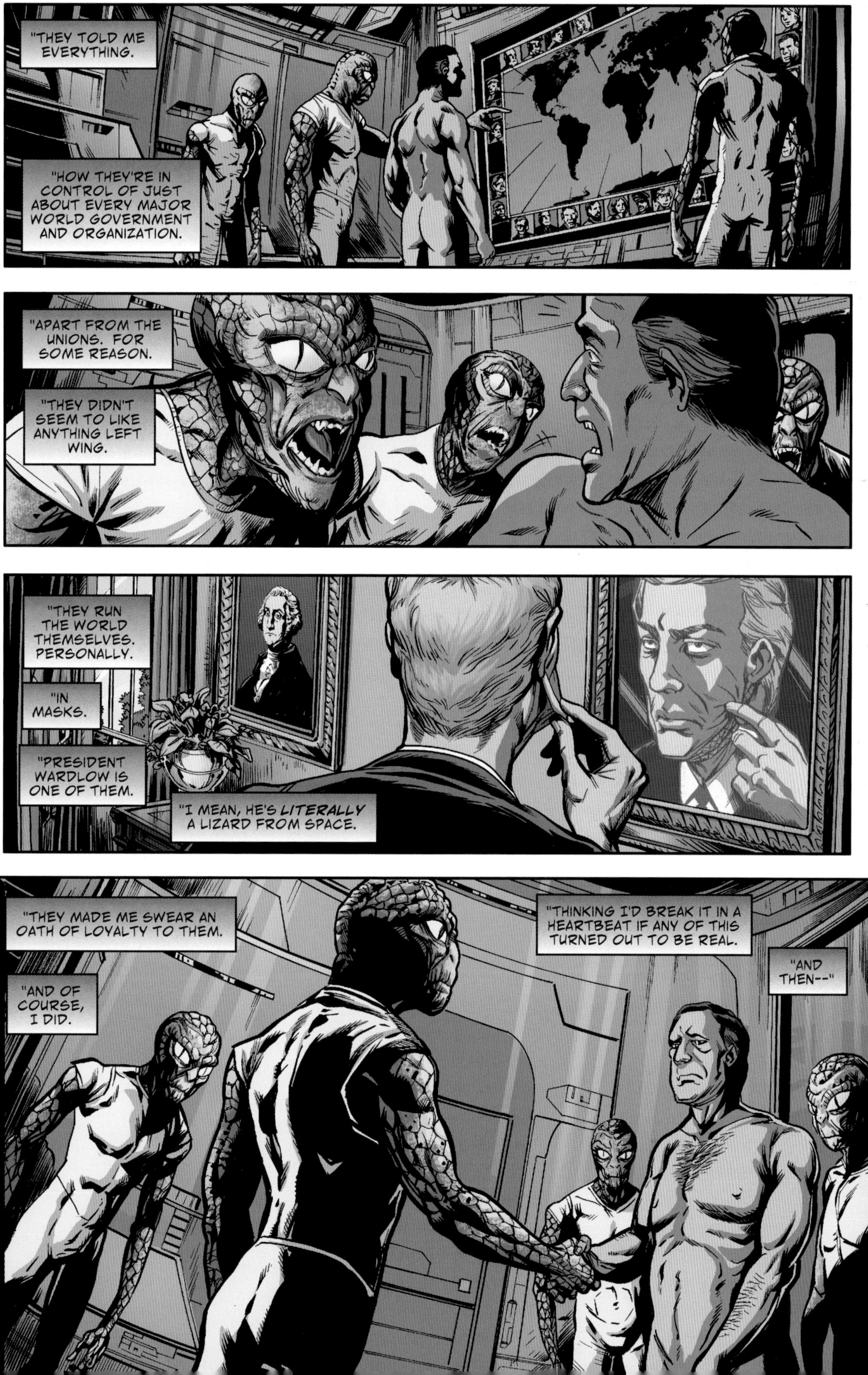
"THEY TOLD ME EVERYTHING.
"HOW THEY'RE IN CONTROL OF JUST ABOUT EVERY MAJOR WORLD GOVERNMENT AND ORGANIZATION.
"APART FROM THE UNIONS. FOR SOME REASON.
"THEY DIDN'T SEEM TO LIKE ANYTHING LEFT WING.
"THEY RUN THE WORLD THEMSELVES. PERSONALLY.
"IN MASKS.
"PRESIDENT WARDLOW IS ONE OF THEM.
"I MEAN, HE'S *LITERALLY* A LIZARD FROM SPACE.
"THEY MADE ME SWEAR AN OATH OF LOYALTY TO THEM.
"AND OF COURSE, I DID.
"THINKING I'D BREAK IT IN A HEARTBEAT IF ANY OF THIS TURNED OUT TO BE REAL.
"AND THEN--"

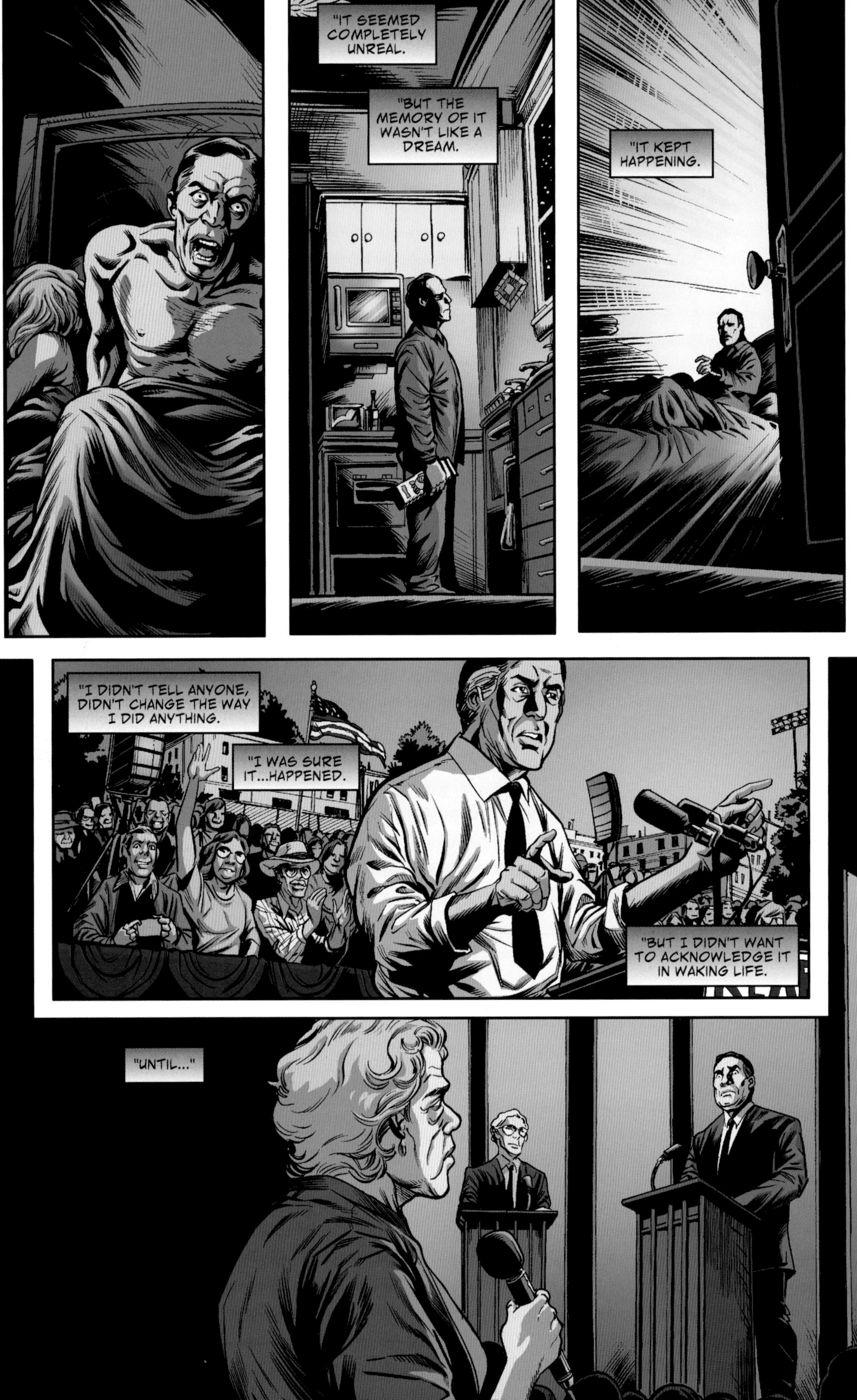
"IT SEEMED COMPLETELY UNREAL.
"BUT THE MEMORY OF IT WASN'T LIKE A DREAM.
"IT KEPT HAPPENING.
"I DIDN'T TELL ANYONE, DIDN'T CHANGE THE WAY I DID ANYTHING.
"I WAS SURE IT...HAPPENED.
"BUT I DIDN'T WANT TO ACKNOWLEDGE IT IN WAKING LIFE.
"UNTIL..."

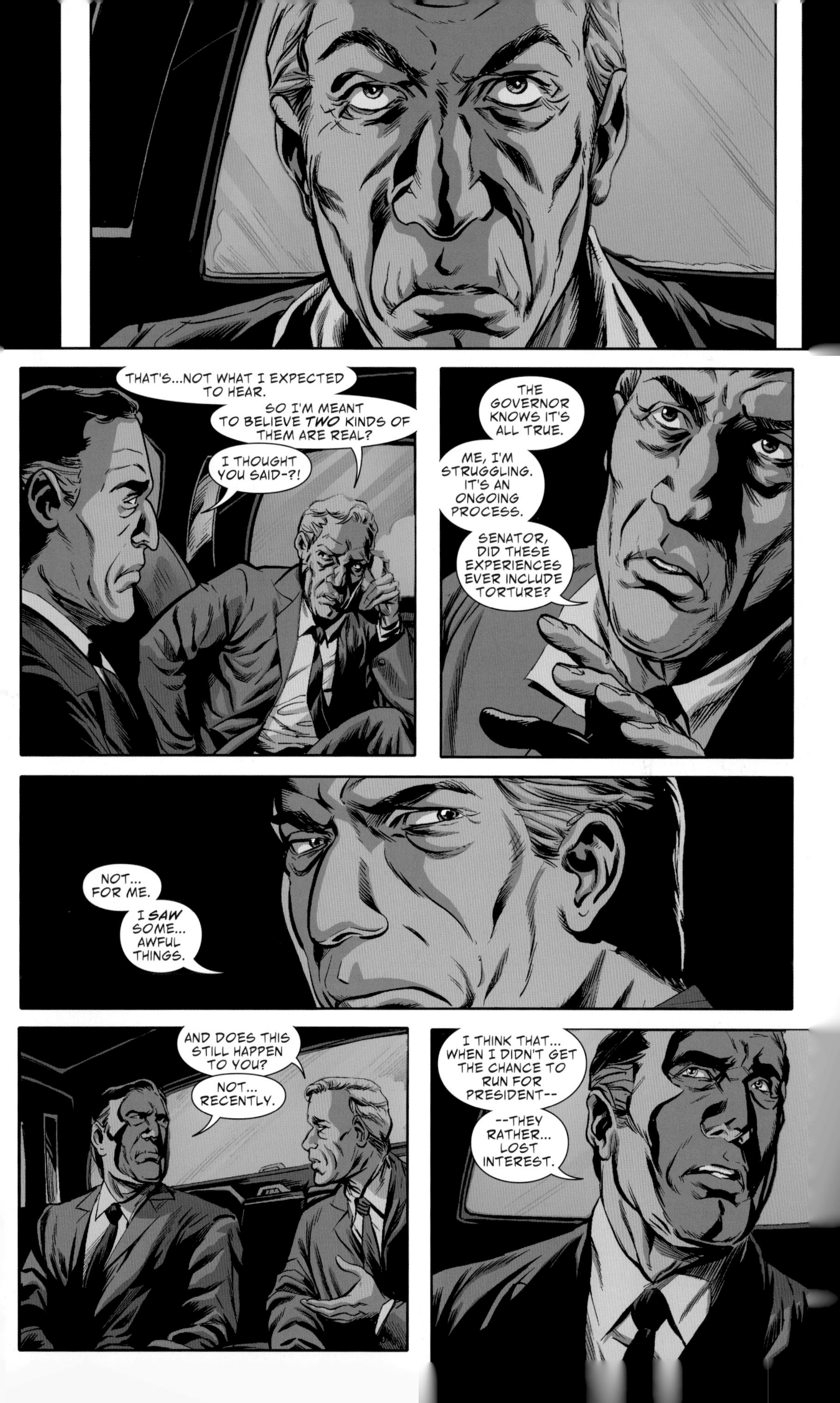
THAT'S...NOT WHAT I EXPECTED TO HEAR.
SO I'M MEANT TO BELIEVE TWO KINDS OF THEM ARE REAL?
I THOUGHT YOU SAID--?!
THE GOVERNOR KNOWS IT'S ALL TRUE.
ME, I'M STRUGGLING. IT'S AN ONGOING PROCESS.
SENATOR, DID THESE EXPERIENCES EVER INCLUDE TORTURE?
NOT... FOR ME.
I SAW SOME... AWFUL THINGS.
AND DOES THIS STILL HAPPEN TO YOU?
NOT... RECENTLY.
I THINK THAT... WHEN I DIDN'T GET THE CHANCE TO RUN FOR PRESIDENT--
--THEY RATHER... LOST INTEREST.

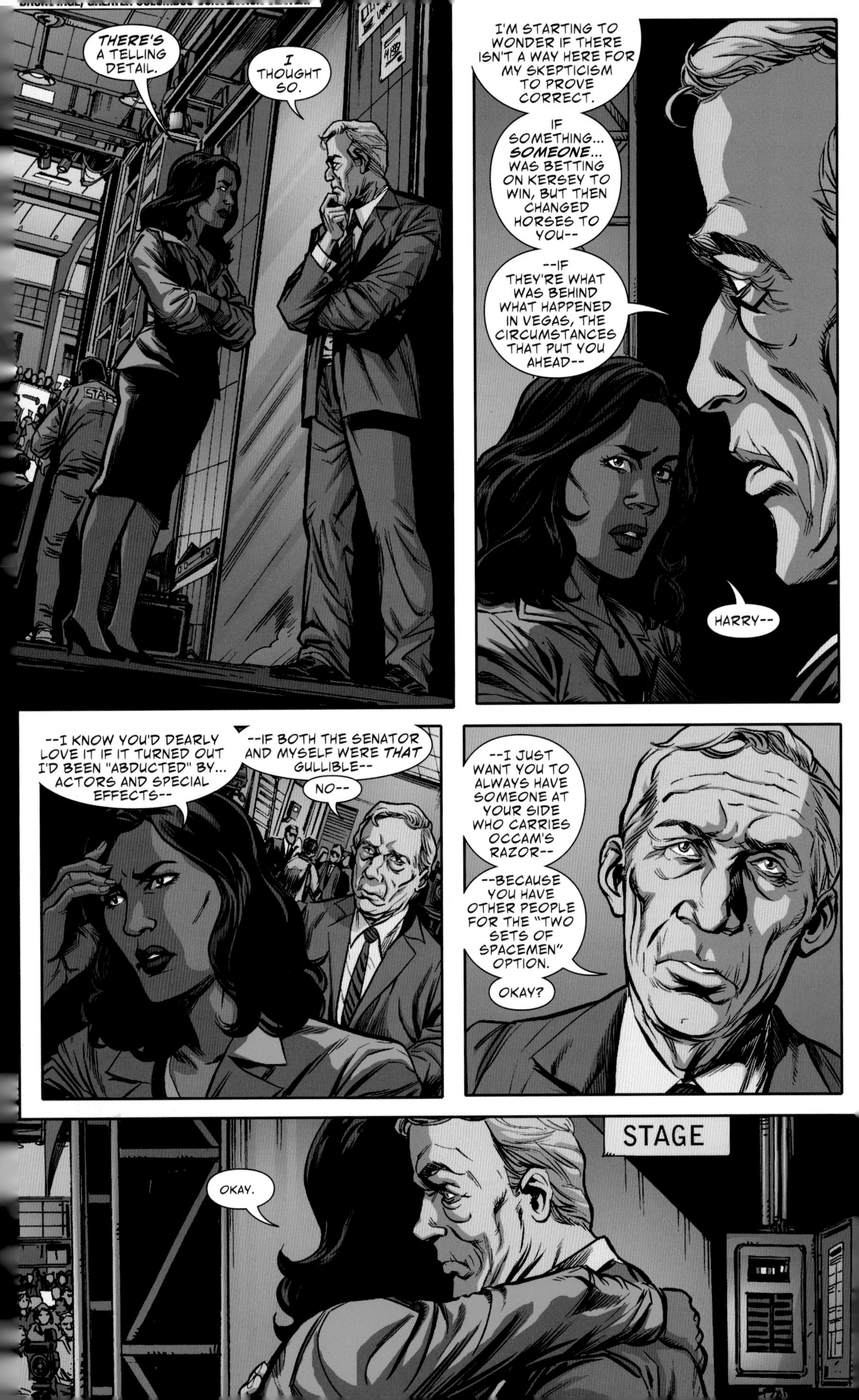
THERE'S A TELLING DETAIL.
I THOUGHT SO.
I'M STARTING TO WONDER IF THERE ISN'T A WAY HERE FOR MY SKEPTICISM TO PROVE CORRECT.
IF SOMETHING... SOMEONE... WAS BETTING ON KERSEY TO WIN, BUT THEN CHANGED HORSES TO YOU--
--IF THEY'RE WHAT WAS BEHIND WHAT HAPPENED IN VEGAS, THE CIRCUMSTANCES THAT PUT YOU AHEAD--
HARRY--
--I KNOW YOU'D DEARLY LOVE IT IF IT TURNED OUT I'D BEEN "ABDUCTED" BY... ACTORS AND SPECIAL EFFECTS--
--IF BOTH THE SENATOR AND MYSELF WERE THAT GULLIBLE--
NO--
--I JUST WANT YOU TO ALWAYS HAVE SOMEONE AT YOUR SIDE WHO CARRIES OCCAM'S RAZOR--
--BECAUSE YOU HAVE OTHER PEOPLE FOR THE "TWO SETS OF SPACEMEN" OPTION.
OKAY?
STAGE
OKAY.

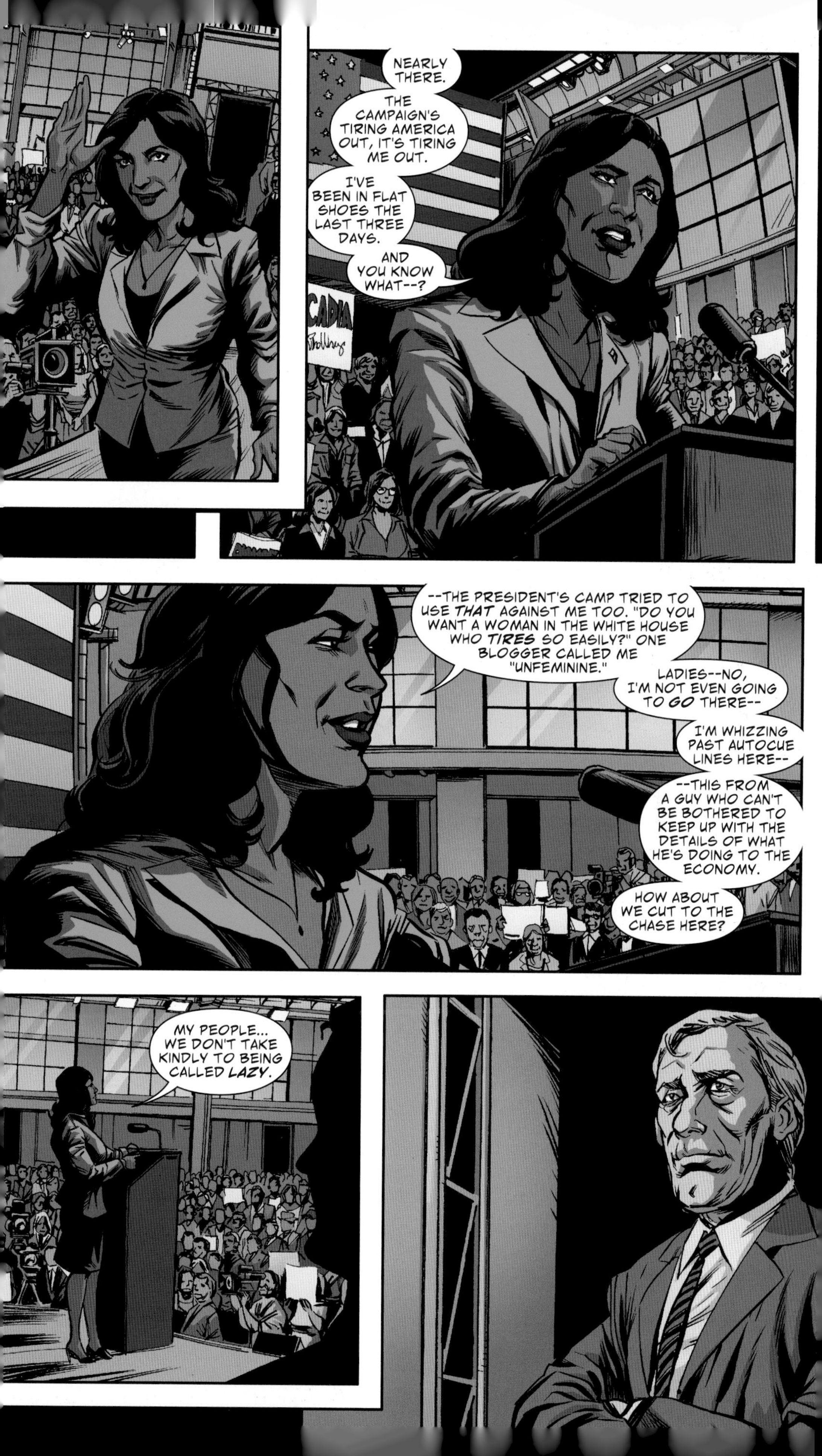
NEARLY THERE.
THE CAMPAIGN'S TIRING AMERICA OUT, IT'S TIRING ME OUT.
I'VE BEEN IN FLAT SHOES THE LAST THREE DAYS.
AND YOU KNOW WHAT--?
--THE PRESIDENT'S CAMP TRIED TO USE *THAT* AGAINST ME TOO. "DO YOU WANT A WOMAN IN THE WHITE HOUSE WHO *TIRES* SO EASILY?" ONE BLOGGER CALLED ME "UNFEMININE."
LADIES--NO, I'M NOT EVEN GOING TO *GO* THERE--
I'M WHIZZING PAST AUTOCUE LINES HERE--
--THIS FROM A GUY WHO CAN'T BE BOTHERED TO KEEP UP WITH THE DETAILS OF WHAT HE'S DOING TO THE ECONOMY.
HOW ABOUT WE CUT TO THE CHASE HERE?
MY PEOPLE... WE DON'T TAKE KINDLY TO BEING CALLED *LAZY*.

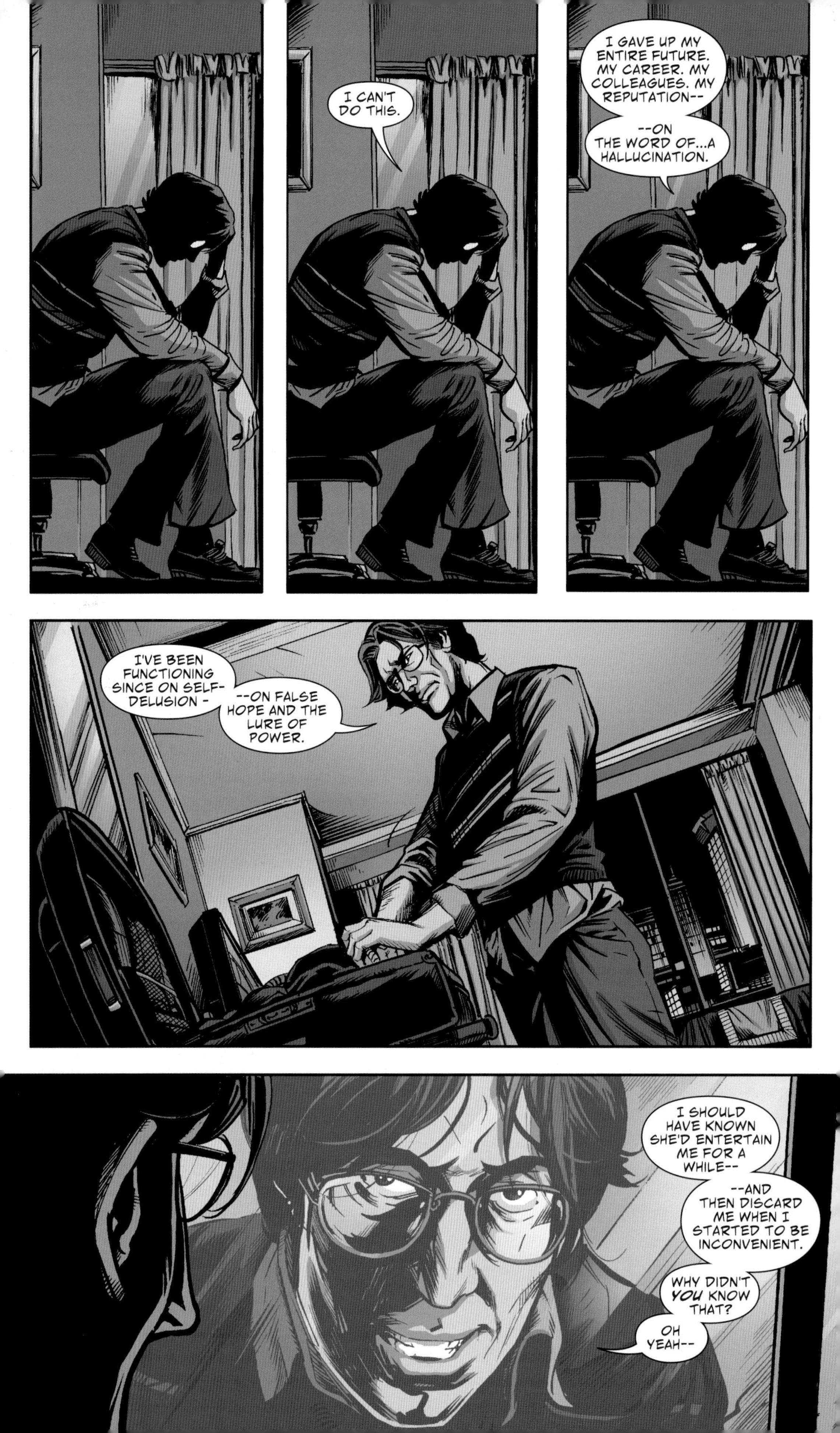
I CAN'T DO THIS.
I GAVE UP MY ENTIRE FUTURE. MY CAREER. MY COLLEAGUES. MY REPUTATION--
--ON THE WORD OF...A HALLUCINATION.
I'VE BEEN FUNCTIONING SINCE ON SELF-DELUSION -
--ON FALSE HOPE AND THE LURE OF POWER.
I SHOULD HAVE KNOWN SHE'D ENTERTAIN ME FOR A WHILE--
--AND THEN DISCARD ME WHEN I STARTED TO BE INCONVENIENT.
WHY DIDN'T *YOU* KNOW THAT?
OH YEAH--

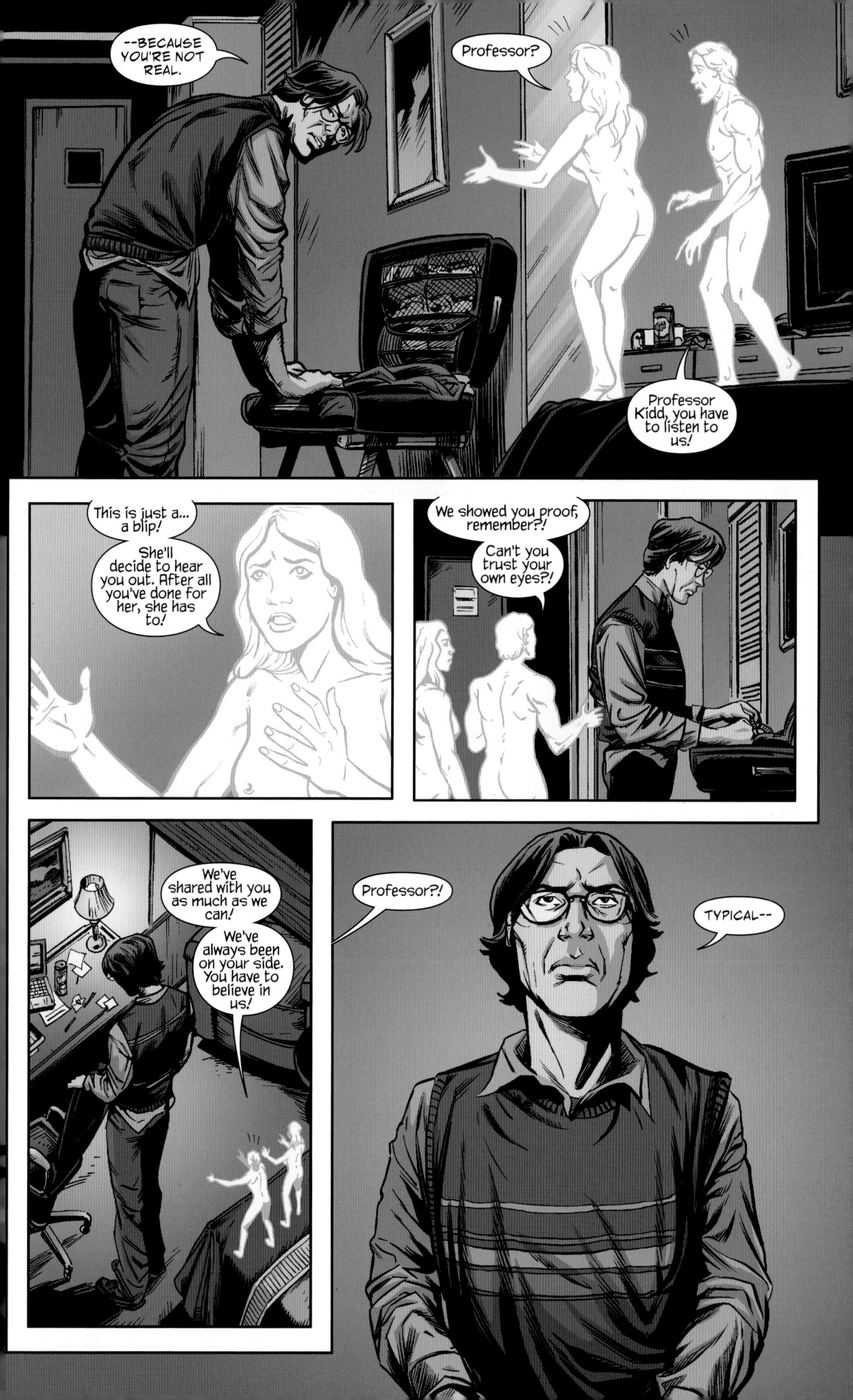
--BECAUSE YOU'RE NOT REAL.
Professor?
Professor Kidd, you have to listen to us!
This is just a... a blip!
She'll decide to hear you out. After all you've done for her, she has to!
We showed you proof, remember?!
Can't you trust your own eyes?!
We've shared with you as much as we can!
We've always been on your side. You have to believe in us!
Professor?!
TYPICAL--

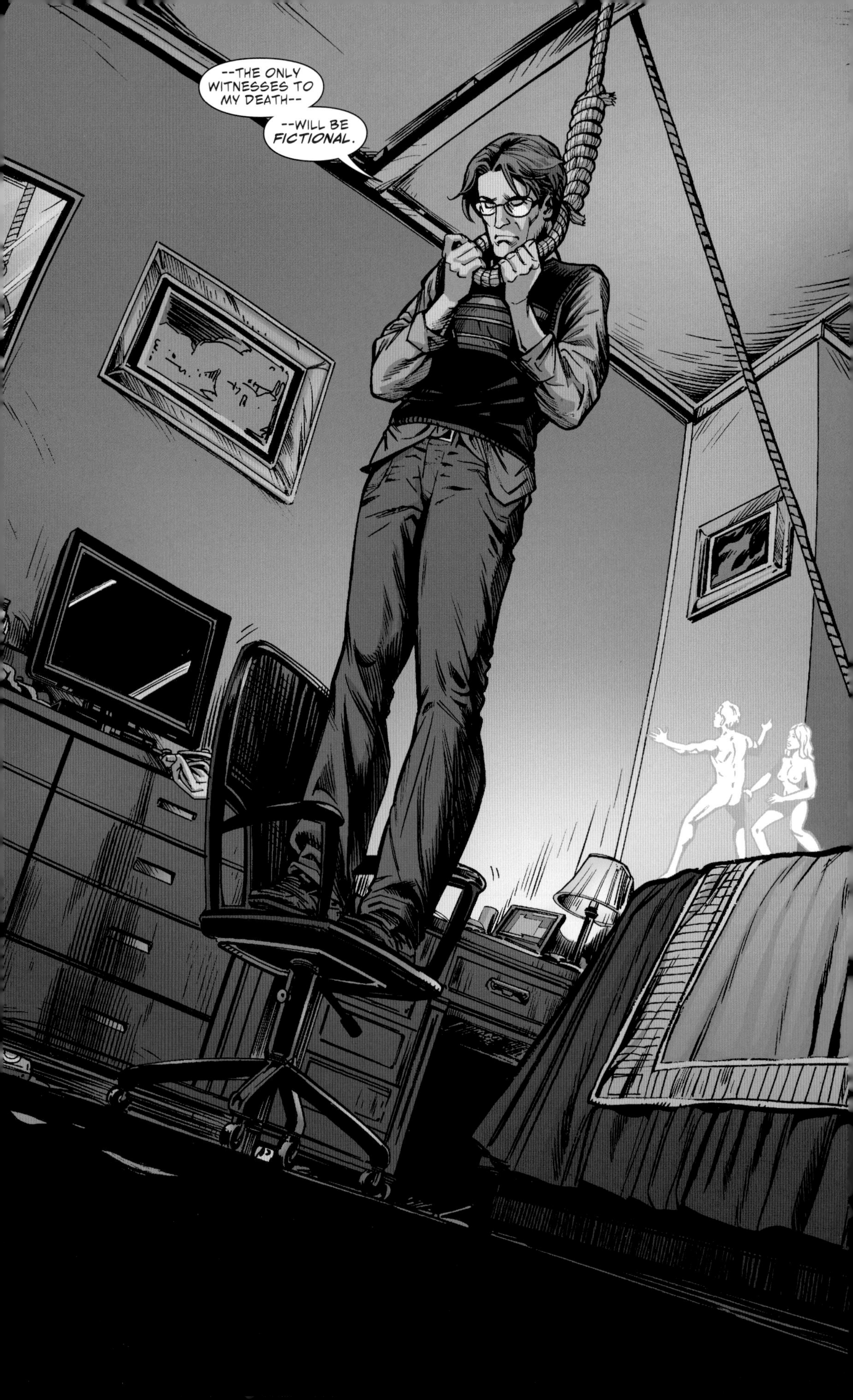
--THE ONLY WITNESSES TO MY DEATH--
--WILL BE FICTIONAL.

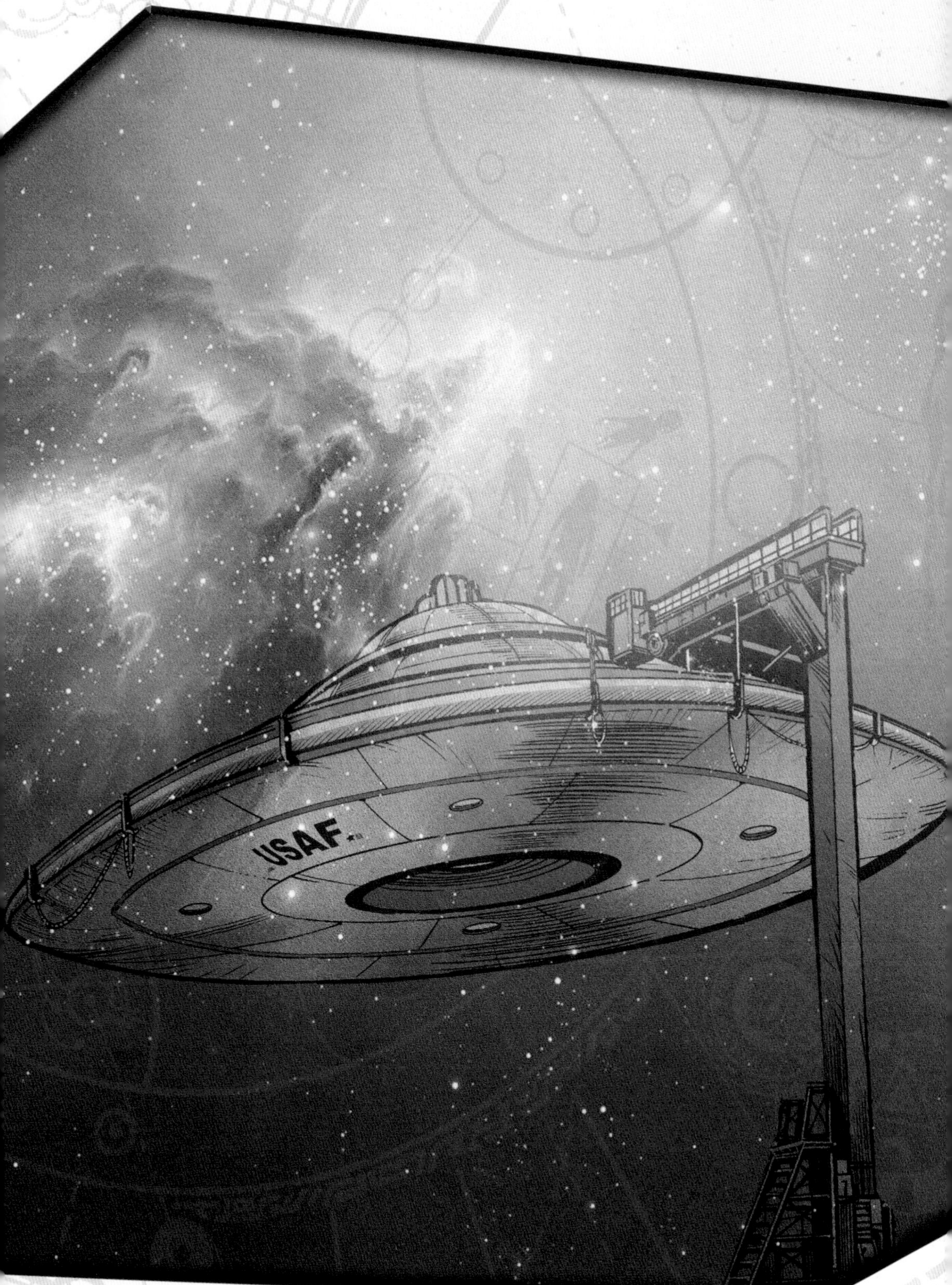
USAF.

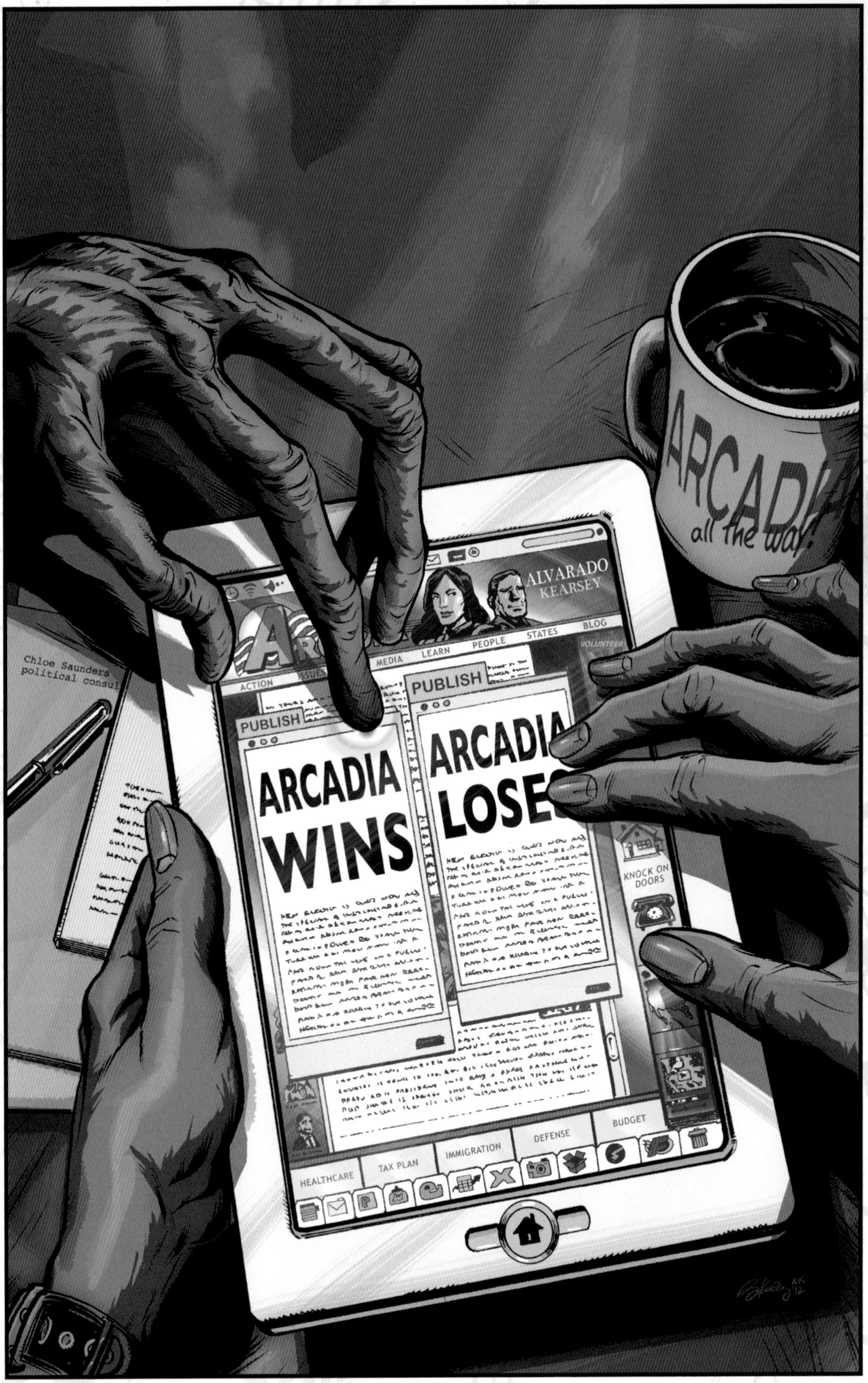

ALVARADO
KEARSEY
ACTION
ISSUES
MEDIA
LEARN
PEOPLE
STATES
BLOG
VOLUNTEER!
PUBLISH
ARCADIA
WINS
PUBLISH
ARCADIA
LOSES
KNOCK ON
DOORS
HEALTHCARE
TAX PLAN
IMMIGRATION
DEFENSE
BUDGET
ARCADIA
all the way!
Chloe Saunders
political consul

COVER ART BY **RYAN KELLY**

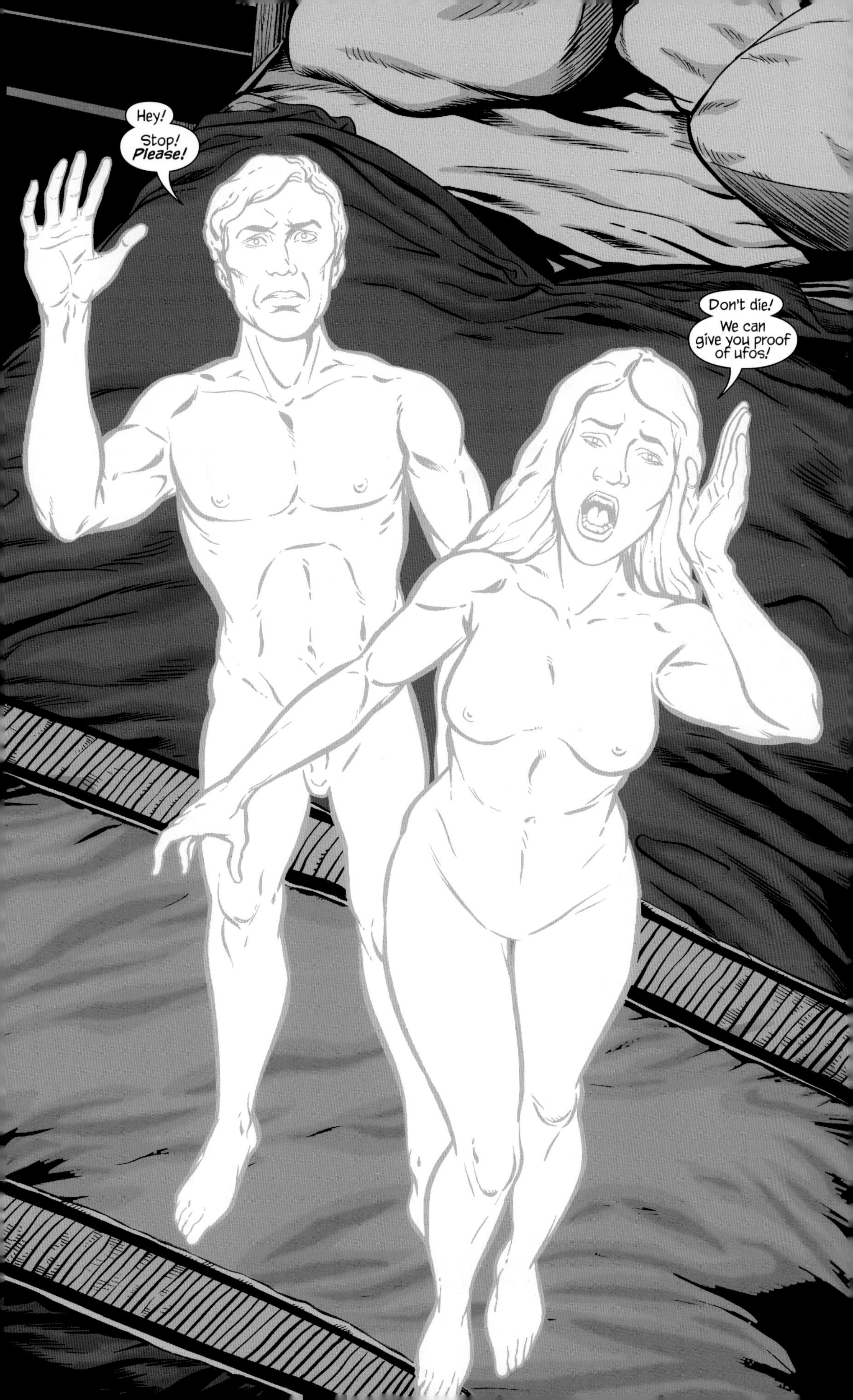
Hey! Stop! *Please!*
Don't die!
We can give you proof of ufos!

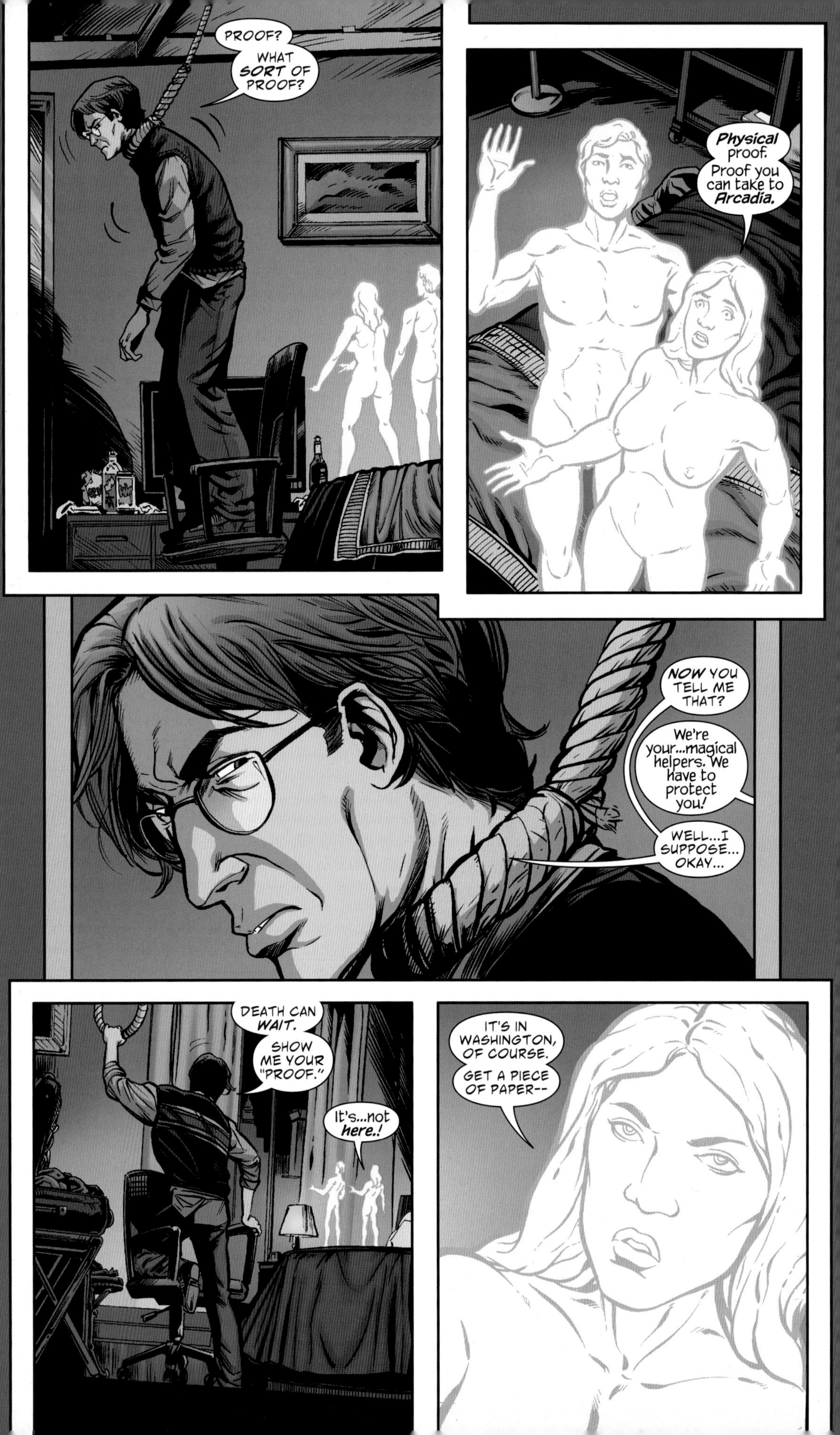
PROOF?
WHAT SORT OF PROOF?
Physical proof.
Proof you can take to Arcadia.
NOW YOU TELL ME THAT?
We're your...magical helpers. We have to protect you!
WELL...I SUPPOSE... OKAY...
DEATH CAN WAIT.
SHOW ME YOUR "PROOF."
It's...not here.!
IT'S IN WASHINGTON, OF COURSE.
GET A PIECE OF PAPER--

"- we'll provide directions."

OKAY, I THINK WE'VE HEARD ENOUGH. YOU KNOW, IT'S A PLEASURE TO MEET SOMEONE ELSE IN MY LINE OF BUSINESS, ASTELLE--

YES, I KNOW YOUR NAME. WE WERE EXPECTING SOMEONE FROM YOUR SIDE TO ARRIVE AT SOME POINT, AND I'M SO PLEASED IT'S YOU.

BY "HER LINE OF BUSINESS," FROM WHAT WE'VE JUST HEARD, I THINK SHE MEANS "LYING."

HOW DARE YOU--?!

THAT'S NOT AT ALL WHAT I WAS GOING TO SAY.

MY LINE OF BUSINESS IS THE CONSTRUCTION AND SALE OF NARRATIVES.

WE DISCOVERED YOUR NAME AFTER PROFESSOR KIDD PROVIDED US WITH A VERY GOOD DESCRIPTION OF YOU.

YEAH, 'CAUSE AS YOU STARED INTO HIS EYES, HE STARED INTO YOURS.

PERHAPS HE'S NOT AS MUCH OF A SHMUCK AS YOU THINK.

AND FROM YOUR NAME, USING RESEARCH RESOURCES THAT ARE PERHAPS MORE POWERFUL THAN THOSE OF MANY COUNTRIES' INTELLIGENCE ORGANIZATIONS, WE LEARNED ANOTHER IMPORTANT WORD--

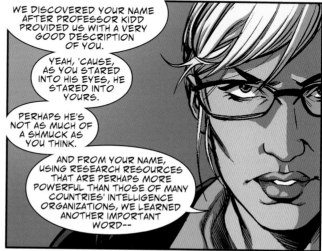

"BLUE-BIRDS."

I...I...

BUT YOU'RE NOT A PROFESSIONAL AT THIS.

YOU WORK IN AEROSPACE. WE COULD NAME THE FIRM. AND YOUR POSITION. AND YOUR BOSS.

AND, OF COURSE--

THERE'S THIS.

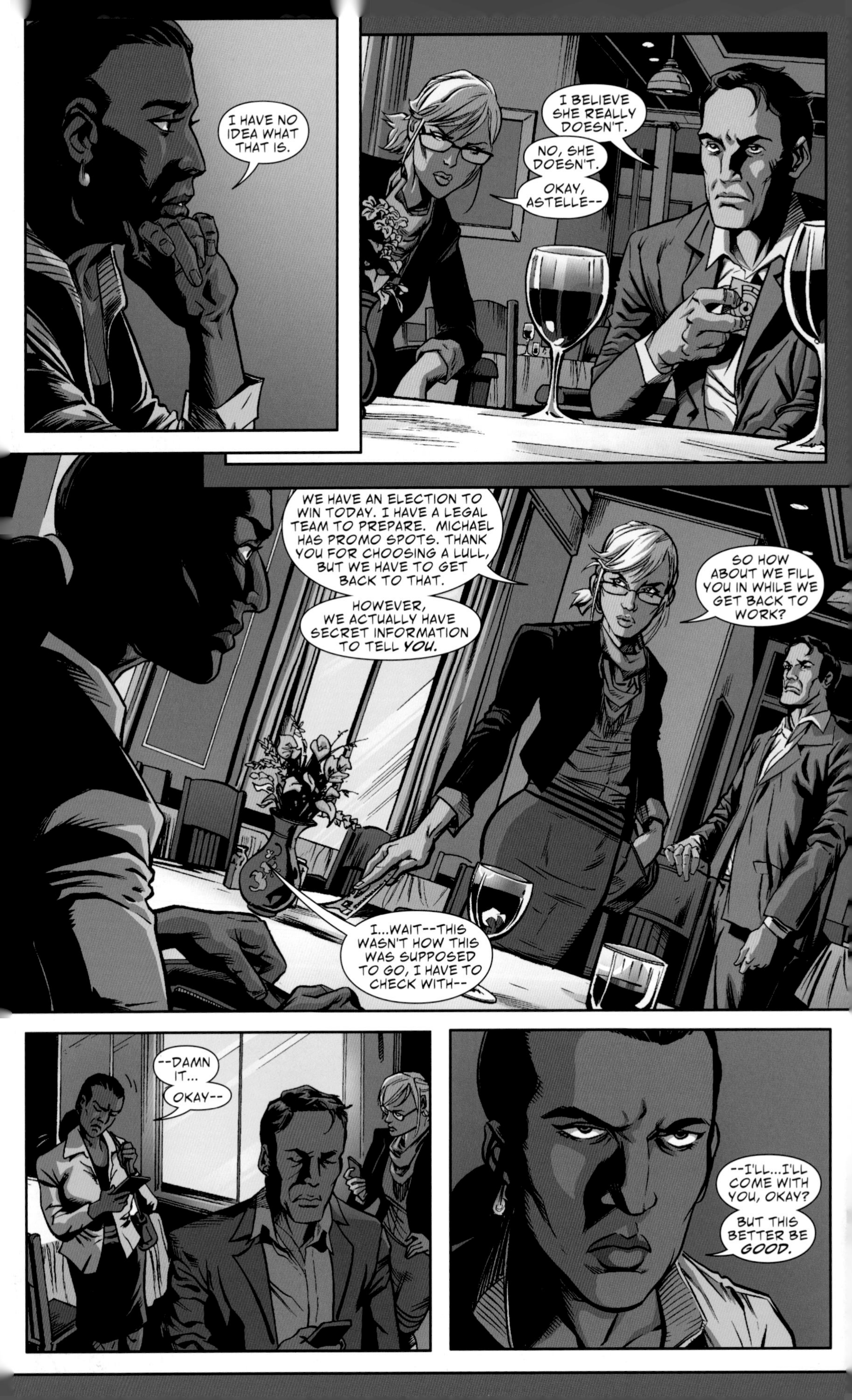
I HAVE NO IDEA WHAT THAT IS.
I BELIEVE SHE REALLY DOESN'T.
NO, SHE DOESN'T.
OKAY, ASTELLE--
WE HAVE AN ELECTION TO WIN TODAY. I HAVE A LEGAL TEAM TO PREPARE. MICHAEL HAS PROMO SPOTS. THANK YOU FOR CHOOSING A LULL, BUT WE HAVE TO GET BACK TO THAT.
HOWEVER, WE ACTUALLY HAVE SECRET INFORMATION TO TELL *YOU*.
SO HOW ABOUT WE FILL YOU IN WHILE WE GET BACK TO WORK?
I...WAIT--THIS WASN'T HOW THIS WAS SUPPOSED TO GO, I HAVE TO CHECK WITH--
--DAMN IT...
OKAY--
--I'LL...I'LL COME WITH YOU, OKAY?
BUT THIS BETTER BE ***GOOD***.

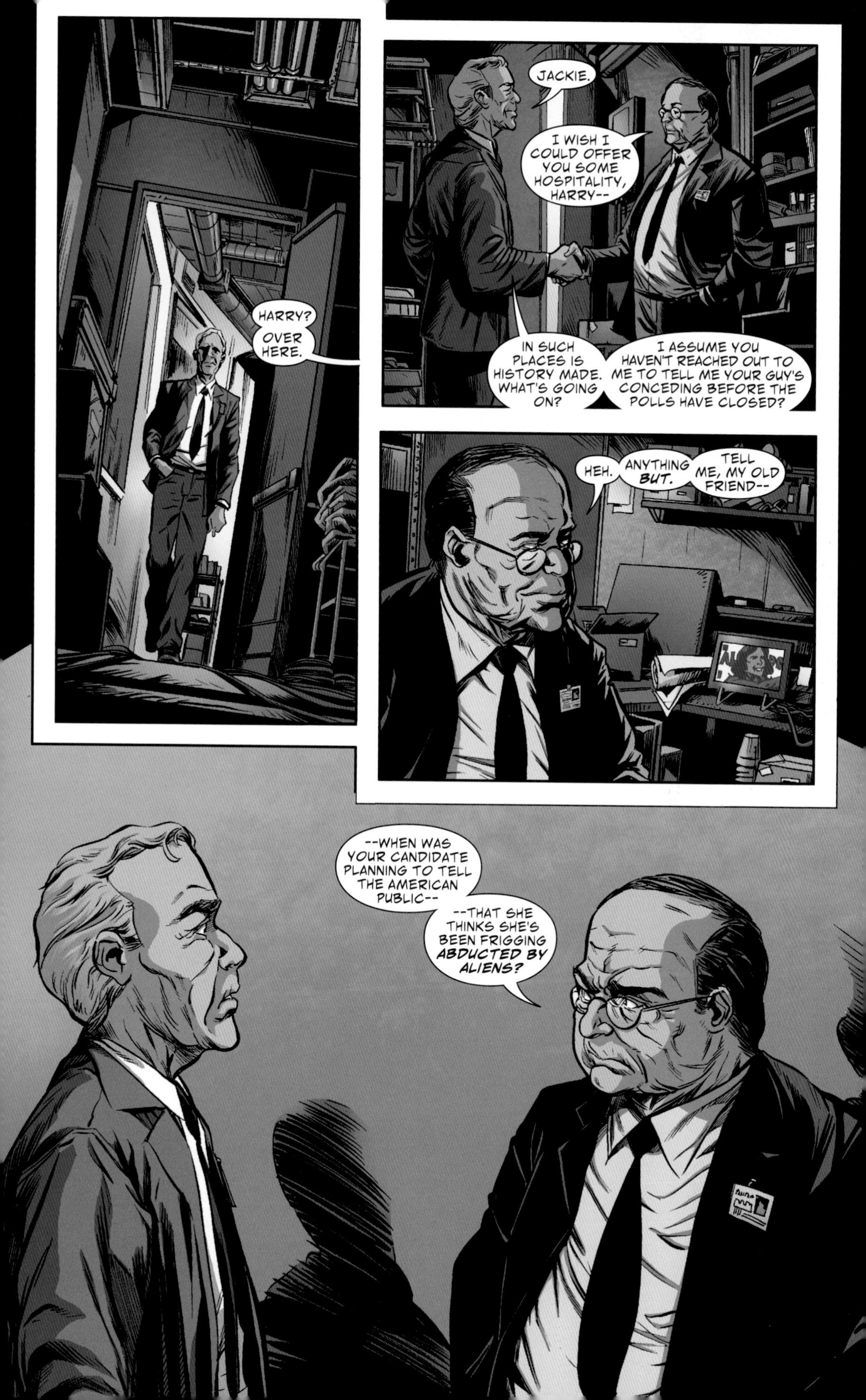
HARRY?
OVER HERE.
JACKIE.
I WISH I COULD OFFER YOU SOME HOSPITALITY, HARRY--
IN SUCH PLACES IS HISTORY MADE. WHAT'S GOING ON?
I ASSUME YOU HAVEN'T REACHED OUT TO ME TO TELL ME YOUR GUY'S CONCEDING BEFORE THE POLLS HAVE CLOSED?
HEH.
ANYTHING *BUT.*
TELL ME, MY OLD FRIEND--
--WHEN WAS YOUR CANDIDATE PLANNING TO TELL THE AMERICAN PUBLIC--
--THAT SHE THINKS SHE'S BEEN FRIGGING ***ABDUCTED BY ALIENS?***

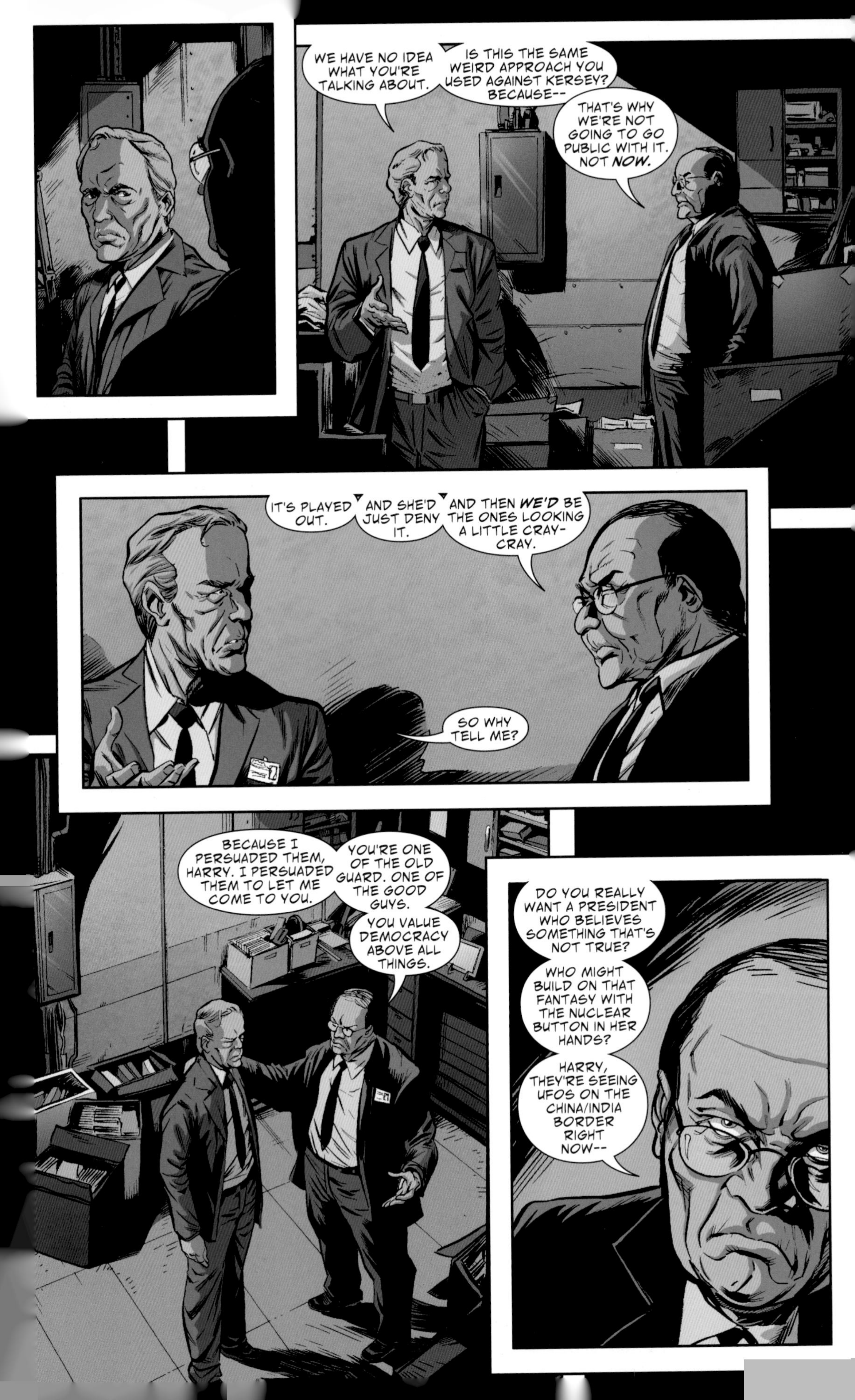
WE HAVE NO IDEA WHAT YOU'RE TALKING ABOUT.
IS THIS THE SAME WEIRD APPROACH YOU USED AGAINST KERSEY? BECAUSE--
THAT'S WHY WE'RE NOT GOING TO GO PUBLIC WITH IT. NOT NOW.
IT'S PLAYED OUT.
AND SHE'D JUST DENY IT.
AND THEN WE'D BE THE ONES LOOKING A LITTLE CRAY-CRAY.
SO WHY TELL ME?
BECAUSE I PERSUADED THEM, HARRY. I PERSUADED THEM TO LET ME COME TO YOU.
YOU'RE ONE OF THE OLD GUARD. ONE OF THE GOOD GUYS.
YOU VALUE DEMOCRACY ABOVE ALL THINGS.
DO YOU REALLY WANT A PRESIDENT WHO BELIEVES SOMETHING THAT'S NOT TRUE?
WHO MIGHT BUILD ON THAT FANTASY WITH THE NUCLEAR BUTTON IN HER HANDS?
HARRY, THEY'RE SEEING UFOS ON THE CHINA/INDIA BORDER RIGHT NOW--

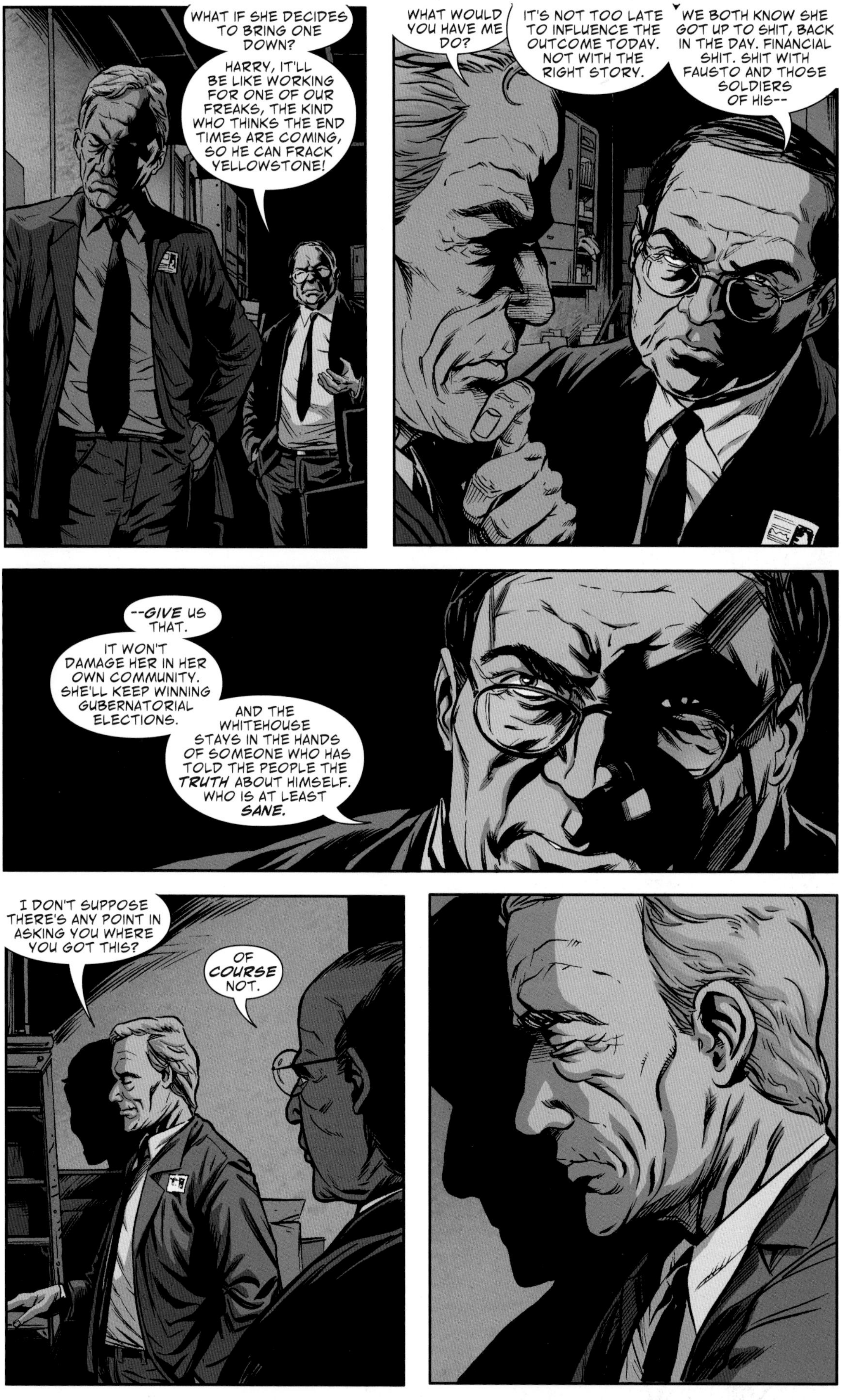
WHAT IF SHE DECIDES TO BRING ONE DOWN?
HARRY, IT'LL BE LIKE WORKING FOR ONE OF OUR FREAKS, THE KIND WHO THINKS THE END TIMES ARE COMING, SO HE CAN FRACK YELLOWSTONE!
WHAT WOULD YOU HAVE ME DO?
IT'S NOT TOO LATE TO INFLUENCE THE OUTCOME TODAY. NOT WITH THE RIGHT STORY.
WE BOTH KNOW SHE GOT UP TO SHIT, BACK IN THE DAY. FINANCIAL SHIT. SHIT WITH FAUSTO AND THOSE SOLDIERS OF HIS--
--*GIVE* US THAT.
IT WON'T DAMAGE HER IN HER OWN COMMUNITY. SHE'LL KEEP WINNING GUBERNATORIAL ELECTIONS.
AND THE WHITEHOUSE STAYS IN THE HANDS OF SOMEONE WHO HAS TOLD THE PEOPLE THE *TRUTH* ABOUT HIMSELF. WHO IS AT LEAST *SANE.*
I DON'T SUPPOSE THERE'S ANY POINT IN ASKING YOU WHERE YOU GOT THIS?
OF *COURSE* NOT.

WOW. YOU GUYS MUST BE FUCKING *TERRIFIED.*

HARRY--

NO, YOU LISTEN TO ME, JACKIE--

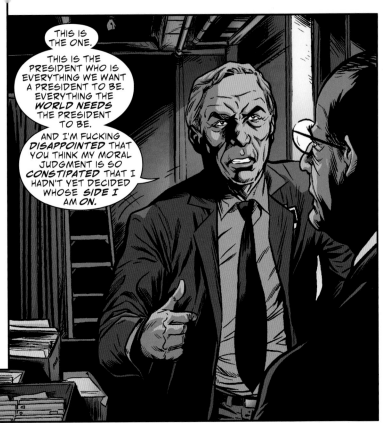

THIS IS THE ONE.

THIS IS THE PRESIDENT WHO IS EVERYTHING WE WANT A PRESIDENT TO BE. EVERYTHING THE *WORLD NEEDS* THE PRESIDENT TO BE.

AND I'M FUCKING *DISAPPOINTED* THAT YOU THINK MY MORAL JUDGMENT IS SO *CONSTIPATED* THAT I HADN'T YET DECIDED WHOSE *SIDE* I AM *ON.*

WE'RE STILL FRIENDS, JACKIE.

YOU COME TO ME FOR A JOB AFTER THE GOVERNOR IS PRESIDENT.

BUT THIS SHIT WAS LOW. THE LOWEST YOU'VE BEEN.

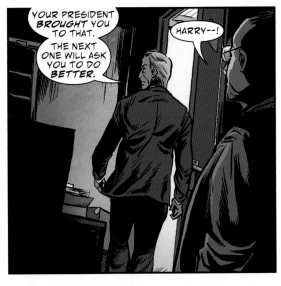

YOUR PRESIDENT *BROUGHT* YOU TO THAT.

THE NEXT ONE WILL ASK YOU TO DO *BETTER.*

HARRY--!

DAMN IT, HARRY--

YOU CAN'T SAY WE DIDN'T *WARN* YOU.

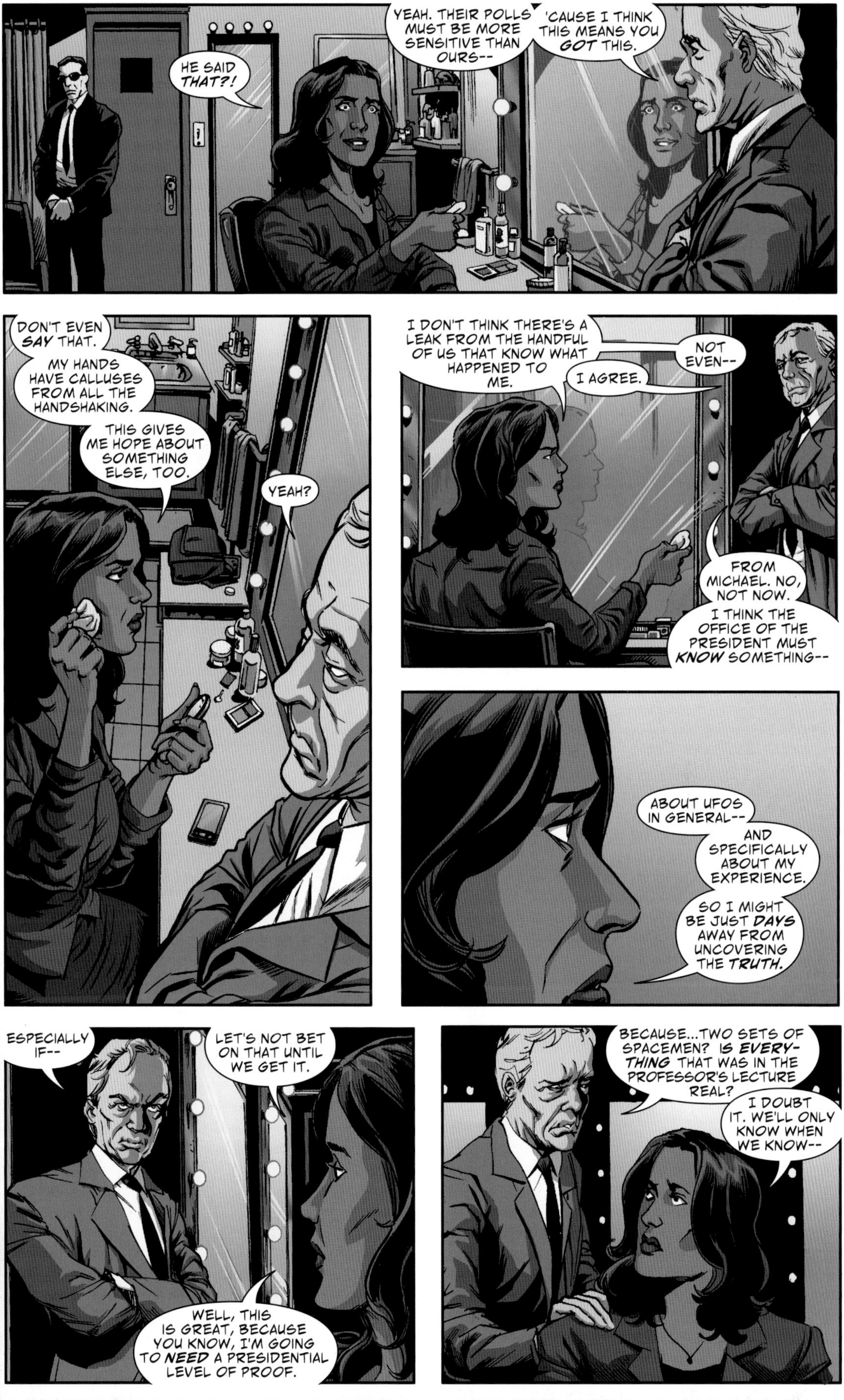
HE SAID THAT?!
YEAH. THEIR POLLS MUST BE MORE SENSITIVE THAN OURS--
'CAUSE I THINK THIS MEANS YOU GOT THIS.
DON'T EVEN SAY THAT.
MY HANDS HAVE CALLUSES FROM ALL THE HANDSHAKING.
THIS GIVES ME HOPE ABOUT SOMETHING ELSE, TOO.
YEAH?
I DON'T THINK THERE'S A LEAK FROM THE HANDFUL OF US THAT KNOW WHAT HAPPENED TO ME.
I AGREE.
NOT EVEN--
FROM MICHAEL. NO, NOT NOW.
I THINK THE OFFICE OF THE PRESIDENT MUST KNOW SOMETHING--
ABOUT UFOS IN GENERAL--
AND SPECIFICALLY ABOUT MY EXPERIENCE.
SO I MIGHT BE JUST DAYS AWAY FROM UNCOVERING THE TRUTH.
ESPECIALLY IF--
LET'S NOT BET ON THAT UNTIL WE GET IT.
WELL, THIS IS GREAT, BECAUSE YOU KNOW, I'M GOING TO NEED A PRESIDENTIAL LEVEL OF PROOF.
BECAUSE...TWO SETS OF SPACEMEN? IS EVERYTHING THAT WAS IN THE PROFESSOR'S LECTURE REAL?
I DOUBT IT. WE'LL ONLY KNOW WHEN WE KNOW--

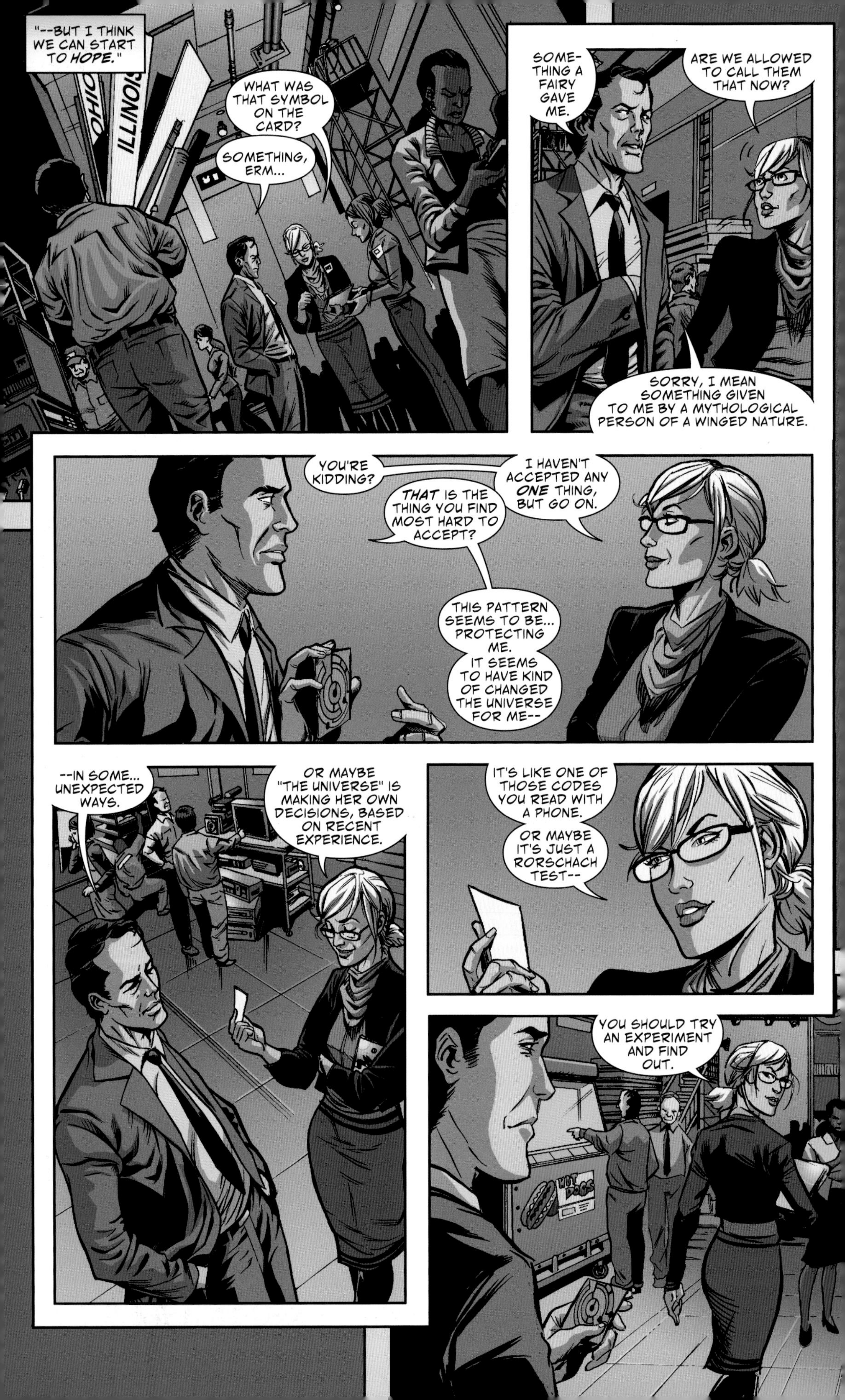
"--BUT I THINK WE CAN START TO *HOPE.*"
OHIO
ILLINOIS
WHAT WAS THAT SYMBOL ON THE CARD?
SOMETHING, ERM...
SOME-THING A FAIRY GAVE ME.
ARE WE ALLOWED TO CALL THEM THAT NOW?
SORRY, I MEAN SOMETHING GIVEN TO ME BY A MYTHOLOGICAL PERSON OF A WINGED NATURE.
YOU'RE KIDDING?
THAT IS THE THING YOU FIND MOST HARD TO ACCEPT?
I HAVEN'T ACCEPTED ANY *ONE* THING, BUT GO ON.
THIS PATTERN SEEMS TO BE... PROTECTING ME.
IT SEEMS TO HAVE KIND OF CHANGED THE UNIVERSE FOR ME--
--IN SOME... UNEXPECTED WAYS.
OR MAYBE "THE UNIVERSE" IS MAKING HER OWN DECISIONS, BASED ON RECENT EXPERIENCE.
IT'S LIKE ONE OF THOSE CODES YOU READ WITH A PHONE.
OR MAYBE IT'S JUST A RORSCHACH TEST--
YOU SHOULD TRY AN EXPERIMENT AND FIND OUT.
HOT DOGS

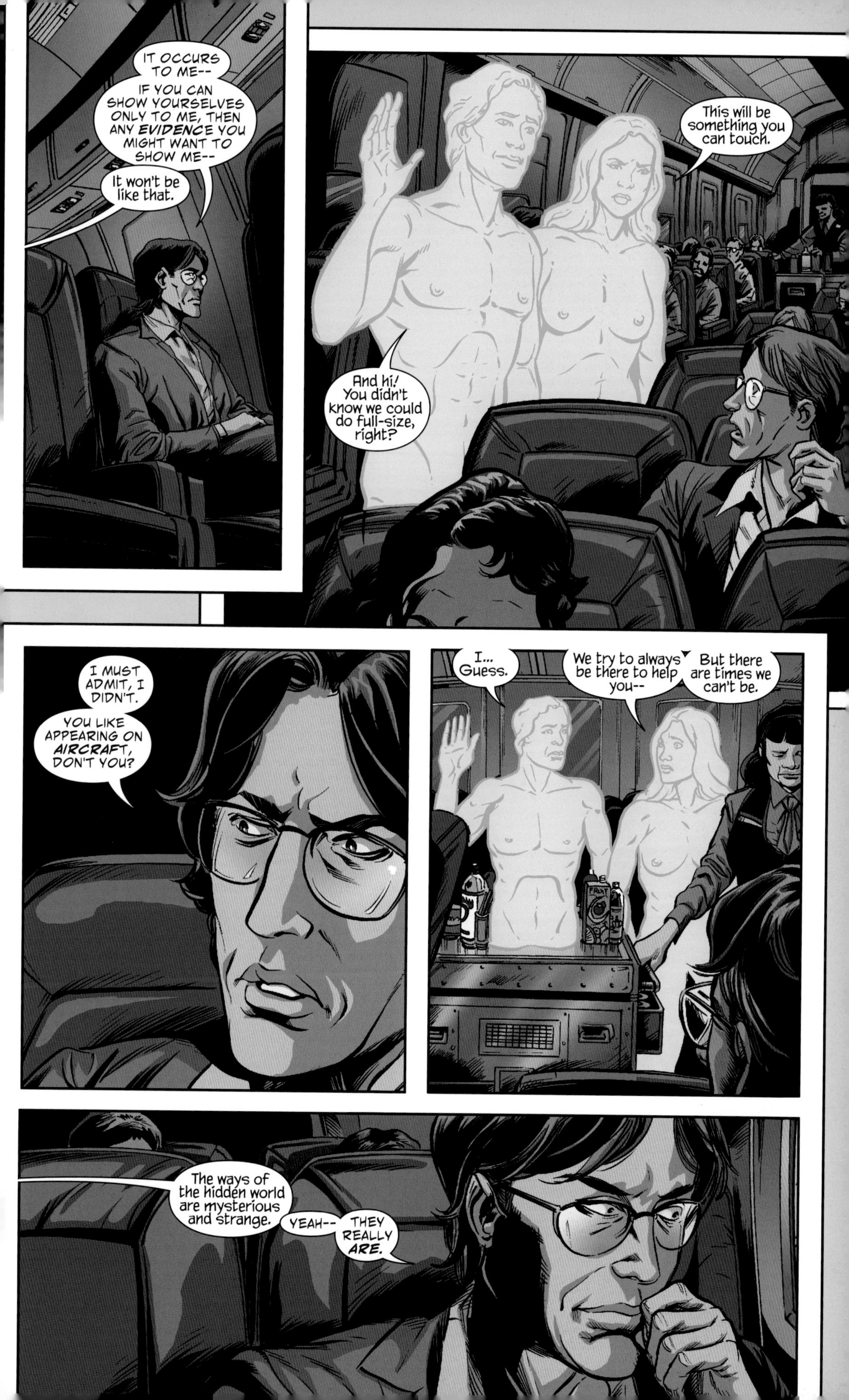
IT OCCURS TO ME--
IF YOU CAN SHOW YOURSELVES ONLY TO ME, THEN ANY EVIDENCE YOU MIGHT WANT TO SHOW ME--
It won't be like that.
This will be something you can touch.
And hi! You didn't know we could do full-size, right?
I MUST ADMIT, I DIDN'T.
YOU LIKE APPEARING ON AIRCRAFT, DON'T YOU?
I... Guess.
We try to always be there to help you--
But there are times we can't be.
The ways of the hidden world are mysterious and strange.
YEAH--
THEY REALLY ARE.

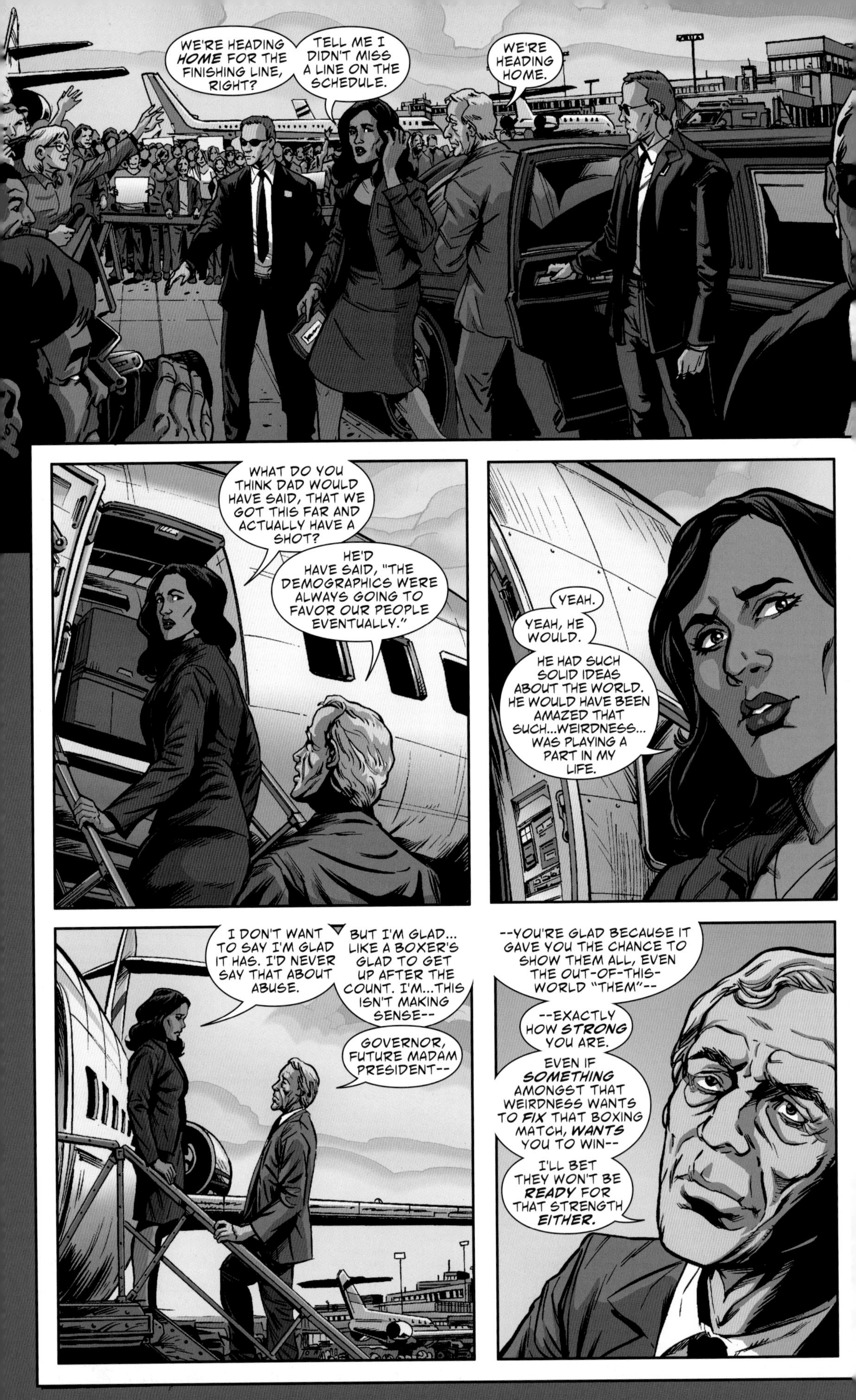
WE'RE HEADING HOME FOR THE FINISHING LINE, RIGHT?
TELL ME I DIDN'T MISS A LINE ON THE SCHEDULE.
WE'RE HEADING HOME.
WHAT DO YOU THINK DAD WOULD HAVE SAID, THAT WE GOT THIS FAR AND ACTUALLY HAVE A SHOT?
HE'D HAVE SAID, "THE DEMOGRAPHICS WERE ALWAYS GOING TO FAVOR OUR PEOPLE EVENTUALLY."
YEAH.
YEAH, HE WOULD.
HE HAD SUCH SOLID IDEAS ABOUT THE WORLD. HE WOULD HAVE BEEN AMAZED THAT SUCH...WEIRDNESS... WAS PLAYING A PART IN MY LIFE.
I DON'T WANT TO SAY I'M GLAD IT HAS. I'D NEVER SAY THAT ABOUT ABUSE.
BUT I'M GLAD... LIKE A BOXER'S GLAD TO GET UP AFTER THE COUNT. I'M...THIS ISN'T MAKING SENSE--
GOVERNOR, FUTURE MADAM PRESIDENT--
--YOU'RE GLAD BECAUSE IT GAVE YOU THE CHANCE TO SHOW THEM ALL, EVEN THE OUT-OF-THIS-WORLD "THEM"--
--EXACTLY HOW STRONG YOU ARE.
EVEN IF SOMETHING AMONGST THAT WEIRDNESS WANTS TO FIX THAT BOXING MATCH, WANTS YOU TO WIN--
I'LL BET THEY WON'T BE READY FOR THAT STRENGTH EITHER.

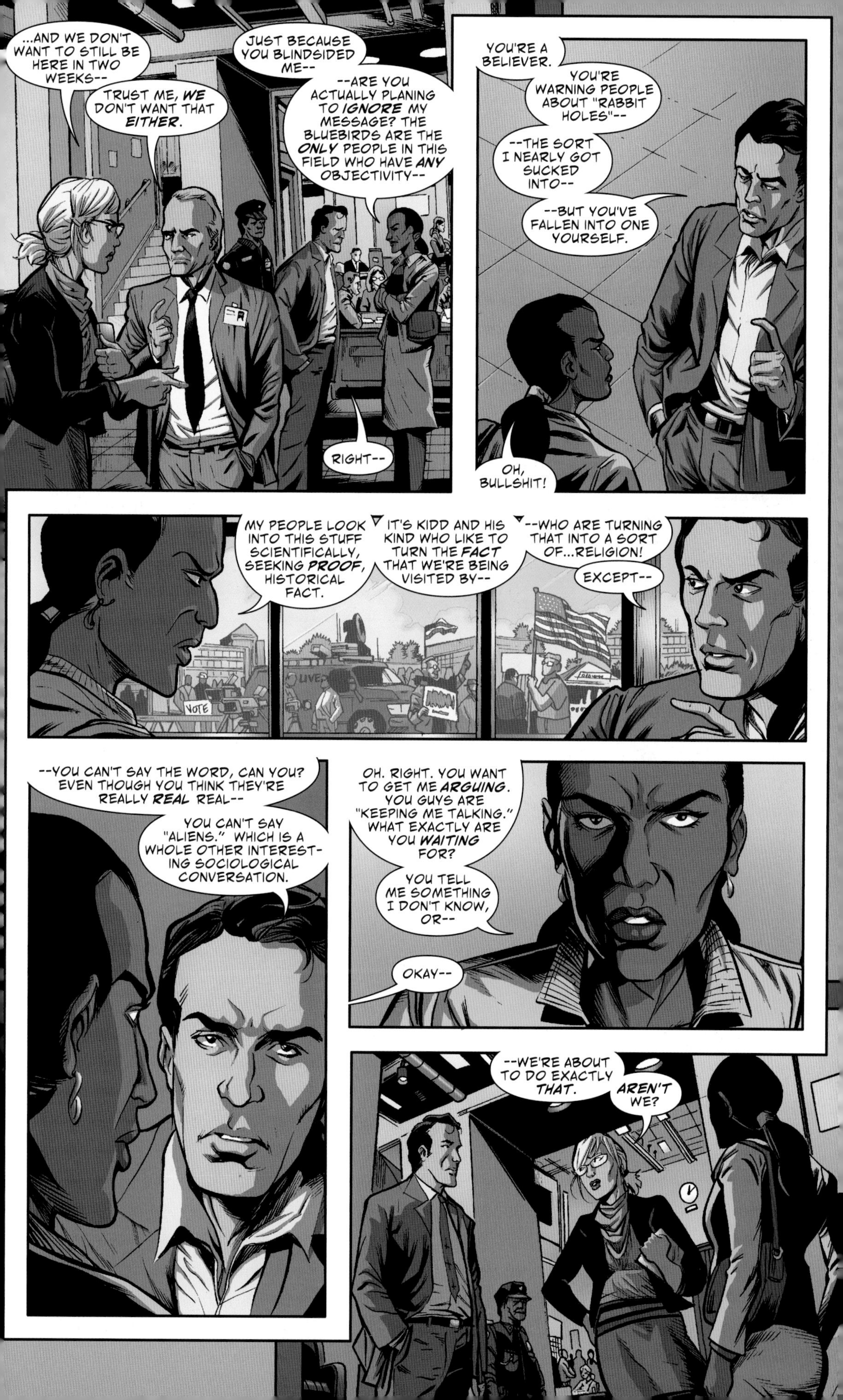

...AND WE DON'T WANT TO STILL BE HERE IN TWO WEEKS--
TRUST ME, *WE* DON'T WANT THAT *EITHER*.
JUST BECAUSE YOU BLINDSIDED ME--
--ARE YOU ACTUALLY PLANING TO *IGNORE* MY MESSAGE? THE BLUEBIRDS ARE THE *ONLY* PEOPLE IN THIS FIELD WHO HAVE *ANY* OBJECTIVITY--
RIGHT--
YOU'RE A BELIEVER.
YOU'RE WARNING PEOPLE ABOUT "RABBIT HOLES"--
--THE SORT I NEARLY GOT SUCKED INTO--
--BUT YOU'VE FALLEN INTO ONE YOURSELF.
OH, BULLSHIT!
MY PEOPLE LOOK INTO THIS STUFF SCIENTIFICALLY, SEEKING *PROOF*, HISTORICAL FACT.
IT'S KIDD AND HIS KIND WHO LIKE TO TURN THE *FACT* THAT WE'RE BEING VISITED BY--
--WHO ARE TURNING THAT INTO A SORT OF...RELIGION!
EXCEPT--
VOTE
LIVE
--YOU CAN'T SAY THE WORD, CAN YOU? EVEN THOUGH YOU THINK THEY'RE REALLY *REAL* REAL--
YOU CAN'T SAY "ALIENS." WHICH IS A WHOLE OTHER INTEREST-ING SOCIOLOGICAL CONVERSATION.
OH. RIGHT. YOU WANT TO GET ME *ARGUING*. YOU GUYS ARE "KEEPING ME TALKING." WHAT EXACTLY ARE YOU *WAITING* FOR?
YOU TELL ME SOMETHING I DON'T KNOW, OR--
OKAY--
--WE'RE ABOUT TO DO EXACTLY *THAT*.
AREN'T WE?

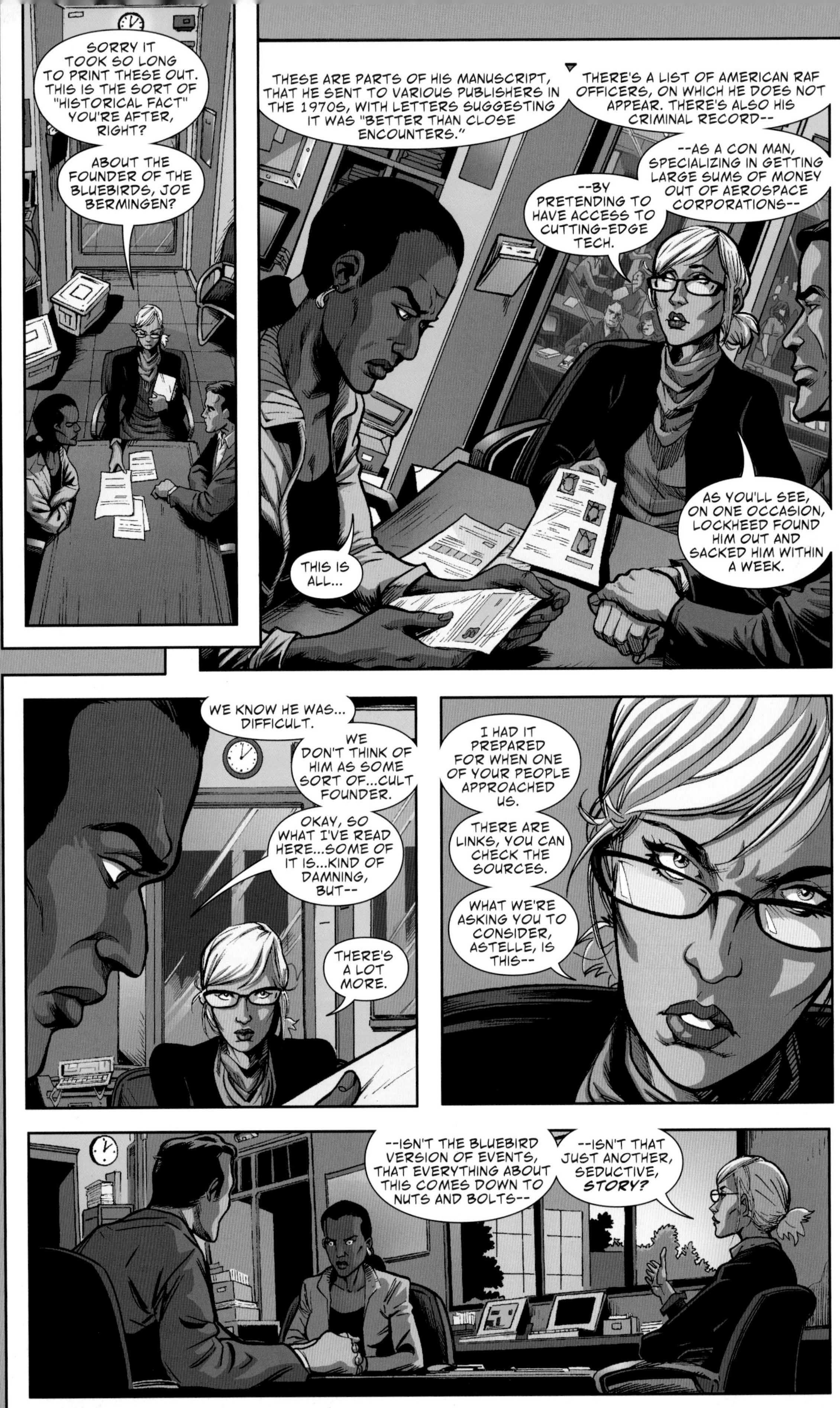
SORRY IT TOOK SO LONG TO PRINT THESE OUT. THIS IS THE SORT OF "HISTORICAL FACT" YOU'RE AFTER, RIGHT?
ABOUT THE FOUNDER OF THE BLUEBIRDS, JOE BERMINGEN?
THESE ARE PARTS OF HIS MANUSCRIPT, THAT HE SENT TO VARIOUS PUBLISHERS IN THE 1970S, WITH LETTERS SUGGESTING IT WAS "BETTER THAN CLOSE ENCOUNTERS."
THERE'S A LIST OF AMERICAN RAF OFFICERS, ON WHICH HE DOES NOT APPEAR. THERE'S ALSO HIS CRIMINAL RECORD--
--AS A CON MAN, SPECIALIZING IN GETTING LARGE SUMS OF MONEY OUT OF AEROSPACE CORPORATIONS--
--BY PRETENDING TO HAVE ACCESS TO CUTTING-EDGE TECH.
THIS IS ALL...
AS YOU'LL SEE, ON ONE OCCASION, LOCKHEED FOUND HIM OUT AND SACKED HIM WITHIN A WEEK.
WE KNOW HE WAS... DIFFICULT.
WE DON'T THINK OF HIM AS SOME SORT OF...CULT FOUNDER.
OKAY, SO WHAT I'VE READ HERE...SOME OF IT IS...KIND OF DAMNING, BUT--
THERE'S A LOT MORE.
I HAD IT PREPARED FOR WHEN ONE OF YOUR PEOPLE APPROACHED US.
THERE ARE LINKS, YOU CAN CHECK THE SOURCES.
WHAT WE'RE ASKING YOU TO CONSIDER, ASTELLE, IS THIS--
--ISN'T THE BLUEBIRD VERSION OF EVENTS, THAT EVERYTHING ABOUT THIS COMES DOWN TO NUTS AND BOLTS--
--ISN'T THAT JUST ANOTHER, SEDUCTIVE, ***STORY?***

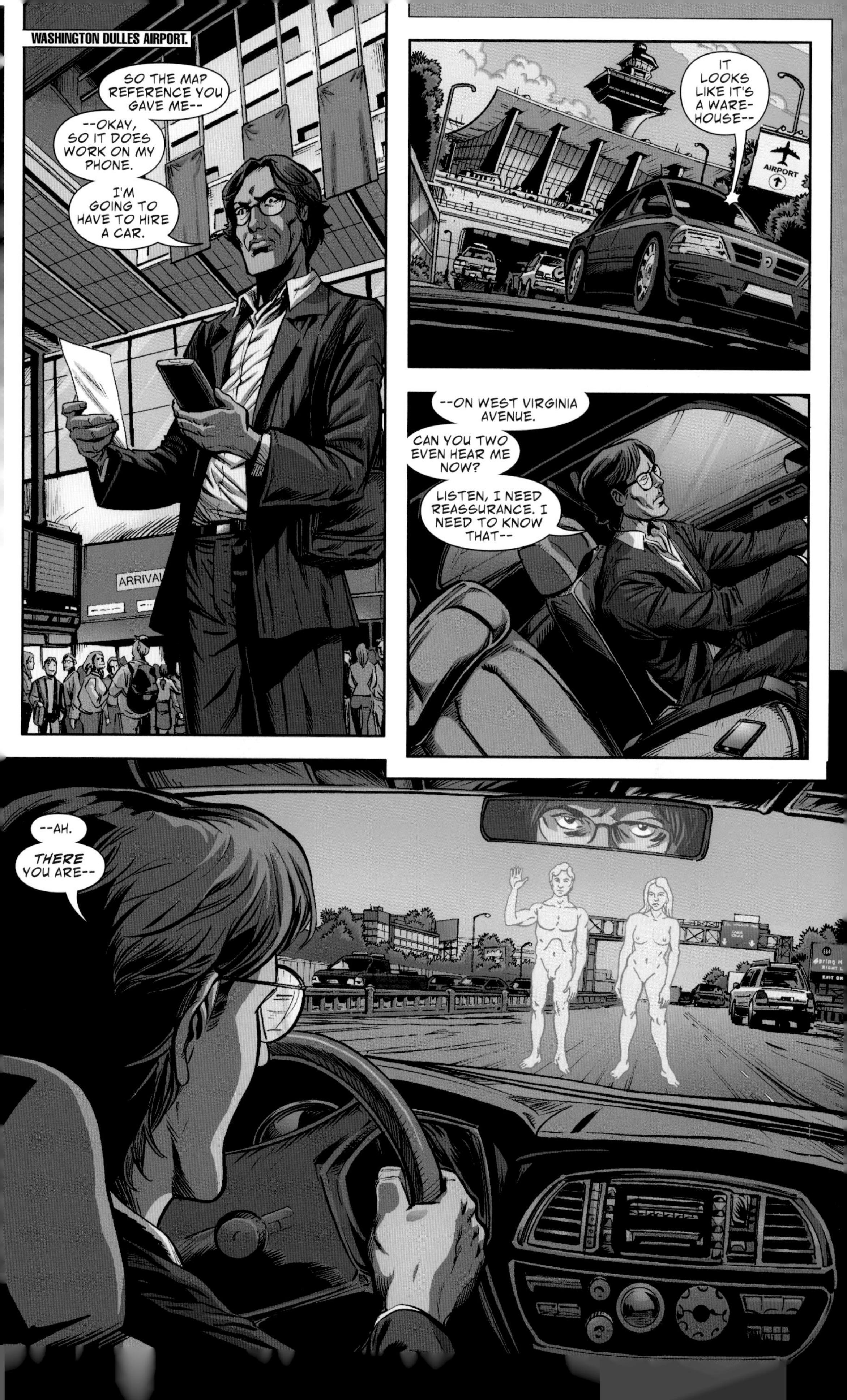
WASHINGTON DULLES AIRPORT.
SO THE MAP REFERENCE YOU GAVE ME--
--OKAY, SO IT DOES WORK ON MY PHONE.
I'M GOING TO HAVE TO HIRE A CAR.
ARRIVAL
IT LOOKS LIKE IT'S A WARE-HOUSE--
AIRPORT
--ON WEST VIRGINIA AVENUE.
CAN YOU TWO EVEN HEAR ME NOW?
LISTEN, I NEED REASSURANCE. I NEED TO KNOW THAT--
--AH.
THERE YOU ARE--

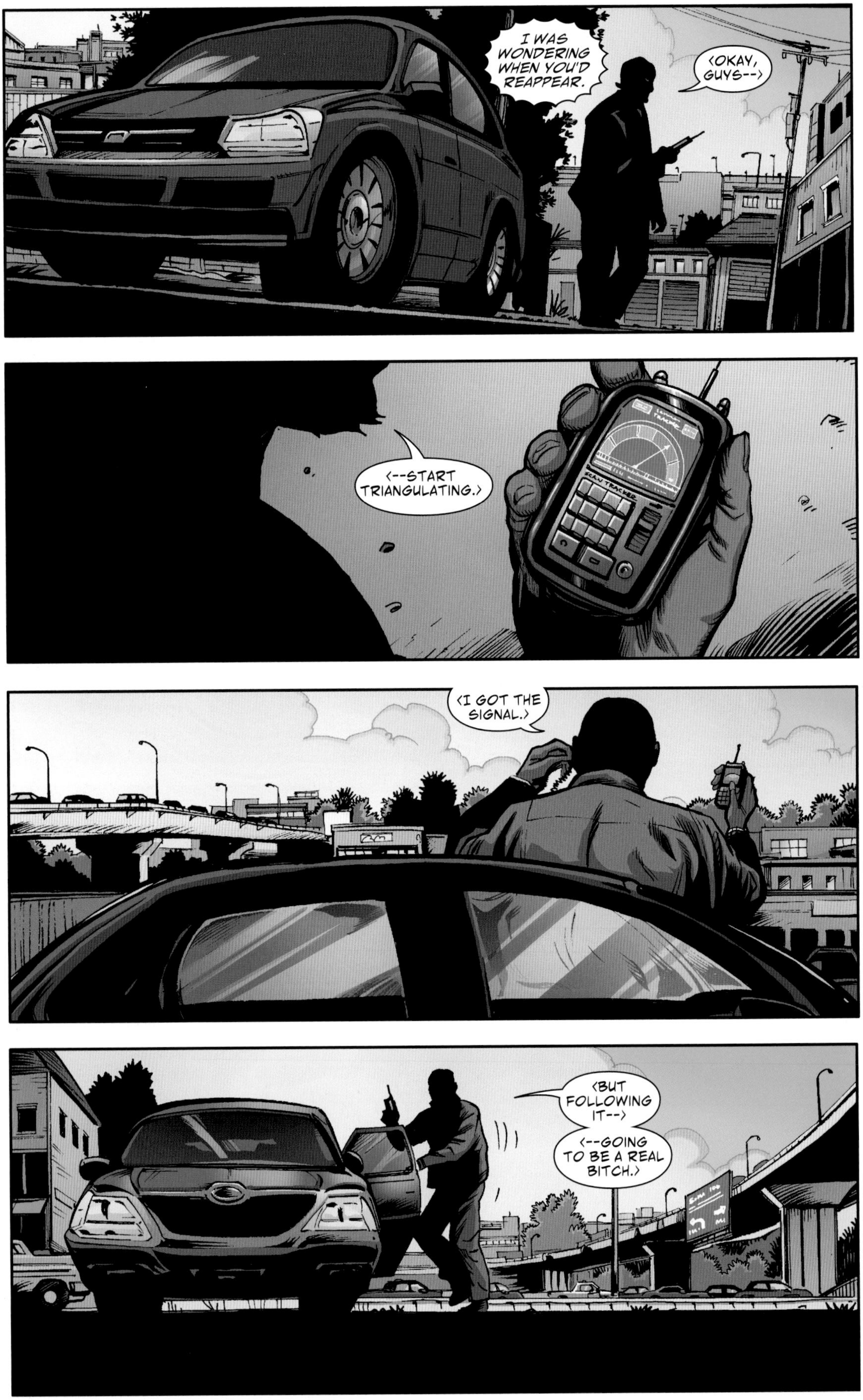
I WAS WONDERING WHEN YOU'D REAPPEAR.
‹OKAY, GUYS--›
‹--START TRIANGULATING.›
SCAN TRACKER
‹I GOT THE SIGNAL.›
‹BUT FOLLOWING IT--›
‹--GOING TO BE A REAL BITCH.›

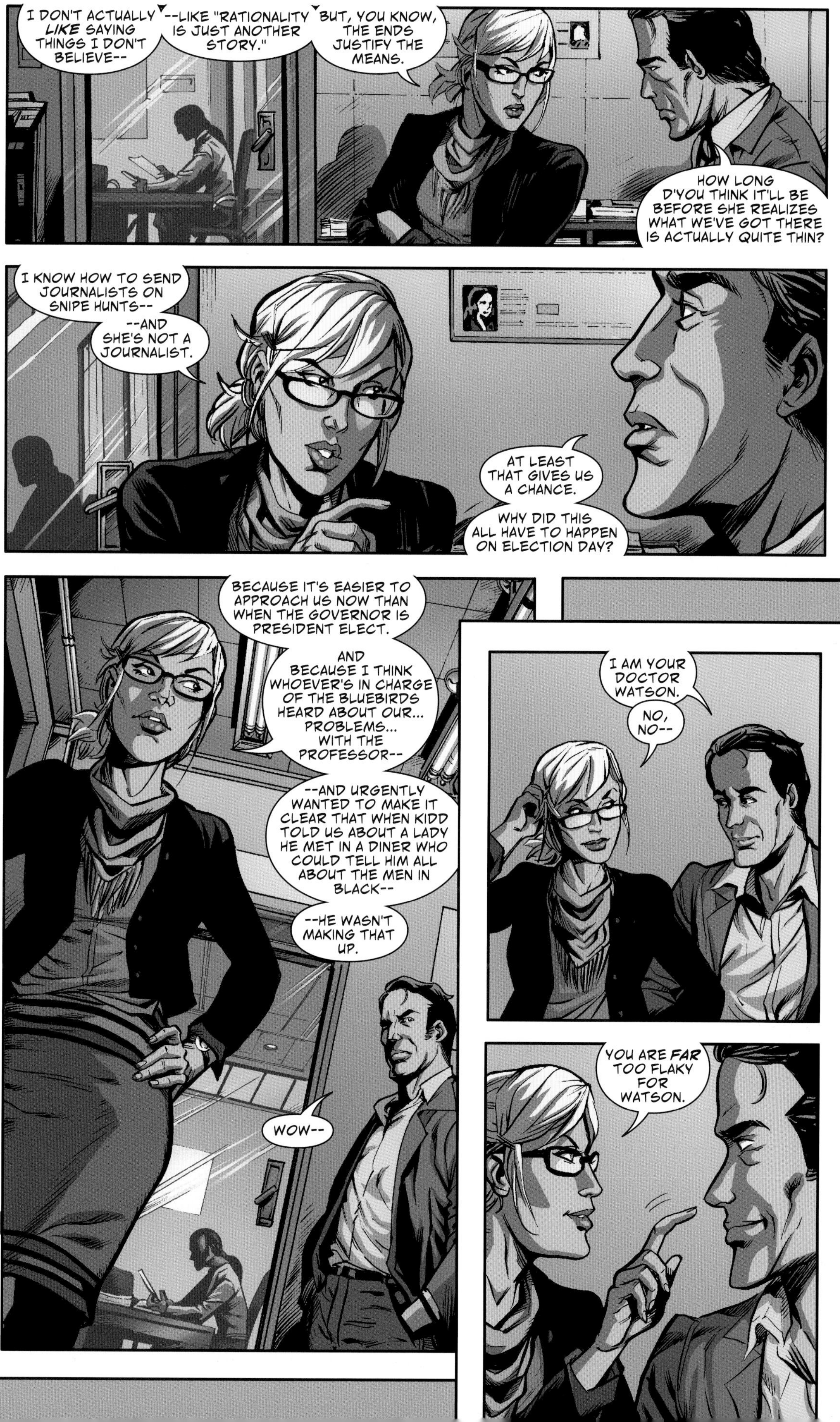
I DON'T ACTUALLY *LIKE* SAYING THINGS I DON'T BELIEVE--
--LIKE "RATIONALITY IS JUST ANOTHER STORY."
BUT, YOU KNOW, THE ENDS JUSTIFY THE MEANS.
HOW LONG D'YOU THINK IT'LL BE BEFORE SHE REALIZES WHAT WE'VE GOT THERE IS ACTUALLY QUITE THIN?
I KNOW HOW TO SEND JOURNALISTS ON SNIPE HUNTS--
--AND SHE'S NOT A JOURNALIST.
AT LEAST THAT GIVES US A CHANCE.
WHY DID THIS ALL HAVE TO HAPPEN ON ELECTION DAY?
BECAUSE IT'S EASIER TO APPROACH US NOW THAN WHEN THE GOVERNOR IS PRESIDENT ELECT.
AND BECAUSE I THINK WHOEVER'S IN CHARGE OF THE BLUEBIRDS HEARD ABOUT OUR... PROBLEMS... WITH THE PROFESSOR--
--AND URGENTLY WANTED TO MAKE IT CLEAR THAT WHEN KIDD TOLD US ABOUT A LADY HE MET IN A DINER WHO COULD TELL HIM ALL ABOUT THE MEN IN BLACK--
--HE WASN'T MAKING THAT UP.
WOW--
I AM YOUR DOCTOR WATSON.
NO, NO--
YOU ARE *FAR* TOO FLAKY FOR WATSON.

Third warehouse along.

YOU BETTER STAY WITH ME--

WHY?

I'M... KIND OF FREAKING OUT ABOUT THIS AREA.

WHAT'S YOUR "PROOF" DOING IN HERE?

ARE YOU SETTING ME UP FOR SOMETHING?

It was... left here.

That one.

OKAY. THAT'S... THAT'S--

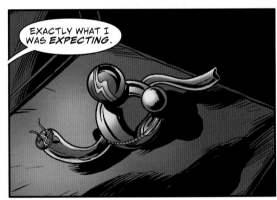

EXACTLY WHAT I WAS EXPECTING.

FAUSTO-- --GO FOR CAPTURE.

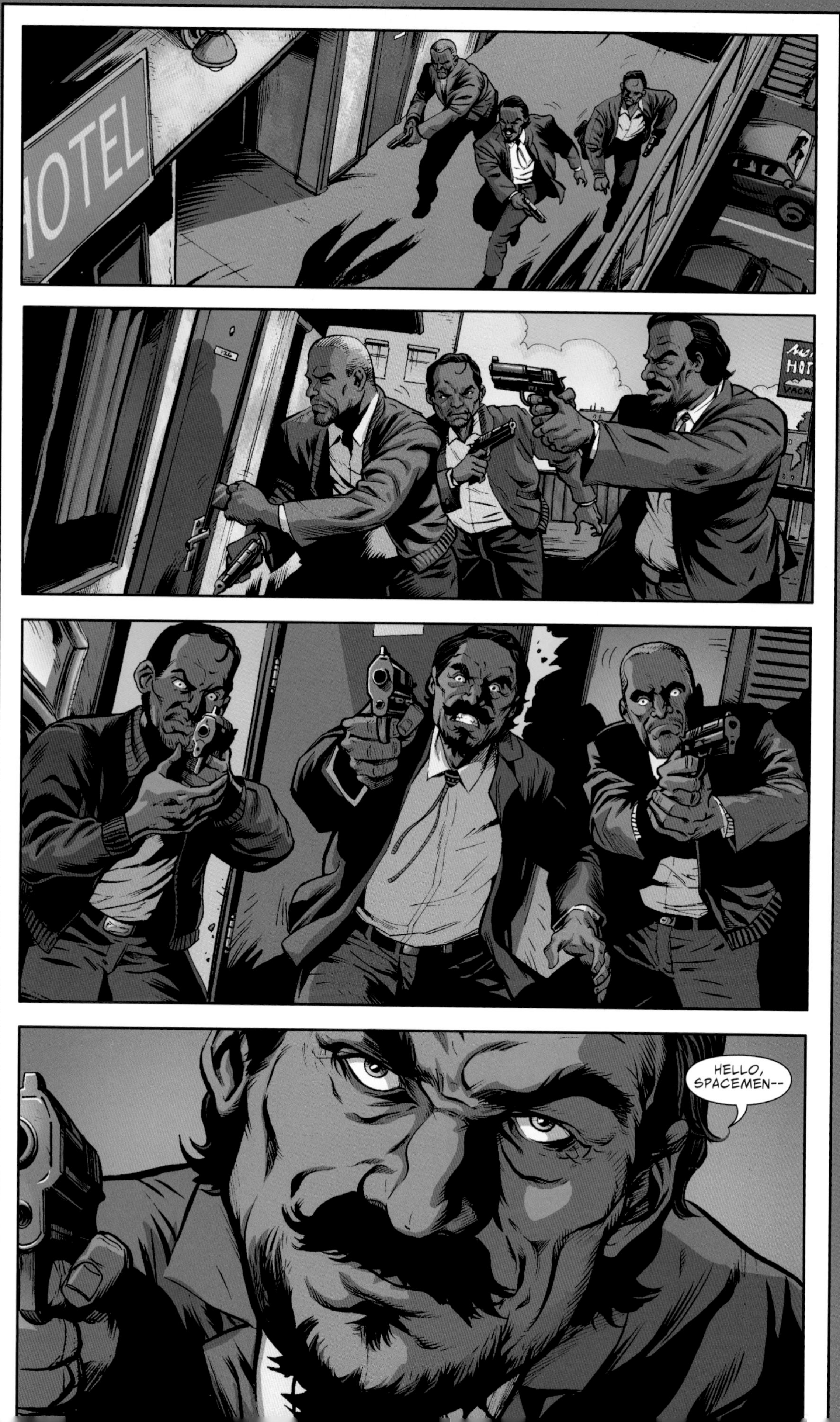
HOTEL
HELLO, SPACEMEN--

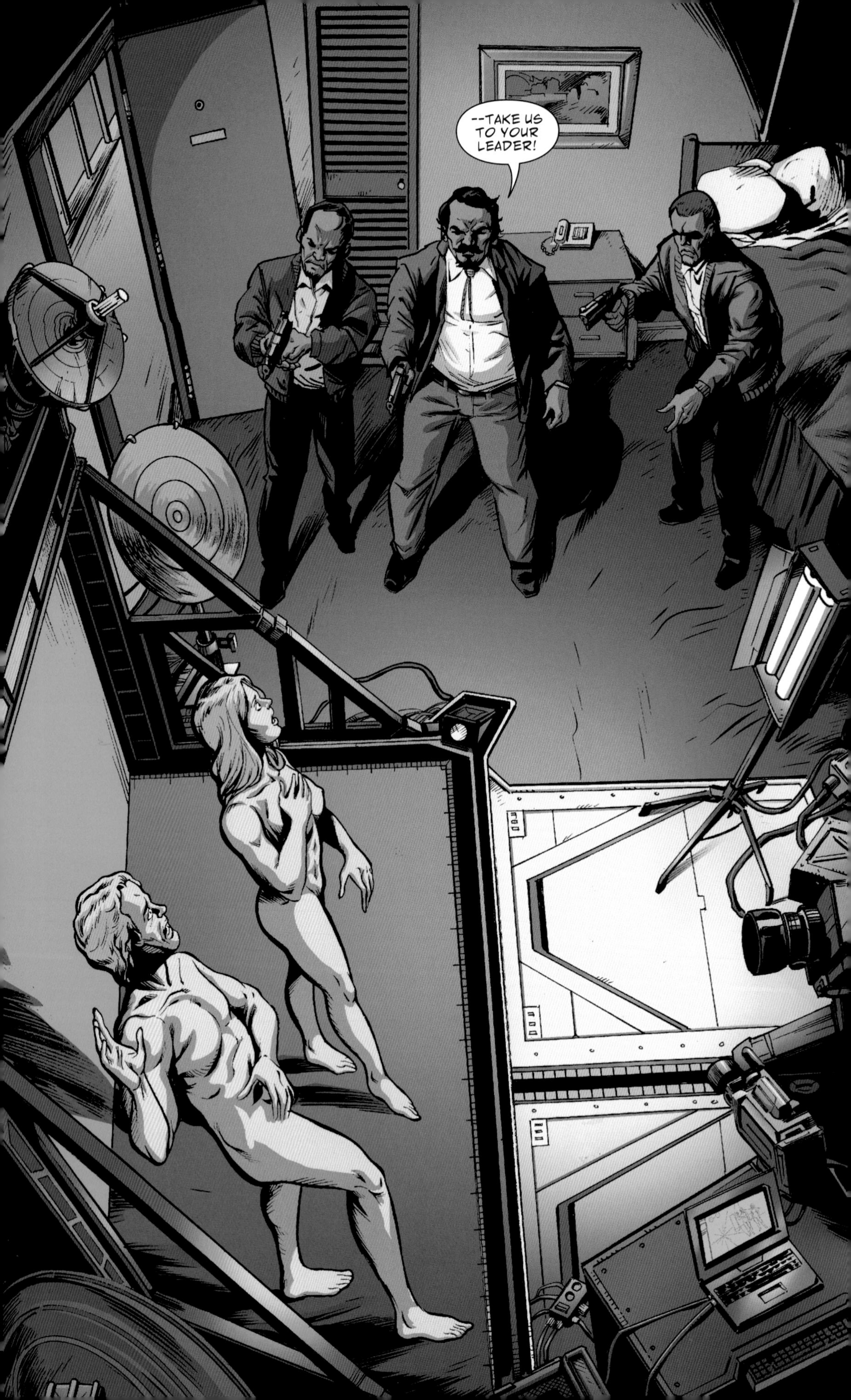
--TAKE US TO YOUR LEADER!

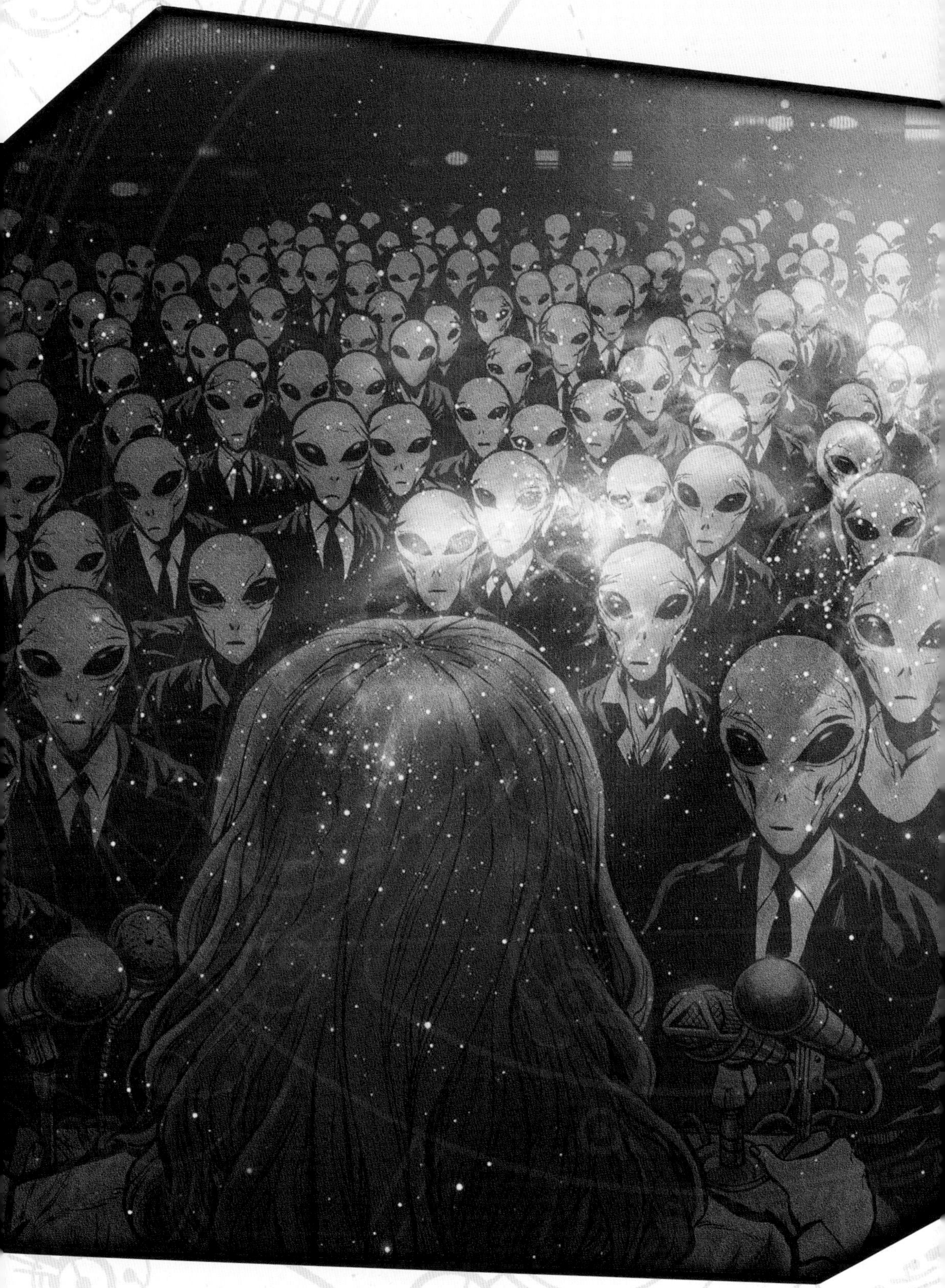

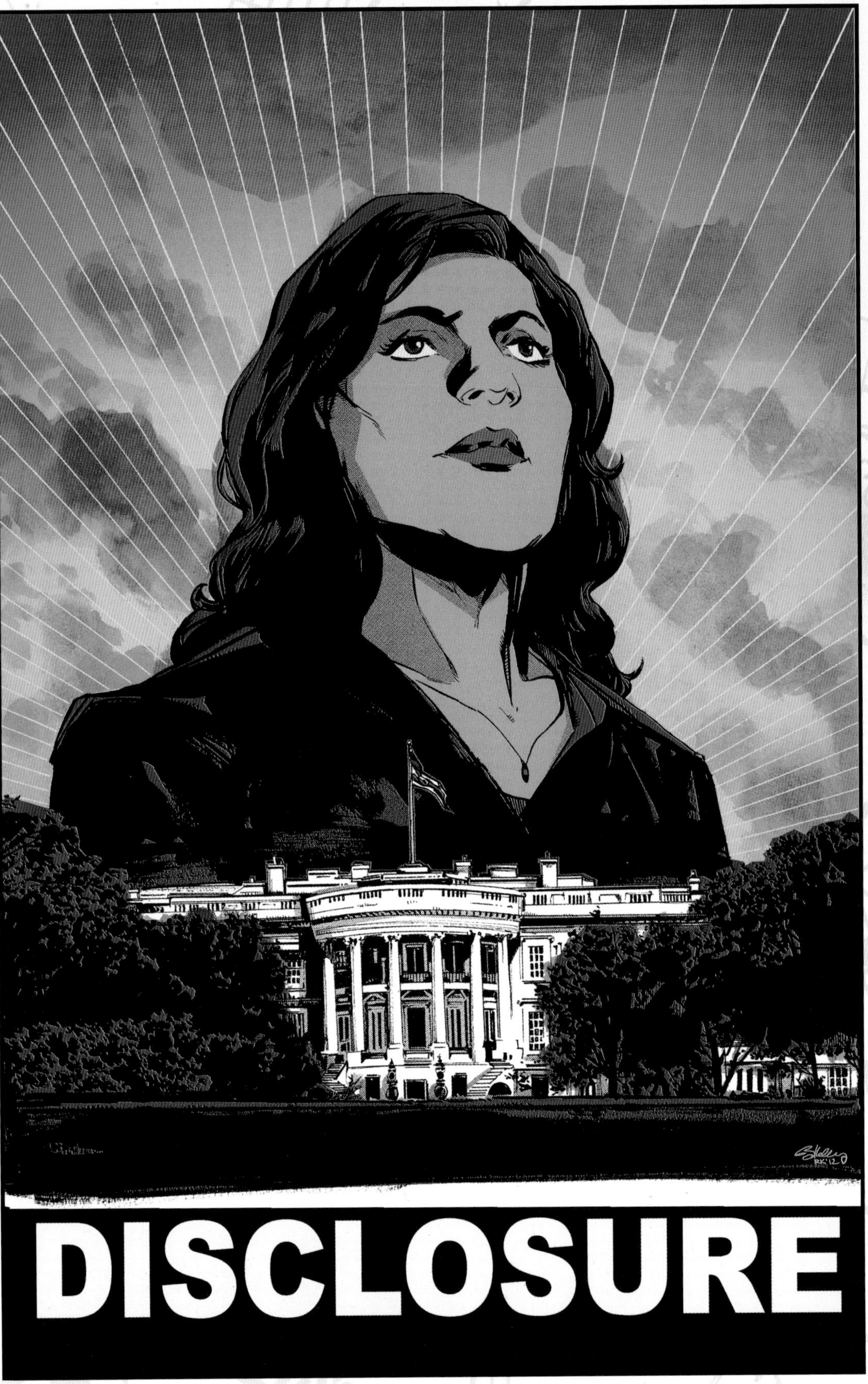
DISCLOSURE

COVER ART BY **RYAN KELLY**

SO I GUESS THIS IS WHAT WAS BEING USED TO PROJECT YOUR IMAGE INTO THE... WHAT, *BRAIN*, OF PROFESSOR KIDD?

WELL, THE INNER EAR ACTUALLY--

BRIAN--!

AH, NOW WE HAVE A NAME!

HE'S NOT THE MESSIAH --

JUST A VERY NAUGHTY BOY!

YOU HAVE NO IDEA WHAT YOU'RE MESSING WITH HERE, AND NO RIGHT TO--

NO RIGHT--?!

WE'RE ACCREDITED DEPUTIES OF THE ARLINGTON COUNTY SHERIFF'S DEPARTMENT. FOR TODAY.

AND WE'RE WONDERING IF THESE *GAMES* YOU'RE PLAYING GOT TWO FRIENDS OF OURS *MURDERED*.

DON'T LET OUR PLEASANT NATURES--

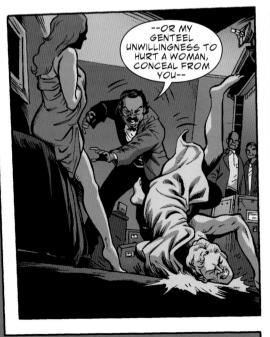

--OR MY *GENTEEL* UNWILLINGNESS TO HURT A WOMAN, CONCEAL FROM YOU--

--THE SHEER *DEPTH* OF THE *SHIT* WHICH WE CAN *DROWN* YOU IN!

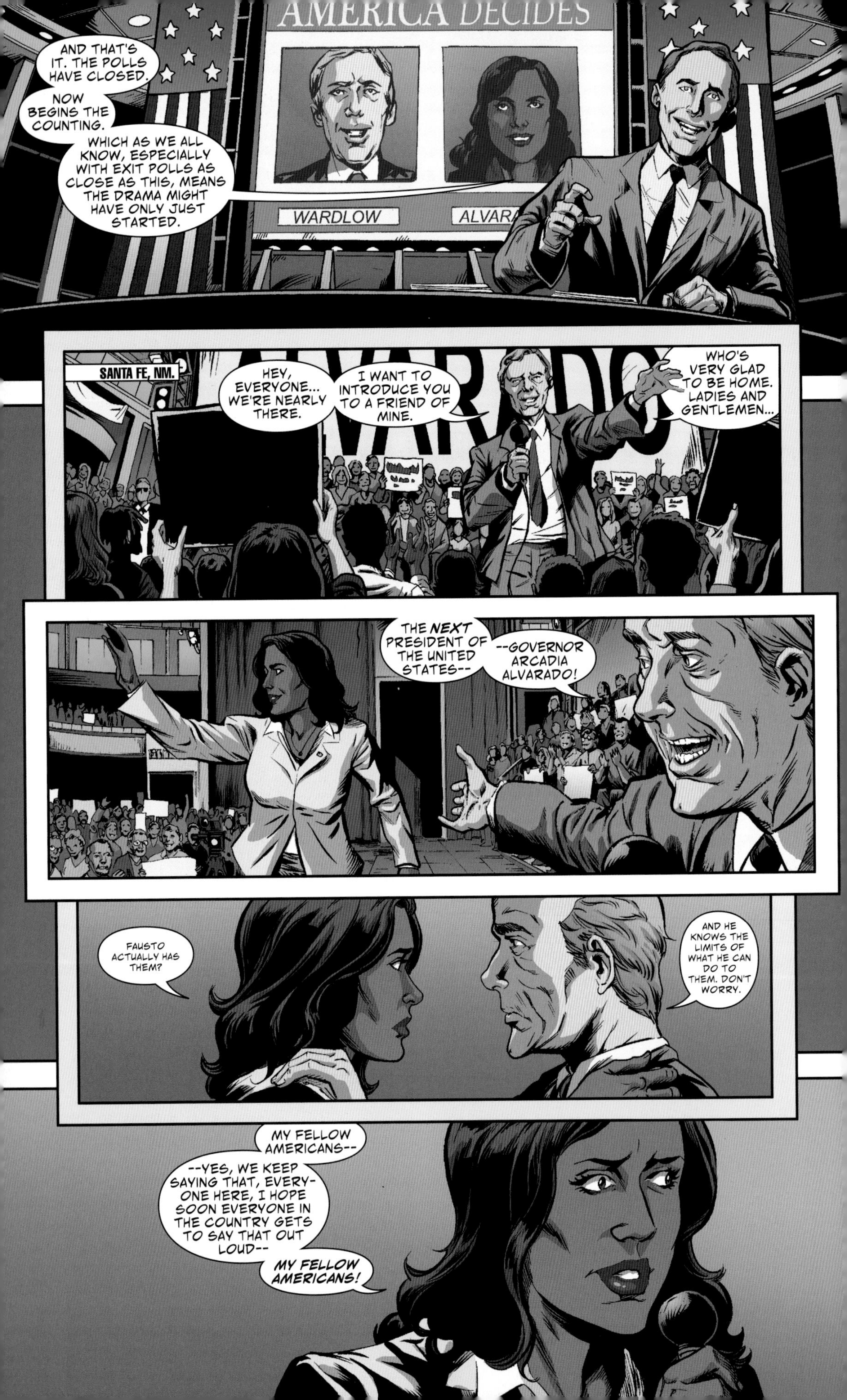
AMERICA DECIDES
AND THAT'S IT. THE POLLS HAVE CLOSED.
NOW BEGINS THE COUNTING.
WHICH AS WE ALL KNOW, ESPECIALLY WITH EXIT POLLS AS CLOSE AS THIS, MEANS THE DRAMA MIGHT HAVE ONLY JUST STARTED.
WARDLOW
SANTA FE, NM.
HEY, EVERYONE... WE'RE NEARLY THERE.
I WANT TO INTRODUCE YOU TO A FRIEND OF MINE.
WHO'S VERY GLAD TO BE HOME. LADIES AND GENTLEMEN...
THE *NEXT* PRESIDENT OF THE UNITED STATES--
--GOVERNOR ARCADIA ALVARADO!
FAUSTO ACTUALLY HAS THEM?
AND HE KNOWS THE LIMITS OF WHAT HE CAN DO TO THEM. DON'T WORRY.
MY FELLOW AMERICANS--
--YES, WE KEEP SAYING THAT, EVERY-ONE HERE, I HOPE SOON EVERYONE IN THE COUNTRY GETS TO SAY THAT OUT LOUD--
MY FELLOW AMERICANS!

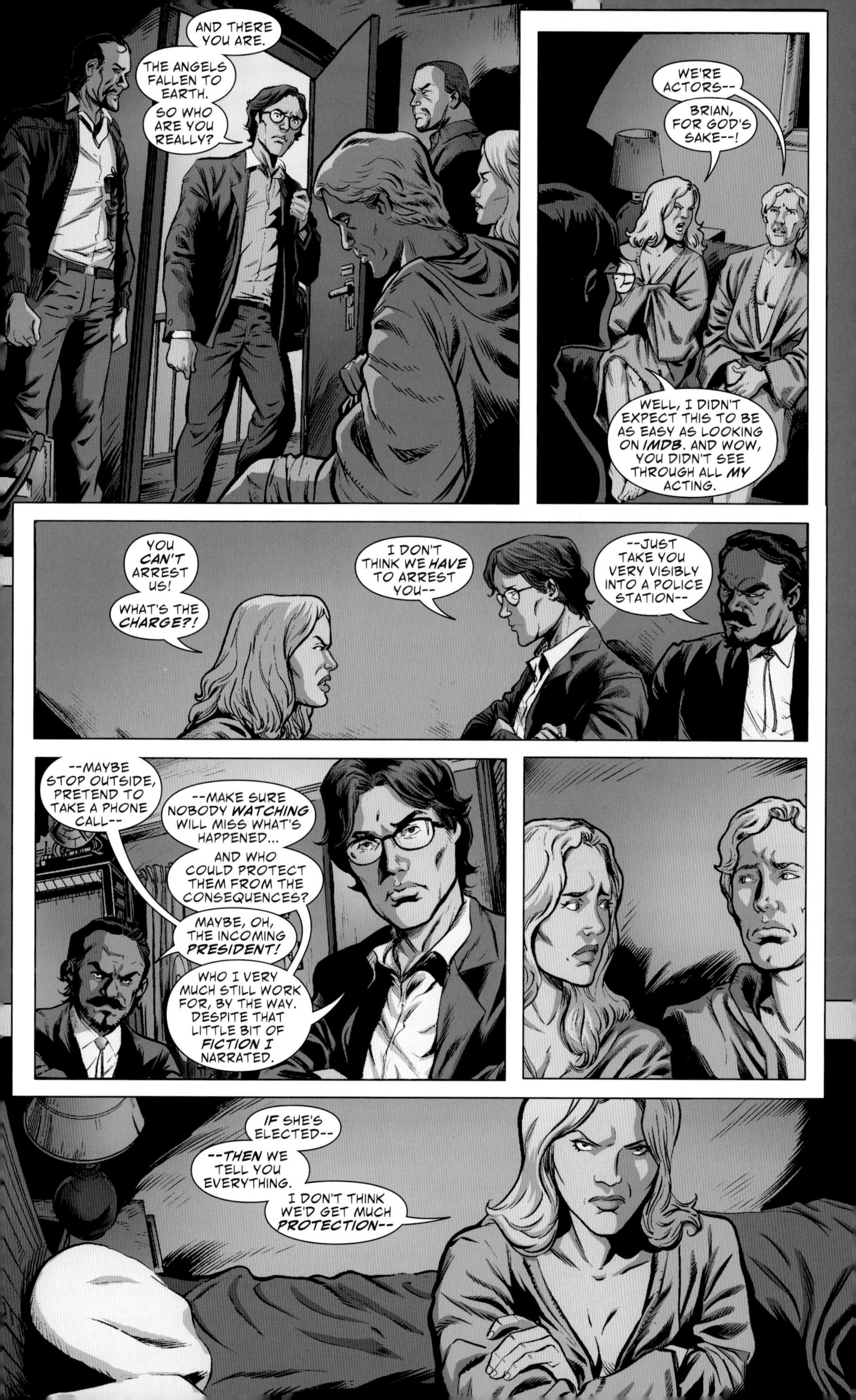
AND THERE YOU ARE.
THE ANGELS FALLEN TO EARTH.
SO WHO ARE YOU REALLY?
WE'RE ACTORS--
BRIAN, FOR GOD'S SAKE--!
WELL, I DIDN'T EXPECT THIS TO BE AS EASY AS LOOKING ON IMDB. AND WOW, YOU DIDN'T SEE THROUGH ALL MY ACTING.
YOU CAN'T ARREST US!
WHAT'S THE CHARGE?!
I DON'T THINK WE HAVE TO ARREST YOU--
--JUST TAKE YOU VERY VISIBLY INTO A POLICE STATION--
--MAYBE STOP OUTSIDE, PRETEND TO TAKE A PHONE CALL--
--MAKE SURE NOBODY WATCHING WILL MISS WHAT'S HAPPENED...
AND WHO COULD PROTECT THEM FROM THE CONSEQUENCES?
MAYBE, OH, THE INCOMING PRESIDENT!
WHO I VERY MUCH STILL WORK FOR, BY THE WAY. DESPITE THAT LITTLE BIT OF FICTION I NARRATED.
IF SHE'S ELECTED--
--THEN WE TELL YOU EVERYTHING.
I DON'T THINK WE'D GET MUCH PROTECTION--

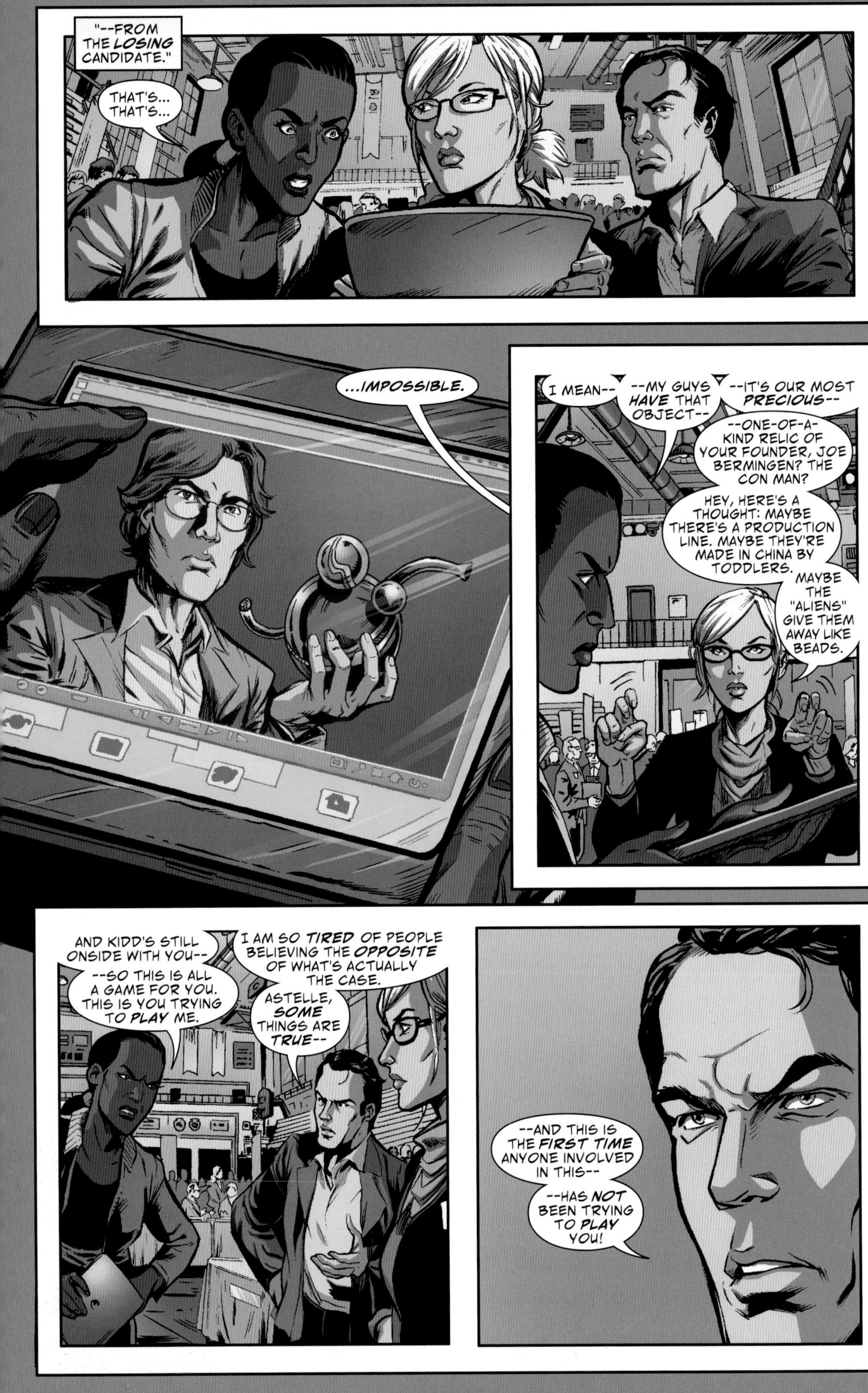
"--FROM THE LOSING CANDIDATE."
THAT'S... THAT'S...
...IMPOSSIBLE.
I MEAN--
--MY GUYS HAVE THAT OBJECT--
--IT'S OUR MOST PRECIOUS--
--ONE-OF-A-KIND RELIC OF YOUR FOUNDER, JOE BERMINGEN? THE CON MAN?
HEY, HERE'S A THOUGHT: MAYBE THERE'S A PRODUCTION LINE. MAYBE THEY'RE MADE IN CHINA BY TODDLERS.
MAYBE THE "ALIENS" GIVE THEM AWAY LIKE BEADS.
AND KIDD'S STILL ONSIDE WITH YOU--
--SO THIS IS ALL A GAME FOR YOU. THIS IS YOU TRYING TO PLAY ME.
I AM SO TIRED OF PEOPLE BELIEVING THE OPPOSITE OF WHAT'S ACTUALLY THE CASE.
ASTELLE, SOME THINGS ARE TRUE--
--AND THIS IS THE FIRST TIME ANYONE INVOLVED IN THIS--
--HAS NOT BEEN TRYING TO PLAY YOU!

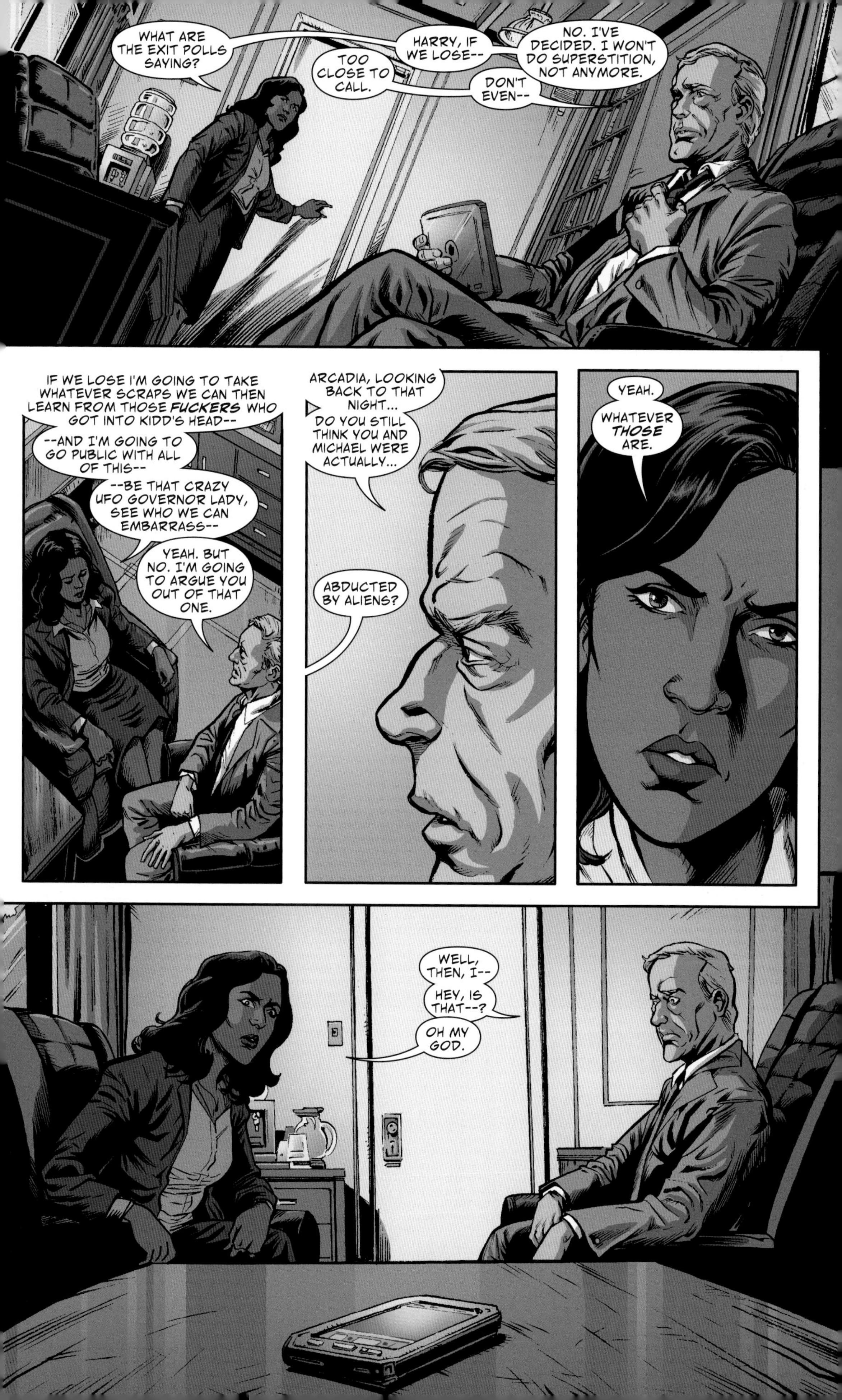
WHAT ARE THE EXIT POLLS SAYING?
TOO CLOSE TO CALL.
HARRY, IF WE LOSE--
DON'T EVEN--
NO. I'VE DECIDED. I WON'T DO SUPERSTITION, NOT ANYMORE.
IF WE LOSE I'M GOING TO TAKE WHATEVER SCRAPS WE CAN THEN LEARN FROM THOSE FUCKERS WHO GOT INTO KIDD'S HEAD--
--AND I'M GOING TO GO PUBLIC WITH ALL OF THIS--
--BE THAT CRAZY UFO GOVERNOR LADY, SEE WHO WE CAN EMBARRASS--
YEAH. BUT NO. I'M GOING TO ARGUE YOU OUT OF THAT ONE.
ARCADIA, LOOKING BACK TO THAT NIGHT...
DO YOU STILL THINK YOU AND MICHAEL WERE ACTUALLY...
ABDUCTED BY ALIENS?
YEAH.
WHATEVER THOSE ARE.
WELL, THEN, I--
HEY, IS THAT--?
OH MY GOD.

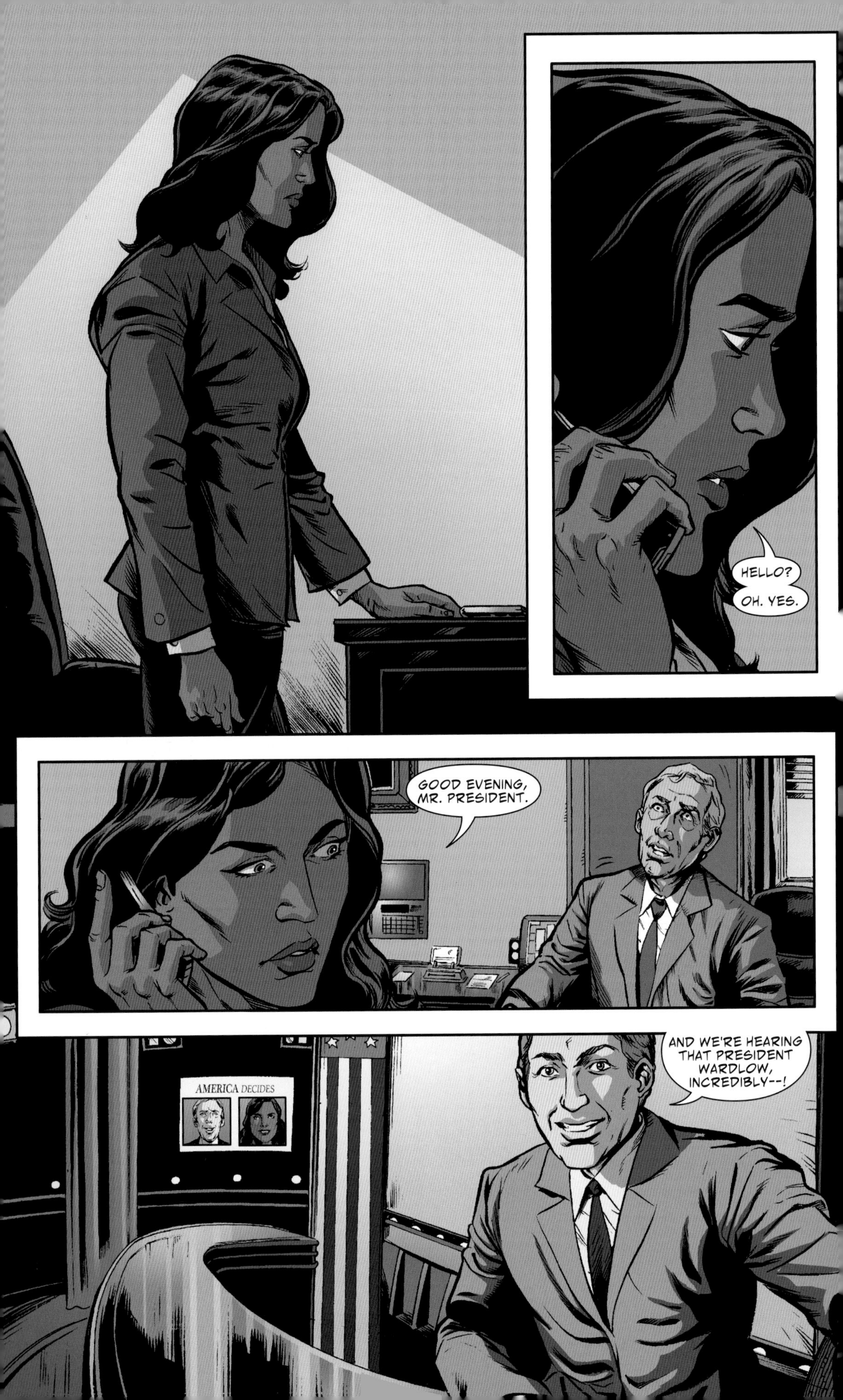
HELLO?
OH. YES.
GOOD EVENING, MR. PRESIDENT.
AMERICA DECIDES
AND WE'RE HEARING THAT PRESIDENT WARDLOW, INCREDIBLY--!

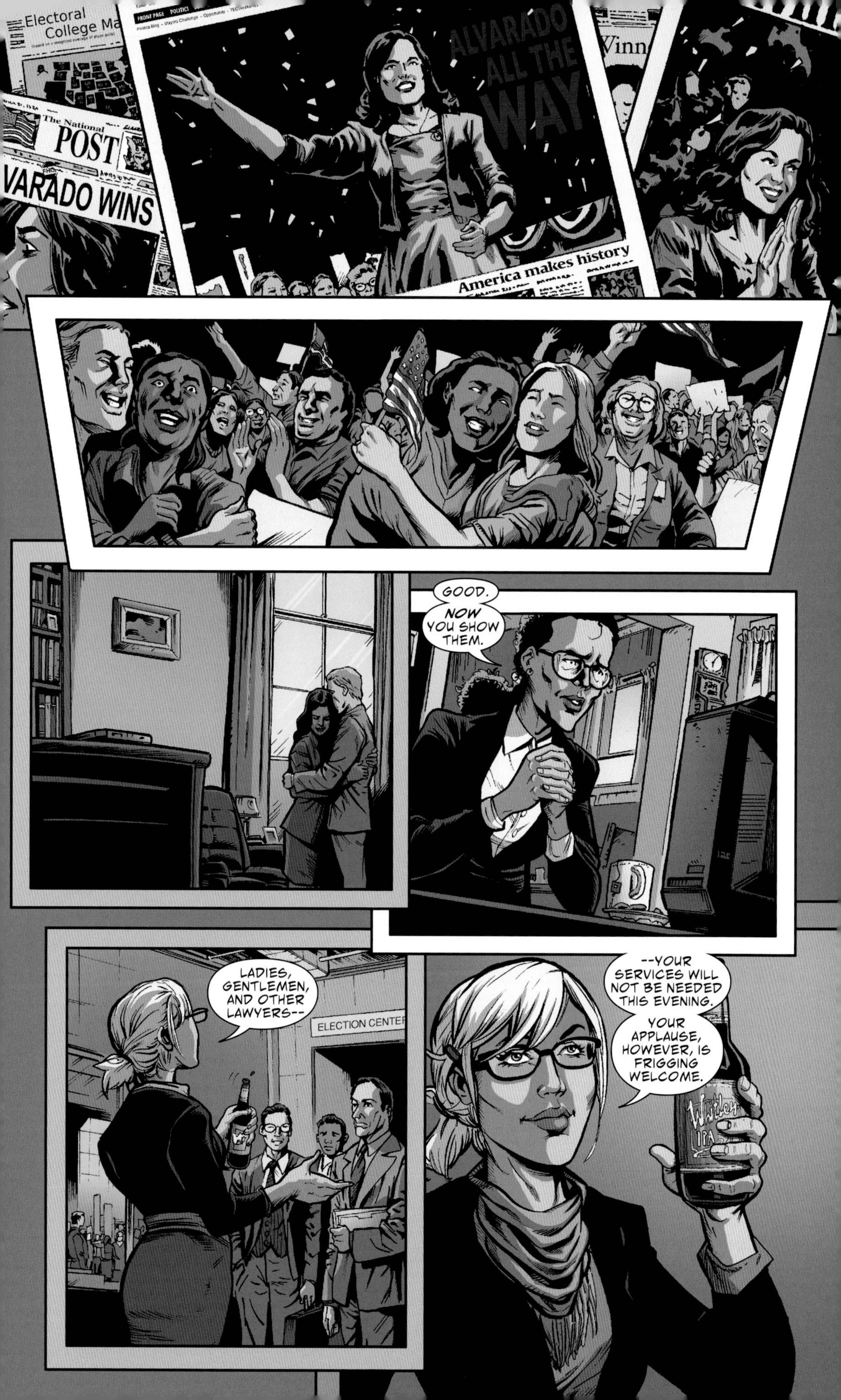
Electoral College Ma
The National POST
VARADO WINS
ALVARADO ALL THE WAY
America makes history
GOOD.
NOW YOU SHOW THEM.
LADIES, GENTLEMEN, AND OTHER LAWYERS--
ELECTION CENTER
--YOUR SERVICES WILL NOT BE NEEDED THIS EVENING.
YOUR APPLAUSE, HOWEVER, IS FRIGGING WELCOME.

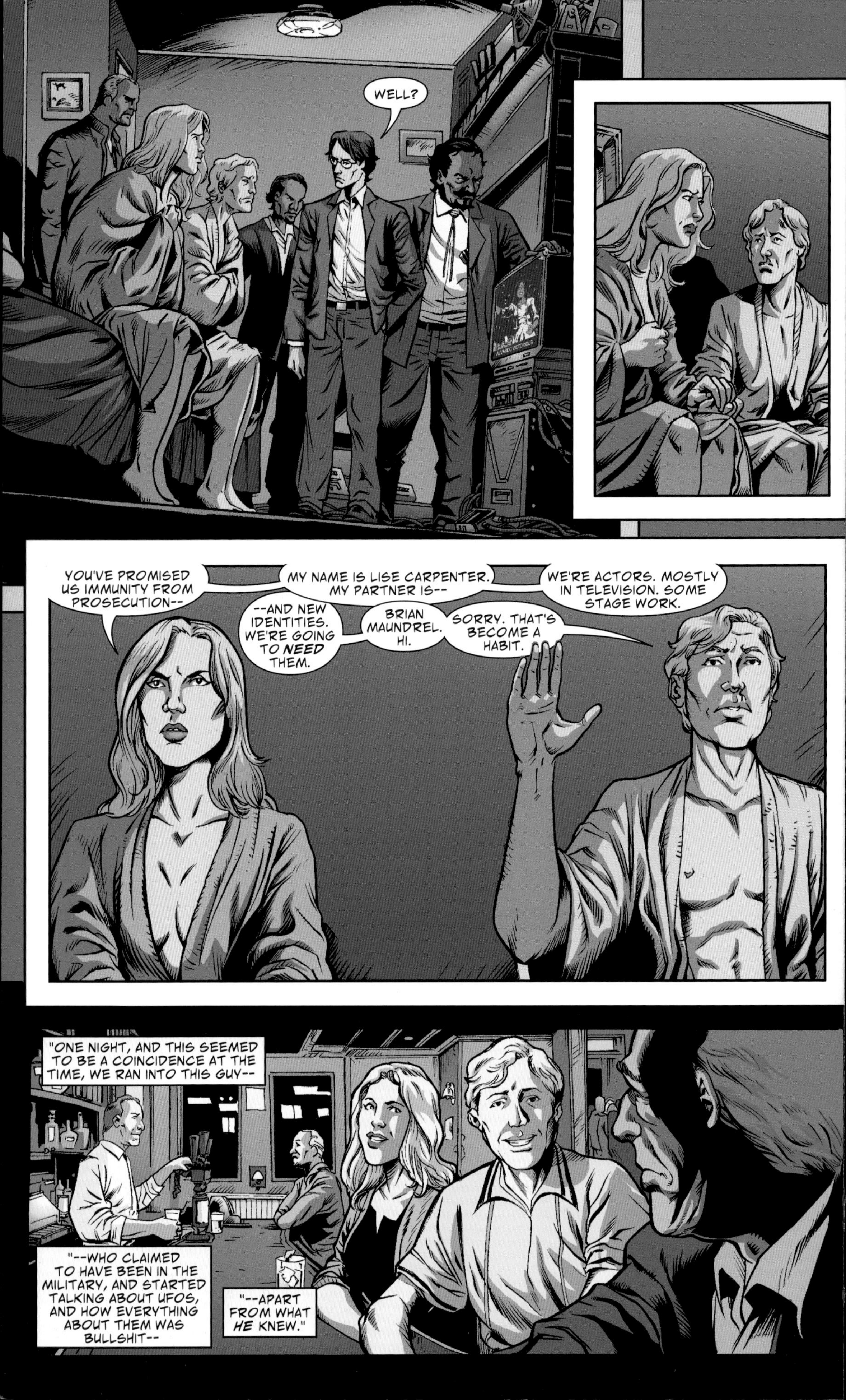
WELL?
YOU'VE PROMISED US IMMUNITY FROM PROSECUTION--
--AND NEW IDENTITIES. WE'RE GOING TO *NEED* THEM.
MY NAME IS LISE CARPENTER. MY PARTNER IS--
BRIAN MAUNDREL. HI.
SORRY. THAT'S BECOME A HABIT.
WE'RE ACTORS. MOSTLY IN TELEVISION. SOME STAGE WORK.
"ONE NIGHT, AND THIS SEEMED TO BE A COINCIDENCE AT THE TIME, WE RAN INTO THIS GUY--
"--WHO CLAIMED TO HAVE BEEN IN THE MILITARY, AND STARTED TALKING ABOUT UFOS, AND HOW EVERYTHING ABOUT THEM WAS BULLSHIT--
"--APART FROM WHAT *HE* KNEW."

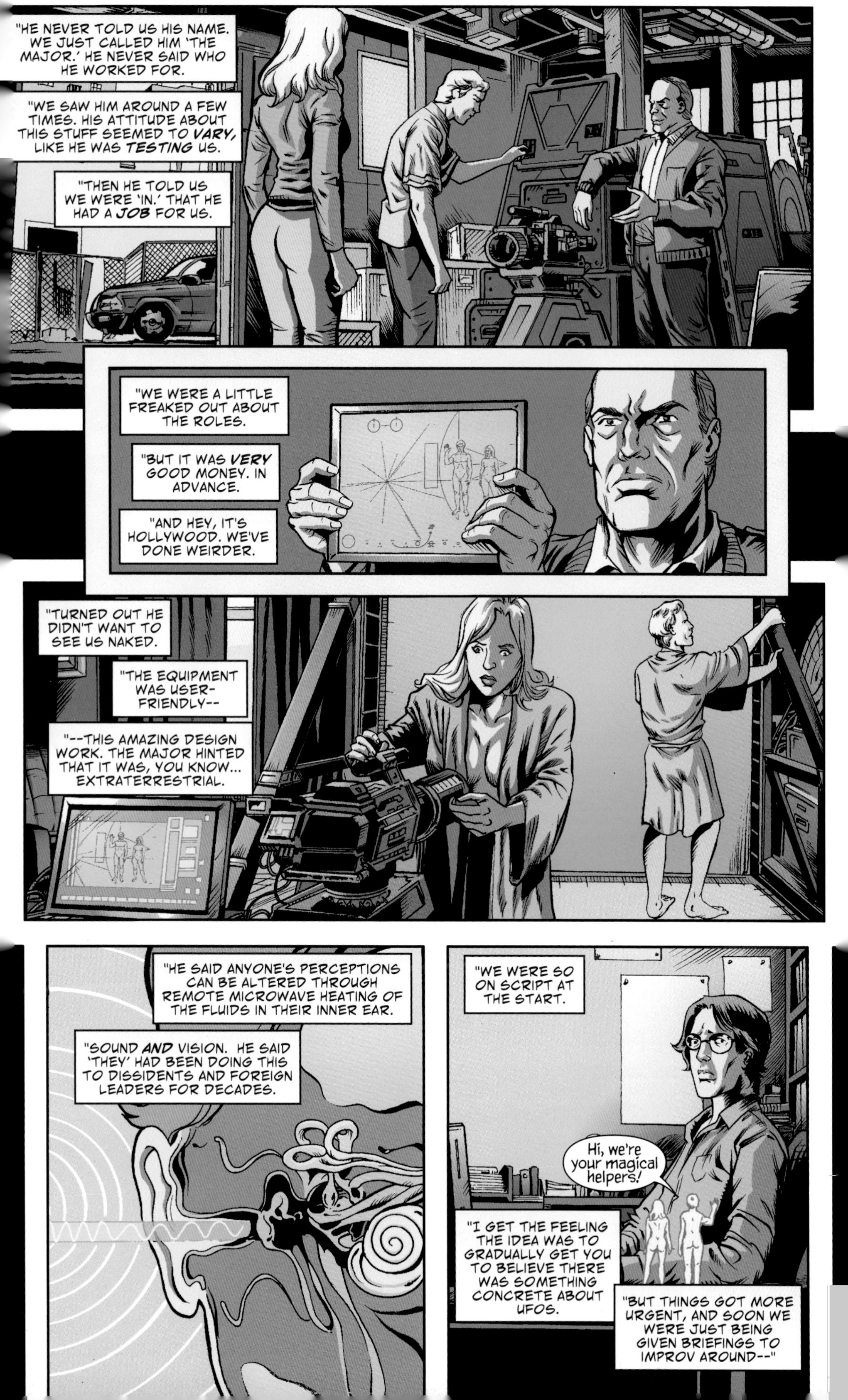

"HE NEVER TOLD US HIS NAME. WE JUST CALLED HIM 'THE MAJOR.' HE NEVER SAID WHO HE WORKED FOR.
"WE SAW HIM AROUND A FEW TIMES. HIS ATTITUDE ABOUT THIS STUFF SEEMED TO *VARY,* LIKE HE WAS *TESTING* US.
"THEN HE TOLD US WE WERE 'IN.' THAT HE HAD A *JOB* FOR US.
"WE WERE A LITTLE FREAKED OUT ABOUT THE ROLES.
"BUT IT WAS *VERY* GOOD MONEY. IN ADVANCE.
"AND HEY, IT'S HOLLYWOOD. WE'VE DONE WEIRDER.
"TURNED OUT HE DIDN'T WANT TO SEE US NAKED.
"THE EQUIPMENT WAS USER-FRIENDLY--
"--THIS AMAZING DESIGN WORK. THE MAJOR HINTED THAT IT WAS, YOU KNOW... EXTRATERRESTRIAL.
"HE SAID ANYONE'S PERCEPTIONS CAN BE ALTERED THROUGH REMOTE MICROWAVE HEATING OF THE FLUIDS IN THEIR INNER EAR.
"SOUND *AND* VISION. HE SAID 'THEY' HAD BEEN DOING THIS TO DISSIDENTS AND FOREIGN LEADERS FOR DECADES.
"WE WERE SO ON SCRIPT AT THE START.
Hi, we're your magical helpers!
"I GET THE FEELING THE IDEA WAS TO GRADUALLY GET YOU TO BELIEVE THERE WAS SOMETHING CONCRETE ABOUT UFOS.
"BUT THINGS GOT MORE URGENT, AND SOON WE WERE JUST BEING GIVEN BRIEFINGS TO IMPROV AROUND--"

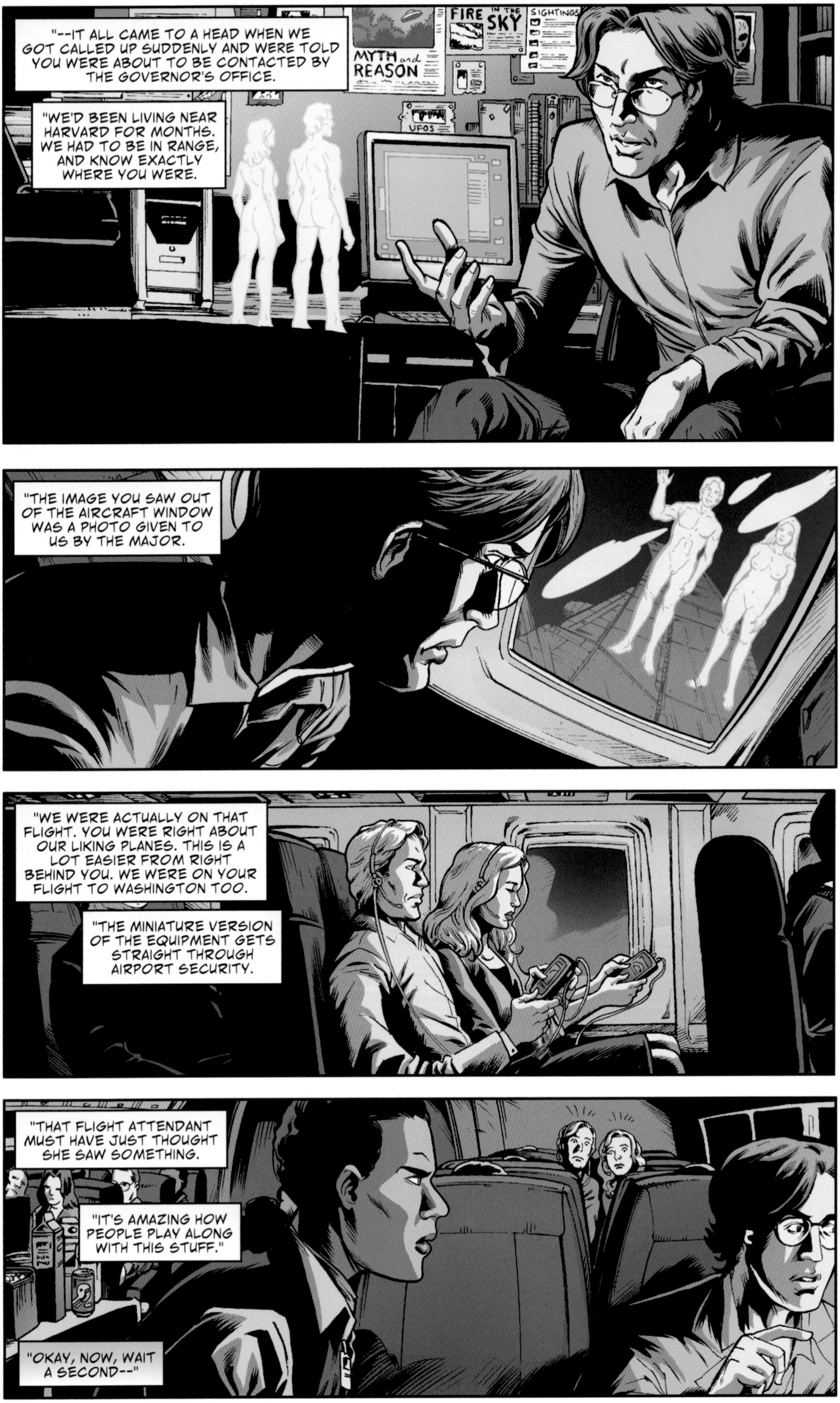
"--IT ALL CAME TO A HEAD WHEN WE GOT CALLED UP SUDDENLY AND WERE TOLD YOU WERE ABOUT TO BE CONTACTED BY THE GOVERNOR'S OFFICE.
MYTH and REASON
FIRE IN THE SKY
SIGHTINGS
UFOS
"WE'D BEEN LIVING NEAR HARVARD FOR MONTHS. WE HAD TO BE IN RANGE, AND KNOW EXACTLY WHERE YOU WERE.
"THE IMAGE YOU SAW OUT OF THE AIRCRAFT WINDOW WAS A PHOTO GIVEN TO US BY THE MAJOR.
"WE WERE ACTUALLY ON THAT FLIGHT. YOU WERE RIGHT ABOUT OUR LIKING PLANES. THIS IS A LOT EASIER FROM RIGHT BEHIND YOU. WE WERE ON YOUR FLIGHT TO WASHINGTON TOO.
"THE MINIATURE VERSION OF THE EQUIPMENT GETS STRAIGHT THROUGH AIRPORT SECURITY.
"THAT FLIGHT ATTENDANT MUST HAVE JUST THOUGHT SHE SAW SOMETHING.
"IT'S AMAZING HOW PEOPLE PLAY ALONG WITH THIS STUFF."
"OKAY, NOW, WAIT A SECOND--"

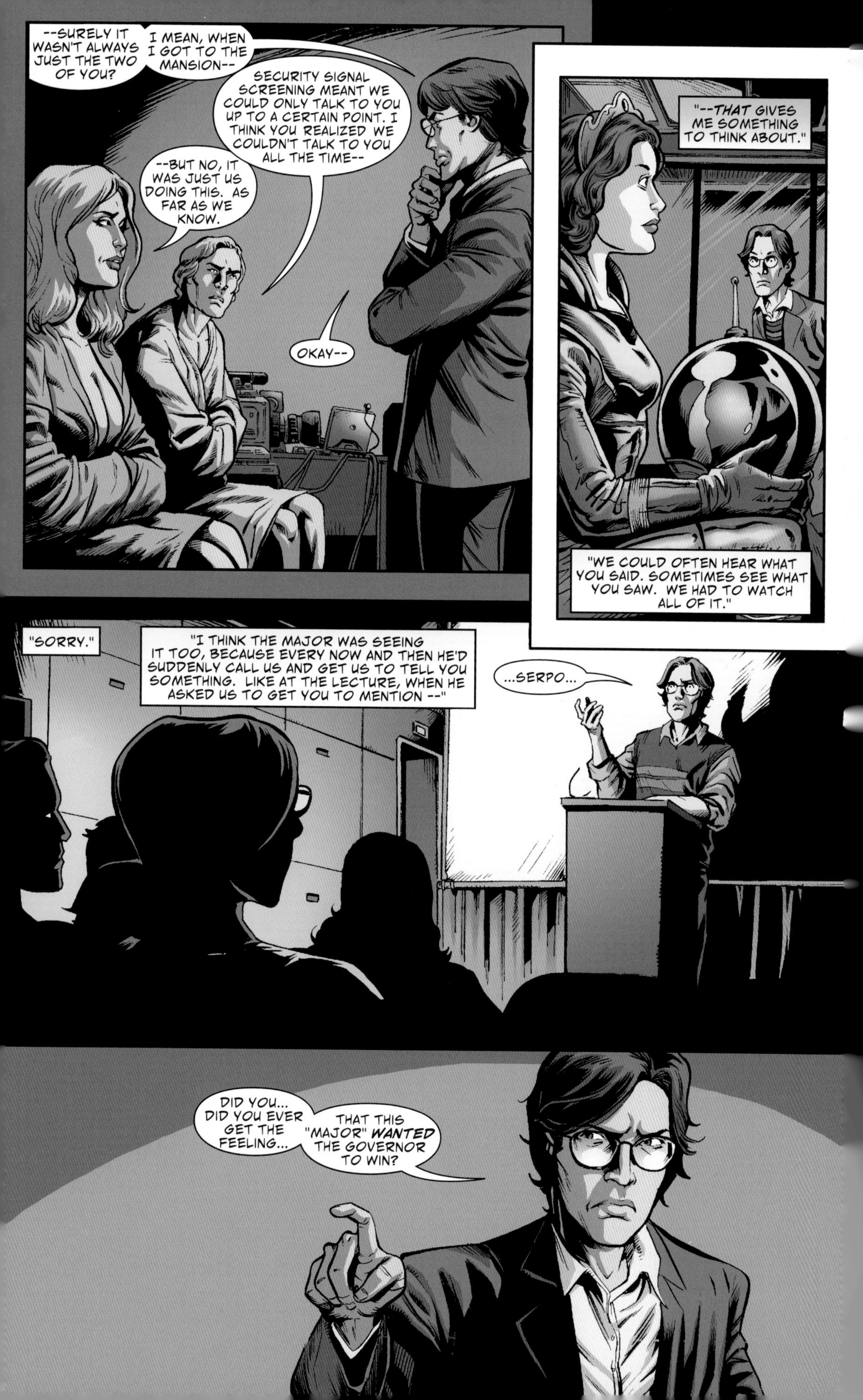
--SURELY IT WASN'T ALWAYS JUST THE TWO OF YOU?
I MEAN, WHEN I GOT TO THE MANSION--
SECURITY SIGNAL SCREENING MEANT WE COULD ONLY TALK TO YOU UP TO A CERTAIN POINT. I THINK YOU REALIZED WE COULDN'T TALK TO YOU ALL THE TIME--
--BUT NO, IT WAS JUST US DOING THIS. AS FAR AS WE KNOW.
OKAY--
"--*THAT* GIVES ME SOMETHING TO THINK ABOUT."
"WE COULD OFTEN HEAR WHAT YOU SAID. SOMETIMES SEE WHAT YOU SAW. WE HAD TO WATCH ALL OF IT."
"SORRY."
"I THINK THE MAJOR WAS SEEING IT TOO, BECAUSE EVERY NOW AND THEN HE'D SUDDENLY CALL US AND GET US TO TELL YOU SOMETHING. LIKE AT THE LECTURE, WHEN HE ASKED US TO GET YOU TO MENTION --"
...SERPO...
DID YOU... DID YOU EVER GET THE FEELING...
THAT THIS "MAJOR" ***WANTED*** THE GOVERNOR TO WIN?

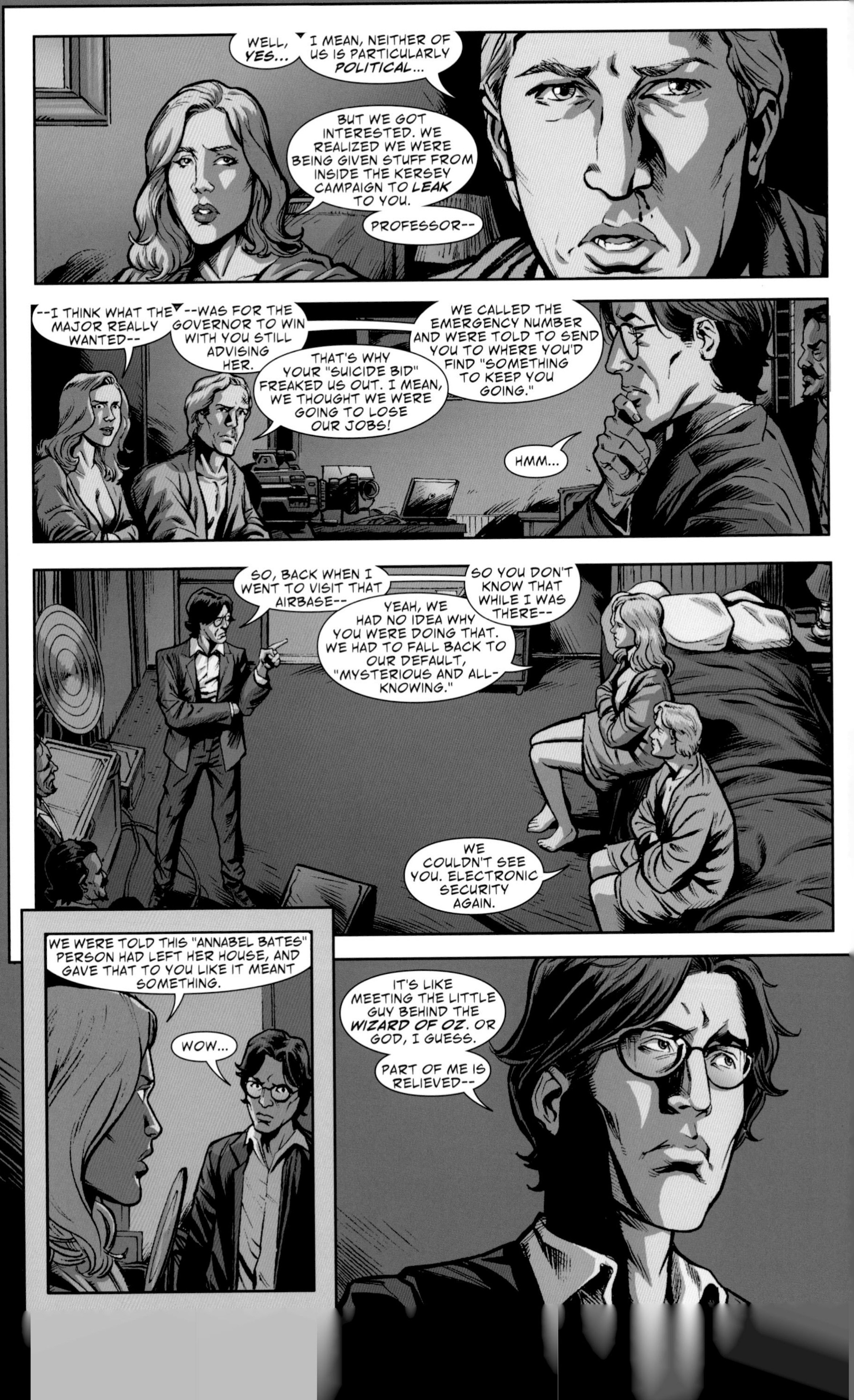

WELL, YES...
I MEAN, NEITHER OF US IS PARTICULARLY POLITICAL...
BUT WE GOT INTERESTED. WE REALIZED WE WERE BEING GIVEN STUFF FROM INSIDE THE KERSEY CAMPAIGN TO LEAK TO YOU.
PROFESSOR--
--I THINK WHAT THE MAJOR REALLY WANTED--
--WAS FOR THE GOVERNOR TO WIN WITH YOU STILL ADVISING HER.
THAT'S WHY YOUR "SUICIDE BID" FREAKED US OUT. I MEAN, WE THOUGHT WE WERE GOING TO LOSE OUR JOBS!
WE CALLED THE EMERGENCY NUMBER AND WERE TOLD TO SEND YOU TO WHERE YOU'D FIND "SOMETHING TO KEEP YOU GOING."
HMM...
SO, BACK WHEN I WENT TO VISIT THAT AIRBASE--
SO YOU DON'T KNOW THAT WHILE I WAS THERE--
YEAH, WE HAD NO IDEA WHY YOU WERE DOING THAT. WE HAD TO FALL BACK TO OUR DEFAULT, "MYSTERIOUS AND ALL-KNOWING."
WE COULDN'T SEE YOU. ELECTRONIC SECURITY AGAIN.
WE WERE TOLD THIS "ANNABEL BATES" PERSON HAD LEFT HER HOUSE, AND GAVE THAT TO YOU LIKE IT MEANT SOMETHING.
WOW...
IT'S LIKE MEETING THE LITTLE GUY BEHIND THE WIZARD OF OZ. OR GOD, I GUESS.
PART OF ME IS RELIEVED--

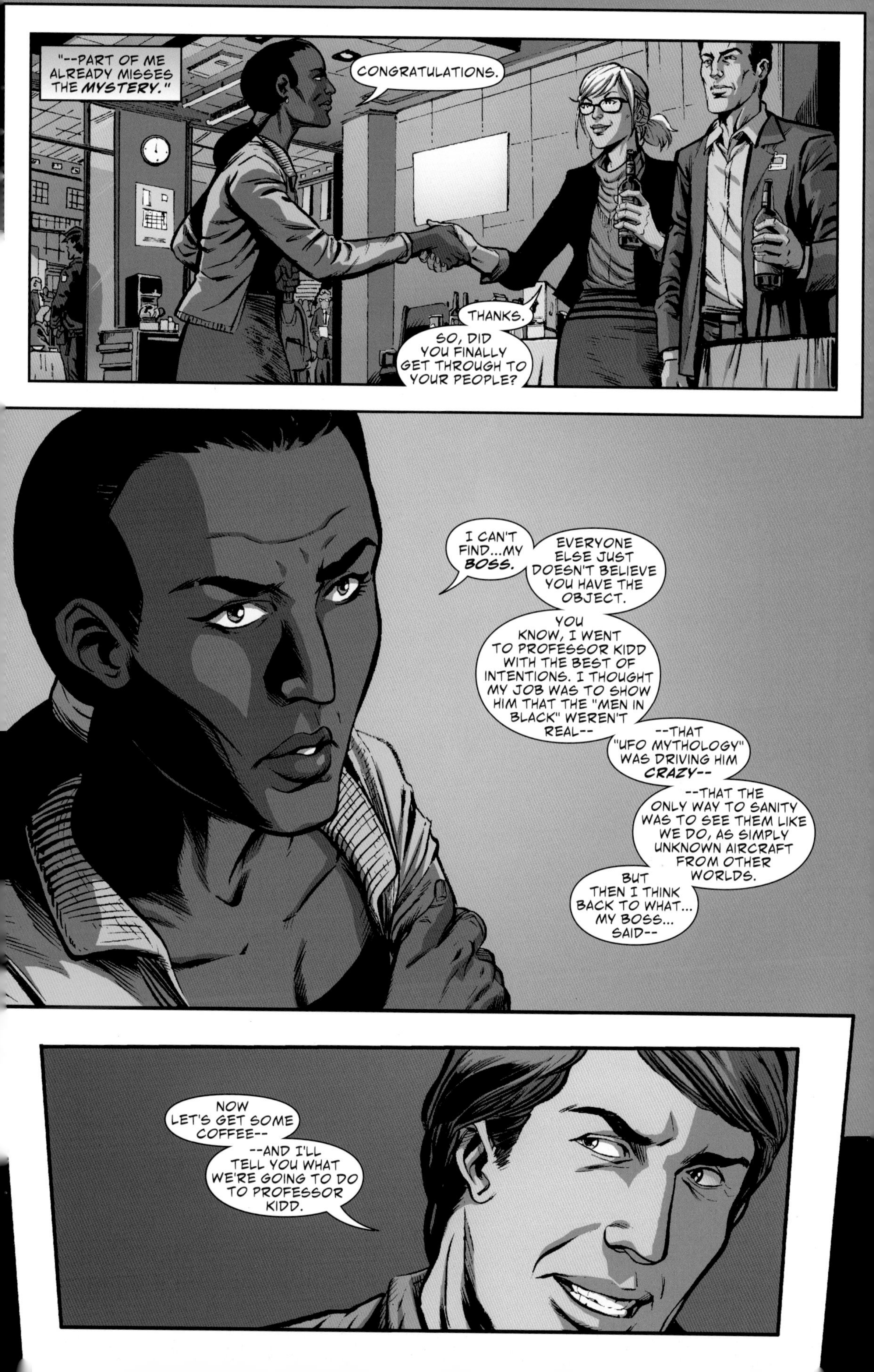
"--PART OF ME ALREADY MISSES THE *MYSTERY.*"
CONGRATULATIONS.
THANKS.
SO, DID YOU FINALLY GET THROUGH TO YOUR PEOPLE?
I CAN'T FIND...MY *BOSS.*
EVERYONE ELSE JUST DOESN'T BELIEVE YOU HAVE THE OBJECT.
YOU KNOW, I WENT TO PROFESSOR KIDD WITH THE BEST OF INTENTIONS. I THOUGHT MY JOB WAS TO SHOW HIM THAT THE "MEN IN BLACK" WEREN'T REAL--
--THAT "UFO MYTHOLOGY" WAS DRIVING HIM *CRAZY--*
--THAT THE ONLY WAY TO SANITY WAS TO SEE THEM LIKE WE DO, AS SIMPLY UNKNOWN AIRCRAFT FROM OTHER WORLDS.
BUT THEN I THINK BACK TO WHAT... MY BOSS... SAID--
NOW LET'S GET SOME COFFEE--
--AND I'LL TELL YOU WHAT WE'RE GOING TO DO TO PROFESSOR KIDD.

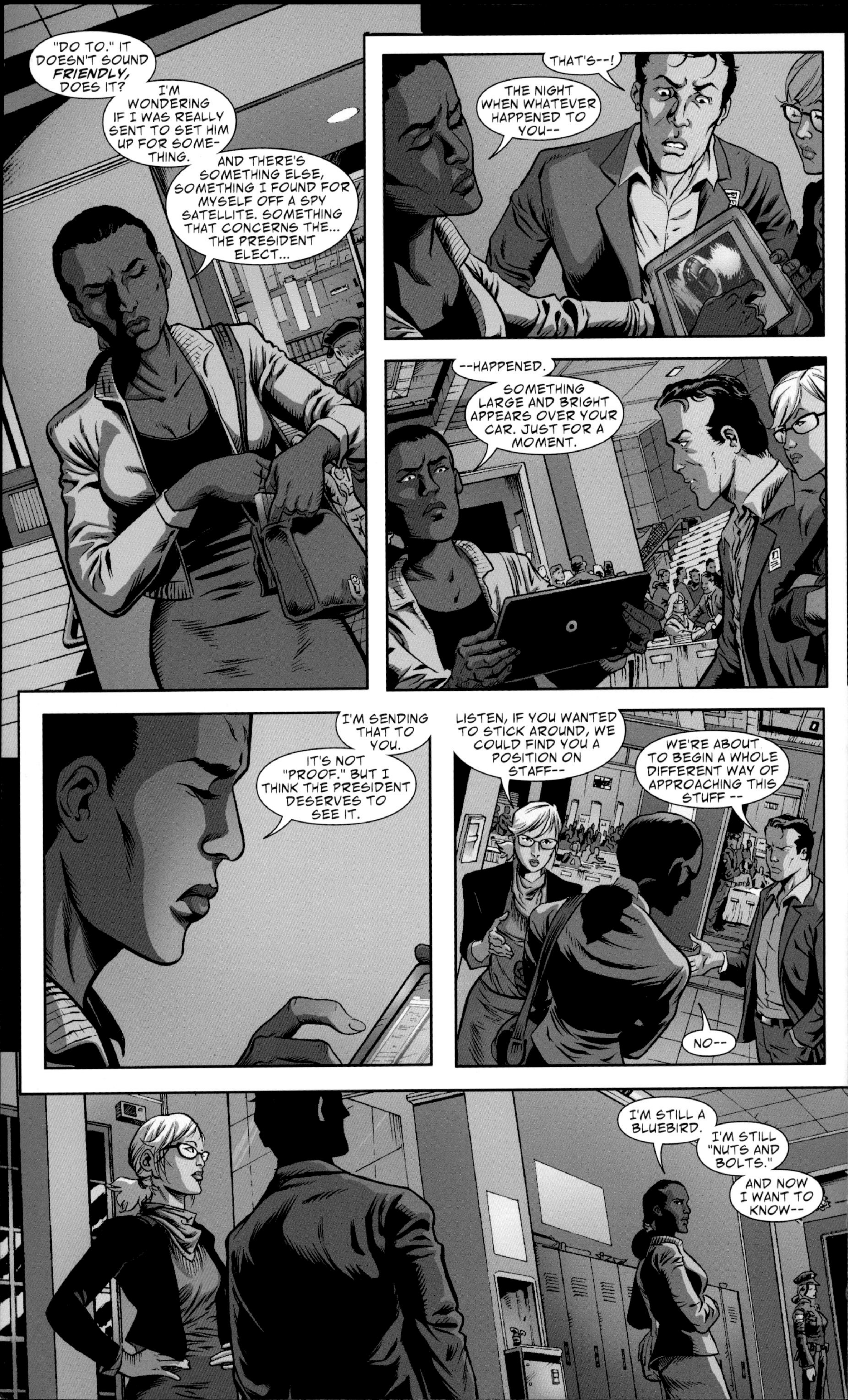
"DO TO." IT DOESN'T SOUND *FRIENDLY*, DOES IT?
I'M WONDERING IF I WAS REALLY SENT TO SET HIM UP FOR SOME-THING.
AND THERE'S SOMETHING ELSE, SOMETHING I FOUND FOR MYSELF OFF A SPY SATELLITE. SOMETHING THAT CONCERNS THE... THE PRESIDENT ELECT...
THAT'S--!
THE NIGHT WHEN WHATEVER HAPPENED TO YOU--
--HAPPENED.
SOMETHING LARGE AND BRIGHT APPEARS OVER YOUR CAR. JUST FOR A MOMENT.
I'M SENDING THAT TO YOU.
IT'S NOT "PROOF." BUT I THINK THE PRESIDENT DESERVES TO SEE IT.
LISTEN, IF YOU WANTED TO STICK AROUND, WE COULD FIND YOU A POSITION ON STAFF--
WE'RE ABOUT TO BEGIN A WHOLE DIFFERENT WAY OF APPROACHING THIS STUFF --
NO--
I'M STILL A BLUEBIRD.
I'M STILL "NUTS AND BOLTS."
AND NOW I WANT TO KNOW--

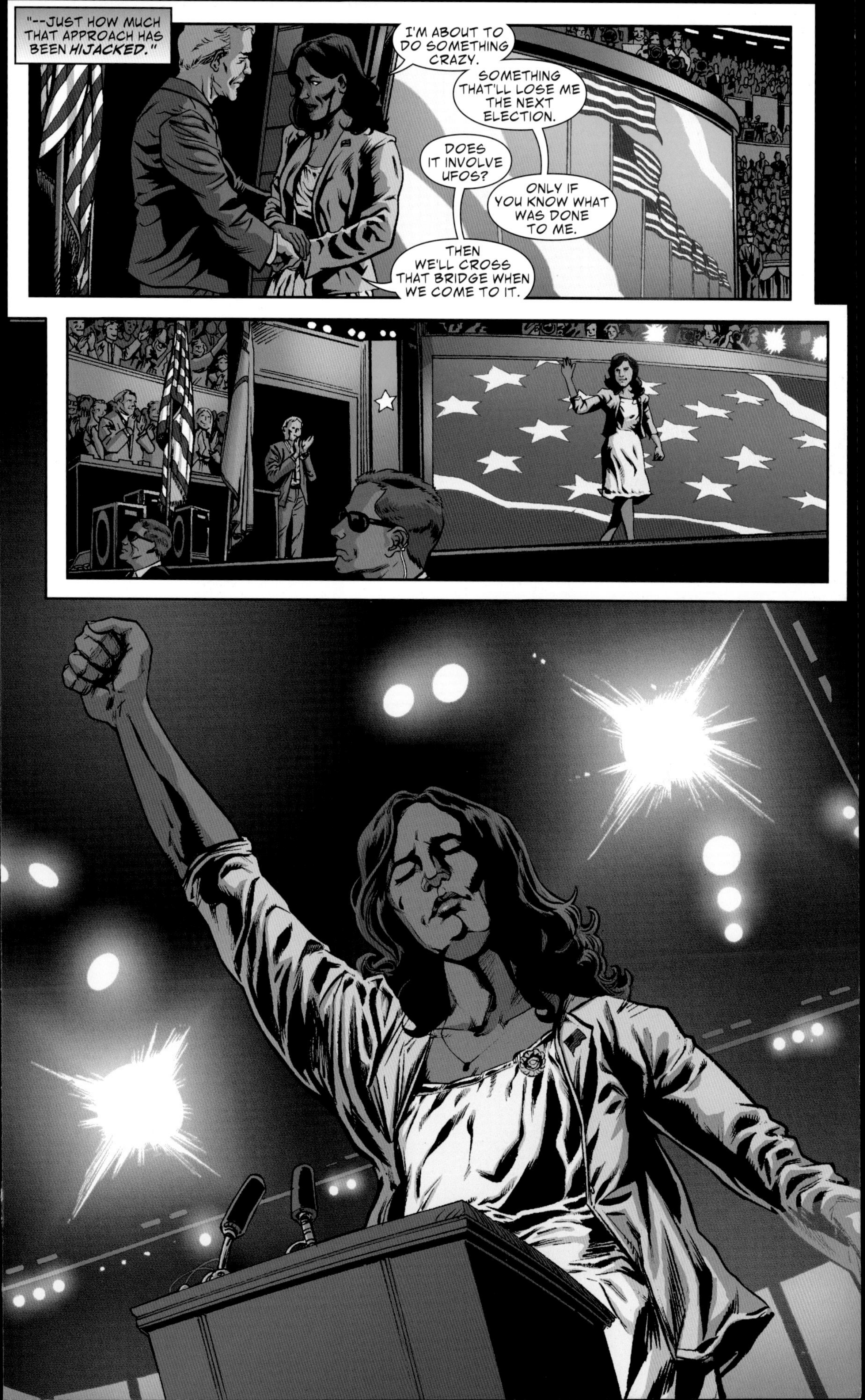
"--JUST HOW MUCH THAT APPROACH HAS BEEN *HIJACKED.*"
I'M ABOUT TO DO SOMETHING CRAZY.
SOMETHING THAT'LL LOSE ME THE NEXT ELECTION.
DOES IT INVOLVE UFOS?
ONLY IF YOU KNOW WHAT WAS DONE TO ME.
THEN WE'LL CROSS THAT BRIDGE WHEN WE COME TO IT.

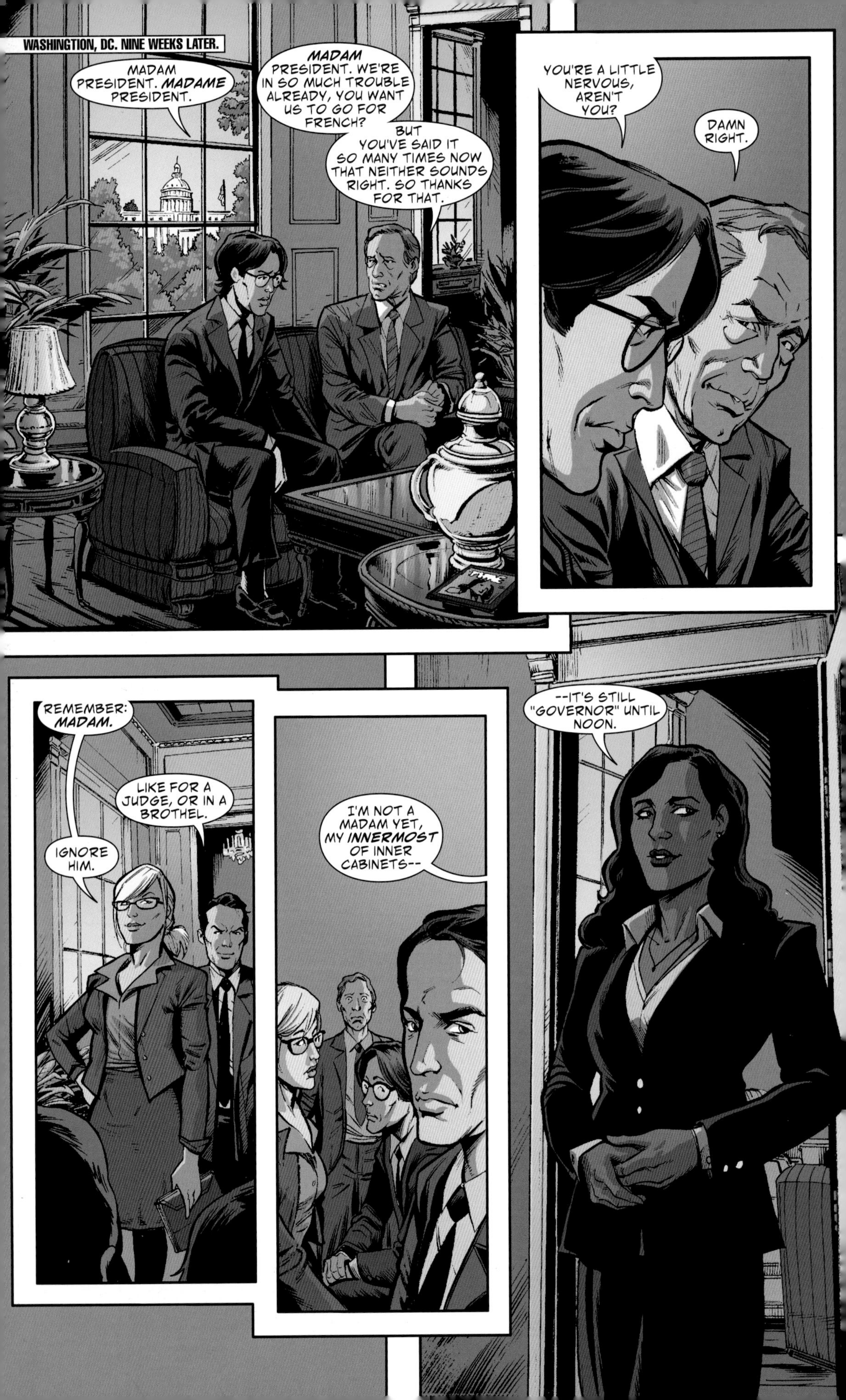
WASHINGTION, DC. NINE WEEKS LATER.
MADAM PRESIDENT. *MADAME* PRESIDENT.
MADAM PRESIDENT. WE'RE IN SO MUCH TROUBLE ALREADY, YOU WANT US TO GO FOR FRENCH?
BUT YOU'VE SAID IT SO MANY TIMES NOW THAT NEITHER SOUNDS RIGHT. SO THANKS FOR THAT.
YOU'RE A LITTLE NERVOUS, AREN'T YOU?
DAMN RIGHT.
REMEMBER: *MADAM.*
LIKE FOR A JUDGE, OR IN A BROTHEL.
IGNORE HIM.
I'M NOT A MADAM YET, MY *INNERMOST* OF INNER CABINETS--
--IT'S STILL "GOVERNOR" UNTIL NOON.

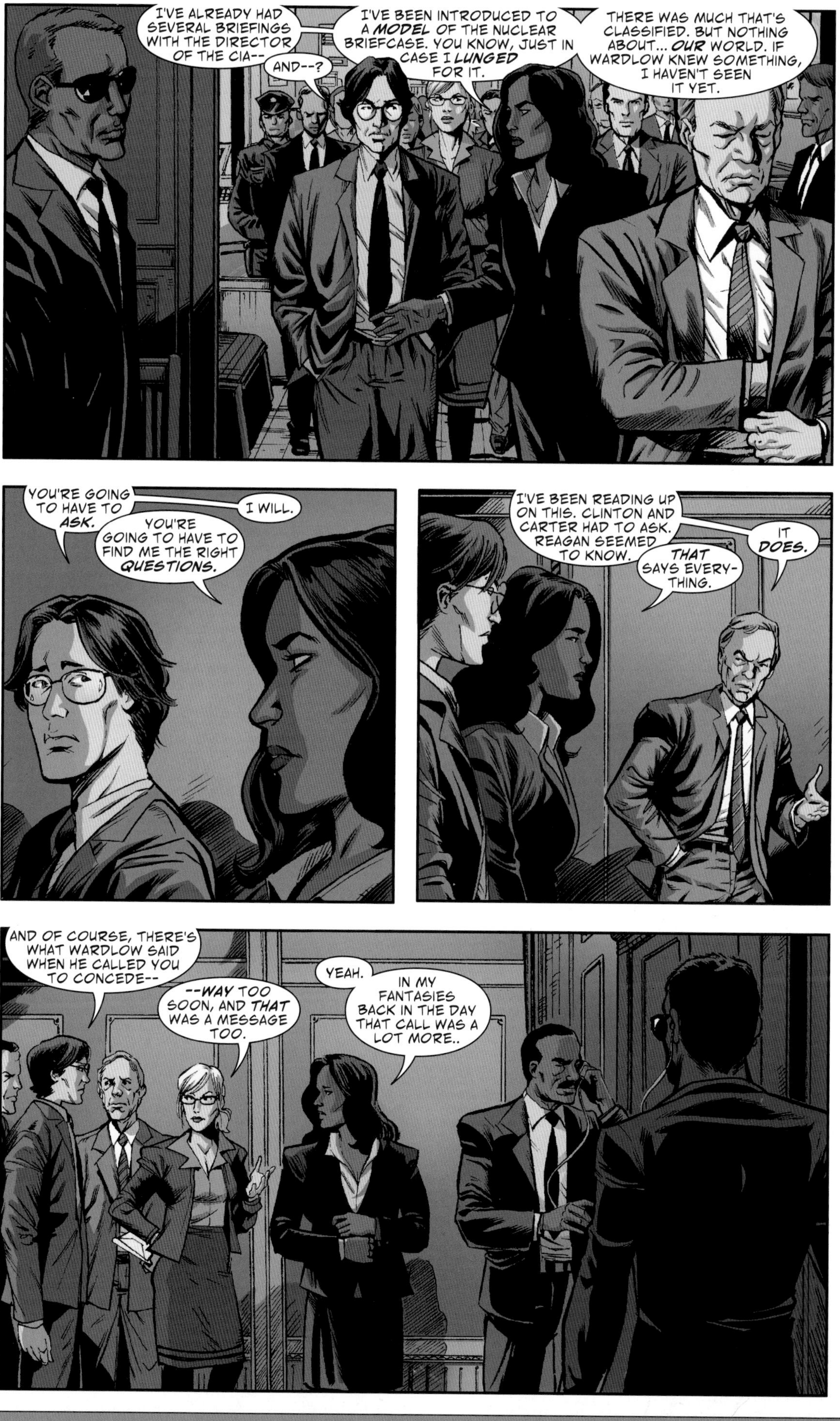
I'VE ALREADY HAD SEVERAL BRIEFINGS WITH THE DIRECTOR OF THE CIA--
AND--?
I'VE BEEN INTRODUCED TO A MODEL OF THE NUCLEAR BRIEFCASE. YOU KNOW, JUST IN CASE I LUNGED FOR IT.
THERE WAS MUCH THAT'S CLASSIFIED. BUT NOTHING ABOUT... OUR WORLD. IF WARDLOW KNEW SOMETHING, I HAVEN'T SEEN IT YET.
YOU'RE GOING TO HAVE TO ASK.
I WILL.
YOU'RE GOING TO HAVE TO FIND ME THE RIGHT QUESTIONS.
I'VE BEEN READING UP ON THIS. CLINTON AND CARTER HAD TO ASK. REAGAN SEEMED TO KNOW.
THAT SAYS EVERYTHING.
IT DOES.
AND OF COURSE, THERE'S WHAT WARDLOW SAID WHEN HE CALLED YOU TO CONCEDE--
--WAY TOO SOON, AND THAT WAS A MESSAGE TOO.
YEAH.
IN MY FANTASIES BACK IN THE DAY THAT CALL WAS A LOT MORE..

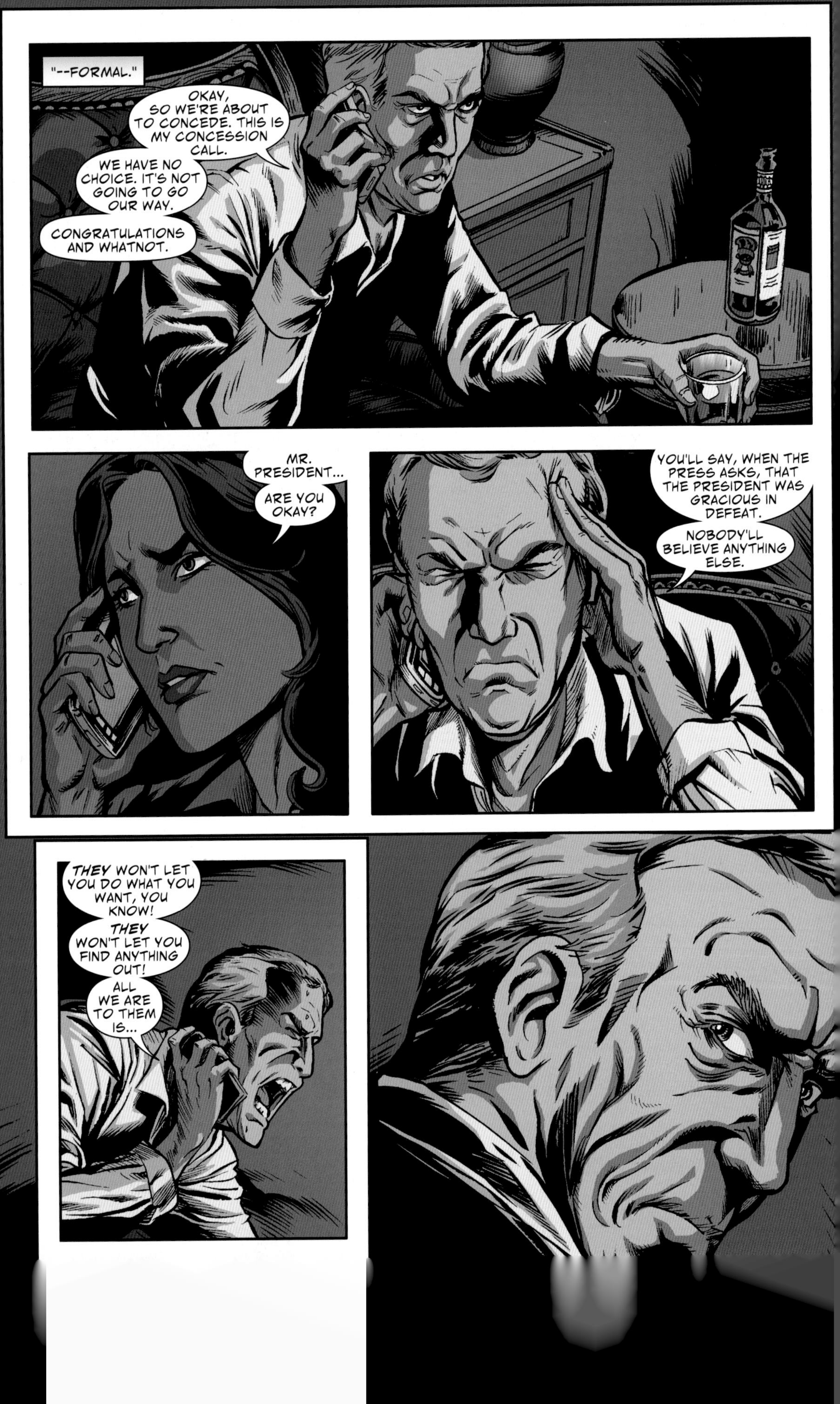
"--FORMAL."
OKAY, SO WE'RE ABOUT TO CONCEDE. THIS IS MY CONCESSION CALL.
WE HAVE NO CHOICE. IT'S NOT GOING TO GO OUR WAY.
CONGRATULATIONS AND WHATNOT.
MR. PRESIDENT...
ARE YOU OKAY?
YOU'LL SAY, WHEN THE PRESS ASKS, THAT THE PRESIDENT WAS GRACIOUS IN DEFEAT.
NOBODY'LL BELIEVE ANYTHING ELSE.
THEY WON'T LET YOU DO WHAT YOU WANT, YOU KNOW!
THEY WON'T LET YOU FIND ANYTHING OUT!
ALL WE ARE TO THEM IS...

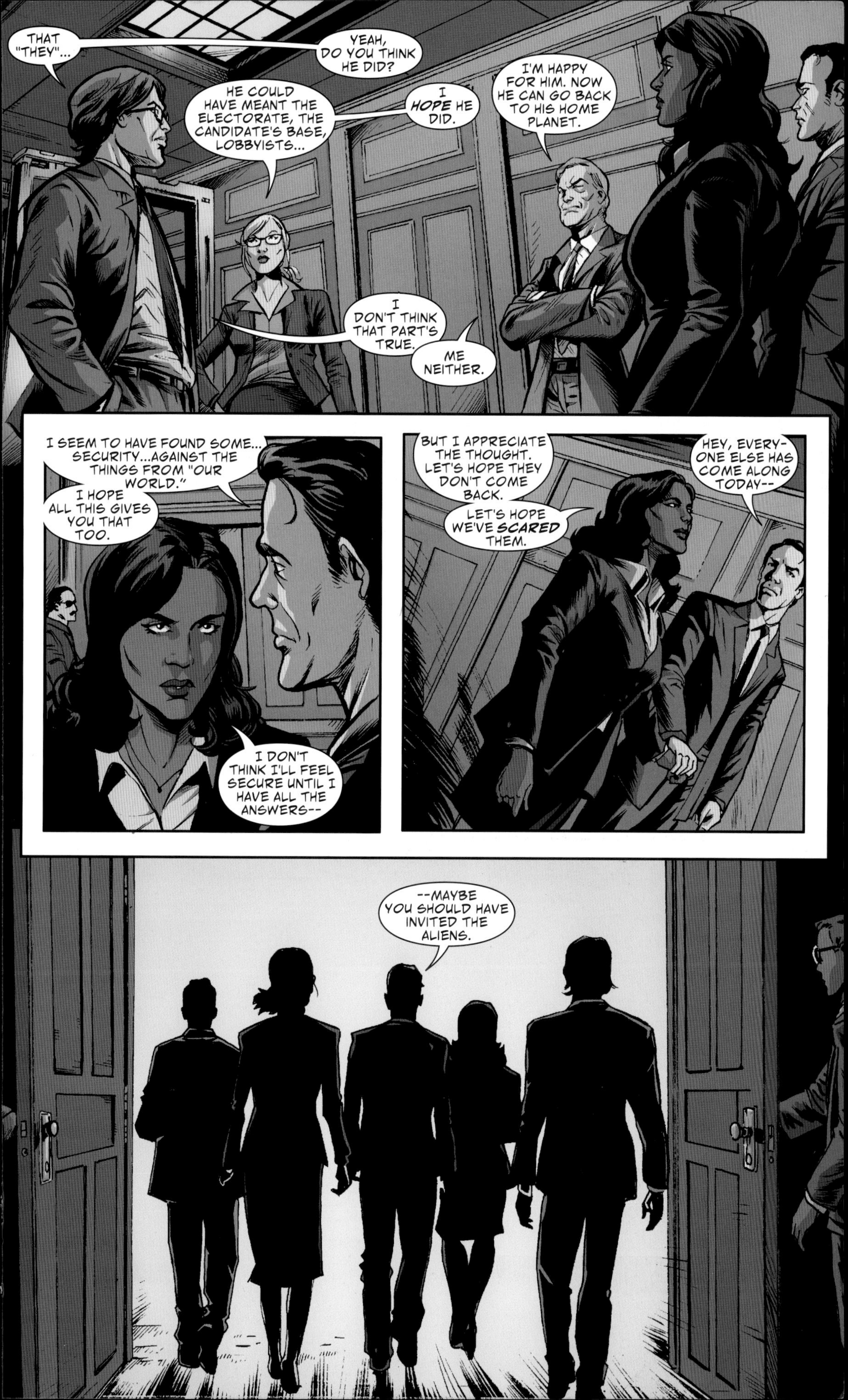
THAT "THEY"...
YEAH, DO YOU THINK HE DID?
HE COULD HAVE MEANT THE ELECTORATE, THE CANDIDATE'S BASE, LOBBYISTS...
I **HOPE** HE DID.
I'M HAPPY FOR HIM. NOW HE CAN GO BACK TO HIS HOME PLANET.
I DON'T THINK THAT PART'S TRUE.
ME NEITHER.
I SEEM TO HAVE FOUND SOME... SECURITY...AGAINST THE THINGS FROM "OUR WORLD."
I HOPE ALL THIS GIVES YOU THAT TOO.
I DON'T THINK I'LL FEEL SECURE UNTIL I HAVE ALL THE ANSWERS--
BUT I APPRECIATE THE THOUGHT. LET'S HOPE THEY DON'T COME BACK.
LET'S HOPE WE'VE **SCARED** THEM.
HEY, EVERY-ONE ELSE HAS COME ALONG TODAY--
--MAYBE YOU SHOULD HAVE INVITED THE ALIENS.

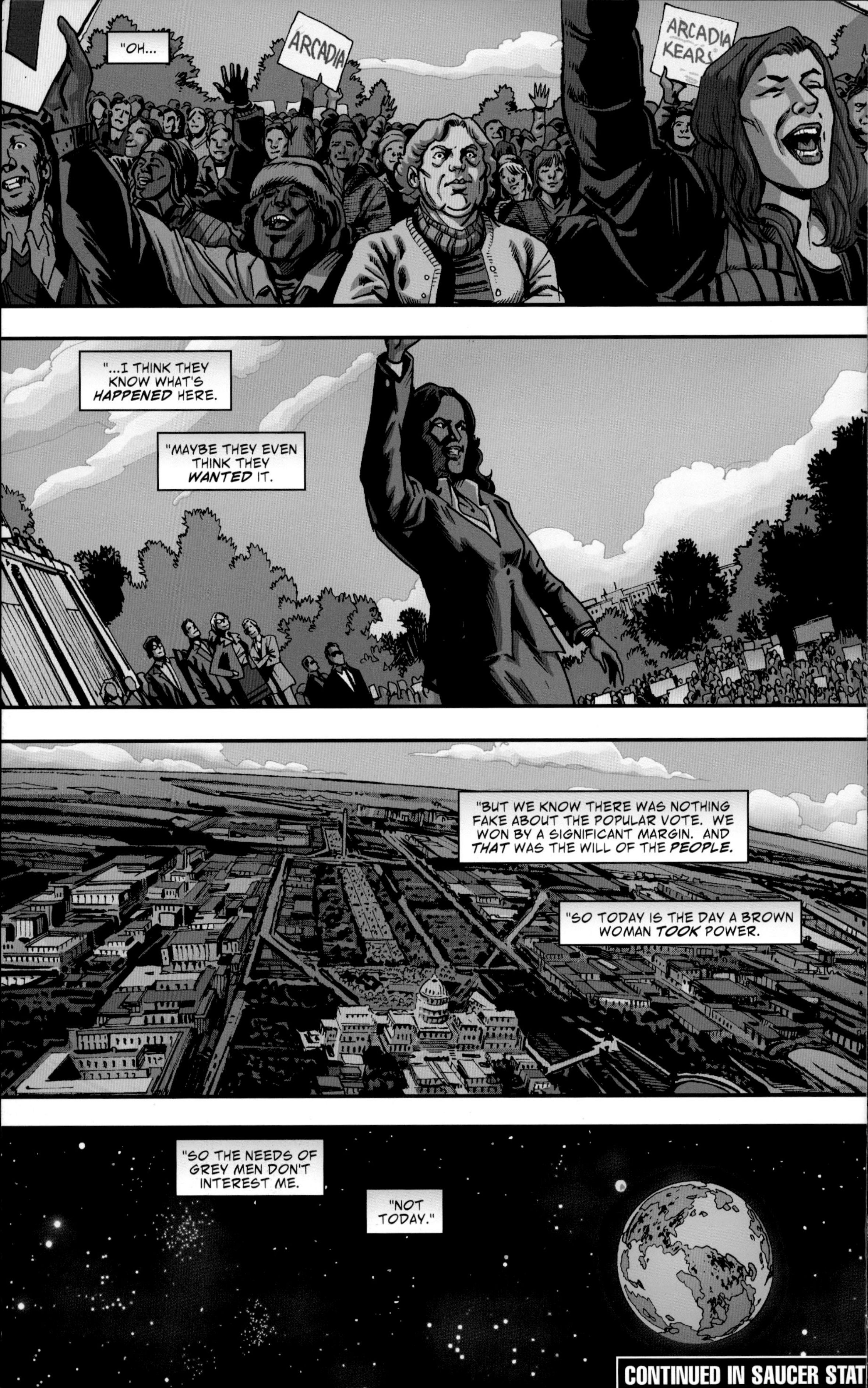
"OH...
ARCADIA
ARCADIA KEARS
"...I THINK THEY KNOW WHAT'S *HAPPENED* HERE.
"MAYBE THEY EVEN THINK THEY *WANTED* IT.
"BUT WE KNOW THERE WAS NOTHING FAKE ABOUT THE POPULAR VOTE. WE WON BY A SIGNIFICANT MARGIN. AND *THAT* WAS THE WILL OF THE *PEOPLE.*
"SO TODAY IS THE DAY A BROWN WOMAN *TOOK* POWER.
"SO THE NEEDS OF GREY MEN DON'T INTEREST ME.
"NOT TODAY."
CONTINUED IN SAUCER STAT

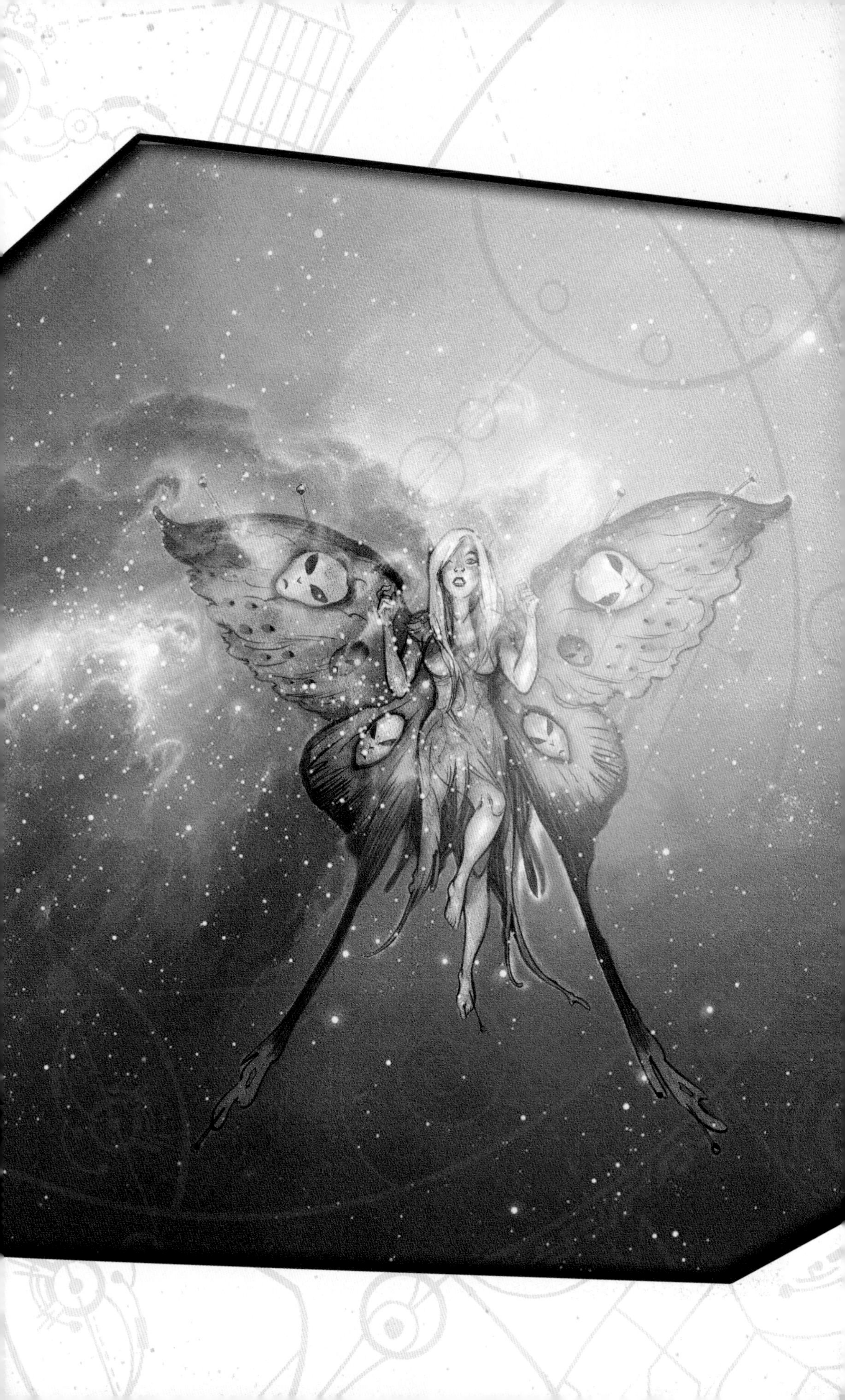

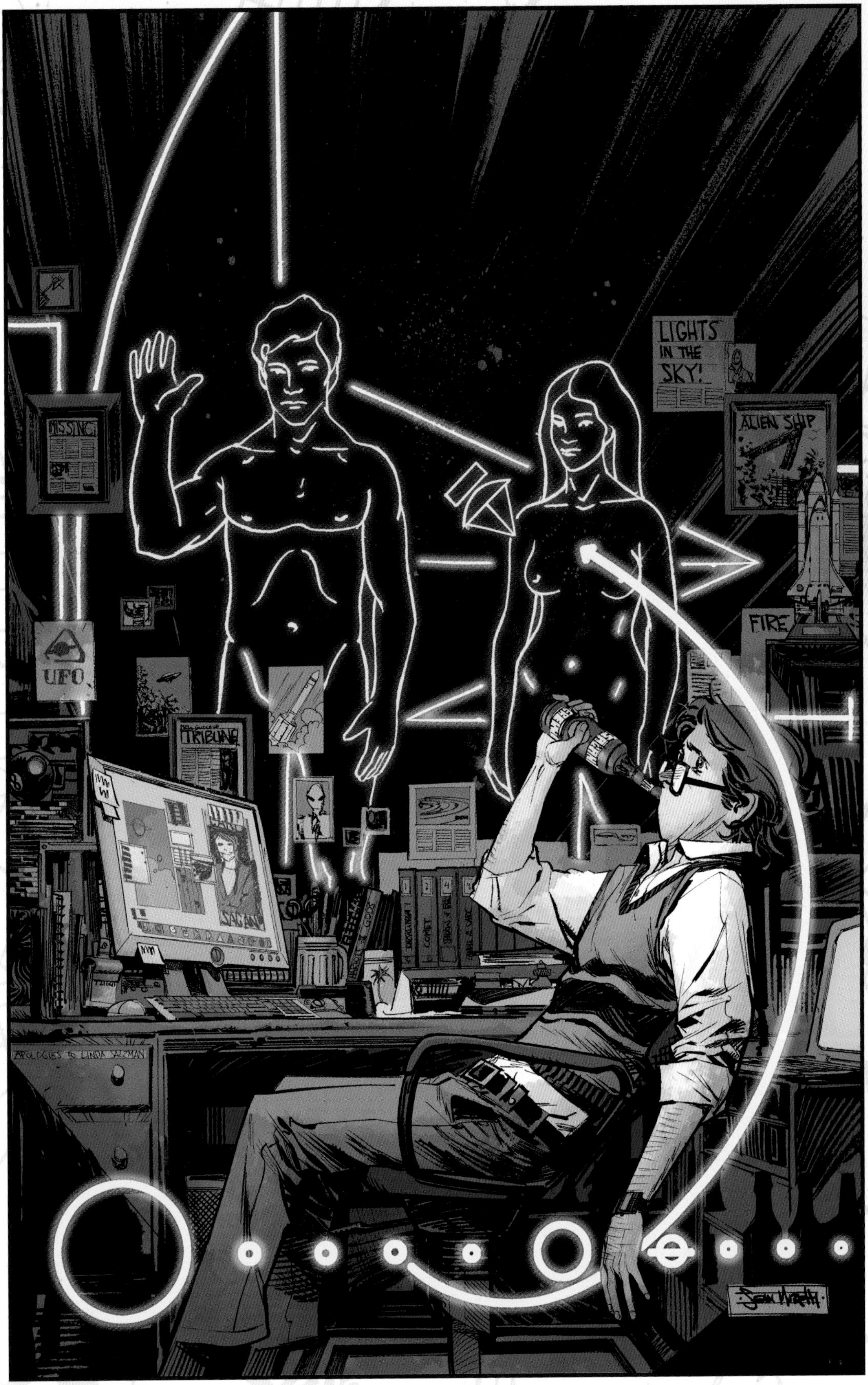
LIGHTS IN THE SKY!
ALIEN SHIP
MISSING
UFO
TRIBUNE
FIRE
SAGAN
COMET
APOLOGIES TO LINDA SALZMAN

COVER ART BY **SEAN MURPHY**

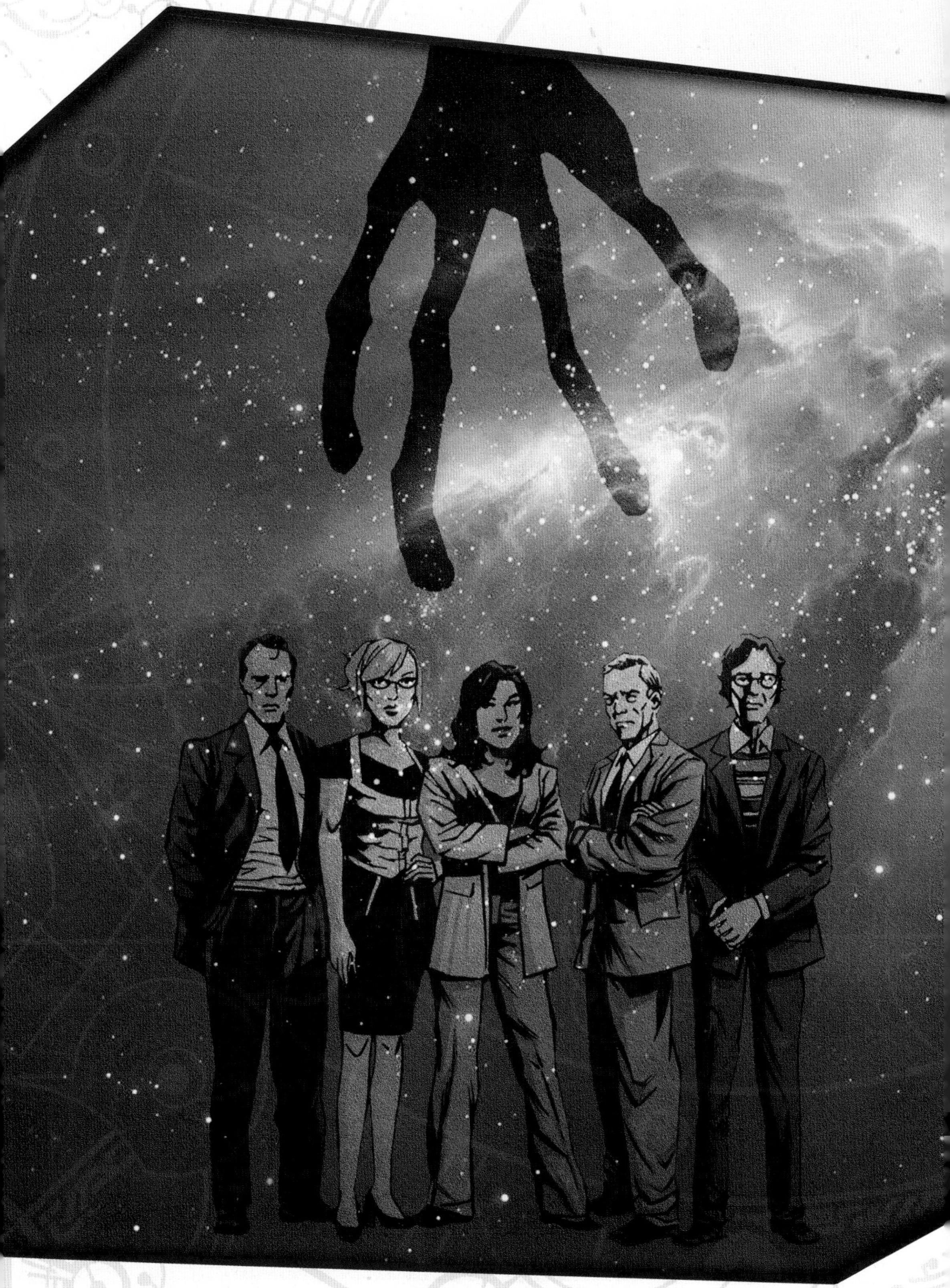

SAUCER COUNTRY